From the first page of *The Eternal Conductor*, I was drawn into the story. Debbie has a knack of weaving the past to the present, making the history of Fair Haven come to life. The wonderful descriptions made me visualize the town and characters. A wide array of emotions that the characters were experiencing felt real to me. There was joy, fear, tension and sorrow all woven together. I found myself both laughing and crying. Debbie is a masterful storyteller, incorporating an unexpected twist at the end. Now, my interest is piqued about the Underground Railroad being used for so long to help slaves in their pursuit for freedom. Wonderful job, Debbie!

—LINDA G.

An historical novel, *The Eternal Conductor* by Debbie Griffin, is her first book, and a great read. She braids the past and present with 200 years of history, intertwining the lives of families who passed through and around the Vermont home in which she was raised. The stories in the book run the gamut from the runaway slaves, wars, speakeasies, to present day and Silicon Valley. It is a page turner and timely tale of struggle, resistance, survival and love, all well worth the investment. I look forward to her next work, as I couldn't put this one down. Bravo.

—SALLY SCHUBB

The Eternal Conductor grabs your heart from the beginning as it passionately shares the heartbreaking story of the horrific battles fugitives endured while trying to gain their rightful freedom along the Underground Railroad. Once I started reading, I was enveloped by the hope, desire and determination the characters were experiencing, and then the joy of the final path to reconnection with protective angels and spirits from above.

—NOLA H.

THE ETERNAL CONDUCTOR

Debbie Garneau Griffin

Disclaimer: This is a work of fiction. Names, characters, businesses, places, events and incidents are either the products of the author's imagination, or used in a fictitious manner. Where real-life historical figures appear, the situations, incidents, and dialogs concerning those persons are entirely fictional and are not intended to depict actual events or to change the entirely fictional nature of the work. In all other respects, any resemblance to actual persons, living or dead, events, or locales, is entirely coincidental.

A note on the town name: Fairhaven, Vermont, was chartered on October 27, 1779, to Ebenezer Allen and 76 associates, and first settled the same year. The post office at Fairhaven was established in 1797. The origin of the name Fair Haven remains a mystery. Up until 1861, the town was written as one word, just as it occurred in the charter. For some unknown reason after 1861, it switched to the two-word format used today.

Editor: Kathleen Strattan
Book cover design: Karen Phillips. PhillipsCovers.com
Text design and composition: John Reinhardt Book Design, BookDesign.com
Published: Write Your Way, United States of America
Printed, shipped and distributed by: Ingram Spark. ingramspark.com

ISBN: paperback: 978-0-578-78247-8
ISBN: ebook: 978-0-578-78249-2
LCCN: 2020920205

Printed in the United States of America

In loving memory of my mother,
Robena Vera Madeline.

A true believer.

Exodus 21:16–

And he that stealeth a man,
and selleth him,
or if he be found in his hand,
he shall surely be put to death.

CONTENTS

PRESENT DAY

Williams' Residence
Cupertino, California
September, 1999

DEEDEE MAKES PLANS

MY HUSBAND MARK scratched his graying beard and asked, "So, what are you going to do with the house?" We sat at the patio table under our covered lanai finishing Sunday breakfast on a warm late-summer day.

That was the burning question I had been agonizing over for years. *What happens when…* "I'm not sure. Maybe rent it out."

He gave me a disapproving look. "Are you sure you want to be a long-distance landlord?"

I shrugged. "Well, no, not really. I'm sure it'd be a pain in the ass. But I could probably find a local property manager to oversee the place for me."

Mark's forehead creased. "Babe, I think you should bulldoze the whole damned thing and put it out of its misery!"

I stared at him. "Geez, Mark! It's my family *home.* I'm not going to freaking *bulldoze* it! Are you crazy?"

"Well, Dee, you should think about it! You've dumped a ton of money into that place—"

"Yeah, so Mom could live safely in her own home!"

"Isn't that house about a hundred years old? It's beat to shit!" Mark waved a hand in the air to make his point.

"Actually, it's over a hundred and fifty years old. But it has good bones! Look at how long it's withstood the harsh Vermont winters!" I shook my head. "I can't be the one responsible for its demise. I just won't do it!" I envisioned my family homestead, with several additions attached to the original farmhouse over the decades, giving it an unconventional floor plan.

Mark continued, "So now you want to pour more money into it to rent it, only to have it trashed by tenants? It's not worth it!" He glared at me. "If we bulldoze it, we could sell the land and be done with it once and for all." He wiped his hands together in an exaggerated fashion, as if discarding something foul.

"Who says it'll get trashed? There are decent people who rent, you know?"

"From what I've seen of folks in your hometown, I doubt that! You need to be practical about this, DeeDee, and not let your emotions get in the way." Mark slapped his hand on the table.

Frustrated at his outburst, I rose from the table, and grabbed my half-full cup of coffee. "You know what? You can take your advice and shove it where the sun don't shine!"

"I'm sorry, Babe. I just…" Mark's voice trailed me as I stomped into the kitchen heading toward the living room.

"I gotta call Mom and give her the bad news. Thanks so much for your goddamn support!" I yelled back.

I plopped into my recliner, and took deep breaths. *Damn him! I own the house, and I'll be the one to decide what to do with it!* I glanced up at the wall clock. Eleven… *twelve, one, two.* Out of habit, I tapped out the three-hour time difference to the East Coast. *Mom should be home from church by now… better get this over with… as much as I hate to do it.*

Sighing, I dialed my familiar home phone number in Vermont.

After three rings, the phone was answered. "Van Dyne residence." I recognized Mom's low, raspy voice. She always answered the phone as if she were the butler of a grand estate, even though she lived alone. It made me smile.

"Hey, Mom! How are you doing today?" I began our conversation with the usual opening, trying to sound cheerful.

My mother, Robbie Van Dyne—born Robena, a name she always hated—suffered from the advanced symptoms of Parkinson's disease, which she was diagnosed with at age fifty. Now, past her eightieth birthday, she had been living alone for over twenty years in the big, two-story farmhouse she had inherited when I was three. As a single parent, she lived there with me until I went off to college. When Mom turned sixty-five, we transferred the property into my name. I was twenty-five when I took sole ownership of our old family farmstead.

Mom answered with her standard reply. "Oh, not too bad for an old lady!" No longer able to drive, she depended on neighbors to go to and from church, doctors' appointments, and other errands.

"How was church?"

"Well, Dear, the sermon was good, but something awful happened."

I pictured her sitting in our regular pew, five rows back from the altar. "Really? What kind of bad stuff could happen in church?" I chuckled.

"Do you remember old Missus Eisley?" I could hear the phone cord rattling in Mom's trembling hand.

"Yeah, I think so. Doesn't she live down on Grape Street?" I tried to picture which of the many little old, gray-haired denizens in town she was talking about.

"Well, she's deaf as a doorknob and crazy as an old coot!" Mom grumbled. "Today she sat at the end of my pew. This nice gentleman and his wife wanted to get by her to go to Communion. The man asked her politely to let them pass, and she wouldn't move a muscle. Damned old broad, I swear!" Mom paused and took a breath. "When the man tried to step over her, she started yelling that he was trying to rape her, and then she hit him with her cane!"

"Oh, my God, Mom. That's terrible!" I stifled a laugh, my mood improving. Trying to delay the bad news, I asked, "So what happened?"

"It was awfully embarrassing, Dear. Everyone in church was staring at them," she said with disgust. "Then the deacons came over, and helped the man into the aisle as old lady Eisley smacked him on the butt." Mom coughed, then continued, "The men pulled her out of the pew, then they lifted her up by the ass. When they carried her out of the church, she was screaming like a banshee, and beating those poor deacons over the head with her cane!"

"That's hysterical, Mom," I said, laughing so hard tears were coming to my eyes. I could envision the parishioners, solemnly lined up for Communion, watching the commotion unfold in the middle of the church. "I guess that'll give all the old biddies in town something to gaggle about for a while."

"They shouldn't let that crazy old bat into church. She's just a trouble-maker!"

Still laughing, I said, "You're right, Mom. Maybe Father Cosgrove can give her Communion at home."

"He can try, but I don't think it'll do much good to save her damned soul!"

"Now Mom, be nice, you just came from church!" As much as I hated to, I had to tell her that my older sister, Ellie, and I had made a decision about her living arrangements.

"Her old soul is going to be damned to hell!" Mom groused.

"Mom, listen, I want to talk to you about something." I took a deep breath. "Ellie and I talked to your doctor. He said you're not doing very well living home alone anymore."

Mom grumbled, "Well, I don't know why he would say that! I'm fine, Dear," she said, still showing her stubborn, independent streak.

I took another long breath. "He's afraid you're going to fall again, like you did last year, because you're still unstable on that new hip. He thinks you need more care than your visiting nurse can provide." I knew this was going to be a difficult conversation, and it broke my heart to give her the bad news, especially over the phone. "Mom, I know you don't want to hear this, but Ellie and I agree with his assessment. So we've made arrangements for you to move to a nursing home in Rutland."

There, I'd said it. I paused to get my emotions in check. I heard Mom's breath catch on the other end of the line.

"Mom, Ellie says the people there are very friendly, and they're looking forward to meeting you! I think they'll take real good care of you." Tears welled in my eyes, and my voice broke, as I waited for her response.

"Oh, dear! Oh, my! Do you really think that's necessary?" There was a tremor in her deep voice, and I thought she was going to cry.

I wished Ellie, who lives forty miles from Mom, had had this conversation with her face to face, and not left it to me to break the news. But because I was the youngest daughter, and had the closest relationship with Mom, we had decided it would be best if I told her.

My stomach was in knots as I pictured Mom sitting alone, trembling, as she absorbed the drastic change that was about to take place in her life. "I'm so sorry, Mom. I know you don't want to leave the house. But you won't be far away, and you can come visit anytime," I tried to reassure her. "We're worried about you, and just want you to be safe."

"But, DeeDee, if I leave here—" her voice caught. "What's going to happen to my house?"

I knew that question was coming, and I was ready. "So here's the good news! I'm flying home to visit you." I hesitated telling her my plans to possibly rent the property. I definitely wasn't going to tell her Mark's take on the situation. "My manager gave me permission on Friday to take a six-week leave of absence. I'll be landing in Burlington next Wednesday, around six, so I'll be in Fair Haven sometime around eight that night."

"Oh, I'm so glad you're coming home, Dear," she responded heavily. "I really miss you!"

My heart ached. "Well, when I get there we'll figure out how we're going to get you moved, and who can help us clean the place out." Mom was a pack rat, and I dreaded what I would find.

Mom sobbed. "You know this is the only *real* home I've ever had, and I don't want to leave!" She mumbled something away from the phone that I couldn't make out. "But if those are the doctor's orders, I guess I don't have much choice, do I?"

I choked up. "I'm so sorry, Mom. But I'll be there to help you every step of the way, you know that!"

"Yes, I know you will, Dear." She sniffled. "I understand you and Ellie are doing this for my own good. I'll leave it up to you to figure things out," she said, her voice getting more raspy. "I love you, DeeDee. Have a good trip home."

"I love you too, Mom. I'll see you next week," I said, and hung up, wiping my tears.

I now faced the daunting prospect of making major changes in both of our lives—Mom moving to a nursing home, and me being a long-distance landlord.

And I desperately hoped that once Mom moved out, the sometimes-not-so-benevolent spirit who shared the house with us would vacate the premises as well.

THE CONDUCTORS

HOPPER FAMILY FARM
FAIRHAVEN, VERMONT
OCTOBER, 1850

A PACKAGE ARRIVES

THREE SHARP RAPS on the back door awoke Gabe Hopper from a light slumber.

Weariness from the day's chores washed over him and he lay quiet for several seconds. Still fully clothed, he sat up in bed and lowered his legs to the floor. A sharp pain shot through his lower back, causing Gabe to exhale with a low groan. He hoped he had not disturbed his wife, Emma, breathing softly in the adjacent bed. Sighing, he ran his fingers through his tangled, longish gray hair, and scratched at his full beard.

Should that be friend or foe? His heartbeat quickened. *I must take precautions. May the Lord watch over us.*

Gabe rose in the darkness of the bedroom. He pulled the straps of his suspenders over his shoulders, hitching them to the front of his trousers, then buttoned the cuffs of his red flannel shirt. A wind gust rattled the window, and Gabe felt the chill swirl through the room.

Gently closing the bedroom door, Gabe stepped into the darkened main room. Immediately to his left was the front door. To the right of the door, he touched the lantern sitting on a table. Groping in the dark, Gabe struck a match and lit the lantern. He paused to load wood into the potbelly stove, centered against the side wall. Grasping his lantern, he moved through the main room and stepped down into the kitchen. Behind him, the mantel clock on a shelf chimed twice.

Three more knocks resonated through the house.

Gabe lit another lantern on the kitchen table. Opening the door to the anteroom, he set his lantern on a shelf next to the back door. With slightly trembling hands, he grabbed his loaded, double-barreled shotgun, propped a few feet to the right. He snapped it shut, and cocked the trigger.

Holding the gun in the crook of his arm, barrel pointed down, Gabe took a breath and called, "Who goes there?"

An undecipherable, muffled voice came from beyond the thick wooden door.

Is this a slave hunter, or the package we have been waiting for?

Bracing himself, Gabe lifted the heavy latch and opened the door just far enough to slide the barrel of the shotgun through, still pointed at the ground. A gust of icy wind swept over him. In the slice of lantern light, Gabe could discern a slight figure, head hung low, draped in an oversized, dark coat. Rain cascaded from the brim of the figure's hat.

"Who is there?" Gabe repeated.

The figure looked up and squinted at Gabe through the sliver of light. "A friend sent me, Suh."

Gabe saw the grim face of a Negro youth staring back at him, and breathed a sigh of relief.

Opening the door wider Gabe asked, "Has thee been followed?"

The boy shook his head. "I don't think so. I am sorry to wake you, Suh."

Gabe peered beyond the boy into the darkness of the rain-soaked farmyard. No other figures were evident. "Very well then, come in." Gabe ushered the shivering boy into the small room, then shut the door behind him.

The Negro boy, of about twelve years, glanced furtively around the room. Chopped wood was stacked in one corner with a pile of straw next to it. Coats, hats, and cloaks hung from hooks on the wall. Muddy rubber boots slouched on the wooden floor. A mop and bucket stood ready for use in the opposite corner. The boy shook some water from his cloak, then removed his drenched hat and dropped it to the floor. He stared at the double-barreled shotgun, crooked in Gabe's arm.

Gabe saw the boy's frightened look. He uncocked the trigger, and cracked the barrel, returning the gun to its position against the wall. "We cannot be too careful these days." Gabe retrieved his lantern and directed the boy into the kitchen, closing the inner door.

Standing in the kitchen, the boy nodded. "Yas, Suh." From inside his coat, he withdrew an envelope, which he passed to Gabe. "I carry a letter from a friend, Suh."

Lifting the lantern to get a better look, Gabe inspected the envelope. It read:

Friend Hopper, Hopper Farm, Fairhaven, Vermont.

On the back of the envelope Gabe read:

Friend Granger, Granville, New York.

This "package" had traveled more than twelve miles since their last stop.

"I thank thee, Son." Gabe set the letter on the table. He would read it in the daylight, but having aided such travelers for over two decades, he already knew the gist of its contents. "What is thy name?"

Samuel paused and glanced back over his shoulder toward the yard. "Ahhhh, Samuel Prescott, Suh," the boy responded with a slight Southern accent.

"I am Gabe Hopper. My wife, Emma, and I shall help thee with thy journey. Where is thy family, Samuel?"

Samuel shuffled his feet, eyes flitting around the small, well-kept kitchen. "They're in the woods behind the farm." Samuel pointed toward the back door, his hand trembling. "And they's mighty scared, Suh."

Gabe nodded. "Very well. Please wait while I awaken my wife." Gabe turned and was startled to see Emma standing in the kitchen entrance, attired in a blue gingham dress and white bonnet. Tendrils from her long gray hair, pulled into a bun, straggled alongside her face. Standing over six feet tall, Gabe towered over her slight frame.

Emma smiled. "I thought I heard voices. I see our package has arrived." Emma gazed upon the rain-soaked Negro boy as he swayed side to side. Wind-driven rain pounded the kitchen window, causing Samuel to startle.

Gabe squinted and followed Samuel's gaze, then turned back. "This is my wife, Emma." He held an outstretched hand, helping Emma step down to the kitchen. "Mother, this is Samuel Prescott." Touching Samuel's shoulder, he said, "Thee is among friends, my Son."

Samuel shivered and nodded. "I thank you kindly, Suh."

Emma stoked the wood cook stove, where a venison stew simmered on the back burner. She motioned for the young boy to come closer. "Come here and warm thyself by the stove, Samuel. Thee must be chilled to the bone."

Samuel trudged across the wooden floor and stood near the heat, wrapping his arms around his thin frame. "Much obliged, Ma'am. 'Tis a cold, wet night, but I must get to my family."

Gabe nodded. "Of course. I shall get ready."

Emma turned away from the stove toward Gabe. "Father, shall we give the Lord a short prayer first?"

Gabe hesitated, then nodded. "Yes, Mother."

Emma guided Samuel to the center of the room and took his left hand in hers. When Gabe grasped the boy's gloved right hand, he heard a faint crackling sound. Gabe thought there was something odd about the boy's grip, but dismissed it.

Emma clasped Gabe's free hand. They bowed their heads, and Emma prayed, "Dear Heavenly Father, we ask Thee bestow upon us courage and strength this night to provide Thy weary travelers comfort so they may continue their journey safely to the land of freedom. We ask this in Thy name, Jesus Christ, our Lord and Savior. Amen."

Gabe lifted his head and responded, "Amen." He peered at Samuel.

Samuel shuffled from one foot to the other, under Gabe's steady gaze. "Umm, Amen!" he finally blurted.

Gabe smiled and nodded at the boy. Then Gabe opened the kitchen door and entered the anteroom where he slid on his boots and rain cloak. Samuel followed the older man, retrieving his hat from the floor.

At the wooden counter next to the stove, Emma scooped tea leaves into the teapot, then filled it with hot water and set it to steep. She stirred the stew on the back burner, which she had prepared earlier, in anticipation of the package's arrival. A tin of fresh-made cornbread, covered by a cloth, rested on the counter.

Gabe watched Emma place the cornbread, a crock of hand-churned butter, and a tea strainer into a wooden crate. "Mother, I shall take Samuel to fetch his family and guide them to the barn. Then I will help thee with this load."

Emma smiled. "Hurry then. Everything should be ready when thee returns, Father."

Gabe slid his hat over his ears, and grasped the lantern. Then he and Samuel stepped into the muddy yard, bowing their heads against the wind and pelting rain. Gabe said, "Samuel, show me where thy family hides."

On their left was the carriage and horse barn, facing the main road. To their right stood the long cow barn. The man and boy slogged through the yard between the barns, wind flapping their coattails. After several minutes, they reached the edge of the woods at the south end of the farm.

Samuel made a warbling, turkey-like call that got lost in the wind. He waited. No response. Samuel repeated the warble louder. Moments later, Gabe thought he heard an unusual sound above the wind. Samuel turned to his right and stepped into the shrouded trees, with Gabe's lantern shining behind him.

Then a hand reached out and grabbed Samuel's arm.

As Gabe watched, two women, hunkered in their cloaks, emerged from under the water-laden branches. The first figure staggered as she struggled to hold a bundle in her arms. The second woman carried heavy satchels in each hand, with another strapped to her back with ropes.

Gabe approached the first, smaller woman, and reached for the bundle. "Here, let me help with thy load."

The young mother yelped and turned away from Gabe's reach. It was then he realized she was clutching a whimpering child close to her chest.

"Nahhh, nahhh, nay!" she wailed. "Ya no take ma boy."

"Do not be afraid, Miss," Gabe said. "Thee is safe and among friends now."

Samuel gently touched his sister's arm. "It's okay, Sarah. He won't hurt Jonah. Please let him help us. You trust me, right?"

Sarah lifted her head and squinted at Samuel with beseeching eyes. The wrapped child squirmed in her arms. She slowly nodded her head.

Gabe turned to Samuel, "Here, take the lantern and lead us to the hay barn behind the house." Gabe struggled to lift the heavy bundle from the frightened woman's arms.

Suddenly, a loud crack caused Sarah to cry out.

Gabe froze. *I should have brought my gun! I hope Samuel was right and they were not followed.* The bundle whimpered in his arms.

Samuel and the older woman stopped where they were.

Gabe turned toward the woods, from where the sound had emanated. Moments later, a thump reverberated under their feet. Gabe exhaled. "I think a branch has fallen. Quickly, we must get thee to shelter."

The two women gathered their traveling satchels, and followed Samuel and Gabe along the muddy row between the carriage and cow barns. When they reached the hay barn, Gabe passed the fussing child back to the young woman. He flipped the door latch and shoved one side of the double barn doors open wide enough for the group to enter. Gabe grimaced as the rusted wheels screeched against their track. Samuel and the two women entered the barn and Gabe pushed the protesting door closed behind them, shutting out the storm.

The older woman sighed as she slid the cloak from her head. "Ahh, my! Praise the Good Lord to get outta that wind."

Gabe's lantern dimly lit farm and plowing instruments propped against the left wall. Two enclosed stalls were stacked to the ceiling with hay.

Through the gloom, at the back of the barn, a stairway climbed to the loft. Shadowed beneath the staircase, a door led to the two-seater privy. Against the right wall sat a row of large, wooden grain barrels.

"Samuel, shine thy lantern here." Gabe pointed to the last grain barrel, situated along the middle of the wall.

Samuel stood next to the tall, stooped man as Gabe grasped the wide, empty barrel, tilted it along its bottom edge, and rolled it out of the way. Then Gabe bent over and tugged at an iron ring embedded in the floorboard. A hatch opened, and he leaned the hinged wooden door against the barn wall.

"Wait here while I get the lanterns lit," Gabe instructed his visitors. He took the lantern from Samuel and descended the ladder. At the bottom, Gabe ducked his head so he wouldn't hit the low ceiling beams. Setting the lantern on the table, he lit a candle and two other lanterns in the underground room, then climbed through the trapdoor, carrying the first lantern.

Leaving the lantern on the barn floor, Gabe motioned to the boy. "Samuel, climb down here." Gabe stepped down the ladder and out of the way as Samuel descended to the packed earthen floor.

Samuel was surprised that the underground room was quite large, almost half the size of the barn. A rough-hewn table and chairs sat against the outer, long wall. A cupboard next to the table contained kitchenware. The three outer foundation walls were constructed from stacked slate slabs. The inner wall, which ran beneath the middle of the barn, was excavated dirt, crisscrossed with supporting timbers. A small potbelly wood stove stood against the outer wall near the table. The stovepipe extended up into the barn floor. A stack of wood was piled next to the stove. Against the back wall were three mattresses laid head to toe in a horseshoe shape. Coarse, gray woolen blankets covered the beds. On the right side of the room, beneath the front of the barn, stood a round, wooden bathtub, partially obscured by a sheet hanging from the rafters. Wooden crates and trunks lined the wall near the tub. On a stand next to the tub sat a water pitcher perched inside a wash basin. In the corner farthest away from the tub was a chamber pot.

Gabe touched Samuel's shoulder. "Will this suffice for thy family?"

A grin spread over Samuel's face. "Yas, Suh! Thank you! It is fine." He removed his hat and placed it on the table.

Gabe turned back to the ladder. "Let us help them down. Samuel, climb up and pass the child to me."

Perched halfway up the ladder, Samuel said to his sister, "It's okay, Sarah. Let Jonah come to me and I'll help him."

Sarah hesitated, then lowered her bundle to the barn floor. She slid the cloak from the boy's head. "Go to Samuel, Jonah," she said, pointing to her brother balanced on the ladder. Jonah whimpered and clung to Sarah's leg. She wrapped her arms around his chest and hefted the boy to Samuel's waiting arms. Samuel grasped his nephew and backed his way down the steps.

Gabe lifted the fussing child from Samuel's arms and sat him on a chair. "Thee is a good boy." He patted the boy's mussed hair. The wide-eyed child stared up at Gabe, and whimpered.

Then Samuel passed the travel satchels to Gabe, who set them against the inner wall. Samuel descended to the floor, then guided his sister and mother down the six steps of the ladder.

"Please make thyselves comfortable while I get the fire going," Gabe said as he pointed to the small kitchen table.

The older woman removed her wet cloak and let it sink to the ground. Then she sat down with a thump. "We's sho' do thank ya, Suh. Praise the Lord for ya kindness." She clasped her hands in prayer. The young woman removed her wet cloak and lifted the soaked blanket off her son, dropping them both to the earthen floor.

As Gabe got the fire started, he studied the child more closely. The small Negro boy, about three years old, with thick, wavy black hair, was light-skinned in comparison to the two women. Gabe noticed a distinct resemblance between the boy and Samuel.

Gabe smiled as he closed the stove door. "There. That should warm things nicely."

The younger woman took the fussing child onto her lap, so Gabe could join the group at the table. When Samuel removed his gloves, pieces of hay scattered on the table. He placed his right hand on the older woman's hand, and turned to Gabe. "Suh. This is my mother, Miss Elsie." Then Samuel turned and smiled at the younger woman. "This is my sister, Sarah." Sarah nodded at Gabe with a sullen look, but said nothing. Then Samuel grasped the child's hand. "And this is Sarah's boy, Jonah."

"I am Gabe Hopper, and my wife, Emma, shall be here shortly," Gabe said as his gaze traveled to Samuel's right hand. He was surprised to see Samuel's first two fingers were missing, almost down to the knuckles. It was then Gabe noticed the finger holes of Samuel's right glove were stuffed with hay.

So that is what I heard when I took his hand. What a horrible injury for a boy to endure. I wonder how he lost those fingers.

Gabe studied the two women at the table. The older was thin and road-weary, her face deeply lined. Gabe guessed she was Emma's age, maybe older. Gray, kinky curls escaped the edges of her soiled bandanna. Her layered skirts were muddy and torn. The younger woman wore a yellow bandanna and a high-collared, button-up shirt. Dried blood caked the fabric where her right sleeve was ripped. Her layers of brown skirts were dirty and tattered.

Gabe smiled at the fugitives. "We are blessed to help thee with thy travels."

Miss Elsie bowed her head. "May the Good Lord bless ya and Miss Emma. We's much abligin' to ya, Suh."

Gabe nodded. "Please get comfortable. I must help Mother with the stew. We shall return shortly." Gabe climbed the ladder to the barn floor and retrieved the lantern. Leaving the barn door slightly ajar, he soldiered through the driving rain to the house. Loud claps of thunder rumbled overhead and the low-hanging clouds glowed momentarily. Gabe stomped his feet and shook the rain from his cloak in the outer room, then entered the kitchen.

"How are they faring?" Emma asked. She set the pot of hot venison stew on potholders in the crate and added the steaming teapot next to the cornbread.

"They are grateful to be out of the rain. The young child is frightened, and shall need comfort. His mother's arm is bloody and will need tending."

Emma nodded. "Very well. Let me fetch my kit." She opened the cupboard to the left of the table and retrieved a well-used, leather-bound, rectangular satchel. Placing it on the table, she unlatched the hook and lifted the top cover. Slim glass tubes containing herbs and pills, closed with cork toppers, were held upright by clips in the panel that separated the top and bottom sections. Emma bent to inspect her apothecary, including the wraps, unguents and implements situated along the bottom of the case. She looked at Gabe. "I believe I have what I need to dress her wounds." She closed and latched the case.

Already wearing her child-sized rubber boots, Emma donned her heavy cloak, and pulled the hood over her head. Then she slung the long strap of her satchel over her shoulder. She hoisted a pitcher of milk and the lantern as she pushed out the door. Gabe followed, carrying the food crate. Setting the lantern on the stoop, Emma closed the heavy door behind them. Grasping the lantern, she stepped off the landing and grunted as her foot sank into oozing mud.

The two conductors slogged through the pounding storm to feed and comfort their weary, late-night visitors.

FARM CHORES

After getting the Prescott family fed and bedded down for the night, Gabe and Emma returned to the house, took short naps, then rose to attend to morning chores. In the kitchen, Emma cooked breakfast of eggs, ham, and porridge.

Sitting on the table next to Samuel's travel letter was the missive Gabe had received three days earlier. While waiting for his breakfast, he re-read the letter.

10 mo, 6th, 1850

My Dearest Nephew Gabriel,

I hope this letter finds thee and thy family in good health. Thy son, Adam continues to be of great assistance, since my quest to serve the Lord and His flock is never-ending. Adam's boundless enthusiasm for our work brings me great joy. Alas, such youth and energy is a gift from the Almighty, which no longer avails me in the winter of my years.

We recently had a lovely visit from longtime friends. I am sure thee remembers grandmother El, along with her daughter, son and grandson. They spoke fondly of the last time thee and Emma stayed with us, and expressed a wish to see thee again.

Adam has graciously arranged their passage to Vermont. I believe they shall arrive at thy farm within a few days. We hope thee and Emma will welcome their visit, and provide them thy gracious hospitality.

With full purpose of heart, may we cleave unto the Lord, for whatever trials and besetments may await us. And may our endeavors in the love of our Lord, Jesus Christ, be forever blessed in His heavenly covenant.

With Sincerest Affection,
Your devoted Uncle,
Isaac T. Hopper
New York City

Being members of the Hicksite Quakers, Gabe's father Jacob, and Jacob's younger brother, Isaac, had been vocal leaders in advocating the abolishment of slavery. The Hopper brothers were credited with organizing a system for hiding and aiding fugitive slaves in Philadelphia, in the late seventeen-eighties. As a young boy growing up in Philadelphia, a hotbed of slave kidnappers, Gabe had abhorred witnessing the inhumane treatment rained upon their captives. He fervently believed that according to God's law, it was a sin for any man to own another.

Now, Gabe, Emma, and their two sons, Luke and Adam, carried on the family legacy by providing aid to those who sought their freedom from tyranny.

The sound of stomping feet caused Gabe and Emma to pause and turn toward the anteroom.

"Mother. Father." Luke yawned and nodded as he entered the kitchen. Tall and lanky like Gabe, with thick, unruly brown hair, Luke, now twenty-eight, leaned over to kiss his mother's cheek where she stood at the stove.

Luke and his wife, Mary, their twin sons, Brian and Bernard, and daughter Martha lived just a few steps away to the north of Gabe and Emma's house. Luke and Gabe jointly owned and worked the Hopper farm.

Emma smiled up at her oldest son. "Good morning, Dear." She set a bowl of steaming porridge on the table.

Luke retrieved the tea kettle and poured the hot liquid into a tea strainer he had placed over the top of a mug. Leaving the used strainer on the counter, he carried his cup to the table, where he joined Gabe.

"Wonder when this rain is gonna let up. 'Tis a muddy mess in the yard," Luke grumbled as he sipped his tea. "Heard those Foley boys down Poultney-way hightailed it for the gold rush." Luke ladled porridge into his smaller bowl. "Guess they're taking a ship from Boston 'round the Horn bound for 'Frisco." Luke had a wistful look on his face. "Gonna be quite an adventure, but I'll bet they won't get rich!" He laughed. "I 'spect they'll be back within a year, tail 'tween their legs, lookin' for work."

Gabe stared out the kitchen window into the dawning light, brow furrowed, thinking of his family's dilemma.

As a young man, Gabe had traveled with Jacob and Isaac from Philadelphia to attend an abolitionist meeting in Glens Falls, New York. It was there Gabe had learned fugitive slaves were using the Hudson River as a connection to Lake Champlain, and a direct route to Canada. At this meeting, Gabe met a man who told him a farm was for sale just across the border in Fairhaven, Vermont. Gabe saw the opportunity to not only have his own farm, but also to be in a position to provide another waystation along the freedom route to Canada. At the age of nineteen, with the financial help of his father and uncle, Gabe had purchased twenty acres of land, one mile south of the town.

Now, more than thirty years later, Gabe was furious. *That coward President Fillmore has bowed to the Southern slave owners by using the full force of government to catch runaways!*

Prior to the Fugitive Slave Act being enacted a month earlier, it was unlikely a master or slave catcher would travel into the free Northern states in search of their runaways, as it was just too much trouble and expense. Most Negroes had been able to move openly in Vermont, with little fear of being accosted.

As Gabe ate, he fretted over the new law.

'Tis absurd that anyone adhering to God's will, could be fined a thousand dollars and spend six months in jail! And that bounty has slave hunters popping up like weeds. I must be ever-vigilant to protect my family and those who seek our aid.

"Father? Did you hear what I said? You seem troubled." Luke studied his father's dour expression.

"Hmmm?" Gabe responded. "Ah, yes, the gold rush foolishness. Hope old Mister Foley can manage the farm without his boys." Gabe scooped a bite of porridge, then halted, spoon poised. "The package arrived during the night."

Luke raised an eyebrow. "Did they now? I thought I heard that old barn door squealing. Then again, it could have been the wind."

Gabe shook his head. "I shall need thy help to grease that old wheel." A worried look played across his face. "'Tis not wise to make such a racket when new visitors arrive."

"How many in this lot? I hope they are doing better than the last travelers we assisted. Those men were in rough shape." Luke took a bite of porridge, then sipped his tea.

Gabe stared into the gloom toward the hay barn, thinking of their new arrivals. "Mother and grown daughter, a young lad and a boy child," Gabe said. "The girl, Sarah, had a decent gash on her arm. She said it caught on a branch as they were running through the woods." Gabe nodded with appreciation in Emma's direction. "Mother dressed the wound before they bedded down."

Luke ran a hand through his tousled hair. "Hmmm. Don't get many of their womenfolk coming through these parts. It's usually just the men. I'm surprised the boys haven't already been sold away."

Gabe shrugged. "The lad is maimed—missing a couple of fingers. Probably was not worth much to the buyers because he could not pull his weight," he surmised.

"Wonder how that happened. How old is the lad?" Luke asked.

"Maybe twelve. Hard to tell for sure. But the finger stumps are well healed. Whatever lost him those fingers happened some time ago." Gabe stared into this porridge bowl, his appetite waning, as he thought of the pain the young lad must have endured.

Emma set the scrambled eggs, ham, and bread on the table, poured herself a cup of tea and joined the men. "The grandmother, Miss Elsie, is a God-fearing woman. I admire her courage to lead her family to safety." Emma passed the eggs and ham to the men, then parceled some food onto her own plate. "I will learn more of their travels when I bring their bath water."

Gabe absentmindedly scratched at his beard, frowning. "Luke, we must keep their arrival quiet. With all the troubles from this God-forsaken law, we do not know who we can trust."

A strong gust of wind splattered rain against the window as the family ate their breakfast.

Luke nodded. "Yes, Father. It will be more difficult moving this lot than in the past. But I believe we'll manage." Luke chewed his eggs. "And don't forget, there's a meeting tonight. I bet there'll be plenty of talk about this damned new law."

Gabe shook his head, a look of disgust crossing his face. "I wish that cowardly President—"

The sound of a horse neighing in the yard stopped their conversation. Gabe and Emma stared at one another, not moving.

"That's probably just Buster," Luke said, referring to their farm hand. Finishing his breakfast, Luke rose from the table. "Time to get to milkin', I s'pose." He touched his mother's arm. "Thanks for the meal, Mother."

Gabe stood up from the table to follow Luke. "When the milking is done, I shall help thee with the water for their baths." He squeezed Emma's hand before he left the kitchen.

The gray light of dawn seeped through the heavy rain clouds as Gabe and Luke donned their outerwear. Gabe's mood was as dreary as the rain pounding the roof. He clasped Luke's arm. "Remember, we shan't speak of our visitors to anyone," he warned.

A SICK CALF

After Emma cleaned the dishes from their breakfast, she retrieved her journal from her bedside nightstand. As daylight slowly emerged from the dreary dawn, Emma sat at the kitchen table in the glow of the lantern. Although she had been raised Methodist, having spent her entire adult life with Gabe, she had naturally adopted some of his Quaker speech patterns for her own. Thus, Emma began a new entry in her many written pages.

10 mo. 11th, Friday, early morning, 1850

A new group of travelers has arrived during the night seeking refuge from the storm. I thank Thee Lord for guiding these weary souls to our doorstep. We shall provide them shelter and sustenance, as Thee would have done. Please shine Thy light upon Miss Elsie, Sarah, Samuel and Jonah so they may travel safely in Thy good graces to the land of freedom. I ask this in Thy name, Jesus Christ, our Savior. Amen.

She returned her diary to her nightstand, and donned her cloak and boots in the anteroom. Gathering her large woven basket, she made her way through the wet, chilly dawn to the long chicken coop located behind the hay barn. The cackling of more than a hundred chickens reached a fever pitch on her approach. Opening the coop door, she stepped inside, closing it behind her, and shooed away the few birds trying to make their escape. Ammonia stench from their droppings assaulted her, making her eyes water. Coughing, she took shallow breaths as she made her way along the lay racks, gathering eggs of varying hues. Hens squawked and chased one another in the enclosed space. One brave hen pecked at Emma's bare leg under her skirt, causing her to jump.

Emma swung her leg in the hen's direction. "Away! Ye old coot," she commanded. The hen squawked and flew a few feet, causing more chickens to erupt in short flight. When Emma had completed her circuit, her basket was heavy with eggs, forcing her to hold the handle with both hands. "Shoo! Shoo! Out of my way," she scolded as she made her way through the gaggle of chickens. After shouldering her way out the door, she set her basket down on the stoop to carefully close the door behind her.

Back in the kitchen, Emma carefully washed and dried the eggs. Retrieving straw from the outer room, she placed a layer along the bottom of a wooden crate and then arranged eggs along the straw. On a piece of paper she jotted down the number of eggs placed. She continued layering straw, then eggs in this manner until they were all safely cradled in the box. Then she summed her egg count. Wedging the top onto the crate, Emma set it on the shelf in the anteroom along with the totaled note, for Luke to take to the town market later in the day.

Not long after Emma finished crating the eggs, Gabe returned to the kitchen. "Luke and Buster are driving the cows out to pasture. Shall I help thee get water?"

"Yes. I would think with all the noise those confounded hens make, our visitors should be awake by now." Emma wrinkled her nose, still stinging from the coop stench.

Emma and Gabe each grabbed a metal bucket and made their way to the well pump, between the house and the hay barn. Gabe primed the handle to get the water flowing, as Emma steadied each bucket along the base of the pump. When both buckets were filled, they each lugged a sloshing bucket to the front of the hay barn. As Gabe pushed open the barn door, the rusty wheel squealed on its track.

Gabe grimaced at the offending wheel and grumbled, "Darn that thing. I must get it greased."

The squeal of the hay barn door caught Buster Slater's attention as he and Luke were returning to the cow barn. Buster, shorter and more muscular than Luke, peered in that direction as he watched Emma and Gabe lugging heavy buckets of water inside. "Why are your parents taking water in there?" Buster asked.

"Hmmm." Luke paused, following Buster's gaze. "We have a sick calf that got out during the night. It's caked in mud so they need to clean it before it can be tended to." Luke grasped Buster's arm and guided him back toward the cow barn. "Let's get this mucked out, then I have to take Mother's eggs to town."

Buster looked back over his shoulder and mumbled, "Sick calf, huh? Seems odd to have a calf this time of year."

"Well, yearling, if you like." Luke handed the farm hand a pitchfork. "Let's get to work."

I hope Buster believes my story. Although we've been friends for years, I'm not sure I can trust him to keep our secrets.

Luke kept his head down and pitched his fork into the dirty straw, ignoring the frown on his friend's face.

THE LEDGER

Gabe helped Emma carefully descend the ladder into the underground room. Emma lit a lantern on the table, since the gray light of morning did not penetrate here. She walked to the back of the room where the family slept. Miss Elsie lay on her side, facing the outer stone wall. Samuel snored softly on the bed against the back and Sarah cuddled Jonah in her arms on the bed next to the reinforced inner dirt wall.

Emma gently shook the matriarch's arm. "Miss Elsie," Emma whispered. "We have brought water for thy baths."

Elsie turned to face Emma. Her head scarf had come off during the night and her thick, gray curls were askew. "Goodness me," Elsie whispered as she ran her fingers through the snarls. "I must look a-fright." She yawned and sat up on the straw mattress, dropping her feet to the floor.

Emma placed an arm on Elsie's shoulder and smiled. "'Tis no matter to me. I believe a hot bath will do thee good."

Emma startled as Samuel bolted upright in bed, his arms waving as if in a fight. "Wha! What? Who's there?" he yelped, still half asleep.

Elsie placed a hand upon Samuel's head. "You'se okay, Son. We's safe now. Go back to sleep." Samuel gave his mother a sleepy nod, then fell back onto his cot and turned his back to the intruding lantern light.

In the bed next to the inner wall, Sarah didn't stir as Jonah grumbled and changed position in her arms.

Emma touched Elsie's arm and guided her to the small table. Elsie looked back at her slumbering family. "I'll let 'em sleep a mite longer. We's all powerful weary from our journey." She straightened her soiled scarf and deftly wound it multiple times around her head, corralling her wild curls, then secured it at the nape of her neck. "There!" She smiled at Emma. "Now's I won't be scarin' none of God's good creatures."

Both women chuckled quietly.

"Mother?" Gabe's deep voice came down through the opening. He had attached one water pail to a rope-and-pulley system attached to the underside of the floorboards.

Emma rose and stepped to the ladder. "I'm ready, Father. Let it down." Emma guided the full pail of water to the ground. Placing a large pot on the stove, she hoisted the water bucket and filled the pot. Then she turned to retrieve the second bucket, as Gabe lowered it to the floor.

Gabe descended the ladder, bowing his head to avoid the wooden beams. He stirred the embers and added wood to the stove. Gabe lifted the second water bucket and poured it into the round, wooden bathtub at the front of the room. Turning back to the women he said, "I will leave thee to thy business." He bussed the top of Emma's head. "I must go tend the horses."

Carrying the empty water bucket, Gabe ascended the ladder to the barn floor. Emma winced as she heard the door squeal shut.

From the shelf next to the table, Emma retrieved a tin of tea and scooped several spoonfuls into the teapot, then ladled hot water from the larger pot and left it to steep. She sat next to Elsie at the table.

The two women sat in silence for several seconds. Then Elsie tentatively reached her hand out to Emma. "Shall we pray?" Emma nodded and grasped the black woman's calloused hand. They bowed their heads and Elsie began, "Dear Heavenly Father. I thank ya for guidin' my family on our journey an' keeping us safe from those who wish to cause us harm. Please shine your grace down upon Miss Emma and Mistah Gabe for the love an' kindness they done showed us. They's put themselves at great risk so's all your children may one day find the Promised Land. We's humble servants in your name, Jesus Christ, our Savior. A-men!"

"Amen," Emma whispered. A tear rolled down her cheek as she squeezed Elsie's hand a bit tighter. Guided by their undying faith, the two women of different races looked into each other's eyes, each feeling a strong bond forming between them.

Emma rose from the table and bent to remove a swatch of cloth from the bottom of the shelves next to the table. From beneath the swatch, she pulled a long, bluish-gray, hard-covered ledger along with a quill and inkwell. Sitting back at the table, she opened the ledger and flipped through many filled pages until she came to one with blank lines available halfway down the page. Dipping the quill into the ink, she turned to Elsie.

"I have been ledgering those travelers who come to our home. I wish to add thee and thy family," she said, peering into Elsie's dark eyes.

Elsie studied the neatly slanted writing filling the lines of the ledger page. "Wish't I knew how to write that purty," she said. "Those be all our run'way folks that done come through here?" Elsie shook her head in amazement. "How many you think there is?"

Emma shrugged. "I do not know for sure. Never did stop to count them all. Gabe and I have been working with thy people for nigh over twenty years now." Emma shook her head thinking about how many desperate fugitives had risked their lives to journey north to an uncertain destiny. "Probably a couple hundred or more." She sighed.

"Lordy! Sure's lots of us niggahs high-tailin' it north!" Elsie glanced at her slumbering children. "Hope we makes it to Canada 'fore them damned low-down slave hunters catches us up." Elsie gripped her hands tight on the table. "'Twas hearin' of that sinful new law that we done run when we did."

Emma placed a hand on Elsie's clenched fist. "I will not lie to thee. It shall be more dangerous this time when we transport thy family." Emma saw the worried look on Elsie's face. "But Gabe and Luke have done this many times with success. We pray the good Lord will guide thy safe passage on Lake Champlain to Canada." Emma squeezed Elsie's hands. "Now, what is thy full name?" Emma asked as she raised her quill over the ledger.

"My name be Elsie Mae Prescott Swaley." Elsie paused, a sly smile creeping across her face. "'Cept Swaley be my Massa's name and I sho' don't be needin' it no mo'!"

Emma smiled at Elsie's declaration and wrote *Elsie Mae Prescott* in her tight, slanted script on a line in the ledger. "Age?" Emma asked.

"Don't rightly know, I s'pose." Elsie shrugged. "Ain't never had no birthin' records. But I seen plenty a-turnin' of the seasons." Her gaze lifted and brow knotted as she spoke.

Emma left a space on the line next to Elsie's name, then, out of habit, wrote Master Swaley to indicate Elsie's slave owner. In the preceding ledger entries, names of slave holders from the South were listed.

Emma said, "Does thee know how old Sarah is?"

Elsie rubbed a hand over her chin, thinking. "I be guessin' she might be eighteen years. Could be more. She be birthin' Jonah not long after she done got her womanhood. And Jonah now 'bout three." Elsie smiled at her sleeping grandson, curled in his mother's arms.

Emma wrote on the next line of the ledger: *Sarah Prescott, Age 18, Datr.* On the line following she wrote: *Jonah Prescott, Age 3, G-son.* On the next line she wrote: *Samuel Prescott.*

"And then there's Samuel. What is his age?" Emma asked.

Elsie stared thoughtfully into the distance. "Le' me think. Sarah was a girl when I birthed Samuel. She done helped the midwife with the birthin'—tryin' to be a big girl an' all. But at the end she got scar't and ran out the cabin a-wailin'." Elsie chuckled as she remembered Sarah's reaction to the birth. "She say later she thought I be a-dyin'. Poor chile. Think she was maybe five or six then."

Subtracting six from Sarah's now eighteen years, Emma wrote: *Age 12* next to Samuel's name. "And does thee remember giving birth to Sarah?" Emma asked gently.

Elsie nodded. "Yas, 'm. I sho' do! I done jumped the broom with my man, Raymond— prob'ly a couple years after I got my womanhood. We both worked Massa Swaley's plantation." Elsie had a faraway look in her eyes. "'Twern't no more room in our cabin 'cause of all us kids. My mammy said I should be movin' on and havin' my own babies. I liked Raymond sho' 'nuf, so off to his cabin I went." She chuckled. "Musta been 'bout a year later I birthed Sarah." She shrugged.

"So, if thee was seventeen when thee gave birth to Sarah, and she is eighteen now, I believe thee is about thirty-five years old." Emma was surprised that she, Emma, was more than ten years Elsie's senior. Elsie's deep-lined face and gray hair made Emma think the weary woman was much older. Next to Elsie's name in the ledger, Emma wrote: *Age 35, G'mthr*

"If ya say so," Elsie said. "'Tis Samuel who knows his numbers, not me."

Emma raised an eyebrow at Elsie's comment, as most of the Negroes who had passed through their property were uneducated. "How is it Samuel knows his numbers?" Emma asked.

"Massa Swaley learned him along with his son, Chester," Elsie said. "Being as Samuel was his son an' all, Massa wanted him edj'cated. Boy can read an' write an' do his numbers, just like them white boys." Elsie sat straighter in her chair, eyes glowing.

"Oh, my!" Emma gasped. "Samuel is thy master's son?"

The teapot whistled gently. Elsie startled at the noise and looked over to the cots to see if her family had awakened. All three still slept soundly.

Grabbing a potholder, Emma set the pot on the table. From the shelf she retrieved two teacups, saucers, and a tea strainer. Elsie held the strainer over the cups as Emma poured the tea.

Sitting back down at the table, Emma stared at Elsie. "I do not wish to pry, but does thee mind if I ask about Samuel?" Her voice was solemn.

Elsie blew on her hot tea, then she shook her head and lowered her voice. "I was the cook in the big house an' when Sarah was old 'nuf, she helped the house girl do cleanin'," Elsie said. "One day, Massa's wife, Miss Priscilla, got word her sister in Boston was taken poorly. When she went travelin' from our plantation in Maryland, they's got caught in a bad rain." Elsie's dark eyes clouded. "'Parently the horses spooked in a river and the carriage done went over. Miss 'Cilla and the niggah driver both got drown't." A tear slid down her cheek as she sipped her cooled tea. "Then, Massa had no wife and the boy, Chester, he be nigh on two years, done lost his Momma."

"Oh, how horrible! That poor boy losing his mother at such a young age." Brow wrinkling, Emma thought of her own two sons at that age and wondered how they would have fared without a mother.

In her ledger, Emma wrote *Maryland* next to Master Swaley's name.

Elsie nodded, her face thoughtful. "Massa was sho' torn up 'bout it. Shut hisself away in his room for days after Miss 'Cilla's buryin'," Elsie recounted. She took a deep breath, collecting herself. "Us house Negras took over raisin' Chester best we could." Elsie looked over to Samuel's sleeping form. "One day, Massa came to the kitchen and told me to bring soup to his room as he be feelin' poorly." Elsie sniffled and wiped her nose. "When I walked in, Massa was looking out the big window to the fields. I's set the soup down next to his readin' chair and turned to go." Elsie paused, her breath coming in little gusts as she stared down at the table.

Emma had a knot in her stomach as she sensed what was coming.

"'Fore I realized what was happenin', Massa moved in front of me an' shut the door. He grabbed my arm an' pulled me to him. I screamed—tried to get away. Massa held me tight—said to me, 'I don't got a wife no more, so's you'll have to do.' I told him it warn't right, that I gots a husban'." Elsie turned away from Emma and dropped her head. "Mo' I fought—stronger he got. Then he punched me and I done fell to the bed."

Emma reached across the table and grasped the woman's hand. "Oh, Miss Elsie. I'm so sorry."

Elsie pursed her lips, holding back tears. "Warn't much I could do. Let him have his way wi' me as he wanted," Elsie said, her voice ragged, shoulders slumped. "When it was over, I done fixed my skirts, and went back to the kitchen to start makin' his dinner." Elsie looked intently into Emma's eyes. 'Tweren't long 'fore I knowed I was with child. When Samuel was born, my man Raymond took one look at that high-yellah boy and knowed 'tweren't his." Elsie glanced again at Samuel who snored softly, his body facing the wall.

Emma sipped her tea and watched Elsie closely. *Another beastly master raping his slave. When will this horrific evil ever come to an end?*

"Raymond was 'raged—wanted to know what white man was the baby's father." Elsie's face crinkled. "Lordy! Ya knows I was fear't to tell him 'cause he gots a God-awful temper—didn't know what he gonna do. He guess it was Massa's—threatened to kill the baby if I didn't tell him the truth. I was scair't for my son's life so's I told him, yeah, Massa had forced hisself on me." Elsie's hands shook as she grasped the edge of the table.

Emma gasped, "Oh, no! What did Raymond do?"

Elsie kept her voice low. "He hollered, 'I'm gonna kill that bastard for touchin' my wife!' and he done ran out the cabin. I pleaded with him not to do nothin' stupid, but he wan't lis'nen to me." Tears seeped down Elsie's face as she recalled that horrible night. She sniffled and wiped her nose on her sleeve.

Emma sat deathly still, stomach churning, unable to speak.

"Raymond didn't come home to the cabin that night and I was worried som'thin' fierce. Next mornin' I gathered the baby an' went a-lookin' for him." She shook her head. "Heard a commotion at the carriage barn. When I looks inside, there was Raymond, face bloody, shackled inside a wooden cage that was latched on top of the wagon. I done screamed an' ran to him." Elsie's voice sounded strangled.

Emma raised a hand to her mouth, her eyes wide.

Elsie took a breath, then a sip of tea. "Massa stood 'side the wagon with his farm hands. His face was purple swolled an' his arm in a sling. 'Take him to the slave auction,' Massa done told the driver. 'Make sho' he gets sold to the Deep South. Don't want him finding his way back to these parts.'" Elsie shook her head. "I screamed an' pleaded with Massa—'No! No! No! Ya can't take him! Please! He's my husban', don't take him!'"

Samuel murmured and turned over in his bed.

Emma grasped the distraught woman's shaking hands. *What a horrible injustice for Elsie and such harsh banishment of her husband.*

"Thee and Raymond were treated very unfairly, Miss Elsie. Master Swaley will have to face the Lord's judgment one day."

Elsie looked at Emma. "I hope's you right, Miss Emma." She paused, looking away. "Raymond done yelled at me, 'Miss Elsie, 'tain't nothin' ya can do. I got my licks an' I gotta take my punishment. Don't make things worse on yo'self. Now get outta here with that baby.'"

Elsie continued, "Massa pulled me out the barn and yelled at me, 'He's right! He's gettin' what's coming to him. Now leave!' An' he pointed to our cabin. The baby was wallerin' so's I went." Her small frame trembled as she recalled the event.

"I wailed when they carted Raymond away. Never did see or hear from him again." Elsie broke down sobbing. "An' Lordy! Lordy! God knows I sho' did love that stubborn ol' niggah."

A moment of silence stretched between the two women. "I'm so sorry thee lost thy husband. What happened after Raymond left?"

Elsie paused and wiped her face. She sipped her tea, collecting herself. In a firmer tone she continued, "Massa Swaley said since Samuel was his son, he wanted the boy edj'cated. Said he didn't want no son of his being a 'lowly, stupid Negro.'" Elsie glanced again toward Samuel as he mumbled in his sleep. "Since I was a big-house niggah, I brought Samuel an' Sarah wi' me every day. When Samuel was old 'nuf, he was learned by the house tutor along with Massa's boy, Chester."

"Oh, my!" Emma said. "I'm surprised Master Swaley took favor on thy boy."

"Yas,'m. 'Cept Chester war'nt none too happy about a niggah boy learnin' his school lessons. An' he was smartin' real bad when he done learn't Samuel was his father's son." Elsie stared at Emma. "Lordy, Miss Emma. I swear to the Almighty! Even tho' us house women be raisin' Chester to be a God-fearin' boy after his Momma died, that boy done got the devil in him." Elsie's eyes had a faraway look. "Hadda keep a close eye on those boys 'cause Chester, he be hurtin' on Samuel every chance he get!"

"Oh, it pains me to hear that! It must have been difficult for thee trying to protect Samuel." Emma rose and popped a finger into the big, two-handled pot of water warming on the stove. "Almost there," she said, as she poured more tea into their cups and sat back down.

For a moment the two women stared at each other. Elsie dropped her eyes first.

Emma sipped her tea. "I believe the good Lord gives us children to bring both joy and sorrow to our lives. My two sons, Luke and his younger brother, Adam, have brought us much joy." She smiled at her visitor. "Adam lives with Gabe's uncle, Isaac Hopper, in New York City, and helps with our cause," Emma said proudly.

Elsie flashed a grin, revealing a gap in her upper jaw where two back teeth had been. "Adam's yo' son?" Elsie said as she recalled part of their journey. "He's a han'some, well-bred boy. Done treat us with respect. Drove us in a fine carriage right out the big city, just like we was important folk. 'Tain't no one bothered us with Adam drivin' them reins." Elsie grasped Emma's hand. "Took us to a farm and gave us a fancy letter to show them folks. Said they was his frien's."

Emma smiled envisioning Adam driving the family out of New York City. "Adam is a good boy, but I worry about his safety with these infernal slave catchers popping out of nowhere," she said, exhaustion creeping into her voice. "I could not bear to lose another child." A look of sorrow crossed Emma's face.

"*Another* chile, Miss Emma?"

Emma sniffed and peered at Jonah, cuddled next to his mother, Sarah. "We had a daughter, Ruth, our youngest. She was frail at birth. But she soon grew stronger and became the joy of our life. She had a God's-light about her that brought us all much laughter." Emma's voice caught at the memory. "Her older brothers doted on her every wish, and Ruth just delighted in giving them silly orders." A wan smile crossed Emma's face as she stared into her tea.

"She die, Miss Emma? I's so sorry for ya," Elsie said, seeing the downcast look on her host's face.

"Yes. She died. Winter of thirty-two was a bad one—bitterly cold and snowed all February," Emma recalled. "Ruth came down with the cough. Doctor came and treated her the best he could. The boys cared for her as did Gabe and I. But she could not shake free of the cough. It got so bad, she could barely eat. Come sugaring time, with the sap just starting to run, the Lord took her from my arms! She was just five years when she became God's little angel." Emma buried her face in her hands and sobbed.

Elsie rose from her chair, walked to the other side of the table and, after a moment of hesitation, touched Emma's shaking shoulders. "Ruth wi' the Lord now, Miss Emma. You knows she'll be waitin' when ya gets to the Pearly Gates."

Emma's sobs slowly subsided. She grasped Elsie's hand and smiled up at her. "I thank thee. I miss her terribly and think of her every day." Emma blew her nose in her hanky and collected herself. "But enough about me, let's get thee in the bath."

Using two potholders, Emma grasped the handles of the pot and poured the heated water into the round wooden tub. "When thy family has finished with the bath, thee can pull the plug and it will drain here." Emma pointed to a drainage culvert that had been dug into the dirt floor and led beneath the stone foundation wall to a cistern.

Elsie looked to where Emma was pointing and nodded.

Emma pulled towels from one of the trunks on the floor, and passed Elsie a bar of handmade lye soap. Pointing at the other trunks Emma said, "There are clean clothes in these trunks that have been donated by our church members. Please take whatever is needed for thee and thy family." Emma reached up and latched the loose section of drape onto the hooks attached to the ceiling in a semicircle, providing privacy around the tub.

"I shall leave thee to it then," Emma said, as she grasped Elsie's hand.

"Bless ya, Miss Emma, for yo' kindness," Elsie said.

Emma lifted the empty bucket and climbed the short ladder to the barn floor, leaving the hatch open for air circulation in the underground room. She struggled to slide the barn door open far enough to make her exit, then muscled it shut. As she made her way back to the house, her heart ached both for what Miss Elsie had endured, and for her own lost daughter.

Oh, how I miss my dear, sweet Ruth. Were she alive, she would be nigh on twenty-three years and probably a mother of her own. And I would have more sweet grandchildren to love.

About to close her prayer, something compelled her to add, *Dear Lord, please keep my sons safe in Thy loving grace as we continue Thy work on this earth to help the poor and downtrodden souls seeking our help. Amen.*

Emma entered the kitchen and gathered the ingredients to bake bread, still haunted by visions of Elsie's harrowing tale.

A TRIP TO TOWN

While Emma was in the barn tending to the needs of Elsie and her family, another farm hand, Enos Adams, arrived on horseback to assist Buster Slater and Luke with the farm chores.

Enos, with sandy brown hair and green-brown eyes, now aged twenty-six, looked up to Luke as an older brother. Enos' father, Joseph Adams, was a partner in the Fairhaven marble-sawing business. Joseph was also the president of the Washingtonian Temperance Society, with over five hundred members in Fairhaven. After Enos had finished his studies at the University of Vermont, he had joined his father and his partners to help manage the marble mill. But Enos also loved farm chores, and since his early teen years, except for his college stint, had been working daily on the Hopper farm.

Enos hitched his horse to the railing next to the main path, dismounted, and went to the cow barn in search of Luke.

After Gabe had left Emma with their visitors, he entered the stables that adjoined the carriage barn. The combined structure was built about thirty steps from the main highway connecting Fairhaven to Hampton, New York, just a mile farther south. Two riding horses and the two draft horses, used for pulling the carriage, buckboard, and sleigh, were housed in four stalls, where Gabe began pouring grain into their troughs.

The younger riding horse responded with a nicker and bobbed its head against Gabe's arm. "Now settle thee down. Here's thy food." Gabe patted the horse's muzzle.

The second, older riding horse came to the front of the stall and nudged Gabe. "Yes, yes, I see thee, too." Gabe poured feed into the horse trough. Peering into the large barrel against the wall, Gabe calculated he had about two days of grain left. He would have to make a trip to town to replenish the stock. Gabe walked out into the barnyard to find Luke.

In the yard, Gabe watched Buster and Enos grasp a handle on either side of a twenty-gallon covered milk jug and haul it to the edge of the path that ran through the center of the farm. A clang echoed as the metal container landed next to several others lined up to be transported to town. A few steps behind the men, Luke struggled to carry one full milk jug alone.

Gabe walked over to help his son. "Set it down and let me help thee." Luke grunted and set the heavy load on the ground. He and Gabe each grabbed a handle and wrestled it to the line of other jugs.

"Did thee already take milk to the cheese house?" Gabe asked.

The cheese-making shed was located behind and to the south of the cow barn. Within the cheese house an iron cauldron hung from the ceiling, suspended over an unburned woodpile. The milk would be boiled and stirred until the curds separated from the whey. Then the curds would be squeezed and molded into cheddar cheese rounds, wrapped in a linen cloth and dipped into hot wax, preserving the rounds. In the far corner stood a wooden butter churn. Emma and her daughter-in-law, Mary, used the cheese and butter to feed their families and also to sell to the town grocer.

To the right of the cheese shed, about twenty paces farther along the edge of pasture, stood the dormant sugaring house. It would come alive in March when the sap began to run in the maple trees surrounding the pastures. Some of the syrup was kept for the families, but much of it was sold to add to the farm coffers.

Luke nodded toward the cheese house. "Yes, Father. Once we get the milk loaded, I'll have the boys get the fire going and work the cheese."

"I must go to town with thee as I need grain. Will thee help me get the horses hitched?"

Luke nodded at his father and then turned to Buster and Enos. "Boys, when we finish loading the milk, will you get the cauldron lit in the cheese house? I need to help my father right now."

"Yep. We'll take care of it," Buster responded, his brows narrowed as he exchanged a nod with Enos. "Go ahead and help your father." The farm hands sauntered back to the cow barn to retrieve another full milk can.

Luke and Gabe walked to the front of the carriage barn and slid open the main door. Inside, they lifted the hitch of the buckboard and began pulling it through the door. Luke glanced at his father, wondering whether he should tell him about Buster. Finally, he decided he should. "Father. You should know Buster saw you and Mother carrying water to the hay barn this morning."

The two men continued hauling the wagon out of the barn. Gabe, frowning across the wagon at his son, said, "Did he? That is unfortunate, now. What did thee tell him?"

"I said we had a sick calf that got out during the night and it was covered with mud. We had to clean it up before we could tend to it." Luke's half-smile faded as he wondered how his father would react.

Gabe finally chuckled. "Oh, my. Quite a lie indeed!"

Luke grinned. "First thing that came into my head."

"Did Buster believe thee?"

"Hmmm…maybe. He thought it strange to have a calf this time of year so I told him it was a yearling." Luke waved a dismissive arm in the air.

Gabe furrowed his brow as they positioned the wagon to hitch the draft horses. "He may be suspicious. We must be careful. Thee knows Buster likes to stir up trouble at his father's tavern."

Luke shrugged. "Yep, he does. But the old man Jeb is usually the one who gets the gents riled up after serving them too much liquor. Guess the acorn doesn't fall far from the tree, does it?"

"No, Luke. I do not believe it does." Gabe stared beyond Luke.

Luke followed his father's gaze. *I wonder who in town might turn against our cause because of this ungodly new law.*

Their wagon now in position, the father and son entered the stables. Each led a draft horse to the front of the wagon and positioned them side by side, facing north. Gabe held the horses' heads, while Luke moved the yoke into place and attached the harnesses to secure them to the wagon. Once they were hitched, Gabe climbed onto the seat and steered them to the left, onto the path between the house and barns. He halted the horses and applied the wagon brake.

As Gabe was positioning the wagon, Luke went into the house. Moments later he emerged carrying Emma's crate of eggs. Loops of rope hung off one arm and an old blanket hung off the other. Luke slid the crate onto the buckboard then climbed onto its bed. Laying the blanket directly under the driver's seat, he nestled the egg crate into the folds. Turning around on his seat, Gabe helped Luke wrap the rope around the crate several times to secure it to the wagon. Then Gabe climbed down and went to the back of the wagon.

"That should hold until we get to town," Luke stated. He walked to the end of the buckboard where the farm hands waited. "Enos, come up here and help me," Luke said.

Enos jumped onto the wagon bed as Buster and Gabe began hoisting up jugs of milk. Luke and Enos dragged the jugs to the front of the wagon and placed them in line. When the ten jugs were loaded, Gabe threw a rope to Luke, who secured them to the wagon frame. Then Luke and Enos climbed down from the wagon and secured its back gate.

While the men were loading the milk, Emma had emerged from the kitchen. "Luke, here is my list for Mister Jones at the grocery. The items on the top are most important," she said, pointing to her neatly written note. "If that old Welshman will not give thee everything in exchange for the eggs, get as much as thee can. Thee knows that infernal man drives a hard bargain." Emma shook her head in frustration.

"Yes, Mother. I'll do my best, I promise!" Luke chuckled at his mother's opinion of the stubborn, foreign proprietor. Out of the corner of his eye, Luke saw Buster approaching Emma from the side of the wagon.

"Mornin', Missus Hoppah. How's that sick calf doin'?" Buster asked, his solicitous question contrasting with his mischievous, lopsided grin.

Emma blinked and stared at the stocky, muscular farm worker, not much taller than she. "Wha—"

Luke quickly stepped in front of Emma, his back to Buster. "You know, Mother. The calf from last season that got out last night. It was muddy and you and Father brought water to the barn this morning to clean it off." Luke stared with raised eyebrows into his mother's eyes, willing her to support his story.

A brief look of confusion clouded Emma's face. Then she smiled. "Oh, yes! The sick calf. Please forgive me, as I am quite exhausted. She fares much better now. A little bruised up, but she shall be fine in a few days."

Gabe grasped Luke's arm. "We must be heading into town, Luke. Day's a-wasting."

"Yes, Sir," Luke said and turned to Buster and Enos. "When the curds are ready in the cheese house, let Mother know and she will finish up."

"Sure, Luke." Enos nodded.

As Gabe and Luke drove off and Emma, humming to herself, returned to the house, the farm hands walked toward the cheese house.

Looking over his shoulder, Luke saw Buster grab Enos' arm, lean close, and whisper something in his ear.

GOSSIP

Luke and Gabe climbed aboard the high seat of the buckboard. The heavy rains of earlier in the day had subsided to a sprinkle, slapped by wind gusts. Low, dark clouds overhung the treetops. The men gathered their cloaks tight and secured their hats. Luke took the reins and directed the horses between their two farmhouses, where he turned left, heading north on the road to the village. About a half-mile later, they arrived at the top of a steep hill that dropped to the bridge crossing the Castleton River, separating the south and north sides of Fairhaven. Beyond the bridge, a two-tiered incline led to the village proper.

Luke brought the horses to a stop at the crest of the hill and surveyed the deep, muddy ruts in the road left by previous carriages and wagons. "It looks rough today, Father. What do you think?"

"Hmmm," Gabe responded as he peered through the gloom at their pending descent route. "I think if thee rein to the left, it may be the smoothest path." Gabe grasped the handbrake. "Just keep them tight and I shall hold the wagon," he advised his son.

Luke lifted the reins and clicked his tongue to get the horses moving slowly. Their hooves immediately sank ankle-deep into the oozing mud, as the wagon began to descend. Gabe kept a strong hold on the brake to steady the wagon's movement. The rig rocked as its left wheel clumped into a deep hole. The men jolted in their seat as the wagon bounced into another pothole on the right. The milk jugs clanged into each other in the wagon bed.

The younger horse shied and whinnied at the jolting of the wagon and banging of the milk jugs.

"Keep them steady, Luke," Gabe yelled.

Luke saw another deep rut directly in front of the horses and sharply reined them to the right. The wagon fishtailed to the left, coming close to sliding over the precipice. The milk jugs rattled and bounced.

"Straighten 'em out or we will go over!" Gabe hollered as he worked the brake to direct the sliding wagon. Luke guided the horses slowly down the rain-soaked, rutted road, while Gabe struggled to control the loaded buckboard.

Luke loosened the reins, pointing the horses toward the middle of the wooden trestle bridge. Gabe released the brake and the momentum pulled the wagon back in line. The milk jugs clunked, then settled back into place.

At the bottom of the hill, Luke reined the horses. He paused to catch his breath as riders coming from Whitehall, New York, to their west, merged into the lane and crossed the bridge. Gabe looked into the back of the wagon, while Luke watched the horses and other traffic trundling single file across the wooden span.

"Everything still hitched back there?" Luke asked as he exhaled.

"Yes, it looks to be fine. Shall we continue?" Gabe raised his voice to be heard over the roar of the lower falls, tumbling just below the left side of the bridge. He faced front again to survey the bridge and two-tier hill leading into town. Both men scrunched their faces against wind-blown spray rising from below the bridge.

Luke reached over to touch the younger horse's flank. "You're doing good, boys." As he let the steeds rest for a moment, an unexpected chill ran down Luke's spine. He looked around, spooked, then shook it off.

Taking a deep breath, Luke said, "Bridge looks slick. I'll take it slow going across. Hey-up!" He hailed the horses and they began a steady trot. The clopping of their hooves echoed off the wooden planks. The wagon wobbled unsteadily as the wheels bit into the deep grooves in the bridge's floorboards.

As they crossed the river, Gabe looked to the left bank at the new slate mill that had been constructed on the burned-out remains of the Fairhaven Iron Works.

The first slate quarry in Vermont had opened two years earlier, along the north end of Caleb Ranney's property on Scotch Hill in Fairhaven. The quarry and mill were owned by the partnership of Ranney, Gabe's good friend, Colonel Alonson Allen, and Judge William C. Kittredge. The pounding of hammers and shouts of men intermingled with the roar of the falls.

"Wonder if the Colonel will make anything out of this slate business. Seems like a big gamble to me." Gabe raised his voice to be heard over the constant drumming of the water cascading below them. He wiped the mist from his face and beard with his sleeve.

Luke glanced at his father. "Don't know. But Colonel Allen is ambitious and determined to get things done his way." Luke laughed as he turned the horses right onto River Street, halfway up the hill into town.

To their right, upstream along the banks of the river, below the upper falls, stood the sawmill. Teams of horse-drawn wagons laden with logs waited to unload their cargo. At the corner of River and Cottage Streets, opposite the sawmill, was the Fairhaven Creamery. Three long, connected barns stretched east along River Street. Luke steered the wagon to the front of the receiving doors along Cottage Street, where an unloaded wagon was just leaving. He halted the horses and Gabe applied the handbrake.

Luke jumped down from the seat and circled around the horses to lend a hand to his father. From the barn opening emerged the creamery owner, John Boardman.

"Hey'ya, Mista Hoppah!" The Irishman grinned, approaching the two men and shaking Gabe's hand. The owner's long, reddish, gray-streaked hair and beard were matted from the rain. "How's that damn'd hill t'day? Heard she's a righ' bitch, with the mud an' all." His high-pitched laughter rang out over the churning inside the creamery, where men worked the various stages of cheese to completion. Thirty-pound rounds of finished cheddar encased in black wax were stacked on shelves along the right side of the barn.

As the three men discussed the weather and muddy roads, Boardman's workers began unloading the milk jugs from the wagon. To the left of the wagon was a tall pole with pulleys attached to two ropes connected to the roof of the creamery. The wide mouth of a funnel protruded through the top of the roof, where four men stood balanced, waiting for the incoming jugs. The men on the wagon attached a grappling hook hanging from the high rope to each handle of a milk jug. When they gave the signal, a man on the ground next to the pole turned a winch, pulling the rope, which hoisted the milk jug up to the waiting men. They detached the jug from the line and the milk poured down the funnel, flowing into the enormous vat on the floor of the barn. The empty pail was hooked to the second rope and pulley, and sent back to the Hopper wagon.

After discussing the weather, the men's talk turned to other pressing events. The Irishman, John Boardman, scratched his beard and stuck his hands into his pants pockets. "So wha'cha think of them Feds crackin' down on the niggers coming our way?" he asked Gabe and Luke. "Heard some boys be lookin' to cash in on catchin' themselves a few of those run'ways."

Luke and Gabe glanced at one another.

Gabe's face flushed with anger. "I think 'tis a damned fool law that just pits folks against one another for no good Godly reason."

Luke placed a hand on his father's trembling arm. "But there's nothing we can do, so we must learn to live with it, right Father?" Luke saw the emotion play across his father's face and squeezed his arm tightly, not wanting Gabe to expound on his convictions any further within earshot of the workers.

Gabe sighed and his shoulders slumped. "Yes, yes. Of course thee is correct, Luke. We must continue into town. Are we finished unloading?" Gabe turned to ask Boardman.

The creamery owner looked up at the pulley lines as the last milk can descended from the roof to the wagon. "Ay'yup, looks like we're done. How many we got, boys?" John asked his workers as they jumped from the wagon.

"Ten pails," one of the men yelled back.

"Lemme get your money, Mister Hoppah," the proprietor said, hitching his pants and disappearing into the creamery.

Gabe glared at Luke who shrugged his shoulders and released his grip on his father's arm. They watched the helpers secure the empty milk jugs in the wagon bed.

John Boardman returned from the creamery and passed Gabe a handful of coins. "Here ya go, Mister Hoppah. Guess I'll be seein' ya 'round."

Gabe counted the coins. *A fair price for the milk.* Although he didn't much care for the Irishman, at least Mister Boardman was an honest businessman and had never tried to cheat Gabe on his milk. Gabe stuffed the coins into his pocket. "I thank thee, Mister Boardman," Gabe said as he mounted the wagon seat. Luke settled next to Gabe, who released the handbrake. Luke clucked his tongue to get the horses moving and they continued traveling along Cottage Street.

When they were out of earshot of the creamery, Luke turned to Gabe. "Father, you have warned us that we must be diligent now. But you have been careless twice today." Luke watched the frown deepen on his father's face. "I don't mean to chastise you, but Buster saw you and Mother taking water to the barn this morning. And you let your emotions get the best of you just now."

Gabe wiped his face, scratched his beard and sighed. "Yes, thee is right, Son. I am tired from the long night and I must watch my words."

"We have always been careful with our activities concerning the cause, so we must not draw undue suspicion to ourselves, especially now." Luke turned the horses left onto Liberty Street, where they mounted the slope taking them to the level of Main Street and the village proper.

"I shall keep my thoughts to myself. I thank thee for the reminder." Gabe folded his arms and looked away.

Almost to the end of Liberty Street, Luke stopped the horses at a hitching post. The men disembarked from the seat, and Luke hitched the wagon team to the rail in front of the feed and grain store. Two other wagons were hitched beside them.

Dropping the back gate, Luke climbed into the bed of the wagon and slid the empty milk cans out of the way so he could untether the egg crate. Handing the crate down to Gabe, he jumped from the wagon and collected the eggs from his father.

"I'll take Mother's eggs to the grocery. I hope none of them cracked from that bumpy ride. Once I get her list filled I will meet you back here." Luke saw the sour expression on his father's face. "We'll be fine, Father. Please don't worry."

"Yes, yes." Gabe mumbled, head slumped as he entered the feed store.

As Luke passed the harness and saddle shop on Liberty Street, he noticed the owner, Zenas C. Ellis, their closest friend and neighbor, at his workbench. Luke nodded and Zenas waved back. Luke turned right on Main Street to deliver the eggs to the grocery store, located at the end of the L-shaped business district.

Carriages, horses, and wagons were hitched along the mud-filled street. Luke passed townsfolk conducting business at the shops occupying the lower floors of the three- and four-story brick buildings lining the thoroughfare. Women chatted on the wooden porch of the milliner's shop, comparing purchases. Men conversed on the steps of the tavern, next to the mercantile and dry goods store. A heavily loaded wagon had become mired in the muck in the middle of town. Luke chuckled as he stopped to watch men shouting and rocking the buckboard to free it, while other men urged the horses out of the mud. Luke passed the meat market, shoe store, and cabinet-maker's shop before he reached the grocery at the corner.

Inside the grocery, a woman and her daughter, whom Luke recognized but didn't remember their names, were at the counter bartering with the Welsh proprietor, John Jones.

When the store owner saw Luke, he tipped the brim of his cap then wiped his hands on his apron. "Be wi' ya in a wee bit, Luke."

Although the Welshman had lived in Fairhaven as far back as Luke could remember, he still had difficulty understanding the man's garbled accent. Luke nodded and stood a few paces behind the women, lowering the heavy egg crate to the floor. As Luke waited, perusing the store shelves stocked with dry goods, he spotted three men sitting in a semicircle in front of the wood stove at the back of the store. The two older men he knew by name. The third, a younger man with a rough-shaven face, and wearing a dark, slouch hat, was a stranger.

Snippets of the men's conversation drifted to Luke.

"…don't want no niggers as my neighbors, no sir!"

"…they can stay down South far's I care…"

Luke stared at the women in front of him, his back to the men, straining to hear more of their conversation. *This is why we need to be ever more careful, Father!*

"…done heard tell that Quaker Zenas Ellis fella out to south side be helpin' them fugitives get to Whitehall…"

Luke stiffened at the mention of their closest neighbor, and his father's good friend.

"…ya talking about that harness fella? Nah, I be doubtin' that. He's a good man—wouldn't be helping them niggers 'scape…"

"…maybe…done heard some boys gonna be keepin' an eye on him though—just in case…"

Just then, two men entered the grocery, their boots and trousers mud splattered. The first man wiped grime from his face. "Dang fool driver! You'd think he'd be able to keep his horses outta those deep ruts. Should'a gone along the edge, like most folks!"

The second man swiped his hands on his trousers. "Yep, but we got 'em moving. Least ways they didn't break a wheel with that heavy load."

The men sitting at the stove lowered their voices at the appearance of the new customers.

Luke caught just snippets of their furtive discussion.

"…posse…" One man mumbled something.

"…cash for niggahs…"

Luke thought the last voice belonged to the younger, unknown companion. To Luke's ear, his accent sounded French-Canadian, but there was something else about the man's speech he couldn't quite identify.

The women finished their transaction with proprietor John Jones, and left the store chatting.

Luke lifted the crate of eggs onto the counter. "Good day, Mister Jones. Here's Mother's list for today." Luke passed Emma's neatly written items to the grocer.

The man crinkled his red, bulbous nose, squinting as he read Emma's note. "Hmmm…sixty-eight eggs…hens layin' pretty good deese days, yah? Lemme see what t'ings I got for yo' Mum." The man stepped out from behind the counter to search the store shelves for Emma's items.

The men standing behind Luke continued discussing the stuck cart in loud voices, and Luke could no longer hear the conversation of the men at the back of the store. Luke tapped his foot impatiently, as John Jones meandered around the store, placing items on the counter. The grocer finally wrapped them all in brown paper, securing the package with twine.

Jones nodded to Luke. "Got'cha 'most eve'thin' on the list. Come back t'morra and get'cha crate, ya?" Jones said.

"Yes, Sir. Thank you. I'll do that," Luke said grabbing the package of goods. Not wanting to dicker with the man, as he had promised Emma, he rushed from the store to find Gabe.

CONCERN

When Gabe finished loading the bags he had purchased from Heman Lawrence at the feed store, he realized he needed to buy more rope. Leaving the horses hitched, he walked to the end of Liberty Street, and turned right onto the Main Street boardwalk, heading for the mercantile, owned by his friend, Colonel Alonson Allen. The Colonel had used profits garnered from the store to invest in the new slate mill being built along the banks of the Castleton River.

The shop was bustling with activity when Gabe entered. Colonel Allen and his fifteen-year-old son, Edward, stood behind the counter helping customers. The Colonel spotted Gabe immediately and greeted him. "Friend Hopper! How is thee?" he boomed.

"Colonel." Gabe smiled, tipping his wide-brimmed hat to the distinguished businessman. "I am well. I thank thee for asking, Friend." Gabe waited a few minutes, then took his place at the counter.

"What can I get for thee?" the Colonel asked.

"I shall need twenty feet of stout rope, please," Gabe said.

Edward, the Colonel's son, who was of slight build, with stringy black hair and a pale, pimpled complexion, responded in a high-pitched voice, "Yes, Sir. I'll fetch it for you." The boy awkwardly loped to the back of the store, where long coils of rope were kept.

While waiting for the boy's return, the Colonel addressed Gabe. "Will thee be attending the meeting tonight? I shall be looking for thy support to protest this infernal Fugitive Slave Act."

Gabe peered down at the sturdy, well-dressed, gray-haired man. The Colonel's clean-shaven upper lip twitched over his neatly trimmed beard. As one of the original founders of the Vermont Antislavery Society, Colonel Allen was a vocal advocate for social reform, including the abolition of slavery.

"Yes, Friend. Luke and I shall be in attendance this evening. 'Tis an unjust law that pits neighbor against neighbor for no good reason. Thee knows thee can count on our support." Gabe scratched his beard, worried about the daunting task he and Luke would face in transporting their current group of visitors safely.

Edward returned to the counter. "Here you go, Mister Hopper, twenty feet." The skinny boy handed Gabe the length of rope, wrapped neatly in a bundle.

Gabe dug two coins from his pocket and placed it on the counter. "I thank thee, Son." Gabe smiled at the awkward, timid boy. "Colonel, see thee tonight." He tipped his hat to the proprietor and exited the front door.

Gabe had barely taken two steps along the boardwalk when he felt his arm being grabbed from behind. Startled, he turned to see Luke by his side.

"Father! We must speak with Zenas immediately!" Luke whispered harshly in Gabe's ear.

"What is it, Son?" Gabe raised a brow at hearing his son's agitation.

"I cannot speak freely. Come! We must hurry." Holding his father's arm, Luke directed Gabe quickly along the walkway until they turned left, back onto Liberty Street, where the wagon was tethered. Luke rushed into the harness shop where Zenas Ellis sat at his work table. Gabe followed his son inside. A quick look around revealed no other customers in the shop.

Zenas rose from his workbench and smiled to greet his neighbors. "Gabe. Luke. What can I do for thee this day?"

Luke stepped close to Zenas and said in a low voice, "We must speak with you in private. It's important."

Zenas saw the alarm on Luke's face. Peering around, he nodded. "Yes, of course. Come into the back room." Zenas walked to his storeroom with Luke and Gabe following. Once inside, Zenas closed the door behind them.

Gabe stared at his agitated son. "Luke? What has happened?"

Luke set Emma's bundle on an open table space, and dragged a hand through his tousled hair. "When I was at the grocery, I overheard three men talking about the fugitives. Zenas, they said you were known in town for helping them escape." He paced a couple of steps. "Sounds like they're going to have men watching your place for any suspicious activity." Luke turned toward his father, then looked back at Zenas. "If they're watching your place, that means they could be watching us, too, Father!"

Gabe touched Luke's arm. "Keep thy voice down." Gabe tilted his head toward the closed door. "There may be customers."

Zenas' long, oval face compressed as he pursed his lips. "I made no secret in the past of my activity in transporting travelers in the open to the canal. So I presume it would be known in town. I have no visitors at present, but we must be more careful now, since there are those who would act against us."

"But we *do* have a package!" Luke blurted, then paced to calm himself. He exhaled, his voice lowering. "We may be detected when we're on the move."

Gabe turned to Zenas. "We may need thy help. What does thee suggest?"

"How many visitors does thee conceal?"

"There are four—two women, a young lad and a boy child," Gabe responded.

Zenas nodded and sighed. "What has worked for us under the new law is to load hay in the wagon, leaving space for the travelers, and cover the load. Then hang fishing poles and buckets from the end. If anyone asks your business, tell them you are going to the canal fishing, and then to deliver some hay to the barges."

Luke paced the small storeroom, whipping his hair out of his face. "I don't know, I don't know. Would anyone believe us?"

"I think 'tis worth a try, Luke." Gabe said, trying to calm his son.

There was a momentary lull, as Zenas crossed to the door, opened it slightly to check that no customers had entered, then quickly closed it. He asked, "When would thee be moving the package?"

"Hmmm…" Gabe pondered, exchanging a glance with Luke, and scratching his beard as he considered his options. "Today is Friday. I think early Sunday morning, before first light, as no one will expect us to travel on the Sabbath."

"I shall help thee prepare the wagon, then, if that is thy wish," Zenas said.

"I thank thee, Friend. Thy help is much appreciated. We must not waver in our resolve to do God's will, despite the risks."

Luke grasped Emma's bundle under one arm as Zenas opened the door for them to exit. Stepping into the shop, Luke noticed a customer perusing the harnesses hung along the wall, near the storeroom. Luke paused… *It's not one of those men I saw at the mercantile, but I hope this fellow didn't hear our conversation.*

Zenas waved at the customer. "Mister Wells. I shall be right with thee." Turning his attention back to the Hoppers, Zenas said, "Well, Gabe, could have sworn I had some back there. I guess I'll have to order it. Should have it by next week sometime."

Gabe nodded. "I thank thee, Zenas. That will be fine."

"Shall I see thee at the meeting this evening?" Zenas asked.

Gabe held the shop door open for Luke to pass. "Yes, we shall be in attendance. Come, Luke, we must head home."

At the hitching post, Luke stowed Emma's bundle of groceries between the lashed milk jugs, so it wouldn't bounce around in the wagon bed. Then he untethered the horses, and the men climbed onto the wagon seat. He steered the horses to Main Street, then turned left and guided the horses south, down the hill toward the bridge.

"Damn those men!" Luke said, relieved to be able to speak freely. "What is that stranger doing here stirring up trouble in our town? I wonder if I should have a talk with the sheriff."

Gabe shook his head. "Best to let this go for now. We may learn more at the meeting tonight. And, Luke, we shan't mention this to thy mother."

The knot in Luke's stomach stayed with him all the way home.

ELSIE'S TALE

After Emma gave Luke her grocery list, she returned to the anteroom where she removed her wet cloak and muddy boots. Stepping into the kitchen, she checked to see if the bread dough she had kneaded a short time ago had begun to rise. Satisfied with its progress, she went into her bedroom and retrieved her leather-bound diary, then sat at the kitchen table. As she waited for the yeast to finish its job, she dipped her quill and began to write.

10 mo. 11th, Friday, mid-morning, 1850

I am conflicted in my thoughts after Miss Elsie spoke of the actions of Master Swaley. It is unforgivable that a man feels he must use his power to force his way with his slave, especially when she was a married woman in the eyes of the Lord. I hope God shall punish him for this evil deed! Yet, how can I criticize Master Swaley's actions when he took Elsie's son into his household and educated the boy alongside his own? I am weary from the long night and I must remember what thee has preached: "Judge not, lest ye be judged." I shall make due diligence to follow Thine instruction and not judge the man too harshly for his abhorrent behavior toward Miss Elsie and her husband, Raymond. Now I must tend to lunch preparations for Thy visitors. In the Lord's name. Amen.

Emma returned her journal to the bedroom. Back in the kitchen, she kneaded the dough, formed it into loaves, put them into greased pans, and then, after giving the loaves time to rise, placed them into the oven to bake. From a smoked hock, she sliced ham steaks, then cut fragrant chunks of cheddar from the black-waxed wheel on the counter. As she prepared the midday meal, she hummed a gospel tune, thinking of the Prescott family.

I am truly blessed to have a solid roof over my head, my family close by, and my dear guardian angel, Ruth, watching over me. I cannot fathom the courage it must take to flee thy home in the dark of night, not knowing what uncertain fate awaits thee.

Then Emma donned her cloak and boots, and went to the well to pump a bucket of water. As she straightened to stretch her back, she heard a familiar voice.

"Gra'ma!"

Emma turned to see her three-year-old granddaughter, Martha, running across the mud-laden backyard, her skirts flapping in the breeze. Emma's daughter-in-law, Mary, tall and naturally slender, though now seven months pregnant, followed several steps behind, her long blond hair swept up under her bonnet.

Emma set the bucket down and scooped the little girl in her arms.

"Sweetheart!" Emma kissed the girl's cheek and untangled a curl wrapped around the child's bonnet string. "How's my favorite girl today?"

Martha wrapped her arms around Emma's neck and giggled. "Mama says Jesus loves me very much, so I'm happy!"

Emma grinned at Mary, then turned to Martha, still in her arms. "Yes, He does. Thy mother is right. Thee should be very happy today." Emma set the girl on the ground, and retrieved the water bucket.

"Good morning, Mother." Mary said. She smiled down upon her petite mother-in-law, then clasped Emma's arm and took Martha's hand.

"Come join me in the kitchen," Emma said, retrieving her bucket. Once in the kitchen, Mary and Martha removed their cloaks and sat at the table.

"Did the boys get off to school today?" Emma asked as she put the ham steaks into a greased skillet to brown them.

Mary smoothed Martha's long, tangled curls. "Yes, but Bernard has a cough and wasn't moving very fast. Fortunately, Brian is feeling well and got his brother going. I worry that Bernard's cough will get worse with the boys walking in this wet weather."

Emma tensed and kept her back to Mary. Memories of her sweet daughter Ruth flooded her. At age eight, the twins were just three years older than Ruth had been when she passed away. "Yes, thee should keep an eye on him. Don't let sickness take one of thy children, Mary!" Emma choked back a sob.

Composing herself, Emma poured two cups of tea for herself and Mary, and brought them to the table.

After sipping her tea, Mary said, "Luke tells me a package has arrived."

Emma raised an eyebrow and nodded toward Martha, sitting between them, playing with tendrils of her hair. "Little pitchers have big ears."

Mary stared at her mother-in-law for a brief moment, bewildered. Then she smiled. "Of course! Martha, Honey. I think your baby doll on Grandmother's sofa is lonely. Can you go sit with her and tell her the story of Baby Jesus?"

Martha beamed up at her mother. "Can I tell her Baby Jesus loves her like He loves me?"

Mary smiled. "You sure can! And don't forget to tell her about all the things Baby Jesus does for us." Mary touched her daughter's hand. "Now go along and find your baby doll."

Martha rose and jumped onto the step leading to Emma's main room. She cuddled her doll on the sofa, and began reciting what she knew about Baby Jesus, in her sing-songy voice.

Mary chuckled at her daughter's recitation. "Well, at least she remembers some of it!" Then, Mary leaned closer to Emma. "So, tell me of our visitors."

Emma briefly told Mary about the members of the Prescott family, but omitted the secrets Miss Elsie had confided in her.

Mary said, "I'm surprised there are women in this lot. It's usually just the men who make it this far north."

Emma nodded. "Yes, that's true. But Miss Elsie is a very determined, God-fearing woman. And her boy, Samuel, can read and write, which I think must help them on their journey."

Emma rose from the table and slid the ham from the skillet onto a plate. Checking her bread loaves, she determined they were done, pulled them from the oven, and placed them on the counter to cool. Then she laid the plates of cheese wedges and ham into a wooden crate, followed by a crock of hand-churned butter. Once the bread was no longer hot to the touch,

Emma sliced it into thick slices and placed them into a basket, covered with a cloth.

Emma turned to Mary. "I could use thy help to bring this to the barn if thee has time."

"Yes, of course, Mother."

"Martha!" Mary called. "Come, Honey. We must be going. Say goodbye to your dolly."

When Martha came into the kitchen, Emma handed her the covered bread basket. "Can thee carry this very carefully, Sweetheart, and not drop it?"

"Yes, Gra'ma. I can do that!" Martha replied, and with a determined look, grasped the basket in both hands.

"Thee is a very good girl!" Emma grinned at her only granddaughter.

Emma led the way to the barn carrying the food crate. Martha followed in her footsteps, focused intently on balancing the bread basket while Mary came after, carrying the water pitcher. Emma set the crate down and, with a heave, slid the squeaky barn door open a crack.

"Thee can leave the bread and water and I will take them from here." Emma motioned to the barn floor.

Martha looked confused and tugged her mother's skirt. "Mama, why are we feeding the barn?"

Emma and Mary smiled at one another over the girl's head. Mary started to speak, but Emma held up her hand and knelt on one knee in front of the inquisitive girl.

"Sweetheart, we have a sick calf in the barn and she's very hungry. So, we have to bring her lots of food." Emma grasped the girl's hands and stared into her crystal blue eyes. "Thee has been very helpful!" Emma kissed her lovely granddaughter's cheek and stood.

"Thanks, Gra'ma!" The girl grinned and did a little twirl.

The two women hugged one another. "If you need anything, let me know." Mary said as she grasped her daughter's hand. "Come, Martha, we have chores to do."

Once Martha waved goodbye to Emma and the mother and child crossed the yard to their house next door, Emma brought the food into the barn and pulled the stubborn door shut behind her. Walking to the open hatchway, she dropped to one knee on the barn floor.

"Hello? Miss Elsie? I have brought thee food. Can thee come to the ladder?" Emma kept her voice low as she beckoned the group in the underground room.

"Yes, I'm here." The earthen chamber flattened and muted the resonance of Elsie's response. "Samuel, go help Miss Emma."

Dropping to both knees, Emma passed the water pitcher, bread basket and crate through the hatch to Samuel who was balanced on the short ladder. Then she climbed down to join the family. Emma noticed they had bathed and changed into fresh clothing.

"Thee look much refreshed. I hope thy bath was satisfactory." Emma nodded toward the empty wooden tub.

Elsie grinned. "Oh, Lordy yes, Miss Emma! Like the Good Book say: *cleanliness is next to godliness,* and I's feelin' right close to the Lord jus' now!"

Both women chuckled as the family gathered around the small wooden table.

"Mmmmm, something smells good," Samuel exclaimed, while reaching into the box sitting atop the table.

Elsie smacked the boy's hand. "Now get yo' fingers outta there, Samuel, and wait yo' turn! I done brought ya up better 'an that."

"Yes, Mama!" Samuel laughed, and sat at the table next to Sarah, who held Jonah in her lap.

Sarah had changed into a pretty yellow and brown gingham dress and matching bonnet, which made her look younger than her eighteen years. But the bright dress only highlighted the dark look on her face.

Emma put the food on the table and set the crate on the ground nearby. She retrieved plates, silverware and cups from the nearby shelf, and placed them on the table.

"Shall we pray?" Emma said, after taking her seat. She clasped her hands together and bowed her head. The family in turn bowed their heads. "Dear Lord, we thank Thee for Thy blessings this day and for providing this food for our visitors. May Thee shine Thy grace upon them and keep them safe throughout their journey. Amen."

Elsie raised her head as a tear rolled down one cheek. "Amen. I thank ya, Miss Emma, for yo' kindness. May the good Lord bless ya."

Emma smiled at the solemn family gathered around her and felt at peace knowing she was doing the Lord's work. "Please, help thyself," Emma said, waving a hand over the small feast.

Elsie placed two slices of bread on her plate and smiled at Emma. "Ahhhh, the bread's still warm. Bless yo' heart!" Elsie buttered her bread and added ham and cheese to her plate. Sarah followed Elsie's lead and, murmuring softly to Jonah on her lap, added a little extra on her plate.

Samuel waited patiently, as instructed, then filled his plate with a sizable helping.

"I swears to the good Lord! That boy could out-eat a grizzly on any given day." Elsie laughed watching Samuel attack the slice of smoked ham.

Emma poured water into their cups as the family ate their lunch.

"Ain't ya eatin', Miss Emma?" Elsie asked.

Emma shook her head. "'Tis all for thee after your long and hard journey, but maybe I *shall* have some cheese," she said, reaching for a piece of the fragrant cheddar. "We make it here on the farm, finest around as far as I'm concerned!" Emma grinned.

Elsie nodded her head in agreement, chewing her food.

Emma waited for Elsie to swallow, then asked, "If thee doesn't mind my asking, would thee tell me of thy journey?"

Elsie took a sip of water. "Yes, 'm. Sure you wanna hear our sorry tale?"

Emma looked into Elsie's dark-eyed gaze and a shiver ran up her spine. *I have heard so many frightening tales from our travelers. Their journey is fraught with danger and I am thankful Miss Elsie and her family have arrived here safely.*

Solemnly gazing at Elsie, she nodded.

Elsie sighed and gave a small shake of her head. "'Member when I told you Chester done had the devil in him? I seen that boy doin' cruel things to animals on the plantation. Just warn't right. And then he be hell-bent to beat up on the slave boys ev'ry chance he done got." She took a bite of bread, her gaze traveling to Samuel, who now munched silently, eyes downcast.

"When Massa would catch him, Chester would get some punishin'. Then he'd mind his ways for a spell. But then he got real good at hidin' his acts so Massa woul'nt fin' out." Elsie shook her head and sighed. "One day I's in the kitchen cookin' an' I done hear a God-awful caterwaulin' comin' from the backyard. Thought some animal bein' butchered alive by that crazy Chester." Elsie reached over to touch Samuel's arm.

Samuel glanced sideways at his mother. "I'm sorry, Mama. Didn't wanna cause you no trouble." He dropped his head and chewed his food more slowly, clenching and unclenching his maimed hand.

Elsie glared at her son. "So I runs out the door an' I sees Samuel covered in blood, his hand wrapped in a rag! Lordy, how my heart done near stopped!" Elsie's voice trembled recalling the horrifying scene. "I finds out 'nother farm boy done helped him to the house. Samuel be a-screamin' somethin' fierce, all hunched over his po' cut up hand. After I got over my fright, it done made my blood boil."

Emma gasped and put her hand to her mouth, gripping her cheese wedge, forgotten, in her other hand.

"I pulled Samuel into the house and took him to the wash basin, thinkin' he done cut hisself. When I unwrapped that bloody rag, I screamed when I sees his first two fingers be gone!" Elsie sat bolt-upright in her chair, shaking with anger. "Just bloody stumps where those fingers once was." She sighed and slumped back in the chair, folding her arms.

Emma stiffened, her eyes wide. *Oh, God! How horrifying for both of them!*

In the chair opposite Elsie, Jonah struggled in Sarah's arms.

The toddler cried, "Wanna down! Down!" pointing at the ground. Sarah let the boy slide off her lap. The three-year-old ran over to the bed where they had slept and curled up under the blanket.

Sarah shrugged her shoulders and glared at the boy. "He's fussy and don' wanna eat. Can't make him." Features taut, she cast her eyes down at her plate and continued eating her midday meal.

Emma watched the light-skinned little boy climb into bed. He reminded her of her own sons when they were young. She turned to Elsie and asked quietly, "What on earth happened to Samuel's fingers?"

Elsie waved her hand in the air dismissively. "Don't rightly know. Samuel was babblin'—couldn't make no sense of his words." Elsie shook her head. "I washed his hand an' wrapped it in clean dressin'. Had the kitchen girl go fetch Massa to get help."

Sighing, Elsie said, "When Massa come in an' see Samuel, he be mad as a wet hen an' wanna know what happen. But Samuel just shook his head an' woul'nt say." She glared at Samuel, who continued eating, eyes downcast. "Massa got the doc to come over an' he done sewed up the stumps best he could."

"Oh, my goodness! How old was Samuel when this happened?" Emma asked, her face ashen.

"He be a young boy, meb'be five or six years," Elsie said, as she stared at the partially eaten food on her plate. "Done broke my heart to have my sweet boy maimed." She touched Samuel's disfigured right hand but he quickly pulled it away. "Samuel won't say nothin' 'bout what happen, even when Massa threaten' to whip his butt. I done 'spected Chester had somethin' to do wi' it—boy had the devil in him." Tears welled in her eyes and she swiped them away. "But then again, guess it mighta been one of the overseers—they all gots a mean streak." She shook her head. "And to this day, Samuel still won't tell me the truth!"

Samuel glanced at his mother, then down at the table and sighed. "Don't matter no more, Mama. I was just trying to protect our family. What's done is done—gotta live with it." He took another bite of ham, avoiding Elsie's smoldering gaze.

Elsie stared at her son, then shook her head in frustration. "That be when I starts thinkin' we needs to leave. I fear't for Samuel's safety and coul'nt be watchin' him every minute, ya know?"

"Yes. I can understand how thee would feel, always worrying about thy son's safety." Emma's hand trembled as she touched Elsie's arm. "But thee didn't leave then?"

Elsie's eyes darkened. "No, Ma'am. After Samuel healed some, he done gone back to his lessons with Chester. I was scair't when them two was together, always worried Chester be doing somethin' behin' my back. Figure since Samuel be gettin' edj'cated, we best stays where we was."

Elsie took a drink of water and stared at Emma. "'Twas what Chester threatened to do after Sarah birthed Jonah, that fine'ly convinced me we had to run, an' run far, to save my gran'son's life!"

SARAH

Absorbed in Elsie's story, Emma had stayed with her visitors longer than she had intended, as Elsie had continued her tale of what finally drove them to escape the plantation. Chores waited, so Emma reluctantly bade her farewell and carried the crate with dirty dishes back to the kitchen. She was shaking with rage at the injustices inflicted upon Elsie's family.

How can men be so cruel to other human beings? May God punish them for their earthly sins!

When the dishes were tidied, Emma retrieved her diary and sat at the table. The intermittent drizzle of the dreary day brought little light through the kitchen window. Emma lit the lantern and pulled it close to better see her journal. She dipped her quill into the inkwell and steadied her hand as she imagined the pain Samuel must have endured when his fingers were severed. *I believe the Lord must have something very special in store for Samuel, as it was a miracle he did not die that day.*

Emma remembered her boys growing up, with all the scrapes and bruises she had tended over the years. She thanked the Lord they still possessed all their fingers and toes.

Recalling more of their conversation, Emma realized it was only when Samuel had excused himself to use the privy upstairs in the barn, that Elsie had confided who Jonah's father was.

*I am aghast at the appalling attack on Sarah Miss Elsie witnessed when
she returned from her errands. Miss Elsie said she was in the kitchen of
the big house, when she heard Sarah's muffled screams. She ran upstairs
and burst into the guest bedroom. Rage overtook her at seeing her young,
virgin daughter, naked and bloody on the bed, held down by*

The clopping of horses' hooves halted Emma mid-sentence. She looked
out the kitchen window to see Luke and Gabe in the buckboard, returning
from town. Hand palsied with suppressed emotion, Emma hastily finished
writing her thoughts.

She closed her diary and returned it to the bedroom, her mind raging.

Donning her cloak and boots and making her way outside to the wagon,
Emma whispered, "Dear Lord, please keep Elsie and her family safe in Thy
loving grace as they continue their perilous travels. Amen."

She gathered her strength to quiet her trembling legs.

RETURN FROM TOWN

Emma huddled next to the wagon, arms crossed to protect herself from
the chill wind.

Luke stood in the wagon bed and handed down the grocery bundle to
Emma. "Here's most of the things on your list, Mother. I'm sorry I could
not get everything, but you know how Mister Jones is." He shrugged his
shoulders and turned back to grasp an empty milk jug.

Emma cradled the brown-paper-wrapped package in her arms. "Yes.
Yes. I know. I thank thee for bringing this much." Emma turned to Gabe,
who stood next to her by the wagon. "How was thy trip to town?"

"Hey'ya, Luke! Need help?" Buster yelled from across the pasture after
he and Enos had emerged from the cheese house.

"Yeah! Come give me a hand." Luke hollered back at the two men.

Gabe peered down at Emma. "It was fine, Mother. A little slippery going
down the hill, but the horses did very well with the load."

Emma stared up at Gabe's troubled face. "Please come in and have supper. Thee must be starved."

"I shall be in shortly after we unload and groom the horses." Gabe
watched as Buster and Enos offloaded the empty milk jugs and began
delivering them back to the cow barn.

Gabe turned to his son. "Luke, we must not tarry. We should leave within the hour to ride back to town for the meeting."

Emma's heart pounded as she carried her bundle back into the kitchen and placed the items on the shelves. *Something's wrong, I can tell from Gabe's expression. I wonder if slave catchers are already here and stirring up trouble. That would not bode well for us or our visitors.*

Her mind racing, she quickly prepared the same meal for Gabe she had fed their visitors earlier in the day.

When the jugs were unloaded, Gabe and Luke drove the wagon to the carriage barn and unloaded the feed bags. Luke unhitched the horses and brought them to their stalls, where he brushed them down and provided feed and water. Then they pushed the wagon into its spot next to the sleigh. Father and son walked together back toward Gabe's house.

"Mother has supper ready if thee would like to join us," Gabe said to Luke.

"Thank you, Father. But I should check on Mary and the children before we leave again. I will get the horses saddled shortly." Luke waved as he crossed Gabe's front yard to his house next door.

Gabe entered the anteroom, removing his overcoat, hat, and boots. Muttering under his breath, he sat at the kitchen table, buttered a slice of bread and added a cheese wedge, then took a big bite of the fare. As he watched his petite, gray-haired wife moving about the kitchen, his worried face relaxed and he smiled, remembering when they had first met.

It was May, 1819, a year after he had purchased the farm. Gabe's closest neighbor, Zenas C. Ellis, had invited him to attend an abolitionist meeting at the Methodist church in Sandy Hill, New York, some twenty miles to the west. Zenas, a founding member of the Vermont Abolitionist Society, had elicited Gabe's help on two previous occasions to transport slaves along their journey to Canada.

At the meeting, Gabe had listened to one orator after another rail against the inhumane practice of slavery. Getting a little restless, his gaze wandered to a lovely young lady with auburn hair, sitting with her mother in the pew across the aisle. He thought she looked like a fragile, porcelain doll with her glowing cheeks and neatly groomed attire. A couple of times during the meeting, out of the corner of his eye, Gabe caught her glancing his way.

When the meeting had ended, folks gathered on the church lawn as the sun rapidly dropped below the budding maple trees. A chill spring breeze stirred through the branches. Neighbors bade their farewells and hurried to their carriages to get home for supper. Gabe wanted to speak to the young lady before she disappeared. He bolstered his courage and awkwardly approached the group of girls she was speaking with.

"Pardon me, Miss," Gabe said, peering down at the top of her lacy, blue bonnet. Gabe's face flushed when the girl's friends giggled, linked arms and walked quickly away. The young lady's long skirts swayed as she turned toward Gabe. Before he could say another word, the girl's mother moved protectively by her side.

Gabe nodded politely to the primly dressed older woman, not much taller than her daughter, but a bit more rotund. "Madam. I would very much like thy permission to introduce myself." Gabe shuffled his feet and his hands twitched by his side.

The woman tipped her head up to peer into Gabe's face. "My, my!" she exclaimed. "You are quite the strapping lad, are you not?" Forcing Emma to take a step back, she said in a stern voice, "What are your intentions with my daughter, young man?"

Gabe blushed at her abrupt question. "No—no intentions, Madam. Thy daughter is lovely and I only wish to know her name." He tried to still his trembling hands.

Out of the corner of his eye, Gabe saw Zenas standing a few paces to his side, arms crossed, watching the scene unfold with great amusement.

The mother briefly nodded her head. "You may proceed."

Gabe turned to the girl. "I bid thee a fine evening, Miss. My name is Gabe Hopper. May I know thy name?"

The young, petite girl smiled and peered up at Gabe. "I am Emma Saunders. My father is the pastor of this church," she said. "That is him over there." The middle-aged man she pointed to stood outside the doorway shaking hands with men as they left the sanctuary. He wore a wide-brimmed black hat, black sack coat, white button-up shirt and thin, black bow tie. Gabe had been impressed with the pastor's passionate oratory to open the meeting, vehemently demanding those in attendance do God's will and abolish slavery at all costs.

"And this is my mother, Missus Rose Saunders." Emma put her arm around her mother's waist.

Gabe had bowed his head to the older woman, then turned to gaze into Emma's startling, light blue eyes. "'Tis indeed my pleasure to make thy acquaintance, Miss Emma. My friend, Zenas, and I are visiting from Vermont." Gabe waved in Zenas' direction. "The hour 'tis getting late and we wish to find lodging and sustenance for the night. Is there a place in town thee might recommend?"

Rose Saunders positioned herself between Gabe and Emma, then pointed in the direction of town. "The Wayfarer Inn is at the end of Main Street, one block over to the left. The innkeeper is Mister Gates. He is a fair man and will prepare you and your companion a hearty supper that should satisfy your hunger. Good evening to you, Sir." Rose nodded at the men, grasped her daughter's arm and started to turn toward their wagon. Emma hesitated.

"I thank thee for thy kindness, Missus Saunders," Gabe said, then turned to Emma. "I hope we shall meet again, Miss Emma. Thou art quite lovely." He blushed as Emma smiled up at him.

"I would like that very much, Mister Gabe," Emma said as she reached out to gently graze his hand. "I do believe Father will hold another meeting in a month's time. Perchance you and Mister Zenas will attend. Good evening." Emma had grasped her mother's arm and the two women walked to their carriage, hoisting their skirts over the muddy ground.

As Gabe watched them drift away in the fading light, he felt a tug on his arm.

"Well, well, Friend," Zenas grinned. "I do believe thee has made an impression on that young lass. She is quite a beauty, is she not?" The men walked companionably to their tethered horses.

Gabe flushed again and turned to his friend. "There shall be another meeting in a month's time. Will thee join me?"

Zenas laughed heartily and slapped Gabe on the back. "But of course, Friend. Thee shall need a chaperone to court such a lively filly." They had untethered their horses, mounted and rode together through town to the Wayfarer Inn.

A year and a half after their first meeting, Gabe and Emma had been married by her father, Pastor Saunders, in the Sandy Hill Methodist Church, in 1821. Gabe's closest neighbor and friend, Zenas C. Ellis, stood up for him. To show his devotion to his new wife, Gabe decided to forsake his Quaker upbringing and join Emma's Methodist congregation. On their wedding day, he was twenty-one and she was eighteen years of age.

Gabe reflected on their life together, watching Emma bringing the teapot to the table. *And some thirty years later we are even more devoted to the Cause, helping our travelers escape the shackles of oppression.*

Emma, watching her husband closely, poured tea into Gabe's cup. "What happened in town? Thee seems upset," she said inquiringly, placing a ham steak on his plate.

Gabe took a sip of tea and peered down at the table. "How do our visitors fare?"

"They are fine." Emma sat at the table and poured herself a cup of tea. "They have bathed, changed into clean clothes and eaten their midday meal. They seem to be in fairly good spirits. Why does thee ask?"

Gabe took a bite of ham, paused and stared at Emma across the table. "Because they will need to be in keen form for our travels." Gabe swallowed and took a sip of tea. The unsettled look on Emma's face prompted Gabe to reach across the table and touch her hand. "We shall be fine, Mother. Please do not fret. Thee knows we have made this journey successfully many times in the past."

"Did thee encounter slave catchers in town?"

"Not that I am aware of." Gabe cast a glance at his plate, not wanting to expound on Luke's encounter at the mercantile.

"And would thee tell me if thee did?" Emma stared at Gabe, suspicion clouding her eyes.

Gabe paused, then chewed and swallowed a bite of bread and cheese. "We have spoken with Zenas and he has offered to help us prepare the wagon," he said, ignoring her question. "We can no longer carry the passengers in the open as we have done before. We will stack hay into the wagon, and they can hide there." Gabe stopped eating as he stared through the kitchen window. "Zenas says we should make our journey appear as if we are going fishing. That has worked well for him whilst transporting visitors since this law was passed." Gabe ran his fingers through his tousled gray hair and shook his head.

"And what does thee think, Father?" Emma asked. Her hand trembled slightly as she held her teacup.

Gabe's forehead crunched and his voice boomed, "I think 'tis a shame we must resort to such trickery to transport our visitors along their journey!" He took a deep breath, lowering his tone. "But I do believe Zenas' plan would draw less attention than having them ride in the open."

Gabe's unexpected outburst worried Emma. "Well, when shall thee leave?" She tried to eat some of her supper, but her stomach had soured.

"If we can get the wagon set, and our visitors are ready to travel, we shall leave before dawn Sunday morning." Gabe peered through the window at the hay barn, gradually fading in the evening twilight.

"But, Father! If thee and Luke are not at Sunday prayers, it may raise suspicion." Emma watched uncertainty play over her husband's bearded face.

Gabe waved a hand dismissively. "Yes, yes. 'Tis possible. But if all goes well, I believe we can make the trip to the canal and be back in time for services. And if we do not return, remember, you can tell people we are tending a sick calf which has made us late."

Emma forced a wan smile at Gabe's reminder of their little white lie.

Gabe scratched his beard, causing small clumps of dirt to scatter on the table. "I must wash before we go to town." He rose from the table and poured water from the pitcher into a wash basin on the counter. Using a bar of lye soap, he scrubbed his hands, face and beard, then rinsed. Emma passed him a cloth to dry himself. Then he sauntered to the bedroom, muttering under his breath.

Emma busied herself cleaning the dishes. When she looked up, Gabe had returned to the kitchen wearing a clean white shirt and trousers, topped with his long, black Quaker coat and wide-brimmed black hat. His tangled hair and beard had been neatly combed. She smiled up at her lanky husband, his shoulders now hunched with age. *When did he get so gray? I still remember that young, handsome suitor who stole my heart so many years ago.*

"Thee is quite presentable for thy trip to town, Father," she said. "Please, do be careful."

Gabe bent over and bussed his wife's cheek. "We shall be fine, Mother. Do not fret thyself. Luke and I shall take care of one another. Now I must be off." In the anteroom, Gabe slipped into his riding boots and waved to Emma as he exited the back door.

With a sigh, she rose from her chair and retrieved her diary from the bottom shelf of her nightstand. At the table, she dipped her quill into the inkwell and pondered the uncertainty of a slave's life. *I cannot imagine the angst of never knowing when one might be ripped away from one's home, or when one might have one's family torn apart.* She imagined the danger of being forced to flee into the woods at a moment's notice, with the hounds of Hades on one's heels.

After writing the account of Elsie's plans to escape the plantation, she finished her entry with:

Dear Lord, please watch over Miss Elsie and her family this evening so they may sleep soundly in Thy loving grace. Amen.

Emma yawned and laid down her quill. She stretched her arms in the air and arched her back against the chair. It had been a long day and she was exhausted. She leaned forward, rested her elbows on the table, clasped her hands together and bowed her head.

"Dear Lord—"

A sharp knock on the anteroom door made Emma jump and squeal. *Oh, my! Who might that be?* Realizing she was home alone with her menfolk gone to town, she cautiously made her way to the outer door. "Who goes there?"

A man's voice said, "Miz Hoppah? It's Bustah. Sorry to bother ya, Ma'am."

Releasing her breath, Emma opened the door. Farm hands Buster and Enos stood on the stoop looking disheveled from their day working on the farm. "Yes, Buster. What can I do for thee?"

Buster's lopsided grin unnerved Emma. "Hope we didn't stahtle ya, Ma'am. We gotta be off to the meetin'. Wanted you to know the curds and whey are separated. They're ready for you to tend to in the mahnin'." He shuffled his muddy boots.

Emma stared at the two young men. She had forgotten they had been working in the cheese house most of the day. "Oh, yes. Of course! I thank thee for the help. I shall finish the cheese first thing tomorrow. Do ride safely to town."

Enos smiled and tipped his brimmed hat. "Yes, Ma'am. Have a nice evening." The two turned away and walked to their horses, tethered by the cow barn.

Emma closed the door and realized her legs were shaking. *Enos Adams is a polite young man. His father, Joseph, has raised him well. But there's something about Buster that makes me uneasy.* She paused for a moment, staring at the closed door. *Perhaps I should express my concerns to Gabe.*

Her heart still pounding from the interruption, she returned to the kitchen table. With her hand trembling slightly, she wrote one last entry.

Dear Lord. I know Thee works in mysterious ways and 'tis not my place to tell Thee how to do Thy work. I ask Thee bestow Thy shining grace upon Miss Elsie and her family. And please give us guidance as we do Thy bidding on this earth. 'Ye who helps the least of those among us, helps me.' 'Tis my prayer those who have committed sin and inflicted harm on Thy most vulnerable children, be made to atone for their sins at their time of reckoning. May Thee show mercy on their damaged souls. I pray this in Thy name, Lord Jesus Christ, our Savior. Amen.

Emma set the lantern and her diary on a table in the main room. She added several large logs to the wood stove, so it would burn through the night. Then she carried the lantern and diary to her bedroom where she changed into her night clothes, got into bed and snuffed the light.

I know Father and Luke have transported visitors to the canal before, but I fear for their safety and for the Prescotts, as the discontented hearts of men may seek to do them harm in the name of monetary gain. Unbidden, her thoughts switched to prayer: *Lord, I ask Thee to grant them a safe journey. Amen.*

RIDING WITH NEIGHBORS

By the time Gabe entered the stables, Luke had finished saddling their riding horses. The dreariness of the overcast day was quickly fading to early evening. Luke had secured a hooked staff to the horn and saddle of each horse. Gabe hung his lantern on the staff and mounted Faith, a gray dappled mare. Luke hung his lantern likewise and mounted Charity, a chestnut Morgan with a white star shape beneath her forelock.

"Is all fine with Mother?" Luke asked Gabe as they led the horses from the stable and began trotting north toward town.

"Yes. She is tired from the long day. Thee knows how she likes to fret about us. I assured her we would be fine." Gabe smiled, appreciating his son's genuine concern for his mother.

As the men passed Zenas C. Ellis' farm on their left, a voice hailed them. Gabe and Luke reined their horses and saw the two elder of Zenas' four sons, Zenas H. and Barnaby, emerging from the barn, leading their horses. Lit lanterns swayed from staffs secured on both mounts. At ages nineteen and seventeen, the boys managed most of the farm chores while their father tended to his harness shop in town.

"Luke! Mistah Hoppah!" Zenas H., the elder, called out. Taller than his younger brother, Zenas' long hair was pulled back with a tie beneath his felt, brimmed hat. "Goin' to the meetin'?"

Luke smiled and waved. "Evening, boys. Care to ride with us into town? We'd be pleased to have your company." He and Gabe sat waiting along the side of the road, while the two Ellis boys mounted and rode toward them.

"Mighty kind of you, Luke," Barnaby said. His long cloak spread over the cantle and onto the horse's rump. "We must find Father at the commons before the meetin' starts."

Gabe tightened the reins to control Faith, his mare, who had gotten skittish as the other horses approached. "We spoke with thy father earlier today and he said he would be there. We must move along so we shan't be late." Gabe relaxed Faith's reins and the horse trotted in the lead. Zenas H. rode next to Luke and Barnaby trailed the group.

Luke turned to speak quietly to his young neighbor. "May need your help tomorrow, Zenas. Father and I must load the wagon with hay. We're planning a trip to the canal."

Zenas raised his eyebrow and grinned at Luke. "You goin' fishin' too? Been on more 'en a few fishin' trips mahself lately. Imagine you gotta deliver hay to the bahge in Whitehall first, though, aye?"

Luke glanced sideways at his neighbor. "Yep. We have four special packages that need to get safely on board. Then we'll have time for fishing."

Zenas' face became serious as he kept abreast of Luke's horse. Leaning closer he said, "Been talk 'round town there might be some posses gathering, looking for folks *goin' fishin'*. Want me and Barnaby to ride on top of the wagon for ya?"

"I thank you for your offer, Zenas, but it won't be necessary. If you boys could come by after sundown and help us load the hay, that should be sufficient." Luke rubbed his chin and thought for a moment. "Oh, yes. If we could borrow two fishing poles and a bucket—I guess we will need those to catch fish." Luke grinned.

Zenas chuckled. "Yep, can't go fishin' without poles. Might look 'spicious."

Night had fallen about a half-hour later when the men arrived in town. The deep chill in the air highlighted the vapor streaming from the heavily breathing horses. The neighbors directed their horses along the trails crisscrossing the town common. To the right of the common was the business district and to the left sat the stately marble mansions of the town's founding families, including those of Colonel Alonson Allen and Joseph Adams, Enos' father. At the northwest end of the common stood the Methodist church, where men were gathering for the abolitionist meeting.

The four men tethered their horses to the split-rail fence bordering the common opposite the church. Gabe snuffed his lantern, but Luke kept his to light their way to the gathering. Zenas H. and Barnaby, each carrying lanterns, approached Luke and Gabe.

"We must locate Father to speak with him before the meetin' starts. I think that might be his carriage over yonder." Zenas H. pointed to a line of horse-drawn carriages hitched to the railing on their left. "We'll see you inside."

Luke touched Zenas' arm and leaned toward the youth. "No mention of our fishing trip to anyone, right? It's our secret."

"Of course, Luke. You know you can trust us. We've been fishin' aplenty!" Zenas grinned and grabbed his brother's arm as they walked toward the parked carriages.

TOWN MEETING

Gabe and Luke approached the steps of the spire-topped church. Men chatted in small groups, their breath billowing around their heads. Luke snuffed his lantern and set it on the ground next to the steps, where other lanterns were stationed, then joined his father to greet friends.

Inside, the two wide rows of church pews were filling fast. Townsmen gathered in groups along the center aisle, their loud discussions echoing off the high ceiling. Lighted wall sconces cast eerie shadows across the stained-glass windows.

The Hopper men viewed the scene. Gabe turned to his right, walking down the open side aisle. He and Luke squeezed into the end of a pew, about halfway toward the front. Arranged in front of the chancel were four chairs set behind a table holding several glowing lanterns. Prominent men of the town stood behind the table, their conversations mingling with the din echoing in the large chamber, which could seat two hundred parishioners. School-aged sons of the men in attendance playfully wrestled one another in front of the pews.

Gabe leaned close to Luke. "Men seem quite agitated this evening. I hope there is no violence," he said, scanning the crowded room. When Gabe looked back to the entrance, he saw his neighbor Zenas C., with sons Zenas H. and Barnaby, moving their way down the left aisle. They sat at the end of a pew, near the back of the room.

Luke followed his father's gaze. "I thought they would find a seat near us. Guess 'tis best we do not mingle, with all these prying eyes," Luke said in a low voice.

Across the center aisle, Gabe spotted Heman Lawrence, from whom he had bought feed earlier in the day. Sitting behind and to the left of Heman was John Jones, the Welsh grocery proprietor. Heman turned his head to view those at the back of the room, spotted Gabe and waved. Gabe tipped his head in acknowledgment.

Several cracks of the gavel by Joseph Adams, president of the meeting, sent men scrambling for seats. The back of the sanctuary was lined with hard-scrabble men, who chose to stand.

"Gentlemen! Please! Quiet down and take your seats." Dressed in a three-piece black suit, white high-collared shirt and black bow tie, the intense look on the leader's angular, gray-bearded face eventually brought an uneasy hush to the gathering.

Gabe watched the men now being seated at the front table. Colonel Alonson Allen, Joseph Adams' business partner in the new slate mill and owner of the mercantile, nodded toward the audience. Then he leaned to his right and said something to his nephew, Ira C. Allen. At age thirty-four, Ira, the short-statured, rotund partner in the Adams & Allen law firm, twisted in his seat to respond to this uncle's comment. At the other end of the table, next to Joseph Adams, sat Judge William C. Kittredge, also in partnership with Colonel Allen and Joseph Adams in the Fairhaven Marble and Marbleized Slate Company. Kittredge's high forehead blended into his peaked, balding pate. The three senior townsmen each owned a stately marble mansion situated along the west side of the common.

To the right of the main table facing the congregation, Colonel Allen's gangly, fifteen-year-old son, Edward, sat at a school desk, which had been brought in for the meeting. In front of the young man was an open leather-bound ledger, an inkwell, quill, and candlestick to light his work. The pinched look on the lad's pale, pimpled face reflected his unhappiness at having been tasked by his father to be the meeting scribe.

Joseph Adams struck his gavel and rose to face the gathering. "This meeting of the Fairhaven Temperance Society is brought to order on this good day, Friday, eleventh October, in the Year of Our Lord, eighteen hundred and fifty. All stand for the benediction," he ordered. The sound of muttering and shuffling of boots filled the chamber.

Adams bowed his head and clasped his hands. "Let us pray. Heavenly Father, please give us the courage and strength to do Thy will on this earth as we gather at this house of worship. Shine Thy loving grace upon Thy children who seek Thy mercy and everlasting forgiveness for our sins. We ask this in Thy name. Amen." Adams peered at the diverse group of farmers, laborers, local businessmen, and potential foes gathered before him. He sighed. "Please be seated."

When the crowd had quieted, Adams, still on his feet, commenced his oratory.

"The great State of Vermont was founded as the fourteenth state of this great Union in seventeen seventy-seven. Our State Constitution declares we shall forever be a free state against the tyranny of slavery!"

"Hear! Hear!" came the shouts of several men in the crowd.

Adams continued, "We have fought to uphold that constitutional status, but it is now being stripped from us without our vote!"

Grumbling erupted around the sanctuary.

Adams raised his hand to quiet the outburst. "President Millard Fillmore has appeased the Southern land barons by passing a most hateful statute, the Fugitive Slave Act, as part of the Great Missouri Compromise. As a free state, we are now required by law to issue arrest warrants, form posses, and return alleged runaways to their masters, with no proof of their status." Adams paced behind the men seated at the table. "And if we refuse to abide by this unjust law, we can be fined a thousand dollars. What a mockery of justice! The free State of Vermont will not stand for such an abomination! We must overturn this rotten law!" Adams' booming voice echoed through the silenced crowd.

A simply dressed man standing in the back of the room shouted. "Well, I sure could use some bounty money for turnin' in those fugitives." Others laughed or rumbled agreement.

Another voice from the nave chimed in. "And if we don't abide by the federal law, we'll all get 'rrested!"

Gabe turned back in his seat to see the speaker, Jeb Slater, standing next to his son Buster, Gabe's farm hand. Then he noticed his other farm helper, Enos Adams, slouching in the back pew. *I wonder why Enos is not in the front row, supporting his father, Joseph.* Gabe thought it odd behavior for the son of the Temperance Society president.

Gabe scrubbed his beard and whispered to Luke, "Jeb appears to be stirring up trouble. I do not like this at all, especially with Buster working at the farm."

Luke glanced at the tavern owner and his son standing against the nave wall. He noticed Jeb talking quietly with Jeremiah Wardwell, the middle-aged, portly town sheriff. Next to Jeremiah, listening to their conversation, was his deputized son, George. Luke had a bad feeling about that cabal.

Turning back to Gabe, Luke whispered, "I will ask Buster not to come to the farm tomorrow for work, if that is your wish, Father."

Gabe shook his head. "No. That would just raise suspicion. We shall give him light chores and ensure he leaves by midday." *I wonder how long it shall take us to prepare the wagon.*

Colonel Alonson Allen rose from his seat at the table. "Gentlemen! Your attention, please! We have been entrusted by the Negro travelers to provide them safe passage to Canada. Our neighbors and friends have always been able to move freely to accommodate their travels. We cannot now betray the trust of our fellow man in his time of greatest need."

One man yelled, "It is our duty to do God's will on this earth!"

Several answered, "Amen!"

Men conversed loudly in their pews.

Edward Allen scribbled rapidly in his ledger.

A thin man, wearing ill-fitting clothes, sporting a scraggly beard, yelled, "If I seen a niggah in town, you can be sure I'll round 'im up and take 'im to the 'thorities. T'ain't my place to decide if he's a runaway or not. I got a wife and kids to feed and I need the damned money!"

Luke recognized the man as a farmer from the north side of town, but he didn't know him well.

"Yup, me too!" another man yelled from the crowd, standing three-deep in the church vestibule.

Jeb Slater called, "It's the law, can't fight it. Might's well make some money. Don't give no truck to them niggahs being my neighbahs."

A lanky, grim-faced farmer from the western end of the parish stood and glared at Slater from across the aisle. "That law ain't nut'in' but a passel o' mischief! We let 'em get 'way with that law 'gainst black men, what's to stop 'em from passin' a law like that 'gainst white men nex' time?"

"'Cause white man t'ain't niggahs an' nevah will be!" Slater yelled back.

A chorus of angry rejoinders arose from both sides of the aisle.

The Colonel grabbed the gavel and pounded it several times. "Gentlemen! Gentlemen! Please take your seats!" He waited until the gathering had quieted. "Now, this edict is turning neighbor against neighbor, friend against friend, and it's not right! It has only been a month since it was signed. We cannot idly stand by and let this evil take root in our land. We must go to the legislature and fight it with all our wits." He waved his hand in the air.

"It was my cousin, General Ethan Allen, who led the Green Mountain Boys in the defeat of the British at Fort Ticonderoga. If he can do *that*, surely we, as steadfast Vermonters, can defeat this unjust law!"

"A great man—Ethan Allen!" William C. Kittredge piped up from his place at the end of the table, his long, narrow nose twitching.

Colonel Allen nodded toward his colleague and continued, "If General Allen's men could defeat the mighty British army, then surely we can stand up to our cowardly government who have forsaken the Northern free states for the riches of the South."

Men in their seats heatedly argued with one another, their voices echoing off the high-ceilinged chamber.

Joseph Adams rose, took the gavel from the Colonel and struck it several times. "Order, I say! Order!"

The men murmured but took their seats. Then Gabe watched as the only woman in the room, across the aisle from him in the second pew, rose to her feet. Wearing a slouched felt hat over her short gray hair, and a men's shirt, she hadn't stood out amongst the men in the pews. The crowd hushed as she strode to the front of the room. Standing a solid six feet tall, her sizable bulk made her an imposing figure. The buttons of her brown flannel shirt strained to corral her ample, drooping bosom.

The woman turned to the president. "Herr Adams. May I speak?"

Adams nodded. "Thee may, Widow Guildersleeve. Please! Quiet down, everyone!" He waved his hand at the gathering.

Luke grinned at his father. "We're in for hellfire and brimstone now. Lord have mercy on our souls!"

Gabe chuckled as Paree Guildersleeve prepared to address the rowdy gathering. He had great respect for the Prussian woman whose husband, Stanley, had been a good-for-nothing drunk, and wife-beater. Gabe remembered that morning back in December of '39, when Stan had been found slumped on the ground beneath a tree in the common, frozen solid, an empty skin of drink by his side. The sheriff concluded he had passed out there, drunk, the night before. The doctor couldn't determine whether the bloody lump found on the back of Stan's head happened before or after he had presumably fallen. No witnesses had seen him go down.

Not having children, Paree had petitioned the court to transfer the deed of her dead husband's land holdings into her name as sole proprietor. In a hotly contested battle—it wasn't proper for a woman to own land—she eventually won her case. Because there were no heirs to work her land, Paree now rented it to sharecroppers who grew grain for their cattle.

Gabe admired how, over the past decade, Paree had gradually bought land adjacent to her original tract west of town. Now her land holdings stretched to the New York border. These acquisitions made her one of the largest landowners and the richest woman in Fairhaven.

Paree addressed the congregation in her heavy Prussian accent. "Any of you men think you're going to form a posse and come on my land searching for fugitives, you've got another think comin'. I vill shoot first and let the sheriff come find you."

"Now Paree. T'ain't no need for violence!" called the north-side farmer.

"Oh no? Vell, 'til now, ve have been using my land to get the fugitives across to New York. And I intend to keep helping those who need to travel north." Her voluminous skirts swayed over her laced-up men's riding boots, as she strode back and forth. "I vill not abide by this unjust law. And may God have mercy on any man who thinks he can arrest me for doing God's vork on this earth. You vill be in the hands of the devil before the Lord knows you are gone!" Her face flushed with exertion.

"You threatenin' us, Widow? Don't sound like a wise thing to do," a man yelled.

Luke turned around to see the speaker, several pews back, was the creamery owner, John Boardman. Luke leaned close to Gabe, "That was Boardman. Those Irish sure do hate the Prussians. Don't think Paree will take much guff from the likes of him."

Gabe nodded at Luke's remark. *At least now I know where Boardman's loyalties are. Luke's right, I must be circumspect with my speech.*

Sitting at his school desk facing the crowd, Edward Allen dropped his head, covered his mouth with his hand and snickered, watching Paree parade in front of the gathering. He made no attempt to scribe her remarks.

Paree's husky voice echoed off the church walls. "I'm just varnin' ya…stay the hell off my land if you be doing the devil's vork 'cause I vill *not* stand for it!" She pointed a fat finger Boardman's way, then walked from the front and plopped down in her pew, facing forward. Crossing her arms in defiance, she ignored a surge of shouts from the rest of the crowd.

Luke murmured to Gabe, "Boardman's a fool if he doesn't take Paree seriously. She could easily beat the tar out of him or any man that steps foot on her land."

President Adams took back control of the meeting. "Gentlemen! Madam! We shall resolve this dilemma without turning to violence. We are a God-loving people and there shan't be need for such disturbances between neighbors."

Ira C. Allen, seated at the end of the table, spoke up. "What, then, shall we do? Our hands are tied by this law. We're damned if we help the runaways, and we're damned if we don't! And challenging this law in court would cost us a lot of money." The young lawyer wrung his hands in frustration.

Several men grumbled in their seats.

Adams raised his hand for silence. "We shall send men to the State Legislature to argue our case to overturn this unjust law and uphold Vermont sovereignty." He stepped several paces to his left and placed his hand on the shoulder of William Kittredge. "I propose the honorable Mister Kittredge lead our delegation, since he is our newly elected judge of the Rutland County Circuit Court. He has spent much time in Montpelier, and I believe he can eloquently state our case. All those in favor?"

A chorus of "Ayes" rose from the audience.

"All those opposed?" Adams asked.

A rumbling of discussion permeated the room. Despite the disapproval of certain men, no formal "Nays" were declared.

Adams continued, "The 'Ayes' have it then. Is this appointment acceptable to thee, Judge?"

Kittredge nodded to Adams and stood. "It is. I shall be honored to represent our interests at the State Capital. And I would request my apprentice, Cyrenius Willard, assist with our appeal." Kittredge waved his hand toward a stoic thirty-year-old lawyer, sitting in the front pew.

The young lawyer rose and ran his fingers though his shoulder-length red hair. "It is my honor to accompany you, Sir." He made a small bow to his mentor and resumed his seat.

Adams said, "That settles it then. I thank thee both for thy service. I wish thee Godspeed and success in thy endeavors to return Vermont to its former status as a free slave state."

"Zat settles nothing!" A man who had been tucked into a dark corner of the nave stepped forward. Glow from the wall sconce highlighted the man's gaunt face. "I'm offering ten dollars to any man who will join my posse to track the fugitives. For 'zere are run-ways zat come through here, *n'est-ce pas?* And I'll give another fifty for every one we bring in, *Oui?*"

A roar of voices erupted bouncing off the sanctuary walls. Suddenly, almost everyone was on his feet, arguing with each other, or gesturing in the direction of the stranger.

Dismayed at the mayhem erupting before him, Edward Allen squirmed at his desk. Hand shaking, he dipped his quill into the inkwell, only to topple the jar off the desk, splattering a large swath of black ink across the altar floor.

Luke gasped and grabbed Gabe's arm. "Father! That's the stranger I overheard today at the grocery!"

"Order! Order! Order!" yelled President Joseph Adams, banging his gavel.

BUSTER AND JEB

As Buster Slater tried to follow his father, Jeb, out the church's double doors, a sharp elbow pushed him to one side and a big boot stomped on his right instep. Buster swore and howled in pain, grabbing his foot. Off balance, he couldn't stop the melee of men swarming out of the church from pushing him through the open doors. Stumbling on the first step, Buster slammed into the backs of two men.

A burly, gray-haired man turned and grasped Buster's arm, yanking him forward. "Hey! Watch it," the man growled at him.

"Sorry! Sorry." Buster said, as he gained his balance and sidestepped the men, stumbling down the remaining marble steps.

Men gathered in groups outside the church, loudly debating the merits of whether or not to form a slave-hunting posse.

Buster scanned the dark churchyard and town commons across the road in search of his father. Several men carried lit lanterns but it was too dark to discern their faces. Limping, he plunged through the crowd and made his way along the railing to where his horse was tethered.

In the dark recesses of the common a familiar voice reached him. "Bustah! Ovah yondah." Buster staggered toward his father. Looking in that direction, opposite the church, he saw the glow of a lantern that had been placed on the ground. Buster could make out the dark forms of men gathered. He slogged his way through the deep ruts, grabbing trees to take the weight off his throbbing foot. When he reached the gathering, Buster leaned heavily against Jeb's shoulder. Nearby, men talked in hushed whispers.

Jeb looked at his son's pained expression. "Whassa mattah with you, boy?"

Buster bent over, rubbed the top of his right foot. "Some id'jit stepped on me! I'll be all right." Gaining his composure, Buster nodded at the man whose outburst had ended the meeting. "Who's that guy?"

Jeb grabbed Buster's arm and pulled him back several paces from the group. "Name's Pierre Duschanne. Says he's from N'Orlans. Huntin' niggahs to bring 'em back to their mastahs so he can get paid." Jeb rubbed his long, straggly beard. "Been seein' him at the tavern for a week or so now. We need to lis'en to what he's gots to say." Jeb pulled Buster closer to the huddled men.

"...be needin' some brave men who can help me uphold the law of the land," Duschanne said, standing in the center of the group. "Got some owners looking for their run'ways. But, *mon Dieu*, don't matter much to me. A niggah's a niggah. All of em's worth money at auction, *n'est-ce pas?*" Pierre waved his hands in the air, his French accent becoming more pronounced.

"Yup, sure 'nuff," one man in the group mumbled.

"Sure could use some money mahself," another chimed in.

Jeb stepped a few paces forward. "You says you're paying ten dollahs to help you out, and anothah fifty for every niggah we catch. Ain't that rayght?"

Duschanne stepped closer to Jeb, his stubbled face sizing up the older man and his long beard. "You're the tavern owner? Zsheb, *n'est-ce pas?*"

Jeb looked to his left and right, trying to read the expressions of the men in the group. He didn't know if they were going to join the posse, but he knew he and Buster were in.

"Yep, and this here's ma son, Bustah." Jeb pulled Buster forward. "We're both with ya and Bustah's a damned good ridah." Jeb's voice rose as he patted Buster's shoulder.

Buster grinned at his father's compliment, trying to keep weight off his damaged foot. "Damned right! And I gotta nose for niggahs! Jus' like them hounds."

The men in the circle laughed.

Loud voices echoed into the common from the church lawn.

"...we shan't fight over this!"

"...still gonna be trouble, no matter what—"

The men paused as Duschanne stared across the common toward the men still gathered in front of the church. Then the stranger turned back to the group and shook hands with Jeb and Buster. "Mais, oui! Most excellent. Glad you can join our cause. And you, *Messieurs,* will you join us?" He swept a hand over the men gathered in a circle.

The other five men shuffled forward to introduce themselves to Duschanne and shake his hand. One of them was the disheveled northside farmer who had complained he had a wife and kids to feed.

Duschanne motioned the men to come closer to him and lowered his voice. "You gents being local, I'll bet you know who's been hidin' ze niggahs, *n'est-ce pas*?" He peered at the men's faces eerily illuminated by the ground-level lantern light. "I will need to know where those farms are. We want teams of two to watch for any suspicious behavior. You see anything out-the-ordinary, then you come back to Zsheb's Tavern and report in. *Comprenez-vous*?"

"Yeah, we understand," one man replied.

A big, burly hulk of a man with a wide, dull face spoke up. "We know them niggahs crossing Paree's land to New Yawk. But she's got a big place—tough to spy on her—and her dogs be jus' plain mean if she sicks 'em on ya." The lout rubbed his right forearm. "Dogs done got me good one nigh' when I was out there huntin'."

The men chuckled and Buster turned to the dim-witted man. "Well, Cyrus, you should'a knowed better than to be messin' with that old hag. Ever'body knows she kill't her husband! 'Cept Sheriff couldn't prove it. You're a damned fool to be on her land, 'specially at night. She coulda kill't you, too!" Buster flashed his crooked grin.

A round of laughter spread through the group. "Yup, Bustah's surely right," another man chimed in. "She's crazier'an a wet hen. Need to steer clear of her."

Duschanne waved his arm in the air. "*Messieurs*! We will try to avoid Paree and her dogs. Now, *ecoutez, s'il vous plait*! Does anyone know of other farms hiding fugitives?"

The north-side farmer spoke up. "I know of a couple places east of here, 'round Lake Bomoseen, where they're bringing niggahs in from Rutland. Them farms should be easy to watch."

Duschanne patted the man on the back. "I thank you, Elmer. I'll put you in charge of showing ze men those farms by ze lake."

Elmer slightly straightened his rounded shoulders and spit a clod of tobacco to his side. Most of his teeth were missing. "Sure 'nuff. Long's I get paid for ma services."

"Yes, *Monsieur*. You shall be well paid, trust me." Duschanne turned to the other men hunched in the group. "Anyone know of other farms where fugitives might be hiding?"

An older man who had been at the grocery with Duschanne earlier in the day spoke up. "We told you today 'bout that Zenas Ellis fella out to south side. He's known to help the niggahs—ain't never made no secret of it. Pro'bly be good to keep an eye on his place."

Duschanne nodded his head. "*Qui! Merci!* Who can watch ze Ellis place for us?"

Buster leaned into the group. "I can do that. I work at the next fahm south, so I can keep an eye on it for ya."

"*Bien*. Good," Duschanne said. "Thank you for your service to ze cause, Buster."

Buster beamed. Jeb patted his boy on the back.

"Any other places you boys know of?"

Carl Yates, a bearded, middle-aged man said, "Yep, there's a fahm west on the Whitehall road, just before the bordah bridge, 'cross from Paree's land. Been known to harbor the run'ways in their bahn."

"*Très bien,* Carl. Can you get another man to cover ze place with you?"

Carl said, "Yep, my son here, Paul, can help since we live ovah that way."

"So when's we getting paid anyhow?" Elmer, the north-side farmer, blurted.

Duschanne pulled Jeb aside and spoke with him quietly for a few moments. Jeb nodded.

Duschanne said, "You gents come to Zsheb's Tavern tomorrow at noon. You'll get your first ten dollahs then." Duschanne paused and looked at the rag-tag group of men. "You're my lead posse, but I could use another five men. Anybody else you bring in, I'll pay 'em five dollahs and twenty-five per niggah. Y'all got that straight?"

"Yup!" "Yes, Sir." "Sure 'nuff. " came the responses from the gathering.

"Hey! You over there!" A shout came from across the common. A large-framed man wearing a stiff brimmed hat illuminated by the lantern he carried, trotted in their direction.

"It's the sheriff. We should get—" one of the men said.

"Don't want no more trouble tonight! Be off with ya now. You boys get on home!" Sheriff Wardwell hollered as the men scattered through the trees.

Buster grabbed Jeb's arm. They circled wide around the lawman, Buster limping on his sore foot, staying out of the lantern glow. When they reached their horses, they crouched and waited, watching the sheriff's progress following a man through the common.

"Let's go!" Jeb said to Buster. Both men mounted their horses and rode the opposite direction from the sheriff's light.

TROUBLED NIGHT

The fifth chime of the mantel clock in the main room awoke Emma to start her day. Gasping from a troubled dream, her thoughts were confused as she came fully awake. *What was I dreaming? Gabe and Luke were there—in some kind of trouble. Why did it scare me so? And were the Prescotts there? Maybe. I cannot remember.* She shook her head to clear her thoughts and let the ghastly images fade.

Peering over to the opposite bed, Emma made out Gabe's bulk under the covers. *I did not hear him come home last evening. He must have been careful not to wake me.* As quietly as she could, she groped her way across the room and made use of the chamber pot in the corner. In the dark, she changed from her nightgown to her day dress, tidied her hair, and donned her bonnet. Not wanting to wake Gabe, she grasped the unlit lantern next to her bedside and gently closed the bedroom door behind her. In the main room, she lit the lantern and stoked the wood stove.

Once in the kitchen, she stirred the remaining embers in the cook stove, added kindling, waited for it to ignite, then added larger pieces of wood. She grasped the water pitcher near the wash basin to fill the tea kettle on the back of the stove. The pitcher was empty. Emma sighed as she remembered Gabe had washed before going to town, and the water buckets were empty. After donning her cloak and boots, she tossed the dirty water from the wash basin out the door and returned it to the counter.

Grasping the empty bucket and the lantern in one hand, she pushed her way through the heavy outer door. East of the house, gray dawn light seeped beneath heavy cloud cover. Emma sniffed the cold, moist air. *Smells like snow.*

The deep, muddy ruts in the yard had hardened with the colder weather. Emma stepped carefully to avoid twisting an ankle on her way to the well. Balanced on the wooden platform, she grimaced as she gripped the frost-covered handle. Grunting, she used all her strength to prime the frozen pump to get the water flowing. When the bucket was full, she grasped it with one hand and held the lantern high with the other, making her way back into the darkened house.

After removing her cloak and boots, Emma filled the pitcher, and poured hot water into the teapot and added loose tea. She then poured clean water into the basin for her and Gabe to wash. Placing a cast-iron pot onto a front stove burner, she poured water and added several pinches of salt. From the shelf, she removed a sack of rolled oats and set it next to the stove to make porridge for Gabe, herself and their guests.

About fifteen minutes later she heard noises coming from the bedroom, boards creaking, then heavy footsteps crossing the main room. She looked up to see Gabe standing in the kitchen doorway, looking every bit of his fifty years. Stooped at the shoulders, with his hair mussed, he looked as if he hadn't gotten much sleep the previous night.

She smiled at her disheveled husband. "Come sit. I shall pour some tea."

Gabe stepped down and shuffled to the table, where he sat down heavily.

Emma set two saucers and teacups on the table, poured tea through the strainer, then joined him at the table. "How was the meeting last night?" She watched Gabe's face for any telltale signs of trouble.

Gabe sipped his hot tea and stared at the table. "Hmmmm," he said. "It was fine, I suppose. Joseph Adams is sending William Kittredge and his apprentice to Montpelier to argue our case against the Fugitive Slave Act in the legislature."

Emma noted Gabe's distracted expression. *Is he just tired, or is there more?* "Kittredge? Did he not just get elected judge in Rutland County? He should represent our needs admirably, I should think."

Gabe waved his hand in the air. "Yes, yes. He is very qualified to state our case. I wish them Godspeed and a fair resolution." Gabe stared out the kitchen window as dawn light slowly brought the hay barn into view. Distracted, he ran fingers through his tangled hair.

"Father, thee seems troubled. What else happened at the meeting?" Emma knew the signs of his distress.

Gabe stared into his tea then looked long and hard at her. "Ummmm—" A long pause ensued, then he cleared his throat. "Nothing happened. Luke and I rode back with the boys to accompany Zenas' carriage. It was late when I got home and I tried not to wake thee."

He's hiding something. "Gabe Hopper! If there is something thee is not telling me to spare my feelings, thee had better speak up now!" Emma's outburst surprised her.

Gabe shook his head. "Very well, Mother. If thee must know, the good woman, Paree Guildersleeve, got to arguing with some uncouth men. Adams got the meeting under control quickly, so all is fine."

"But what were—" Emma stopped at hearing the clock chime and the clopping of horse's hooves coming into the yard.

Gabe rose and cracked open the outer door to see Buster and Enos arriving for chores. He returned to the kitchen and bussed the top of Emma's head. "'Tis five-thirty and the boys are here so we need to get to milking. Please do not fret thyself, Mother." Gabe reached down and squeezed her hand. He returned to the anteroom, donned his boots and cloak, then exited to meet the workers.

That infernal man! I know he keeps secrets. He does not fool me. I shall talk with Luke later.

Emma peered out the kitchen window to see Luke passing behind the house to meet Buster and Enos. She watched Luke and Gabe help the farm hands unsaddle their horses and put them out to pasture. Then the four men, bundled against the cold wind, made their way toward the cow barn in the steely morning light.

In the outer room, Emma slid on her rubber boots, donned her hooded cloak and grasped her egg basket. A cold wind slapped her face once she entered the yard and she moved quickly beyond the hay barn to the chicken coop.

Back in the kitchen, Emma went through her daily routine of laying the eggs in layers of straw in the wooden crate. "Only forty-two today," she mumbled to herself as she made note of her count. "'Tis getting colder and the hens aren't laying like they do in the summer." As she covered the crate to be taken to town, she felt disheartened at the thought of winter looming.

Turning her attention to the boiling water, she added rolled oats to the pot, then she poured a healthy serving of maple syrup into the mixture along with cinnamon, and stirred the mixture. Using potholders, she slid the heavy pot to the back of the stove to simmer.

Grasping the lantern from the table, Emma stepped up into the main room and opened the cellar door directly to her left. She carefully made her way down the steps in the darkness to the dirt floor. Shelves of canned goods lined two walls and root vegetables filled bins along the opposite walls. Emma selected two jars of applesauce, then slowly climbed the steep stairs back to the main room.

While preparing breakfast, scattered visions from Emma's dream floated in and out of her mind. A flash of Elsie struggling in churning water made Emma gasp. She closed her eyes and gripped the counter to steady herself. Opening her eyes, she saw her hands trembling.

Is this a premonition, or has this already happened? Dear Lord, what has me so troubled today? Why is my stomach sour? My hand trembles and I cannot help but feel trouble is on the horizon. I do not think Gabe is being forthcoming with me. I must speak with Luke when chores are done. He will tell me the truth!

Emma placed a large bowl of porridge, a ladle, jars of applesauce, and the empty water pitcher into a wooden crate. Peering out the kitchen window, she could just make out light snowflakes sputtering to the ground in the dim morning light. Once again, she donned her heavy cloak and opened the outer room door. She looked toward the cow barn to make sure she wasn't being watched. Lantern light glowed from the open barn door. *Good. Milking is in progress.*

She carried the crate into the yard and lightly kicked the door closed behind her. At the pump, she refilled the water pitcher. "Dear Lord. Please keep us all safe in Thy loving grace," she muttered, walking to the barn to wake and feed their visitors.

BOYS ARGUE

Luke sat with his wife, Mary, at their kitchen table, lit by lantern glow, eating breakfast. It being Saturday, Mary had let the children sleep a bit later than usual.

Mary yawned and rubbed her pregnant belly. "This one had a busy night and kept waking me up. I just might go lie down after you leave."

Luke grinned at this wife. "Don't worry, I won't tell your secret." Then his smile faded. "And I would appreciate it if you don't tell Mother the secrets I told you about our trip to town yesterday and the meeting last night." He waved a hand toward Gabe and Emma's house. "You know how she worries."

Mary touched Luke's hand. "I worry, too. But no, I won't tell Mother about the slave hunter in town. I know it would just upset her."

Hearing horses approaching the house, Luke rose, walked into the living room and peered out the front window. Buster and Enos rode together, arriving for the day's chores.

Luke donned his coat, boots, and hat, then kissed Mary's cheek before heading for the back kitchen door. "Go enjoy your nap before the children get up. You need your rest now more than ever."

Mary smiled at her tall, handsome husband. "I will!" she said, rising to set their dirty dishes on the counter.

Outside, Luke tightened his coat against the chill wind, as snowflakes swirled in his wake. Moving between Gabe's house and the hay barn, his mind replayed the events of the meeting the previous evening. *I hope our boys didn't get swayed by that rabble-rouser. He's just out to cause trouble and get folks riled up for the sake of a dollar.*

Luke greeted his workers as they rode into the yard, "Morning, boys. Looks like we're getting a touch of snow."

Buster and Enos dismounted and wrapped their reins around the rail.

"A mite early for snow if you ask me," Enos said, looking chipper and clean-shaven. "Hope it doesn't stick." Enos unbuckled the girth straps holding the saddle, lifting it off the horse's back.

At that moment, Gabe joined the group in the yard.

Luke grabbed the pommel and helped Enos perch the saddle over the rail, then crossed behind Enos' horse to help Buster tend to his tack.

Buster's straggly brown hair hung from his felt hat in odd directions. Grinning, he rubbed a hand over his stubbled beard. "Mornin', Luke. Mornin', Mistah Hoppah. So, what did ya think of the meetin' last night?"

Luke helped Buster hoist his saddle onto the railing. "I think it did not end well." He shook his head. "Any idea who that stranger was that got everybody so riled up?"

Buster pulled the blanket from his horse's back and flopped it over the fence. Not making eye contact, he said, "Nope. Sure don't, Luke. But I can always ask my fathah. Bet he'd know, being at the tavern an' all."

Luke held open the gate for Buster and Enos to send their horses into the pasture, then closed and latched it. The four men crossed the yard behind the carriage barn, then walked to the south end of the cow barn on their right. The early light of the cloudy dawn barely lit their way.

Walking next to Enos, Gabe scratched his beard and said, "That stranger is just causing trouble and pitting God-fearing neighbor against neighbor. We do not need such rabble-rousers in this town."

Enos Adams nodded. "Yes, Sir. My father was roaring mad about the way the meeting ended. Said he's going to talk to Sheriff Wardwell to see if we can run that man outta town before he causes more trouble."

Buster, following behind with Luke, spoke up. "Mistah Hoppah. If I find out who that strangah is, I'll be sure to let you know, Sir."

Gabe entered the dark cow barn and lit four lanterns, then turned to Buster. "I thank thee, Buster, but do not trouble thyself unnecessarily. I am sure Sheriff Wardwell shall apprehend the scoundrel in good order."

Gabe handed a lantern to each of the men. Luke and Buster walked to the south end of the barn. Luke turned left, pulled up a stool and began milking the first cow on the row. Buster turned right and began milking that row. Gabe and Enos walked to the north end of the barn and each began milking the cows from the opposite end of the rows. Cows mooed, plopped, swished their tails and shuffled their feet as the milking began.

Several hours later, when the milking was done, Luke retrieved Emma's crate of eggs and secured it under the wagon seat. Then he and Gabe helped the farm hands tie down and secure the milk jugs. The snow squalls had temporarily subsided, leaving the day overcast and chilly. Buster and Enos retrieved their horses from the pasture, saddled them and rode alongside Luke, who drove the buckboard into town.

When they finished unloading the milk jugs at Boardman's creamery, Luke addressed his workers. "We won't need your help again until Monday, boys. Father and I will take care of the milking tomorrow before worship."

Enos' brow wrinkled. "You sure about that, Luke? We'd be happy to help."

"I thank you, Enos. With the weather turning cold, tomorrow's milk will hold a day and we'll make a double delivery on Monday, so take the day off."

Buster shuffled his feet and flashed his crooked grin. "Sure 'nuff, Luke. I got somewhere I need to be anyhow. See you Monday."

Buster and Enos mounted their horses and started to ride away. Luke yelled after them, "You boys stay out of trouble tonight, ya hear!"

Buster turned back in his saddle and broadly doffed his hat, "Sure, Luke! You know us bettah 'an that!"

Luke chuckled, knowing full well Buster would probably spend Saturday night at Jeb's tavern. He mounted to his seat, released the brake, and directed the horses around the block from the creamery to Main Street. Navigating among riders, carriages, and wagons along the wide thorough-fare, he found a hitching spot near John Jones' grocery. He untied Emma's egg crate and delivered the lay to the proprietor.

A few minutes later, Luke returned to the boardwalk, carrying Emma's empty crate from yesterday's delivery and her credit slip from today's eggs. Unhitching the horses, he noticed Buster and Enos, facing one another, engaged in what looked like a heated discussion. The men stood in front of Jeb's tavern, halfway down the business district. Luke couldn't hear their conversation over the din of the townsfolk around them, and resisted the temptation to move closer. As he watched, Buster said something, force-fully stabbing his forefinger into Enos' chest, causing Enos to take a step back. Enos, looking surprised, shook his head, raising his hands in the air in a gesture of exasperation or defeat—Luke couldn't tell which. Then Buster roughly grabbed Enos' arm and pulled him through the front door of the tavern.

I wonder what that was all about. Those boys don't usually argue.

Luke secured Emma's crate beneath the wagon seat and turned the horses to head south on Main Street. The horses startled as the daily noon whistle, atop the highest building in town, wailed its high-pitched screech.

"Easy! Easy!" Luke reined the horses to settle them down. After the horses slowed, Luke noticed the dim-witted man, Cyrus Wilmington, grinning vacantly as he held open the door to Jeb's Tavern. The man's imposing bulk blocked most of the entrance.

Why in heavens name is Cyrus wearing such a fancy black top hat in the middle of the day? He looks ridiculous and people are staring at him.

As Luke rode by, he saw several men pat Cyrus on the back and scurry into the darkened tavern.

Isn't that the farmer from the north of town who was at the meeting last night? What was his name? Elmer, I think. Wonder what business he's got at Jeb's place. Thought he was dead broke.

With a goofy sneer on his face, Cyrus followed the men into the drinking establishment.

Because Luke's wagon had crested the hill on his way south to the bridge, he did not see Sheriff Jeremiah Wardwell and his son, George, entering Jeb's Tavern a moment later.

LETTERS

When the morning chores were done, Gabe returned to the house to have his breakfast. Entering the anteroom, he brushed the snowflakes from his cloak before he hung it up, and removed his muddy boots. In the kitchen, he rubbed his cold hands together above the stove as the circulation returned.

He saw Emma had added clean water to the wash basin and he silently thanked her. He scrubbed his hands and bearded face then ran wet fingers through his long gray hair to remove the tangles. When he straightened, a spasm of pain in his back made him gasp. He massaged the offending muscle.

Ahhh, those chores make my bones weary.

He ladled a bowl of porridge from the pot, poured a cup of tea, then set the items on the kitchen table. In the main room, Gabe retrieved two pieces of paper, envelopes and his seal stamp from the desk beneath the mantel clock.

Sitting down heavily at the table, Gabe sighed, rubbed his eyes and ate a spoonful of porridge. *I still cannot believe that slave hunter had the gall to disrupt our meeting last evening. Joseph Adams and the sheriff should have dragged him out of there by the scruff of his neck for causing so much trouble.*

He rubbed his weary eyes.

Heard one man say the stranger was from Savannah, another said he was from N'Orleans. The only thing I know is he is a Southerner here stirring up a hornets' nest.

Gabe took a sip of tea and another bite of porridge.

Wonder if he got any of the men to join his cause. Probably did—lots of ne'er-do-wells who would sell their souls for thirty pieces of silver, just as Judas betrayed Jesus. I can only hope Sheriff Wardwell tracks him down and sends his evil soul packing back down South. Any man who would sell another human being is nothing but a disciple of the devil himself!

Gabe's outrage made his hands shake and he clasped them together atop the table. He expelled a deep sigh to calm his thoughts. Scenes from the previous night's meeting flashed through his mind as he ate more porridge. He remembered Paree Guildersleeve's dire warning to stay off her land. Smiling, he thought of the men in town who steered clear of her. He and Emma had always enjoyed a cordial relationship with the strong-willed, like-minded woman.

I have often wondered if the rumors are true about Paree killing her husband. She certainly did not look overly grieved at Stan's funeral. She was probably glad to be done with his drinking and slovenly ways. I guess only she and her Maker know the truth. He briefly glanced to the ceiling. *It would be a fool's errand to challenge that woman to a head-to-head duel, because, as Luke said, she could beat the living tar out of nearly any man in town.*

Gabe sipped his tea, thinking of the task he and Luke were about to undertake.

Paree has done well for herself as a widowed woman. I cannot help but worry how Emma would fare, should I pass to the Lord before her. But I am thankful she has Luke and Adam to care for her in her old age.

Gabe ate the last of his porridge as he stared out the kitchen window to the hay barn. His thoughts turned to Emma, who was currently tending to their fugitive visitors in the underground room.

*She is under great strain of late to care for our travelers and still keep
our secrets. I know she worries about my welfare, and Luke's too. I must not
increase her concerns by telling her of the unrest in town.*

His porridge now finished, he set his dirty bowl on the counter next to
the wash basin and sat back down at the table, grumbling to himself as he
continued to ponder.

*President Fillmore is nothing but a coward to sympathize with the
Southern-held Congress! What did he think was going to happen in the North
when he signed this infernal law? He must have known there would be an
uproar. And for him to threaten to send the military to Vermont to enforce
the law, 'tis just a madman's folly!*

Gabe sighed and rubbed his beard.

*Ahhh. Times have changed. There is ever more danger in the work we do
on behalf of the Lord's will. But we must be steadfast in our faith and not
allow the greed of evil men to distract us. Our mission is too important to flag
in zeal, so all of God's children shall know the grace and dignity of freedom.*

The honking of Canada geese flying overhead prompted Gabe to peer
out the window and watch them pass low over the farm.

*We must be careful in our preparations to travel. I pray to the Lord that
Thee will watch over our party and deliver us safely to the canal.* He looked
down at the blank paper in front of him. *I cannot dally longer. I must prepare these letters for the Prescotts to travel north on the morrow.*

Gabe lit a candle next to the lantern to enhance his light. He dipped the
quill into the inkwell, and, steadying his hand, began to write.

10 mo. 12th, 1850

My Dearest Friend Titus,

*'Tis my sincere hope this letter finds thee and thy family well. I can
only presume thy travels on the steamship Saranac II to and from
Burlington are keeping thee busy cooking favorable meals for their
passengers.*

*As a free man devoted to the cause of liberty, espoused by our Society
of Friends, I must once again enlist thy help, in the name of our Lord.*

*On this day, I entrust unto thy care four friends who seek passage on
Lake Champlain.*

*I ask thee shepherd their journey and deliver them safely to our Friend
in Ferrisburgh, whom I trust will assist with their passage farther north.*

I thank thee for thy dedicated service in our quest to do God's will so that all His children will know the freedom of His loving grace.

With My Sincerest Gratitude,
Friend Gabe Hopper
Fairhaven, Vermont

Gabe finished his tea, now cold, and re-read the letter. He admired Titus Battis, a slave who had made his way to Whitehall. Titus had bought his freedom and that of his wife and two daughters with the money he had earned working on the steamship. Gabe estimated Titus had been working with him and Luke to move fugitives along the lake to Canada for about ten years.

I hope there shan't be trouble at the canal. 'Tis a known point for slaves to embark upon the lake for Canada. There could be new slave catchers lurking on the dock because of this infernal law.

Gabe folded the letter and placed it in the center of the unfolded envelope. He wrapped the four pointed ends of the envelope around the letter, then dripped candle wax onto the center of the envelope. Using his seal, he secured the four points together. On the front of the envelope, he wrote:

Friend Titus Battis, 45 No. Williams Street, Whitehall, New York

On the back of the envelope, beneath his seal, he wrote:

Friend Gabe Hopper, Fairhaven, Vermont

With one letter complete, Gabe stood and stretched. The spasm in his back made him wince and he again massaged the sore spot. *Ahhh, my aches and pains do increase as I add more years.*

Placing another piece of paper before him, he dipped his quill and began the second letter.

10 mo. 12th, 1850

My Dearest Friend Rowland,

May this letter find thee and thy lovely wife, Rachel, in abundance with the grace of our Lord. I have recently learned thee has increased thy Merino sheep herd by a hundred-fold. May this undertaking be a success for thy family at Rokeby Farm.

My uncle, Isaac T. Hopper, sends his fondest regards. Now over age eighty, Isaac is still very active in the support of our Friends in New York

City. My youngest son, Adam, lives with Isaac and assists with daily affairs. In these dark days, their work is more important than ever before. Upon Isaac's behest, a package recently arrived at our farm in Fairhaven.

It is my intent to entrust unto thee the acceptance of this package. Perhaps it may be of use to thee on thy farm with the increased sheep herd. If not, I request thee ensure this precious cargo arrives safely with our Friends to the north.

Emma and I wish to pay thee a visit soon and partake of the breathtaking views of the lake from thy veranda. Until then, I pray for thy health and well-being and thank thee for thy committed service in the name of our Lord.

Thy Devoted Friend,
Gabe Hopper
Fairhaven, Vermont

Gabe re-read the letter and was satisfied. He thought about how nice it would be for him and Emma to take a well-deserved respite on Friend Robinson's farm along the beautiful shores of Lake Champlain.

I shall give both letters to Samuel for safekeeping. He is a smart young man and does read and write. He has done a fine job guiding his family on their journey and I have faith the Lord will lead them safely to reach freedom in Canada.

Gabe wrapped the envelope over the folded letter and added his seal. He addressed the front:

Rowland T. Robinson, Rokeby Farm, Ferrisburgh, Vermont

Then he signed his name beneath his seal on the back. He set both letters on the table.

I must speak with Samuel privately once they have finished their morning meal. I do not want the women to worry about the imminent dangers we may face on this journey.

SLAVES JOURNEY

Hovering over the open trapdoor in the barn floor, Emma called down to awaken the Prescotts. A moment later, Samuel climbed the ladder partway to assist with delivering breakfast to his family.

Making her way down to join her visitors, Emma's mind swirled from the stories Elsie relayed to her the previous day. She was particularly appalled Chester had wanted to have poor little Jonah trampled to death. *How could anyone be so cruel? 'Tis no wonder Miss Elsie decided to run away.*

As the family rose from their cots, Emma stoked the small stove to heat water. She placed bowls, spoons, and cups on the table and ladled porridge into each dish.

Elsie grasped Emma's free hand. "May the Good Lord shine His light upon ya this mornin', Miss Emma."

Emma smiled. "And may He bless thee and thy family also!" She joined the family as they settled around the table. After their prayer of thanksgiving, Emma turned to Elsie and said, "I am anguished from what thee has told me about thy life and it has troubled me all night." She looked at the sleepy boy just coming awake in Sarah's lap. "I understand thee was rightfully concerned about Jonah. So, tell me, how did thee manage to escape the plantation in Maryland and make it to Vermont?"

Between bites of porridge, Elsie told Emma, "My brother, Robert Watkins, done joined the Navy to earn his freedom. He was sailin' on the ship the *U.S.S. Vermont.* Lord above! Ain't that somethin'?" Elsie chuckled and waved her hand in the air.

Emma smiled. "Oh, my goodness. That was fortunate for him."

Elsie nodded. "Yas 'm. I be right proud of 'im." She paused and glanced at Samuel. "Robert and Samuel wrote letters to each other when they could. Ya knows we grew tobacca on the farm. One of the old, hobbled slaves, Ernest, drove the wagon with his boy Clyde, to deliver the loads to the dock." She smiled wistfully. "That Ernest, he be a good ol' fella. On their way back, they's pick up the mail waiting at the dock for the plantation." She sipped her tea. "Us niggahs not suppos' to be getting no mail. So old Ernest, he done stop the wagon befo' he gots home, and had Clyde, who could read a bit, find any mail that be coming for Samuel. Then Clyde tuck it away in his shirt, and deliver it to us late at night when no one be lookin'."

Emma scooped loose tea into the teapot, added hot water to let it steep, then returned to the table. "Oh, Miss Elsie. I never realized slaves would not be allowed to receive mail."

Elsie glanced at Samuel as he ate his breakfast. "We's had to be careful. So's when I fear't for Jonah, I had Samuel send a letter to Robert and let him know we's be needin' help to get off the plantation righ' soon. We done give the letter to Ernest to take to the Navy office next time he make a delivery."

Elsie sighed. "Seem't like it took nigh onto forever to hear back from Robert. When Samuel done read his letter, we learn't his ship would dock in Chesapeake Bay in four days. Lordy! Robert said we needed to be at the dock and ready to board when the ship got in."

Emma gasped. "That did not give thee much time. How did thee know where to travel?"

Samuel swallowed his food and spoke up. "When I was about eight, Massa started bringing me and Chester with him to the dock when he did business with the wharf-masters. Massa wanted us to learn how to get the best price so the dock workers would load our tobacco onto the ships first 'cuz if the bales sat in the rain, they would get moldy and be ruined."

Elsie smiled. "'Twas the good Lord lookin' over us that Samuel knowed the way."

Samuel said, "Well, I knew how to get there by carriage and it took 'bout a day's ride. But running and hiding in the woods was different. I figured it would take us two days, maybe three, if nothing bad happened."

Leaning forward, Elsie turned to Emma. "We's left the cabin with our satchels and started through the tobacca' field. Then I hears a thud and Jonah cried out. Scair't the bejesus outta me! I done figured we'd been captured befo' we's even got started." She wiped her brow. "Then I turns back in the dark and I hears Samuel whisper my name." Elsie glanced at her daughter. "Sarah had fallen and dropped Jonah. They was okay, just muddy."

Sarah looked morosely at her porridge.

Samuel continued Elsie's story. "We heard a dog barking and knew we had to hurry. So I carried Jonah, and Mama and Sarah grabbed our satchels. Mama led us in the dark, stumbling through the tobacca' field." Samuel grinned. "Then Mama let out a grunt when she walked into a tree."

Elsie shook a forefinger at her son. "Now don'cha be mockin' me. I got us to the woods, didn't I?"

Samuel snickered. "Yes, Mama. You sure 'nuff did."

Emma touched Elsie's hand. "Thee must have been terrified." Emma rose, poured tea into their cups, then returned the pot to the stove.

Elsie nodded. "Yas, 'm. Sho' was. But I knowed once we got started, there was no turnin' back. So's we pushed on into the woods."

Emma asked, "Did the dogs follow you?"

"No, 'm. Not right then. But they did a mite later." Elsie's hands trembled as she remembered hiding from the hounds.

"Mama had me take the lead in the woods," Samuel said, "so I could keep us close to the road. We walked through the trees all night and just as it was starting to get light, I thought I heard something. So I put up my hand to stop.”

“Sho’ surprised me,” said Elsie. “’I ask’t Samuel why we’s be stoppin’. Then Samuel said, *Shhh! Lissen!*” Elsie wrung her hands. “That’s when I heard horses comin’ toward us ’long the road. I could barely see Samuel through the trees as he turn’t right deeper into the woods.”

Samuel nodded. “I had Jonah on my back and it was still pretty dark, so I made sure Sarah and Mama followed me. After fighting through branches, I found a downed log, and it seemed like a good place to hide.”

“Don’cha know, Miss Emma. I was powerful tired and just fell on the wet ground. Sho’ did feel good to sit down.” Elsie paused. “And no sooner ’an we done slid behind that log, we done heard them riders passin’ us by.” She looked to Samuel. “I’s just ’bout to let out my breath, when we hears the hounds start barkin’. Lordy! My heart done be in my throat!”

Emma watched the play of emotions on Elsie’s face. “Oh, my goodness! I am so sorry, Miss Elsie. I cannot imagine what that must have been like for thee.”

“I told everyone to lay on the ground and cover up with leaves,” Samuel said. “I thought it might throw off our scent with the hounds.”

“Oh! Miss Emma,” Elsie cried. “When we done heard the hounds barkin’ and crashin’ through the trees, I’s thought we’d be catch’t for sho’!” She wrung her hands. “We done laid on that wet ground for what seem’t like an eternity. Finally, we heard the whistles calling the dogs off. Lordy! Don’cha know! I done be prayin’ somethin’ fierce for the good Lord to protect us.”

Emma nodded. “And He was protecting thee Miss Elsie. I believe He heard thy prayers.” She momentarily bowed her head. “What did thee do next?”

Samuel said, through a mouthful of porridge, “We walked through the woods all day, hiding when we heard riders or carriages on the road. At least the rain had stopped, so it was a little easier walking.”

“When it be gettin’ dark,” Elsie said, “I sho’ was mighty tired and hungry. So’s we stopped in a grove of trees away from the road. We done ate some of our food, so’s we lighten our load.” She sighed. “We tried to rest a bit, but Jonah be fussy ’cause he be wet and dirty. We had to shush him to keep him from givin’ us away.”

Samuel continued, “Come morning, I heard shouts, and then the hounds barking again. I knew we were coming near the swamps, but I didn’t want to go in there.”

Sarah piped up. “Yeah, the swamps stink real bad!”

"Out of decency for ya, Miss Emma," Elsie said to her host, "I'll spare ya the details of us hiding in that nasty swamp." She dipped her head with a look of disgust. "But once we broke out the swamp—praise the Good Lord—we could see the Drinking Gourd. Ya know, Miss Emma, the great star guiding our journey north to the Promised Land."

Emma nodded. "I do. We call it the Big Dipper."

"We done traveled north 'til we comes to the road again. Samuel said we was suppos' to be at the dock in the mornin' so's we best hurry." She paused to wipe her brow. "When it was gettin' light, I started smellin' dead fish, so I's figured we's be gettin' close. That's when we done moved fast as we could to get to the bay."

Samuel, sitting with his back against the slate wall, facing Emma, said, "I was worried the ship would leave without us. Then we'd be in big trouble. I carried Jonah best I could, but we was still moving mighty slow." Samuel glared at Sarah, sitting opposite Elsie and holding Jonah in her lap.

Sarah squinted at Samuel and shrugged her shoulders, "Don't be blamin' me. Did the best I could in that nasty swamp."

Emma looked at Elsie and said, "That must have been terrifying. But thee did make it to the ship."

Elsie grimaced. "When we reached the harbor, Lordy, I was nerved-up with all those people runnin' 'round. Ships and boats be docked everywhere." She shook her head. "Men be shoutin' out orders, unloading cargo, and some folks be tryin' to load lumber onto another ship. Fancy folks, they be boardin' a steamship. Ain't never seen so many people in one place befo'." She wrung her hands. "We fought our way 'long the docks lookin' for the *U.S.S. Vermont*. 'Twas all we could do to hold onto Sarah and Jonah."

Samuel wiped his mouth. "That's when I saw a broadside in a warehouse window. It said Massa Swaley was offerin' a thousand dollars for the capture of a runaway slave family—two women a boy and a child. It said the boy was missin' the first two fingers from his right hand." Samuel rubbed his right hand with his left. "I got real worried and stuffed my hand into my pocket. When we got to the end of the warehouse, I found an old pair of gloves on the ground. I grabbed some hay from a horse's stall and stuffed two empty holes, then put them on. I thought it would hide my missing fingers and it musta worked."

Elsie smiled at Samuel, "'Twas a mighty smart thing to do, Samuel. You was usin' your head then."

Samuel grinned back, then turned to Emma. "At the end of the dock, past where cargo was being loaded, I saw a large gathering of black folks next to a big ship with tall masts. I grabbed Jonah and we ran as fast as we could to the group."

Elsie clasped her hands, as if in worship. "I praised the Good Lord when Samuel done tol't me the ship was the *U.S.S. Vermont.* We done pushed through the noisy crowd and their bags to the front of the railin' so's I could find my brother Robert. Black folks was being led up the gangplank by the sailors and sent along the ship deck. I was worryin' somethin' fierce as I searched the faces of the Navy men, tryin' to find my brother."

Elsie shifted in her seat, hands on the table. "Suddenly, someone grabbed my elbow from behind, and I scream't. When I turns 'round, I saw a tall, bearded black man, dressed up real nice in a sailor's uniform. I near jumped outta my wits when he kiss't my cheek." Elsie chuckled at the memory. "'Twas only then that I knowed my big brother Robert. Lordy, Miss Emma! But di'nt he look wonderful, bein' a free man!" Elsie's tears swelled. "I gave him a big hug and coul'nt help but cry to see him. It'd been so long."

Elsie recalled, "Robert smack't Samuel on the back and said, *You must be Samuel. You was in nappies last time I done set eyes on ya.* Then he told us, *Quick. Get up the gangplank. Our captain is an abolitionist and won't send you back once you're on board.*" Elsie wrung her hands again. "We hurried after Robert up the gangplank. Sarah was behind me carrying Jonah, who was fussing at all the commotion at the dock. Samuel came up last, carrying our travel satchels."

Samuel added, "All of a sudden we heard the shouts of white men on horses, racing along the dock. They were knocking people out of their way and stopped at the group huddled in front of the ship. A yell went up from the crowd and all the black folks started fighting their way up the gangplank. I guided Sarah and Jonah onto the ship before we got trampled. Some folks got knocked off the plank and fell screamin' into the water."

Elsie's voice was strained. "Robert took us around to the right side of the ship and found us a place to sit next to one of those huge black funnels. He yelled at us, *Stay here! I gotta help the others board befo' it's too late.* Then he ran off to the other side of the ship."

Samuel said, "I thought I could help, so I followed Robert and watched from the railing. The white men were grabbin' black folk from the crowd and throwin' them to the ground. I saw one of our men get stabbed in the back. His wife screamed and went to help him, but her head was bashed with a club."

Emma let out a small cry and covered her mouth with her hand.

Samuel shook his head in disgust. "As I watched, Robert and the other sailors were pulling the slaves up the gangplank as the slave hunters tried to drag them back down. A white man punched a slave in the face. The slave wrestled with him and they both fell into the water." Samuel took a breath and continued, "I was scared the slave catchers would storm the ship and kill us or drag us all back to the dock. Then a group of sailors returning to the ship saw what was happening. The captain yelled at them to block the entrance to the gangplank, but get the blacks on board." Samuel's voice rose in pitch as he recalled the scene. "A big fight broke out with the sailors and the slave hunters. I thought those white men were gonna kill each other, 'cause of us black folk."

Emma gasped. "Oh, my! That must have been dreadful."

Samuel exhaled, "Then the ship's horn blasted—nearly jumped outta my boots, and the gangplank began to rise. The fighting sailors jumped onto the plank, knocked the rest of the slave hunters into the water and ran to the deck where they tied up the plank. The other slaves on the dock screamed and ran in different directions with the slave hunters on horseback chasin' 'em. I felt horrible and wanted to help, but there weren't nothin' I could do. It was only then I thought we might get away."

Elsie said, "Yas 'm. That horn blast done scair't the be-jesus out of us! Poor Jonah wailed bloody murder, and if it wasn't for me and Sarah holdin' onto that boy for dear life, he would'a jumped over the railin'."

Emma peered at Jonah sitting in Sarah's lap. "Oh! The dear boy. I imagine he was horribly frightened."

Samuel said, "I ran back over and joined the family on the right side of the ship. I slumped onto the deck and squeezed my knees to my chest to stop shakin'. Mama hugged me and I tried not to cry." Samuel smiled at his mother.

Elsie grinned mischievously. "Lordy, Miss Emma! That boy sho' was shook up. Thinks he's all growed up, but ya know, he needed his Mama then." Elsie grasped Samuel's damaged hand, but he pulled it away. "But we was treated real well on the ship. We was givin' blankets and hot food, and I got to visit with Robert." She smiled. "Ahhh...the stories he done told of the adventures he's had. Sho' am proud of him." Elsie smiled and sipped her tea. "Then we sailed for two nights and docked in New York City the next mornin'. Befo' we left the ship, Robert done give me a letter for Mista' Isaac T. Hopper, and wrote down some street names for us to folla'. Samuel was real good at readin' those street signs and we finally did find Mista' Hopper's place. A fine three-story home, on a shady street in the city."

Elsie smiled and touched Emma's hand. "A tall, handsome young man brung us into the house and made us feel welcome. Now I knows it was your son, Adam, who done treated us with such kindness."

Emma smiled wistfully. "I'm so glad Adam was of help to thee. He is a good son with a strong belief we are all created equal in God's eyes."

Elsie grasped Emma's hand a bit tighter. "Yas 'm. 'Tis our sons who care for us in our old age." Elsie glanced at Samuel, who looked away.

Sarah adjusted Jonah on her lap and said, "Mista' Isaac sure was sweet to Jonah. After we ate, he told us stories of other runaways he done helped, and bounced Jonah on his lap the whole time."

Emma had a faraway look thinking of Gabe's beloved uncle. "I'm not surprised. Uncle Isaac is a humble Quaker, full of love and compassion. He always says, *The rich and poor shall meet together, and the Lord is the Father of us all.* I should hope to visit with him again one day." Emma turned back to Elsie. "How long did thee stay with Uncle Isaac?"

Elsie thought for a moment. "We was there for two days, and slept in the purty bedrooms upstairs. Then Adam says we's be leavin' that second night, once it got good and dark." She grinned and shook her head. "Sho' did hate to leave, but I knowed we had to keep movin'. So we gathered our satchels. Then Adam gave Samuel a letter and said it was for his friends we would be meetin' next." Distracted, she turned to Jonah. "Lord's sake, boy! Eat the food that's done bin given ya, an' stop fussin'!"

Elsie stared off at the cots in the corner of the cellar as she re-gathered her thoughts. "Adam be drivin' a fancy carriage led by two horses, right up to the front of the house. We climbed in just like we was white folks. 'Magine that! Then Adam drove the carriage out the city and we rode for a long time. I think we musta dozed cause it be plenty bright when we done stopped in the country. To my left, through the trees, we could see a big river, with steamboats goin' yonder. Adam said it was the mighty Hudson and it'd be our guide going north. Then he pointed to a path leading from the road and told us to follow it 'til we come to the farmhouse."

Elsie continued, "We done thanked Adam for his kindness. He tipped his hat and said, *You're welcome, Ma'am. Glad I could be of service in your journey. Please travel safely and may God bless you.*" She heaved a sigh. "What a fine young man he is, Miss Emma. You must be very proud of him."

Emma beamed at Elsie's praise of her youngest son. "Yes, I am proud. And I do miss him so. I hope he comes home to visit us soon."

We walked the long road, then Samuel spotted the freedom quilt we was told to look for, hanging in a farmyard. I saw the black-diamond pattern of flyin' geese and knowed we'd found our safe house!"

Elsie let out a sigh and rubbed her wrinkled face. "We hid in the trees while Samuel done give our letter. Imagine my surprise when I done sees a black woman come out the door and wave us to the house!"

Emma eyes went wide. "Oh, my! Who was she?"

"When we's all in the kitchen, the white woman said her name was Miz Higgins and the black lady was Miss Harriet." Elsie grinned. "Lordy! That Miss Harriet—she sure was a bitty thing—'bout Samuel's size. But when I saw that deep look in her eyes, I knowed she be a strong woman. When we sat to eat, Miss Harriet 'splained she be a runaway from Maryland, same as us. Told us she done helped slaves escape and was on her way back down South to get others." Elsie wiped her brow. "That Miss Harriet! She sho' be a fine, courageous woman."

Emma said, "How very brave of her to go back again and risk being captured."

Elsie said, "Yas 'm. Sho' was. Miz' Higgins tol't us we was in a place called Albany and there were plenty of abolitionist friends who would help us along the way. That night, Sarah, me and Jonah done slept in real beds, and Samuel slept on a sofa in the parlor. In the mornin', Miss Harriet done warned us there might be slave catchers 'bout. So's to disguise us, Miz Higgins done helped us dress Jonah like a little girl." Elsie chuckled.

Sarah grumbled, "Yeah, Jonah war'nt happy at havin' to wear a dress. All's I could do to keep him from yanking that stupid bonnet off."

Elsie grinned at Jonah playing on the cot. "Yep, that boy sho' was makin' a fuss when Miz' Higgins and Miss Harriet took us—in broad daylight, mind ya!—in a carriage driven by a colored man down to the river." She sighed, pausing as her expression became serious. "I was a'worryin' when we got to the docks we'd be catched-up. Lots of folks were millin' about." She shook her head. "Jus' as we was gettin' ready to board the canal boat, two fancy-dressed white men done come up to us and demanded to see our papers. 'Course, we didn't have none. A straight-standin' older man had a broadside, and he be lookin' us over real careful like. I looked at Samuel, and praised the Lord he be wearing his gloves." Elsie touched Emma's hand. "Lordy! Miss Emma, don'cha know my heart be pounding out my chest and I's ready to grab Jonah and run! Then Miz' Higgins and Miss Harriet done stepped in." Elsie shook her head, recalling her amazement.

"Miss Harriet, she done squared her shoulders, stood tall, and stared that big ol' white man right in the face. I was worried he gonna smack her down. She done stuck her pointy chin right up at him when she tol't him I was her cousin and we's be free blacks from New York City." Elsie mimicked Harriet's protruding chin and laughed. "That woman sho' gots the gumption of a little bull dog, I prays to the Lord! Then Miz Higgins showed those big men a letter. She says we had jobs a waitin' for us at the Wagner boardin' house and stables in Fort Anne."

Elsie frowned. "I be thinkin' we was gonna be let us on the barge, when all of a sudden, the younger man took the broadside and started reading from it real loud, *One thousand dollar reward for slave family. Negro boy aged twelve, missin' first two fingers on his right hand.* That's when my heart start beatin' outta my chest and I's be lookin' for any place we could run." The fear showed on her face. "There weren't no place to go but the canal. Miss Harriet grabbed my arm and twisted me to her. Then she gave me the God-awfullest stare I ever done seen, 'cuz she knowed I be panickin'. I took a deep breath and prayed, but my legs be shakin' like an old banty rooster."

Samuel continued, "I was standing behind Mama with my hands behind my back. The tall man came to me and demanded, *Boy, lemme see your hands.* I wasn't sure what to do, so I held out my gloved hands. Just as he started to grab my gloves, the horn on the boat blared and we all jumped. Next thing I know, Miz' Higgins got me by the arm and is pushing me onto the boat. She said to the mean man, *Please excuse us, good Sir, but these folks need to get on board. Now!* I figured those men were going to start shouting and come after us. But when they turned around, I heard the man say to the other, *I saw his hands, boy's got all his fingers. Guess it ain't them.* So they let us board."

Elsie took a breath. "Lordy! Don'cha know, my heart be pounding outta my chest. Thought fo' sho' they was gonna nab Samuel." Elsie placed a trembling hand over her heart. "Befo' I gots onto the boat, Miz' Higgins give me the letter of our employment. Then Miss Harriet give me a strong hug, and told us to go down below and stay outta sight 'til we reached Fort Anne."

Emma learned forward, propping her elbows on the table, listening to Elsie's spellbinding account of her journey.

Elsie let out a heavy sigh. "Lordy, Miss Emma! Can you 'magine my shock when we gets into that dark cargo hold, and I see's it's full of our folk?"

FUGITIVES ARRIVE

"Oh, my goodness!" Emma exclaimed as she poured more tea into their cups. Replacing the teapot, she sat back down at the table and grasped Elsie's hand. "What did thee think when thee saw thy folks in the ship's hold?"

"Honestly, Miss Emma, I be thinkin' we'd have to sit on somebody's lap!" Elsie laughed, then her face turned serious. "I heard a lady calling us, 'Ovah here'. We stumbled through the group and found a space on some boxes where we's could sit."

"Were they all bound for Canada?" Emma asked.

Jonah squirmed in Sarah's arms. The young mother lowered him from her lap. The three-year-old grinned as he plunked down onto the dirt floor, dancing a rag doll Sarah had found in the charity trunk.

Elsie smiled at her grandson's antics, then responded to Emma's question. "Far's I know they's all headin' north. Some said they's be goin' to Fort Edward—next stop after Fort Anne—said folks there would be helpin' 'em along. I ask't where they's all be from. Couple of the men said they be travelin' for months from the Deep South." Elsie's soulful eyes widened and she shook her head. "Lordy, Miss Emma! But we's sho' be a smelly bunch of niggahs packed in that hold. Whew!" Chuckling, Elsie fanned her hand in front of her scrunched nose.

Emma couldn't help but laugh along with Elsie at hearing the account of the canal boat ride. "So what happened when thee reached Fort Anne?"

Elsie sipped her tea and replied, "When we gots to the dock, a tall, skinny white man all dressed in black, with a big hat, come up and asked if we be the Prescott family. Lordy! That man be so skinny I done think he was a skel'ton, I swear!" She waved her pinky finger in front of Emma. "Man say his name was Pastor Wagner, and the boy with him was his son, Sheldon— looked to be 'bout Samuel's age. I done felt real bad for that po' boy, 'cause he be the spittin' image of his father!"

Emma covered her mouth to suppress a giggle.

A sly grin spread over Sarah's face. "Yeah, dat white boy sure was God-awful ugly, with his flappy ears and big beak nose. Looked like some crazy bird 'bout to peck yo' eyes out!" She flapped her arms in the air and cawed. "Someone should'a fed him some cornpone and grits to fatten him up."

Elsie laughed. "You'se got that right, Sistah. Boy sho' was a sight! Well, that pastor fella and his son done loaded us in their wagon and took us to their boardin' house. Guess there weren't no rooms for us black folk, so they took us to the back of the stables. There be two stalls with blankets on the floor. Pastor said to make us-selves comf'table." She shook her head. "Now I ask ya, Miss Emma, how comf'table can any creature be in a stinky stable? Even those horses don't wanna be there!"

Emma chuckled. "Not very, I would imagine."

"But we be grateful for any help they's be givin' us, so we's stayed quiet."

Sarah glanced at her son. "Jonah had ripped half of the dang dress off hisself, so we changed him into boy's clothes, then we rested."

Elsie carried on, "That ugly boy, Sheldon, done woke us up in the afternoon and brought us some vegetable soup and bread. We's hungry so's we ate it, but, I swears Miss Emma, that was the wors' tastin' soup I ever done had!" She pursed her lips at the distasteful memory. "'Tis no wonder those white men be so dang skinny, eatin' cookin' like that! Wish't I coulda stayed longer and fixed 'em some good ol' Southern fried chicken." Elsie laughed again and waved an arm in the air. "Sheldon done told us we need to be ready to leave again, soon's it got dark."

Emma looked sympathetically at Elsie. "Thee must have been exhausted with so little rest. I don't know how thee could have kept going."

"Yas,'m. We be mighty tired, but as the good Lord says, there's no rest for the weary." Elsie rubbed her eyes and yawned. "When it got dark, Pastor Wagner and his bird-boy had us lay down in their wagon. Sho' woulda been nice if they'd put some hay down for us, but we be jus' on the bare boards. Then they covered us with some blankets so's we wouldn't be seen."

Elsie shook her head as she recalled their ride. "That musta been the worst wagon ride I ever done took. We be bounced all over and kept bangin' into each other. Jonah was wailin' 'cause Sarah was crushin' on him. Pastor yelled at us, *Shut that boy up!* So's we had to cover Jonah's mouth to keep him quiet." Elsie looked at her grandson playing on the floor and sighed.

Samuel chimed in, "Now I know why they call it a buck wagon! Seemed like we bounced around for hours, and we was mighty bruised up when the pastor finally stopped. He gave Mama a letter—said we was in a place called Granville, and we had rode about fifteen miles. Felt like we'd traveled a hundred! He gave us directions to Friend Granger's farm, and said to tell them Friend Wagner sent us."

Elsie rubbed her elbow. "Yup, still bruised up from that ride. We went through the woods and found the Grangers' farm, just as the pastor done told us we would. 'Twas startin' to get light, so I gives Samuel our letter, and we waited in the trees. Don'cha know, Miss Emma, them Granger folks sho' was kind to us." Elsie smiled, remembering their visit.

Emma nodded. "Yes. The Grangers are dear friends of ours and devoutly committed to our cause. I am glad thee met them."

Elsie took a drink of tea, then set her cup down. "They's got lots of barns on their farm, so I sho' was surprised when Miz Granger done brung us right into the main house and sat us down at the kitchen table." Elsie shook her head in amazement. "She and her daughter done fixed us a fine breakfast, then they sat right down at the table and ate with us. When Mista Granger done come in from chores, don'cha know, he tipped his hat to us, just like we was reg'lar visitors and said, *Howdy folks.* Then he done joined us for breakfast, too." She shook her head. "'Scuse me for saying so, Miss Emma, but I's just can't 'magine a white man doing that!"

Emma shrugged and raised an eyebrow. "Well, Vermont is not the South, though the Lord knows many of our people are not yet as enlightened as we would hope."

Sarah continued the story. "After breakfast, Miz Granger took us upstairs to a pretty bedroom with a view of the farm. She poured us each a bath that smelt real good, then we done slept in some fancy beds. Sho' was mighty kind of 'em to care for us." She reached down and patted Jonah's head.

Emma touched Sarah's hand. "Sarah, thee might like to know Missus Granger has been helping us move fugitives to Canada for nigh onto twenty years now. She is the kindest, most God-fearing woman I have ever known."

Sarah nodded in acknowledgment. "Yas, 'm."

Then Samuel continued their tale. "When it got dark, Miz Granger woke us up. She said it was time to go, and gave me a letter for Friend Hopper." Samuel ate a spoonful of porridge. "She said we should look for the pillow with the black-diamond geese pattern that set on the rocking chair on the porch. Said it was the sign of a safe house, same as the quilt we saw on our way here."

Elsie looked at Samuel. "We gathered our satchels and said our goodbyes to that nice family. Then we's done climbed into the back of their wagon. This time there was hay for us to sit on, so the ride warn't too bad. When we done stop, Mista' Granger said we be at the Vermont border and we needs to walk 'bout a mile 'long the road. Tol't us to stay outta sight best we could, and to look for your carriage barn and stables. So's we set out walkin' in the rain."

Elsie folded her arms and shivered. "We ain't walk't long befo' we done heard horses comin' on the road. It be so foggy, we couln't tell where they be. Samuel led us off the road and we's fought our way through the woods, goin' tree to tree. Couln't see a darn thing!"

Samuel leaned forward. "I tried to keep us close to the road, but it was hard in the dark. We stopped and waited until the horses passed, then we moved on slowly."

Elsie chuckled. "Lordy, Miss Emma! Next thing we knows, we hear a gaggle of hens cluckin' somethin' fierce. Then we done bumped into the hen house, right in front of us! Couln't see it befo' 'cause fog be all 'round us."

Sarah waved a hand in the air. "Yeah. Then a gunshot went off and we done heard a man hollerin' 'bout a bear gettin' into his chickens again. I got scair't and tried to run with Jonah in my arms. But my sleeve caught on a damned branch and I fell and dropped him. He done landed real hard on the rocks and started a wailin'.'"

Elsie picked up the story. "We tried to quiet the boy, then we heard the farmer yellin' *Who's there? You best be leavin' my chickens alone! If youse niggahs, you betta get off my land befo' I shoots you.*" She raised a shaking hand to her chest. "Lordy, Miss Emma, my heart be beatin' somethin' fierce thinkin' that man gonna shoot us dead!"

Emma let out a sigh. "Oh, I'm so sorry, Miss Elsie. I believe that was Mister Pritchard thee startled. He is not one for supporting our cause. Thee was right to be afraid of him and move off his property."

Sarah grinned. "Guess the good thing 'bout being a niggah is it's hard to see us at night in the fog and rain."

Emma let out a small gasp at Sarah's self-deprecating humor. "Gosh, I had not thought about that, but I believe thee might be right, Sarah!"

Elsie shook her head. "Miss Emma, we be fear't for our lives, so Samuel pick't up Jonah and I help't Sarah get to her feet. We grabbed our bags and went fast as we could to get away from that crazy man."

Samuel peered at his mother. "As we were weaving through the woods, we heard another gunshot and the man hollerin', but I couldn't make out what he was saying. We just kept moving and I was just guessing we were close to the road." Samuel rubbed his right hand out of habit and continued, "We came to a little clearing in the woods. By then the fog had cleared some. When I looked across the road, I thought I saw a big carriage barn, just like Mista Granger said. I told Mama and Sarah to stay put. Then I walked up the road a bit and saw a house. I looked for a rocking chair on the porch, but couldn't see that far in the dark. So I ran across the road real quiet-like, and got close to your porch. And there it was, the fancy-stitched geese pillow on the chair, just like we was told."

Elsie clasped her hands in prayer. "Don'cha know, Miss Emma! I done thanked the Good Lord when Samuel come back and said he'd seen the geese pillow, 'cause I knowed we done found another safe house!" She momentarily bowed her head, then peered at Emma. "We done crossed the road, then went into the trees behind your barns and waited while Samuel presented our letter. We's sure sorry to be wakin' ya kind folks up in the middle of the night." Elsie touched Emma's hand with a grateful look in her eyes.

Emma squeezed Elsie's hand tighter and smiled. "I am so glad thee made it here safely, despite thy perils. Gabe and I are pleased the Lord has chosen us—"

The squeal of the barn door abruptly stopped the conversation. Emma twisted in her seat to stare at the open portal above her head.

GABE TALKS TO SAMUEL

The barn floorboards creaked under the weight of his heavy footfalls. A dim glow from the underground room seeped into the gloom of the barn. He reached the trapdoor opening, and slowly lowered himself to his hands and knees. Melting snow dripped from his cloak to the dirt floor below. Peering down into the chamber, he saw Emma staring back at him.

"Mother? Is thee busy?" Gabe spoke to the group gathered at the table.

Emma gasped to see Gabe's face looming above her. "Oh my, Father! Thee has startled us!" A flush rose in Emma's face. "Dear me! I believe I have lost track of time. My apologies." She rose from the table and quickly gathered the dirty dishes, putting them into her wooden crate.

"I shall bring the dishes up presently," Emma said as she bade her good-byes to Elsie's family and donned her cloak.

"Mother, please have Samuel bring the crate up as I need to speak with him," Gabe requested, his face solemn.

Emma raised an eyebrow and glanced sideways at Samuel, sitting with his back to the outer stone wall. Samuel nodded, got up and grasped the crate.

Approaching the bottom of the ladder, Samuel called up to Gabe, "I'm coming up, Suh." Lifting the crate with both hands, wincing a bit at the discomfort caused by his missing digits, he balanced on the ladder and started to climb. Once he was halfway up, Gabe took the crate from his outstretched arms where he set it aside and offered Samuel a hand as the boy clambered onto the barn floor.

A few moments later, Emma's head appeared in the opening and Gabe grasped her arm to help her up. "Goodness me! I have been shirking my chores this morning. I was so involved with Elsie's story, I have forgotten myself." Emma grasped the crate of dirty dishes and moved toward the door. "Father, if thee will open this for me, I shall get on with my work."

As Emma hurried out of the barn, an icy gust of wind blew through the opening. Gabe closed the door behind her. He motioned for Samuel to sit next to him on the low wooden wall of the hay mow stall. Behind them, loose, dried hay was stacked almost to the ceiling. A long-handled, multi-pronged hay rake hung on the wall to Gabe's left.

Reaching into his jacket pocket, Gabe produced the two letters he had written earlier that morning. "Samuel, here are thy travel letters. I am giving them to thee because I believe as the man of thy family, thee has the fortitude to lead them to freedom."

Samuel grinned, his white teeth flashing in the dusky light. "I thank you, Mistah Hopper. I've done my best, but it's been a hard journey."

Gabe placed a hand on Samuel's arm and sighed. "I know that, Son, and I'm afraid there may still be perils ahead." Gabe tapped one letter. "This is for my friend, Titus Battis, who lives in Whitehall. Titus is a free black man who works on the steamship *Saranac II*."

Samuel's eyes widened at the mention of a free black man.

Gabe continued, "Luke and I shall transport thy family to Titus' house. He will make arrangements for thee to board the boat at the canal. Then he will help thee disembark at McNeil's Landing at Charlotte's Point on Lake Champlain."

Gabe presented Samuel the second letter.

Samuel grasped it and read the name and address. "Friend Rowland T. Robinson?" he asked.

Gabe nodded. "Yes. Friend Rowland, and his wife, Rachel, are members of the Society of Friends. Their Rokeby farm is about one mile inland from the Point. They usually have a man waiting at the ferry for any fugitives who might land, and he will take thee to the farm." Gabe looked thoughtful then rubbed his beard. "Perchance, if no one is there to transport thee, follow the road from the shore north about a mile. The farm name *ROKEBY* is on their cow barn."

"Yes, Suh. We can do that," Samuel answered.

Gabe stared at the glow emanating from the underground room and dipped his head.

Samuel touched the older man's arm. "Suh, you look troubled."

Gabe straightened and looked into the boy's dark, inquisitive eyes. *He is still just a child, really. Such a large burden he carries to lead his family on this perilous journey. I doubt my boys would have had his courage at that age.*

Gabe took a long breath. "Samuel, thee must know there is a slave hunter in town, trying to stir up trouble. I do not wish to fret the womenfolk about this. But I want thee to be prepared to protect thy family, should something untoward happen during our travels." Gabe grimaced and scrubbed his gray beard.

Samuel stared back at Gabe's wrinkled, weary visage. "Suh, we have waded through swamps, avoided their hounds, made it safely aboard a naval ship, hidden in a cargo hold and managed not to get shot on our way here." Samuel flashed a wan smile at Gabe, and ran his fingers through his thick black hair. "I do believe we shall make it to freedom safely, with God's help. And I thank you and Miss Emma for your kindness."

Gabe nodded, looking directly into the young man's eyes. "Thee is a brave boy, Samuel, and the Lord has blessed thee with the strength and courage of a grown man. I pray thee has a successful journey."

Samuel nodded. "When will we leave, Suh?"

Gabe replied, "Before first light tomorrow. Our neighbor, Friend Zenas Ellis, and his two sons, will come visit this evening. We will load the wagon with hay and make space for thy family to lie inside. We must keep thee hidden from any strangers that may be about."

Samuel wrinkled his forehead. "Then you *are* worried we may be followed!"

Nodding, Gabe said, "We shall take every precaution, but unfortunately it is a possibility. Please gather thy belongings and be ready to travel before the night is over." He reached into his pocket then gave Samuel a handful of coins. "This is for thy journey."

Samuel stood and slid the envelopes into his jacket pocket, then retrieved the coins from Gabe. "I thank you very much, Mistah Hopper. You are indeed a good friend." Samuel pocketed the coins. "We will be ready tonight, Suh, and are anxious to reach the Promised Land. I will not mention your concerns to Mama."

Samuel walked to the trapdoor portal and lowered himself down the ladder, his head disappearing beneath the barn floorboards.

Gabe rose slowly, and rubbed his aching back. Peering up into the darkness of the barn rafters he murmured, "Dear Heavenly Father, I ask for Thy guidance as we seek to do Thy will on this earth. Please protect us from those who may wish us harm. I pray all Thy children may one day enjoy a life of freedom in Thy loving grace. Amen."

After closing the stubborn barn door, Gabe left the barn, pulled his collar tight, and strode toward the stables to muck out the stalls. The wind-blown snow quickly covered his footprints.

ENOS ADAMS

Saturday afternoon, after their heated discussion on the boardwalk, Enos reluctantly followed Buster into the backroom of Jeb's tavern. Pausing as he entered the smoke-filled, windowless room, he let his eyes adjust to the dim light cast by the wall sconces. Several men sat at poker tables, smoking cigars and drinking ale. Others stood chatting. As he scanned the room, Enos noticed in the far corner Sheriff Jeremiah Wardwell and his son, George, conversing quietly with someone hidden by George's broad shoulders. When George stepped aside, Enos saw the stranger who had caused the uproar at the meeting the previous night.

Buster grasped Enos' arm and pulled him toward the three men. "C'mon," Buster said. "I wanna introduce you."

Enos hesitated. In a low, strained voice he said, "Buster, my father was furious with that man last night. He completely disrupted the proceedings and showed no respect to my father as the president of the Temperance Society." He stared at the sheriff's back. "And if my father finds out I'm here, he'll have my hide!" He swept a hand around the room.

"He won't find out unless you tell him!" Buster leaned in. "Enos, we've known each othah a long time, right? We're friends and I need your help."

At twenty-six, Enos respected Buster, though a year younger than he. While Enos had been a studious child, Buster had learned outdoor survival skills from his father, Jeb, beginning at an early age. It was Buster who had frequently dragged Enos from his studies, and taught him how to hunt and shoot. "I don't—"

"Enos, I'm just askin' you to stay and listen to what this Duschanne fellah has to say. That's all. After he's done, if you don't wanna get involved, then that's up to you."

Enos stared at his friend. *What am I doing here? I should just leave now and be done with it. But maybe it would be good to hear what this stranger has to say, then I could let my father know.* "Okay, Buster. I'll stay. But I don't want to be introduced to him."

Buster shrugged. "Your choice." He motioned to a card table. "Heah, let's take a seat." They joined two other men at the table.

Sheriff Wardwell and his son George ended their conversation and went to sit at a small square table at the front of the room.

Duschanne stood next to the sheriff's table and clapped his hands to get everyone's attention. "*Messieurs!* Please take a seat! Let's get started."

Enos listened as Duschanne stated his case. The Southerner reminded the men that regardless of how Vermonters felt about slavery, federal law now required anyone not aiding in the capture of fugitives could be fined and jailed. Those abolitionists who had freely helped runaways before the Fugitive Slave Law passed a month ago, were now criminals breaking the law. Duschanne argued it was the duty of law-abiding citizens, like the men gathered in the room, to round up these fugitives and return them to their rightful owners.

A round of "Hear! Hear!" went up from the assembled group.

Enos sipped the ale the barmaid had delivered, then leaned back in his chair and folded his arms, pondering Duschanne's words. *I've always believed, as the Lord says, that all men are created equal in His eyes. And I commend my father for his devotion to the cause to end slavery in our lifetime. But, if Duschanne is right, father could now be arrested for helping runaways get to Canada.* He shook his head in frustration. *Dammit! What a mess this hateful law has made of everyone's lives!*

Then Sheriff Wardwell stood before the group. "Any man who wants to be deputized, please raise your right hand."

All men raised a hand except Enos. *I can't betray my father, nor my own beliefs.*

"Repeat after me," Wardwell said, "I, state your name, do hereby swear to uphold the law of the land." The men murmured his words. "I will identify and report the whereabouts of any fugitives," he paused as the men repeated, "so the constables may take appropriate action. So help me God." The men stated the phrase in response.

"You are now deputized under the laws of the State of Vermont," the sheriff declared.

After the oaths were taken, Enos saw Buster scowling at him. Turning away from his friend, Enos rose and started to leave the room. A tug on his arm stopped his progress. Turning, he found himself face to face with Buster. Enos stumbled as Buster yanked him toward the wall.

"Enos, listen to me! Please! I need your help." Buster peered around to see who was close by, then lowered his voice. "I told Duschanne I'd watch Zenas Ellis' place out to south side for any fugitives. Ya know damn well he's a sympathizer and moves runaways to the canal in Whitehall!" Buster pointed in the general direction of New York. "I need you to keep me company. We don't even know if there's any slaves at his place right now."

"I don't know, Buster." Enos looked around the room at other men talking in small groups. "I probably shouldn't get involved in any of this, my father being the head of the Temperance Society and all. What if something happens?"

Buster grinned lopsidedly and put his arm around Enos' shoulder. "My friend, we're just supposed to be lookouts. Ain't nothin' gonna happen. If we see anything suspicious, you heard Pierre, we're just supposed to report back and let him and his posse handle it. I'm just looking for a friend to keep me company and I'll pay you ten dollahs if you'll help me out." Buster pulled some bills from his pocket and offered them to Enos.

Enos raised an eyebrow. "Where'd you get that money from, Buster?"

Buster pointed his thumb toward the Southerner. "Pierre gave each of us ten bucks to help him catch the fugitives. Says he'll pay us anothah fifty per head that we bring in." Buster's eyes gleamed as he spoke of his potential payday.

Enos took the notes from Buster and turned toward the light to inspect them. One was from a bank in New Orleans, another from a bank in Atlanta, and a third from Memphis. Enos shook his head. "Buster, these are wildcat notes! They ain't worth the paper they're printed on. Duschanne doesn't plan to pay you guys shit—can't you see that?" He handed the bills back to Buster. "You can keep it, Buster. I don't need your damn money."

"You're wrong, Enos!" Buster huffed as he stuffed the bills back into his pocket. "Duschanne will pay us 'cause he needs us to round up those niggahs for him. Who else he got that'll do it?"

Enos glanced around the room, seeing a couple of men he knew by name and others by sight. Throughout the meeting, he had noticed men giving him sideways glances. It made him feel like an enemy spy. He couldn't help but wonder if any of them would mention his attendance to his father.

"I don't know, Buster. I just don't feel right spying on the Ellises. What if there's trouble?" *And what if my father finds out?*

Buster gave him one last pitch. "Enos, there won't be any trouble, I promise. It'll be just like when we were boys huntin' that big ol' buck you brought down. Remembah how long we waited in the blind until that beauty came into view? It'll be fun, just like back then." Buster patted Enos' shoulder and grinned.

Enos let out a long sigh. "All right, Buster. I'm in. When are we going up there?"

Buster leaned in close. "You won't regret it, Enos. We're going tonight, before it gets dark. Meet me at the clearing by the mill next to the bridge at five, and we'll ride up togethah. Wear warm clothes 'cause we may be there all night."

Enos felt a creeping dread as he bade farewell to Buster and left the tavern. *Have I just made a deal with the devil?*

Stepping out of the tavern door, swirling snow slapped Enos' face. He grunted, tightening his collar and lowering the brim of his hat.

Walking quickly along the boardwalk, he sidestepped shoppers making their way in and out of the shops. Now that he had reluctantly agreed to join Buster to watch the Ellis farm, he would need a heavy blanket to stay warm. Since nothing indicated any fugitives were being hidden there, he had no idea how long they would be watching the farm.

How will I explain my absence from the house to my father? He'll surely wonder why I'm not home for dinner. Hmmmm, maybe there's a young lady who might invite me to dine with her family this evening… He let his thoughts wander.

At the end of Main Street, he turned left onto Liberty Street and entered Colonel Alonson Allen's mercantile. A cold rush of air followed him inside and he quickly closed the door. The Colonel's son, Edward, who had been the reluctant scribe at the meeting the previous night, stood behind the counter. Enos saw the Colonel at the back of the store, helping a male customer.

Edward leaned across the counter, his tousled black hair partially hanging over his eyes. "Afternoon, Enos. Bit of a blow out there today, aye?" The slender fifteen-year-old chuckled.

Enos nodded his head, distracted. "Yeah, pretty early to be getting snow." He walked down the center aisle in search of blankets.

"Help you find something, Enos?" Edward called from behind the counter.

"No, thanks," Enos mumbled under his breath as he searched the shelves. Toward the back of the store, on an aisle to the right of where Colonel Allen was conversing, Enos found a stack of woolen blankets folded on a bottom shelf. He examined them quickly and chose two woven with a dark gray yarn. He carried the blankets to the front of the store, where Edward waited at the counter.

Edward's pale, pockmarked face grinned up at him. "Gettin' ready for a cold night, eh? That'll be two dollars for two blankets." Edward pulled brown wrapping paper from beneath the counter, then wrapped and tied the blankets in a bundle.

Enos shrugged. "Yeah, need to add an extra layer for the horses so they don't get chilled." He retrieved two coins from his pocket and paid the young merchant. "Thanks, Edward. Say hello to your father for me."

Enos grabbed the bundle and pushed the door open against the wind, then turned right on Liberty Street. Before he reached Main Street, where his horse was hitched, Enos heard his name being called. He turned around to see Edward hailing and hurrying toward him.

"Edward? Did I forget something?" Enos paused, frowning at the clerk.

Edward shuffled his feet in the light snow. "No, no." The boy looked around furtively. Coatless, he hugged himself against the cold wind. "It's something else. I wanted to ask…what you thought 'bout the stranger at the meeting last night."

Why is he asking me this? "I think he's out to cause trouble. Why do you ask?"

Edward glanced beyond Enos' shoulder, then back up at him. "Ummm…well…" The boy ran a shaky hand through his tangled hair. "It's just—it seemed to me—that Jeb and Buster wanted to form a posse with that guy."

Enos raised an eyebrow and stared at him. "Yeah, what of it?"

Edward said, "Well—I know you and Buster are friends, and…" The boy shivered and looked down at his shuffling feet. "I was wondering—well—if you planned to join them." Edward flicked a glance back to the entrance of the mercantile.

Enos stared at the nervous youth. *Both of our fathers are staunch abolitionists. Does he want to join a slave hunting posse?*

"Edward, I don't know why you're asking *me*. I haven't heard of anyone forming posses."

The fifteen-year-old blurted in his high-pitched voice. "I don't believe you! I wanna go! My father is breaking the law by aiding and abetting those no-good runaways and I want to help catch 'em." The boy's eyes were bright as he looked quickly about.

Scowling, Enos moved closer and lowered his voice. "Edward, you are too young to get involved in these matters. You need to leave this bad business to the men in town."

Edward's voice turned petulant, "But I AM a man! My father still treats me like a child, but I'm a *man* and can ride and shoot as good as any of 'em."

Enos patted the boy on the arm to calm him. "I'm sure you can, Edward, but hunting fugitives is dangerous and you could get hurt." Enos waved his arm in the direction of the store and started to walk away. "'Tis best for you to stay at the mercantile with your father."

"You're going, aren't you, Enos? I knew it! You and Buster and that stranger fellah with the funny accent." Edward's eyes blazed and his voice rose as he got more agitated. "Tell me more—I wanna help!"

Enos adjusted the bundle under his arm, walked back to the youth and, with his other hand, pushed him to the side of the building. A man, with a woman clutching his arm against the wind, hurried down Liberty Street and entered the mercantile. When the door closed, Enos leaned toward Edward's ear. "Edward, are you sure you want to do this? What will you tell your father? He'll be mad as hell if he learns you've gone slave-hunting against his wishes."

Edward nodded furiously. "Yes, yes, I want to be involved! I won't tell my father a thing. I'm a *man* and don't need to report my every move to him." Edward put his hands on his hips and looked at Enos defiantly.

Enos wondered why Edward was so insistent. "So, Edward, tell me, what do you have against fugitives? Why do you want to catch them? You know our fathers want them freed."

Edward's pale face flushed and he looked away. "It's because she—" He stepped away from his inquisitor and folded his arms across his chest. "It's not your business, Enos. I just wanna go, that's all!" His voice cracked.

Enos shook his head and exhaled, his breath steaming in the cold air. "I think this is a very bad idea, Edward. But if you insist on coming along, then it's your choice. Mind you now, I won't be baby-coddlin' ya."

Edward grinned and picked at a pimple. "You won't have to, Enos. I can take care of myself. I promise!"

Enos shook his head in defeat. "Very well, then. Do you know where the mill clearing is at the bottom of the hill before the bridge?"

Edward nodded.

"Meet me and Buster there at five tonight. Dress warm and don't come armed. We'll be watching Zenas Ellis' farm out to south side. We need to see if there are any signs of fugitives hiding there." Enos adjusted the blanket bundle he held. "We may be there all night—you'll need to think up a good story to tell the Colonel so he doesn't come looking for you." Enos shook his head again, angered he had let himself be convinced to bring the eager boy along.

I hope Buster is right and nothing happens.

Edward did a little quick-step on the sidewalk. "You're right, Enos. I don't want Father worrying about me. I'll make up a story to explain my absence. Thank you. I know I will make you proud!" Edward clasped Enos' arm and scurried back into the mercantile, the wind blowing his hair straight out behind his head.

Enos made his way to Main Street, where his horse was tethered. Wiping snow from his saddle, he secured his bundle, then untethered his horse. After mounting, he shook his head, staring back at the entrance to Jeb's Tavern.

What in hell have I gotten myself into? If anything happens to that fool boy, it'll be my head on the damned chopping block.

BOYS MEET

Fifteen minutes before Enos was scheduled to meet Buster, he left the Adams' marble mansion on the west side of the common. Bundled against the chill wind, he watched light flurries float to the ground. Underneath his formal wool overcoat, he wore multiple layers of work clothes, including a heavy flannel shirt. He had told his parents he would be dining and playing charades with Miss Mathilda Sharron and her family. Mathilda's father, Simon, was a well-known carpenter in town, and had built homes for some of the prominent members of the community. Although not actively involved in the abolitionist movement, Simon was sympathetic to Joseph Adams' efforts.

Mathilda had recently turned eighteen and was earning her teaching credentials. Unbetrothed, she was actively courted by a number of eligible boys in town.

I hate lying to my parents, but I'm glad they believed me. Don't know what I'll tell them if we're out all night. And if Simon ever found out I used his daughter's name in a lie… he didn't even want to consider the consequences.

In the stables, Enos hung his wool coat on a hook and donned a travel-ing greatcoat. He replaced his felt hat with a tattered, wide-brimmed hat that would keep snow from melting down his neck. In one travel satchel were cheese and bread, a canteen of water and his monocular. In a second, smaller satchel, he packed his flintlock pistol, a powder flask, bag of minie balls and short tamping rod.

I hope I won't need to use the pistol, but it's best to be prepared.

Earlier in the day, when he had returned home from the tavern, he had fed and watered his gelding, Beldon, but had left the horse saddled and the new blankets secured, so he could leave quickly. Now, Enos attached one satchel to each side of the cantle and secured his lantern staff in the pouch slung from the horn. He mounted the horse and retrieved the lantern from its hook on the wall, then balanced it on the hooked staff.

Squeezing his legs against the horse's sides, Enos urged Beldon out of the stables. Horse and rider turned right and cantered around the town common, where they reached Main Street. Turning right, Beldon trotted through the quiet town and headed south toward the bridge. Snow had been falling off and on all day. Although cart tracks had worn grooves into the mud, the slope down to the bridge next to the slate mill was still slip-pery. Enos slackened the reins and let his horse pick his way down the hill. Halting before the bridge, he paused, listening to the drumming of the falls on the craggy rocks below. Steering Beldon off to the right of the main road, he made his way around a small copse of trees and entered a clearing about twenty feet away from the edge of the steep riverbank.

A voice called from deeper in the trees. "Enos! Ovah heah!"

Enos turned his horse slightly and followed Buster's voice. Moments later, he saw his friend standing beneath a tree, next to his tethered horse. Enos dismounted, unhooked his lantern and secured his horse next to Buster's.

I must tell him about Edward. I hope he isn't mad. "Hey, Buster." Enos nodded to his friend.

Buster's lopsided grin took on an eerie cast in the glow of the lantern. "You ready to have a l'il fun t'night?" His chuckle sounded a bit ominous.

"Buster, I have something to tell you. There's someone else who's going to join us." Enos shuffled his feet as his horse sidestepped toward him.

Buster's eyes narrowed. "Yeah? Who's that?"

Enos cleared his throat. "Ummm…Edward Allen."

Buster snarled. "What! Edward? Colonel Allen's son? Are you crazy? Why in the hell would you wanna bring him along? Christ, Enos! What the hell were you thinkin'?"

Enos held up his hand to his agitated friend. "I know. I'm sorry, Buster. But I went into the mercantile today to buy some blankets, and Edward came after me on the sidewalk when I left. He said he thought you and I were joining a slave posse and insisted he wanted to help."

"Damn, Enos! He's just a kid. I won't be coddlin' him. And what if he tells his fathah about this? You'll be in deep trouble and that boy'll get a strappin' he won't never forget."

"That's what I told him, Buster. But Edward insisted he was a man and his father wouldn't find out. So against my better judgment, I told him to meet us here." Enos shrugged his shoulders in frustration. "What else could I do?"

The sound of a horse nickering near the bridge caught their attention. "That's probably Edward, I'll go get him." Glad for an excuse to escape Buster's wrath, Enos walked through the dripping trees to the edge of the road. He recognized the boy in the glow of the lantern swinging from his horse.

"Edward, this way," he called quietly.

Edward turned his horse from the main road and followed Enos across the clearing into the cluster of trees to where Buster waited.

Buster stood in the gloom next to Enos' horse, both hands on his hips. The glow of Enos' lantern lit Buster's disgusted face. Buster hissed at the young interloper. "Come down, Edward. We need to talk."

Edward dismounted and held the reins, the lantern swinging from the staff, as the horse shied away from the others. "Whoa, boy. Whoa." Edward reached out and stroked the horse's neck to calm him.

Buster positioned himself directly in front of Edward and glared at the interloper. Edward shuffled his feet and looked away. Enos watched from one side.

"What are you doing heah, Edward? Are you crazy, or what?" Buster grabbed the boy's arm and squeezed.

Edward let out a small yelp, then composed himself. "Enos said I could come! I'm sorry, Buster, but I thought I could help you guys."

Buster asked, "Do you know what we're doin' t'night?"

Edward nodded several times. "Yep! We're catching nigger runaways! It's the law!" His voice rose enthusiastically.

Buster leaned into the eager boy. "Shhh. Keep your voice down. And *no*! That is *not* what we're doin', Edward!" Buster's spittle splashed the boy's face. "We're watchin' the Zenas Ellis farm to see if there's any signs he *might* be harborin' fugitives. If we see anythin' suspicious, we're just supposed to report back to Jeb's Tavern. Do you understand?" Buster jammed his finger into the boy's chest for emphasis.

Edward stumbled back and looked sheepishly at Buster. "And then what? We go hunt 'em down and catch 'em, right?"

Buster shook his head and laughed dismissively. "No, Edward. You ain't huntin' nobody. If we see anything, the men'll form a posse and do the huntin'. I don't even want you heah, and Enos shouldn't have let you come. Now, go home!"

Edward straightened his shoulders and glared back at Buster. "I'm a *man*, Buster, just like you and Enos. I can hunt niggers just as good as any-one." He turned toward Enos. "If you don't let me come, then I will tell *both* our fathers what you're up to. You'll be in big trouble then, Enos!"

Enos wished with all his might he hadn't let Edward talk him into letting the boy accompany them. He had a bad feeling that kept getting worse. With his breath coming rapidly, Enos grabbed Edward and pulled him toward the brink of the deep river chasm. "I swear to God, Edward, if you mention this to anyone, I will throw you over the falls!"

Edward squealed, yanking away from Enos' grasp. He looked petulantly back toward Buster. "Take me along. I won't be no trouble, I promise!"

Buster glanced over his shoulder at Enos and shook his head.

Enos shrugged and raised an eyebrow. "I told you, Buster. He's deter-mined. Might's well let him come along. Like you said, nothing's gonna happen."

Buster rubbed his days-old stubble and glared at Edward. "Edward! If you so much as mention a peep of this to anyone, I'll *gladly* help Enos throw you to your death! Do you understand?"

Edward vigorously nodded his head. "I promise, Buster, honest!"

"I don't like it, but let's get goin'." Buster lit his lantern, untethered his horse and mounted.

Enos mounted Beldon and hung his lantern on the staff crook, tucked his collar under his hat to keep the snow out, then motioned for Edward to follow Buster. Reaching the road, they turned right and rode their horses slowly across the slippery wooden bridge. Spray from the roaring falls slapped their cloaks.

Once across the bridge, Buster clucked his tongue to trot his horse up the rutted, snow-covered hill.

Enos watched from below as Buster, then Edward and his mount, crested the steep slope. Enos leaned to his gelding. "You ready, Beldon?" He squeezed his legs against the horse's side. "Let's go!"

The horse trotted three-quarters of the way up the hill, then Enos felt the horse's front legs slipping in the muck. Enos leaned forward in the saddle and lifted the reins on the horse's neck. "C'mon, boy. You can make it." The horse did a sidestep, regained his footing, and joined the waiting riders. Enos reached down and stroked the horse's neck. "Good boy, Beldon! Good boy!"

Buster flashed his lopsided grinned when Enos reached him. "Didn't think you were gonna make it there for a minute. Beldon got himself a l'il spooked."

Enos nodded. "Oh, he's a good horse. Just needs more confidence, that's all." Enos rubbed the horse's neck again.

Buster and Enos rode side by side along the stretch of flat road leading south toward the New York border. Edward followed closely behind the two men. On two occasions, riders heading north toward town passed them. Brief greetings were exchanged. A few hundred yards before the trio reached the two-story, brick farmhouse of Zenas Ellis, Buster held up his hand for the party to halt. To their right spread fallow fields and grazing pastures of the Ellis farm. To their left, dense forest reached to the roadway. Edward halted his horse on Buster's left, and Enos stopped on Buster's right.

Pointing to a snow-covered path about the width of a wagon, its angled ascent through the woods barely visible, Buster said, "We're going up yondah where Zenas' sugaring house is. Douse your lanterns, mine will be enough. Follah me." Buster steered his horse left through the rough opening in the trees.

Enos and Edward both extinguished their lanterns as instructed. Edward followed Buster's horse and Enos brought up the rear. Low-hanging branches forced the three to duck their heads. About a hundred yards up the incline, the path switchbacked sharply to the left. Buster quietly urged his horse into a trot up the steeper section of the path. Edward and Enos followed closely behind. They quickly reached the sugaring barn, built on top of a ridge that paralleled the main road.

"We'll hitch the horses heah," Buster said as he dismounted. He wrapped his horse's reins around the hitching rail along the right side of the barn. From behind the saddle, he untied an old horse blanket and one satchel with a tamping rod protruding from its top. He removed a short-barreled, muzzle-loading rifle, hanging along the side of his saddle. Taking his lit lantern from the staff, he turned to his companions. "Leave your lanterns, we'll only need one. And bring whatevah else you need to set up watch," he told them.

Edward and Enos dismounted and tethered their horses. Enos detached his packet of blankets and his satchel. Edward also carried one satchel.

"Follah me," Buster said grasping his horse blanket and lantern in one hand, rifle in the other. The blanket shielded the lantern so the light wouldn't be seen from the road. Enos and Edward followed Buster single file down the path's steep slope until they reached the switchback. Buster turned to his left and carefully walked through several inches of snow along a slate ledge, then stopped. "We'll wait here." He pointed to the ledge they stood on. "Enos, hold the lantern and keep it shielded." Buster passed his friend the lantern and blanket. Then he used his feet to scrape snow from the stones to establish a place to sit. Buster turned to the boy. "Edward, cleah some space for you and Enos."

The boy obeyed, using his feet and satchel to clear a large swath of snow from the uneven rock of the ledge.

Enos passed the lantern and blanket back to Buster, then laid one of his blankets on the cold ground before sitting down. Edward plopped down on the bare stones to his left. "Edward, didn't you bring a blanket?"

Edward responded petulantly, "Nope—didn't think of it when I was packing. *Sorry!*"

"Keep your damned voices down," Buster hissed. "They carry on the night air."

Enos glanced over at Buster's exasperated face in the lantern glow and sighed. Enos moved to the right side of his blanket. "Here, Edward, sit here with me so you won't freeze your bottom."

Edward slid onto the blanket close to Enos. "Thanks."

"You boys done playin' around?" Buster growled. "Good, 'cause I'm dousin' the lantern."

Suddenly they were thrown into near complete darkness. Enos heard Buster lay the lantern on the ground. Then he felt his friend's hand on his shoulder.

"Enos, grab an end of my blanket," Buster directed.

Enos felt around then grabbed the edge of the blanket, while Buster spread it on the ground. With a grunt, Buster settled himself along the ledge. A moment later, Enos heard Buster rustling through his satchel. As his sight adjusted to the darkness, he saw Buster holding a long spyglass in front of his face.

"Wha'dya see?" Enos whispered.

The bulk of the brick, two-story Ellis farmhouse across the road below them was just visible in the twilight.

Buster swept the eyepiece in a side-to-side motion, peering through the scattered trees between their perch and the roadside. "I see lantern light in the house and barn. But I ain't seein' no movement."

Edward leaned across Enos and grasped Buster's arm. "Lemme see!"

Buster shook off the boy's hand. "No! Just calm down, Edward."

Enos asked quietly, "Now what?"

Buster lowered the spyglass to his lap and turned to the others. "Now we wait."

GABE AND LUKE PREPARE

Saturday night, after the family had finished their supper, the two Ellis boys, Zenas H., the elder and taller, and Barnaby, two years younger, exited their farmhouse carrying lanterns. They walked about thirty paces to the barn behind the house. Inside, Zenas collected two fishing poles, and Barnaby loaded some basic fishing tackle into a bucket. The boys left the barn and met their father, Zenas C., who waited for them next to the house. The three men, with Zenas Senior in the lead, followed their driveway and turned right onto the main road. The Hopper farm was approximately a quarter mile to the south of their farm, so there was no need to ride their horses.

Intermittent snow had been falling throughout the day and had changed to a light, cold rain, turning the several inches of snow into a slushy mess. The brothers walked a few steps behind their father.

Barnaby turned to his older brother. "Seems strange to be carrying fishin' gear this time of night."

Zenas chuckled. "Ay'up. Ain't nobody goes fishin' 'til dawn. But Luke asked us to bring it along, so we need to help him out."

"I'd say we've done pretty good on our fishin' trips. T'ain't one of 'em's been caught!" Barnaby exclaimed.

Both boys chuckled at the fugitive innuendo.

Suddenly, Zenas Senior stopped in the road and held up his hand. "Quiet, boys!" he hissed.

The young men stepped to their father's side. "What is it?" Barnaby whispered.

Zenas C. turned to his left and shined his lantern onto the leafless trees across the road. "Thought I heard something." He walked to the opposite edge of the road and peered into the dark depths, moving his lantern left and right. "Humpf. Sounded like a grunt. Might be a buck in rut, but seems it's a little early in the year though. Let us keep moving." He waved an arm ahead as he returned to his sons waiting on the other side of the road.

The three men silently passed in front of Luke's house and then Gabe's front porch, where they turned right into the path separating the house from the carriage barn. At the back, south-facing side of Gabe's home, Zenas Senior knocked on the outer door. The boys set the fishing poles, bucket, and lanterns on the stoop to the left.

Emma stood at the sink cleaning dishes from the supper she had prepared for Gabe and the Prescott family. Having finished the evening repast with his own family, Luke had joined his parents and now sat at their kitchen table. He and Gabe discussed their pending travel plans. Lanterns on the table and the wooden countertop provided ample light for the family's activities.

Responding to the knock on the door, Gabe rose and entered the anteroom. Opening the door, he welcomed his neighbors into the kitchen.

"Good evening, Friend Gabe, Friend Emma," Zenas C. said.

"Evenin' Miz' Hoppah, Mistah Hoppah," both Zenas H. and Barnaby chimed in.

Emma stepped away from her washing chores, wiped her hands on a towel, and smiled at their neighbors. "Good evening, gentlemen. I trust thee have eaten a satisfactory supper."

"Yes, Ma'am." Barnaby grinned. "Mothah always feeds us well."

Gabe waved his hand. "Well, since thee are well fortified, shall we get started?"

Luke stood and turned to Zenas the younger. "Did you bring the fishing tackle?"

"Sure did." Zenas H. nodded toward his brother. "We brought two poles and a bucket, just as you asked. They're on the stoop."

Luke patted the oldest son on the back. "Good. Thank you."

Assured the fishing gear was ready, Luke grasped a lantern from the kitchen table and set it on a shelf in the anteroom. He and Gabe donned their winter cloaks and boots, then Luke held the outer door for his neighbors. The brothers stepped outside and retrieved their lanterns and fishing gear. Zenas Senior followed, with Gabe and Luke exiting last. The men made their way to the hay barn directly behind the house.

At the barn door, Gabe turned to the Ellis men. "Please wait here, so I can alert the family to our arrival." He unlatched the lock and with Luke's help, slid the barn door open. Not having had a chance to apply grease, Gabe sighed as the wheel squealed in defiance. He stepped to the right of the wagon and approached the open trapdoor, where dim light seeped from the cavern.

Dropping to one knee, he quietly called, "Miss Elsie? Samuel? 'Tis I, Gabe."

Feet scuffed in the dirt, and Samuel's head popped into view at the bottom of the stairs. "Yas, Suh?"

"Samuel, my neighbor Zenas Ellis and his sons have arrived to load the wagon. Would thee be able to help with the hay?"

Samuel nodded. "Yas, Suh. I heard the wagon come in earlier. Let me put my shoes on and I'll be right there." Samuel's head disappeared to the left of the opening.

Gabe straightened and returned to the open barn door. "Thee can enter. They know we are here and Samuel shall assist us with the loading."

Luke and the Ellis boys entered the barn and stepped to the left of the wagon where the hay mow stall was located. Zenas C. entered last and yanked at the offending barn door. When it squealed once more, Zenas left it open a few feet to avoid making additional noise.

"Thee must get that wheel greased, Gabe." Zenas said to his friend. "'Tis a frightful noise."

Gabe nodded. "Yes. Yes. I know. Just have not had time to address it."

To light their work, the men hung their lanterns on wall nails, spread at intervals around the barn. At the back of the barn, beyond the stacked hay, five slatted wooden rail sidings leaned against the wall. The four side railings were approximately four feet long and three feet high, consisting of three horizontal boards nailed to two vertical wooden stanchions that protruded from the bottom. The fifth header railing was six feet wide and the same height. Metal hinges flapped along the ends of each set of railings. When hoisted above the wagon's existing sides, the stanchions slid into brackets protruding from the inside wall of the wagon, then buckled closed. When completely installed, the railings doubled the height of the side and headboard walls.

Luke motioned for the Ellis boys to follow him to the back of the barn. "Here, Zenas," he said, "grab one end." Luke and Zenas H. lifted the widest of the railings and carried it to the front end of the wagon behind the seat.

Just then, Samuel appeared at the right of the wagon and stood next to Gabe and Zenas C. "How can I help, Suh?"

The men stopped to look at the young Negro boy. Zenas H. and Barnaby both smiled at him. The younger brother walked around the wagon to greet the visitor. "Hey! I'm Barnaby. Nice ta meet'cha." He held out his hand to Samuel.

Samuel nodded and extended his right hand in greeting. "I'm Samuel."

As Barnaby looked down to grasp Samuel's hand, he exclaimed, "Whoa! What happened to your hand? Your fingahs are missin'!" Barnaby blushed at his outburst. "Oh, I'm so sorry—didn't mean to be rude."

Samuel's eyes crinkled. "It's a long story and happened when I was just a child. I can manage without them."

Barnaby shook his head. "Gee, that must be rough."

Luke called to the boys. "Barnaby, Samuel, get into the wagon and help us with this head railing."

As instructed, the two jumped onto the bed and positioned themselves at the head of the wagon. Luke and Zenas hefted the heavy, six-foot-wide wooden frame over the wagon side. Barnaby and Samuel lifted it above the headboard and slid the stanchions into the brackets. From the side of the wagon, Luke wiggled it a bit and it settled with a thump on top of the wagon frame.

"That looks good. Let's get the sides attached," Luke said to his helpers.

He and Zenas H. lifted one of the four-foot side railings up to Barnaby and Samuel, who positioned and slid it into place. When all four of the side railings were attached, Luke fastened down their end hinges, thus securing the four railings to the headboard for stability.

Gabe and Zenas Senior looked on in approval as the wagon took shape.

Zenas turned to Gabe and said, "What did thee make of the proceedings last evening? I felt badly for Joseph with the way the meeting ended. I bet he was furious with that interloper."

"I think the rabble-rouser is causing trouble and has pit neighbor against neighbor. 'Tis the devil's mission he is on!" Gabe grimaced and shook his head.

Zenas looked around the barn, then asked, "When shall thee leave?"

"Before first light. I wish to arrive at the canal just after dawn. We shall deliver the packages to Friend Titus, to board the steamer that will take them to Friend Robinson for passage to Canada."

Zenas nodded. "Yes. Friend Titus has been of great service to our cause. He will ensure their safe passage." The older neighbor rubbed his chin in thought. "The weather is foul, Gabe. Thee must pass slowly across the New York bridge with your heavy load." He waved his hand toward the wagon. "Thee knows the bridge will be perilous from this freezing rain and snow."

Gabe scratched his beard and nodded. "I thank thee for the reminder, Friend. We shall travel with utmost care as we cross the border." He looked at his longtime friend. "'Tis a shame to have snow this early in the season. The Lord certainly does work in mysterious ways." He shook his head.

Zenas chuckled, "That Friend, is our lot in this life!"

Luke retrieved two pitchforks leaning against the back wall of the barn, handed one each to Gabe and Zenas C., and grinned. "All hands on deck, gentlemen! Let's get this hay loaded." Luke walked around the back of the wagon and lifted from the wall a curve-handled hay rake sporting long horizontal tines. He turned to the younger men in the barn. "Boys, you'll have to use your hands."

Over the next hour or so, the six men established a work routine. The older men pitched mounds of hay into the wagon, while the three younger boys crawled around the wagon bed stacking the hay in layers against the extended headboard and sides. When the outer walls of hay were about a foot thick, Luke called a halt to the stacking. "Zenas, Samuel, climb down. Barnaby, stay up there and help us spread hay along the floorboards."

As the men shoveled mounds of hay onto the wagon bed, Barnaby spread it from the front to the rear of the wagon, creating a thick layer for the travelers to rest upon. Then he jumped down to the barn floor. A cavity of about four feet wide and six feet long, surrounded by hay, now existed in the bed of the wagon.

Luke turned to Samuel. "Do you think this will be sufficient room for your family to travel after we cover the load?"

Samuel looked at the result of their work. "Yas, Luke. It's fine. We've ridden in wagons a lot worse than this and we sure do appreciate all you've done for us."

Zenas H. tapped Luke's arm and pointed to the front corner of the barn. "Don't forget the fishin' gear when you get loaded up."

Luke nodded. "All right, boys. Let's call it done."

Zenas C. and his sons bade their farewells to Samuel and wished him and his family safe travels.

Before Samuel descended to the underground room, Gabe said, "We shall leave before first light. Please be sure thee are ready to travel."

As the men approached the barn door, Gabe frowned when he noticed it had been left a few feet ajar. With a sharp tug, the door slid open, making a light squeal. The five men, lanterns in hand, left the barn and Gabe closed and latched the door behind him. Zenas C. and his two sons bade goodbye to Luke and Gabe, then made their way north along the road back toward their farm.

Wearily, Luke and Gabe entered the anteroom of the Hopper house.

No one noticed the dark-cloaked figure crouching along the side of the hay barn.

BOYS GET A SURPRISE

Buster, Enos, and Edward had been sitting on the slate ledge for about an hour. The earlier snow had turned to a drizzling rain. Enos wrapped the second blanket over his shoulders for added warmth, and munched on the bread and cheese he retrieved from his satchel. Buster pulled his collar up and his hat down over his ears to keep the rain from dripping down his back. Edward, sharing Enos' blanket, seemed impervious to the wet conditions. His constant prattle grated on Buster and Enos, who did their best to ignore their unwanted companion.

"So what did you'ah fathah say when you told him you were having din-nah with Mathilda?" Buster asked Enos and chuckled.

Enos shrugged. "He said he had great respect for Simon Sharron and wished the man would join the abolitionist movement. You know my father: you're either with him or agin' him," he said, waving his hand in the air. "And of course, he asked what my intentions were by visiting Mathilda."

Buster laughed, mimicking Enos' father, Joseph Adams. "*Yes, my good son. What are thy intentions, indeed!*" In a lower voice, he added, "Wouldn't he like to know where you are right now!"

Enos chuckled at the imitation of his father. "I told him Mathilda was a friend of mine and we'd be playing charades after dinner, so I'd probably be late coming home. Mother thought it a fine way to spend a Saturday evening!"

"And it does sound like a *fine* way to spend a Saturday." A note of mischief entered Buster's voice. "But s'posing your fathah gets to asking Simon Sh—"

"Buster. Enos," Edward whispered urgently.

Buster ignored Edward. "—Simon Sharron 'bout tonight? You'll be in a heap of—"

"Buster! Enos!" Edward gave Enos a dig in the ribs.

Exasperated at another interruption, Buster leaned around Enos and glared at Edward. "What!"

"Look! Down there!" Edward pointed toward the road.

Buster and Enos peered down the hill through the barren trees toward the Ellis farm. Two indistinct figures carrying lanterns were entering the barn. Buster grabbed the spyglass and extended it to full length, focusing on the Ellis barn. Moments later, he saw Zenas H. and Barnaby Ellis coming out of the barn. Moving the eyepiece to his right, he spied the boys' father, holding a lantern, waiting by the house, where the sons joined him. As he watched, the three figures left the yard and turned south along the main road, where they would soon pass in front of their location on the ledge.

"Hmmm, wondah where they'ah going this time of night," Buster mumbled to himself.

"Wha'da ya see? Who is it?" Edward asked, his voice a bit too loud.

Enos squeezed the boy's arm to quiet him.

Buster whispered, "Looks like Zenas and his sons are out for a walk. That's odd in this weather. I'm gonna follow 'em. Stay heah!" he hissed to his companions.

Buster handed the spyglass to Enos and inched his way off the six-foot-high precipice, landing in the slushy snow below. As quickly as he could in the dark, he scrambled down the slope. Suddenly, his foot hit a boulder and he lost his balance. Flailing his arms, he tumbled a few yards until his back thumped into a tree. Involuntarily, a grunt escaped him. He lay still, wincing at the impact, trying to catch his breath.

On the ledge, Edward started to call out, "Bus—".

Enos threw his hand over the boy's mouth to quiet the outburst.

Squirming as quietly as he could to right himself, Buster saw lantern light penetrating the woods, illuminating the snow-covered, forested slope to just a few feet below where he had landed. Despite the pain in his back, he tried not to move.

A man's deep voice at the bottom of the slope said, "…sounded like a grunt. Might be a buck in rut. . ."

Buster stayed perfectly still, holding his breath.

After what seemed like an eternity, the figure holding the lantern moved to the other side of the road. Buster assumed it was Zenas Senior, with his two sons following. He exhaled and got to his feet and did a quick check to make sure he hadn't broken anything. Then he continued his slide down the remainder of the slope to the edge of the road. As he watched the backs of the three figures move away, he caught a glimpse of something in one of the son's hands.

What is he carrying? Fishin' poles? Why are they going fishin' this time of night? Somethin' ain't right heah.

When the Ellis men turned right into Gabe's yard, Buster quickly crossed the road to traverse the fallow fields adjacent to the two Hopper houses. Staying at a safe distance so as not to be seen, he passed behind Luke's house and worked his way through the uneven, terrain to the north side of Gabe's hay barn. He crouched halfway along the wall and watched the Ellis men enter the Hopper kitchen.

A few minutes later, Buster heard voices coming from outside the back door. He stood and flattened himself against the side of the barn. Then he heard Gabe's voice very close by, "Please wait here so I can alert the family to our arrival." Buster heard the barn door squeal open.

Family? Shit! The Hoppahs are haborin' fugitives! I would've thought it would be Zenas Ellis. I wondah if that's why Miz' Hoppah was confused when I asked her about the sick calf yesterday. I thought there was something off about that story. Buster took shallow breaths and waited.

Gabe's voice reached him. "Thee can enter. They know we are here and Samuel shall assist us with the loading."

Buster remained motionless as the barn door squalled. His heart pounded and his breath quickened. *Damn! I had no idea the Hoppahs were involved. I guess I found what Duschanne wanted, but it's just the wrong family. Now what am I gonna do?*

After waiting for several minutes, Buster crept to the front corner of the barn. Lantern glow spilled onto the ground in front of him and he realized the barn door was partially opened. Silently, he positioned himself against the front wall of the barn, next to the opening, and quickly peeked inside.

Damn! That's a niggah boy talking to Barnaby. He flattened himself back against the front wall.

Buster's heart thudded and he put his hand over his mouth to control his breathing. Snippets of conversation drifted through the open barn door.

"...your fingahs are missin'!"

"...I can manage without them..."

Peering through the drizzling rain, Buster could see Emma inside the kitchen moving about. Then she sat at the kitchen table in front of the window, bent forward and tilted her head, focused on something in front of her.

Realizing Emma might see him if she looked out, Buster slid to the side of the barn out of the reach of the lantern light, and crouched beneath the dripping eaves. While he strained to hear the conversation, a thump came from the barn and the wagon hinges squeaked.

"...I think the rabble-rouser is causing trouble..."

"...before first light. I wish to arrive at the canal just after dawn..."

That sounds like Mistah Hoppah. They're movin' the fugitives later tonight!

"...Yes. Friend Titus has been of great service to our cause..."

"...We shall travel with utmost care as we cross the border..."

They're takin' 'em to the canal! I gotta alert Duschanne so he can get his posse ready. But I'd bettah wait until they're done. Maybe I can learn more.

Buster moved to the front of the barn and risked one more peek through the open door. He saw the black boy and Barnaby in the wagon, attaching railings to the side walls. When he pulled back from the door, he noticed Emma staring intently out the kitchen window in his direction. He scurried to the dark side of the barn, where he pressed himself against the wall, trembling.

Shit! I wondah if she saw me!

After what seemed like an eternity, Buster heard Luke's voice.

"All right boys. Let's call it done."

Buster slid to the back end of the barn, where he bent to a crouch, ignoring the cramping in his legs. The door squealed shut and he heard the men bid their farewells. He stayed in position until he saw the Ellis men, carrying their lanterns, pass in front of Luke's house, heading north along the road. Stumbling in the dark across the fallow fields, Buster followed the men at a distance and watched until they entered the Ellis house. Then he crossed the road and went cautiously into the dark woods. Slowly he made his way at an angle through the trees up the slope, until he felt the slate ledge in front of him. He hoisted himself onto the edge, then walked north, being careful not to slip off the uneven surface. At one point he stumbled on a rock and his foot landed hard, breaking a branch.

Edward called out, "Buster? That you?"

Buster heard Enos chastise their unwanted guest. "Edward, shush."

Buster peered straight ahead along the ledge, and could just make out two dark forms hunched together. Catching his breath, he joined the others and plopped down on the horse blanket to Enos' right.

Enos asked, "You okay?"

Edward leaned past Enos and asked eagerly, "Buster? What happened? Did you find any niggers we can go catch? Where are they? Let's go!" The youth pulled a revolver from his satchel and flailed it wildly in the air.

Enos grasped Edward's arm, and yanked the gun from his hand, setting it on the ground out of the boy's reach. "Edward! Goddammit! I told you not to come armed. You're dangerous with that thing. Just shut up and calm down!"

Buster removed his drenched hat, and ran his hands through his hair, then replaced the hat and took a couple of deep breaths. Ignoring Edward's question, he turned to his good friend and said in a strained voice, "Enos, you're not going to like this, but the Hoppahs are hidin' fugitives."

"What!" Enos hissed. "You must be mistaken! We work there every day. We would've known!"

Buster held up his hand. "Honest to God, Enos! I ain't lyin'. I saw the niggah boy with my own eyes! I sweah!" He put his hand over his heart. "Heard the niggah's name is Samuel, and there's somethin' about him missin' fingahs. Mistah Hoppah said there's a whole family there—don't know how many."

Enos shook his head in disbelief. "Are you sure, Buster? I can't believe this!"

"Yep, and heah's the thing," Buster took a breath. "Best I could tell, they're planning to leave before first light in the mornin' to transport the fugitives."

Enos said, "They're leaving tonight? But that's impossible—tomorrow's Sunday. They'll be missed at services."

Buster grunted. "That's what I heard, Enos. They were in the barn fixin' up the wagon with hay, and gettin' ready to go to the canal."

Edward chimed in, "So whatta we waitin' for, Buster? Let's go get 'em!" He reached for his revolver in the snow. Enos blocked him.

Buster shook his head several times. Scowling, he turned to the overeager boy. "Edward, shut your mouth for once and put that damned gun away!" He sighed. "Enos. Much as I hate to do this—'cuz I like the Hoppahs—we gotta turn 'em in to Duschanne!"

GUNS ARE LOADED

As Emma moved about the kitchen finishing chores, she hummed a favorite hymn. Gathering slices of smoked ham, bread, cheese wedges, and fresh apples. she wrapped them in reused brown grocery paper and tied the package. Placing the bundle in a clean flour sack, she cinched the string.

I hope this shall sustain Miss Elsie and her family until they reach Friend Robinson's Rokeby farm.

She walked into the bedroom, retrieving her diary from the nightstand, and returned to the kitchen table. Her well-used pen and ink pot were positioned next to the window. Pulling the candle closer, Emma began a new diary entry.

10 mo. 12th, Saturday evening, 1850

'Tis been a hectic day as we prepare to transport the Prescotts to the canal in Whitehall, so they may continue their journey north. Gabe and Luke will leave before first light on the morrow with the family covered in the hay wagon. The weather has been foul—snowing, raining and now freezing. I fear there may be difficulty for the horses pulling that heavy load.

I ask the Lord's forgiveness as I was remiss in my chores this morning. Miss Elsie and her family imparted to me more of their difficult journey to reach our farm. I am continually amazed by their fortitude and determination to reach the Promised Land.

When Miss Elsie saw her grandson, Jonah's life was in danger, she knew they must leave the plantation. She spent months trying to contact her brother, Robert, in the Navy. Finally, she learned when his ship would be in dock at Chesapeake Bay. In the stealth of night, the family slipped away from the plantation and spent days wading through swamps, and evading the hounds, to reach the dock. Thank God, Elsie was able to find her brother, who took them on board the naval vessel and provided them protection.

Emma looked up from her writing and flexed her fatigued wrist. *The Lord was watching over them. What would their fate have been had they not found Robert at the dock?* She continued her diary entry:

I am grateful that when the family reached New York, my son, Adam and Uncle Isaac T. Hopper provided them comfort and sustenance.

Emma smiled as she pictured Uncle Isaac, weaving his fanciful stories, bouncing three-year-old Jonah on his lap. Though Isaac was small-statured, he stood with the dignity of a much taller man.

She dipped her pen in the inkwell. *In the spring, I shall ask Gabe if he would like to visit his dear uncle. The sweet man is gaining years and I wish to pay my respects before the Lord takes him home.*

Sighing, Emma turned to a blank journal page and wrote of how Adam drove the Prescotts from the city to a safe house in the country, and of the two women there who welcomed them. As Emma turned to her right to dip her long-feathered pen into the inkwell, she thought she saw movement near the shaft of light spilling from the partially open barn door. Moving the lantern and candle away from the window, she leaned closer to peer through the rain-splashed pane. Fog and rain swirled in the eerie glow.

I wonder why Father has left the barn door open. 'Tis not like him.

She stared more intently into the darkness, trying to determine what might have caught her attention.

Hmmm…thought I saw something. She rubbed her forehead. *Must be my tired, old eyes playing tricks on me.* She yawned, then continued writing Elsie's account of the family's journey up to when they had arrived at the Hopper farm. Emma ended her diary entry:

I thank Thee, Dear Lord, for guiding the Prescotts on their journey and
they have arrived safely into our care. We seek to do Thy will on this earth
in Thy Loving Grace. Amen.

As Emma closed the diary, she heard Gabe and Luke talking quietly as they entered the anteroom. After removing their outer garments and boots, they set their lanterns on the kitchen table and joined her.

Emma placed her folded hands atop the closed leather-bound diary, and looked at Gabe. "Has thee prepared the wagon for travel?"

Both men nodded. "Yes, Mother," Luke replied. "The side boards are secured and Samuel helped Zenas and Barnaby stack the hay."

Emma raised an eyebrow. "Is that so? What did the Ellis boys think of Samuel?"

Gabe chuckled. "Barnaby was surprised to see Samuel's missing fingers and asked what happened to them."

"Oh, my goodness!" Emma placed a hand to her heart, shaking her head. "That boy certainly does speak out of turn. What did Samuel say?"

Gabe said, "Samuel laughed off Barnaby's inquiry, and said he could manage just fine without them."

Luke nodded. "And he was right. Samuel worked hard to help us get the hay loaded."

Gabe added, "I told Samuel to make sure the family was prepared to travel before first light and he assured me they would have their satchels packed."

Emma stared out the window, then turned back to Gabe. "Why did thee leave the barn door ajar? I saw lantern light shining into the yard."

Gabe looked toward the now-closed barn door. "Ahhh. 'Twas Zenas C. who left it open because of that infernal squeal. With the wagon in the way, I did not notice until we left. Why does thee ask?"

Emma shrugged. "Thought I saw something moving near the barn."

Luke and Gabe stared at each other.

Gabe's brow knitted and he reached over to touch Emma's hand. "What did thee see, Mother?"

"Oh, my! I must say I do not know," a flustered Emma exclaimed. "It may have been the rain playing tricks on my failing sight." She rubbed her eyes. "'Tis not important. Shall we pray?"

Emma grasped Gabe's hand and reached for Luke's. The three bowed their heads at the table and Emma prayed, "Dear Heavenly Father, please watch over Thy travelers on this dreary night and keep them safe in Thy loving grace as we seek to do Thy will on this earth. Amen."

"Amen," Gabe and Luke chimed in.

Emma pointed to the full flour sack on the counter. "I have prepared a food satchel for the family. Please wake me, so I may bid my farewells before you leave." Emma gathered her diary and lantern, said good night, and made her way to their bedroom.

Once Emma had closed the bedroom door, Gabe leaned close to Luke and spoke quietly. "Does thee think we had an unwanted visitor tonight?" *I wonder who might spy on us—could be anyone.*

"I don't know. I certainly hope not." Luke peered into the darkness beyond the window. "Probably just a skunk or 'coon stalking the hen house." He bent closer to Gabe. "Father, I know you abhor violence, as do I. But I am concerned about the presence of the slave catcher in our midst. I believe we have been diligent in concealing our visitors, but I think 'tis prudent to be well prepared for our journey."

"What does thee propose?" Gabe asked, his deep voice cracking with weariness.

"When we travel, I usually have my Colt revolver. But I think you should also consider bringing your shotgun." Luke waved his hand toward the outer room.

Gabe scratched his beard. "Hmmm…maybe. But would we not look suspicious going on a fishing trip fully armed?"

Luke stared at the rain weeping down the pane and caught the reflection of his tousled brown hair. Half-heartedly, he ran his fingers through it. "Yes, perhaps. But I can conceal the Colt under my cloak, and we can wedge the shotgun behind our legs on the wagon. Traveling at night, it won't be seen."

The creases in Gabe's forehead deepened. "I do not like it, but I understand thy concern. This infernal law is raising the devil himself from the pits of hell. I deem 'tis wise to be prepared to ensure our travelers reach their destination."

Luke rose from his chair. "I'll go collect my gun and bid good night to Mary and the children. I think it best if I rest on your divan, so I don't wake them when we leave."

Gabe followed Luke into the anteroom, where Luke bundled into his cloak and boots, retrieved his lantern and left for home. To Gabe's right, still propped in the corner from the previous night, was his loaded shotgun, the double-barrels cracked open. He retrieved the firearm and, returning to the kitchen, set it gently on the table.

Moving into the main room, he gathered a flask of black powder, sheets of paper, a wooden dowel, a small leather satchel with a long strap, and a pouch of round lead balls from a drawer in his rolltop desk.

That Southerner is stirring up a hornets' nest. But if it wasn't him, it would be someone else eventually. Those bloody Washington politicians are being cowed by the rich plantation owners so they can keep their slaves. And Fillmore is nothing but their string puppet!

Back at the table, Gabe folded then ripped the paper into twelve equally sized squares. He wrapped one square around the end of the wooden dowel. Holding it firmly with his finger, he dripped candle wax along the side of the paper roll and secured the loose end into the wax. He squeezed the roll for several seconds while the wax hardened.

I wonder which of our good neighbors shall betray our trust and follow Satan's lead? And did Sheriff Wardwell run that scoundrel out of town, or are they in cahoots? I wish the Lord would provide me with more answers!

Slipping the roll partially off the dowel, Gabe twisted and crimped the end. Cupping the closed end of the paper cylinder in his palm, he added a lead ball, then poured a measured amount of gunpowder into the cavity. When the top of the roll was twisted and crimped, he had a fully contained charge.

I have the utmost respect for those who have escaped from their oppressive, greedy owners. I cannot imagine my entire life spent in bondage! 'Tis against God's will, and a sin, for any man to own another. Why cannot those politicians, who claim to be of the Christian faith, adhere to that simple truth?

Brow knotted and muttering to himself, Gabe continued forming and crimping twelve shotgun charges. Wanting to ensure his previously loaded charges were secure, he extracted the rod from its gun sheath, then tamped the long barrels. Pulling a cloth from the counter, he wiped any loose residue from the stock and barrels.

Of course, 'tis not surprising that Christian beliefs would play second fiddle to greed and power! It has always been the way of mankind Jesus preached so ardently against.

As he stashed the crimped charges into the leather satchel, footsteps on the stoop pulled Gabe from his troubled thoughts.

After hanging his wet cloak, Luke joined Gabe. He placed his revolver and a small box of gun-loading gear on the table. "Looks like you have ample charges for the journey, Father."

Gabe glanced at the satchel. "I hope I shall use nary of these. But the shotgun is loaded for travel." He secured the flap over the satchel full of charges. "Is all well with Mary and the children?"

Luke nodded. "Yes. The baby tires her, but she manages." Luke opened the revolving chamber and poured a measured amount of powder from a flask into each hole, then looked at Gabe. "Naturally, she frets over our impending travels. I have reassured her we will take every precaution for a safe journey." Next Luke placed a felt wad over one open chamber and added a .44 caliber round ball on top of the wad. He turned the cylinder until it met the loading lever, compressing the ball into the chamber.

Luke chuckled as he continued loading the gun. "Brian and Bernard wanted to ride along in the wagon."

Gabe leaned his loaded shotgun against the wall and furrowed his brow. "I hope thee told them *no*."

Luke kept his gaze fixed on his work. "Didn't have to. Mary made it very clear to the boys they were not allowed on this journey, and they weren't to discuss our visitors with their classmates." Luke half-cocked the hammer and placed a percussion cap into the nipple of four of the five chambers. The last nipple he left empty. He rotated the cylinder within the gun until the open nipple faced the hammer, which he uncocked, then let it rest against the uncharged cylinder as the safety. When ready to shoot, Luke would quickly add a final percussion cap to the fifth chamber, and the firearm would be fully loaded.

While Luke finished loading his revolver, Gabe returned the extra paper, dowel, and remaining round balls to his desk drawer in the main room. Sitting back at the table he asked Luke, "When thee was in town, did thee learn the name of the Southerner who disrupted Joseph's meeting?"

Luke used a soft cloth to wipe the barrel clean. "No, I didn't hear his name. But I did see Buster and Enos having what looked like an argument outside Jeb's Tavern."

Gabe's face wrinkled more deeply. "That is unusual for those boys. They seem quite cordial to each other."

Luke nodded. "Yep, I thought it was odd, too. Then they went together into the tavern. A few minutes later, I saw the north-side farmer go into the tavern, and that big, dim-witted Cyrus followed him."

Gabe shook his head. "This worries me greatly. What does thee think they were doing?"

"If I had my guess, I'd bet Jeb was gathering a posse, probably working with the Southern rabble-rouser. But I wouldn't expect Enos to be involved. Can't say the same for Buster though, being Jeb's son and all." Luke peered through the window toward the barn.

Gabe ran his fingers through his long, gray hair and sighed. "I hope those boys imbibed heartily and do not get motivated for many days—if ever."

Luke's wan smile poorly concealed his personal angst, even though his father was trying to make light of the situation. He changed the subject. "I heard Zenas warn you about the New York bridge."

"Yes. He said the bridge would be perilous with this snow and to cross carefully. Do not know why railings were not built," Gabe grumbled. "I am always leery of that bridge, even in good weather."

Shrugging, Luke said, "Who knows? Politicians probably ran out of money to finish the darn thing!" He returned the gun-loading gear to the small box and set the loaded revolver near the edge of the table, muzzle pointing toward the window. "At least the horses have made the trip many times, and the crossing no longer spooks them. Plus, we have a heavy load, which is easier to keep on track."

Gabe squeezed his hands together. "With Mary and Mother praying for us, and with the Good Lord watching over us, I am confident our mission will succeed." Gabe bowed his head and whispered a quick prayer.

Luke whispered, "Amen. And I am glad we are armed just in case anything untoward should happen." He rose from the table and stepped up into the parlor. "Still, who's going to be out on the roads looking for trouble at an early hour on the Sabbath?"

"Aye, that is what I hope as well. I shall wake thee when the clock strikes four." Gabe watched Luke curl his long limbs on the small sofa and pull a blanket over himself.

Gabe blew out the candle and doused the lanterns on the kitchen table. By the glow of the fire in the wood stove, he made his way to the left side of the parlor and slowly opened the door to the small master bedroom. Emma breathed gently in her bed to his right. He slid off his suspenders but did not undress, instead lying quietly on the bed, and pulling a woolen blanket over his shoulders. To still the thoughts racing through his mind about the pending journey, Gabe sought solace in prayer.

Dear Lord. I am eternally grateful to be blessed with a wonderful wife and two strong, healthy sons. 'Tis my honor to seek to do Thy will on this earth and help Thy oppressed children gain freedom to live in Thy everlasting Grace. Amen.

POSSE GATHERS

About 9:00 p.m. that Saturday night, after hitching their horses, Buster led Enos and Edward into his father Jeb's tavern. Soaked and chilled to the bone after hours of sitting in the inclement weather watching the Ellis farm, they found the smoky warmth of the tavern a welcome haven.

Patrons gathered at the bar, laughing and talking loudly. Jeb manned the closest end of the bar, and a small, wiry, bearded fellow poured beers for those at the opposite end. A big fire blazed in the hearth, in front of which four men played dice at a low table.

Situated against the back wall, two men played fiddles, while a third smacked a raucous beat on his tambourine. Other folks sat at tables facing the band, drinking and tapping their feet to the music. The sickly-sweet smell of pipe tobacco permeated the room.

Buster sidled up to the bar and waved his hand to get his father's attention. "Hey, Pop! Busy night, eh?"

Jeb came closer, bending across the bar toward Buster. He glared at the three shivering boys. "What in tarnation have you been doin'? Y'all look like hell!"

Buster leaned closer to his father, not wanting to be heard by the other patrons. "We've been on patrol. I'll tell you moah latah."

Jeb straightened, placing his hands on the bar, a sly grin spreading across his face. "Well, then! What can I get you boys?"

"Beahs for me and Enos, and a pop for Edward. This here fellah is too young to be drinkin'!" Buster grinned and slapped the despondent boy on the back. Edward recoiled from Buster's touch.

With freshly poured drinks in hand, Buster led the way past the bar with Enos and Edward following, leaving a trail of drips and small puddles in their wake. Buster approached the closed door on the left leading to the card room. A hand-printed sign on the door said: *Private meeting. Knock first.* Without hesitation, Buster gave it three smart raps.

"Who goes there?" a deep, male voice came from beyond the door.

"It's me, Bustah, with friends."

The door opened and Buster entered the smoke-filled, windowless chamber, followed by his companions. Pierre Duschanne, Sheriff Wardwell and the sheriff's son George sat at a table along one side of the room, drinking ale. Eight other men were gathered at nearby card tables. Their loud conversations stopped when the three disheveled boys entered the room.

In the afternoon some hours earlier, when the first meeting had ended, the teams enlisted by Duschanne had left for their assigned watch locations. Buster, Enos and Edward were the last to rejoin the group.

Duschanne stood and greeted them. "Well! Well! *Bien, retour a durer.* Welcome back, boys. We were wondering where you 'ad been, yah? Ze others 'ave been back for *un moment*—a while now. How did your watch go, *Messieurs?*"

Buster set his beer on the table next to Duschanne, dropped his water-logged coat and hat on the floor, and sat down. Enos and Edward stood behind Buster's chair and removed their cloaks.

"We done fou—" Edward piped up, only to be silenced by a sharp jab in his ribs from Enos.

George, the sheriff's son, sneered, "Looks like all you fellas did was get caught in the weather!"

Sheriff Wardwell and Duschanne chuckled.

Buster squinted at George, but otherwise ignored the remark. Frowning, he motioned for Duschanne, Wardwell and George to lean in closer.

Buster's eyes gleamed. With his voice lowered, he told Duschanne, "We done found us some niggahs!" He grinned mischievously at seeing the others' surprised looks. He took a long drink of his beer, then belched and laughed.

"*Très bien!*" said Duschanne, his eyebrows raised as he rubbed his hands together.

Sheriff Wardwell asked, "Are they at the Ellis farm like we thought?"

Buster shook his head. "Nope. Ya ain't gonna believe this, but they're at the Hoppah farm."

George exclaimed, "What! The Hoppers? You mean Gabe and Luke Hopper? That can't be right. Are you sure?"

Buster sat up a little straighter, placing his hands on the table. "Yep, I'm shoah. Done seen the niggah boy with my own eyes in the Hoppah barn."

The sheriff's forehead furrowed. "Thought you were watching the Ellis farm. How'd you end up at the Hoppers instead?"

Buster pointed his thumb back at his two companions. "We *was* watchin' the Ellis farm. Then we seen Zenas and his boys walkin' past us on the road."

"I saw 'em first!" Edward stated loudly, leaning over Buster's shoulder, defiantly putting his hand on his hip.

Edward's outburst caught the attention of the other men in the room, who quickly rose and gathered around Sheriff Wardwell's table.

Buster turned to see the men approaching and glared at Edward. Turning his back to the boy, he said to the sheriff, "Yes, Edward saw them first. But I followed them and they went directly to the Hoppah house. So I hid beside their hay barn to watch."

Duschanne lit his pipe and puffed out the smoke. "An' what did you see? Tell us everythin'" The Frenchman stared intently at Buster.

Buster felt the heat rising on his neck and squirmed in his chair with the men staring at him. *Everything? Shit! I like workin' for the Hoppahs and feel bad about spyin' on 'em.* Suddenly he regretted telling what he had seen inside the Hopper barn. *Shoah do wish they weren't helpin' the runaways. Should I tell 'em or should I…* His lips moved as he struggled with his response. *I can't just shut up now—I've already said too much. Damn!… But the Hoppahs are breakin' the law, and I guess they need to be stopped.* Still hesitating, he stared at Duschanne.

The Southerner took another puff on his pipe. "Well? Speak up, *Monsieur!*"

Buster glanced at Sheriff Wardwell for any guidance the lawman might provide.

The sheriff nodded to Buster. "You can tell us what you saw, Buster. All these men here have been deputized and will keep our secret."

Buster jumped when he felt a hand on his shoulder, then heard Enos whispering in his ear. "You don't have to do this, Buster. The Hoppers are friends of ours. Maybe there's another way."

Conflicting expressions crossed his face, then, finally Buster pulled away from Enos' grasp and took a breath. Leaning toward Duschanne, he said, "When I was hidin' by the side of the barn, I heard the men comin' out of the house. Then I heard Mistah Hoppah say, *Please wait so I can alert the family.* I figured he was talkin' 'bout some fugitives."

Duschanne and the head lawman glanced at one another.

Buster took a drink of ale, his hand trembling, and continued, "The Hoppahs' barn door was left open a bit, and I peeked inside. That's when I saw the niggah boy. Done heard somethin' 'bout him missin' fingahs."

"Is zat so?" Duschanne asked with considerable interest, his accent thickening in his excitement. "Tell me, *Monsieur,* 'bout how old would you say ze boy was?"

Buster shrugged. "Can't say for shoah. Maybe eleven or twelve."

Duschanne laid his pipe in the ashtray, then pulled a handful of broadsides from his satchel on the floor. He laid the posters on the table in front of him. All had the word WANTED in big letters across the top. Whistling softly through his teeth, the Southerner quickly flipped through five or six, then stopped. He loudly read the broadside he was holding to the men gathered around the table. "*Wanted. Fugitive slave family. Two women, one boy, one boy-child. Older boy missing first two fingers of right hand. One* thousand *dollar reward for capture and return alive to Mitchel Swaley, Esquire, Swaley Manor, Bryantown Hundred, Charles County, Maryland.*"

Several of the men gathered around the table commented to one another. Duschanne looked up from his reading and stared at Buster. "How many were in ze family, Buster?"

"I—I—I don't know. Nevah did heah 'em say." Buster fidgeted in his chair, and took another gulp of his ale.

"*Eh bien.* What else did you hear?" Duschanne gave Buster a stern look.

Buster hesitated at the direct interrogation. "Ahhh...I heard 'em say they was leavin' befoah first light in the mornin'. They were loadin' hay into the wagon. I heard 'em say they was goin' to the canal in Whitehall." Again, he felt the back of his neck burning.

The sheriff said gruffly, "They're traveling on Sunday? That seems unlikely." He waved his beefy hand. "You sure you heard 'em right, Buster?"

Buster peered at the sheriff through his still damp, tousled hair. "Yes, Sir, best I could tell, that's what they said. Heard Mistah Hoppah mention some guy named Titus."

Sheriff Wardwell nodded. "Duschanne, I know of this Titus fella. Free black man who works the steamships going up to Burlington. He's been rumored to help fugitives stow away. Gotta believe Buster's telling the truth." He gave the young man a nod.

Buster let out a breath and sat back in his chair, a wan smile on his face. *Well, I've done it now. Shit! Guess I won't be workin' for the Hoppahs no moah. I hope no one gets hurt during all of this.*

Duschanne turned to the sheriff. "We'll need to intercept 'em before zey reach ze New York bridge, *n'est-ce pas?*—'cause your boys are only deputized in Vermont."

Enos, his face shining from sweat in the closed, cramped room, stepped next to the sheriff and set his beer down. "Sheriff. Please! Even if the Hoppers are harboring fugitives, they're just following their religious beliefs, as we all have done before this damned law got passed!" He waved his arm at the gathered men. "Just because it's the law doesn't mean it's right!" Enos stared intently into the sheriff's eyes. "Why can't you just let them make their delivery, then go talk to Gabe tomorrow and give him a warning not to do it again? The Hoppers are good folks, I'd hate to see anything bad happen to them!"

"With a *thousand* dollars on ze line, I will *not* let those niggahs slip through my grasp!" Duschanne growled as he puffed his pipe and raised a hand in the air.

"I understand your concern, Enos, and Gabe is a friend of mine," Wardwell said. "But the Hoppers are knowingly breaking the law." He waved his hand. "Remember, it is my duty to uphold the law—whether I like it or not."

Duschanne grinned. "*Très bien!*"

Elmer, the north-side ne'er-do-well farmer, shuffled into the group. "An' what 'bout that Zenas Ellis fella? Betcha he's got slaves at his place, too. They's naybahs ain't they? They's prob'ly helping each othah out. How's 'bout it, Bustah?"

Several of the men echoed Elmer's sentiment.

Buster sputtered, "I—I—don't know about the Ellises. Didn't heah 'em say nothin' 'bout havin' runaways."

The sheriff held up his hand to silence the group. "Men. We have a mission, but I'm warning each of you, there will be no violence. Do you understand?"

The men alternatively nodded or said, "Yep. Sure, Sheriff."

Wardwell continued, "I am reminding each and every one of you…" he paused to look in the eyes of each onlooker in turn, making a point of holding Enos' gaze in particular, "…that you are bound to secrecy as to all that has been said and done here tonight. Anyone who breaks that bond will be deemed interfering with the course of justice, and dealt with accordingly. Am I clear?" Again, his narrowed gaze swept the room, lingering once more on Enos and Buster. Other men shuffled their feet and voiced agreement to the sheriff's order.

Wardwell got to his feet, tucking a thumb beneath his belt. "Now, listen up! We will gather at the mill bridge at two this morning. Half of the men will station along the north of the Whitehall road and half along the south. When the wagon approaches, George and I will command it to halt. Then we'll search it before they reach the bridge. If all goes well, and Gabe cooperates, Duschanne and you boys can capture the fugitives. Then George and I will take Gabe and Luke into custody."

Cyrus, the big simpleton growled, "I ain't goin' on the north side of that road! That's Paree Guildersleeve's land and I don't want no part of her vicious dogs. They almost ripped my damned arm off!"

Several men in the room chuckled, as they'd heard Cyrus' complaint about Paree's dogs before. Carl Yates and his son Paul, who owned a farm near the bridge, came closer to the circle of men. Carl spoke up, "Paul and I know Paree's land pretty well. We'll set up along the north. Any dog that comes near us is a dead dog, right, Paul?"

Paul nodded his agreement, his long red beard swaying with the movement.

Too late, Enos was realizing the full implications of the plan to intercept his employers. *I've got to try to stop this!* Enos stood face to face with the lawman. "Sheriff! I beseech you. Please don't do this! You know Gabe and Luke—we all do!" He swung his arm toward the men behind him. "They are upstanding citizens of this town. What harm have they ever done any of you? I say let's go to the farm right now and talk to Gabe peaceably. I think we owe him that much respect."

"Sheriff," Duschanne took his pipe from his mouth. "Ze law was broken when ze Hoppers gave these *escapers*—these fugitives shelter, *n'est-ce pas*?"

"That's right," the sheriff agreed. Hands on his hips, he stepped closer to the young man. "Enos, you have a choice. You can join the posse, or you can go home and keep your mouth shut about what you've heard here tonight. If I get any inclination you've tipped off the Hoppers, I'll have you arrested for breaking a federal law! Do I make myself clear?" He scowled at Enos.

Enos felt Buster tugging at his sleeve, and he bent over to his friend at the table. Buster whispered, "You gave your *word* you would help us!"

Enos straightened and stared at the sheriff, conflicting emotions playing across his face. *Should I walk away and warn the Hoppers? They've always treated me fairly. What if something bad happens? And if I join the posse, eventually my father will find out and he'll be furious I went after his good friend. But if I don't go, this could mean the end of my friendship with Buster.* He felt himself quailing under the unfriendly stares of men gathered about him. *Shit! What a mess!*

Enos took a deep breath. "Very well. I don't like it, but if you can promise there'll be no violence, then I'll come along."

The sheriff nodded. "Good. I have every intention to apprehend them peacefully."

"But Sheriff! I wanna kill me some niggahs tonight!" Edward blurted, standing behind Buster.

Sheriff Wardwell looked at Edward, seemingly seeing the teen boy for the first time. "Edward! What in hell are you doing here, anyway? You're too young to take part in any of this. And what do you want to kill fugitives for? The Colonel's gonna tan your hide if he finds out you're here! Plus, these slaves are worth a lot of money to their owners. They'll come hunt you down if you shoot their property!"

Edward pouted and stuck his chin out defiantly. "I have my reasons! And I am a *man* just like everybody else here. I can take care of myself! And those niggahs deserve to die!"

For a big man, Wardwell moved quickly. He rounded the table, grasped Edward's arm and pulled it up and tight behind the boy's back. Edward let out a cry and bent over from the pain.

"There won't be any *killin'* tonight!" the sheriff hissed in the petulant boy's ear. "Do you men understand that?" He yanked Edward away from the table, turned him around and marched the boy to the closed door. "Go home, Edward! You're not welcome here. And if you don't, I'll be paying a visit to your father forthwith! And you keep that silly, flapping mouth of yours shut! I hear of you saying one peep about what went on tonight, you'll have me *and* your father to deal with!" Wardwell opened the door and pushed Edward into the noisy bar room, then slammed the door behind the whimpering boy.

Wardwell turned back to the men staring at him, returned to his seat at the table, took a drink of his ale and shook his head. "Seems the devil's gotten into that boy. Don't know how the hell that happened, with Colonel Allen being a staunch abolitionist and all." Wardwell glared at Buster. "Why was he even here at all? You should've known better than to involve him, Buster."

"I—I—" Buster faltered, his glance sliding from the sheriff to Enos.

Enos spoke up. "It was my fault, Sheriff. After I left the mercantile Edward followed me into the street. He guessed Buster and I were going to be part of the posse and insisted on coming along. Said he was gonna tell my father if we didn't let him join us." He shrugged. "So we let him ride out to watch the Ellis place. Didn't think there'd be any problem."

Sheriff Wardwell waved his hand in the air in a dismissive fashion. "Well, what's done is done. The boy's gone and if he has a lick of sense, he'll keep his damn mouth shut. Now, let's finish up our business here and get a few hours rest before we meet."

He turned to Duschanne. "We'll have to make arrangements to transport the fugitives back to town…"

As Edward stumbled through the open door into the bar room, he grasped for the closest table to get his balance, knocking over a man's beer.

"Hey, watch it, kid! What the hell you doin'?" The man lurched for Edward's arm.

He reeled away from the man's grasp and bumped into the back of a woman at the bar.

She swung around and cuffed Edward in the chest with her arm. "Get your goddamn hands off of me!" she bellowed.

Her drinking partner turned toward Edward. "Get on your way, boy! You ain't man enough for a woman like Sally!" Laughter erupted from other patrons at the bar.

Edward staggered away from the woman, stumbling his way toward the main door. Customers turned to glare at him, their laughter exploding in his head. He gasped for breath in the smoky confines. *Gotta get outta here. Lemme outta here!* With a grunt he pushed through the heavy tavern door and slid on the icy boardwalk, catching his fall against the horse railing. He inhaled the chilly night air, breathing heavily. His clothes were still very damp from the night spent outside, and he shivered.

Damn them all! I AM man enough to be part of this posse, and by God I WILL be, whether the sheriff likes it or not!

Still shaking from his encounter, Edward mounted his horse and rode to his family compound on the opposite side of the common, two properties south of Enos Adams' family mansion. Dismounting, he led his horse into the stables and lit a lantern hanging on the wall. He unsaddled the mount, gave the dappled gray a quick brushing, then led him to his stall. Edward fed the horse some hay and filled the water trough.

"They think I'm an idiot," he said as he nuzzled his horse's nose. "But I'll show them. You just wait and see!"

Shivering, Edward removed his wet outer garments and threw two horse blankets on top of a stack of hay. He checked his pocket watch: 9:45 p.m. *At least my father thinks I'm spending the night at my friend Anthony's house, so he won't miss me. I'll just rest for a couple of hours, then I'm following them to the New York bridge.* He doused the lantern, curled up on the hay and threw the blankets over himself.

As his mind slipped into a troubled sleep, Edward repeated his mantra: *Gonna kill me some niggahs tonight…gonna kill me some niggahs…*

HOPPERS TRAVEL

"Mother! The eggs must be gathered," a voice called to her.

Emma grabbed her lantern and rushed out of the anteroom door. She moved quickly past the hay barn toward the hen house.

"Mother! The horses must be fed," the same urgent voice hailed her.

Immediately, Emma pivoted and returned the way she had come, her lantern swaying from her quick movements. She headed for the stables next to the road.

"Mother! The cows must be milked," came the voice, more insistent.

Confused, Emma lurched to her right and jogged along the path between the stables and the cow barn, lantern swinging wildly. Cows mooed mournfully as she reached the door.

"Mother! The cheese is curdling. Hurry!" the voice shrilled.

Breathless, Emma ran to the south end of the path beyond the cow barn and turned right to reach the cheese house along the edge of the back pasture. She doubled over, trying to catch her breath at the door. The lantern dropped from her grip and shattered on the ground.

"Mother! The sap is boiling over! Heeelllp!" came the voice, now panicked.

Staggering toward the sugaring house in complete darkness, Emma felt a hand grasp her shoulder from behind. She screamed.

When the mantel clock struck the fourth chime, Gabe awoke from an uneasy rest. Yawning, he sat up, swung his legs to the floor, and groaned. His joints ached and an offending muscle in his back twinged. He lit the two lanterns on the bedside stand, then reached across the void to the adjacent bed and gently shook Emma's shoulder.

"Mother. Time to rise. We must be on our way," Gabe said.

At his touch, Emma screamed and her eyes flew open, her arms flailing about.

Gabe stumbled back. A look of dismay crossed his face at this wife's outburst. "Mother! What has upset thee?"

Emma gasped, breathing hard. She squinted up at Gabe looming over her in the lantern light. Catching her breath, she sat up in bed. "Oh, dear! I had a most horrible dream." She shook her head and swiped stray tendrils of gray hair from her eyes. "Someone was yelling at me to do all the chores at once!"

She swung her legs off the bedside and attempted to stand. Lightheaded, she sat back down and dropped her head to her hands.

Gabe studied his wife closely. "Here, let me help thee."

Emma grasped Gabe's outstretched hands as he lifted her to her feet. She leaned against his tall body to get her balance. Gabe placed an arm around her waist to stabilize her.

"Is thee better?" Gabe looked at Emma's flushed face.

"Yes, yes. I shall be fine. I thank thee, Father. I am just overwrought. I shall join thee shortly." She wiped a trembling hand across her forehead.

Gabe nodded, trying to read Emma's emotions more clearly. She turned from his gaze and made her way to the wardrobe to dress for the day. Not knowing how else to help, he picked up a lantern and left the bedroom. In the parlor, Gabe paused to observe his oldest son snoozing on the sofa. Luke's long legs curled toward his chest, and his knees hung over the edge of the two-seat divan. *He has grown into such a good, God-fearing man, loving husband and father. I am proud to call him my son. I thank Thee, Lord, for blessing me with Luke's constant support and friendship. Please keep him safe in our travels this day.*

Gabe leaned over and gently shook Luke. "Time to rise, Son."

Luke grumbled and rubbed his rough beard, then rolled off the divan, landing on his hands and knees. "Uggh, I hate that thing! No room to stretch my legs." He slowly stood and ran his hands through his tousled hair.

Gabe turned from Luke and stoked the wood stove just as Emma emerged slowly from the bedroom. She was dressed in a brown and beige woolen dress, and her gray hair was neatly combed into a bun, which peeked from the bottom of her white bonnet.

"Good morning, Mother." Luke saw her flushed cheeks and gave her a questioning look. "Are you getting sick?"

She waved her arm in the air, dismissing both her strange visions and the question. "I am fine. Just an odd dream." Holding her lantern in one hand, Emma put her other arm around her tall, handsome son and gave him a light hug. "Shall I make tea?" She turned to Gabe.

Gabe shook his head. "Not today, Mother. Best we get moving." He made his way to the kitchen and Emma and Luke followed, stepping down from the main room.

Emma set her lantern on the table and her eyes went wide when she saw Luke's revolver resting there. Then she noticed Gabe's double-barreled shotgun leaning against the wall. She looked up at her husband with concern. "Father? Thee is taking the shotgun? Does thee expect trouble?"

Luke raised his brow and looked at Gabe for direction.

Gabe placed his hand on Emma's shoulder. "No, Mother. We do not expect trouble. This is just a precaution. Do not worry thyself. We shall be fine with thy prayers guiding us."

Emma stared at Gabe, trying to read his expression. *I hope he is being truthful, but that does not keep me from worrying.* Still unsettled from the vestiges of her distressing dream, she held her hands out to the men. "Shall we pray, then?" There was a knot in her stomach she could not ignore.

Standing in a circle, the three held hands in the middle of the small kitchen. The table lantern cast eerie shadows across their bowed heads. Gabe spoke quietly, "Dear Heavenly Father, on this day we shall seek to do Thy will to help Thy downtrodden children gain their freedom from the oppressions inflicted upon them. We ask for Thy holy grace to guide our journey, so we may deliver them safely along their voyage. In the name of our Savior, the Lord Jesus Christ. Amen."

Emma and Luke chimed, "Amen."

"Let us be on with it then," Gabe said beckoning Luke and Emma to follow. After donning their outer cloaks, the three returned to the kitchen.

Emma retrieved the food sack she had prepared the previous evening. Gabe grabbed his shotgun leaning against the wall and the satchel full of charges. Luke stuffed his Colt revolver into his right coat pocket, his charges into the other.

Emma carried one lantern and Luke the other as the three made their way across the backyard through the pitch-black darkness to the hay barn. The earlier winds had subsided and light snowflakes cascaded to the ground. Gabe unlatched the sliding barn doors. Emma waited as Gabe slid one door open to the right. She grimaced as its wheels squealed against the railing. Luke slid the other door to the left, until both were fully opened.

Gabe turned to Emma, "Mother, please get the Prescotts ready to travel forthwith. Luke and I shall return soon with the horses." Still carrying one of the lanterns, Gabe and Luke turned and made their way to the stables south of the house.

In the barn, Emma inched her way around the loaded hay wagon and reached the open trapdoor. Darkness filled the cavern below. Setting her lantern on the floor near the opening, Emma dropped to her hands and knees and called into the underground chamber. "Miss Elsie? Samuel? Sarah? 'Tis Emma. I am coming down."

She set the food sack next to the wagon, then lowered herself down several steps of the ladder, balancing the lantern as she descended to the dirt floor. Looking to the left of the cavern in the dim light, she saw Samuel was sitting up on the middle cot. Elsie and Sarah rested on the other cots, but Jonah had awakened, and he peered at Emma from under Sarah's arm.

Emma took several steps toward Samuel. "Will thee wake thy family? Thee must be moving soon." Emma placed her lantern and sack on the table then walked to the ladder. "I shall give thee some privacy, and return shortly."

Nodding, Samuel got up and gently shook his mother and sister.

Emma climbed to the barn floor and walked around the wagon, inspecting the men's handiwork in the gloom. *They have done a good job and this should protect our travelers from any prying eyes.* After a suitable amount of time, Emma climbed down the ladder and joined the fugitive family.

Sitting at the small table, she watched Samuel lace his boots. Then he lifted Jonah from Sarah's arms and set the boy on his empty cot. Crouching, he struggled to fit the small shoes to the boy's feet. Jonah squirmed and giggled at Samuel's efforts.

Emma smiled at Jonah's antics. *My boys hated to put their shoes on, too. Oh, how they loved to run barefoot in the summer.*

Elsie groaned, straightening her scarf over her tangled gray curls. "Mornin' Miss Emma." The disheveled matriarch smoothed her wrinkled skirts, then joined Emma at the table. "Praise the Lord for a new day! Guess it's 'bout time we be movin' on, eh?"

With the commotion around her, Sarah rose from her cot. Yawning, she raised her arms in the air to stretch. Seeing Jonah already had his shoes on, she picked him up and sat at the table, balancing the boy on her lap. Samuel sat in the empty chair next to the outer wall.

When the family had settled, Emma smiled at Elsie. "It has been through the grace of God, and my honor, to assist thy family on thy journey. I have brought thee food for thy travels. I hope it shall be enough sustenance until thee reach the next safe haven."

Elsie patted Emma's hand. "We can't never thank ya and Mistah Gabe enough for yo' kindness and gen'rosity, Miss Emma. The grace of the Good Lord is with ya."

Sarah nodded as she repositioned her head scarf. "Yas, Ma'am. We sho' do appreciate all ya done for us. Y'all ain't like the white folks we knowed down South. You done treated us real nice, like we's reg'lar folks."

Emma looked deeply at the young mother. "Sarah, thee knows the Lord says, 'Do unto others as thee would have them do unto thee.' I believe all God's children deserve to be treated with respect."

Sarah groaned, "Yeah, well, those slave hunters ain't got no respect, the way they capture and kill our people."

Emma nodded. "I agree. 'Tis a travesty, Sarah. And I sincerely wish it was not so. I can only do my small part to help thee travel as safely as possible."

"You'se a good woman, Miss Emma," Elsie said. "Me'be someday the Lord will allow us to meet again on this earth. But if not, we shall come together in His glorious Kingdom. Praise the Lord!" Elsie clasped her hands together, fingers pointing upward.

Samuel added, "And when we reach Canada, I shall write and tell you of our journey. Perhaps you and Mistah Hopper can come visit us when we get settled."

"I should like that very much, Samuel. I thank thee. Shall we pray?" Emma reached out her hands to Elsie and Samuel on either side of her at the table. Sarah grasped Elsie's other hand and Samuel held Jonah's. "Dear Heavenly Father, we ask Thee to shine Thy loving grace upon us this day, as Thy children continue their journey to the Promised Land. Please watch over Miss Elsie, Sarah, Samuel, and Jonah, and guide them to Thy safe harbor. In Thy name, Our Savior, Jesus Christ. Amen."

"Amen," the family echoed.

The sound of horses nickering filtered into the lower chamber and Emma looked up to the open trapdoor. "Gabe and Luke have arrived with the horses. Time to go."

Elsie and Sarah quickly stuffed a few stray items into their travel satchels and secured their four bags. Sarah bundled Jonah in a coat a bit too big for the small boy, then draped a cloak over her own shoulders. Elsie bundled herself in a heavy wrap, and Samuel donned the long coat he had worn when they had first arrived.

Samuel climbed partway up the ladder. "Pass me the bags," he said to the women. Sarah passed each satchel up to Samuel, who laid them on the floorboards to his right. Then he climbed onto the barn floor. Sarah lifted Jonah so Samuel could pull him through the hatch. Then Sarah climbed up the ladder, with Samuel giving her a hand up.

Lingering in the chamber Elsie turned to Emma. "I'll never forget ya, Miss Emma. In 'nother life, I believe we would'a been friends." The two older women hugged, both holding back tears, as they bade their farewells.

Emma pulled back and smiled at the black woman. "I consider you a friend, now, Miss Elsie. I wish thee Godspeed and a safe journey. I shall never forget thee, either."

The women smiled at one another as they wiped their eyes. Then Elsie climbed the ladder with Samuel helping her up onto the barn floor.

Emma paused and looked around at the somewhat messy underground room. *I shall clean later to prepare for our next visitors.* With lantern in hand, Emma climbed to the top of the ladder and Samuel helped her ascend to the barn floor. Then she closed and latched the trapdoor behind her.

Elsie reached out to touch Emma's arm. "Can I borrow ya lantern, Miss Emma? We gotta use the privy befo' we go." Emma nodded and passed Elsie the lantern. Elsie and Sarah, with Jonah in her arms, edged their way around the back of the wagon and dipped beneath the loft staircase to enter the two-seat outhouse, attached to the back of the barn.

As the Prescotts were emerging from the barn cellar, Gabe and Luke positioned the draft horses in front of the wagon and hitched up the harnesses. While Gabe finished securing the horses, his son gathered two of the travel satchels and walked to the back of the wagon. "Samuel, climb up and I'll hand these to you," Luke said.

Samuel hoisted himself into the hay-covered wagon bed and positioned the bags along the base of the headboard. Luke passed up their two remaining bags and the food sack to Samuel, who placed those next to the others.

Elsie, Sarah, and Jonah emerged from the outhouse and Elsie passed the lantern to Samuel who had jumped off the wagon. He quickly used the privy, then returned the lantern to Emma.

"Sarah, let me help you up," Luke said to the young mother. He gave her his hand and helped her into the wagon. Then Luke hoisted Jonah up next to her. "You'll want to get comfortable against your satchels," Luke told her. Sarah sat with her back against the travel bags at the head of the wagon, and Jonah settled between her legs.

Luke turned and smiled at the fugitive matriarch standing next to Emma. "Miss Elsie, your turn."

Elsie squeezed Emma's hand one last time and walked to the back of the wagon.

"Turn around and I'll lift you up," Luke said.

Elsie turned her back to the wagon. Luke placed his hands on her waist and lifted her to the wagon bed.

Elsie grinned, "Sho' is a strong boy ya got there, Miss Emma!" Elsie crawled across the hay to the head of the wagon, sitting next to Sarah and Jonah.

Luke motioned to Samuel standing nearby. "Come over here, Samuel. I need your help."

Samuel followed Luke to the front of the barn where the fishing gear rested against the wall. Luke handed the poles to Samuel and leaned in to whisper to the boy. "Samuel, we may have trouble tonight. As Father told you, there's a posse in town. I want you to sit at the back of the wagon and keep watch behind us. If you see any riders, can you give your bird whistle?

Samuel nodded. "Sure, Luke. I'll keep a good lookout."

"And don't mention this to your womenfolk. We don't want them to fret."

Samuel nodded again.

Standing near the open barn door, Emma watched Luke lead Samuel to the opposite side of the barn. Luke passed Samuel two fishing poles, then leaned over and whispered something in the boy's ear. Samuel nodded and whispered something back. Emma looked askance at their exchange, feeling unexpected anxiety. *What might they be discussing? We should not have secrets.* Remembering she had awoken from a troubled dream, she gripped and twisted her hands together. *They shall be fine. As Father says, I worry too much.*

Gabe approached Luke and Samuel, "'Tis time for us to move on, boys."

Samuel nodded in solemn assent. "Yes, Suh. I do believe it is."

Luke picked up the fishing bucket and led Samuel, carrying the poles, to the back of the wagon. Speaking loud enough so the women could hear him, Luke motioned to Samuel. "You should sit near the rear so we have the wagon balanced." Samuel climbed aboard and sat with his back against the hay stacked along the left side. Luke lifted the back gate and secured it to the side rails.

While Luke was loading the family into the back of the wagon, Gabe quickly secured the shotgun onto two hooks attached beneath the wagon seat and slung the satchel of charges across his chest. Then he grabbed a large tarpaulin from the floor and threw one side to Luke, and they secured it to the headboard. They unfolded the tarpaulin over the heightened rails, covering the Prescott family, and fastening it to the wagon sides. A gap of about three feet between the gate and the covering left a small view out of the back of the wagon.

Luke grabbed the two fishing poles left by the Ellis brothers and wedged one on each side of the wagon gate. He wound a rope several times around the fishing bucket, securing it so it wouldn't bounce around.

"We are ready, Father," Luke turned to Gabe.

Both men walked to where Emma stood by the barn entrance. Gabe gave his petite wife a long look, then leaned over and kissed her now-paled cheek. "We shall return in time for morning worship, Mother. Do not fret thyself."

Luke hugged his mother. "I love you, Mother. We'll see you soon."

Inexplicably holding back tears, Emma gripped Luke, the knot in her stomach growing tighter. The men climbed onto the wagon seat, and Gabe hung his lantern on a staff behind him. Luke took the reins and flicked them lightly to get the horses moving. The floorboards creaked as the heavy wagon slowly rolled out of the barn. Emma followed behind the travelers. When the wagon was clear of the barn, Luke jumped down and closed the barn doors with a loud squeak and clank of the latch. Climbing back onto his seat, he took the reins in one hand, and waved at Emma with the other.

"Safe travels!" Emma said, as the horses pulled the wagon along the snow-covered path.

Holding her lantern, Emma stared up into the dark, dreary night. *How many times have I seen them off on this journey? 'Tis been many years and I have not overly worried for their welfare. But this feels different, and I cannot help but fear for their safety.* Snippets of the shrill voice from her troubled dream floated in her mind as light snowflakes landed on her face.

Shivering, she moved quickly toward the kitchen and murmured, "Dear Lord, please keep them all safe in Thy loving grace."

Emma wondered if her prayers would be heard on this frigid night.

WEST TO WHITEHALL

After waving goodbye to Emma, Luke directed the horses left onto the road, heading north toward town. The wagon swung in the turn, then settled behind the horses. Turning to Gabe, he spoke in a low voice. "Snow's starting to stick. Too bad it's coming so early this year. Would've been better to make this trip on dry roads."

Gabe murmured, "Yes. Zenas cautioned me about going slow across the New York bridge. Still wish those builders had put railings on that span. Would have been safer for travelers." He rubbed his beard and stared straight ahead into the darkness.

The creaking of the swaying wagon lulled the two men into a comfortable silence. Snow flurries swirled around them on a light breeze. Although the lantern light did not extend beyond the front of the horses, the steeds stayed on a straight path, with Luke's light touch on the reins.

Having traveled about fifteen minutes, Luke drew the wagon to a stop. Angling below them was the hill that dropped to the bridge over the waterfall. The road north led up the opposite hill into town. On this trip, Luke would turn left before reaching the bridge, and follow the Whitehall road to the west.

Luke exhaled. "Wish I could see where we are going. This is worse than driving blind." He leaned to his right, trying to peer beyond the horses.

Gabe pulled the lantern from its perch and held it out to his side, casting a glow just beyond the precipice. "Yes, 'tis difficult to see the ruts with the snow cover. We just need to trust the horses and take it slow." Gabe returned the lantern to its staff behind him, and held up a hand for Luke to wait.

Turning in his seat, speaking in a hushed tone, Gabe addressed their travelers. "Miss Elsie? Can thee hear me?"

A quiet voice from beneath the canvas replied, "Yas suh."

"We are moving the wagon down a steep hill. Please brace thyselves, as it may be a bumpy ride."

A few moments later, the voice responded, "Okay. We's ready."

Gabe turned forward in his seat and rested his left hand on the wagon brake.

"Ready?" Luke asked.

"Yes." Gabe nodded.

Luke flicked the reins, guiding the horses over the edge of the berm. The wagon lurched and began its descent. Gabe gently lifted the handbrake to prevent the full weight of the wagon from bearing down upon the draft horses. Snow-filled ruts caused the wagon to jolt first to one side, boards creaking, then to the other.

"Keep 'em steady," Gabe said in a hushed tone.

Luke kept a solid grip on the reins, trusting the horses to pick their way down the slick slope in the dark. When they were almost at the bottom, the front left wheel punched into a large pothole, tilting the wagon, almost bouncing Luke and Gabe out of their seat. A child's cry emanated from behind them.

"Dammit!" Luke swore under his breath. A stricken look on his face, he shook his head, glancing at Gabe.

Gabe turned to the back, warning in a harsh whisper, "Thee must remain silent!"

Luke brought the horses to a halt at the bottom of the hill to give them a quick rest and catch his breath. "We cannot have them crying out," he whispered to his father.

Gabe nodded. "I know. I hope they shall stay quiet."

Luke swung the horses to the left onto the Whitehall road, traversing the southern side of the riverbank. Spray and fog erupting from the roaring falls intermingled with the lightly falling snow. Luke swiped the freezing moisture from his face.

About a quarter mile past the slate mill, they approached the incline leading them away from the meandering river to level pasture land. Gabe held up a hand for Luke to halt the wagon. Turning, he called quietly to their passengers. "Miss Elsie. We shall climb a steep hill, so be prepared. And thee must keep Jonah quiet."

Elsie's voice rose softly from underneath the tarp. "Yas, suh. Sorry. We'll do our best."

Gabe turned forward in his seat and nodded to his son.

Luke shook the reins to get the horses into a trot. The draft horses strained against their yokes as they pulled the heavy wagon. More than halfway up the hill, the young, lighter horse in front of Luke started to lose his footing, the weight of the wagon dragging him backward. Luke pulled the reins left, trying to distribute the weight to the sturdier horse. The wagon skewed sideways in the snow.

"Hee-aw," Luke called softly as he slapped the reins hard across the horses' backs. The skittish horse stomped to regain purchase, getting back in line with his partner. With another slap of the reins, the horses worked together to drag the heavy load over the crest of the hill.

Luke stopped the horses so they could catch their breath. The wagon creaked and settled on its wheels. He dropped the reins onto his lap, took a deep breath and stretched his arms in front. "At least the rest of the way is fairly level," he whispered.

Gabe nodded. "And our passengers were silent."

Taking the reins, Luke got the horses walking at a slow pace along the rough, snow-covered road. To their right, toward the north, stretched the pastures and barns of Paree Guildersleeve's many leased parcels. To their left, several individual farms adjoined one another. One of these farms was owned by Carl Yates and his red-headed son, Paul. In the snowy darkness, none of the barns along either side of the road were visible. A coyote howl echoed through the trees.

Luke maneuvered the wagon as it rocked and creaked along the frozen road. Occasional wind gusts blew the lightly falling snow sideways into Luke's face, causing him to wipe his eyes with his sleeve. *The bridge can't be far now. I hope we don't have any unwanted company. Maybe this trip will be a success as so many others have. I'm probably worrying for naught.*

As Luke turned to Gabe to express his thoughts, a swooping bird call rang out behind him. Luke stiffened. "What was that?"

Samuel's voice from inside the wagon reached them. "It's me, Luke. Look!"

Gabe turned in his seat and peered intently into the darkness. "I can barely see two lanterns." He paused, tipping his head to listen. "Sounds like they are riding hard."

Luke touched the revolver resting in his coat pocket. Squinting ahead through the snow and mist, he tried to locate the end of the bridge. *I know we're close. Should I urge the horses over the bridge? It'll be a difficult crossing in the dark with this heavy load.* He turned to his father. "Should we make a run for it?"

Samuel's strained voice responded, "Yes, Luke. Run for it!"

Gabe shook his head. "We would never make it. Best to be safe with this load. If we are approached, we shall stop." Reaching below his legs, Gabe quickly unwrapped the ties securing the shotgun beneath the seat. The gun now rested propped on the two protruding hooks. Then he unlatched the satchel of charges still slung over his shoulder.

Luke clucked softly to hold the horses at a lumbering pace. Glancing back, he recognized the two riders overtaking the wagon. *The sheriff and his son!*

Moments later, Sheriff Wardwell reined his heavily breathing horse next to Luke's right-hand seat, and George slowed his horse up next to Gabe. *Damn! How are we going to talk our way out of this?* Luke looked over to Gabe, who had turned toward George.

With both the sheriff and his son alongside the wagon, Luke brought the horses to a halt. The wagon lurched, then settled on its wheels.

The sheriff tipped his hat to the Hopper men. "Morning Gabe. Luke. Where you heading this early?"

Luke replied, "Mornin' Sheriff. Just delivering a load of hay to the barge in Whitehall. Got a buyer in southern New York who needs it right away."

Sheriff Wardwell glanced toward the back of the wagon. "Oh, yeah? You boys planning to break the Sabbath by going fishin', too?"

Gabe flashed a wan smile at the sheriff and shrugged. "Well Jeremiah, we thought after we delivered the load, we might have a little time to fish and still get back for morning worship." He swiped at his beard, staring at the sheriff. "Of course, I will ask the Lord's forgiveness for our transgressions should we catch a big one." Gabe bowed his head slightly.

The sheriff's lips curled into a half-smile as he took a longer look at the covered wagon. "It's not that I don't believe ya, Gabe. But there's talk fugitives are being smuggled into New York. Sorry, my friend, but we're gonna have to check your wagon."

Luke spoke up, "Sheriff, with the bad roads, we have traveled at a slow pace. If you don't mind, we'd prefer to be on our way, so we don't miss the barge sailing."

George responded, "It shouldn't take long, Luke. I can help you un-cinch your tarpaulin. We just need to take a quick look, that's all." George turned his horse and approached the back of the wagon.

Luke turned to watch George's movements. *Now what? After all the work we've done, the Prescotts are going to be captured. I can't let that happen! Maybe we can make it…*

"But I think it's best if—"

Suddenly, a gunshot blast echoed.

"What the hell?" the sheriff shouted.

"Where's that comin' from?" George yelled as he pivoted his horse away from the wagon.

Luke felt the wagon lurch. Turning forward in his seat, he saw the younger draft horse rearing. He yanked the right rein to control the startled creature. The bigger horse snorted, then bolted forward, pulling the younger horse in line with the attached long pole. Luke glanced quickly at his father. Gabe nodded solemnly, now cradling the shotgun in his lap.

"Let's go!" Luke slapped the reins harder on the horses' backsides, encouraging them forward. "We must be close to the bridge," he yelled at Gabe. "We're gonna hit it hard—hold on!"

As the horses struggled to reach a gallop, Luke could see the entrance of the bridge through the gloom. The wagon rocked and slid on the rough road. Gabe grabbed the back of the seat with one hand to keep from being ejected. Muffled cries of alarm and dismay erupted from the back. Luke strained to guide the frightened horses straight on toward the span's threshold. Taking a quick glance behind, he saw the sheriff and his son gaining on them.

Then Sheriff Wardwell hollered, "Stop! Or I'll shoot!"

ENOS

Enos shivered and wrapped his collar tighter against a cold blast of wind. Having met the sheriff and the posse more than two hours earlier, he now huddled against farmer Carl Yates' hay barn, waiting for Gabe's wagon to pass. He hugged Beldon's neck to get some warmth, and murmured, "Think they'll do the run, boy? Or are we gonna freeze to death first?" Beldon nuzzled his hand.

Near Enos' position on the Whitehall road, spread throughout the trees were Pierre Duschanne, Cyrus the big, slow-minded man, and Elmer, the pauper farmer from the other side of town. Across the road to his north, stationed in the line of trees separating the road from Paree's pastures, were Buster and farmer Carl with his son, Paul, along with their horses.

The sheriff had said he and George would position themselves closer to the bridge, but Enos didn't know their exact whereabouts.

The plan Sheriff Wardwell had discussed with the men was that he and George would stop and search the Hoppers' wagon. Then he would blow his whistle three times to signal Duschanne and the posse to move in and take the fugitives into custody. The sheriff said he wanted it to go "real nice and peaceful."

It's a good plan, but will it work? Enos pondered the many scenarios where things could go wrong. *I should have brought some whiskey from Jeb's tavern. I wonder if Duschanne packed any in his saddlebags. Who knows how long we're going to be here? And what if the Hoppers changed their minds? But what if they do show up? Should I jump out and warn them about the posse? Maybe they decided to wait for better weather to travel. I'm gonna try to find Duschanne—*

The sound of slowly plodding hooves approaching his position brought Enos to attention. Staying within the trees, he moved along the short cart path toward the main road. Halting, he watched Gabe and Luke, their grim faces lit intermittently by the swaying lantern, drive the hay wagon past him at a lumbering pace. Conflicting thoughts raced through his mind.

So they are *going to the canal! I hope the sheriff's plan works and all goes peacefully. I wish I had not agreed with Buster to join the posse. I should not be going against Gabe and Luke's plans. Maybe I'll just wait here with Beldon for the sheriff's whistle.*

As Enos turned back toward the barn, the pounding of a horse's hooves caused him to halt. *Who in heavens could be riding that hard this time of night?*

Quickly moving to the edge of the road, he saw a rider approaching from town at a full gallop. From the erratic, pitching glow of the lantern swinging wildly on its staff, Enos recognized the rider. *Edward! What the hell is he doing here?*

Passing Enos' hiding place, Edward dropped the reins and pulled a shotgun from its holster along the horse's side. Balancing awkwardly on the galloping horse, he cocked it and fired a shot into the air, then howled a banshee wail as he flew by.

What's he shooting at? Shit! I need to stop him. He's gone mad!

Enos ran to the side of the barn, untethered Beldon, then mounted and kicked his horse into a gallop to pursue the unhinged youth.

From his left, Enos heard Duschanne yell, "*Ah! Mon Dieu! Merde! Stupide!* Mount up! Let's go, men—I wan'em taken alive!"

EDWARD

"Ahhh, shit!" Edward cried out in the darkness. A pressure in his groin awoke him from an erotic dream. Instinctively, he grasped his throbbing penis pressing against his trousers. Pain shot through his lower region, causing him to roll over into a ball.

Heart pounding and disoriented, he lifted his head to glance around the gloomy stables. He grimaced as another pain shot through his stiff neck, then fell back against the hay mound. His pulse raced as visions of the girl's striking blue eyes floated in front of him. The memory of his disastrous encounter with her came flooding back.

It was the previous May, when Ester and her father, Justice, had arrived at their house seeking refuge. Justice needed work to earn their passage to Canada, so Edward's father, Colonel Allen, hired them. While Justice worked in the stable with the horses, Ester helped Edward's mother, Kathleen, with the house and kitchen duties. The fugitive family had stayed in their downstairs bedroom, behind the kitchen.

When Edward had first seen Ester, he was stunned by her crystalline blue eyes. All the fugitive slaves he had met before were dark-eyed. Ester was petite in stature, with light brown skin, her soft, black curls gathered by a red ribbon at the nape of her neck. He thought she was the most beautiful girl he had ever seen. He estimated she was about his age, maybe a bit older.

Whenever possible, Edward made attempts to talk to the shy girl, but often ended up tongue-tied. Ester would smile at him, lower her gaze, and walk away to continue her work. About a week after the fugitives' arrival, Edward saw Ester walking through their backyard, an empty egg basket in her arms, making her way to their small chicken coop. He decided to follow her.

When she was out of sight of the house, he made his move. "Hello, Ester!" he said as he rushed up behind her.

Ester let out a small cry and whirled around, startled at Edward's sudden appearance. "Oh, my goodness, Edward. You scared me." She glanced at him briefly, then dropped her eyes, taking several more steps toward the chicken coop.

Edward had followed her closely. "Can I help you gather eggs?"

Ester turned her back to the coop door and stared at the ground. "Gosh, Edward. That's very kind of you, but I can manage." She looked up, flashed him a polite smile, then started to open the door.

Mesmerized by her blue eyes and the curve of her lips, he grabbed her shoulders, pushed her against the door, and kissed her. Ester gasped, dropping her empty basket, struggling against Edward's grasp. She swung her head away from his forceful kiss and tried to push his body away. Edward's strength outmatched hers and he slammed his body directly against her. The feel of her small breasts pushing against his chest aroused him, and he tried to kiss her again.

Ester twisted her head away and started to scream. His heart pounding, Edward slammed his hand over her mouth. "Shush, Ester! I just want to kiss you," he panted, pinning her body. "Please don't scream."

Edward saw her eyes go wide as his erection pressed against her abdomen. She twisted her head side to side trying to escape his grip. "Ester, don't fight me. I won't hurt you. I just want to love you," he panted, as he felt lust surging within him. Then he released his hand from her mouth and bent to kiss her again.

A sudden pain shot up Edward's leg as Ester stomped on his instep. He gasped in pain and lost his grip on the girl. She swung her arm, hitting him in the side and throwing him off balance as she slipped from his grasp. Edward staggered on his good leg and reached out to grab her dress. She twisted away as he tumbled to the ground. Gasping and crying, calling out for her father, Ester ran toward the corral where Justice was shoeing one of the horses.

"Ester," Edward cried. "Come back!" Getting to his feet and lurching a pace or two on his injured foot, he paused.

When Justice heard Ester calling his name, he straightened from his ministrations. Seeing his daughter in distress, he exited the corral just as Ester ran into his arms, sobbing.

Then Edward saw her gesture wildly in his direction.

That bitch! She's gonna get me in big trouble. Goddamn her and the rest of her kind. All I wanted to do was kiss her and love her!

Now, months later, as he gasped in the cold, night air of the stable, he could still remember the sting from the belt-whipping the Colonel had inflicted upon him because of his indiscretions. After that degrading humiliation, Edward had vowed to get his revenge on any slave he came in contact with, despite his father's most precious ideals.

Damn that girl! I hate her! Yet here I am waking up with another goddamn stiffy. Will I ever get that niggah bitch out of my dreams?

As his vision of Ester's unusual blue eyes faded, and his erection shriveled, a horse nickered in the stable.

What am I doing here—? Oh, shit! The posse.

Scrambling from the haystack, he floundered in the dark to locate the lantern hanging on the wall. Digging into his pockets, he found matches, and, with shaky hands, lit the lamp. Then he opened his pocket watch clipped to his shirt, and tipped it toward the light.

Four-thirty-five! Dammit, I've overslept! The posse's long gone by now. I've got to catch up to 'em if I'm gonna kill me some niggahs today!

LUKE

Fleeing the sheriff and his deputy, Luke could feel the wagon fishtailing behind him as the galloping horses approached the bridge. "Father! Straighten it out!" His ears still rang with Sheriff Wardwell's shout ordering them to stop. He hoped the sheriff wouldn't start shooting.

Gabe pumped the wagon brake up and down several times trying to get the side-slipping load in line with the horses.

A few yards before entering the wooden bridge, Luke pulled hard on the reins to slow the horses down. But the spooked horses ignored his command and hit the bridge span at a full run.

"Get 'em under control, Luke!" Gabe yelled at his son.

Luke felt the front wheels of the wagon thump hard onto the wooden bridge planks. The horses skidded on the slippery surface, sending the back of the wagon fishtailing to Luke's right.

"Brake! Brake!" Luke yelled at Gabe.

As the wagon skidded to the right, the back left wheel thumped onto the bridge. The back right wheel skidded on the snow and missed the entrance, bouncing into the rough ground along the side of the span. The wagon jerked and slewed to the right, slowing the straining horses. Cries from their covered passengers erupted from the back.

"Stop the horses!" Luke threw the reins to Gabe and leaped from his seat onto the slippery bridge.

Gabe dropped his shotgun onto the seat and grabbed the reins with both hands. "Whoa! Whoa!" he yelled, as the horses skidded, whinnying against the weight of the wagon pulling them off balance. Glancing back, he saw the sheriff and his son stop their horses a few feet before the bridge. The revolver in the sheriff's hand pointed directly at him.

Scrambling to maintain his balance on the icy bridge, Luke moved to the back of the wagon. He saw the right wheel slowly sliding down the snow and loose rocks of the embankment, tipping the weight of the wagon toward the edge of the wooden span.

Samuel, hearing Luke's muffled curses, poked his head from beneath the tarpaulin. "Luke! What should we do?"

Luke was frantically pushing his weight against the right corner of the wagon, trying to free the wheel, when he heard Samuel's cry. He looked up into the panicked boy's face. "Run! And take Jonah. I'll get Elsie and Sarah."

Samuel climbed over the wagon gate, landing on the bridge. Sarah lifted Jonah's legs over the edge of the gate so Samuel could grab the boy. Jonah squirmed in Sarah's arms, gripping his mother's neck and yelling, "Mama!"

"Let him go!" Samuel yelled as he grasped the boy's legs. With an anguished cry, Sarah yanked her son's grip from her collar. Jonah whimpered as Samuel hugged the boy tight to his chest. As Samuel turned from the wagon, he saw the sheriff pointing a gun in his direction, and could hear other riders fast approaching. "Where to, Luke?" he screamed.

Luke took a quick glance at the bridge. With the horses askew and the wagon fishtailed, passage was blocked. Meanwhile, the shouts and gestures from the dim forms of other approaching riders seemed to have distracted the sheriff and his son. Thinking fast, Luke pointed north along the Vermont side of the rushing stream closest to them. "Follow the tree line. I'll find you later. Go!"

Clutching his nephew to his hip, Samuel slid down the embankment next to the bridge and disappeared into the trees.

Realizing his efforts to straighten the heavy load were futile, Luke unlatched and dropped the back gate. "Elsie, Sarah! Get out now!"

With the movement of the family, the midline of the wagon now teetered along the edge of the bridge. The wagon tipped precariously to its right.

Sarah slid her feet over the edge of the gate and jumped to the slippery, frozen ground, landing on her hands and knees near the entrance to the bridge.

"Elsie! Hurry!" Luke yelled, as the wagon continued its treacherous slide.

Another gunshot pierced the air.

THE LAWMEN

Sheriff Jeremiah Wardwell and his son George reined their horses to an abrupt halt just feet before the bridge. As they watched, the Hoppers' wagon started to fishtail on the slippery wooden span.

"Gabe! Luke! I order you to stop in the name of the law! We must search your wagon," the sheriff commanded, aiming his revolver at the men.

"They're not going to make it. Look!" George pointed at the right rear of the wagon sliding into the rough. "They missed the bridge."

As the lawmen watched, Luke jumped from the wagon and ran to the back right side. He strained and rocked the heavy load to get the wheel back onto the bridge bed.

"Stop what you're doing, Luke," the sheriff yelled. "I don't wanna shoot you!"

Suddenly, the head of a Negro youth popped out of the back of the wagon. Luke said something to the boy they couldn't hear. Then, to the lawmen's surprise, the boy jumped off the tailgate, grabbed a child in his arms and bolted into the woods along the stream.

Seeing the Negro boy running away, the sheriff hollered, "Halt! I order you to stop right there!" He fired one shot into the air as the two boys disappeared into the darkness. *Dammit! Duschanne's gonna be mad that the slaves are escaping. But I don't want anyone to get killed.* "Luke! You're under arrest for transporting—"

A wild banshee-like scream echoed around them.

George turned his horse east toward town and saw a rider coming at a dead run. "Who the hell is this? Is he the one who fired?" Behind the lead rider were the silhouettes of dark figures on horseback rapidly approaching.

The sheriff roared, "Goddammit! I didn't whistle for the posse." He pointed at the oncoming rider. "George, stop that sonofabitch!"

George steered his horse toward the oncoming rider, then swung into a wide U-turn, galloped to the rider's side, and grabbed the horse's bridle. The other horse grunted and swung his head at the intrusion.

The agitated rider held tight to the reins with one hand, and his shotgun with the other. "Nah! Nah! No!" he screamed. "Lea'me 'lone. Ya can't stop me! Gotta kill niggahs!" He swung the long gun wildly in the air.

George held fast to the panicked horse's headstall, struggling to halt both mounts just before they reached the bridge.

Who the hell is this causing trouble against my orders? The sheriff rode to the pair and recognized the agitated rider. "Edward Allen! What the hell are you doin' here, you li'l shit? Didn't I tell you to go home and stay outta trouble? You stupid sonofabitch!" The sheriff swung his arm toward the disabled wagon. "Look at the damned mess you've caused! Now the fugitives are escaping!"

Edward's eyes were wide, his mouth gaping like a caught fish. He waved his shotgun toward the wagon. "Ain't nobody gonna 'scape, 'cause I'm gonna shoot me some niggahs—"

George swung his beefy arm and punched Edward in the face, knocking the boy partway off his saddle. Then he yanked the gun out of Edward's hand and flung it into the trees. "No you're not, Edward. Not today! Now calm the hell down!"

Edward squealed and grabbed his bloody nose, babbling, "Hate 'dem nigs! No goo' ta-me!" He didn't resist when George snatched the shotgun.

The sheriff snarled at George. "Keep him under control!" Even as he finished speaking, he saw Buster, followed by Enos, Duschanne, and the rest of the posse, arrive at the melee taking place at the bridge.

"Look!" Buster yelled, pointing toward the fleeing figure. "The niggahs are escaping!"

ZENAS C.

The three male riders had just crested the hill out of town beyond the slate mill when they heard a gunshot. The elder rider turned to his sons. "Sounds like trouble. Let's go!"

The riders kicked their horses into a gallop with the eldest rider in the lead. They rode toward the New York bridge, covering the three-mile stretch as quickly as their horses could run on the road's rutted surface. As they rode, the sounds of men shouting reverberated back to them in the pre-dawn gloom. Another gunshot rang in their ears.

Realizing Gabe and Luke might have trouble on their journey, Zenas C. had enlisted his sons to join him to follow the Hoppers in case they needed help. Approaching the bridge, Zenas C. saw through the bouncing lantern lights a number of men on horseback, jockeying for position as the sheriff shouted commands. Reining their horses a short distance behind the agitated group, the three riders tried to make sense of the chaotic scene. The Hoppers' wagon was tipped askew along the right side of the bridge, with Gabe trying to control the panicked horses from his seat. Luke was at the back side of the wagon trying to right the off-set wheel. In front of the trees off the road to his left, Zenas watched George struggling to keep Edward Allen's horse in line, with Edward, his face smeared with blood, in the saddle.

Shaking his head in disbelief, Zenas C. said to his sons, "Boys! Go help Gabe with the horses!"

Zenas H. and Barnaby slid from their mounts, threw the reins to their father, and ran onto the bridge, slipping and sliding past the left side of the wagon.

"Stop! Or you'll be arrested!" Sheriff Wardwell yelled, seeing the Ellis brothers crossing the bridge.

Ignoring the sheriff's warning, Zenas H. yelled at his younger brother, "We need to unbuckle the traces!"

Zenas C. maneuvered their horses off the road to his left and positioned himself along the upstream side of the riverbank. He hollered to his friend. "Gabe! We are here to help thee!"

Gabe turned and quickly nodded at his neighbor, then refocused his efforts on controlling his panicked horses.

"You shouldn't be here, Zenas. We can arrest you for aiding and abetting the fugitives!"

Zenas C. turned to see George ride up beside him, leading Edward, slumped atop his horse. The Ellis boys' horses whinnied and pranced sideways, disturbed at the proximity of the two unknown horses.

Spooked by the four other horses jostling around him, Edward's horse pushed backward, banging his rump against a tree. Rearing partway in surprise, the horse sidestepped, bumping into Barnaby's horse, who nipped at his face, causing him to bite back in defense.

Zenas, seeing the horses tussle, tightened the reins of his sons' mounts and pulled them in an arc to get away from George and Edward.

Edward's horse leered, pawing the ground, then lunged at his attacker. George yanked the spooked horse's bridle, "Whoa, boy. Whoa!" He pulled the horse's head in line to avoid more confrontation.

Zenas C. kept his distance with his captive horses and waved a hand in the air toward the teetering wagon. "Don't do this, George! It's not right," he yelled. "Gabe and Luke are friends. We need to help them, not stop them!"

"You know we're sworn to uphold the law, Zenas, and that's what we're doing." George clung to his saddle, keeping Edward's agitated horse in line behind him. "We wanted to take them peacefully, but this idiot fired his gun." He turned, glaring back at Edward's horse. The rider was gone.

"Goddammit! Where the hell is he?" Instinctively, George reached for his revolver. His right holster was empty. "Shit! That bastard stole my gun!"

Zenas C. watched as George rode to the sheriff, who was barking commands to the posse stationed along the road. George threw the second horse's reins to his father. George yelled, "Edward stole one of my guns and took off. I'm goin' after that little shit!" The deputy pulled the other revolver from his left holster, and rode into the woods along the south side of the road, where he thought the deranged boy had run.

Zenas turned toward the bridge and saw his sons struggling to unlatch the traces of Gabe's draft horses, straining against the weight of the back-sliding wagon.

"Dear Lord! Please help us all!" Zenas C. cried out.

GABE

The close proximity of a gunshot caused the already panicked horses to try to bolt across the icy bridge. With the strain of the tipping wagon, they neighed, pawing the slippery surface as they were being pulled off balance.

"Easy, boys. Easy!" Gabe commanded, yanking the reins in each hand to get the horses back in line.

Suddenly, Gabe heard a familiar voice hailing him. "Gabe! We are here to help thee!" He turned toward the riverbank and could barely see his neighbor, Zenas C., lit by lantern glow, calling to him. Moments later, to his surprise, he saw the Ellis brothers making their way alongside the wagon. They gained solid footing in front of the struggling horses.

Zenas H. yelled at his younger brother. "We need to unbuckle the traces!"

Gabe dropped from his seat onto the bridge and joined the brothers. He grasped the lines on each nose guard, urging the horses forward to steady the wagon.

"Hurry!" Gabe said. "Get 'em unhitched." *I hope Luke can get the Prescotts out of the wagon quickly.*

Barnaby moved around Gabe to the younger horse, Zachary, hitched to the right side of the wagon. His cold fingers fumbled with the buckle connecting the trace to the hame on the horse's collar. Spooked by Barnaby's appearance, Zachary sidestepped into him. Barnaby grabbed the long mane to keep from falling off the bridge.

"I can't get the buckle!" he called to his brother.

Zenas H. leaned against the older horse's neck, trying to release the taut line. "I can't get this one, either. It's frozen solid."

Holding the horses' heads forward, Gabe shouted. "Thee must cut the traces!"

Zenas pulled a knife from the sheath attached to his belt and started slicing the two-inch-wide leather strap along the outer neckline of the bigger horse.

Barnaby also pulled out his knife and began slicing the line on the right side of Zachary's neck. The horse whinnied and moved into Barnaby again, leaving him little room to maneuver on the slippery bridge.

Gabe yanked on Zachary's bridle, forcing the horse to take a step forward and straighten his body. "Try again, Barnaby."

Barnaby spread his legs for balance and took his position next to the panicked horse, and frantically slashed at the tight line with his dulled knife.

Zenas, wielding a bigger blade, sliced through the first trace. "I've got this one. Hurry, Barnaby! I'm going to cut the second line." Zenas ducked below the spreader bar and squeezed his body between the horse's side and the attached wagon long pole. He quickly began sawing at the taut trace attached to the inner side of the horse's collar.

Seeing Zenas between them, Zachary swung his backside, slamming the long pole into Zenas' legs, causing him to stumble.

"Dammit!" Zenas exclaimed, quickly grabbing the other horse's collar to keep himself from dropping beneath the stomping hooves.

"Keep 'em steady, Mistah Hoppah!" Regaining his balance between the horses, Zenas continued slicing at the strap stretched thin between the horse and wagon.

Barnaby called to his brother. "I can't cut this line. My knife isn't big enough!"

"I've almost got this one," Zenas replied. "Duck under and unhook the spreader bar, so we can get one horse free."

Barnaby crouched between Gabe and the spreader bar connecting the two horses at their chests. He fumbled, trying to untie the multiple knots in the rope holding the bar at the base of the older horse's collar.

Seeing Barnaby crouched below him, Zachary dropped his head and bit the boy's shoulder.

"Dammit!" Barnaby cried out as he dropped to his knees. "Hold on to him, Mistah Hoppah!" Barnaby pushed the horse's head away, giving himself more room to maneuver. Still on his knees, Barnaby pulled the loose end out of several loops of the tight knots, making progress, all the while glancing at Zachary's prancing hooves.

"Hurry, Barnaby! I'm almost done," Zenas called.

"Luke! We're releasing the horses. Stay clear!" Gabe yelled at his son, guessing he was somewhere near the back of the wagon.

Barnaby released the rope holding the spreader bar to the horse collar just as Zenas cut through the second trace.

"Watch out!" Zenas yelled as the older horse swung to his left, pulling free from the traces that had pinned him to the center pole. Now the wagon's weight was carried solely by the younger, lighter horse.

Barnaby dropped to the ground as the spreader bar, still attached to Zachary, swung wildly, just missing his head. The horse staggered backward, pulled by the weight of the tipping wagon.

Struggling to control both horses, Gabe called to Zenas, "Hold Zachary!"

Zenas gripped the bridle, as Barnaby scrambled to his feet, evading the pounding hooves.

Gabe held tight to the older horse's headgear as it lurched sideways, almost sliding off the left side of the bridge. Then he yanked the horse forward, stepped to the side and released his grip. Smacking its shoulder, Gabe yelled, "Haw!" The freed horse bolted across the remainder of the bridge span, trotting along the road toward Whitehall.

Zenas, grasping both sides of the bridle, urged Zachary forward, as the horse struggled with the weight of the load pulling him off balance. The horse neighed and stomped his front hooves, struggling for a foothold on the bridge's slippery wooden planks.

But with the stronger horse gone, Zachary could not carry the load alone. Gabe grabbed the bridle from Zenas. "Cut the traces before the wagon goes over!"

A man's shout echoed in the darkness. "Go find 'em…"

Barnaby glanced over his shoulder at the rushing water before he braced himself along the narrow, right-hand edge. Using his small knife, he continued slicing at the notch he had already made in the taut strap. At the same time, Zenas cut frantically at the trace line along the left side of Zachary's collar.

"Elsie! Hurry!"

Gabe jerked at hearing Luke's frantic plea from behind the wagon. *He's got to get them out NOW. Dear Lord, help us!* Then he saw the wagon tipping slowly sideways, its weight pulling it beyond the edge of the bridge. "Look out!" he yelled.

Barnaby lunged, sliding hands-first along the bridge. Zachary's front right hoof hit him in the ribs, causing the youth to cry out in pain. Zenas skidded backward away from the wagon.

Gabe held the panicked horse's head, as Zachary back-stepped along the edge. The wagon continued its slow roll off the bridge. Zachary squealed in fright trying to get his footing. At the last second, Gabe shouted in frustration, "Oh, God! Help us!" releasing the horse's bridle. The weight of the falling wagon yanked Zachary sideways into the river.

BUSTER

Buster, Carl Yates, and Carl's son, Paul, were positioned in the line of trees separating the road from Paree's pastures to the north. They watched Luke and Gabe drive the covered wagon past their location.

"See!" Buster whispered to his companions, "I was right!" A lopsided grin spread across his face in the darkness. "I hope the sheriff can stop them peacefully like he planned. Hate to see anything go wrong."

Carl responded, "Yeah, I hope so, too."

Buster swung his hand in the air. "Well, I think we should—"

Suddenly a rider tore into view. Then a gun blast pierced the air.

"Who the hell is that?" Paul blurted, as lantern light rapidly flashed past the leafless branches.

Buster grabbed the reins of his horse and mounted. "Dunno. Com'on! Let's go!"

Carl and Paul, atop their mounts, followed Buster to the road. Buster saw Enos astride his horse emerge from the path across from them, his lantern swinging wildly, as he pursued the lead rider. Buster pressed his horse into a gallop.

Other riders emerged from their hiding places, joining Buster and Enos. Duschanne shouted, "Don't shoot! I want 'zem alive! Don't shoot!"

Buster rode abreast of Enos' horse and hollered. "What happened?"

"It's Edward!" Enos yelled back. "He fired his shotgun. I think he's gone crazy!"

"Oh, shit!" Buster spurred his horse slightly ahead of Enos.

Quickly covering the half-mile to the bridge, Buster saw Sheriff Wardwell, his revolver pointed toward the bridge, yelling at Luke and Gabe to give themselves up. Near the sheriff, George Wardwell struggled to detain Edward's horse as Edward screamed incoherently.

Atop the bridge, Luke strained at the skewed right wheel of the Hoppers' wagon. From the driver's seat, Gabe smacked the reins to control the panicked horses, as the wagon pulled them off balance.

Suddenly, the black boy Buster had seen in the Hoppers' barn poked his head from the back of the wagon. Moments later, the boy scrambled off the tailgate, grasped a child clinging to a woman in the wagon, and disappeared into the trees along the riverbank.

"Look!" Buster yelled, pointing toward the fleeing figures. "The niggah's escaping!"

"Go find 'em, Buster!" the sheriff commanded.

"Let's go!" Buster hollered to the men beside him.

Carl and Paul backtracked a short distance from the bridge, with Buster in the lead, then directed their horses north through the dense grove of trees lining the bank.

Within a few yards of the road, they were trespassing on Paree Guildersleeve's land.

PIERRE

Pierre Duschanne circled his horse around his men arriving on the chaotic scene at the bridge. "Don't shoot! I need 'zem alive! *Merde!* They're worth money!" He watched in dismay as a black boy ran toward the riverbank, clutching a child in his arms. Then he saw Buster, Carl and Paul take chase through the woods. "*Bien. Allez, messieurs!*" he yelled after the departing riders.

As the wagon continued its treacherous slide off the bridge, Pierre saw a wiry Negro girl jump off the wagon gate, landing on her hands and knees in the rough ground next to the bridge. She scrambled to her feet, hesitating as she watched the posse chase after the other fugitives. Looking around frantically, she bolted to her left, sidestepping through a line of trees into Paree's pasture.

Holding his reins tight, Pierre pointed at the fleeing girl. "*Attention!* Cyrus! Elmer! Don't let her get away!"

Following orders, the two men turned their horses, making their way through the trees in pursuit.

Sarah ran through the rough-hewn field. Gasping for breath, she stumbled, caught her balance and continued groping her way in the darkness. A voice behind her bellowed, "Don't let her get away!" The pounding of hooves made her run faster. *Where can I hide? I can't be caught!* Sensing trees close by, she veered to her right.

Before she could duck into the woods, a horse pulled to an abrupt halt in front of her, blocking her path. Dropping to her knees, she cried out, then righted herself and swung around the horse's rump. As she regained her balance, someone grabbed her from behind and squeezed her into a bear hug. She screamed, pounding her fists against her captor's bulky arms. Gasping for breath, she tried to squirm out of his crushing grip.

"I got her! I got her!" her captor hollered, huffing.

Then another horse arrived and the rider called, "I'm here, Cyrus. Lemme help ya."

I've got to get away! Sarah kicked her foot backward and down hard onto Cyrus' shin, causing him to howl and loosen his vice grip around her chest. She slid beneath the wailing man's bulky form and bolted for the trees.

"Goddammit! Get her, Elmer!" Cyrus cried.

Sarah's hot breath rasped in her chest as she escaped Cyrus' death grip. Flailing her arms in the darkness, she bounced from tree to tree. A change in the terrain caught her by surprise and she slammed to her knees. Gasping in pain, she scraped her hands along the ground, grasping rocks and ice. Crawling, she propelled herself up a small embankment. Clambering to her feet, she quickly looked around and saw the lanterns moving erratically near the bridge. Realizing she was back on the road, she turned and ran in the opposite direction.

Within moments, Sarah heard heavy footfalls, and a man grunting behind her. As she risked a quick glance over her shoulder, her foot landed on a rock and her ankle twisted. A sharp pain shot up her leg, causing her to cry out. Careening on one leg and cartwheeling her arms, she tumbled forward and slid into the dirt-encrusted mush. Then her pursuer jumped on top of her. Sarah screamed, twisting beneath the attacker, and rolled onto her back. His soiled face and bad breath assaulted her. Repulsed, she smashed her fist into the white man's nose. The sound of cracking bone made her stomach churn, but brought a brief flash of satisfaction.

Elmer screamed, blood gushing from his broken nose. "You niggah bitch!" he roared. As he lifted his left hand to staunch the bleeding, Sarah plunged two fingers into his right eye. Elmer's eyeball sank back into its socket, muscles ripping and blood vessels bursting. He howled, lashing out with his other hand, smashing Sarah in the head.

With Elmer straddling her, Sarah started pumping her knees to dislodge the vile, putrid man. She pummeled his stomach mercilessly with both fists as he tried to stop the blood flowing down his face. With a combination roll and kick, she shoved the emaciated man off her body. He rolled over groaning, and slumped into the snow.

Breathless and woozy, Sarah rose to her feet, stumbling away from her attacker and hobbling along the slippery, uneven surface.

From his position near the bridge, Pierre heard someone yell, "I got her!" *Bien! At least ze id'yets caught one of ze escapers.* Then a man's howl echoed into the night. *Merde! What the hell?* Pierre turned his horse and trotted east back along the road.

"Cyrus! Elmer! Where are you?" he called into the gloom.

A commotion from the tree line to his left caused him to halt his horse. "Over here!"

Cursing, Duschanne directed his horse through the bare-limbed row of trees toward the man's voice.

"Pierre!" the voice called. Duschanne emerged onto the edge of the pasture and saw Cyrus lying on the ground, whimpering, cradling his injured leg. Cyrus' horse sidestepped away, but stayed near his downed rider.

I swear zeese stupid farm boys are useless! "Where's the niggah girl?" Duschanne's horse pranced around the injured man.

"She went thataway," Cyrus whined, pointing toward the road. "Elmer chased her."

"*Bon Dieu!*" Duschanne grumbled. He directed his horse back through the trees onto the road, then urged him into a restrained trot. Within a few hundred yards, he saw Elmer rolling in the ditch, grasping his face. Dark pools of blood stained the snow. Duschanne slowed his mount. "Goddammit! You id'yet! Where's the niggah girl?"

Hands cradling his bloody face, Elmer cried, "By'ch b'oke ma nose and stab't ma eye."

"I don't give a *sheet*, you moron! Where the fuck is she?" Duschanne roared at his incompetent helper.

Elmer pointed along the road back toward town.

The Southerner kicked his horse into a gallop. Within moments, he saw a dark form limping along the roadway in front of him. *There she is—niggah whore!* Holding the reins in one hand, he used his free hand to pull a long stretch of thin rope from his pocket. In a long-practiced maneuver, he gripped the slipknot tied at one end and, using his teeth, extended the loose end to open the loop.

Slowing his horse, he rode up behind the fleeing girl. As she turned to glare at him, fear flashed on her face. *Bien! She should be afraid.* He flung the noose over her head and yanked it tight, then dug in his heels, abruptly halting his horse. The girl staggered, her feet flew out in front of her, and she thumped backward onto the roadbed.

Duschanne quickly dismounted, keeping the rope taut around her neck. Heaving for breath, the fugitive frantically clutched her fingers around the line. The slave catcher rolled the spasming girl onto her stomach, hog-tying her wrists and ankles with another line he pulled from his pocket. Then he released the rope around her neck.

She coughed and sucked for air, spitting into the snow. "You evil bastard!" A hoarse scream escaped her.

Très bien! She is still alive. The Southerner's tanned, weathered face crinkled as he grinned at his hard-won prize.

"Call me whatever you like, *Ma Chérie*, but you are gonna make me a lot of money!"

LUKE

Luke was furious to see Buster and his men ride into the woods chasing Samuel. *Damn them all to hell!*

Then the Ellis brothers' shouts from the bridge reached him. "We need to unbuckle the traces!" *What are they doing here?* Luke had not seen them run onto the bridge.

Recovering from her jump off the wagon gate, Sarah righted herself and scrambled through the trees toward Paree's pasture.

"Run!" Luke called after her.

As he braced the tottering wagon, voices came at him from all directions.

"*Luke! We're releasing the horses…*"

"*…I'm goin' after that li'l shit!*"

"*…Don't let her get away!*"

"Elsie! Com'on!" Luke reached into the wagon, trying to grasp the woman huddled on her hands and knees, leaning against the tipping side of the wagon. She was just out of his reach. "Crawl forward. Hurry!" He lunged for her hand and missed.

Gabe yelled, "Haw!" Luke felt the thump of hooves shaking the wooden bridge. *Oh, no! One of the horses is free. We're going over!*

Luke braced himself against the bridge as the wagon skewed back and sideways. A horse's squeal mingled with shouts from the front of the wagon. "Cut the lines…"

Moments later, Gabe shouted, "Look out!"

"Noooo!" Luke screamed, jumping out of the way, as the back right half of the wagon dangled in the air momentarily, then the front right wheel slipped off the edge. A horse's panicked whinny reached Luke as the wagon crashed to its side in the streambed.

Oh, God. Elsie!

"Luke!" Gabe's voice pierced the mayhem.

"I'm okay!" Luke yelled back. "I've got to get Elsie!"

Crawling on her hands and knees through the hay clods in the wagon bed, Elsie heard Luke cry out. She lunged and grabbed the left-side railing as she felt the wagon slide violently sideways. Suddenly, she was momentarily weightless. Then the right side of the wagon smashed into the river. The jolt caused her to lose her grip, and she fell into the jumbled hay. More clods landed on top of her, as the icy water flowed through the cracks in the wagon.

"Dear Lord, Jesus! Please help me!" she cried.

Sheriff Wardwell, atop his horse a few yards from the bridge, watched the disaster unfolding. Still holding the reins of Edward's riderless horse, he hollered, "Gabe and Luke, you're under arrest! Surrender now!"

Duschanne, reining his horse close to Wardwell, shouted, "Ziss is your fault, Sheriff! Ze fugitives, zey are escaping!"

Luke ignored the shouts and slid down the embankment to the crashed wagon. He waded through the waist-deep, frigid water to the wagon gate. The entire hay load had tumbled to the bottom side of the wagon, getting soaked from the rushing water.

"Elsie!" Luke yelled as he crawled into the wagon, balancing on the submerged side rails. In the freezing darkness of the wagon interior, he clawed through the wet hay, moving farther into the wagon bed.

"I's stuck, Luke!" A muffled voice came from directly in front of him.

He pawed thick hay clumps aside until he felt something like clammy skin. Groping with both hands, he touched a face, then frantically freed it of cloying grass.

"Praise the Lord, it's me, Luke!" Elsie exclaimed, thrown sideways against the tarp.

"Are you hurt?"

"Don' think so, but I can't move."

Luke knelt beside Elsie, the icy water rushing over his legs. Breathing hard, he continued to pull heavy, wet hay away from her body.

"My arms are free," Elsie cried, grasping Luke's head.

Struggling to get to his feet under him, Luke crouched in front of her. "Grab my arms," he directed as he thrust both hands under her armpits. Using all his strength, he yanked Elsie's body free of the heavy load that had buried her. They both thumped back against the tilted wagon bed, causing it to wobble, then resettle against the submerged rocks. Luke crawled to the open back end, turned around and pulled Elsie toward him. With a final effort, they both fell backward off the wagon into the streambed. A sharp pain shot through Luke's back as he landed on a rock. Momentarily paralyzed, he inhaled a mouthful of water, coughing it out. Elsie sputtered and flailed in his arms while Luke held her head above the icy stream. With a grunt, he struggled to his feet and hoisted Elsie so she could lean against him.

"We need to get to the bank," Luke said, bracing his legs against the rushing, frigid current.

With his arm guiding her, they took a step toward the Vermont side of the stream. Landing on a slippery rock, the weight of Elsie's water-logged skirts threw her off balance. She stumbled, slipped from Luke's arm and sank below the surface. Luke grabbed the back of her cloak and pulled her up. Elsie coughed and spit water as she wrapped her arms around his waist.

"Can you make it?" Luke yelled at the panicked woman.

Shivering violently, Elsie nodded. Righting herself in the current, she held tight to Luke.

Through all the shouting and mayhem happening along the bridge, Luke suddenly heard a familiar voice nearby yell, "Luke! Look out!" He turned toward the bank to see a dark, shadowy figure looming above him.

"Gonna kill me some niggahs!" The scream rose into a high-pitched cackle.

Luke instinctively twisted around and pulled Elsie down with him. A banshee squeal rang in his ears just before the gun blast. Then a searing heat penetrated the back of his neck. He lost his grip on Elsie and grasped his throat, feeling warm liquid rushing through his fingers. *Oh, God! No!* Stumbling on the slippery boulders, his legs went numb and slid out beneath him.

I've been shot! Lord, help me. I don't wanna die here!

Moments later, another shot echoed in the darkness. The screaming figure near the bank dropped to the ground.

Fighting against the current pulling him downstream, Luke tried desperately to keep his body from sinking below the surface. Water flowed over his face, and he thought he would drown. Suddenly, he felt something grab his right arm.

"Luke, I'm here!" the familiar voice called, directly above him.

Arms wrapped around his chest and he felt his body being dragged. He struggled against his rescuer, trying to get to his feet, but his legs wouldn't respond. Then his body thumped onto solid ground, his head cushioned against the other's chest.

The man called his name. "Luke! Luke! Stay with me!"

Who's calling? Leave me alone! I'm so tired and cold.

"Luke! Open your eyes!"

Luke struggled to obey—blurry shapes swirled around him. *Who's there?* He tried to speak but only gurgles escaped the gaping wound in his throat. He gulped for breath as blood spurted down his chest and oozed from his mouth.

"Stay with me, Luke. I'm going to help you."

Luke felt a pressure against his neck. He struggled to push it away but his arms were limp.

"Help!" Luke's friend cried. "Someone help us!"

Luke's eyes fluttered shut. *I'm so cold.*

"Here, warm yourself by the fire, Dear." Luke saw his wife Mary sitting by their wood stove, a babe in her arms. Their children, Brian, Bernard and little Martha gathered around her.

She had the baby! "Boy or girl?" he asked.

Mary held the infant up for him to see.

"Come join us, Daddy. We love you," Martha reached up for a hug.

Luke tried to touch his little girl, but his arms were still.

"Come to us Luke. It's warm here," Mary pleaded, waving to him.

His body spasmed as he struggled to join his family.

Then Emma's voice echoed, "We ask Thee, Lord, for Thy holy grace to guide our journey…"

The blinding glow of the firelight engulfed him. Comforted by its warmth, and released from pain, he hugged his family to his chest and smiled.

The sound of a man's screech and a gunshot terrified Elsie. Immediately, pain seared her cheek, and a hot fragment pierced her eye. She screamed, gripping her face, as Luke relaxed his grasp on her body. The current pulled at her heavy skirts and she tumbled sideways. Holding her breath, she sank below the surface.

Elsie flailed her arms under water to right herself in the churning flow. Then her body slammed against a large boulder and her head popped to the surface. Chest heaving, she gulped for air. Blood oozed from her nose and the deep gashes in her face.

"Oh, Dear Lord! Help me! Help me!" She sputtered up water and blood.

Clinging to the slippery rock, her legs numbing from the frigid water, she tried to get solid footing in the mud. Frantically looking around in the gloom, Elsie could just see the dark reaches of the embankment to her right.

I can make it. I's gotta try! "Jesus be with me!"

Taking deep breaths to steady herself, she slid slowly along the waist-high boulder and stepped her right foot into the flow. Bracing her arm against the rock for balance, she followed with her left foot. The current sucked her sodden skirts between her legs and pulled her feet first into the middle of the icy, rushing, water.

Elsie screamed and gasped for breath as her head went under the current.

She tumbled downstream in the direction Samuel and Jonah had run just minutes earlier.

GABE

"Luke!" Gabe yelled to his son as the wagon toppled off the bridge.

"I'm okay!" Luke called back. "I've got to get Elsie!"

God in heaven! Help us all!

Distraught at seeing his horse Zachary land along the riverbank, hind-quarters partially submerged in the frigid water, Gabe ran to the New York end of the bridge and skidded down the embankment.

The smashed wagon lay on its side in the river rocks. Pressure of the stream against the wagon bottom caused it to wobble precariously. The long pole still attached to the wagon frame pinned the frantic horse as he tried to right himself.

"We'll help you!" Barnaby and Zenas yelled as they followed Gabe down to the edge of the stream.

Seeing the brothers by his side, Gabe directed, "Try to lift the pole! I must pull the collar off him."

Barnaby and Zenas positioned themselves along the edge of the stream-bed behind the horse. Using all their strength, they hoisted the wagon pole out of the water. With the force of the water pushing against the hay-loaded wagon, the horse pulling to free himself, and the boys putting pressure on the pole, the wooden pin connecting the doubletree to the front of the wagon snapped loose. The wagon jerked free, its back end wobbling against the boulders. Relieved from the weight of the wagon, Zachary lurched forward, his hooves sinking into the muddy riverbank. Whinnying, he slid and fell sideways, the loose longpole still hindering his progress.

With the traces now loose, Gabe yanked the collar over Zachary's head, extracting the horse from the spreader bar and dangling pole. Then he grabbed the bridle and yanked upward as the panicked horse struggled to his feet in the mud.

"Look out—he's free!" Gabe yelled at the brothers, who scrambled up the bank so they wouldn't be trampled.

Stepping to the horse's side, Gabe released the bridle and slapped Zachary's shoulder, yelling, "Haw!" The injured horse hobbled up the steep slope.

Suddenly, Gabe heard a shout from across the river. "Luke, Look out!" A shriek and a gunshot rang out in the darkness.

"Oh, God! Who's shooting?" Gabe clawed his way on hands and knees up the slippery embankment.

"Gimme your hand!"

Gabe looked up to see Zenas H. offering help from the top of the bank. He grabbed the young man's arm and took the last few steps to dry land. Breathing heavily, Gabe righted himself as a sharp pain shot through his lower back.

"Ahhhh," Gabe murmured, rubbing the spasm.

Then another shot rang out from across the river.

Several moments later, a voice rose in the woods. "Help! Someone help us!"

Zenas H. turned to his brother Barnaby. "Somebody's in trouble. Let's go!"
"Luke! Luke!" Gabe yelled. "Where is thee?"

ENOS

Enos slowed and halted his horse on the road, a few yards from the sheriff, who was positioned just before the bridge entrance. Moments later, the rest of the posse arrived behind him. To his left, in front of the line of trees hugging the road, Enos saw George had taken control of Edward's horse. The crazed youth sat in his saddle, babbling nonsense. *Good. George has him in custody. At least Edward won't kill anyone tonight.*

The other riders jockeyed for position along the road as the sheriff yelled threats to Luke and Gabe.

Lifting his gaze to the bridge, Enos saw Gabe in the dim lantern light, seated on the wagon, struggling to control the straining horses. The back of the wagon sagged to its right at the end of the bridge. Then he heard Luke yell something from behind the sinking right wagon wheel. With the other horses jostling one another, the commotion on the bridge, and the sheriff shouting commands, Beldon pranced sideways, almost dislodging Enos. Cursing under his breath, Enos stepped his horse off the road along the south side of the tree line, several yards away from where George held Edward and his horse. Beldon pranced and fought the reins, turning Enos to face east.

Peering down the road toward town, Enos saw an erratic lantern glow illuminate three riders approaching him. *I thought all the men were already here. Who could that be?* When the riders slowed their mounts, he recognized Zenas. C. Ellis, followed closely by his sons, Zenas H. and Barnaby. *Oh, no! What are the Ellises doing here?*

Zenas yelled, "Boys! Go help Gabe with the horses!" The Ellis brothers jumped from their mounts, throwing their reins to their father. They bolted past the shouting sheriff and onto the slippery bridge. Working their way to the front of the wagon, they approached the panicked horses.

Enos sat frozen in his saddle, watching the unexpected scene unfold. *Damn! What a mess. Should I go help them? Or should I help Luke? Will the sheriff arrest me if I do? Best to wait for his command.*

Zenas C., leading his sons' horses, rode a few yards past George and Edward to the southern edge of the riverbank, just upstream from the bridge. Zenas yelled to Gabe he was there to help. George warned Zenas not to interfere, or he'd be arrested.

Enos pulled Beldon's reins tight to keep his skittish horse from bolting. Staying yards away from the commotion, he watched as George and Zenas C. tried to control their mounts and keep the other three horses separated. Suddenly, Edward's horse backed into a tree and bucked in surprise. As the horse partially reared, Enos saw Edward slip over the cantle and slide down the horse's rump, narrowly missing the tree. The boy crouched close to the ground, then slipped into the undergrowth as the restrained horses tussled with one another.

Enos yelled at the deputy, "George! It's Edward. He's getting away!"

George and Zenas C. were struggling with the nipping horses, and Enos realized with frustration George wasn't paying attention to Edward. *Damn! He didn't hear me.* Enos turned to his right and saw Edward's dark, crouching form emerge from the woods. The boy furtively dashed across the road behind the posse, who were focused on the sliding wagon. *Where the hell is he going?* Enos lost sight of Edward as the boy dashed into the trees along the northeast side of the river. *I better go after him.*

Enos pulled his flintlock pistol from his satchel, tamped a charge into the muzzle, quickly loaded the firing pin and rode after the mad boy. Just as Beldon entered the trees, Enos heard Luke's cry of dismay, and the crash of the wagon into the stream.

Oh, God! I hope nobody got hurt.

Ducking low-hanging branches, he emerged a few moments later into a small clearing along the riverbank. He saw a dark figure standing along the bank, aiming a revolver toward the water. *Oh, no! Where'd he get the gun?*

Enos reined Beldon to a quick stop. From his angle, Enos could just make out Luke's lanky form struggling to help a woman by the fallen wagon. "Luke! Look out!" he screamed at his friend.

"Gonna kill me some niggahs!" The deranged boy let out a high-pitched squeal. Then the gun went off.

Enos watched Edward stumble backward from the kick of the blast. "Edward! You fucking bastard!! What the hell?" Enos roared.

Steadying Beldon with his knees, Enos fired at Edward's back. Beldon jerked at Enos' movement, throwing off his aim. The shot hit the boy in the leg. Edward shrieked and slumped to the ground. Enos jumped off his horse, threw the reins over a branch, ran past the writhing boy and slid down the riverbank. Luke's body was slowly sliding downstream. Gasping at the icy water flowing around his legs, Enos quickly grasped Luke's arm, slowing his friend's tumble. He wrapped his arms around Luke's chest and, fighting against the current, tugged him to the muddy bank. Enos landed on his backside against the up-sloping bank, cradling Luke's head against his chest. Seeing blood spurting from his friend's throat, Enos pulled his bandanna from his neck and pressed it against the wound to stem the blood flow.

"Luke! Luke! Stay with me!"

Luke's head rolled to the side, his eyes closed. Enos cradled his friend's cheeks with both hands. "Luke! Open your eyes!"

Enos saw the confused, glassy look on Luke's face as he partially opened his eyes. He thought Luke was trying to say something, but only a gurgling croak came from his torn throat.

"Stay with me, Luke! I'm going to help you." Enos pressed his handkerchief tighter over Luke's neck. Luke's legs dangled in the frigid river, his body spasming in Enos' grasp.

"Help!" Enos cried. "Someone help us!" *Oh God! Luke can't die. I can't believe Edward shot him. That crazy bastard. What if he tries to shoot me?*

Then he heard Gabe's voice from the opposite bank. "Luke! Luke! Where is thee?"

Enos twisted to look back up the bank. He could hear Edward howling in pain but couldn't see him. *Good. At least he's down.* Then he heard crashing through the trees and suddenly two figures appeared above him.

"Luke! Enos!" A cry rose into the night as the Ellis brothers skidded down the slope to Enos' side.

"Luke's hurt real bad!" Enos said. "Help me get him to the top!" Enos moved from beneath Luke's form and cradled his friend's head as the three men lifted his body from the water. Barnaby grabbed Luke's legs while Enos and Zenas H. lifted Luke's limp upper body. They slipped and struggled carrying him up the muddy slope. Breathing hard, the three laid Luke on the top of riverbank, just yards away from Edward.

Enos dropped to the ground and cradled Luke's head. "Luke! Luke! Open your eyes. Com'on! Open your eyes!" Zenas and Barnaby knelt along either side of Luke, watching Enos' efforts to revive their neighbor.

As Enos shook Luke's shoulders, Luke's head lolled to the side. Enos saw the anguished pain on his friend's face just moments before was gone. A benign smile crossed Luke's bluing lips.

"No! No! No!" Enos screamed. "Luke! Don't die on me!"

Barnaby and Zenas H. each grasped one of Luke's hands and bowed their heads.

Overcome with grief, Enos let out a blood-curdling wail, rose to his feet and staggered to Edward's prone body. "I'm gonna kill you, you son-of-a-bitch!" He kicked Edward in the head and chest repeatedly until Zenas H. tackled him and yanked him off the screaming boy.

PAREE

Paree sat at her kitchen table, eating a light breakfast, illuminated by lantern light. She sipped her tea, recollecting the contentious town meeting two nights earlier. She had been more than willing to help fugitives and their conductors use her land to travel to New York. But with this new Fugitive Slave Law in effect, she worried the Southern slave hunter was stirring up trouble and trying to gather a posse to hunt the runaways.

If that bastard offers enough money, who knows how many men might join him. Damn him all to hell! Thinking of armed men trespassing on her land brought back painful memories of her traumatic childhood in Prussia.

Napoleon's soldiers didn't knock, they just barged through the door of the farmhouse. Paree screamed as the men swarmed the kitchen where she and her mother, Katarina, were eating a spartan dinner. One soldier grasped her mother in a headlock and pulled her to her feet, as Paree was yanked from her chair by two others.

At fifteen, Paree had grown to her adult height of over six feet, and she towered above the French soldiers holding her captive. As she fought against the two holding her, another soldier slapped her face. She screamed again as she was forced to her knees, her arms held in a vice grip.

Then the commander, dressed in a highly decorated uniform, entered the room and declared, "We are taking control of this farm until we are called to fight. You will cook for us and obey my commands!"

Paree sobbed, staring at her captive mother who was weeping. She realized there was no way to escape the despised soldiers' intrusion.

When Paree had been seven years old, in 1806, Napoleon and his army had invaded Rhineland and taken control of the capital city Cassel. He then renamed the region Westphalia, imposing French rule across the kingdom, which encompassed their family farm just three miles outside the city. Paree's father, Gustav, an officer in the Prussian army, opposed Napoleon's rule, and had led local skirmishes against the French forces. Against her father's vehement opposition, both of her older brothers were forced to join Napoleon's guard when they turned sixteen. In 1812, Napoleon had led an ill-conceived invasion of Russia, and the Russian and Prussian allies decimated his forces. Paree was heartbroken and her childhood devastated, when she learned both her beloved older brothers had been killed in the fighting.

Two years later, in October, 1814, her father now fought with the Prussian army and its allies to overthrow Napoleon's forces in Cassel, and regain control of Rhineland for Prussia. So she and her mother had been left to manage the family farm.

Following orders, she and Katarina fed the dozen soldiers with what little provisions they had in their stores. After finishing their meal, the commander stood and waved his hand. "Now is ze time for fun, *Oui?*" The soldiers cheered and guffawed.

Paree's heart sank as she stood at the stove next to her mother. Before she could react, she was yanked backward and pushed into a chair. Her arms were tied behind her back. Two soldiers grabbed her mother, who fought against their grasp, and pushed her down on the cleared table. Katarina screamed as still more soldiers held her arms, and lifted her skirts.

Being forced to watch as one soldier after another raped her mother horrified Paree. Silently vowing revenge, she memorized the commander's features as he smoked a cigar and cheered on his men. Then she shut her eyes to the carnage being inflicted. Her mother's wretched wails, intermingled with the grunts of the men abusing her, bounced off the walls of their small cabin. Paree cursed the soldiers for their heathen brutality. She knew they would take her next, and she steeled herself not to fight her attackers now, but get revenge later.

Lord! I beg you! Commit their damned souls to burn in hell for eternity!

For three days, the dozen French soldiers pillaged their farm. Pigs and chickens were slaughtered. Paree seethed while she and Katarina were forced to cook and feed the army. After eating their fill and becoming belligerent drunks, the soldiers forced themselves on the unwilling women. On the morning of the fourth day, the commander ordered his troops to get ready to march on the capital of Cassel.

While Katarina and Paree were preparing breakfast, the commander stepped behind Katarina and said, "You have served us well, *Madam. Merci.*" Grabbing her long hair, he pulled her head back and slit her throat with his bayonet.

Paree screamed seeing her mother slump to the floor, blood spurting from her neck. Then a blinding pain ripped through Paree's head, her vision blurred and she felt her body drop as everything went black.

A loud crackling sound had brought her back from oblivion. She took a breath and coughed acrid smoke. Her head pounding from the blow, she slowly opened her eyes. Flames streaked across the ceiling. *Oh, God! They've set the house on fire. I need to get out!* Woozy and nauseated, choking for air, she crawled on hands and knees, dragging herself through the burning door into the muddy yard where she collapsed.

Sometime later in the day, she heard male voices around her. She curled into a ball to protect herself from their assault. A hand touched her shoulder and she cried out in fright.

"We won't hurt you," the deep male voice said in her native tongue. She opened her eyes to see several Prussian soldiers peering down at her.

"Is there anyone else here?" the officer asked, indicating the burned ruin of her home.

Paree gasped, seeing the house burnt to the ground. She shook her head. "No. They killed my mother. My father fights with your army, and my brothers are dead. I am the only one left."

The sympathetic officer asked, "What is your father's name and rank?"

Paree wiped soot from her face and sat up, arranging her skirts about her. She propped her arms on her knees and peered up at the officer. "He is Lieutenant Gustav Gerber. He fights to regain our capital."

The officer nodded to the men around him. "Very well then. We shall see you get medical aid."

The soldiers lifted her from the ground and helped her settle in the back of a wagon. As the group moved out, she glanced back at the smoldering house and barns of their once-prosperous farm.

I can't even give my mother a proper Christian burial. May her loving soul rest in the Lord's arms. She wrapped her arms about her chest and sobbed in the rocking wagon. *I swear to God! I will get revenge against those who have committed such evil against my family!*

The Prussian troops transported her to the soldiers' field hospital outside the city, where she was treated for her wounds. The battle between the French and the Prussian allies raged on for three more weeks. Finally, Napoleon and his forces were cast out of the capital, and the land returned to Prussia.

Being underage, with no family nearby to take her in, Paree was sent to a Catholic orphanage on the outskirts of Cassel. Several months after arriving, and suffering from daily nausea, Paree was informed by Mother Superior that she was probably pregnant. Horrified at hearing the news, she cursed the invaders. *This baby is from those bastard French soldiers. Damn them all to hell!*

But as the months went by and the baby began to move in her womb, Paree began to embrace the idea of being a mother and having an infant to love. At age sixteen, in the summer of 1815, after a horrendous and painful labor, Paree gave birth to a baby girl. The baby was immediately whisked from the hospital room, with Paree only catching a brief glimpse of the baby's head. She assumed the nuns were cleaning the child and it would be returned for her to suckle. When hours had passed, and there was no sign of her baby, she began to loudly demand to see her child.

The nuns, in a panic at Paree's outbursts, brought in Mother Superior. "Where is my baby?" Paree demanded. "I want to see my child!"

The head nun grasped her hand. "My dear girl. A good family has adopted your baby. You can rest assured she will be given a good home. It is best if you do not have any contact with the child, for your own good."

"Noooo!" Paree wailed. "I never agreed to this! You cannot take my baby! I won't allow it!"

Mother Superior shook her head and walked out of the room. Paree sobbed in her soiled delivery bed, her tender breasts leaking milk for a baby she would never feed.

Two days after giving birth, Paree saw two Prussian officers entering Mother Superior's office. One officer had gray hair and appeared to be in his fifties. The other was younger, with a thin mustache. Noticing the door wasn't completely closed, Paree hid behind the outer corner of the office, listening to the conversation.

Mother Superior said, "We have a two-day-old baby girl who is strong and healthy, from good Prussian stock. The grandfather was an officer in your army, and I have recently been informed he has been killed in the siege."

Oh, no! Father is dead! Now I truly am an orphan. God help me!

A deep, gruff voice, which Paree attributed to the older officer, said, "I have two families who have offered handsome sums for a baby girl. One is more generous than the other, and I would recommend this family. They are loyal to the Prussian cause."

Mother Superior responded, "Thank you, Colonel Schleswig. Of course, we wish the child to be raised by a respectable family. And a generous donation helps us support the poor orphans in our care."

The younger officer said, "Mother Superior, my wife and I had a young son, who died of illness at the age of three. My wife cannot bear another child and we desperately wish to adopt a baby girl."

Mother Superior sighed. "I see. And tell me, good Sir. Would you be able to match or exceed the generous donation being offered by the colonel's family?"

From her hiding place, Paree gasped. *They're selling my baby girl to the highest bidder! How can they do this? It's not Christian and it's not right! I want to raise the baby myself.* Taking a chance of being seen, she peered around the corner through the partially opened door. The colonel was writing something on a piece of paper.

"This is the offer from my first family," he said, sliding the slip across the desk to the nun.

Mother Superior tilted her head toward the younger officer. "Can you match that amount, Sir?"

Glancing at the figure on the paper, the man shook his head. "No. I'm sorry, Sister, I cannot. It would take my wife and me many years to save that sum."

"Very well, then," the head nun nodded at the commanding officer. "It is decided. The baby will go to your family once the donation is received. And may the Good Lord bless you for your generous contributions to our ministry over the years."

Paree's stomach was in a knot and her body trembled. *I can't let them sell my baby! And how many others have they sold?* Enraged, she burst into Mother Superior's office, pushing aside the Prussian soldiers.

Standing tall in front of the desk, Paree's voice shook. "Mother Superior! She is MY baby girl. You cannot sell her! I want to raise her myself. I *know* I will be a good mother. PLEASE! I beg you. The Lord would not want you to do this!" Paree fists thumped on the wooden desk, her tears flowing and her body trembling.

Mother Superior's stunned look rapidly changed to anger. She moved quickly from behind her desk, grabbed Paree's arms and shook her.

"Paree! You have given birth to a bastard child and you have no say in these matters. You are too young to raise this baby and you have no family to support you. You would NEVER be a good mother!" Mother Superior glanced behind Paree and nodded.

"But—"

Suddenly her arms were yanked from behind and she felt herself being dragged from the office. The young officer was standing to one side, a look of surprise on his face, so she assumed it was the colonel who had her in his grasp.

The head nun yelled, "Because of this intrusion, you are confined to your room for one week. Now go, before I have Colonel Schleswig arrest you!"

Paree was pushed out of the office and the door slammed shut behind her. Staggering up the stairway, she ran down the hallway to her second-floor room, fell on her bed and cried wracking sobs.

Now, in her dimly lit kitchen, Paree's hand trembled as she sipped her tea. The anguish she had felt at sixteen over losing her daughter flooded her fresh and anew. *I wish I had been able to hold and love her for just a minute so she knew who her mother was. It was cruel of the nuns to rip her from me. I swear on the life of my baby daughter, I will do everything in my power to never let another person be sold to the highest bidder!*

At age eighteen, Paree was released from the orphanage and given a job as a secretary in the government offices in the capital city. She earned enough money to afford a small two-room flat in a boarding house.

Then in 1820, at the age of twenty-one, she became the nanny for a government official. She was paid well for overseeing their four children, and moved in with the family at their villa near the seacoast outside of Cassel. Paree enjoyed caring for the children, yet her heart ached, not knowing what had happened to her own daughter.

Less than two years later, the government patriarch was transferred to New York City to advocate for the Prussian homeland. He asked Paree to accompany the family on their journey. She was conflicted about leaving her homeland. But with the seemingly never-ending war between France and Prussia raging on, and no family to hold her back, Paree accepted his offer.

One beautiful spring day, about a month after getting settled into their apartment in New York, Paree decided to take the children for a walk. Pushing the toddler in a pram with the three older children walking alongside her, she ambled toward the waterfront. Here, a stage of sorts had been erected and a group of well-dressed men and women were gathered around. Curious, she sat on a bench on the outskirts of the group and gathered the children around her. She hoped there would be entertainment they might enjoy.

As she watched, more adults milled through the crowd, their voices becoming louder and more raucous. Shortly, a man in a frock coat and black top hat came on stage. He smartly announced the auction was about to begin and the crowd quieted. Then, from behind the cloaked stage, another man led a line of disheveled black men, women and children to the podium. The captives shuffled awkwardly, limited by the chains shackling their feet and necks.

Paree's heart pounded and her stomach lurched. *What is happening here?* This was not what she was expecting.

The top-hat man lifted the arm of the first man in line. "Good lookin' specimen right here, Ladies and Gentlemen! Strong arms, and," he opened the man's mouth. "Good teeth. Would make a fine slave." Waving his hand toward the gathering, he shouted, "Do I hear a bid for fifty dollars?"

Murmurings swirled through the crowd. A man raised his hand and called, "Fifty!"

Another man called, "Fifty-five."

Top-hat hollered back, "Do I hear sixty?"

Men jockeyed one another, then the first man countered with sixty.

The auctioneer waved his gavel toward the second bidder, "Do I hear seventy?" The man shook his head.

"Going once! Going twice! To the gentlemen in the brown overcoat, for sixty dollars!" His gavel banged on the table in front of him. His helper unshackled the half-naked, slouching, young black man, and helped him down the stairs to the waiting bidder. Two men alongside the new owner grasped the slave and half-dragged him to a waiting wagon. Then the buyer disappeared behind the stage, presumably to finalize the transaction.

Paree was horrified as each of the captives was auctioned off. Her body trembled as she watched mothers scream and fight at being separated from their children. The raw memory of her own daughter being sold to the Prussian colonel flooded back to her.

This is horrible! The Lord said it's against His law for one man to own another. How can they do this? Aren't these people Christians?

Disgusted at the sight of the slave auction, she hustled the children back to the apartment. *I wonder if there is anything I can do to help these poor people escape their bondage. I have to try.*

A distant gunshot echoed in the pre-dawn stillness.

Paree jolted from her childhood recollections, her heart pounding. Running her hands through her short gray hair, she swore in her native language. *Who the hell is that? Poachers? Or those damn fool slave catchers? They better not be on my land!*

Already dressed for her day's chores in men's trousers, lace-up boots, and a thick muslin shirt, she threw on her winter coat and felt hat, then tucked her always-loaded revolver into her pocket. She grabbed her short-barreled shotgun, also loaded, positioned next to her back door, and slung the satchel of charges over one shoulder. Lifting the lantern from her table, the tall, middle-aged woman swung her bulky frame out the back door, where she paused on her stoop. Intermittent shouts came from the direction of the road, quickening her heartbeat. Light snow flurries fell on the already snow-covered ground as she stomped toward the stables. In the yard, her four herding dogs, leashed to their dog houses, barked furiously.

I wonder if they've found fugitives. I'll bet that damned Southerner is causing trouble.

Quickly harnessing and saddling her horse, she slipped her shotgun into its holster, strapped the lantern to a staff hooked to the horn, and led her horse from the stable. After unleashing her barking dogs, she mounted her horse and yelled at the pack, "*Ferse!* Heel!" The pack leader, Bruno and his mate, Hilde, took up positions behind her horse's right flank. Their young, full-grown progeny, Gunther and Fritz, followed behind the horse's left flank. Paree trotted with her dog pack toward the southwest side of her property, where the gunshots and shouts had come from.

She halted her horse in a section of trees separating two of her pastures, the first of which bordered the Whitehall road.

Then another gunshot came from the direction of the bridge. A man shouted, "Don't let 'em get away!"

Scheisse! Someone's on the run!

She hissed at her dogs,"*Bleibe!* Stay!" The pack, panting, stood alert along either side of her horse. She pulled her shotgun from its holster, cocked it and waited.

If there's a posse on my land, there's going to be trouble.

Moments later, the glow of a rider's lantern flashed through the bare tree branches. Her heart pounding, she yelled, "Get off my land or I vill shoot!"

A voice yelled back, "We're after niggahs! Stay outta the way!"

Cursing under her breath, Paree directed her horse into the open pasture. As the rider approached, she hollered, "I vill not varn you again! Get off my land! Now!" Waiting a moment to see if the rider changed direction, she took a deep breath, steadied the shotgun against her shoulder, aimed at the rider's midsection and fired. A small amount of satisfaction rushed over her, imagining she could have stopped Napoleon's soldiers from occupying her family farm.

The shot slammed into Buster's right shoulder, jerking him back in the saddle, causing him to drop his shotgun. He screamed and twisted to grab his injured arm. At the unexpected movement of his rider, the horse reared and Buster toppled sideways from the saddle, hitting the ground with a grunt. The lantern swung from its staff and shattered with a hiss, just inches from Buster's head.

Carl and Paul Yates, following a short distance behind, reined their horses to a halt where Buster had fallen. Carl called to his son, "Find the runaways! Go!" Then he dismounted and dropped to Buster's side.

Paul hesitated in the pre-dawn darkness, not knowing where the shot had come from. Cursing under his breath, he kicked his horse into a gallop and went north following the stream bordering Paree's property.

Seeing the rider fall from his mount, Paree called to her lead dog, "Bruno! *Toten!* Kill!"

Following his master's command, Bruno charged toward the two men. With the smell of fresh blood in his nose, he lunged for the body on the ground, sinking his razor-sharp canines into the man's neck. Growling and swinging his head, he ripped a chunk of flesh from the man's throat. Then a sharp kick in his side knocked him from his prey. Bruno growled and scrambled to regain his footing in the slush. As the other man started to kick him again, Bruno leaped, clamping the hand in his mighty jaws, crunching through bone.

The man howled and grabbed Bruno by the nape of the neck, yanking the dog off his arm, as he dropped to his knees and cradled his mangled hand. The lust for blood turned Bruno back to his first prey, where he buried his muzzle into the man's neck, ripping out another chunk of flesh. Blood immediately gushed from a severed artery, splashing the dog's face.

Bruno shook his head to clear the blood from his eyes and backed a few paces away.

While the dog continued mauling Buster, Carl struggled to remove his revolver from his holster. He clutched the gun against his chest with his right arm as blood gushed from the wound. Using his shaking left hand, he pulled a percussion cap from his pocket and loaded the last chamber, then dropped the hammer. With the dog temporarily disoriented pawing blood from his eyes, Carl grasped the handle of the gun with his trembling left hand and pulled the trigger, hitting the dog in the head at close range.

Bruno yelped and dropped to the ground, a few feet from Buster's bloody head. Buster and Carl's horses bolted into the pasture, spooked by the blast.

As Bruno charged toward Buster and Carl, Paree heard another rider gallop past her, heading north. *Damn! Where is he going?* She commanded her second dog, "Hilde! *Angriff!* Attack!" Paree pointed in the direction of the uninvited rider. Hilde barked and took chase. Then Paree rode toward where Buster had fallen. Another man was crouched near him. Moments before she arrived, in the pre-dawn gloom, she saw Carl shoot Bruno and the dog drop to the ground.

"You evil bastard!" she screamed.

After shooting the dog, Carl struggled to his feet. He fumbled with his good hand to revolve the chamber and re-cock a new load. Looking up, he saw Paree and two dogs fast approaching.

"Gunther! Fritz! *Toten!*" Paree pointed at the intruder.

Before Carl could steady his aim at the heavyset Prussian woman, Gunther launched his muscled, ninety-pound body into the air and slammed into Carl's chest, knocking him to the ground. The revolver flew out of his hand. Fritz, joining his brother in the kill, sunk his teeth into Carl's leg, twisting his head violently on his prey.

Carl screamed and fought the dog on his chest to keep its sharp teeth from biting his neck and face.

At closer range, Paree recognized the two men. *Buster and Carl! I'll bet they're part of a damned posse!* Memories of Napoleon's sadistic soldiers pillaging her family farm enraged her.

"Gunther! *Aus!*" Paree called her young dog off Carl's body. Still growling with teeth bared, the attacking animal released his grip on his prey, and returned to Paree's side. Fritz continued gnawing on the man's leg.

Paree circled her horse around the men, both splayed in the blood-soaked snow. "I varned you to get off my land! This is for Bruno, you bastard! *Verrotte in der hölle!* Rot in hell!"

Then the face of the sadistic French colonel, memorized so long ago, grinning and smoking his cigar as his men ravished her mother, came full center in her mind. *Revenge!* She took aim and fired her shotgun, blowing a gaping hole in Carl's chest.

Scheisse! God-DAMN you! She holstered her empty shotgun and grabbed the loaded revolver from her jacket pocket.

"Gunther! Fritz! *Ferse!*" Both dogs, with blood dripping from their jowls, returned to their position on the horse's left flank. Paree screamed at Buster. "You stupid shit! You should have stayed away."

Writhing on the ground, Buster grasped his mangled throat. Blood gushing through his fingers slathered his face.

Following the streambank, Paul heard another gunshot, and his father's scream. Turning his horse in the woods, he made his way out to the second open pasture. Kicking his horse into a gallop, he started to ride back to where Buster had fallen. Suddenly, his horse jerked and almost threw him. Paul heard growling and turned to see a dog with its muzzle buried in his horse's flank. The horse flailed his back leg and the dog fell, ripping a chunk of flesh in her mouth. Paul struggled to stay in the saddle as the horse fought off its attacker. When the dog dropped, Paul slapped the reins and kneed the horse, who took off in a lopsided trot, trying to outrun the chasing dog.

Approaching the spot where Buster had fallen, Paul reined his horse to an abrupt stop. In the early morning light he saw his neighbor, Paree, on horseback, pointing her revolver directly at him. He held up both hands in surrender, then glanced at the bloody bodies on the ground. Staring at the imposing, angry woman, Paul shook his head in disbelief.

"Stay vhere you are, Paul," Paree commanded. "Now, vhat is happening on the road?"

Paul balanced in his saddle, hands still in the air. "My father! He's hurt!" He swung his arm toward the wounded, gurgling man. "I need to help him. Please!" He started to dismount.

Paree, positioning her horse just feet away, kept her revolver pointed at his head. "You dismount, you're dead! Now, tell me!"

Paul stayed in his saddle, and pointed toward the road. "The sheriff caught the Hoppers transporting slaves. But their wagon got caught—"

"The Hoppers? Are you sure?" *Damn! I would have thought it was Zenas Ellis. He is known to harbor fugitives.*

Paul nodded. "Yes, yes! Gabe and Luke. Their wagon got stuck on the bridge and the fugitives are escaping!" He pointed north along the river bordering Paree's land. "Sheriff is trying to arrest them and sent us to find the runaways."

Carl, writhing on the ground and clutching his chest, mumbled Paul's name.

Staring at his injured father, tears welled in Paul's eyes. He looked to Paree. "Please, let me help him. He's dying!"

Paree shook her head. "No! You're trespassing. Now get the hell off my land before I shoot you, too!" Gunther and Fritz bared their teeth and growled.

Just then Hilde ran up behind Paul's horse, launched herself into the air and sunk her sharp teeth into its right haunch. The horse squealed, rearing in pain, almost throwing Paul to the ground. Ripping more flesh, Hilde circled the horse, growling. The rider grabbed the reins, trying to control his panicked mount. Then the horse bolted with its rider across the pasture into the line of trees separating Paree's land from the Whitehall road.

"Hilde! *Ferse!* Heel!" Paree commanded. The dog took her place along the right flank of Paree's horse, still chewing on the raw horse flesh.

"*Scheisse!* Shit!" Paree yelled. *I will probably be arrested for shooting them, but they were trespassing. And Carl did shoot Bruno, so I was defending my property.* With steely determination, she turned her horse north. *Now that the Hoppers are in trouble, it is my sworn duty to help the runaways.*

Kicking her horse into a trot, her remaining dog pack followed by her side as she went in search of the fugitives on her land.

ENOS

Enos dropped his hands in defeat. "Get off me!" he yelled at Zenas H., who had pinned him to the ground. A few feet away Edward wailed, his arms protecting his head from Enos' attack. Zenas released his grip on his friend.

"Edward, you stupid bastard!" Enos spat at the downed boy. Dazed, he crawled on his hands and knees back to Luke's stiffening body, then sat in the snow, pulling his friend onto his lap. Sobbing and distraught, he cradled Luke's head. "Oh God, Luke! I'm so sorry. It's all my fault! I never should have let him come with us!"

Barnaby, still holding Luke's hand, stared at Enos. "Let who come with you where?"

Zenas H. crouched down by Enos after hearing his brother's question. "What are you talking about, Enos?"

Enos shook his head in dismay. "I—We…" Enos quickly glanced at Zenas, then bowed his head. "We spied on you last night."

"You *what*?" Zenas' face flushed.

Enos spoke in a hushed tone. "I am *so* sorry. It was just supposed to be me and Buster. Then Edward insisted on coming with us. Didn't think it'd be a problem."

Barnaby's face twisted. "You didn't think spying on us was a problem? What the hell, Enos? We thought you were our friend."

Zenas H. stood, arms crossed, towering over Enos. "Well? What did you see, then?"

Enos tenderly wiped blood from Luke's slack face. "Nothing, really. We saw you on the road—it was Buster—he followed you to the Hoppers'." Enos paused and ran his sleeve over his dripping nose. Vaguely he heard shouting and commotion from elsewhere, but he ignored it. "Buster came back and said he saw the wagon being loaded and a Negro boy helping you."

Barnaby raised himself from the ground and stood next to his brother. "And you turned us in? How *could* you? Look what you did—Luke's dead! He was your friend and gave you work. You are a goddamned traitah!" Barnaby bent and slapped Enos in the face.

Zenas grabbed his younger brother's arm to keep him from inflicting more harm. "*Why*, Enos? Why did you do it? Did that Southernah offah ya money?" Zenas backed away a few steps and pointed his finger at the distraught man. "You're just like Judas—betraying us for thirty pieces of silvah! I hope it was worth it, 'cause you gotta live with this for the rest of your life!"

Enos, despondent, dropped his head and swiped blood dripping from his nose. "You're right. You're right! I never should have gotten involved. Ahhhh! Jesus! God forgive me! I am so, so sorry." He covered his face with his bloodstained hands and sobbed.

"So, what happened with Edward?" Zenas H. asked after a minute.

"I didn't trust Edward. He'd gone crazy. Kept sayin' he wanted to kill some niggahs. We tried to get rid of him. Honest! The sheriff warned him at the meeting last night to go home otherwise he was going to tell the Colonel." Enos coughed and spat blood from his split lip. "Just now, I chased after Edward when he ran into the woods. Then I saw him point the revolver toward the wagon, and I yelled at Luke to warn him. But I was too late!"

Barnaby asked, "So you shot Edward?"

Enos' body trembled. "Yes! I wanted to kill that sonofabitch! But Beldon spooked and my aim missed. Oh, God! What have I done?" Enos shook his head.

The sound of their names echoing through the woods caught the brothers' attention.

"Over heah, Fathah," Zenas H. called through the trees.

Moments later, the Ellis patriarch emerged into the small clearing, the brothers' horses following his lead. He reined to a stop, dismounted, tethered the three horses to limbs and grabbed his lantern from its staff.

No sooner had Zenas dismounted then Edward began whining, "Enos shot Luke—shot me! Help me! Help me!"

Zenas glanced at the boy flailing on the ground, then turned to his sons. "Oh Jesus! What in the good Lord happened? Thee boys hurt?"

Barnaby shook his head. "No, but Luke is dead. Enos said Edward shot him!"

Zenas C. turned his back on Edward, walked to the edge of the riverbank and, holding up the lantern, knelt beside Luke. Seeing the gore and shattered cartilage protruding from Luke's throat, Zenas dropped his head and said a silent prayer. "Oh, God! No! Gabe will be beset with grief." He looked at Enos. "So, what is Edward babbling about? He said thee shot him and Luke."

Enos erupted. "He's lying. That little shit! I saw him shoot Luke, then I shot Edward to stop him."

Zenas Senior stood and walked to Edward's twisting form, crouched, and pulled his lantern closer to see the boy's wounds. He noticed blood soaking the slushy snow beneath Edward's right leg, and the bruises rising on the boy's pockmarked face. Ripping open Edward's pant leg, Zenas saw the shinbone was shattered. Blood welled from the wound and fragments of bone jutted at odd angles. Zenas pulled off his belt and wrapped it tightly above the knee to stem the flow of blood. Then he wrapped his handkerchief tight around the shredded hole in the boy's leg.

Edward howled at the movement of his leg. He lifted his head slightly and glared at Zenas C. "I watched—Enos shoot Luke." The boy gasped.

"Then he tried to kill me!" He dropped his head into the snow and he coughed up a mixture of sputum and blood.

Zenas C. turned to the struggling boy. "That's not what Enos says, Edward. He says thee shot Luke. Why should I believe *thee*?"

Zenas H. came to his father's side and held Edward's shoulders down. "Father, Enos said he didn't trust Edward and followed him when he saw Edward run into the woods here. He saw Edward shoot Luke, and he fired at Edward to stop him." Zenas H. waved his hand in Enos' direction. "I believe Enos. He told us that he, Edward and Bustah were spying on us last night. They turned in the Hoppers to the sheriff, but they tried to get rid of Edward. Even Sheriff Wardwell had warned Edward to go home."

"Goddammit!" Zenas C. raged, uncharacteristically swearing. "How could they be so stupid?" He pounded his fist on the ground. "Barnaby, run across the bridge and tell Gabe Luke's hurt pretty bad, but don't tell him Luke is dead. Let him know we will get Luke home. But make sure Gabe stays on the New York side of the bridge, so the sheriff does not arrest him. And don't let anybody stop thee, hear me?"

"Yes, Sir." Barnaby sprinted through the woods toward the bridge. He could just make out the tall, imposing form of Deputy George Wardwell riding in the opposite direction, a few yards to his left.

GEORGE

Having given the reins of Edward's riderless horse to his father, George ventured south into the woods where he thought Edward had escaped. The sound of a gunshot coming from the opposite direction made George wheel his horse around. He trotted back through the woods toward the bridge.

With half the posse chasing Samuel and Jonah along the riverbank, and Duschanne and the others tracking Sarah back toward town, Sheriff Wardwell guarded the bridge alone. As George reached his father, another shot rang out directly to the north.

"Goddammit! Now who's shooting?" the sheriff bellowed. "George, go find out what the hell is going on!" The sheriff struggled to hold the reins of Edward's horse, which was trying to bolt from its captor.

George, holding his second revolver pointing upward, directed his horse north through the trees next to the riverbank. He heard shouts and cursing, and quickly came upon a bloody scene. From the glow of his lantern, he saw Edward whimpering in the snow, grasping his smashed nose. Blood soaked the ground beneath the boy's lower right leg. At the edge of the riverbank, Enos sat, legs splayed, cradling Luke's head in his lap. Zenas Senior held his lantern over the men and his elder son crouched along the side of the body.

"What the hell happened here?" George yelled at the Ellis patriarch.

Before Zenas C. could answer, Edward swung his arm in Enos' direction and wailed, "Sheriff! Enos shot Luke—tried to kill me. Arrest him!"

Enos screamed, "That's a fucking lie, George! Edward killed Luke! And I shot that stupid sonofabitch before he did more harm!" he added, pointing at Edward. Then he subsided, grasping Luke's body closer to his chest.

George moved his horse between Edward and Enos. "Enough of this bullshit. Now who the hell shot Luke?"

Enos turned and pointed. "Edward did. He's mad! You gotta believe me! I think he was aiming for the Negro woman Luke was helping out of the wagon. He screamed he 'wanted to kill some niggahs,' but he shot Luke instead. Now Luke's dead!" A deep sob escaped him. "I was so mad I kicked the hell out of him. Zenas H. pulled me off before I killed him."

"Negro woman?" George asked. "Where did she go?"

Enos pointed downstream. "Don't know. Luke lost his grip on her when he got shot and she disappeared."

As George was interrogating Enos, a distant gunshot from the north echoed through the trees. George's horse stomped sideways and he pulled the reins to calm his mount. Turning in the direction of the shots, he realized they were coming from Paree's land.

"Shit! You boys stay here!" George turned his horse and rode back to the bridge. Just then he saw Barnaby sprinting across the bridge as he pulled his horse next to his distracted father. "Pa, Look!" George pointed at the fleeing boy.

Having heard the shots from Paree's land, the sheriff had his back to the bridge. Swinging his horse around, he pointed his revolver toward the bridge. "Barnaby! Stop, or you'll be arrested!"

The youth ignored him and kept running toward Gabe, who was tending his injured horse along the New York riverbank.

Sheriff Wardwell turned and growled at his son. "Dammit! Someone's shooting over on Paree's land. Now, what's happening by the river?"

Catching his breath, George said, "It's bad, Pa. Luke's been shot—not sure who did it. But Enos says he shot Edward. Plus the fugitive woman is gone and Luke is—"

Suddenly, a horse bolted out of the woods near them, with Paul screaming, "Pa's shot!…dogs got him…crazy woman!"

Sheriff Wardwell turned to his son. "His Pa got shot? A crazy woman? What's he yellin' about?"

The frantic steed plowed into George, causing his horse to rear, the hooves crashing down on the rump of Paul's injured horse. The sheriff snagged the spooked horse's bridle and pulled it around to face him. The sudden jostling of the animals caused him to lose his grip on Edward's empty mount, who took off down the road leading back toward town.

"Shit!" Wardwell grabbed the distraught man's arm. "Paul! What the hell happened?"

Paul pointed north across the road and gasped, "Chasin' the niggahs—dogs—got Buster. Paree shot Pa—dogs after me!"

The sheriff shook his head and turned to George. "What a goddamned mess! I cannot believe this! I said *no violence,* didn't I?"

Paul blathered in his saddle as Wardwell squeezed the man's arm tighter. "Where are Carl and Buster now?"

Paul flung his arm in the direction of Paree's land. "On the ground—dead!" He choked and cried. "Paree did this. That hag killed them—arrest her!"

George stared at his father's anguished face.

The sheriff ran his hand over his chin. "You say Paree shot the men and set her dogs on them? Damn! They were deputized to uphold the law." He shook his head. "I'm going to have to get Paree's side of the story before I can arrest her for protecting her land."

"What happened to the fugitives?" George asked.

Paul scratched at his matted, red beard. "Don' know! Don' know! Never did see 'em. Oh, Pa!…Oh, Pa!" His body shook from his wrenching sobs.

George heard Gabe yell from the opposite side of the bridge. "Sheriff! Where is Luke? Where are the Prescotts? An—" His shouts became inaudible.

The senior lawman yelled back. "Gabe! I order you to come over here right now." He motioned to the Vermont side of the bridge. "You are under arrest. Do you understand me?"

After a fruitless yelling match with Gabe, the sheriff turned to his son. "George, stay with Paul and don't let Gabe outta your sight. He's under arrest." He waved in Gabe's direction. "I need to go see what's happening by the river."

Sheriff Wardwell wheeled his mount, crossed the road on the Vermont side of the bridge, and rode through the tree line, his gun at the ready.

SHERIFF

Riding through the trees along the riverbank, Sheriff Wardwell heard their voices before he saw the men. Halting in the small clearing, he saw the three Ellis horses and Enos' horse tethered to trees. They nickered and jostled at the arrival of another mount.

On the ground just a few feet from him, he saw a dark figure. The boy called out, "Sheriff! Help! Enos shot me!—shot Luke—arrest him!"

Wardwell lifted the lantern from its staff to better view the whimpering figure.

"Edward! What the hell are you talking about?"

Swinging his light toward the river, he saw Zenas C. holding his lantern over Luke, being cradled in Enos' lap. Zenas' eldest son crouched nearby.

"Zenas!" Wardwell called out to the Ellis patriarch. "What the hell happened here?" The sheriff looked down at Edward. A belt tourniquet had been applied to the boy's naked leg and a bloody handkerchief was wrapped around his shin. The beginnings of a black eye puffed his bloody face.

Zenas C. left his lantern near Luke's body and approached the sheriff several yards away. "Jeremiah," he said in a hushed voice. "Luke's dead. And we think Edward shot him." Zenas waved his hand toward the wailing boy.

"Oh, Jesus! I didn't want any violence. I cannot believe this!" Holstering his gun, Wardwell dismounted and tethered his mount away from the other agitated horses. The glint of a revolver, half-buried in the snow to Edward's right, flickered in the lantern light. He stooped to pick it up, then sniffed the end of its barrel.

With Zenas C. by his side, he confronted Edward. "This is George's gun you stole!" He waved the revolver in front of the boy's bruised face. "Smells like it's just been fired." Reaching down, he gripped the boy's arm. "Did you shoot this gun, Edward?"

Edward howled and tried to squirm away from the sheriff's firm grasp. "Nah, Nah!" He screamed. "Enos shot me and Luke. Arrest 'im!"

Zenas touched the sheriff's shoulder. "I don't think that's the truth, Jeremiah. Thee should speak with Enos."

"Goddammit! Somebody tell me what the hell happened!" Wardwell tucked George's revolver behind his holster strap, and strutted to where Enos sat at the edge of the riverbank. Zenas C. followed closely behind.

With the sheriff's arrival, Zenas H. left his vigil at Luke's body and took up a position guarding Edward.

Standing taller than the others, Wardwell peered down at Luke's stiffening body, illuminated by both lanterns. Caked blood covered Luke's face and chest. "Enos! What the hell? Who shot Luke?" he bellowed. "There wasn't supposed to be any violence. Those were my orders!"

Enos choked on his tears. "It was Edward! Honest to God, Sheriff! He went crazy. I saw him slip off his horse while George was holding it, so I followed him." He took a deep breath and looked up at the lawman's imposing figure. "Luke was helping an old Negro woman get out of the wagon before she drowned." He shook his head. "I heard Edward scream, *Gonna kill me some niggahs,* then he fired and hit Luke in the back of the neck."

Hearing Enos' story, Edward started yelling, "Not true! Lyin'!…killin' niggahs…ain't no good…Enos killin' niggahs!"

Wardwell turned toward the babbling boy. "Edward! Shut the hell up or I'll shoot you myself!" Wardwell rubbed a hand over his face. "Oh, Christ! Whoever shot Luke, there's gonna be hell to pay. And Gabe is going to be inconsolable!" He turned back to Enos. "Where'd the woman go?" The sheriff peered into the gloomy, pre-dawn woods along the river.

Enos released his grip on Luke's head and swung one hand in the air. "I don't know! I guess she got caught in the river when Luke lost hold of her."

"Goddammit! Another fugitive on the run! What a bloody mess!" The sheriff paced near the men. "So who the hell shot Edward?"

"I did!" Enos screamed. "I wanted to kill that bastard for shooting Luke. He's crazy, Sheriff. You know that! Now look what's happened—Luke's dead and the fugitives are gone. Ahhh, I never should have gotten involved in this." Enos dropped his head into his bloodstained hands.

Passing his lantern to Zenas C., the sheriff dropped to one knee. He held Luke's wrist, waiting for a pulse. After a few seconds, he shook his head. "Enos, until I can get to the bottom of this, you and Edward are both under arrest."

Zenas C. exclaimed, "Now, Jeremiah! Does thee think this necessary? What if—"

The lawman grunted as he stood and wiped his hands across his rotund belly. "Zenas, I've got a huge mess here to deal with. Luke's body needs to be sent home. Edward needs to go to the doctor, and something's happening over at Paree's place. Plus, I need to round up the runaways, or Duschanne will have my hide!" The sheriff shook his head in frustration and blew out a breath. "I'll tell you what, if you and your boys can get Luke's body home, I'll want Enos to come by my office tomorrow and give me his statement. I'll decide then whether he's under arrest."

Enos nodded. "Thanks, Sheriff. We'll do our best, I promise." He peered toward the river. "We'll need Gabe's help with Luke's body."

Wardwell snapped. "Nope. Gabe's under arrest for transporting fugitives. He's coming with me to jail."

"Jeremiah! Please! Don't do this," Zenas C. implored. "You know Gabe. He's not a criminal. Please!"

"I'm sorry, but Gabe knew he was breaking the law. I gotta do my job and bring him in." Wardwell waved his hand over Luke's body. "You boys get Luke outta here. May he rest in peace. I'll have someone get Edward to the doctor. Now move!"

The sheriff retrieved his lantern, walked away, mounted his horse and trotted into the woods in the direction of Paree's pastures, just as another gunshot echoed in the distance.

GABE

After hearing the two successive gunshots from across the river, Gabe scrambled up the embankment with the help of Zenas H. Breathing hard, he bent and grabbed his knees, then shouted in a raspy voice, "Luke! Luke! Where is thee?" Waiting, he got no answer.

Why is there shooting? Where is Luke? Where are the Prescotts? Who needs help?

His heartbeat wasn't slowing, and he felt a tight pressure in his chest. Massaging the area, he gasped to slow his breathing. As he straightened, he could just make out the dark forms of the Ellis brothers slipping and sliding across the bridge, then ducking away from the sheriff into the trees.

Intermingled shouts from the Vermont side of the bridge reached him.

"*Let's get 'em!*"

"*What a goddamned mess!*"

"Bien! *What the hell?*"

"*Gabe! You're under arrest.*"

Taking a deep breath, Gabe hollered across the bridge. "Sheriff! Where is Luke? Where are the Prescotts?"

He got no response to his call amidst the continuing commotion on the opposite bank. Then a nicker got his attention and he turned to see his young draft horse, Zachary, hobbling toward him. He walked a few steps from the bridge to investigate the animal's injuries. A gash on the right shoulder bled but didn't look too deep. Gabe bent and ran his hands down Zachary's uplifted right front leg. When he moved the joint, the horse flinched, bobbing his head and pulling away from Gabe's grasp. *Oh, no! I hope it's not broken, as I couldn't bear to put him down.* Standing from his ministrations, Gabe peered across the bridge toward Vermont.

From the erratic glow of Zenas C.'s lantern, Gabe saw his neighbor leading two horses, following his sons into the woods along the opposite streambank.

Then he heard Deputy George yell, "I'm goin' after that li'l shit!" The lawman rode off on his mount.

Oh, dear Jesus! Someone's going to be hurt. Please protect Luke and the Prescotts. It was then Gabe remembered his shotgun. *Where is my gun? Did it go over with the wagon?*

Taking advantage of the confusion, Gabe carefully trod onto the slippery bridge searching for his shotgun. About halfway across, he dropped to his hands and knees, sliding his hands back and forth on the icy planks, but he couldn't locate his weapon. *I hope it's not in the river.* He crawled several more feet along the edge to where the wagon had gone over. Suddenly his hand hit something cold and hard and he gasped, "Thank you, Lord!" Gabe grabbed the shotgun, but its trigger guard was wedged between the wooden bridge slats. Yanking hard, he pulled it free, then stood and retreated back to the New York side of the bridge. He still carried the satchel of charges slung over one shoulder.

More distant gunshots rang out from the north, in the direction of Paree's land. In the gray morning light, Gabe could identify the sheriff's form atop his horse, now alone near the edge of the bridge. "Jeremiah! What is happening? Where is Luke?"

The preoccupied sheriff didn't seem to hear Gabe's plea. Moments later, George halted his horse next to his father.

Wardwell demanded. "Dammit! Who is shooting—"

Gabe heard more shouting and confusion then a voice rang out, as a rider plowed into the two lawmen. "Pa's shot!...dogs got him..."

Oh, God! I need to know what's happening and where Luke is!

Suddenly, Gabe saw a crouching figure running across the slippery bridge toward him.

The sheriff warned, "Barnaby, stop or you'll be arrested!"

Gabe grasped Barnaby's arm as the boy skidded to a stop in front of him. "Jeremiah!" Gabe yelled back. "Who is hurt? Tell me!"

Then Wardwell hollered, "Gabe! I order you to come over here right now. You are under arrest. Do you understand me?"

Barnaby gripped Gabe's arm. "Don't do it, Sir. Fathah sent me to tell you to stay here, so you won't get arrested."

Gabe glared at the disheveled boy. "Barnaby, does thee know where Luke is? What has happened?"

Barnaby looked to the ground, then back at Gabe. "Luke's been hurt, Sir."

"He's hurt? How? Where is he? I must go to him!" Gabe started to step onto the bridge.

Barnaby scurried in front of his elder neighbor, stopping his progress. "He's been shot, Sir. Fathah said to tell you we'll get him home. But you must stay here." Barnaby touched the elder man's arm.

"Ahhhh, God! No! No! Please protect him!" Gabe threw his hands to his face, then grasped Barnaby by the shoulders. "Who shot him? Is he alive? And where are the Prescotts?"

Barnaby looked into his neighbor's wrinkled, distraught face. "I'm not sure who shot him, Sir. But father says we need to get him back to the farm."

Gabe felt his heart racing, in fear for his son.

Barnaby continued, "I didn't see none of the Prescotts, Sir, so I can't say. Lots of commotion at the bridge, and I think the posse is out chasing 'em."

Dear Lord, this is my fault! Luke thought there would be trouble today. I must go to my son.

Gabe composed himself in front of his young neighbor. "Barnaby. I must get to Luke, but I cannot ride Zachary because he's hobbled. And if I cross the bridge, I shall be arrested. What does thee suggest?"

Barnaby looked down the embankment at the crippled wagon lying on its side. The stream pulsed and eddied around the large obstacle. Several yards downstream, a large boulder loomed in the middle of the flow. Barnaby dropped his gaze, his face slackening with futility as to how to help his neighbor. The nickering of a horse behind him caused him to turn. He stared at Zachary, who was milling nearby, keeping his weight off his injured front leg. The long traces that had attached the horse to the wagon dragged on the ground behind him.

"I have an idea, Sir." Barnaby went to the horse and disconnected the reins still attached to the halter. Crouching next to the horse, he untangled the twisted lines, then presented one to Gabe.

"Sir, Luke is just on the othah side of the bank from the wagon. I think we could cross the rivah before it gets much lightah. If we tie these lines to our bodies, we could help each othah across." Barnaby pointed to the wagon. "I think we can pass downstream of the wagon and the current won't be so strong. We could probably make it, Sir."

With the deep darkness of night fading to a lighter gray dawn, Gabe squinted down through the low mist rising from the river between the wagon and the boulder. "Yes. I believe thee is correct, Barnaby. And perhaps we shan't be seen from the bridge. Shall we try?"

"Yes, Sir." Barnaby pulled the two ends of one long rein together. Using his knife, he sliced through the leather strap, cutting it into two pieces of about equal length. After he tied one end of the rein around Gabe's waist and the other end around his own, about four feet of slack drooped between them.

The shouts of men stopped their conversation. Gabe saw a rider, carrying something bulky across his saddle, approach George, who was guarding the bridge alone.

"*Ahhh. Mon Dieu!*" the voice echoed. "Done caught me 'ze niggah bitch!"

Oh, God! One of the women has been captured. I must help her. 'Tis my duty. The wave of the unfolding disaster fully washed over him. *How could everything have gone so wrong?*

A few moments later, two other riders reached the Vermont side of the bridge. Both men were whooping and hollering.

"*Bi'ch b'oke ma nose—*"

"*She stomped my leg—*"

"*We caught her—*"

Their horses pranced, sidestepping into one another. George barked commands to the boisterous men. Another voice reached Gabe and Barnaby as they watched the commotion.

"*I gotta go to Pa—*" The rider left the group, turning his horse back toward town.

George yelled, "Paul! Get back here! Goddammit!"

Barnaby tugged Gabe's arm. "Sir. Your son. We should go now."

Gabe hesitated, looking at Barnaby, then back across the bridge. *I am so sorry, Sarah. I cannot help. May the Lord watch over thee.* Gabe nodded at the boy and grabbed the shotgun he'd left leaning against a tree when Barnaby had arrived.

Barnaby led the way down the rocky, brush-strewn embankment, waiting at the river's edge for Gabe to join him. Barnaby pointed to a small inlet beyond where the wagon was slowly breaking apart. "We can go in here, Sir."

Barnaby stepped into the rocky streambed and gasped as the frigid water rushed above his waist. He took a few tentative steps, maintaining his balance, then reached his hand out to Gabe. "Careful, Sir. It's slippery." Holding the shotgun high in his left hand, Gabe gave his right hand to Barnaby and stepped into the current. The water rushed past Gabe's thighs and he, too, gasped at the cold.

Taking slow, deliberate steps through the rushing current, Gabe followed Barnaby's path toward the wagon. Barnaby grabbed the half-submerged seat to steady himself. Moments later, Gabe joined him, breathing hard.

A concerned look on his face, Barnaby waited to let Gabe catch his breath. "The current is not so strong behind the wagon, Sir. We shall go slowly."

Grasping the side rail of the toppled wagon for balance, Barnaby moved from one rock to the next, checking his footing each time. Gabe held the shotgun aloft as he followed in Barnaby's footsteps. They reached the back end of the wagon, the current flowing in eddies around the obstruction. About ten feet of turbulent water stretched between them and the opposite bank.

A voice reached them from beyond the wagon. "Zenas! What the hell happened?"

Barnaby turned and whispered to Gabe. "Oh, no! That's the sheriff. We cannot let him see us." Barnaby pointed to the north edge of the river, downstream from the sheriff. "If you can make it to the bank, we can hide under those tree branches."

Gabe nodded. "Yes. Let us go quickly before we are spotted."

Barnaby took a tentative step into the fast current and threw his arms out for balance. He took a second step, balanced his weight, then a third. Gabe moved into the rushing flow but the force of the icy water caught him by surprise and his right foot slipped on a rock. He sidestepped to his left to keep his balance. The current pushed against his thighs and he slipped backward trying to gain his footing. The rein connecting him and Barnaby pulled taut and Barnaby grunted, straining against Gabe's weight. Stumbling forward, Gabe flailed his arms as the rushing water pushed him toward the huge boulder. Swinging his left arm to brace himself, he smashed the shotgun into the chest-high rock with a clunk.

Lord! Do not let me lose this gun. With his right hand, Gabe grasped the boulder, his chest pressed against it by the current pushing against his body. He felt a tug on the rein and looked back to see Barnaby, struggling to keep his balance, finally join him at the boulder.

The boy braced himself. "Mistah Hoppah. Are you injured?" He spoke urgently to the older man.

Gabe grimaced. "No, Son. Just lost my footing. I am fine."

Barnaby nodded. "Sir, grab my shoulder and we'll cross togethah." Barnaby pointed several yards away where a downed tree lay against the water's edge. "To that log, Sir."

Barnaby and Gabe moved cautiously into the rushing stream, holding one another. Struggling for balance with each step pushing against the torrent, they reached the opposite bank. Barnaby climbed over the fallen log and gave Gabe a hand to help him up. Both men sat with their feet dangling over the log, under overhanging branches, catching their breath. Gabe rested the shotgun on his lap. The river mist swirled over them.

Barnaby untied the line and threw it into the bushes. "I don't think we were seen, Sir." Barnaby peered toward the top of the riverbank.

The sound of men's voices filtered to them but were unintelligible until they heard, "*Edward! Shut the hell up or—*"

Gabe vigorously rubbed his numbed legs to get the blood circulating. "Edward?" He whispered to Barnaby. "Is that Edward Allen? Why is the boy here? Is he part of the posse? And where in the good Lord's name is Luke?"

"Luke is just yonder on the bank, Sir." Barnaby pointed in the direction of the voices. "And, no. Edward wasn't part of the posse. Enos told me Edward was the one who fired the first shot that spooked your horses. I believe the sheriff is going to arrest him."

"Oh, my!" Gabe rasped. "This is terrible indeed. We have brought such trouble. But I must go to Luke." Gabe started to rise, but Barnaby put a hand on the older man's shoulder.

"If you will permit me, Sir. Please stay here and let me see what is happening. I shall stay hidden and report back as quickly as I can."

Desperate to see his son, but not wanting to be arrested, Gabe reluctantly nodded. "Yes, yes. But thee must hurry." Gabe watched as Barnaby crouched and made his way into the undergrowth following the riverbank upstream. He lost sight of the boy in the thicket.

Dear Lord. I ask Thee for a miracle to keep Luke alive. He's a fine man, with a loving family that needs his strength. Please keep him on this earth, Lord, so he may continue to do Thy work. And Lord, please watch over the Prescott family and keep them safe in their quest to reach the Promised Land.

While he waited, Gabe focused his attention on his shotgun. He ran his hand halfway down the left barrel and stopped. He felt something unusual. In the gloom of the river mist, he lifted the shotgun to inspect the barrel. He felt a dent and a deep crack in the steel. *Oh, no! Now I've cracked the barrel. I did not want to bring it anyway, but Luke convinced me.* He settled the disabled shotgun across his lap. Realizing his boots were filled with cold water, he lifted one leg and then the other, to let the boots drain.

A few minutes passed as Gabe shivered in his wet clothes, struggling with his thoughts. *What if Luke is dead? What if the Prescotts are dead or captured? This trip has been such a failure!* He shook his head. *Why in heaven did that trouble-making slave hunter have to come to our town?*

A noise coming through the woods pulled Gabe from his thoughts. Then he saw Barnaby emerge from the thicket. "Well. What did thee see?" Gabe asked, as the boy crouched next to him.

Barnaby took several deep breaths. "The sheriff has gone, Sir. Now is our chance to get to Luke." Barnaby stood and helped Gabe, still cradling his shotgun, to his feet.

Gabe grasped the boy's arm. "How is Luke? Is he alive?"

"I really can't say. Just follow me, Mistah Hoppah." Barnaby braced himself against the tree trunks to ascend the slope, helping Gabe with each step. When they reached the crest of the bank, they stayed in the cover of trees while they hurried toward Luke's location.

Emerging from the trees, Gabe saw horses milling about in a small clearing. A wail came from a dark figure lying on the ground, where another man appeared to be guarding him. "Luke!" Gabe cried, moving quickly toward the downed man.

Suddenly, someone grabbed his arm and swung him around. Gabe stood face to face with his good friend and neighbor. "Zenas! I need to get to Luke! Please!"

"Gabe! That's Edward. He's been shot, but he'll be fine. Zenas H. is guarding him." Then Zenas pointed to Enos, sitting on the bank, his legs splayed and his back to the men. A slumped body lay cradled in his arms. "I'm so sorry, Gabe, but Luke is over there."

"Luke!" Gabe gasped as he rushed toward the two figures. Laying his damaged shotgun on the ground, Gabe dropped to his knees. He saw the blood-soaked handkerchief on Luke's throat and stared into his son's bloody, yet serene face.

Shaking his son's shoulder, Gabe called out, "Luke! Luke! I am here." He shook his son more vigorously. "Open your eyes, Luke. Please! I'm here for thee!" Yet, his son's body lay inert.

Enos and Zenas C. reached out to lay hands on Gabe as he sobbed over his fallen son.

"Oh, no! No! God, why has Thee *forsaken* us? Luuuuuuke!" An animal-like keening pierced the air as Gabe threw himself onto his son's chilled body.

PAREE

Getting revenge on the men trespassing on her land did not make Paree feel better. They were not Napoleon's men, after all, and killing them did not assuage her anger against the pillagers of her childhood home. And she was furious her lead dog, Bruno, was dead.

Damn those men! I warned them at the meeting to stay clear. Those bastards got what they deserved. They should not have been on my land, and they knew it!

In a foul mood, she rode along the edge of the tree line between the river and her pastures. Her three remaining dogs, obeying her heel command, followed on each side of the horse's flanks. In the distance she could make out the bulk of her hay barn silhouetted against the dawning sky. Not knowing whether there were fugitives or more of the posse on her land, Paree called to her pack. "*Suche!* Search!" She swept her arm in a circle and pointed forward.

Hilde bolted into the lead, smelling the ground directly in front of Paree's horse. Gunther followed his nose into the woods toward the river and Fritz, the youngest, howled and ran into the pasture to Paree's right, his head swinging rapidly, nose to the ground.

Paree clucked her horse into a trot following Hilde's lead. Suddenly the dog snarled, lifted her head and charged toward the barn. Paree heard Gunther crashing through the underbrush near the river, then saw his form bolt from the trees behind the barn. Then he joined Hilde, pacing back and forth behind her. The lead dog, poised in an attack position, bared her teeth, growling at the closed barn door.

Halting her horse, Paree unholstered her shotgun from the saddle, and dismounted. She pulled a charge from her satchel, ripped off the top with her teeth, poured the gunpowder and lead ball into one barrel, tamped it hard, then threw the casing on the ground. She repeated the process with the second barrel, cocked the first trigger and pointed the gun at the barn door. "Who goes there?" she called. "Come out now, or I vill send my dogs on you." She turned to see Fritz had joined the pack, growling.

Grasping her lantern from the horse's staff, Paree waited as her dogs continued to growl, but there was no movement at the barn door. "I'm varning you! Come out now, or ve are coming in!"

Still no movement.

She slid the barn door partially open. Aiming the shotgun into the barn, she quickly ducked into the first stall.

"Hilde! *Suche!*" she directed.

Hilde charged into the barn, her progeny following her lead. The dogs moved around the barn growling, smelling the hay mows, farm equipment and wagon parked to one side. "Who's there? Come out!" Paree called from the stall.

Having not been shot at upon her arrival and carrying her light, she took several steps inside, her shotgun at the ready.

At the back of the barn, Hilde growled in her attack stance, snarling up at the ladder climbing to the loft. Stepping to Hilde's flank, Paree hung the lantern on a wall hook and pointed her shotgun toward the rafters. "You better come down now, before I shoot!" she called up to her possible trespassers.

In the faint glow of the lantern light, a dark figure appeared above the ladder. His hands reached high into the air. "Don't shoot. Please! We need help." His voice trembled.

Paree turned to her dogs, "Hilde. Gunther. Fritz. *Bleibe.*" She gave them each the open palm signal to stay. The dogs sat, panting. When she looked back up to the loft, she saw two dark heads peering down at her. The younger figure was whimpering.

"How many of you are up there?"

"Just me and my nephew," the older boy called.

Paree lowered the muzzle of the gun to the floor. "Come down here. Let me see you."

"What about the dogs? He's scared of 'em," the boy responded.

Paree saw the smaller figure hug the taller one. "They vill not hurt you unless I tell them to. Now climb down."

The older boy took a few steps backward down the ladder, his long coat swaying behind him. Then he guided his nephew onto the steps in front of him, where they slowly descended. When they reached the barn floor, the older boy faced Paree, clasping the small boy to his side.

Paree laid her shotgun on the floor, muzzle facing the wall, and stepped closer to get a better look at the shaking, disheveled boys. An oversized coat slouched over the older boy's thin shoulders and hung below his knees. The younger boy's muslin coat had a large rip along the shoulder seam. She watched his wide eyes flicker, watching her panting dogs.

These must be the fugitives the posse is chasing. I have vowed to help those who are in trouble.

Addressing the older boy, Paree asked in a softer tone, "Vat is your name, Son?"

Samuel looked nervously at the three large dogs surrounding him, saliva dripping from their mouths. He tightened his arm around Jonah. "Samuel, Ma'am. And my nephew is Jonah."

"You boys part of that trouble at the bridge?" Paree swung her arm in the general direction.

Samuel nodded. "Yes, Ma'am. The Hoppers were taking my family to Whitehall. But something went bad and the wagon slipped on the bridge. I grabbed Jonah and we ran into the woods." A sob escaped Samuel's trembling lips.

Ah mein Gott! With the Hoppers in trouble, I must help these boys escape to freedom. She dropped to one knee to face the scared duo.

"Do you know where my mother and sister are? They were in the back of the wagon, and I don't know what happened to them." Samuel brushed tears from his eyes. "I've heard an awful lot of shooting, an' I'm mighty worried. Please, we need to find them!"

Paree shook her head. "I am sorry, I do not know. But you can't vorry about that now. Ve need to get you boys 'cross the border before the rest of the posse comes looking for you. I downed a couple of them, but there vill be more—mark my vords!"

Jonah trembled in Samuel's arms as the older boy's eyes went wide. Samuel said, "But I can't leave my family. Please! We must save them."

Paree nodded toward Jonah, then peered at Samuel. "Samuel, you seem like a smart boy, and probably don't vant to scare your nephew even more."

She reached out to the frightened little boy. "Let's get you boys 'cross the river, den I'll go looking for your family. Who are you to meet in Vhitehall?"

Samuel pulled Gabe's letter from his inside coat pocket and handed it to Paree. Hilde growled at Samuel's movement, causing Jonah to whimper, and hug Samuel's leg more tightly.

"Hilde. *Bleibe.*" Paree held her open palm to stay the dog. Letter in hand, Paree walked to the lantern and read Samuel's travel orders. She returned to the boys, who stood rigid staring at the three panting dogs. "You're supposed to meet Titus Battis at his house. Then he vill get you on-board a ship at the canal. I can lead you there. Can you ride?"

Samuel looked up at the imposing bulk of the Prussian woman. "Yes, Ma'am. I suppose I can."

"*Goot.* Ve vill need to move fast. I have to saddle another horse. But I'm going to leave Hilde here to protect you." She beckoned to the two boys. "Samuel, Jonah, hold out your hands and valk to me slowly."

Paree called her lead dog. "Hilde. *Kommen.* Come." The boys tentatively approached the woman as the eighty-pound, brown mottled dog stood and walked forward. Hilde pressed her long snout, smelling the outstretched hand of first Samuel, and then Jonah. The small boy let out a whimper at the dog's touch.

"Don't try to pet her. Let her get to know your scent," Paree cautioned as she ran her hand down the dog's back.

After inspecting their hands, the shepherd sniffed their feet and legs as the boys stood stock still. Standing muzzle-to-face with Jonah, the dog licked the frightened boy's cheek. Jonah gasped, staring directly into the dog's emerald-green eyes.

"Hilde. *Schützen.* Protect." Paree commanded. Hilde swung her body around and sat directly in front of the amazed boys, looking up at her master. Paree stood, pointed at the boys then touched the tips of her fingers together, forming a circle. She raised her hands up and down deliberately three times in front of the dog. "*Schützen,*" she said again. The dog raised her paw in acknowledgment. "*Braves mädchen!* Good girl!" She patted Hilde's head.

Paree pointed to the hay mow next to the door. "Samuel, you and Jonah bury yourselves in there. I vill be back soon. If anyone comes, stay quiet and Hilde vill protect you. Do you understand?"

Samuel nodded. "Yes, Ma'am. Thank you." He pulled Jonah to the hay stack and dug a space they could crawl into, leaving an opening for them to breathe.

Paree gathered her shotgun, doused the lantern, and walked to the barn door. "Gunther. Fritz. *Kommen!*" The dogs followed her out of the barn and she closed the door behind her.

In front of the occupied hay stall, Hilde sat at attention protecting her charges.

GABE

Shivering in his wet clothes and in shock at finding Luke dead, Gabe barely noticed when Zenas C. removed his cloak and placed it around his shoulders. Zenas, holding back his emotions, crouched next to Gabe. His son Barnaby stood by his side, while Zenas H. guarded Edward.

Gabe felt a strong arm steadying his back, and he heard Zenas say, "I am so sorry, Friend. The Good Lord has taken Luke home to be by His side."

Gabe sat up, his face crumpled with anguish. "Why?" he wailed. "Why has He taken my firstborn son? He is *not* a good Lord. He is a *vengeful* Lord!" A tortured sob escaped him. "I did not offer Luke in sacrifice, as Abraham did Isaac. And the Lord spared Abraham's son. What sins have we committed?" He shook his fists toward the sky. "We only wished to do His work on this earth. Oh, God! Mother shall be desolate when she learns of Luke's death. Why have *we* been so cruelly punished?" Gabe wrapped his arms to his chest, gulping air.

Zenas C. shook his head. "I do not know the answers, Friend. But the Lord does work in mysterious ways. Perchance Luke's work on this earth was done."

"No! No! 'Twas not! He had so much life ahead of him!" Gabe, still kneeling beside Luke's body, rubbed his weary face. "Why was it not me? I am old and would have willingly given my life for Luke's." The grieving father choked on his tears. "Now what will happen to Mary and the children? They are without their father."

Zenas C. slumped to his knees and pulled Gabe to his chest. Gabe sobbed on his neighbor's shoulder, lost in misery.

The Lord has shunned me and Emma. Has our faith in His guidance been all in vain? We sought to follow His word, helping those seeking freedom. And this is how we are rewarded? By taking our firstborn? We have not sinned. Why are we being punished? 'Tis not just!

As his raspy sobs subsided, Gabe lifted his head in despair. "Zenas, what happened? Will thee tell me? Who shot Luke?"

Once Gabe had arrived, Enos moved away from Luke's body and now stood next to Barnaby. Hearing Gabe's anguished questions, Enos said, "Edward shot him, Sir." He knelt next to Gabe. "I saw Edward slide from his horse, and I followed him here." Enos dropped his head. "I'm so sorry! Edward was screaming he wanted to 'kill some niggahs'. He pointed a gun toward the woman Luke was helping from the wagon. When I yelled at Luke to warn him, he turned his back to protect her as Edward fired." Enos said, trembling. "I was too late, Sir. I tried to save Luke, and Luke tried to save the Negro woman."

A whine came from behind Gabe. "Lyin! He's lyin! Enos shot Luke—shot me. Arrest him!"

Gabe glanced toward Edward, curled on the ground several yards away, then turned back to Enos with a questioning look.

Enos shook his head. "No, Sir. That's not the truth. Edward's mad, and wanted to kill all the fugitives. I shot him to stop him from doing any more harm."

Zenas H. kicked the downed boy in the side. "Shut up, Edward! No one believes you!"

Gabe stared at the dim shape of the half-submerged wagon through the early morning mist. He rubbed his hands over his ragged face and spoke to Enos. "Where's the woman Luke was helping? Did she escape?"

Enos took a deep breath. "Sir, after Luke got shot, he lost his grip and she disappeared into the darkness. I don't know what happened to her." Enos waved a hand toward the river. "I jumped in and pulled Luke to the bank before he was swept away." Choking back tears, Enos said, "I tried to save him, Sir, but I'm so sorry, Luke died in my arms."

Gabe sobbed. "Oh, God. No! Why? Why Luke? This is all my fault. 'Tis pride that goeth before the fall." Gabe took racking breaths. "And where is the rest of the Prescott family?"

Barnaby spoke up, "We don't know, Sir. But I think the posse is searching for them."

Gabe sat in the snow, holding Luke's cold hand. He glowered at Enos, his trusted farm hand. "And why is thee here, Enos? Is thee part of the posse? And how did the sheriff know of our travels?"

The Ellis men fell silent, all eyes on Enos. Enos dropped his head and sighed, then looked at Gabe. "I'm so sorry, Mister Hopper."

"Tell him the truth," Barnaby demanded. "Tell him what you did!"

Enos turned his anguished face to Gabe. "Luke was good to me, Sir. I should not have done it. I blame myself for everything." Enos shook his head and took a breath. "Buster, Edward and I spied on you last night. But it was Buster who told the sheriff he saw a Negro boy in the barn, and when he thought you would travel."

I have known Enos his entire life, and he has always been a good boy. Why would he spy on us after we have treated him well?

"Ahhhh, no! Why, Enos? Why would thee betray us? We have been kind to thee and Buster, and given thee work." Gabe glared at his trusted farm hand. "With thy father leading the cause, how could thee act against us?"

Enos dropped his head in his hands and sobbed. "I didn't know this would happen. I'm so very sorry, Sir." Wringing his hands in despair, Enos stared at Gabe. "The sheriff warned the men he didn't want any violence. He planned to take the fugitives into custody peacefully." Enos pointed in the direction of Edward. "Sheriff Wardwell sent Edward home—told him to stay out of trouble or he'd tell the Colonel. But Edward's crazy—kept sayin' he wanted to 'kill some niggahs'. None of us knew he was going to ride out here and start shooting!"

Gabe shook his head. "May the Lord forgive thee for thy sins, Enos, because I shan't!" He turned from the sobbing young man and grasped Luke's hand to his heart.

And how can I forgive the Lord for taking Luke too soon? Emma shall be inconsolably grieved, and I cannot bear her pain, or to live without my son.

The subdued group were interrupted by the sound of a horse breaking into the clearing.

The men turned toward the approaching rider.

"Gabe Hopper! You are under arrest!" the lawman yelled, pointing his revolver at Gabe's head.

GEORGE

George watched his father, the sheriff, trot north into the woods along the riverbank. Moments earlier, a frantic rider had collided with George's horse. Wrestling with the reins, George shouted, "Paul! Calm down. Tell me what happened to your Pa."

Paul coughed and spat on the ground, his horse bumping into George's again. George pushed the other horse away and grabbed Paul's arm. "Paul, Tell me!" George commanded the hysterical man.

Paul threw an arm in the air toward Paree's pastures. "She shot Buster—dog ripped him up." His head swung back and forth. "Pa stopped to help him—told me to go catch the fugitives." A deep-seated gurgle escaped him. "Ah, Jesus! Pa!"

"Paul!" George said in a stern voice. "What happened to your Pa?"

Paul replied, "Dunno. Heard two shots, then heard him screaming. Paree must'a shot him!" He wiped his face. "I was by the stream—started to ride back—dog attacked my horse."

"What dog? Thought you said the dog got Buster? You're confused." George stared at the shaken man.

"Nah, nah. Pack of dogs—everywhere—chasing me!" Paul scanned the ground frantically.

George squeezed the man's arm. "Paul! There are no dogs here. Where was your Pa?"

Paul rubbed his swollen eyes. "He was on the ground—shot—blood everywhere. Dog's head blown off, lying next to Buster. I wanted to help Pa—he's hurt real bad! But she said she'd shoot me too, if I dismounted." Paul turned in his saddle, staring at his horse's rump. "Dog attacked my horse, he bolted—I almost fell off."

George released his grip on Paul's arm but kept a tight hold of the frightened horse's reins. He noticed the raw wounds in the horse's flank, so assumed Paul was partially telling the truth. "Paul, listen to me. This is important." George stared at the man, who was now a bit calmer. "Did Paree warn you to get off her land?"

Paul nodded. "Yah, yah. She warned us. Buster tol' her we was chasin' niggahs and to stay outta the way." Paul, voice now hoarse, said, "She shot Pa. You gotta arrest her!"

George sighed and shook his head. "Paul, we'll find Paree and talk to her. Right now, I don't know if we can arrest her for protecting her property, even though you were acting under the law."

"Ah. *Mon Dieu!* Done caught me a niggah bitch."

George recognized the Frenchman's voice. As the rider reined to a halt, George saw a slight figure flung across Duschanne's saddle. Following their leader, Elmer and Cyrus halted their horses in front of the bridge. Both men were whooping and hollering.

Elmer, "Bi'ch b'oke ma noz'—"

Cyrus, "She stomped my leg—"

Elmer, "We caught her—"

The horses nickered and sidestepped into one another.

In the early morning gloom, Duschanne turned his horse and peered downstream to the crushed, partially submerged wagon. "*Merde!*" he screamed at the deputy. "Where are ze slaves? Did you let zem get away? You are losing my money!"

George saw Sarah squirming in her slumped, hog-tied position across the slave hunter's saddle. "Lemme go, you bastard!" she yelled.

Her body started to slip off the horse, but Duschanne grabbed her hair and yanked her back into place. Sarah cried out at the assault.

Duschanne smacked the girl in the head. "*Tais-toi!* Or I will gag you, too."

George watched with revulsion as the bounty hunter grasped the back of her dress to keep her body splayed against his horse's neck. Disgusted, he finally responded to the Southerner's inquiries. "We don't know where the fugitives are. The sheriff has gone to investigate. We've heard several shots, and we know two men are down." George waved his hand toward the downstream bank. "And there's been some shooting over on Paree's land."

"Goddammit!" Duschanne lashed out. "Zis was to be an easy arrest! *Non?* Now ze runaways are scattered, and you've lost me a lot of money!" He flung one arm in the air toward the river. "*Tu êtes très stupide! Ah, mon Dieu!*"

George positioned his horse next to the agitated Southerner and leaned close. "I am not stupid! We're doing the best we can, but everything went wrong when the wagon slid on the bridge. We will apprehend the fugitives, I promise you!"

Duschanne glowered. "You had better, *Monsieur.* And you and your father had best remember our *arrange'mon'.*"

George sighed and shook his head. *Yeah twenty percent of the bounty ain't going to be much without the rest of the slaves. Shit.* "Yeah, I remember. Father is searching for them now."

Then a faint shout emanated from Paree's pastures. The men at the bridge jostled their horses to look in that direction. Next to George, Paul yelled, "I gotta go to Pa!" He yanked his horse's reins from George, and galloped east along the road then north through the copse of trees onto Paree's land.

"Paul! Get back here!" George yelled. "Goddammit!"

"George!" the Frenchman demanded. "Why are you not chasing ze runaways? You are ze deputy, *non?* Go do your damned job!"

George grunted, regarding the Frenchman sourly. "Because Father wants me to stay here and arrest Gabe when he crosses the bridge." With his back turned to the bridge, George swung his arm toward New York.

In the light of early dawn, the full span of the bridge and opposite bank were now visible. Duschanne peered in that direction and shrugged his shoulders. "Zere is no one! Who you gonna arrest, the hobbled horse?"

George swung his horse to face the bridge. Before the posse had arrived, Gabe and Barnaby had been standing along the New York bank. Now they were gone.

"What! Where the hell did they go?" *I didn't see them cross the bridge. Did they sneak into the woods? I'll bet Gabe is trying to get to Luke. Damn! Father will be furious with me for losing them!*

The belligerent Southerner bared his teeth in a sneering grin. "George, *Je répète: Tu êtes très stupide!* Now go find my cargo! *Jésus Christ!*"

George seethed. *Damn him for ordering me around.* "Duschanne, stay here with Elmer and Cyrus. I'll be back soon."

George rode away from the bridge, and entered the trees to the north. Within a few moments, he emerged into the small clearing by the stream. There he saw Zenas H. guarding Edward, who was lying on the ground. As he rode past Edward, a group of men turned toward him.

Is that Barnaby standing next to his father? How the hell did he get here? Then he saw Enos and another man crouched on the ground near Luke's body. *It's Gabe! I don't know how in hell he got past me, but now is my chance.*

He withdrew his revolver and pointed it at the lawbreaker. "Gabe Hopper! You are under arrest!"

SHERIFF

Jesus! What a mess.

Sheriff Wardwell maneuvered his horse through the line of pine and dormant maple trees separating the Whitehall road from Paree's five pastures. Each grazing pasture boundary was marked by a similar line of trees. As far as Wardwell knew, Paree's property stretched at least three miles along the river marking the border between Vermont and New York.

For a woman, Paree has done well for herself since Stan died. I always suspected she had something to do with her husband's death, but could never prove it. I know she's helped fugitives escape across her land before, but this time she may have gone too far if she attacked the posse. I need to question her, and fast!

Having emerged from the first copse of trees, Wardwell rode north, paralleling the woods along the river. As the gray light of an overcast dawn spread around him, he saw a portion of Paree's farmhouse through the second line of trees. No lights glowed from the windows. Behind the dwelling stood the stables and barn.

I wish to hell Duschanne had never showed up in our town! He's caused nothing but trouble, and now Luke is dead because of that damned, unjust Fugitive Slave Law! I'm sorry Gabe and Emma have lost their firstborn. They don't deserve this. But the law's the law, and Gabe is stubborn. I need to enforce order and bring Gabe in, though I hate doing it since Gabe and Emma are my friends.

Riding another twenty yards along the pasture, in the freshening light, Wardwell spotted two still, dark figures lying on the ground. Reining his horse a few feet away from the bodies, he dismounted.

God only knows what happened here! I only have Paul's word about Paree and her dogs. And where is she now?

Walking to the closer body, he recognized Carl Yates, Paul's father. Blood soaked the bullet-shredded clothing on the man's chest, and his eyes were glazed. Taking a deep breath, Wardwell grunted as he dropped to one knee next the body. Lifting Carl's arm, he placed two fingers on the man's wrist and waited for the feel of a pulse. Nothing.

Dammit! Sorry, Carl. I didn't mean for this to happen. May you rest in peace.

Pushing his hands against his knee, Wardwell lifted himself to a standing position and walked several yards to his right, where he peered down at Buster's form. Inspecting the body from the feet and along the torso, he saw a bullet wound had shattered the right shoulder. Then he looked closer at Buster's oddly shaped neck.

Oh, Jesus! The stench of fresh blood roiled his stomach. Lurching away from Buster's ripped-apart throat, still oozing, he bent with his hands on his knees, taking shallow breaths. *Christ! A dog did that? It looks like a mountain lion got him. Shit!*

Straightening, he wiped his mouth on his sleeve and stepped around Buster's body. Lying in the snow a few feet from Buster's head, he saw the body of a large brown and black dog, its head mostly gone. Wardwell gulped down rising bile and turned from the grizzly scene to catch his breath.

Knowing Jeb, he's gonna want revenge for his son's death, and I'm gonna have a vigilante mob on my hands. Damn!

Squinting into the distance along Paree's pastures, he hoped to see some sign of the woman on horseback. Early morning bird caws could be heard above the noise of the white-water.

Three dead men on my watch! And where are the rest of the fugitives? We've caught one, but two boys are on the run, and the woman Luke tried to save may or may not be dead. Our deal with that devil Duschanne was twenty percent of the bounty, but that won't amount to much with only one in custody. He swiped spittle from his chin. *Damn Edward Allen all to hell! What in God's name possessed him to come here, shooting off his gun and causing such havoc? Colonel Allen is gonna be furious when he hears of Edward's involvement! The boy is nigh due for a serious whippin'! And did Edward kill Luke, as Enos said? Or did Enos shoot Luke for some reason?* He let out a tortured sigh. *Could this get any damned worse?* He shook his head in frustration. *I've gotta find Paree before there is more trouble.*

Lifting his wide-brimmed hat, the sheriff ran a hand through his tousled gray hair, and repositioned the hat on his head.

Can I arrest her for protecting her property? She warned us to stay off her land at the meeting. But then again, she also threatened to shoot anyone who trespassed. Maybe the threat would hold up in court since there were witnesses. But we were lawfully chasing runaways, so that would be in our favor. And what if Jeb decides to go after her? I won't be able to protect her from a gang blood-thirsty for vengeance. What the hell was Paree thinking?

Staring at Paree's house, he considered going there first to find her.

I know the fugitives ran this way. Did they make it across the river, or is Paree helping them? Dammit! I can't go searching for them now. I've got to get Carl and Buster's bodies back to town. And I've got that fuckin' idiot, Edward to deal with, then Luke's body...Christ what a night! If it wasn't for money-grubbing Duschanne, none of this would have happened! I'll find Paree later.

The sound of a man's cry made him jump. *What the hell?* Whirling around, he saw Paul Yates on horseback galloping toward him.

"Pa!" Paul cried out as he reined to a halt and slid off the saddle, dropping next to his father's lifeless body. "Oh God! He's dead. He's dead! Whatta we gonna do without him?" The distraught son pulled his father's body into a sitting position and hugged him.

Wardwell walked to Paul's side and laid his hand on his shoulder. "I'm so sorry, Paul. Carl was a good man. I wish this hadn't happened." The sheriff shook his head, then reluctantly said, "Paul, I need your help getting Carl and Buster home."

Turning, he surveyed Paree's land and noticed two saddled horses grazing in the pasture to the east. Wardwell let out a high-pitched whistle to get the horses' attention. When they didn't respond, he whistled again. Both horses trotted toward him. He grabbed the reins of each animal and led them to where Paul cradled Carl's body.

Distraught and sobbing over his father, Paul ignored the sheriff's orders.

"Paul!" Wardwell commanded. "Get up. I need your help."

Paul lifted his head and stared at the sheriff. "Pa! Oh, Pa!" he wailed.

Wardwell squeezed Paul's shoulder. "We need to get the bodies on the horses, so we can get them home. Now get up and help me with your father. Which mount belongs to Carl?"

Paul slowly laid his father's body down, stood and pointed at the Appaloosa as it pawed the ground.

Wardwell nodded and passed the reins to Paul, then walked a few feet to his own horse and wrapped the reins of Buster's horse around the pommel. Returning to Paul, Wardwell lifted Carl's body to a sitting position. Bracing himself behind the body, he grabbed it by the waist and hoisted it upright.

"Hold the horse steady," Wardwell said. With Paul grasping the reins close to keep the horse still, Wardwell grunted as he hoisted Carl's body, head first, over the animal's back. Crossing to the opposite side, he centered Carl's body over the saddle, the arms dangling against the side. The horse snorted and back-stepped, adjusting to the new weight.

Then the sheriff unwrapped the reins of Buster's horse, and maneuvered it next to Buster's body. "Paul, come hold him while I get Buster up."

Appearing dazed as he followed the sheriff's orders, Paul lengthened the reins of Carl's horse and slowly walked toward Buster. He stared down at his boyhood friend, shivering at the sight of his mangled throat. With his other hand, Paul grasped the reins of Buster's horse to steady him for the sheriff.

As the sheriff tried to lift Buster's limp body, the horse whinnied and pulled away, causing Wardwell to stumble. The body slipped from his grasp and slumped to the ground. "Dammit, Paul! Hold it steady!" he growled.

Paul lifted his head, numbly staring at the sheriff. "Yeah, hold the horse," he mumbled, tightly holding the horse's head.

On his second try, Wardwell successfully balanced Buster's body, across the saddle. Stepping in front of Paul, he retrieved the reins. "Paul! Listen to me." He waited for the despondent man to raise his head and look at him. "Mount up and take your father home. Do you understand me?" Wardwell pointed toward the copse of trees along the Whitehall road. "I'll come see you and your mother later."

"Take Pa home," Paul parroted the sheriff's orders. He stiffly climbed to his saddle, then the sheriff passed him the reins of Carl's horse. Moving slowly, Paul directed both animals toward the road.

Wardwell watched as Paul maneuvered through the trees. *Paul's going to be the man of his house now, whether he likes it or not.*

ZENAS C.

Zenas C. rose from his kneeling position next to Luke's body. He approached George, who was pointing his revolver at Gabe. "George, please! Let Gabe take Luke home to Mary." Zenas held his palms open and forward, showing he was unarmed, as he stepped next to George's horse. "I promise we shall accompany Gabe to the sheriff's station, once Luke is home safely."

George looked down at the elder Ellis and shook his head. "Sorry, Zenas. I'm following Father's orders to take Gabe in now."

"This is an ungodly way to treat a friend and neighbor, George." Zenas pointed to Gabe, huddled next to Luke's body. "Look at him! He is no threat to anyone. Does thee doubt my word we shall bring him in?"

George looked over at Gabe's bent figure. "I must insist he come with me, Zenas. I trust you and your boys can manage Luke's body."

Zenas C. scowled at the lawman, then turned to his younger son. "Barnaby, bring your horse here and help me with Luke's body."

Barnaby walked to the three Ellis horses lightly tethered to tree branches. He unwound the reins of his horse and led it next to Gabe.

Zenas C. placed his hand gently on Gabe's shoulder. "Come, Friend. We must get Luke home to Emma."

Gabe made a guttural noise, then grasped Luke's cold hand to his heart. "Ahhh, Jesus! Why? Why has Thee abandoned us?"

Zenas grasped Gabe's arm and helped his friend to his feet.

Gabe staggered, caught his balance, then turned to George, who was still pointing the revolver at him. "May I help with Luke's body?"

George nodded. "Make it quick!"

Zenas C. and Gabe lifted Luke's shoulders as Barnaby and Zenas H. raised Luke's legs. Together, they carried the body to Barnaby's horse. Gabe positioned himself behind Luke's back and grasped the waist. With a grunt, he swung his son's lanky body up into the saddle. The Ellis brothers hoisted Luke's legs. Barnaby stepped to the opposite side of the horse and pulled Luke's torso until the body lay centered across the saddle.

Before Zenas could stop his son, Barnaby rushed to the berm and slid down the embankment. When he climbed back up, he was carrying Gabe's shotgun under his arm.

"Stop right there, Barnaby!" George pointed his revolver at the young man balancing on top of the bank.

Zenas frantically waved his arms in front of the lawman. "George! Don't shoot him!"

Barnaby halted. "It's Mister Hopper's shotgun, Sir. I wish to bring it home for him."

George shook his head. "Unload it first, then bring it to me."

Barnaby pulled the tamping rod from the gun sheath and cracked the gun to open both barrels. He slid the rod into the top of one muzzle, and pushed it through the barrel, causing the lead ball to drop to the ground. When he pushed the rod into the second barrel, it stopped partway down. He rammed the rod up and down several times, but could not clear the charge. "It's stuck, Sir." Barnaby said as he inspected the gun. "Looks like the barrel's cracked." He held the side of the barrel up, so George could see it more closely in the slowly growing light of early morning.

Frowning, George dismounted. Holstering his revolver, he took the shotgun from Barnaby and tried to dislodge the round. Unable to do so, George closed both barrels and re-sheathed the rod. He secured the firearm behind his saddle, then turned to the gathered men. "We'll need this as evidence while Gabe's in custody."

A low moan from a few yards away halted their conversation. George peered over at Edward lying in the snow. "Looks like I'll have to take Edward back to town on my horse." He turned to Enos. "Enos, come help me get him up."

Enos blurted, "Why in the hell should I help that good-for-nothing little shit? He can *die* here, as far as I'm concerned!"

George exploded. "Enos! Either you help me now, or I'll arrest you, too!"

Enos eyed George with disdain, shaking his head, but slowly walked to Edward's supine figure, as George positioned his horse next to the boy. Edward had lost a good deal of blood from his shattered leg, and was in a semi-conscious state.

George bent down to the injured youth. "Edward, we're going to get you onto my horse." George motioned for Enos to grasp Edward's opposite shoulder. "On three, lift. One…two…three." The men shifted Edward to a sitting position, then pulled him up to balance on his uninjured leg. Edward's head rolled forward onto his chest, and he grunted in pain. George wrapped his arm around the boy's chest to hold his weight.

"We need to get him seated in the saddle," George said to Enos. "Go on the other side. I'll lift him up, then you pull his leg over."

Enos did as instructed. After George hoisted Edward's torso head first over the left side of the saddle, Enos grabbed the boy's right arm and damaged leg and pulled Edward so he sat facing forward. Edward howled with pain at the force of the movement, then slumped forward onto the horse's neck.

"Edward!" George yelled. He slapped the boy's left thigh hard. Edward lifted his head and turned toward George. "Edward! Sit up!" He grabbed the back of Edward's shirt and pulled him upright in the saddle. George pressed both of the boy's hands onto the saddle horn. Reaching into his saddlebag, he extracted a short length of rope and wound it around Edward's wrists, securing them to the pommel. Then he brought the reins forward so he could lead the animal.

With Edward and Luke both secured on horseback, George turned to Gabe, who stood next to Zenas Senior. "Gabe, I'm going to trust you to come with me, so I'm not going to tie your hands. Will you agree not to run?"

Gabe stared at the young lawman for a long minute, then glumly nodded his head.

George pointed through the trees toward the bridge. "Lead the way, Gabe."

Gabe reached out and grasped Zenas C.'s hand. "Please take care of Emma and Mary. I hope I shall be home soon."

Zenas C. nodded. "I will, Friend. May the Good Lord shine His light upon thy family." He watched his longtime friend and neighbor, head bowed, under arrest, shuffle through the trees.

Leading his horse with Edward slouched in the saddle, George followed Gabe toward the bridge.

Zenas C. untethered the two idle Ellis horses and handed the reins to his sons. "We shall walk together with Luke's body."

A touch on his left arm caused Zenas to turn and see Enos standing next to him. "I would like to accompany you to take Luke home, Sir."

The Ellis patriarch narrowed his eyes, looking at the traitor. "I do not think it wise, Enos. Thee has betrayed our trust and should repent thy sins!"

Enos dropped his gaze. "I am so sorry, Sir. Truly I am." His voice was hoarse with emotion. Disheartened, he stepped a few feet away and untethered his horse, Beldon, then rode away.

GABE

Gabe walked slowly through the trees and up the slight incline leading to the main road. Deputy George followed, leading Edward balanced on his saddle. When they reached the entrance to the bridge, Gabe saw Duschanne holding Sarah captive across his saddle. Rushing toward Duschanne's horse, he gasped, "Sarah! Is thee injured? Release her!"

George grabbed Gabe's arm to keep him from getting any closer to the captured girl.

Duschanne laughed. "*Non, non, Monsieur.* She is my mine now."

Sarah lifted her head from her slouched, bound position across Duschanne's saddle. "Mister Hopper, help me!" she cried in a hoarse voice. "Where's my baby? Where's Jonah? Is he alive? I want my baby!"

Duschanne smacked the top of Sarah's head, bouncing her face against the horse's shoulder. "Quiet, *ma Chérie!*" he admonished.

Squirming under Duschanne's restraint, Sarah turned her head toward Gabe, blood dripping from her nose. "Where's my Mama and Samuel? Please, Mister Hopper, you must find them!" she pleaded.

Duschanne hit her again and pressed her head down.

Disgusted at the Southerner's action, Gabe lashed out. "Thee is a soulless evil man. Thee shall pay for thy crimes for all eternity! Leave this girl her freedom if thee wishes to escape hellfire and damnation!"

Duschanne cackled at Gabe's attack. "Ah, my good man. 'Tis you who are breaking ze law and should be ashamed! You are delusional and do not speak for ze Good Lord. I must earn a living, *non*? And I will not burn in hell for doing so."

Ignoring the interloper's reply, Gabe looked into Sarah's distraught face. "Sarah, I am so sorry. I do not know the fate of thy family." The lines of distress deepened on his face. "We obeyed God's law, and He has *forsaken* His faithful children! I have failed thee, and I can only ask for thy forgiveness."

Sarah sobbed on Duschanne's horse. "Jonah! Ah, Jesus, please keep my baby safe."

Sheriff Wardwell led the horse carrying Buster's body and reached the gathering of men at the bridge. Duschanne had the slave girl in custody as she wailed for her son, Jonah. Duschanne and Gabe were engaged in a heated argument, with George restraining Gabe by the arm. *Well, at least we have Gabe in custody. Now Duschanne won't think we are totally inept.*

Not having heard the whole conversation, he winced as Duschanne hit the captive girl's head and pressed her against the horse's neck.

I need to take control before anyone else gets killed!

"George, take Buster's horse!" Wardwell commanded. He dismounted and stepped between the agitated men, in an attempt to defuse their quarrel.

Gabe saw the sheriff arrive at the bridge leading a horse with a body slung over the saddle. Staring, Gabe suddenly recognized the slack features of the corpse. *Oh, no! 'Tis Buster! Not another life lost. How can a loving God allow such evil to exist in this land?* He felt wrath rising within him.

Zenas C. led his horse by the reins toward the road. Barnaby followed, leading his horse, which carried Luke's body. Zenas H. and his horse brought up the rear.

Before the Ellis men reached the bridge, Zenas C. glanced past the embankment to the shattered wagon lying on its side in the rushing stream. *It could have been us transporting fugitives, and my boys may have been killed. This is an evil law, and I shall take every action to abolish it!*

Zenas C. glared at the men positioned near the bridge. Along the southern edge of the road, he saw a disgruntled Duschanne holding Sarah firmly in place on his saddle. Zenas shook his head. *May the Good Lord save her from his abuse.*

Seeing Sheriff Wardwell standing between Gabe and Duschanne's horse, Zenas' anger suddenly overcame him. "Jeremiah, thee should be ashamed!" He swung his arm toward Luke's body. "This is *thy* fault! Thee shall have to answer to the Lord for thy sins!"

Caught off guard by the vitriol of the respected town elder, Wardwell blanched, but kept silent.

Gabe clutched his hands to his chest and dropped to his knees. "Oh, Lord! 'Tis a great injustice thee has wrought upon Thy devoted servants." He angrily pumped his fist into the air. "And now Thee has taken Luke, even as he sought to do Thy will on this earth! What sins have I committed to give Thee cause to inflict such unjust punishment upon my family?"

The gathered men watched in silence as the Ellis men walked slowly, leading their horses east along the road toward town. Gabe grimaced at the sight of his son's lifeless body slouched over the saddle. *I shall love thee and seek justice for thy slaying, Luke, until my dying day.* His deep-throated cry rose in the air.

Then Gabe felt a pressure on his shoulder and looked up to see the sheriff at his side. "I have to take you into custody, Gabe. I'm sorry for this." Both of Gabe's hands were pulled behind his back, and he felt the tight clamp of the iron handcuffs thudding into place.

With the sheriff's assistance, Gabe rose to his feet. He took a deep breath, stood tall, and stared at Wardwell. "I shall abide by thy laws." Gathering his wits in the early morning light, Gabe turned to peer across the bridge toward New York. "Jeremiah, I wish to get my horses home. Emma will need them at the farm. Would one of thy men go search?"

"If you will allow me, Sir, I'll round up your horses," Enos said, having arrived at the bridge.

Gabe glared at the young man who had worked on his farm for years, yet had betrayed his family, with disastrous results.

"It's the least I can do for you and Luke, Sir." Enos said. "I'll take the horses back to the farm."

Gabe nodded. "Very well, Enos. If thee insists. Zachary is hobbled and shall need attention."

"I'll see to it, Sir."

Gabe watched as Enos rode across the bridge to New York and disappeared into the trees along the west bank in search of his missing horses. *I should forgive his betrayal, just as Jesus forgave Judas. I hope he can bring the horses home, but I cannot yet forgive him his trespasses against us.*

Sheriff Wardwell grasped Gabe's arm and directed him toward the posse waiting on horseback along the edge of the road. "Cyrus, dismount and let Gabe ride to town," the sheriff commanded.

Cyrus shook his head back and forth. "Nah, nah. My leg hurts," he whined. "I can't walk. Bitch kicked me!" He pointed to Sarah held across the neck of Duschanne's horse.

Gabe stared at the whimpering, dim-witted man crouched in his saddle. Then Gabe noticed the dried blood, misshapen nose and bruised, swollen-shut eye of the north-side farmer, sitting on his horse next to Cyrus. *Looks like Sarah gave Elmer quite a fight.* A small smile crossed Gabe's face. *Good for her! I hope she shan't be horribly mistreated by her captors.*

The sheriff addressed the posse. "Cyrus, I swear to God, you are the most worthless son-of-a-bitch I have ever met!" He turned to the bruised farmer. "Elmer, get down and give Gabe your horse!"

"Ahhh, Sheriff," the farmer grumbled, but dismounted as instructed. Elmer led his horse a few steps to where Gabe waited next to Wardwell. Elmer held the horse's bridle as Wardwell helped Gabe mount with a leg up. Gabe nodded glumly at the sheriff as he settled into the saddle, hands shackled behind his back.

Sheriff Wardwell looked around at the assembled men and held up a hand. "Listen up! We need to get everyone back to town, and Edward to

Doc Sweeney." He motioned toward the injured boy atop George's mount. "I'll lead the way and I want everyone to follow. Do you understand?"

Duschanne brought his horse from the edge of the road to block the sheriff's path. "Wardwell!" he exclaimed. "What of ze fugitives? We must find zem. *Merde!* I do not care about your injured men or dead bodies. I must track ze runaways. I am losing money as we delay ze search. *Incompétent!*"

Wardwell stepped to the Southerner's horse. "Duschanne, right now I do not give a damn about the fugitives or your money! These are good and decent men, and they need to be returned to their families." He pointed at Sarah, on Duschanne's horse. "You have your captive. That should do for now."

Duschanne glowered down at the senior lawman. "You and your *stupide* son have broken our *arrangemon', Monsieur,*" he raged. "Zhere will be no bounty for you!"

Their exchange made Gabe furious. *So Jeremiah made a deal with the devil to receive part of the bounty? He betrayed our trust, and it cost Luke his life!*

Wardwell responded, "I don't care about the bounty, Duschanne. I'm in charge here, and you will do as *I* say. Now, follow me back to town and take the girl to my office. I will meet you there once we get Edward to the doctor's." He glared at the steely kidnapper. "*Comprenez vous, Monsieur?*" he said sarcastically. "I don't want any more trouble out of you!"

Wardwell turned his back and went to George, who was holding the reins of their horses. "Let's go," he ordered. The sheriff mounted, then, leading Gabe's horse, proceeded east toward town.

Gabe dug his heels into the stirrups and balanced in the saddle as the horse lurched forward. George motioned for Duschanne to go ahead of him. Duschanne glared at George, but moved his horse into the road behind Gabe. Then George got in line behind Duschanne, walking his horse with Edward slumped over the saddle. At the rear, Elmer ambled, half-blinded, holding the bridle of Cyrus' horse.

Gabe's mind raced as the party made their slow trek toward town. *How will Emma manage the farm? Now she has no one to help with chores. She is a strong woman and a Godsend, but she cannot do it alone. Ahhh, why has God sent His vengeful wrath upon us? 'Tis His laws we were serving, not the unjust laws of man! Emma should not have to suffer so mightily for my mistakes!*

Gabe turned in his saddle to look back at the muddy, rutted road that led to New York. Images flashed through his mind of the many journeys he and Luke had undertaken over the past twenty years. Although they had taken extra precautions to keep their guests concealed, many had ridden openly with other conductors, who had successfully transported fugitives to the Whitehall canal. There had been no violent posses pitting neighbor against neighbor and no one had lost their life.

This Fugitive Slave Law is an abomination of God's will! We must find a way to abolish it. And now here I am under arrest—Luke and others dead, and the Prescott family torn asunder. I vowed to protect them and deliver them safely, and I have failed miserably!

His borrowed horse bobbed its head and grunted at being led by the reins. Gabe adjusted his position to stay upright in the saddle.

Losing Luke is too great a sacrifice to help those seeking freedom, and I shan't ever take that risk again. If the Lord will not protect my family, then I must bear the brunt of protecting them from all evil that roams this land. I shall not permit anyone to betray me or my family ever again!

As Gabe squinted through the morning mist, he spotted Enos crossing the slippery bridge, with both of Gabe's draft horses in tow.

ZENAS C.

Zenas heard Gabe's pain-filled cry echo behind him as he and his sons led their horses away from the bridge. *May the Lord watch over him and Emma.*

After walking two miles toward town, with rays of sun breaking the intermittent clouds, the men reached the ridge that overlooked the riverbank and led past the slate mill. Zenas H. turned to his brother. "Barnaby, go slow, and I'll hold Luke in place." Zenas C. led his horse down the incline, followed by Barnaby and his steed's burden. Zenas H. held Luke's form on Barnaby's saddle with one hand as he led his horse with the other. At the bottom of the hill, the three men walked next to one another as the cortege passed the slate mill, eerily still on this Sunday morning. The pounding of the rushing waterfall drowned out any conversation. At the bridge which led north to town, the solemn procession turned right and slowly ascended the steep hill leading to the flat farmlands stretching along Fairhaven's south side.

At the top of the hill, the men paused to catch their breath. Zenas C. glanced up at the morning, overcast sky. *What time is it? Seems like it's already been a long, horrible day, and it's only going to get worse.* The men continued another mile, then Zenas C. halted in front of their farmhouse.

"Barnaby, I want thee to go change into dry clothes, then come meet us at Gabe's house. Make it quick!"

"Yes, Father," Barnaby answered as he passed the reins of his horse to his brother, then sprinted into the house.

Zenas and his elder son continued leading the horses past Luke's house. Zenas C. could see the glow of a lantern shining from within. They led the horses beyond Gabe's front porch and turned right into the cart path between the Hopper house and stables. *I hope Emma does not hear our approach. I must prepare her before she sees Luke.*

They tethered their mounts to the railing along the pathway.

Lord! Give me the courage to deliver this dreadful news to my dear friend on this most grievous day. I ask Thee to shine Thy loving grace upon Emma and her family.

He turned to his son. "Zenas, give me your neckerchief." The son complied, and Zenas C. gently wrapped the cloth around Luke's shattered throat to cover the worst of the damage.

"Please stay here whilst I speak with Friend Emma."

In the chilly morning air, Zenas walked up the two wooden steps and knocked reluctantly on Emma's back door.

PAREE

Paree stood next to the closed barn door where she had just left Hilde protecting her charges. Intermittent shouts reached her from the direction of the bridge, over a half-mile away. Through the early morning mist, she squinted toward the line of trees separating her first two pastures. *Where's the sheriff and the posse? They must be close.* Not seeing any riders charging toward her, she mounted, and Gunther and Fritz followed her horse's left flank. To conceal her movements, she quickly rode along the northern tree line forming the boundary of her third pasture.

Paul has probably told the sheriff about his father by now. It won't be long before Wardwell comes looking for me.

Reaching her stables, she dismounted and threw the reins over the barn rail, then commanded her dogs to stay. Once inside, she led a second horse from his stall and positioned him close to the saddle rack. Moving quickly in the dim light, she located the blanket, saddle and bridle. Within a few minutes she had the horse outfitted to ride. Paree led the horse from the stables and gently closed the door behind her. As she mounted her horse, she heard a high-pitched whistle ripple through the trees. She tensed in her saddle. A second whistle followed.

Is that a signal for the posse to come after me? I've got to get those boys across the river or we'll all be captured.

Commanding her dogs to heel, she rode north away from her farm, maintaining her concealment.

A yell filtered through the trees. "*Paul! Get up. I need your help.*"

That sounds like the sheriff. I hope he stays busy for a while longer.

Crossing into her third pasture, she led the riderless horse on a short trek to the west toward the river, where she doubled back and approached the hay barn from the opposite direction of the fallen men. As she reached her barn, she could hear Hilde's low growl coming from within. Quickly dismounting, she stood in front of the door and called to her lead dog in a quiet voice, "Hilde. *Bleibe.* Stay." She didn't want the dog to start barking when she entered. When the growling subsided, she slid the door open and led both horses into the center of the barn, with the dogs following. "Hilde. *Kommen.*" She motioned for the dog to join the rest of the pack.

Stepping next to the hay mow, Paree whispered to the fugitives. "Samuel, come out here."

She watched as Jonah crawled out of the haystack with Samuel close behind. Samuel brushed off pieces of hay stuck to his nephew's coat and hair, then wiped his own clothing as best he could.

"Ve must hurry. The sheriff is close!"

"Ma'am? What has happened to my mother and sister?" Samuel implored. "I don't want to leave without them. Please!"

Exasperated, Paree replied, "I don't have time to look for them now. Ve need to get you across the border before the posse gets here. I vill do my best to find them later, I promise. Now mount up!" She pointed to her second horse.

Jonah whimpered as Samuel stepped away from the boy and mounted the horse. Paree grasped Jonah by the waist and lifted him up to Samuel, who slid back in the saddle to settle the squirming boy in front of his lap. Looking in both directions as she peered out the barn door, Paree saw no sign of riders. Leading both horses from the barn she commanded her three dogs to follow. Then she slid the barn door shut and swung up into her saddle.

Turning to Samuel, she said, "Ve vill ride north along the stream to put some distance between us and the lawmen. You must be silent in case ve are being tracked."

Samuel nodded and followed her lead, the dogs at her horse's flanks. They made their way downstream along a narrow path through trees. The stream took several twists and turns, and suddenly dropped over a steep rock waterfall. The ground dipped beneath the horses, then gradually rose over a rocky section to more level ground.

After riding for about ten minutes, Paree held her fist in the air to indicate a stop. The stream narrowed and took a sharp bend to the left, gouging the opposite bank. Paree turned in her saddle to Samuel. "This is the narrowest part so ve need to cross here."

The fast-moving water rushed and sloshed around the bend. "Ma'am. We can't swim," he called quietly.

Paree saw the frightened look on Samuel's face. "Loosen the reins and give the horse his head. He vill follow me. Just hold onto Jonah, because I don't vant to have to rescue you."

Samuel nodded, letting the reins go slack. Paree stepped her horse from the muddy bank into the rushing current. Samuel watched as her mount fought against the flow to keep its footing. The water reached the bottom of the horse's belly before the animal lunged up the opposite bank. Paree's three dogs jumped into the river and paddled furiously, emerging onto the bank several yards downstream from where Paree waited. Gunther and Fritz shook the water from their coats and returned to Paree's side. Hilde shook her coat, growled, and suddenly ran through the trees and around the bend in the river. Paree watched the dog go, cursing under her breath.

"Easy, now," Paree said a moment later to Samuel, then let out a low cluck to urge her second horse to ford the stream. Carrying both riders, the horse stepped his front legs into the river and slid his back legs down the embankment. Jonah let out a small cry as the horse jostled to maintain his balance against the current.

Samuel wrapped Jonah's hands on the pommel, grasping the boy's arm with the thumb and last two fingers of his right hand. He held the loose reins with his left. As the horse struggled with its footing in the rocky streambed, the water rose steadily to the bottom of Samuel's feet.

Jonah squirmed in the saddle as Samuel held the boy tighter to keep him from sliding into the rushing current. "It's okay, Jonah. Just hold on," he whispered to his nephew.

Paree held out her hands to guide her horse. "C'mon Boy. You can do it. C'mon…" The horse, guided by Paree's voice, sloshed through the deepest part of the stream and scrambled his way up the opposite embankment. Paree grabbed the horse's bridle to steady him.

"Good Boy!" she whispered in the horse's ear. "You can take his head, now, Samuel," she pointed at the slack reins. Moving a few yards into the concealment of the trees, she turned and beckoned the boys following her. "I vant you to stay here. I need to find Hilde."

Paree rode her horse around the downstream bend. Several trees had slipped from the muddy embankment and fallen partially across the widening riverway. Then Paree spotted Hilde in her attack stance along the edge of the bank, just above the first fallen tree. Peering through the deep shadows, she noticed a large, dark lump entwined in the partially submerged branches. Hilde crouched growling, as the other two dogs took up a position on either side of the lead dog. "Hilde! *Bleibe*," she hissed at her dog. The dog turned from the river and trotted to Paree's side, followed by her two offspring.

Dismounting, Paree tossed the reins over a tree branch. Grabbing a large stick for balance, she sidestepped down the few feet of slippery, snow-covered embankment. *Vhat could this be?* Grasping the fallen tree trunk, she stretched the stick as far as she could reach. When she poked the dark form, it jostled slightly against the tree branch. She watched as brown fabric, caught in a whirl of rushing water, flopped over the form.

"Oh, mein Gott!" she gasped. Paree could just make out the bottom end of a torso, legs dangling into the stream. *Is that one of the fugitives?* Hearing the second horse snuffle behind her, she looked upslope to see Samuel and Jonah staring down at her.

"What is it?" Samuel asked.

Paree shook her head. "Samuel, I need you to dismount and tether your horse in the trees behind you. Leave Jonah in the saddle, then come here and stay quiet."

Samuel hesitated, staring at the dark form tangled in the tree branches. He whispered to his nephew. "Jonah, I'll be right here, don't worry. You'll be good, right?" He squeezed the boy's arm. Jonah turned in the saddle, his eyes wide looking up at Samuel, and nodded. Samuel dismounted and secured his horse several yards back from the embankment.

Grasping the tree trunk, Samuel slid down the embankment to Paree. "What is it, Ma'am?"

"I don't know exactly. I need your help," she said. "I'm going to try to dislodge it so you can help me get it out of the stream." She removed her overcloak and threw it up onto the bank.

Paree slid her feet into the stream using the tree trunk for balance. *Mein Gott! Das wasser ist kalt!* Shivering, she stepped over several submerged branches as the frigid water swirled around her waist. Reaching out, she grabbed the back of the body and yanked. The form swayed, but held fast to the tree branches. Paree took a step closer, holding onto the dead trunk with her left arm. The current pushed at her legs and splashed her face. She reached beneath the body and freed the arm tangled in a branch, hefting it over her shoulder. As she freed the weight, the body started to float around the tree branches. Paree grabbed the arm, holding the swinging form, and back-stepped until she had her balance and better footing amongst the submerged rocks. Turning, she dragged the body several steps to the river's edge. Breathing hard, she lay the water-logged form before Samuel.

"Mama! Mama!" Samuel gasped as he looked down upon the woman's sodden body. "Oh, God! She's dead!" he wailed.

Paree gripped Samuel's arm. "Samuel! You must be quiet. Ve vill be found," she hissed. "Quickly, let's get her up the bank."

Once the lifeless form had been lifted from the river, Samuel hugged the soaked body to his chest and sobbed. He gently pushed the wet, gray curls back from her sunken face. "I'm so sorry, Mama. I should have saved you!" He dropped his head as his tears fell upon his mother's frozen face. "You were so strong to lead us this far! I'll try to make you proud and reach freedom. I can only pray you and the Lord will guide our journey."

Paree laid a hand on Samuel's shoulder. "I know you're upset, Samuel, and I'm so sorry. But ve must keep moving."

Samuel stared up at the Prussian woman. "But we can't leave her here. The animals will rip her up!"

Paree nodded, then said gently, "After I deliver you and Jonah to Titus Battis' house, I vill come right back here and take her body to my home, I promise you." Paree looked around and spotted a clump of bushes a few yards uphill from the bank. "Here, help me." She lifted Samuel to his feet. "Let's hide her over there." She pointed to the bushes. Paree lifted Elsie's torso, and Samuel grasped her legs. They laid her under the bushes, then Paree packed loose wet leaves, pine needles and snow around the body, so it couldn't be seen from the narrow trail.

Sobbing, Samuel knelt next to his mother's body, bowed his head, and said a silent prayer.

Paree laid a hand on the distraught boy's back. "Ve must go. I am chilled to the bone and cannot stay out here much longer." She retrieved her cloak from the bank and threw it over her shoulders. "I vill return for your mother, I promise you, Samuel. She vill get a decent Christian burial. Vhat is her name?"

Samuel looked up at the tall, broad-shouldered woman and paused. "Elsie Watkins Prescott…Swaley. But you can leave off the Swaley, as that was Massa's name. She's free with the Lord now, and no longer anyone's property." He turned to Elsie's covered body, "I love you, Mama," Samuel said quietly as he stood and backed away, wiping tears. He walked a few yards through the trees, then untied and remounted his horse.

Jonah turned to look back at Samuel. "What was dat?" the child asked.

Samuel took a deep breath and hugged his nephew. "Nothing. We gotta go."

Paree untethered her horse, mounted, called softly for her dogs, then rode west on a narrow, snow-covered path leading away from the stream. They trotted at a quick pace, zig-zagging through the dense forest. Paree had brought fugitives along this route before, so she kept a lookout for the notches she had cut into the trees, to ensure she was on the right course.

Hearing grunts behind her, Paree turned to see Samuel ducking low-hanging branches, and grasping Jonah, to avoid being knocked off their horse. She slowed her pace to allow the pair to reach her.

After wending their way through the dense woods for over thirty minutes, the sound of a ship's horn brought Paree to a halt. Samuel reined his horse behind her dogs. Through the morning overcast, Paree saw the forest had become sparser. Intermittent shouts, and the sounds of cargo being loaded at the canal, wafted through the trees. The clomping of hooves and creaking of carts on the thoroughfare running along the east side of the canal echoed about them.

Paree motioned for Samuel to come beside her. "Ve will go on foot from here."

Samuel dismounted, leaving Jonah in the saddle, and followed Paree's lead. Interspersed through the trees Samuel could see the roofs of houses and barns that lined the road. He tensed and gripped the reins more tightly as they grew closer to the raucous activity along the canal.

Paree pointed to the back of a barn several yards farther. Beyond the barn, a house stood facing the street. "Samuel, that's Titus' barn. Let's go quickly."

Leading her horse through the trees and across a narrow cart path to the back of the barn, she wrapped her horse's reins over a side railing. Unlike most barns, Titus' had sliding doors on both ends, allowing easier through-transport of the hay wagon. Paree slid open one of the double doors and motioned for Samuel and her dogs to follow her.

Samuel led his horse into the middle of the barn and peered around in the near-darkness.

Paree slid the door shut behind them and turned to Samuel. "Get Jonah down and stay here. You need to be very quiet. I vill be back soon."

Samuel nodded. "Yes, Ma'am." He lifted his arms to his young nephew and pulled the boy off the saddle. The two stood facing Paree and her panting dogs.

"I vill leave the dogs with you. Do not be afraid of them." She turned to her pack. "Hilde, Gunther, Fritz," she commanded. They stared up at her. She pointed to the boys, then touched the tips of her fingers together, forming a circle. She raised her hands up and down deliberately three times. "*Schützen*. Protect." The three dogs took positions in a half-circle, and sat with their backs to Samuel and Jonah. Each dog raised a right paw in acknowledgment of their job. As Paree patted each dog on the head and mumbled "*Guter,*" the paw was lowered.

Paree exited the barn through a side door. Shivering, she walked quickly across the backyard and knocked lightly on the kitchen door.

A stooped, middle-aged black woman, wearing a stained apron, her hair wound in a turban, answered the door. A surprised look crossed the woman's round face. "Miss Paree! Lordy! You looks like somethin' the cat done dragged in. Won'cha come in?"

Paree removed her tattered felt hat and cloak, nodding to the woman. "Morning, Miss Millie. Sorry to bother you on Sunday, but I have brought a package for your husband, Titus."

Millie leaned out the door, peering around. "Did ya now? I *am* surprised to see ya on the Sabbath, but it's fine. How many of 'em?"

Paree followed Millie's glance. "Two boys: one's older, one's a child. They are in the barn with my dogs. Told them to be quiet."

Millie stepped into the kitchen and motioned for Paree to follow her. "Well, come in and let me get'cha some tea ta warm your bones. Your clothes be wet through!" Millie moved to the kitchen stove where a pot of tea was brewing.

Entering the cluttered kitchen, the smell of fresh bread baking made Paree's stomach lurch uncomfortably. Visions of Elsie's body floated in her mind. A lantern on the table and assorted candles lit the room. "Thanks, Miss Millie. I vould love some tea, but I cannot stay long. There is an urgent matter I must attend to." Paree sat at the table and pulled Samuel's letter from her cloak. "Here's the travel letter from Mister Hopper for Titus."

Millie brought the steaming teacups to the table and sat next to Paree. She glanced at Titus' name on the front of the envelope. "Welp, you knows Titus be gone already. 'Dat ship sails at first light. But he'll be back t'night." Millie blew on her tea. "You'se folks usually get the packages here much earlier. Pretty late today." Millie gave Paree a questioning look. "And where's Mistah Hoppah—why ain't he here hisself?"

Paree shook her head. "Ve had some big trouble with the slave hunters and—"

Millie inhaled and held her hand to her mouth. "Oh, no! Dear Lord! I was a'feared 'dat time was a'comin, with that infernal law an' all!" She leaned over the table. "What has happened?"

Looking down at the gouged wooden table, Paree said, "Can't say I know for sure. Samuel, the older boy, said the posse was chasing them, and the vagon fell off the bridge. He escaped into the voods with the younger boy, Jonah. I found them hiding in my barn." Paree's hands trembled as she clutched her hot tea.

Millie's eyes narrowed as she listened to Paree's account.

"I killed two of the slave hunters after I varned them to get off my property." Paree shook her head. "One of the bastards shot my lead dog, Bruno, and it made me furious!"

Millie reached across the table to touch Paree's arm. "Ahhhh, Miss Paree! I's so sorry. Do ya think the sheriff gonna be comin' after ya, 'cause of this?"

Paree shrugged and looked into the kind woman's shiny, worn face. "Yep, most likely. I vill have to defend myself." Paree looked toward the barn. "Samuel said his mother and sister are missing and vanted me to go find them. But vith the posse on my land, I vanted to get the boys safely across the border first." Paree sighed and sipped her tea. "Unfortunately, ve found his mother's body drowned, tangled in some branches downstream." Paree bowed her head.

Millie gasped. "Oh, my! That's terrible. 'Dose boys must be devastated." She clasped her hands together and bowed her head in prayer. "May the good Lord take the dear sister's soul to freedom in His Kingdom."

Paree waited for Millie's prayer. "Samuel was pretty upset, but I don't think he told Jonah—ve needed to keep the younger boy quiet. I told Samuel I vould make sure his mama got a decent Christian burial. That is vhy I have to go. I need to get her body before the coyotes find her."

"Oh, yes. O'course. But what of his sister? Did she escape?" Millie asked.

Paree shrugged her shoulders. "Can't say. I think she might have been captured. I told Samuel I vould find out and try to get vord to him." She sighed. "Terrible thing vith these cutthroat slave hunters roaming the land."

Millie's face clouded. "Yes, 'm. Sho' is. And what of the Hoppahs? Mistah Hoppah and Luke always been good to our folk helpin' 'em get to the canal. What's happened to 'dem?"

Paree shook her head. "I don't know that either, Millie. I'm sorry. It was dark—lots of shouting and gunfire. I didn't see everything—I was protecting my land."

"Dear Jesus! What a terrible night this has been." Millie clasped her hands in anguished prayer.

Paree gave Millie a stern look. "Millie, listen to me! You and Titus must be very careful. These slave hunters could be at the dock looking for the boys. They have lost two of their own, and maybe more, and are gonna be out for blood and vengeance, I'm sure of it." Paree grasped the woman's hand. "Just because you're free blacks, it don't make you any safer than us vhite folks from these killers! That terrible law doesn't give you any chance to defend yourself, if you're taken. Please be careful."

Millie's eyes went wide. "This unjust law is a curse on God's scriptures, and puts all of us in great danger! I's be sure to warn Titus when he gets back. We'll keep 'dem boys well-hidden."

Paree looked toward the barn. "They vill need food and a change of clothes. They lost everything vhen the vagon fell into the stream." She paused for a moment. "Samuel's a smart boy—speaks good English. I think he might be educated."

Millie lifted an eyebrow. "Hmmm…Massa's son, maybe?"

Paree shrugged. "Could be. Looks like he might have mixed blood. I think he vas the one responsible for guiding his family this far. I hope Titus can get him and Jonah to safety. They deserve it after all those boys been through."

As Paree rose from her seat, Millie stood and grasped the woman's hands. "We'll take good care of 'em, Miss Paree, rest assured. Thanks for helping our folks in their time of need. You'se a good woman. May the Lord shine His light down upon ya, and guide ya safely on the journey home."

"Thank you, Miss Millie. I think all God's children should live free." Paree grasped her cloak and hat.

"Amen to that!" Millie said as she guided Paree out the kitchen door. "Tell the boys I's be out shortly with some porridge and bread. May God bless ya."

The kitchen door closed quietly behind Paree. She made her way back to the barn and entered through the side door near where her horse was hitched. Samuel was sitting on the floor with his legs crossed. Jonah perched on his lap with Samuel's arms wrapped around him. The dogs sat in a semicircle, their backs to the boys, protecting their charges, watching attentively as their master approached. Paree motioned for the dogs to come to her and stay.

Then she dropped to one knee in front of the frightened boys. "Samuel, Mister Titus has already left on the steamship, but he vill return later tonight. His wife, Miss Millie, vill bring you food and clothing very soon. You vill stay here tonight, but you must be quiet and stay out of sight. Titus vill get you to the ship before first light. Do you understand?"

Samuel, his eyes downcast as he listened, looked up at Paree, tears welling in his eyes. "Jonah and I thank you, Ma'am." He ruffled his nephew's hair. "I don't even know your name, and you've been so good to us!"

Paree grasped a hand of each boy. "I am Paree Guildersleeve," she said looking deep into Samuel's dark eyes. "I am from Prussia, and have found freedom in this land. And I believe all God's children should be free to live their lives as they so choose." She rose to her feet and swung an arm in the air toward the east. "And I hate slave hunters. They are an evil curse on this land and should all be dead!" *Verrotte in der hölle!*

After wiping his own tears, Samuel lifted Jonah to his feet. "And you'll take care of our business?" He wrapped an arm over Jonah's shoulder, who was staring at the panting dogs.

Paree nodded. "I promise you. I vill talk to Miss Emma and ve vill see to it." Horrific memories rose in her mind of her own mother's body left behind in their burned family farmhouse. "I am so sorry for you, Samuel, but you are a strong boy. I believe you and Jonah vill gain your freedom!"

"I thank you, Miss Paree. You are a good woman and remind me of Mama. And I beg you to try to find my sister, Sarah! I hope you could get word to me through Mister Titus so I know what's happened to her," he implored.

Paree nodded. "I vill do my best, Samuel." Walking to the back of the barn she slid one door open. She grabbed the reins of her spare horse and led him out to the yard. "Hilde, Gunther, Fritz. *Kommen!*" she commanded the dogs, who followed her.

"I vish you Godspeed." She slid the door closed on the two frightened black boys clutching each other in the center of the barn.

Paree untethered her horse from the barn rail, mounted, and commanded her dogs to heel. Leading her second horse, she rode east back along the path into the woods to gather Elsie's remains.

EMMA

Emma lay in bed, tossing fitfully, trying to put her mind to rest after Gabe and Luke had left with the Prescotts hidden in the wagon. She felt as if she had just dozed off when the mantel clock chimed six. Realizing she would get no more sleep, she slowly lifted herself out of bed. Still fully clothed from the previous evening, she threw a shawl over her woolen dress and pulled a bonnet over her mussed hair. In the main room, she stocked the wood stove. Moving into the kitchen, she added more wood to the burner compartment of the cook stove. Adding loose tea to a metal round ball strainer, she dropped it into a large cup, looping the metal chain over the handle. After the water in the kettle had heated sufficiently, she poured it into her teacup and carried the steaming brew to the table.

Emma stared out the window toward the barn as she waited for the tea to steep. Heavy clouds seemed to hang just over the treetops, but the snow flurries had stopped. Several inches of newly fallen snow covered the ground. As she took in the beauty of the soft white blanket that had engulfed the farm, Emma's troubled thoughts turned to the travelers.

'Tis been hours since their departure. The wagon should have reached the canal by now. But with this early snow, their going will be rough. I pray the good Lord has guided their journey, and the Prescotts are safely aboard ship. I wish them Godspeed on their quest for the Promised Land. If all goes well, Father and Luke should be home in time for church services.

Emma sipped her tea and thought about Miss Elsie's courage in leading her family on such a perilous journey to gain their freedom. It didn't seem fair a person's birth should determine whether they lived in freedom or in bondage. *All of God's children, no matter their birthright, should be free to live their lives dedicated to His glory. May the Lord bless and keep them in His holy grace.*

She sighed and rose from the table. "I must get to the chores," she mumbled to herself. Opening the door to the anteroom, she shivered in the morning chill of the unheated room. After sliding on her boots, Emma donned a heavy cloak and grabbed her egg basket. She grunted as she forced the thick outer door open, and closed it behind her with a thump. Wrapping herself in the cloak, she made her way past the hay barn to the chicken coop. As she approached the coop, she heard the hens making a squawking ruckus and she rushed to the door. *'Tis odd. What has them roused this early?*

Arriving at the door in the early morning light, Emma saw medium-sized paw tracks in the snow. Deep fresh gouges had been scratched into the wooden door. She walked a few steps along the side of the coop, following the prints that circled the building. An uncomfortable shiver ran through her.

Something was stalking the chickens. A fox or coyote? Did it get in? Or has it gone? That may have been what I glimpsed out the kitchen window last night.

Emma carefully opened the coop door wide enough for her to slide in and close it behind her. The chickens squawked and swirled away from her. Heart pumping in her chest, she let her eyes adjust to the darkness. Peering around the outer walls of the coop, she tried to identify an intruder in their midst. Watching the hens, she could see they were agitated but not avoiding any particular area. She took a deep breath to calm her nerves, then made her way across the floor to the laying boxes on the opposite end of the enclosure.

Reaching into each box, she retrieved whole eggs, but also felt slippery yokes and shell fragments mixed in. *The hens must have panicked and jumped into their nests, breaking some of the eggs.* She continued gathering slimy eggs from the row of laying boxes until her basket was almost full. After setting the basket on the floor next to the door, she added scoops of grain to the feeders along the side wall. As the hens herded toward the food she grasped her basket and made her way out the door, then slung the long wooden bar into the metal latch to secure it.

Thank you, Lord, for protecting our hens from intruders. She breathed a sigh of relief that she had not been forced to confront a wild animal alone.

Back in the kitchen, Emma cleaned the eggs. Then she pulled a wooden crate from the stack in the anteroom and set it on the table. Grasping a bundle of straw from a pile in the corner, she dropped it on the floor next to the crate. Then she patted a pile of straw into the bottom of the crate and nestled a row of eggs into the padding. She counted the eggs in the layer and jotted the number down on a piece of paper. Alternating between a layer of straw and a layer of eggs, she found the crate was not quite full when she finished. After tallying the numbers, she figured she was about twenty-five eggs short of an average day's lay.

Something spooked my hens. They did the best they could. Shaking her head, she added an extra-thick padding of straw along the top and latched the wooden cover so it wedged firmly into the crate. She hefted the bulky crate and set it on the floor in the anteroom, along with her tally. *There. 'Tis ready for Luke to take to market on Monday.*

Emma swept the straw debris from the floor and dumped it onto the pile in the outer room. From her pantry she gathered flour and other ingredients to make bread dough. She hummed her favorite spiritual as she thought about Elsie and her family. Memories of her own children's antics when they were young brought a smile to her face as she folded and kneaded the dough. When she peered out the kitchen window again, she realized it was now fully light in the yard.

Hmmm. I wonder when Buster and Enos shall arrive to start the milking? 'Tis not like those hands to be late.

Emma left the bread dough wrapped in a flour cloth on the counter to rise. *I must wash and dress for services.* She grabbed the water bucket, pushed through the outer door, and filled it at the well pump. Struggling with the heavy load, she lugged the bucket back along the yard and into the kitchen. Placing the metal wash basin on the top of the stove, she poured water into it to heat. While she waited, she prepared herself another cup of tea and set it on the table. Then she went to her bedroom and retrieved her diary which she brought back to the table, and began to write.

10 mo. 13th, Sunday, early morning, 1850

Father and Luke have left on their journey to deliver the Prescott family to the canal in Whitehall. I pray the good Lord shines His guiding light upon the family and delivers them safely to freedom in the Promised Land. Yet, I cannot help but worry. I do not believe Father has been forthcoming about the risks surrounding us because of this infernal new slave law.

Emma sipped her tea and thought about the guns she had seen at the table before Gabe and Luke left.

'Tis not like them to travel armed when transporting fugitives. Perhaps they expected trouble might be coming and did not want to worry me. I pray they are ever-vigilant in their mission to do God's will on this earth to help

His downtrodden children. May the Lord hold and keep His travelers in His ever-loving grace and guide Gabe and Luke home safely. Amen.

A small frown furrowing her brow, Emma put down her pen. When the water was hot in the wash basin, she unbuttoned the front of her dress and let it drop to her waist. Using a washcloth and lye soap, she gasped as the hot water touched her cool skin. She vigorously scrubbed her face and partially clothed body, then dried her skin. Carrying her diary, she returned to her bedroom, where she changed into a light blue muslin dress she saved for Sunday services. Removing her soiled white bonnet, she unbraided her long, gray hair, brushed it thoroughly and re-braided it so it hung over her shoulder. Pulling a clean blue bonnet from her wardrobe, she centered it and tied the ribbons under her chin.

Back in the kitchen, she pushed open the anteroom door. Gloomy morning light engulfed her. Enos and Buster's horses were not at the hitching rail. *Did Father ask the farm hands not to come today because of the trip with the Prescotts? If so, he did not inform me. The cows shan't wait much longer. I hope Father and Luke shall be home soon to milk before services.* The uncomfortable gnawing in her core since the Prescotts' arrival grew more pronounced.

Wringing her hands, she went back inside, sat down at the table and sipped her cooling tea. Staring out the window toward the hay barn, a heavy sense of foreboding engulfed her. Memories of the shrill voice from her recent dream rattled her nerves. *Should I start the milking, or wait?*

A knock at the outer door startled Emma from her thoughts. *Oh, thank heaven! They have finally arrived.*

Pushing open the door, Emma started to scold the errant farm hands. "Buster! Enos! Where—"

Her neighbor, Zenas C. Ellis, stood on her stoop.

"Friend Zenas! Oh, my. Thee has startled me." She tried to look beyond him, but he blocked her view. "Why is thee here? Where are Gabe and Luke?"

Zenas stepped into the anteroom and closed the bulky door. Unexpectedly, he grasped Emma's elbow and directed her to the kitchen, closing the inner door behind him.

Emma looked closely at her neighbor. His face was solemn, his cloak askew, and his pant legs were caked with mud. A thick swipe of dirt ran across his forehead. *Something's gone wrong. Oh, God!*

Zenas gently directed Emma to the table. "Emma, please sit down. I have brought news."

She pulled her arm from his grasp and stepped away from the table. "Zenas! What has happened?" She wrung her hands. "Where are Gabe and Luke? Tell me!"

Zenas dropped his head, then looked at Emma as she stood rigid, awaiting his news. He took a breath, then continued, his voice low and strained. "Very well. There has been an accident. The sheriff's posse was chasing the wagon—it slid off the bridge. I'm so sorry."

Emma gasped and put her hands to her mouth, staring at Zenas. "Oh, dear Lord!" She pictured the family tucked into the wagon bed. "What of the Prescotts? Were they hurt? Are they safe? And where are Gabe and Luke? Zenas!" Her body trembled, and she began to sway.

Zenas reached out his hand to steady her. "Emma, won't you please sit?" He motioned to the chair.

Emma stepped away from his grasp and pressed her back against the counter. She shook her head. "I shan't, Zenas! Just tell me."

Zenas nodded, his face pained. "Emma, Sheriff Wardwell has arrested Gabe and taken him to jail for illegally transporting fugitives."

"What!" Emma exploded. "That is ridiculous! Jeremiah knows Gabe well. How on earth would he arrest him?"

Zenas took a step closer. "Emma, there's more. Sarah was captured by the slave hunters. I think Samuel and Jonah may have escaped, and I do not know the fate of Miss Elsie. It grieves me sorely to bring these tidings."

Emma let out a gasp. "Oh, no! That poor family! Zenas, we must help them. What can we do?" She folded her hands in prayer. "Dear Lord, please shine Thy loving grace upon the Prescotts and keep them safe."

Zenas grasped her arm.

She looked up into his anguished face. *He has not told me everything.* "Zenas, does thee know where Buster and Enos are? They should have been here before first light for the milking."

Zenas nodded. "They were part of the sheriff's posse, Emma. They—"

"Sheriff's posse?" Emma cried, eyes wide.

"Yes, Buster and Enos have betrayed our trust. They told the sheriff about the Prescotts' presence on your farm. Buster and Enos shan't be coming for chores."

Emma wavered and grasped the counter. "That's not possible. How could they turn against us? They work here!" Snippets of her horrible nightmare again floated through her mind.

"I'm sorry, Emma, but thee should really sit down." Zenas stared into her troubled eyes as he wrapped an arm around her back.

Emma hesitated, staring into her neighbor's eyes. "Where's Luke, Zenas?" Her legs tingled and wobbled. She let him guide her to where her half-empty teacup rested on the table. Her shaky legs caused her to drop into the chair. "Zenas!"

Zenas bowed his head, not looking her in the eye. "It grieves me more than thee could ever know, Emma, to tell thee this. . ." he paused then looked up, "but Luke is dead."

The gnawing in her exploded and gripped her heart. Ringing in her ears sounded like she was directly under the bell in the church steeple—she thought her head would burst. Visions of Gabe and Luke leaving the barn just hours earlier flooded her. She felt Luke's warm hug in the barn. "*I love you, Mother. We'll see you soon,*" he had whispered. She had watched Luke take the reins of the wagon, and had waved and called to him, "*Safe travels!*"

I should have stood in front of the wagon and stopped them right there! I knew in my heart something evil was looming. Oh, dear Lord! How could this happen? 'Tis all my fault!

She threw her hands over the ringing in her ears and screamed. Seconds later, she leaned over and vomited.

Zenas averted his eyes respectfully as Emma got up and bolted for the sink. She poured water into a glass and rinsed her mouth.

"Ahhhh, God! This cannot be true!" Emma turned toward Zenas, her face anguished.

"I am so sorry, Friend. I know thee is grieved. Thee should know the boys and I have brought Luke home—"

"Where is he? I must go to him!" Emma threw open the kitchen door and bolted through the anteroom into the chilly morning air.

"Emma! Wait!" Zenas called after her fleeing form as he followed her into the yard.

While Zenas C. was speaking with Emma, Barnaby had arrived in dry clothes and taken up position on one side of his horse, with Zenas H. guarding Luke's body from the other side. Barnaby stepped aside as Emma ran to the horse and grasped Luke's bloody head against her chest.

"Luke!" she shook his shoulders. "Luke! Pleeeaaasse wake up!" Her forlorn wail pierced the early morning quiet.

Zenas gently guided Emma a few steps from the horse and let her wail on his shoulder until her sobs subsided. "Friend Emma, I know thee is distraught. Please let us get Luke into the house so we can tend to him properly."

She nodded, not taking her gaze off Luke, as Zenas' sons slid the body off the saddle. "What happened? How did he die?" Emma choked on her tears. "Why, Zenas? Why has the Lord taken another of our children? What sins have we committed to deserve such wrath?"

Zenas stared down at Emma's contorted face. "We shall never know the Lord's plan, dear Friend. But we must abide by His will on this earth." He gently led her toward the door, following Zenas H. and Barnaby who were carrying Luke's body into the house.

In the kitchen Emma pulled away from Zenas' grasp and steadied herself against the kitchen counter. As she watched the Ellis brothers transport Luke's body into the main room, her mind swirled. *What will happen to Mary and the children without Luke?*

"Zenas? What about Mary? Does she know?"

Zenas shook his head. "Not yet. I shall go to her presently."

Then the shrill voice of her dream, demanding she do all the chores immediately, came rushing back to her. *Oh, God! What shall I do? I cannot manage the farm alone. And how long will Gabe be in jail?* She gulped air and hugged her chest tightly.

Zenas stood watching with concern.

Emma shook her head and exclaimed bitterly, "The Lord warned me this would happen. I should have stopped them from transporting the fugitives! I should have *listened* to Him! This is all my fault, and now we have lost both our men."

Zenas grasped her shoulders. "There was nothing thee could do, Emma! 'Tis not thy fault. Gabe and Luke have made the trip many times. Thee could not have predicted the posse attack. 'Twas that evil Southerner who stirred up all this trouble!"

A grunt from the parlor caused Emma to turn. She watched the brothers wrestle Luke's lanky body onto a blanket they placed on the floor between the stove and the divan. Barnaby grabbed a pillow and gently laid it under Luke's head.

Emma stepped into the main room, dropped to her knees and squeezed Luke's stiff hand. She stared at his thick, brown hair, now matted and tangled. Rivulets of blood had run down his face and frozen in place. A bandanna had been wrapped around his shattered neck, but frozen, blackish clods splattered his clothing. She let out a cry, and held her other hand to her mouth.

"Why has Thee taken my son from me? 'Tis more than I can bear!" She looked into Luke's mottled face as she held his chill hand to her rapidly beating heart. "Never more will I feel thy tender hugs, nor hear thy gentle laughter or see thy smiling face!" She gazed upward. "Why is Thee punishing us? We only wanted to do Thy will on this earth!" Her body shook violently. "Oh, God! *Why?*"

Zenas C. stepped away from Emma to give her privacy, and motioned for his sons to join him in the kitchen. In a low voice he said, "Barnaby, I must inform Mary of these tragic tidings. I want thee to stay here and comfort Friend Emma." Then he addressed his older son. "Zenas, Come with me so thee can stay with Mary's children."

Both boys answered, "Yes, Sir."

Zenas C. and Zenas H. walked through the Hopper backyard and approached Luke's house, just a few yards to the north. As he drew closer, Zenas C. saw movement through the kitchen window. A few moments after he knocked, Luke's wife Mary opened the door. A look of concern spread across her face. Zenas C. hadn't seen Mary recently, and was surprised at seeing her advanced pregnancy.

"Mary." Zenas C. nodded his head. "May we come in?"

Mary peered behind the two men into the yard. "Yes, come in," she said as she held the door open. "What brings you here on the Sabbath?"

The father and son entered the warm, messy kitchen. Twins Brian and Bernard sat next to each other at the table laughing, as they smacked their porridge spoons in a pretend sword fight. Martha sat opposite the table eating her porridge with a bemused smile, watching her big brothers' antics.

Zenas C. grasped Mary's elbow and pointed to their living room. "Mary, we must speak privately. My boy here will watch over thy children." He turned and nodded to Zenas H., who sat at the table and asked the twins what game they were playing.

Mary looked back over her shoulder as Zenas C. directed her to the living room and closed the kitchen door behind them. He steered her toward the front door, where their conversation wouldn't be heard.

With a frightened look on her face, Mary turned to her unexpected visitor. "What has happened, Zenas? Where are Luke and Gabe?"

Zenas looked into her flushed face and touched her arm. "There has been an accident, Mary. The sheriff's posse was chasing Gabe's wagon, and it slid off the Whitehall bridge. It grieves me to bring these bad tidings."

Mary's Irish complexion became more flushed as she hugged her burgeoning belly. "Oh, no! Luke was worried there were slave hunters in town. Are Luke and Gabe hurt? Where are they? We must go to them!"

Zenas shook his head. "Gabe has been arrested and jailed for transporting fugitives."

"Oh, God, no!" Mary's face twisted. "And where is Luke?"

Gripping her arm tighter, Zenas took a breath, then sighed. "Luke has been shot, Mary. I am so dreadfully sorry, but he is dead."

Zenas watched Mary's face go from shock to horror and her body begin to tremble. As she started to collapse, Zenas guided her into the chair next to the door.

Mary gasped. "No! No! It must be a mistake. Not Luke! Are you sure, Zenas?" She gripped her belly and stared at their neighbor.

Zenas nodded, his face stoic.

Mary stared up at him, her tears flowing. "Who shot him?"

"We do not know the details, Mary. The sheriff will have to investigate." He waved his arm in the direction of town. "We have brought Luke's body back. He is at Emma's now."

"Oh, God! Emma! She must be devastated!" she cried into her cupped hands.

Zenas gently touched her shoulder. "Thee must come with me. Zenas H. will stay with thy children until thee is ready to share this with them."

"Yes, yes. Of course." Mary sighed, wiped her tears and lifted her pregnant frame from the armchair with Zenas' assistance. She stared at him for a long minute. "What shall I tell the children?"

He gripped her hand. "For now, I think 'tis best to say thee is going to visit Emma. 'Tis prudent to wait until thee has seen Luke first."

Mary straightened her skirts and nodded. Zenas followed her back to the kitchen. The children stopped their play and stared at their mother's grim face. Little Martha asked, "Mommy? Are you sick?"

Mary patted Martha's bonnet and said in a strained voice, "No, Honey. But I need to visit your grandmother with Mister Ellis right now. Zenas H. will stay with you." Bernard and Brian sat stock still, their dueling spoons suspended in midair. Mary turned to the Ellis son. "Zenas, help yourself to some porridge," she pointed in the general direction of the stove.

Zenas H. stood. "I thank you, Miz Hoppah. I s'pose I am a mite hungry."

"We must go." Zenas C. said, wrapping his cloak over Mary's shoulders, as he led her out the kitchen door. He felt Mary shivering under his arm while he guided their path across the yard and into Emma's kitchen.

Barnaby, sitting at the kitchen table, stood respectfully as they entered. "Miz Hoppah." He bowed his head. "I'm so sorry, Ma'am."

Mary, overcome with grief, nodded at the young man.

Zenas C. directed the sobbing woman past his weary son to the main room. "Luke's in here."

The sound of a woman's gasp caused Emma to pause in wiping the grime and blood from Luke's face with a damp cloth. She turned to see her tall, very pregnant daughter-in-law standing in the doorway, her expression inconsolable.

Emma lifted her bloodstained hand to the weeping woman. "He is with the Lord now, Mary. And 'tis *all* my fault!"

ADAM HOPPER FARM
FAIR HAVEN, VERMONT
MAY, 1861

ADAM

BRIAN HELD UP the front page of the Sunday *Rutland Herald*. "Grandfather, did you see this?" He read the bold headline spread across the top of the page: "***Lincoln Calls for More Troops.***"

"Lincoln's a fool!" Sitting at the head of the oval, maple table in his youngest son Adam's dining room, Gabe shook his head. "'Tis not right for the North to wage war with the South. Let those damned Confederates secede and make their own country! They shan't survive without the North and they'll find that out." He sighed and rubbed his long, gray beard. "The plantation owners are just fighting to keep their slaves—an abomination of God's Law!"

The patriarch glanced around at the family gathered for the midday meal. Emma sat directly to his right, her Sunday bonnet perched pristinely upon her wrapped gray braid. Seated next to Emma were her daughter-in-law, Mary; her granddaughter, Martha, now fourteen; and Luke's youngest son, George, now ten. George had been born on Christmas Eve, some two months after Luke's tragic death.

To Gabe's left sat his twin grandsons. Brian had grown tall and lanky like Luke, but Bernard was a head shorter than Brian, stocky and muscular. They were now nineteen years old. Next to Bernard sat Thomas Rogers, Adam's business partner, who shared the rambling farmhouse with him. Adam, Gabe and Emma's youngest son, now thirty-six, sat at the opposite end of the table facing Gabe.

Earlier in the day, the Hopper clan had attended Sunday services at the Methodist church, along the northwest side of the common on the corner of West Street. Abolitionist meetings were still held there weekly. After services, the extended family had made their weekly visit to the Hopper family burial plot at the nearby West Street Cemetery. After placing flowers on baby Ruth's and Luke's graves, Emma walked slowly to a plot not far from Luke's. She placed her final bouquet on its gravestone, bowed her head and said a silent prayer.

The inscription on the headstone read:

Miss Elsie Prescott, d. 1850.

She found freedom in her Lord's arms.

Emma spoke quietly, "'Tis a beautiful spring Sunday, Miss Elsie, and I know thee would love it. I have brought thee the first blooms of our purple lilacs. I hope their fragrance reaches thee in the Lord's Kingdom, as they are my favorites." Emma laid her hand atop the curved stone. "I think of thee often, my dear friend. May the good Lord keep thee safe by His side."

"Are you ready to go, Mother?" Adam offered his arm, guiding her out of the cemetery gate and into the carriage, where she was joined by Mary and Martha. Then Adam helped Gabe step up to the carriage seat. Brian, Bernard and George mounted their individual horses and rode in front of the carriage heading west.

Leaving the cemetery, the riders and carriage continued along West Street, the bumpy road leading toward the New York border. Modest houses, barns and farmland stretched along both sides. The road ended as they passed beneath a large, stone-pillared entrance gate with the letters *Freiheit Bauernhof - Freedom Farmhouse,* etched into its wooden archway. The party continued up the long drive to the front of Adam's house. The three riders dismounted and tethered their horses.

Adam helped his elderly mother, Emma, step down from the carriage, then assisted Mary and Martha to the ground. Next he secured the draft horses to the hitching rail. Standing next to the carriage seat, Adam held out both arms as he guided Gabe's fragile frame to solid footing. Adam retrieved a cane from the floorboard and passed it to Gabe.

At the arrival of the family, the ornate, stained-glass front door had flown open. "Welcome, everyone!" Thomas, tall and thin, in his mid-thirties, shouted a greeting. Wearing a dark gray Sunday suit covered by a white apron, he gestured toward the dining room. "Dinner is almost ready. Please come in." He ran a hand through his sandy blond hair.

The Hopper family had climbed the steps to the covered veranda stretching the width of the white clapboard house. They filed through the entry, each greeting Thomas as he stood in the doorway. Inside, they lingered in the high-ceilinged foyer. To the right, a curving, engraved, wooden staircase led to the upper floor where Thomas had his apartment. To the left, a long hallway led to Adam's suite of rooms. Bypassing the stairs, Adam led the family into the large dining room at the back of the house, where the table was set for Sunday dinner.

Now, as Brian continued to read from the newspaper, bowls and platters of meat, smoked duck, potatoes, vegetables, bread and cheese were passed from one family member to another.

"*On Friday last,*" Brian intoned, "*the third of May, President Lincoln issued a second proclamation calling for United States Volunteers to serve three years in the Union Army, with regiments to be organized by the state governments, unless sooner discharged.*" Brian turned to his brother Bernard, and raised an eyebrow. "Says he's adding forty-two thousand more men to the ranks."

Bernard caught his twin's eye and nodded. "Obviously the first regiments Lincoln called up weren't fit to quell the Confederates. We must stop the war of rebellion by the Southerners!" Bernard grasped Brian's arm. "It is our duty to defend our father's honor! He died trying to help the escapees reach freedom. We must fight for what is right and just under God's Law."

Gabe pounded his fist on the table, immediately silencing the conversation. He partially rose from his seat, leaning on the table. "Thee will *not* join the Union Army. I shan't allow it! I have lost one son and will not lose my grandsons to fight a war for an unholy cause! If the South wants to keep their slaves and secede from the Union, then so be it! May God have mercy on their heathen souls!" Gabe's face flushed as he wheezed for breath, dropping hard into his chair.

Emma, now almost sixty, reached out and touched Gabe's trembling, arthritically bent hand. She gazed kindly at her grandsons. "Brian, Bernard, thee know we need thee to work the farm. Grandfather is not as strong as he once was, and George is still a boy. We cannot manage without thy help." *I am grateful Gabe finally forgave Enos for his trespasses against us. It was with God's grace that Enos, now with his wife, Mathilda, and their young son, Luke, has been managing the farm for all these years.*

George piped up from his seat at the far end of the table. "I can do chores, Grandmother! Honest I can."

Mary patted her youngest son gently on his back. "Of course you can, Dear. But you can't do it alone. Mister Enos needs all our help to manage the farm."

Brian turned to Emma. "Yes, Grandmother, we know, but look what is says here." He read another section of the article. "*Governor Holbrook has immediately ordered all uniformed militia organized under the laws of the State of Vermont, to man their companies to their full quota.*" Brian turned to Bernard and raised an eyebrow once more.

Gabe grumbled, "Where will it end? Just let those heathens go their separate way, I say."

Brian looked at his grandfather's wrinkled face and sighed. "The Governor says all able-bodied men over the age of eighteen and under forty-five are encouraged to enlist immediately in the Second Vermont Infantry Regiment. The article goes on…*recruits should present themselves at the county fairgrounds in Burlington. The Second Vermont will be mustered into the U.S. Army at the end of June hence, under the command of Colonel Henry Whiting.*" Brian paused, looking at his uncle Adam for support. "That's next month."

Bernard rose, face reddened, and roared, "If we had joined the First Vermont Regiment back in April when Lincoln first ordered the call-to-arms, we could have beaten those bastards, and the war would be over by now!" He waved a hand in the air.

Again Gabe pounded the table, and all eyes shifted to the aged patriarch.

"Our family has struggled for decades in the abolitionist movement to assist those oppressed by their masters, and look where it has gotten us—nowhere! I was arrested for doing God's will and I have lost my son to the cause. We never saw justice served and never will!" Gabe's voice broke into a wrenching sob.

"Ahhh, God!" Gabe took a labored breath. "'Tis not right! Now Lincoln wants to recruit thousands of men to fight to free the slaves. The Southerners will never abide, and have already seceded from the Union." He waved his arthritic fist. "'Tis a hopeless cause, I say! I shan't lose more family members because those damned heathens refuse to change their sinful ways and abide by God's Laws."

Adam glanced sideways at his partner, Thomas, then gazed at the family members gathered around the table, all quiet, staring at their plates. "Father, if I might say, we *have* made a difference. Look at how many slaves

Uncle Isaac and I helped travel through New York City to freedom in Canada. And you assisted many of them on their journey." He stared at his father, seated at the opposite end of the table. "You know Uncle Isaac dedicated his life to help those seeking freedom, and I promised him on his deathbed I would continue his work for the cause."

Adam looked at Emma, who was nodding her head in agreement. "Mother, I understand the reasons you and Father no longer risk yourselves for the cause. But you know Thomas and I still work with Zenas H. and Barnaby Ellis to transport fugitives to Whitehall. The need is greater now than ever before."

Shaking his head, Gabe rubbed his beard and dropped his gaze.

Adam continued. "Father, think about it. If the boys do not support our homeland and quell the Southern rebellion, the slaves might never have a chance to be freed." He swung his hand across the table. "Regardless, we must continue to do God's work in Uncle Isaac's memory, transporting fugitives, even if we put more abolitionists' lives in danger."

Gabe slowly got to his feet. Now in his early sixties, his scraggly, thin gray hair was swept back from his troubled, weathered face, covered by a drooping, grizzled beard. His crippled fingers pressed the table for balance. Rising to his full, stooped-shouldered height, Gabe looked around the family gathered for the Sunday meal. All eyes were upon him.

"I shan't discuss this further! Thee knows my feelings. As the head of this family, I will not allow my grandsons to fight this God-forsaken war!"

GUNTHER AND FRITZ

Furious and shaking from the heated conversation with his family, Gabe grasped his cane, turned from the dining room, limped through the kitchen, and exited to the back porch. Descending two of the four stairs leading down from the porch, he grasped the railing and lowered his tall, stooped frame onto the step, laying his cane next to him. He exhaled as his aching joints settled.

Directly in front of him, about thirty paces away, were the stables. Gabe gazed beyond them to the verdant pastures stretching in front of him. The pasture farthest to his left bordered the Whitehall road. A thin line of trees separated it from the middle pasture, where cows grazed on tender shoots in the warm spring sunshine. To his right, another grove separated a third pasture, where three of Adam's four horses roamed freely, also grazing.

Through those trees, Gabe could see the slate roof line of the hay barn built along the edge of the river defining the Vermont and New York state line. The spring snow melt had swollen the flow and the sound of white-water crashing over boulders reached Gabe's ear. The warmth of the midday sun on his back helped ease his aches.

As he pondered his grandsons' eagerness to join the U.S. Army, the distant sound of horses' hooves and clunk of wagon wheels crossing the arched New York bridge span brought back painful memories of that tragic night more than ten years earlier, the last time he had transported fugitives.

Upon seeing Gabe settle on the stoop, Gunther, the aging shepherd, lying with his brother Fritz on a rug in the shade of the stables, wagged his tail and slowly rose to his feet. With a yip and a low growl, the dog limped to Gabe, favoring his left hip. Gunther laid his gray muzzle on the old man's knee and Gabe gently scratched the dog's ears. "Thee is a good boy, Gunther. Yes, I feel thy pain. My joints ache, too."

Hearing his brother getting attention, Fritz rose from his bed and wobbled a meandering course away from Gabe. "Over here, boy." Gabe's voice guided the dog to him. Fritz smelled the ground, then sat down next to his brother. Gabe looked down at Fritz's gray muzzle. The dog's right eye was missing and his eyelid had been sewn shut. The past eleven years had left the other eye clouded by cataracts, providing very little sight for the dog to navigate. Gabe petted the dog's head and sighed.

"I cannot let my grandsons go to war, now can I boys?" Gabe stared at the aged dogs, who peered back up at him.

"I know thee both miss thy pack. Thee fought bravely when thy mistress was attacked!" He scratched Gunther's ear.

Gabe smiled at the faithful siblings sitting next to him. "But thankfully, Adam and Thomas kept thee on as good guard dogs when they came home from New York City and bought Paree's farm."

The sound of children's laughter wafted on the gentle breeze as another carriage out for a Sunday ride crossed the distant bridge. So much had happened since their wagon crashed. Gabe was forever grateful to his good neighbor, Zenas C. Ellis, for posting his bail, after he'd spent two nights in jail.

Peering down at his canine companions, Gabe murmured, "Did thee know Vermont was the first state to overturn the hideous Fugitive Slave Law by enacting the Habeas Corpus Law? This gave the fugitives the right to a fair trial and to defend themselves." He scratched Fritz's ear. "Lucky for me, it was overturned just a month before my trial."

He watched the horses frolic in the pasture to his right. "It was my fellow abolitionist, Judge Kittredge, who found me not guilty of breaking the current law, thank heaven." He scrubbed his bearded cheek with one hand. "But, alas and alack, I paid a steep fine for transporting fugitives against the law of that time." He sighed. "So be it."

Gabe stretched his legs over the edge of the steps below him. Grasping the railing he slowly lifted himself to a standing position. Joint pain in his right hip shot down his leg, causing him to groan. Grabbing his cane, he took a couple of steps to balance himself. Looking back at the dogs he said, "Let's go for a walk, boys. Heel."

Gunther and Fritz rose to take positions on each side of Gabe. He turned to his left and slowly made his way beyond the stables into the pasture. Cows meandered away to give him and the dogs free passage through the moist grass and spring clover. Gabe's hand trembled as he leaned on his cane.

If Luke were here, I wonder if he would be in favor of the twins enlisting. For that matter, if Luke were here, might I even support this unholy war? I do not know. He sighed. *But I cannot allow my grandsons to risk their lives for a futile cause which will never succeed!*

He bent to gently rub Gunther's head. *But Luke is gone, and God has torn us asunder! I must remain devoted to protect my family and property from evil.*

As Gabe was brooding, he paused in the trees to watch two jackrabbits chase each other through the wildflowers. Fritz growled at the sudden movement, but made no attempt to chase the fleeting flashes. Gabe patted the old dog's head. "I know, boy. They are much faster than we are these days."

Leaning on his cane, Gabe walked out into the pasture bordering the road. He picked his way around cow patties as he made his way toward the riverbank. Fritz and Gunther kept his slow pace.

Gabe found himself standing on the verge of the streambank, staring at the wooden bridge spanning the state line between Vermont and New York. He watched the rushing water tumble over the rocks where his wagon had landed more than a decade before, and where Luke had been slain. *This is where God cast me and my family aside!*

Still gripped by his bitter memories, he sighed and lowered himself to sit on a boulder in the shade some ten feet from the wooden span. Gunther and Fritz found comfortable spots in the piles of leaves near Gabe's feet. Still no attempt over the past decade had been made to erect side rails because neither Vermont nor New York wanted to foot the bill.

The bridge is still treacherous in the winter months. It's a crime no one will do anything about it.

Suddenly Fritz growled, perked his ears, and turned his head back toward the pasture. The dog may have been nearly blind, but Gabe knew his senses of smell and hearing were acute. Gabe turned his gaze back toward the way they had come.

"Father!" came a distant call on the breeze.

Then he saw a figure emerge from the line of trees and enter the pasture bordering the road. "Father!" Gabe recognized Adam's voice and long stride.

"Looks like we have been found, boys," he said to the dogs. Both of their heads turned toward the oncoming visitor. "Time to move on." Gabe grasped his cane and grunted as he lifted his stiff body from the boulder. Gunther and Fritz rose and followed at Gabe's side as he turned from the bridge and entered the open pasture. He waved his cane at his youngest son. "Over here, Adam."

Adam trotted up to Gabe and the dogs. "Father! We were worried about you. You didn't finish your meal." Adam grasped Gabe's free right arm. "Are you unwell?"

Gabe shook off Adam's help. "No, no. I am fine. The dogs and I just needed some fresh air and to stretch our legs."

Adam looked into his father's gaunt, wrinkled face, and sighed. "Well, let's get you back to the house then, shall we?" He gently laid his arm on Gabe's stooped shoulder, and guided him across the pasture, through the bordering copse of trees, and to the back stoop of the farmhouse.

Gabe patted both Gunther and Fritz's heads. "Thanks for the walk, boys. 'Twas great talking with thee. Now go lie down."

Adam grinned and raised an eyebrow at his father as they slowly ascended the back stairs.

The gray-muzzled dogs wagged their tails. Gunther limped off, leading his nearly blind sibling, Fritz, to their blanket in the shade of the stables. They curled up back-to-back to resume their afternoon nap.

GOD'S LAW

When Gabe returned to his seat at the head of the table, he saw his dinner plate had been replaced by a slice of fresh-baked apple pie. The spicy-sweet aroma made his stomach rumble, and he began to eat.

Adam placed a new cup of tea in front of his father, then took his seat at the other end of the table. Patting Thomas' hand, Adam said, "We were just saying, Father, it isn't right those slave hunters have become rich doing the dirty work those Southern landowners refuse to do."

Bernard spoke up. "Which is all the more reason we should fight to abolish slavery!"

Gabe took a sip of tea and addressed the extended family. "I remember after Sheriff Wardwell arrested me, he left me waiting at the constable's office while he delivered Buster's body to Jeb's Tavern." Gabe shook his head. "Not long afterward, the Southern slave hunter came in with Sarah Prescott. Her hands were bound behind her back, and her face was bloody. He made Sarah sit on the floor as he took a seat on the bench along the opposite wall to wait for Wardwell. I was furious at him for keeping her in custody!" His palsied hand slashed the air.

All eyes at the table were on Gabe. Emma reached over and gently touched his arm.

Gabe glanced briefly at his petite, aging wife, then back toward the gathering. His deep voice wavered as he remembered the horrible aftermath of the posse attacking their wagon. "I asked that devil why he felt compelled to capture fugitives. Did he not believe it was against God's Law to own another human being?"

George, Mary and Luke's youngest son, spoke up. "What did the devil say, Grandfather?"

Gabe peered down the table at the gaping boy. "George, he looked me right in the eye and said in his fancy French accent: *it doesn't matter to me how I make my money, long as someone is willing to pay for my cargo.* He called Sarah, *cargo,* like a damned crate of beans!" Gabe eyes went opaque with rage.

"As I argued God's Law with this godless man, Sarah spoke from where she sat on the floor next to her captor. I shall never forget her words: *you can chain my body, but you can never chain my soul. It will always be free to fly!*" He paused to rub his beard, then continued, "The Prescott family had more courage and determination than I have ever seen in my lifetime. I can only hope Sarah has found peace somewhere in her heart."

Young George stared intently listening to Gabe's story. "What happened then, Grandfather?"

Gabe glanced at his grandson, so reminiscent of Luke at that age. "Well, George, I was furious with the Southerner and wanted to kill him right there and then. 'Twas a good thing I did not have my gun." Gabe shook his head. "So I did the next best thing—I walked over and slapped his face!"

George gasped. "You slapped the devil and you're not burning in hell?"

Martha giggled at George's outburst. Adam smiled with good-natured tolerance, having heard the story many times.

Gabe nodded. "The devil swore a cursed streak, grabbed me by the shoulders, and threw me to the ground. Sarah screamed. It was only because the sheriff arrived and pulled us apart we did not kill each other right there and then!"

"What did the sheriff do?" George asked, enthralled by the tale.

"Well, Son, he locked me in the jail cell to separate us," Gabe said. "Then he and the Southerner argued about how much money they would get for Sarah on the auction block. It wasn't the thousand dollars they had hoped to get for the whole family, so the Southerner said he wouldn't share it with the sheriff." Gabe rubbed his tired eyes. "Sheriff Wardwell got very angry and told the rabble-rouser to take Sarah, get the hell out of his town, and never come back!" Gabe didn't notice the quick flicker of astonishment passing across the others' faces at hearing his casual use of profanity. Instead, he bowed his head and sighed. "I wish I could have saved her."

Emma pursed her lips as she touched Gabe's palsied hand. "Thee never told me the sheriff was to be paid."

Gabe glanced apologetically at his wife, her wrinkled face showing her dismay. "I know, Mother. I did not want to worry thee after all the troubles we have endured. 'Twas a terrible time." He used his fork to fiddle with his half-eaten pie. Then he glared at the twins. "This conflict will not accomplish anything except rip our country asunder. Boys, I beseech thee! Reconsider enlisting to fight this terrible war."

Brian, sitting to Gabe's left, changed the subject. "Grandfather, Bernard and I saw Wardwell at the tavern last night. He sends his deepest respects."

Gabe looked at Brian with a pained expression. "Yes, yes. Well…how is Jeremiah? I have not seen him in quite some time."

Brian shrugged. "'Bout the same. Still drinking. I don't know how he manages to run the tavern, being drunk all the time."

Gabe sighed. "Jeremiah never forgave himself for not keeping the peace when the slave catcher was in town. He was devastated so many good folks got killed during the attack on our wagon." Gabe reached for Emma's hand.

Emma's face flushed as she turned to Gabe. "Jeremiah cried like a baby at Luke's funeral. He said how sorry he was he could not protect Luke, and he never wanted any violence. At the time, I felt much sympathy for the man for admitting his failings." Emma's face crunched as she held back tears. "Had I known Jeremiah was to receive payment to capture the Prescotts, I would have told him to burn in hell!" she blurted, then held her hand over her mouth at her own unexpected outburst.

George giggled. "Grandmother! You said a bad word!"

Emma turned to her grandson. "George, I will not tolerate liars, and those who are not committed to upholding their faith."

Gabe nodded at his wife. "Jeremiah said after Luke's death, he could no longer faithfully do his job, and passed his duties over to his son George. That's when he retired and bought the tavern. Said he wanted to keep an eye on any troublemakers in town." Gabe looked mournfully at Emma. "But that drink shall be the death of him. 'Tis the devil's elixir, and will ruin any man who partakes!" Gabe slapped his hand on the table.

Brian gave Bernard a questioning look and Bernard nodded. Brian broached the touchy subject. "We also spoke with Edward at the bar."

Gabe took a bite of pie and raised an eyebrow at the mention of Edward Allen.

Exchanging a glance with his brother, Brian continued, "You might be surprised, Grandfather, that Edward agrees with your stance on the war. He says the Southerners should be allowed to secede and keep their slaves captive. Edward thinks all slaves should be kept under lock and key for eternity."

Gabe's haggard face flushed. "I have never said that! The slaves *should* be freed, but I also must keep my family safe." He rubbed his anguished face. "Edward is a vengeful, bitter scoundrel. After he lost his leg, Jeremiah took pity on the boy and hired him as his bartender." Gabe's cough rumbled in his chest.

Brian nodded. "When we told Edward we wanted to enlist in the Union Army, Edward said if he were fit for duty, he would join the Confederates to fight against us."

Gabe dropped his fork. "Ahhh! Dear Lord Almighty! Our family has already suffered too much sorrow." He raised his eyes to the ceiling. "Lord, despite all that has befallen our family, do not fail me in this: keep my grandsons safe from all harm during this terrible war!" He pointed a bent finger toward the twins. "I shan't allow myself to be in the same league with the likes of evil-minded Edward. He is a curse on this town, breeding hatred! The Colonel was right to disown his mad son." Gabe roughly pushed aside what was left of his pie, then squeezed his trembling hands together on the table.

Brian looked kindly on the old man. "Grandfather, we know the heart-break you have endured with the loss of our father. But this is the Lord's cause you and Grandmother have risked your entire lives for! Now is the time for us to get justice, so Father's death will not have been in vain." He reached over and touched Gabe's clasped hands. "We would like your blessing to defend our homeland."

Gabe shook his head and stared at his tall, lanky grandson, who reminded him so much of Luke: young, determined, and headstrong. "I cannot in good faith give thee my blessing." He paused, looking deep into Brian's eyes. "But I also cannot stop thee from doing what thee feels is right." He grasped Emma's hand and bowed his head. "Thy grandmother and I shall pray for thy safe return."

Brian turned to his stocky twin brother, Bernard, and smiled. "Thank you, Grandfather. We will help Mister Enos hire new workers immediately."

HOPPER FAMILY FARM
FAIR HAVEN, VERMONT
DECEMBER, 1862

EMMA

16th December, 1862

Dear Mrs. Mary Hopper,

It is with my deepest regret I must inform you your son, Infantryman Brian Hopper, fought valiantly at the battle of Fredericksburg, Virginia and gave his life on the 13th December, 1862, defending the cause of this great civil strife to keep our country united. His ultimate sacrifice should bring honor and valor to your family.

My sincerest sympathies on your loss of this dedicated Patriot.

General Edwin H. Stoughton
2nd Vermont Regiment
United States Army

Emma wiped her tears after reading the letter twice. *Oh, no! Not our beloved grandson Brian, too! And now what will dear Mary do?* Emma stole a look at Mary's ashen face, her eyes red with grief, as she leaned against the still-open door. She hugged her daughter-in-law, and the women wept in each other's arms. Then Emma ushered Mary to the kitchen table, followed by her children Martha and George. The three removed their winter coats and draped them on the chairs.

Emma grasped Mary's cold hand. "I am so sorry, Dear. This is such a tragedy for our family. Thee has been very brave since Luke's death. I know this is a terrible blow for you!"

Mary looked at her forlorn children sitting at the table, their eyes downcast. "It's difficult for all of us, Mother! I can only pray Bernard does not meet the same fate and he comes home to us when this horrible war is over."

Emma nodded. "So if I might ask, what did the officer say shall become of Brian's remains?"

Mary wiped her eyes and stared at Emma. "The sergeant said Brian was buried near the battlefield in Fredericksburg with other fallen Union soldiers. He delivered Brian's hat, boots, medals—" The distraught mother gulped for air. "—his sword, and firearms. I don't know what I will do with them."

Emma grasped Mary's hands. "We shall keep them in remembrance of our brave son who fought to defend his homeland and his father's honor."

Mary nodded, unable to speak.

Emma said, "We shall have a stone laid for him in our plot next to Luke. He will never be forgotten, Mary. And thee must have faith Brian is now at the Lord's side."

Mary covered her face with her hands. "Ahhh! How can we—cele— celebrate Christmas…with this terrible news? How can I rejoice at the birth of Baby Je—Jesus, when my own son is dead?" She wept into her hanky.

Emma leaned from her chair and caressed Mary's back. "I know 'tis difficult to understand God's plan when terrible things happen. Our family is strong, and the Lord does not give us more than we can endure." Sighing, she glanced out the window at the mid-morning winter sun casting long shadows across the snow-covered farmland.

Martha, now almost sixteen, grasped her mother's hand and blurted, "Mother, I must *do* something to honor Brian! I want to go to the front lines. With Grandmother's medicines and training, I know I can nurse our boys. Please! It's the least I can do!"

Mary dried her eyes and looked at her sweet, caring daughter, now almost a grown woman. "I know you want to help, Dear. But I simply cannot allow you to leave. We need you now more than ever to help with the farm." She smiled wanly, seeing the little girl she had nurtured to adulthood. "The battlefront is no place for a young, lovely girl like you. It would cause us untold anguish worrying about your safety!" Mary squeezed her daughter's hand.

Martha cast a furious glance at her mother, then turned to Emma. "Grandmother! Can't you talk some sense into her? You know I am good with your medicines. I've learned so much from you. I want to make a difference in this war. Who knows? I may even bring my brother Bernard home safely."

Emma shook her head, gazing at her spirited blond, blue-eyed granddaughter, who had grown to her mother's stately height. "I'm sorry, Martha, but no. Thy mother is right. 'Tis no place for a young woman. And this is no time for discussing such plans! At least not until…" she stifled a sob, "…until there has been a memorial service and a headstone carved for Brian." Emma reached across the table to touch her granddaughter. "Thee must stay with the family until thee finds a husband, as we need thy helping hands. But I shall continue with thy medical training. Perhaps one day thee can attend formal schooling to become a nurse."

Martha harrumphed, crossed her arms, and slumped back into her kitchen chair, frowning. "That's not fair—the war will be over by then!" Then she grumbled under her breath. "How will I ever avenge Brian's death?"

Mary stared out the window overlooking the backyard and hay barn. Paths had been trodden into the foot-deep snow leading to the pump, barns, and chicken coop. "Well, Martha, I suppose maybe you won't. We just have to do our very best in his absence." She patted her pouting daughter's hand, then looked to Emma, her face clouded with anxiety. "When will Gabe and Enos return from town?"

Emma glanced into the main room at the mantel clock. "If they do not encounter troubles getting the sleigh up the hill, perhaps within the next hour. Thee knows Father will be devastated when he learns this news."

Mary nodded. "I know, Mother. Gabe did his best to keep the boys home. But they were determined to fight for Luke's honor! And I could not blame them for their dedication to the cause, even though they knew it might cost them their lives." Mary choked as she struggled to control her weeping. "I pray the good Lord has taken Br…Brian home to His Glorious Kingdom." Mary sobbed into her hands. "And I pray Bernard returns to us safe and sound." Now subdued, Martha leaned over to pat her mother's back.

George, one day shy of his twelfth birthday, turned to Emma. "Grandmother? Can you teach me the medicines, too? I would like to grow up to be a famous doctor and save everyone's life, even after the war!"

Martha snipped at her younger brother. "You can't save everyone, George. That's ridiculous!"

George, now almost Martha's height, responded, "No it's not! I can save people, can't I, Grandmother?"

Emma looked at her impetuous grandson. "Yes, George. I can teach thee the medicines. And mayhap one day thee can become a famous doctor." Emma turned from the table and scanned her pantry shelf. "I do not have everything I need, but I can begin thy training on the morrow, if thee wish."

George glared at his older sister, then turned to Emma. "Yes! I wish!" He rose from his side of the table, grasped Emma from behind and hugged her. "Thank you, Grandmother!"

Emma smiled wanly at George's outpouring of affection, much needed on a day bringing such sorrow.

Finally, Mary rose from the table and wiped her eyes. "Mother, we have chores to attend. But we can stay until Gabe and Enos return, if you would like."

Emma shook her head. "No, no, Dear. That shan't be necessary. I shall deliver the news to Father alone. 'Tis better this way."

Mary looked at Emma's dour expression. "Do you think Gabe and Enos saw the Union officers in town who delivered the letter to our house?"

Emma shrugged. "'Tis possible. But there have been so many lately, I doubt they would have thought much of it."

After donning their winter coats, Emma reached up to hug her tall daughter-in-law and granddaughter. Then she squeezed George to her.

"I'll be here early tomorrow to begin my training, Grandmother," George said earnestly.

Emma patted the boy on the back. "Thee be sure to get all thy chores done first, George. Does thee hear me?"

"Yes, Ma'am!" the boy replied.

Mary exited the outer room and stood on the stoop as her children followed her. "Will you and Father join us for supper tonight?"

Emma pursed her lips, then replied, "Possibly. It will depend upon how Father reacts when he gets this news."

Mary nodded. "I understand. Hopefully we'll see you later today."

Mary and her children turned to their right and walked along the snowy, trodden path. Emma stepped back into the kitchen and watched the family pass by the window and enter through their own kitchen door. She poured herself another cup of hot tea and sat at the table, glancing again at the letter delivered to Mary earlier in the day. To settle her nerves, and needing to express her grief, Emma went to her bedside table and retrieved her diary. Back at the table, she opened to a new page and began to write.

12 mo. 23rd, Tuesday, mid-morning, 1862

Dear Heavenly Father, why has Thee punished our family once again by taking Brian from our lives? Have we not suffered enough? We have only sought to do Thy work on this earth by helping those who seek freedom. Where is Thy mercy and compassion for Thy faithful followers?"

Emma paused, her mind in shambles. Then she dipped her quill in the inkwell and continued,

I plead with Thee to guide our grandson, Bernard, home safely to us. Please do not let us lose another child to this unholy war!"

Snippets of events over the past decade floated through her mind. After Luke was killed and Gabe arrested, she had realized her detailed entries of their travelers could put their family at even greater risk if they were ever found. She had enlisted Brian and Bernard to help her hide the ledger in a safe place. The twins had also helped her remove some evidence of their visitors from the underground barn room. Everything else was left behind. Then they had hastily latched the trapdoor and covered it with a heavy grain barrel.

It was Brian who suggested I should also hide my journals because they might be incriminating. I remember him scolding me: "Grandmother! You write too much!"
    I am thankful Adam and Thomas came home from New York City, when they received my letter about Luke's death. I would not have been able to manage the farm and Luke's burial without them.

Emma peered over at the freshly baked loaf of bread cooling on the counter. *I must get to making Gabe's lunch.* She remembered Miss Elsie exclaiming over how much she loved Emma's bread. Emma's hand trembled as she recalled her shock when Paree had told her Elsie's body had been recovered.

So many good, God-fearing people have passed from our midst, whose only mission was to do God's will. I hope I shall reunite with them one day in His Kingdom.

Emma sighed, closing her diary, and returned it to her bedside stand. Then she busied herself preparing a midday meal for Gabe when he returned from town. Humming her favorite psalm calmed her mind. She finished peeling and cutting potatoes and dropped them in a pot on the back of the wood stove to boil. Then she began cutting ham from a smoked hock and arranged the slabs on a large platter. Gently she sliced wide swaths from the loaf of fragrant, still-warm bread.

Within the hour, the sound of men's voices outside filtered into the kitchen. Wiping her hands on her apron, Emma opened the anteroom door. A cold wind blew over her as she watched Enos steer the horses and sleigh around the corner of the house to stop in front of the hay barn. Enos jumped down from his seat, then positioned himself on the opposite side to assist Gabe's descent. Gabe grabbed his cane and walked slowly through the snow toward Emma. *I wonder if he saw those Union officers in town.* She searched his grizzled face for some sign.

With the sleigh's arrival, the two farm hands Brian had hired, Jeremy and Ricky, emerged from the cow barn. They trudged along the snow-packed path between the stables and barn to unload the cargo.

Enos addressed the young men. "Let's get these milk jugs to the barn, then you can help me get the horses and sleigh stowed."

"Yes Sir, Mister Enos," Jeremy, the older of the two, said as he climbed into the sleigh to pass down the milk jugs to his helper, Ricky.

Emma called to their farm manager. "Enos! Please join us when thee has finished with the horses."

Enos nodded. "Yes, Ma'am. I'll be there soon."

Emma held the door wide as Gabe trudged up the steps into the anteroom, where he removed his outer garments and boots. When they were both in the kitchen, she closed the door behind him, then poured them each a cup of tea. Setting the platters of food on the table for their midday meal, she settled into her chair.

Gabe limped to the table, where he dropped hard into his seat and let out a moan. "Ahhh, that darned old hip is being a witch in this cold weather." He sipped his hot tea and sighed.

Wanting Gabe to relax before she gave him the bad news, Emma asked, "How was thy trip to town?"

Gabe grumbled, "I wish we did not have to travel those slopes in the winter. Hard on the horses with the sleigh loaded." He helped himself to the ham, bread and potatoes.

Emma clasped her hands together at the table and watched Gabe eat, trying to keep her emotions in check.

In between bites, Gabe mumbled, "We saw Union officers as we were leaving. There are many of them in town lately, usually bearing bad news."

Emma dropped her head and stared at her clenched fist, propped in front of her plate of food.

Gabe peered across the table at his wife. "Mother? What is wrong? Thee is not eating."

Emma lifted her head, her tears glistening. Unable to speak, she shook her head and handed Gabe the letter Mary had received.

Gabe did not immediately take the letter from her hand. "What is this?" he demanded.

Emma took a deep breath. "It was delivered today. Please read it." She watched him closely, her face careworn, fearing his reaction.

Gabe grasped the letter. His palsied hand shook as he read the short message. "Goddammit!" He pounded his other fist on the table, his weathered face flushed. "I *knew* those boys should not have gone off to that God-forsaken war! I tried to stop them! Why did they not listen to me?" The distraught old man put his hands to his face and wept. "How many more of our family has to die to convince those Southern heathens to free their fellow man? Is this what God wants? And *why us*? What have we done to deserve such sorrow and heartache?" Gabe pounded his fist again, making Emma jump.

Emma wiped her eyes and went to Gabe, laying a hand on his shoulder. "Father, I am so sorry! Of course thee was right. But the boys did what they thought was right to honor their father. And they knew the possible cost." Emma sniffled. "We are all grieving Brian's loss, but he is with the Almighty Lord now."

Gabe pulled away from her touch and faced her, his face bitter. "And how does thee *know* that, Emma? What if he isn't? What if Brian is in hell? We do not know what is in the afterlife. Or even if there *IS* a God!" Gabe's hands trembled violently. "Why would God let this war happen? Why would He let our fellow countrymen slaughter one another for this sinful cause? 'Tis not right or just!" Gabe pumped his crippled fist toward the ceiling.

Just then there was a quick knock on the outer door, and a gust of cold wind filtered into the kitchen as Enos entered. After removing his cloak and boots, Enos stepped close to the table. Seeing Gabe's distraught face, he asked, "What is it? What's wrong, Sir?"

Emma's voice quavered. "Our dear Brian has been killed in battle. We just received the letter."

Enos saw tears welling in Gabe's eyes. "Oh, no! I am so sorry, Sir. I know you were disappointed when the boys went against your wishes and enlisted." Enos moved to Gabe and laid a hand on the older man's shoulder. "I guess that explains the officers we saw in town."

Emma placed a cup of tea and a dinner plate at the table and Enos sat between Emma and Gabe.

"And what of Bernard?" Enos asked. "Do you know his whereabouts?"

Gabe shook his head and wiped his eyes. "We do not know. The last Mary heard from him, he was with the Vermont Brigade somewhere in Pennsylvania."

Enos put food on his plate and turned to Emma. "Perhaps there is a way Mary could appeal to the generals to have Bernard sent home due to family hardship. I've heard of other families who have tried it."

Emma patted Enos' hand. "Yes, perhaps thee is right, Enos. I shall speak with Mary about it." She smiled wanly.

Gabe shouted, "It shan't do any good! Those generals do not care about one man!" Gabe's hand shook as he drank his tea. "Why, Enos? Why has the Lord seen fit to punish our family with His wrath? We have dedicated our lives to doing His will, and *look* how the Lord has repaid us!"

Enos shook his head. "I don't know, Sir. It does seem terribly unfair."

Gabe rubbed his long, gray beard. "All I know is I must do everything in my power to protect my family and my property, because God has *forsaken* us!"

Emma and Gabe

March, 1863

AS EMMA FINISHED COOKING their breakfast, Gabe stepped into the kitchen. A lantern glowed next to the stove, and a second lantern lit the table. He yawned and bent to buss her cheek.

"I am feeling much better this morning, Mother," Gabe said. He uncorked the brown elixir bottle on the counter and took a swig. Scrunching his nose, he closed his eyes and swallowed the concoction. "This medicine Doc Sweeney gave me could cure an elephant of whatever ails him." He coughed to clear his throat. "'Tis foul tasting, but seems to be working."

Emma chuckled seeing the grimace on Gabe's face.

"Here, sit and drink some tea. It will help get rid of the nasty taste." She poured two cups of tea as Gabe took his place at the table. Then she set out their pre-dawn breakfast of porridge, scrambled eggs, sliced bread, and smoked fish, and joined him.

Gabe took a drink of tea, swishing it in his mouth before swallowing. "Ahhh, 'tis much better." He began to eat his scrambled eggs and stared out the window toward the hay barn. Turning back to Emma, his expression turned somber. "Now that Lincoln has signed the Emancipation Proclamation, I wonder if the freed black men will be joining the Union Army." He took another sip of tea. "With such heavy losses on both sides, this war probably will not end until there are no more men left to fight! All Lincoln will have are boys like George to take up arms!" Gabe took a bite of fish and bread, and glowered at Emma.

Emma nodded at Gabe's diatribe. "I know it upsets thee, Father. But I can only hope now the slaves are freed, the war will end soon, and Bernard shall come home to us." She took a small bite of her porridge.

"Was it worth it for so many men to die?" Gabe shook his head. "And what if, heaven forbid, those bloody Confederates win the war? Then what? They only follow Jefferson Davis, and *he* hasn't freed any slaves!"

The sound of voices in the yard stopped their conversation.

Finishing his bread and fish, Gabe turned toward the anteroom door. "That's Enos and the boys. Time to get to milking." He covered his mouth as a deep cough rattled his chest.

Emma worried as she watched Gabe rise from the table and grasp his cane. "Father, I know thee feels better. But I still wish thee would stay in until sun-up and let the boys handle the milking. The cold wind shall only make your cough worse."

Gabe dismissed Emma with a wave of his hand as he made his way to the anteroom. "I shall be fine, Mother. But I appreciate thy concern. We must get the cows milked, then tap the maples, since the sap shall start running soon."

Gabe slid on his rubber boots, and slipped into a heavy cloak, and warm hat. Emma passed him a lantern as he opened the outer door. "Thee is a stubborn old man, Gabe Hopper. I wish I knew what to do with thee!"

Gabe smiled, bent and kissed Emma's cheek. "Thee knows how much I love thee, my sweet bride. Please do not fret over me. I am a tough old bird."

Emma blushed at Gabe's show of affection. As she closed the door behind him, an inexplicable cold chill rushed over her.

Gabe braced himself against the frigid wind, and held the lantern so he could see his way across the icy surface. He approached Enos and their two farm hands, who were unsaddling the horses against the hitching rail.

"Mornin', boys." Gabe hunched away from the wind and coughed.

Enos nodded to Gabe. "Morning, Sir. Mighty cold again today. Your cough doesn't sound good. Maybe you should stay in 'til sun-up."

Gabe chuckled and shook his head. "Thee sounds just like Emma! I am fine, Enos. Do not fret thyself."

Enos looked closely at Gabe's weathered face. "If you say so, Sir. It should warm later, and we can get those sap buckets hung."

"Mornin', Mister Hopper," Jeremy and Ricky, the workers hired two years earlier before Bernard and Brian had joined the Army, chimed in.

Gabe acknowledged their greeting, then spoke to Enos. "Yes. I think the sap should start flowing soon with these warmer days. Hoping we have a good run this year."

Once the horses were tended, Gabe held the lantern high as the four men made their way along the icy path between the stables and the cow barn. At the end of the row, Enos slid open the double-wide doors. Gabe followed Enos into the barn and hung his lantern on a hook on the right-hand wall. Enos lit four more lanterns, passing one to each man. Each took an empty bucket and a wooden stool, heading for their milking stations. Leaving his cane propped against the barn wall, Gabe took up position next to the first cow at the south end of the barn across from Enos. Jeremy and Ricky walked to the stalls at the north end of the barn.

While milking his first cow, Enos called to Gabe across the aisle. "Did you hear Lincoln is letting rich boys buy their way out of the draft for three hundred dollars? Guess those bigwigs in Congress pressured him so their precious sons don't have to fight this damned war."

Gabe grumbled. "Lincoln's a fool! And that does not surprise me. He has fought this war on the backs of our farm boys and local militias—leaving our women and children vulnerable." Gabe pumped the cow's teat, and milk splattered into the bucket. "I do not trust the government to help our families. I shall remain determined to protect them and our farm."

After milking two cows, Gabe lifted his almost-full pail and started to walk to the south end of the barn to dump it into a large jug. Suddenly a crushing pain exploded in his chest, then shot through his left shoulder and down his arm. Staggering, he reached for his missing cane. Panting for breath, he dropped the heavy pail. Milk sloshed onto the floor and into the troughs. He grasped his left arm, and then a sharp pain seared through his chest, causing him to land on his knees with a thud. His deep-chested wheeze echoed throughout the barn.

In an instant, Enos dropped to the floor next to him. "Sir! Sir! Gabe! What is it?" Enos wrapped his arm around Gabe's back.

Gabe heaved for breath as the flame ripping through his chest engulfed him. His face flushed an unhealthy red. Now on his hands and knees, he dropped his head, trying to take shallow breaths.

Enos yelled to the men at the end of the barn. "Jeremy, quick! Run to the house and get Miz Hopper. Tell her Gabe is sick! Ricky! Get Gabe some water from the pitcher over there." He pointed to the shelf where the lanterns were kept.

Jeremy immediately ran out through the north-end barn door. Ricky left his milk pail and ran the length of the barn to the shelf near Gabe. He quickly poured water into a mug and held it out to Enos.

Enos sat on the caked, dirty floor and spread his legs. "Sir, lean against me. Let me help you." He guided Gabe into a sitting position and braced the old man's head against his chest. "Ricky, kneel down here and hold the cup to help Gabe drink."

Gabe struggled to breathe, clutching his chest as he took a sip of water.

Enos said, "Hold on, Sir. Emma is on the way."

Ricky, the younger hand, turned to Enos. "What's happening to him?"

Enos shook his head. "Not sure. Could be his heart." He leaned forward, listening to Gabe's rasping breath. The old man's face twisted in anguish, his eyes mutely imploring Enos to help. Enos tried to take a breath to calm himself, but the foul barn odor made him cough. Gabe responded to Enos' movement and tried to right himself.

"Just relax, Sir. You're going to be fine. Emma should be here presently." He hefted Gabe up a few inches to a better sitting position.

Moments later, Emma burst into the barn, guided by Jeremy. She dropped to the dirty floor next to Gabe, and lifted the opened elixir bottle in front of him. "Gabe! I'm here. Do you want this?"

Glancing at the bottle, he shook his head. "Mother…no…" A deep rattle escaped his parched lips.

Emma gave Enos a frantic look as she set the medicine aside. "What is happening?"

Gabe grasped Emma's arm. "…heart…I think…" he wheezed. "…so…sorry…"

"Gabe Hopper, stay with me! Lord! Please don't let him die. Please!" Emma's tears erupted as she gripped Gabe's hand.

The memory of cradling Luke in a similar position after his friend was shot, flashed through Enos' mind as he supported Gabe's weight. "Sir, we're getting Doc Sweeney. Just rest easy." Sweat stood out on Enos' forehead despite the cold. "Jeremy, ride and get the doctor! Now!"

Jeremy nodded and ran out of the barn, following Enos' order.

Ricky moved to the opposite side of Gabe, bent, and offered another drink of water.

Gabe grimaced and squinted at Emma as a deep cough shook his body. Taking irregular, shallow breaths, with much effort, he gasped, "I…shall…"

Emma leaned closer to hear his whispers.

"…forever…" He gripped her hand.

"Shhhh, stay still."

"…protect thee…" His eyes fluttered shut.

Knowing Gabe was dying, Emma soothed him. "Thee shall soon be in the Lord's Kingdom, Father."

"…from evil…"

Emma gently placed her other hand on Gabe's chest.

Gabe's eyes flew open, and a smile crossed his bearded face as he stared at his wife. "…my love…" He exhaled a long, rattling breath, then his body went still.

She cradled her husband's head with both hands and gently kissed his lips. "I love thee, my dear, sweet man. May God take thee swiftly home." Emma let his head loll against Enos' chest. Weeping, Emma peered up at Enos and cried, "Ahhhh, God! How shall I survive without him?"

Enos gently touched Emma's back and bowed his head in sympathy, as she keened over her dead husband's still-warm body.

Emma's anguished sobs and the mournful lowing of the cows were the only sounds in the chill, dim barn.

EMMA

The mourners at Gabe's funeral had filled the Methodist church where Emma and Gabe had attended Sunday services. Emma was grateful her son, Adam and daughter-in-law, Mary, had been by her side during the overwhelming service and burial in the family plot. She worried because Gabe had renounced his belief in the Lord after Luke's death, Gabe's soul might not go to heaven. She could only pray he had been forgiven for his trespasses.

Enos Adams, their farm manager, had hired a new farm hand after Gabe's passing. Even with the new helper, Emma had taken on more of the farm chores. Those additional tasks were taking their toll on her aging body.

Now, having barely eaten any dinner, and still grieving Gabe's passing six months earlier, Emma sat at the kitchen table with the glow of the lantern and candle illuminating the exhaustion on her face. More bad news had been received by the family this day, and her heart was heavy. She dipped her quill into the inkwell and sighed. Murmuring aloud, she added another entry to her diary.

9 mo. 2nd, Wednesday, mid-evening, 1863

*We have received word our beloved grandson, Bernard, has succumbed
of his wounds, sustained on the 28th August of this year at the Battle of
Gettysburg. Mary is distraught, and the children, Martha and George, are
even more determined to get involved in this horrible conflict. May the
Good Lord shepherd Bernard to His Almighty Kingdom and reunite him
with his brother Brian, father Luke, and grandfather Gabe.*

Emma looked up from her writing to stare out the window into the
darkness, then wiped her eyes. *When will this horrible war finally end?*
Dipping her quill, she continued writing.

*'Tis such heartache and sorrow our family has endured in this cause to
free the slaves. Even though I miss him terribly, I am thankful Father is
not here to learn of this devastating news. He would be full of wrath and
anguish, should he have learned of Bernard's untimely fate.*

Emma rubbed her eyes, weary from crying and writing sorrow-laden
lines.

*When shall this never-ending Civil War be put to rest? How many more
of our brave young men must lose their lives? The slaves have been freed!
This must come to an end. Please, Dear Lord, I beseech Thee! Bring love
and peace to men's hearts on both sides of this battle, so our country can
heal these grievous wounds.*

As Emma gripped her quill, a gust of cold wind whipped past her,
fluttering the pages of the journal. The distinct pungent odor of the cow
barn permeated the air. The candle on the table snuffed out, leaving only a
wavering trail of smoke. Then the lantern flame danced violently, making
the shadows of objects jump and distort strangely on the far wall.

"Oh, my!" Emma exclaimed, falling back in her chair at the unexpected
disturbance. Folding her arms across her chest for warmth, she looked
around the kitchen for the source of the draft. Noting the window was
closed and the door to the anteroom was shut, her voice cracked as she
cried out, "What brings this chill wind?"

A sudden thud made her turn toward the stove and wooden counter,
the cold wind still swirling around her. To her amazement, the newly

tipped-over flour sack slid to the end of the counter and smashed to the floor, spreading a long, white swath in its wake.

Eyes wide, Emma gasped, drawing her hands to her mouth. "What is happening?" she cried. "What devil does inhabit my house and bring this evil?"

She watched in awe as the tea kettle rose and slammed against the iron stove, then rose and banged again. "Stop! I say be gone! Whatever thee is, leave my home!"

Then a wooden spoon and soup ladle lifted simultaneously from the stove, flew across the room in front of her, smashing into the wall, then clattered noisily to the floor.

Shaking, Emma bowed her head, clasped her hands, and began to pray loudly. "Oh, Dear Lord! What loathsome devil does enter my midst? Why is it here, and what does it want from me?" She gulped for breath. "What have I done to bring this wrath? I have forever remained Thy faithful servant and followed Thy will to do good on this earth. Please! I ask in Thy Holy Name—banish this angry demon from my home!"

Her heart thumping, Emma raised her head. The cold air swirling about her had subsided and warmed slightly, and the unusual odor she had smelled earlier was less noticeable. The lantern flame had stopped flickering. Peering around the kitchen through the gloomy light, she saw nothing moving. She finally exhaled, gripping the edge of the table.

Suddenly she felt a light pressure on her cheek, and a tingling warmth spread through her body. She touched her cheek gently and turned. It was then she noticed two familiar, worn rubber boot prints in the spilled flour.

Gabe's last words, *I shall forever protect thee from evil, my Love,* reverberated in her mind. A vanishingly faint echo of those words seemed to sound in the very air of the kitchen.

Emma's face flushed and her heartbeat quickened. She sighed, folded her hands and bowed her head. A small curl formed on her lips.

Then a single tear dropped onto her open diary page.

ROBBIE

HOPPER FAMILY FARM
FAIR HAVEN, VERMONT
SEPTEMBER, 1999

ROBBIE CONTEMPLATES

ROBBIE HUNG UP the phone after speaking with her daughter, DeeDee, and slumped back into her wingback chair. Her walker stood perched in front of her legs. Tears slowly rolled down her cheeks. She squeezed her right hand, trying to calm the violent tremor. *How can this be happening? Leave my house? How will I survive? It's the only place I've ever called home. Dear Lord, what will become of me now?*

Robbie's forehead wrinkled with effort as she turned in her chair to stare out the window into the big backyard. Tightening her lips to quell a sob, she raised her right hand a little. Try though she might to steady it, it still shook. Although her mind was still alert, she knew, to her great disappointment, at the age of eighty, her old body was failing her. *That old devil is winning the fight, and it makes me so damn mad!*

Losing her freedom and the thought of living the rest of her days in a cramped nursing home room terrified her. She'd been a strong, hard-working woman her entire life. It broke her heart to have to give up her independence and her home. She was eternally grateful she had had a special guardian angel in the house watching over her all these years. But as far as she knew, even this spirit hadn't been able to help her when she had fallen last year.

Watching the robins flit in the maple trees on this warm, late-summer day, she berated herself. *It was stupid, really—just a little lapse of concentration.*

She had just gotten out of bed with her cane in hand, and started to step down into the kitchen to make coffee. Her cane hit the leg of the chair next to the doorway, causing her to lose her balance. She stumbled, grabbing the chair as she felt herself going down. She landed on her side on the floor with a thump. A searing pain shot up her back. Her head bounced, and the chair landed on top of her.

Oh, no! Oh, dear. Oh, Jesus! Now what have I done?

She lay on the floor, gasping, waiting for her head to stop pounding, and tried to catch her breath. Her hands trembled uncontrollably from the stress of the fall. When she pushed the chair aside and tried to prop herself up, an excruciating pain shot from her left hip, across her back and down her leg, causing her to fall back. "Ahhhh! Dear Lord! Help me!"

Now what am I going to do? How am I going to get help? She couldn't reach the phone perched high on the kitchen wall. She had to think. *Who will check on me, and when? What day was it? Friday. The first Friday in September—Labor Day weekend.*

Ellie and her family had gone to the beach in Maine for the long weekend. Her next-door neighbors, Howard and Betty Greene, were gone to a Fiddlin' Contest at Craftsbury Commons in northern Vermont. And her dear friends, Lynn and Vince Granger, had taken their kids to Disney World in Florida. She wouldn't have any visitors until the ladies came to take her to church on Sunday.

How can I survive that long in this pain? And what will happen if I don't take my medication? Will the Parkinson's cause my body to seize up?

She was furious at herself for making such a stupid mistake and falling in her own kitchen. Slowly, she inched herself close enough to a kitchen chair, despite the sharp pains causing her to gasp for breath. She grabbed a seat cushion and slid it under her head. It made her a bit more comfortable, but not much.

She must have dozed off, because the sound of footsteps on the front porch jolted her awake. *The mailman.* "Help! Help me!" she cried, her voice hoarse. But with the main room and the closed screen and storm doors separating them, he didn't respond to her calls.

Robbie collapsed back onto the pillow, trying to catch her breath. Her throat was bone dry and she desperately wanted a drink of water. Then she remembered a trick her Mamma had taught her as a girl: if you were thirsty, suck on a button. She twisted and turned the top button of her pajama top until she could pull it loose, then popped it into her mouth and began to suck. Almost immediately saliva formed in her mouth, which she swished around and swallowed, bringing some relief to her aching throat. Feeling herself getting drowsy and not wanting to choke, she removed the button and set it on the floor where she could easily reach it again.

Gabe watches the elderly woman fall and knows she is badly injured. He positions himself in the upstairs bedroom facing the neighbors' house. Summoning his energy, he touches the lamp in front of the window so it shines brightly. When he releases his touch, the lamp winks out. *I hope someone will see the lamp flashing and come help.* Gabe continues his vigil, touching the lamp on and off throughout the day and night, hoping desperately someone will come to the fallen woman's aid.

When Robbie awoke again on the kitchen floor, it was dark. She didn't know what time it was because the clock was on the wall above the phone, behind her head. Then she realized she had to pee. She tried her best to hold it, but she felt a leak escape and drizzle down her bottom.

"Oh, dear Jesus, I don't want to wet myself. Please help me!" she prayed. The more she concentrated on holding her bladder, the worse the pressure got. Finally, the pain was more than she could bear, and she let her water go. She was humiliated at the thought of lying in her own wetness. She felt around the floor and found her button, popped it into her mouth and quenched her thirst temporarily.

I've endured a lot of pain and hardship in my life. I can get through this, too.

She pulled the button from her mouth, then shifted her position ever so slightly on the floor to take some of the pressure off her injured hip, and dozed off to dreams of her Mamma and Poppa, now gone from this life.

Birds chirping brought her out of her slumber and back to the sharp pain in her hip, as dawn lightened the kitchen window. Her stomach gurgled, and she felt her bowels rumble.

Oh, no! It's bad enough I've wet myself. I don't want those church ladies to find me wallowing in my own poop like some filthy old pig.

She squeezed hard, holding back the bowel movement, causing a sharp pain to shoot across her back. She popped the button in her mouth, giving her something to concentrate on besides the pain.

She had lain on the floor, drifting in and out of consciousness, for another whole day and night. At one point, she had thought she heard the mailman on the porch again, but was too weak to cry for help.

Why has no one responded to my signal? She is in terrible pain and I wish there was more I could do to help her. In frustration Gabe moves to the bedroom to the left of the stairs with windows facing the street. Although his energy has weakened considerably, he continues his vigil of flicking a lamp on and off. *Someone passing by must see the lights!*

Voices and footsteps on the porch awoke Robbie from dazed near-sleep.

"Yoo-hoo? Robbie? You ready for church?" a woman shouted, as the front doors opened.

"Help me!" Robbie croaked, her voice harsh.

"Robbie? Where are you?" She heard footsteps crossing the main room.

"Kitchen. Help!" She saw her church friend Mildred's face hover above her.

"Oh God, Robbie! What happened? You all right?" she asked, eyes wide.

"No…my hip! Can't get up…call ambulance."

"Oh, my God! Sure, hold on! I'll call right now," Mildred said as she bustled to the wall and grabbed the phone.

Mildred's adult daughter, Sandra, sat on the floor next to Robbie and held her hand. She noticed the stain on Robbie's pajama bottoms and saw the wet puddle oozing from beneath her. "Robbie, when did you fall?"

"Friday. Tripped over my cane…mad at myself." Her throat was so dry, she could barely get the words out.

"You've been lying here since Friday? Oh, Robbie, I'm so sorry! We should've checked on you," Sandra said, looking aghast.

"Thirsty…water!"

Sandra went to the sink, poured a half-full glass of water, and tipped Robbie's head slightly so she could drink. The cool water was like honey on her cracked lips and raw throat.

A short time later the paramedics arrived, started an IV drip, stabilized Robbie on the floor, and gently transferred her to the stretcher. Before they carried her out, she asked, "Mildred, Ellie is on vacation but will you call her on Monday and let her know I'm in the hospital?"

The damage to her hip had been so severe the surgeons had performed a total hip replacement surgery. That was more than a year ago. She had been in the hospital for five days, then was sent to a nursing home for three months of rehabilitation. After her temporary internment, she was not looking forward to spending the rest of her days in confinement.

Propping herself up in her wingback chair, Robbie's gaze rested on the big plot of land to the left of the house. She had tended a vegetable garden here every summer and canned the harvest to feed herself and DeeDee through the winter. She remembered the fragrant aroma of the old lilac bushes blooming every spring with purple and white blossoms. She loved to place bouquets around the house, filling the space with their heady perfume for weeks.

Surrounding the house were several tall sugar maples, just now tinged with the first signs of fall color. Beyond the lilac bushes, three ancient apple trees, barely surviving, still produced small, wormy McIntoshes every September.

She stared farther into the back field, and thought about the small, wild strawberries that grew there in the early summer. It was always a great day when she and DeeDee would take their bowls, crawl along the ground, and gather the harvest. Sometimes they'd have enough berries to make jam, but usually they'd just eat them, still warm from the summer sun, with sugar and cream.

How she missed those days spending precious time with her youngest daughter, the only one she had actually raised to adulthood. Circumstances in life had forced her to make heartbreaking decisions about what she thought would be best for each of her three older girls. She wished her life had turned out differently, and she could have raised each of them as their full-time mother. How wonderful that would have been.

Directly behind the house, Robbie saw the old two-story hay barn, listing to its right, like a ship wrecked on an unseen sand bar. She envisioned the old farm implements hanging from the walls and stacked willy-nilly in the side bins. The floor of the barn was overloaded with broken-down farm equipment, furniture, boxes, old appliances, and other items discarded over the years. The barn, part of the original Hopper farm, was built sturdily with hand-hewn timber, and supported heavy slate roof tiles. She felt bad DeeDee would have such a big job ahead of her cleaning out the mess. All she had wanted to do was lend a helping hand to her neighbors, when she had let them store their belongings in the barn.

The warm, late afternoon sun streamed through the window as Robbie dozed off in her easy chair, dreaming of her Mamma and Poppa.

SCRIBNER FAMILY FARM
MONTICELLO, MAINE
MAY, 1930

POPPA FRANK

THE DEEP, DRY, HACKING COUGH of Poppa Frank penetrated the thin wall of the bedroom, keeping Robbie awake. She heard the gentle mumblings of her mother, probably giving him a drink of water to soothe his throat. Worried Poppa's illness wasn't getting better, she didn't know what would happen to her family if he died.

Robbie shifted her position on the mattress she shared with her two younger sisters, Gladys and Phyllis, sleeping head to toe, trying not to wake them. Two of her younger brothers, Paul and Frank Jr., snoring loudly, shared a bed on the other side of the room. The third bedroom was occupied by her older siblings, Pauline, Marjorie, and Howard.

She was born Robena Vera Madeline, the sixth child out of eleven to Frank Scribner of Dutch descent, and Alvarette Flewelling of Irish descent. Sleeping arrangements were cramped in the small, three-bedroom house on their potato farm in northern Maine, along the Canadian border.

Favoring Poppa's side of the family who were tall and lanky, Robbie had experienced a growth spurt recently and would soon reach her adult height of five-foot-nine inches. On her Mamma's Irish side of the family, Robbie had inherited her thick, unruly, deep red hair and green eyes. Her fair skin was covered with freckles, which she hated because she thought it made her look like a leopard. Being the only girl inheriting her mother's red hair until baby Helen was born, she always thought she was Poppa's favorite daughter, because she resembled her mother.

Poppa had been sick on and off all winter with this cough, chills, and fever. The country was grappling with the effects of the Great Depression and Robbie, now fourteen, had left school two years earlier to work on the family farm and help care for her younger siblings.

She carefully slid off the mattress so as not to not wake her sisters, donned a ratty robe and worn slippers, then tiptoed into the main room. Here were the kitchen, with a wood-fired cook stove, the only heat source in the house; the dining table and chairs; several worn, stuffed armchairs; her mother's weaving loom; a pedal sewing machine; and an old sofa. There, snoring like a freight train, was her oldest brother, Wilmot, now twenty-four. Hanging on the wall above the sofa was a faded painting of Jesus at the Last Supper. Poppa would gather the family in front of this picture every evening to say prayers before bedtime.

The floorboard creaked as Robbie opened the door of the stove to add more wood to take off the early morning chill. She tucked her feet beneath her nightgown as she sank into an armchair and wrapped a blanket around her shoulders. *I love Poppa so much. I so wish he'd get better. I don't know what's going to happen if he dies, and we have to go on the dole!*

Poppa Frank's deep voice echoed in her mind.

Those damned bums on the dole are nothing but a bunch of sinners! The Lord said it's a man's duty to care for his family and a mortal sin to take charity from others. When you've got two good hands you can do an honest day's labor. God will punish those bums, you mark my words. They'll burn in hell with fire and brimstone for their lazy and slothful ways!

The cries of baby Helen came through the wall of her parents' room. Then Robbie heard her Mamma singing faintly, putting the baby back to sleep,

> *Lul-la-by and good night*
> *Thy mother's delight*
> *Bright angels beside*
> *My darling abide.*
> *Lay thee down now and rest*
> *May thy slumber be blessed*
> *Lay thee down now and rest*
> *May thy slumber be blessed.*

The creaking of the baby cradle continued for several minutes, then the door to her parents' room opened with a light squeak. Robbie watched her

Mamma, shoulders hunched, frail and tired, looking much older than her forty-three years, as she quietly closed the door and pushed straggling gray hair from her face. When Alvarette turned toward the kitchen, her eyes widened as she noticed Robbie watching her from the chair.

"Oh, Robbie. I didn't see you there, Honey," she whispered. "What are you doing up at this hour?"

"I couldn't sleep because of Poppa's coughing," Robbie replied quietly.

Alvarette nodded, making her way to the kitchen. She poured water from a pitcher on the counter into a tea kettle, and set it on the stove to heat. She motioned to Robbie to come to the table. "Come sit with me."

Robbie arose, blanket wrapped around her shoulders, and carefully bypassed Wilmot's body sprawled on the sofa, then sat next to her mother. "Mamma, is Poppa gonna die?" She swallowed hard to suppress her anguish.

"I don't know, Honey. The doctor says he's very ill."

"If he dies, will we have to go on the dole?" Her voice trembled. "Poppa says those damned bums on the dole are a bunch of sinners and are going to burn in hell. I don't want to burn in hell!"

Alvarette touched her daughter's hand. "Oh, Robbie. I'm sure the good Lord will provide for our family, and we won't burn in hell."

"I don't want Poppa to die, Mamma. What are we going to do?" Robbie said, as tears started down her cheeks.

"Shush now, Honey," Alvarette said as she leaned over and hugged her. "I'm sure we'll manage somehow."

Alvarette poured them both a cup of tea, took Robbie's hand, bowed her head, and prayed aloud for her husband to get well. By their second cup of tea the other children had straggled into the kitchen, jostling one another for a place at the table. Wilmot awoke, grumbling at the noise. He plopped down at the farthest end of the table and ran his fingers through his tangled hair. Mamma fixed a pot of porridge to feed her brood, and the pungent aroma of cinnamon flooded the room. Robbie helped the younger ones get dressed, then changed the diapers of baby Helen, now eighteen months old. The firstborn sister, Mae, supposedly died at the age of three before Robbie was born, but no one ever talked about her.

It was a cool, overcast morning, with winter's chill lingering on the breeze as Robbie guided her younger brothers and sisters to the road toward school. Then she followed her older siblings to the barn, where they collected bags of potato spuds, and walked into the furrowed rows ready for planting. Robbie made her way to the row where she had left off the previous day, and continued the tedious job of placing starters about two feet apart. She lost herself in daydreams of someday becoming a nurse, so she could save her beloved Poppa. She mumbled a prayer to herself. *Dear Lord, please don't let my Poppa die. I love him so much, and don't want to go on the dole and burn in hell!*

As the day warmed, Robbie removed her heavy jacket and continued planting. She was a considerable distance from the barn when she heard the dinner bell ringing, but it wasn't yet time for the noon meal. As she straightened up to stretch her back, she saw Doctor Riley's black Model A Ford parked in front of the house. Her oldest brother, Wilmot, was waving his arms and yelling something from the barn.

Something's happened to Poppa! A sickening feeling hit the pit of Robbie's stomach, and her legs started to shake. She willed herself to run, but could only stand rooted to the spot, afraid to know the truth. When she heard her brother calling her name, she forced herself to slog through the muddy field toward the house.

Before she could reach the door, Wilmot wrapped her in his arms. She struggled to free herself. "Robbie, Robbie, Poppa's dead," he told her.

"Oh, no! He can't be dead! I want to go see him," she screamed, sobs racking her thin body.

She struggled to get away, but Wilmot held her tight. "You can't go in there, Robbie. Mamma's in there now, helping Dr. Riley with Poppa's body. They'll bring him out when they're ready."

Robbie cried uncontrollably, shaking in her brother's arms. Her worst fears had come true—her beloved Poppa was gone, and they would have to go on the dole. "Oh, Dear Lord! Why did you let him die?" she wailed. "I asked you to save him, but you didn't. It's not fair!" *What am I going to do without Poppa? How will we survive? We're all doomed to burn in hell!*

Pauline and Marjorie, her older sisters, came out of the house with Marjorie holding baby Helen. Her other older brother, Howard, followed them into the yard. Pauline directed Howard to run to the schoolhouse and bring the younger children home. He took off running along the muddy road.

Facing her sisters, Robbie said, "Did you see him? Why can't I go in? I'm grown-up, too!" She lunged for the door, only to be yanked back by Wilmot.

Pauline, her oldest sister hissed, "Robbie! You quiet down now! They don't need you in there. They'll be out soon."

Slipping from Wilmot's grasp, Robbie collapsed to the ground, put her head in her hands and sobbed. Her next younger brother, Paul, kneeled and put his arm around her shoulder for comfort. Within a few minutes, Howard returned, leading the younger siblings to the farmhouse. Robbie stood as the family gathered, forlorn, in the front yard.

Pauline, the oldest, gave them the news. "Poppa's gone to be with the Lord. Let us gather hands and pray," she commanded as the children shuffled in closer. The girls cried, but the boys were stoic, as their Poppa had taught them. "Dear Lord, please take our Poppa Frank to your eternal Kingdom and give our Mamma strength to take care of our family. We pray this in Your name, Amen."

"And don't make us go on the dole, Lord!" Robbie added.

"Now Robbie, you shush up!" Pauline scolded. "Stop being a trouble-maker!"

The front door opened, and Doctor Riley called Wilmot to help. Moments later, the two men emerged carrying the sheet-draped body of Poppa Frank. Alvarette followed, wiping her eyes with her hanky.

Robbie pleaded. "I want to see him. Please let me see him one last time."

The doctor nodded and Wilmot pulled the sheet from his face as the other siblings looked on. Robbie stared at her Poppa's longish hair, prematurely white for his forty-five years. Usually clean-shaven, the growth of gray beard on his thin face made him almost unrecognizable.

Robbie bent over and kissed his forehead. "I love you, Poppa," she said, trying to etch his face into her mind forever.

Paul opened the back door of the doctor's car, and Frank's body was folded gently onto the seat. Alvarette, her mussed hair hanging in her face, stood in the yard silently weeping as her children gathered round her.

"I'll be back tomorrow to discuss funeral arrangements with you, Mrs. Scribner," Dr. Riley said. He reached over and hugged her. "I'm so sorry. Frank was a good man."

As Robbie watched Doctor Riley drive away with her Poppa's body, she imagined she felt the fires of hell licking at her heels.

MAMMA ALVARETTE

In mid-September, just four months after Poppa's death, the family was pushing to get the potato crop harvested before the weather turned cold. Robbie was doing the back-breaking work of picking potatoes and filling bushel barrels her brothers loaded into a mule-drawn wagon. The price of a bushel had dropped again this year due to the Depression. Robbie fretted as she watched her brothers wend their way to the barn. *I hope we get a good price for the harvest, or we'll all starve to death this winter.*

The simple pine box they had buried Poppa Frank in took most of their savings, and they had been struggling all summer to put food on the table. Robbie noticed her mother getting pale and thinner, and heard her deep, hacking cough at night, the same as Poppa's had been. She didn't want to think about what would happen to her family if Mamma died, too. She had been praying, but she wasn't sure how much good it did, since her prayers hadn't saved Poppa. The fear of going on the dole was never far from her mind.

A week later, Robbie and her siblings were at her mother's bedside as she was dying of consumption, the affliction she had contracted from Frank.

Robbie sobbed as Alvarette took her hand. "Robbie, you're a big girl now," she whispered. "I want you to look after the young'uns. I know you can take care of the kids and get them off to school." A deep, rattling cough shook her frail body.

"No Mamma! I don't want you to go," Robbie cried. "I don't want to take care of the kids. I want you here! I love you, Mamma. Please don't die on me!"

"Now Robbie, don't you be sassing back," her older sister Marjorie reprimanded. "You know Pauline and I gotta work the farm, so you gotta take care of the young'uns like Mamma said."

"Honey, the Lord is taking me to be with your Poppa, so don't you worry about me." Alvarette took a shallow breath as she held in another cough. "You do as I tell you. I'm counting on you, my sweet Robbie. Now promise me you'll do it."

Robbie dropped her head to her mother's chest and sobbed as Mamma put her thin arms around her daughter and hugged her. "Okay, I promise, Mamma. I'll take care of them!" Robbie kissed her mother's forehead and ran from the room, too distraught to stay any longer.

Her worst fears had come true; they were now orphans, having lost both parents within mere months of each other. *What will happen to us now? Will we all be sinners and burn in hell if we have to go on the dole? If we can't stay together, where will we go?* The only family member she knew was her Uncle George, her father's brother, who had a potato farm down-country. But he had a big family too, and couldn't take them all in. She feared the thought of going to Uncle George's, because she couldn't face her older cousin, Leroy, after the terrible thing he had done to her when she was nine. Leroy had threatened that if she ever told anyone, he would hurt baby Helen. To protect her sister, Robbie had cleaned up the blood as best as she could and explained away the bruises to her mother by saying she had fallen down.

The congregation did their best to chip in for Alvarette's pine-box coffin, and the undertaker took their offering as full payment. She was buried next to her husband, Frank, on September 26, 1930, aged forty-three. Her epitaph read: *A fine Irish lass who loved God and family.*

To Robbie's dismay, the harvest sold for forty cents a barrel, while just two years earlier they had earned fifteen dollars a barrel. It was a devastating blow for the family. All of them together wouldn't survive the winter; she knew they would have to be split up. A week after the harvest was sold, Uncle George came to visit, accompanied by Pastor Pelletier. The four younger children plus Robbie were sent off to their rooms, while Uncle George and the pastor gathered at the table with the older siblings— Wilmot, Pauline, Marjorie, and Howard.

Robbie tried to listen to the mumbled conversations through the door of her room, but couldn't make out the details. They were trying to figure out what to do with the kids, and she was angry they hadn't included her in the decision. *Dear Lord, please don't send me away from my family. I promised Mamma to take care of the children and I can't break my promise to her!* Her fate rested in the hands of others.

The next morning, her oldest brother Wilmot, weather-worn and haggard for his twenty-four years, gathered the family around the table for a meeting. No one had made breakfast, and their faces were glum. Robbie, scared and shaking, held fretful baby Helen in her lap, and worried about their fate.

"You know we're orphans," Wilmot began. "And we didn't get nearly enough from the harvest to feed all of us for the winter." Everyone was silent as they stared, waiting for him to continue. Wilmot ran a calloused hand through his tangled hair. "We either have to go on the dole or break up the family. And you know how Poppa felt about being on the dole. He'd rather have us all burn in hell first!" He sighed. "So, for all of us to survive, we'll need to split up."

Robbie's stomach lurched.

"Here's what we've decided to do. Pauline, Howard, Marjorie and I are going to stay and work the farm," Wilmot continued. "Robbie, you and Gladys are going to stay with Mamma's sister, Jeannette, in South Boston. She has small kids, and you and Gladys can help take care of them. The

Thornton family in town offered to take Phyllis and baby Helen. Pastor Pelletier has already made the arrangements." He paused, looking at the grim faces. "Frank Jr. and Paul will live with Uncle George and his family. Uncle George said he'll get the boys in school down-country, and put them to work on his farm. When they're old enough, they can come back and help with our fields."

"But Wilmot," Robbie cried, "Mamma told me to take care of the little ones and I promised her I would. I can't break my promise to her! You can't send them away!"

Pauline gave Robbie a withering look. "Robbie, that's enough out of you. We have to make difficult decisions that are best for everyone. You just want to cause trouble and I've had enough of it. Now be quiet!" Robbie hugged whimpering baby Helen to her chest as the rebuke of her eldest sister washed over her.

Wilmot touched her arm, trying to soothe her. "I'm so sorry, Robbie, but the decision has been made. I know you want to honor your promise to Mamma, but there's nothing else we can do."

Robbie felt desolate. She had heard of Mamma's younger sister Jeannette, but had never met her. All she knew was Jeannette had four boys, and her husband, Seamus, worked at the docks in South Boston. Robbie packed the few clothes that still fit her into a clean flour sack and helped her sister Gladys, two years her junior, do the same.

At the last minute, Robbie remembered the lovely pendant her Mamma used to wear on special occasions, and decided she wanted to keep it. She quietly entered her parents' room, which was still full of her mother's belongings. Her tears welled as she stepped to her mother's jewelry box, perched on top of her chest of drawers. In the bottom drawer of the box, wrapped in a small square of white linen, was an ornately carved ivory cameo necklace. Robbie lifted it gently and held it to her chest.

"I'll keep this forever, Mamma, so you will always be next to my heart," she whispered. She closed the drawer, took a deep breath, and with one more look around the room, said a silent farewell. She'd never be back here again, the only place she'd ever known as home.

Pastor Pelletier, who had paid for their bus tickets, waited in his car to drive Robbie and Gladys thirteen miles to Houlton, where the girls would board the first of several buses to reach South Boston. The sisters hugged their siblings outside the house.

Robbie dropped to her knees and pulled her younger sisters, Phyllis and Helen, to her. "You remember what Mamma taught you now. You mind your manners and don't sass back."

Phyllis nodded in agreement, crying, and clung hard to Robbie.

Robbie kissed both sisters on the cheek. "I love you! Don't you ever forget!"

Heartbroken to leave their family, she and Gladys climbed into the backseat and waved goodbye, as the car rumbled down the dirt driveway, taking them to an uncertain future.

Boston

October, 1932

BUMS ON THE DOLE

ROBBIE TRIED TO IGNORE the four boys wrestling and grunting at her feet as she peered out the front window of the two-bedroom brownstone on East 3rd Street in South Boston. A stiff ocean breeze blew the fall leaves along the narrow lane on that October evening in 1932. She noticed a figure slumped against the wind making his way along the sidewalk. Her Uncle Seamus, in his mid-thirties, exhausted from working at the docks all day, slowly pulled himself up the steep staircase. The porch lantern cast a harsh shadow on his lined, grimy face, and his torn, greasy trousers. Before reaching the door, he pulled off his cap and ran bloodstained fingers through his snarled hair.

As the door opened, the boys stopped their fighting and ran to their father. "Daddy! Daddy! Come play with us!" They hugged his legs and grabbed his arms, halting his progress.

Seamus bent and hugged his boys, giving them each a wan smile. "Not now, boys. Daddy's tired and needs to sit down." Removing his worn boots, he dropped into a sagging easy chair. "Where's your mother?" he asked his eldest son.

Just then, Robbie's Aunt Jeannette, wearing a stained apron, made her way from the kitchen. She sidestepped the mattress tucked into the corner of the living room where Robbie and Gladys slept, and stopped next to Seamus. She bent and kissed his cheek. "You look exhausted. Tough day?" She lightly grasped his hand.

Seamus rubbed his aching shoulder. "You have no idea. Can you get me a drink?"

"Sure, give me a minute." Jeannette disappeared into the kitchen.

Robbie rose from her window perch and motioned to Gladys, who was picking up toys on the opposite side of the room. "Let's go boys," Robbie said. "Leave your father alone now and let him have some peace." Robbie and Gladys herded the rambunctious siblings into their room, then shut the door. Then the two girls returned to the cramped living room, and sat on the sofa across from Seamus.

Robbie, now sixteen, stared at her disheveled uncle, remembering the last two years of living with his family. Money was tight, and even though Seamus still had a job working at the docks, his paycheck never stretched far enough for a family of eight. So each day Aunt Jeannette and her four boys, along with Robbie and Gladys, stood in line for hours at the soup kitchen run by St. Brigid's Parish on East Broadway, two blocks from their brownstone.

On her first trip to the soup kitchen, Robbie had been shocked to see *those damned bums on the dole,* as Poppa had called them. An old man, in a shabby overcoat and floppy hat, emerged from the soup kitchen, gnawing a chunk of bread in his toothless mouth. A younger man, wearing a tattered Red Sox cap, stepped out of line in front of them and hit the old man in the head, knocking him to the ground. Robbie had cringed at seeing the violence and squeezed Gladys' hand.

The downed man had grasped the bread with both hands, kicking at his assailant, trying to roll away. The younger man yelled and kicked the old man in his side, causing him to howl in pain. The old man curled into a fetal position, protecting his precious bread. The crowd hooted and hollered, cheering the attacker. Another man jumped out of line and kicked the old man in the face, breaking his nose which gushed blood, knocking him unconscious. The two men wrestled the old man's arms apart, grabbed the bit of bread, and sprinted down the street as the cops chased after them. Several women ran to the old man on the ground and tried to revive him.

Dispirited, Robbie watched the old man get beat up over a just a morsel. She could understand how the attackers would burn in hell.

But what about all the women and children who are in line just like us? Will God make them burn in hell, too? Is it a sin to be hungry? Is it horrible to accept charity from others, like Poppa said? She didn't have the answers, but her stomach had gurgled, and all she had known was she was terribly hungry.

Aunt Jeannette brought a drink to Seamus, then sat on the torn sofa between Robbie and Gladys. "We were able to get a little extra meat today. So we'll have a decent supper tonight." She waved her hand toward the kitchen.

Seamus took a big drink of rum, then swallowed with a grimace. Robbie thought he seemed to stare right through Jeannette, and she was worried. *How will we survive if Uncle Seamus loses his job? Will we have to live like bums on the street?*

The drink seemed to revive Seamus, and he sat up a little straighter. He stared at his wife, then turned his attention to Robbie. "I was talking with one of the ship owners today. His name is Kostas. He mentioned to me his wife could use some help with their kids. I guess she has a bum leg." Seamus paused and sipped his drink. "Robbie, I think it would be a good job for you."

Robbie sat stunned and speechless, her heart thumping.

Aunt Jeannette, her long, red hair hanging in tendrils around her face, responded. "But, Seamus, Robbie and Gladys are caring for *our* boys. And they're family!"

Seamus ran a hand over his head. "I know. I'm sorry." He dropped his gaze, then looked back at Robbie. "But I just can't afford to feed all of us. Robbie could make a little extra money, and Gladys can stay with our boys. What do you think, Robbie?"

Robbie gathered her thoughts and glared at her uncle. "I don't want to leave Gladys here alone." She remembered her promise to her Mamma to take care of her younger sister, now fourteen.

Seamus nodded. "I understand. But we're family, and we'll take care of Gladys. Kostas' wife, Maria, has a bad leg that was injured in an earthquake in Greece when she was young. They have three girls, and you'd be a great help to her. Plus, you could live with them."

I hate to leave Gladys. But I guess I could make a little money to help the family. And I could still honor my promise to Mamma by caring for their daughters.

"Okay, I guess—if you want me to. As long as you promise Gladys will be taken care of, I'll do it for you, Uncle Seamus." Robbie was not at all certain she had made the right decision.

The following Sunday afternoon, after returning from church, Robbie gathered her spare belongings in a satchel. After bidding farewell to Gladys and the family, she and Seamus boarded the local bus for the one-and-a-half-mile ride to Telegraph Hill in Dorchester Heights. Staring out the bus window, Robbie watched the neighborhoods change from the tightly packed brownstones where they lived, to small separate homes, then to manicured lawns and what she considered stately mansions. Her heart pounded. She had never seen such lovely homes in her entire life. *Is this where I'm going to live? Oh, my!* She followed Seamus off the bus, then they walked a block north and stopped.

"Here we are," Seamus said, reading the address from a slip of paper. A walkway led through the large front lawn to the wide veranda. The white clapboard two-story house stared back at Robbie. They climbed to the front door and Seamus knocked. The porch rocking chairs creaked in the fall breeze.

Moments later the door opened and Robbie got her first glimpse of Kostas Tsoukanis. He had a slim but muscular build and was about Robbie's height. His light brown hair swept back from his face, touching the back of his shoulders. He was dressed in a white button-down shirt, and gray trousers. His azure eyes had a twinkle as he greeted them with hearty laugh.

"Seamus! Welcome to my home!" He patted her uncle's shoulder, then turned toward her. "And you must be Robbie. It's wonderful to meet you." Kostas shook her hand. "Please come in!" He held the door as Robbie followed Seamus into the foyer.

Directly in front of them was a great room with a high ceiling. Furniture groupings separated different sections of the room. Robbie noticed three child-sized rocking chairs and a blackboard in the far-left corner. An adult-sized rocking chair sat nearby. Dolls, books, and other toys were splayed on the floor. Robbie smiled. *The children's corner. How nice.*

To her right, Robbie saw a door leading to a formal dining room. She could just see one end of a heavy oak table surrounded by three chairs. On the opposite end of the dining room was a closed door, which Robbie assumed led to the kitchen. At the back of the great room, a staircase led to the second floor, where Robbie supposed the bedrooms were located. She had never been in such a large, beautiful house before, and she couldn't help but stare in awe.

Kostas led them to an area with a sofa, coffee table and matching armchairs. "Here, please take a seat. I'll let Maria know you are here." Then he disappeared into the kitchen.

Robbie carefully sat on the sofa, not wanting to get anything dirty, and dropped her satchel on the floor.

Seamus sat in a facing armchair and grinned at her. "See, Robbie, this isn't so bad, now is it? I think you'll do fine here and will be well cared for."

Robbie felt overwhelmed being in such an opulent home. "I don't know, Uncle Seamus. What if they don't like me? I don't know anything about caring for rich folks." *And what if they kick me out on the street, and I become a homeless bum?*

A few minutes later Kostas held the kitchen door open, and Robbie watched Maria enter the room. She had a petite build and wore a flowered dress dropping just below her knees. Her thick, curly brown hair swirled in a mass around her shoulders. As Maria limped across the room, Robbie couldn't help but stare at the heavy, black metal brace wrapped around her lower left leg. It appeared to be attached to a special shoe with a thick sole. *How horrible it must be to live with that every day.*

Robbie and Seamus both rose to greet the woman. She turned to Seamus, "I'm Maria, and I am so glad you are here!"

Robbie was immediately smitten with Maria's quick smile and her red lipstick glowing in the afternoon light.

Maria gripped Robbie's hand. "You must be Robbie." She looked up at Robbie with her dark eyes. "My, you are a tall girl, aren't you? And I just love your red hair!"

Robbie blushed.

"Please, take a seat," Maria said, as Kostas guided her to an armchair, then helped her swing her legs onto an ottoman. Maria smiled at Seamus and Robbie. "I'm more comfortable with my legs up. I hope you don't mind."

Robbie shook her head.

Kostas touched Maria's shoulder. "I'll be right back with tea."

Maria peered up at her husband. "Thank you, Dear."

They must be very much in love, Robbie thought as she watched Maria and Kostas together. They reminded her of her Mamma and Poppa when they were younger, and she silently felt their loss.

"So, tell me about yourself," Maria said to Robbie.

"Well, I—"

Seamus interrupted. "Robbie's parents passed away about two years ago. With ten siblings still living on their potato farm in Maine, they couldn't manage to keep the family together. So Robbie and her sister Gladys moved in with our family and have been caring for our boys. My wife, Jeannette and Robbie's mother, Alvarette, were sisters."

A look of concern crossed Maria's face. "Oh, I'm so sorry to hear about your parents, Robbie. That must have been terribly hard on you to lose them."

Grief flooded Robbie as she thought about her beloved parents' deaths and having to leave her family behind. Unable to respond, she nodded and dropped her gaze.

"Oh, gosh! I didn't mean to upset you. I'm so sorry," Maria said kindly, her face stricken.

Just then Kostas returned and set a tea tray, which included a plate of cookies, on the coffee table. He poured four cups and passed each with a saucer to his visitors. Robbie admired the delicate, pastel flower design on the fine china.

Maria focused her gaze on Robbie. "You can see I have a bad leg, so it is difficult for me to get up and down the stairs. I could use your help getting the girls bathed and into bed, then getting them dressed in the morning." She waved her hand toward the stairs. "And of course, I would love your help in the kitchen!" Maria grinned, her lipstick gleaming.

Robbie nodded. "I think I can do that. And I can help you clean, too. I'm really good at cleaning!"

"Yes, that would be a great help as well, if you don't mind," Maria said, her eyes sparkling.

Kostas rose. "I'll go round up the girls and bring them down." He walked to the back of the room and climbed the stairs.

Robbie stared at the wall paintings, then turned to Maria. "You have a beautiful home! I've never seen anything like it."

Maria followed Robbie's gaze. "Thank you. We have been very fortunate with our family business, even in these tough times. Kostas' father, Constantine, owns two trading ships. An old friend of his from Greece captains one ship to and from Europe. And Kostas' brother, Theo, is the captain of the other, which travels to the West Indies." She sipped her tea. "Constantine and Kostas manage the loading and unloading of the ships at the dock."

Seamus added, "And that's how I met Kostas, when I was unloading one of his ships. We started talking about our children, and Kostas mentioned you could use some help with your daughters. Because our boys are getting older, we thought Gladys could manage alone, and Robbie might be of help to you."

Maria smiled. "I thank you, Seamus. I'm sure Robbie will be a blessing to our entire family!"

The sound of children's voices got everyone's attention. Three young girls, adorned in their Sunday dresses, came bounding down the stairs. Robbie's heart leaped. *Oh, how I miss my younger sisters. I hope they are being well cared for.*

In the main room, the three sisters stood holding hands next to Maria, grinning at their visitors. Seamus returned to his seat and sipped his tea.

Maria pointed to each girl as she introduced them. "This is Elena, and she's seven." Elena made a slight curtsy. "This is Grace, who is five." Grace waved at Robbie. "And this is our little one, Isis, who is two and a half." Her chubby cheeks were rosy red.

Maria extended her arm toward Robbie. "Girls, this is your new nanny, Robbie."

Robbie's heart ached for her baby sister, Helen. Holding a hand toward Isis, Robbie asked, "May I hold her?"

Maria nodded. "Of course!"

Robbie stood and reached out to Isis. "Can I give you some love?" The little girl grinned and nodded. Robbie lifted the child and sat back onto the sofa and cradled Isis in one arm.

Isis began playing with Robbie's long braid. "Hair! Hair!" she exclaimed. Everyone laughed.

Kostas stood and took Isis from Robbie's arms. "Girls, will you show Robbie to her room?"

"Sure, Daddy." Elena grasped Robbie's hand. "C'mon!"

MY room? I have my own room?

Robbie grabbed her satchel and followed Elena and Grace up the staircase. At the top, a hallway ran the length of the house. The girls turned left and opened the last door at the back of the house. Robbie stepped in and saw a small room with a single bed covered by a lavender flowered bedspread. A nightstand and lamp were positioned next to it. Against one wall were a four-drawer dresser and a chair. Peering out the small window, she looked down onto their big backyard. A four-seater swingset shaded by tall pines looked inviting. Because there were no fences, she spotted children playing in the yards of their neighbors.

To Robbie, her room was a little slice of heaven. It was the first time in her life she ever had a bedroom to call her own.

It wasn't long before Robbie learned to prepare Maria's favorite Greek dishes. She worked hard cooking, cleaning, and caring for their three girls, who were much more well-behaved than Aunt Jeannette's boys.

Robbie was paid five dollars a week. And she diligently gave two of those hard-earned dollars to her aunt and uncle, so their family would not end up as homeless bums on the dole.

TAXI DANCER

It was early afternoon on a cold, blustery day in late January, 1933. Robbie had just put Isis down for a nap, Elena was attending school, and Maria was in the kitchen making a pie. Robbie sat in the big rocking chair in the children's corner, and pulled five-year-old Grace onto her lap. Just as Robbie began reading a children's book aloud, the front door flew open, causing her to jump.

Kostas stormed through the door and slammed it behind him.

Robbie stopped reading and stared at Kostas' pained face. She hugged Grace a little tighter.

"Maria!" Kostas called, his voice booming off the high ceiling.

Moments later, Maria emerged through the kitchen door, and limped to her husband. "What is it? What's wrong, Kostas?" Taking his coat, she hung it in the closet, then sat in her chair.

After quickly removing his winter boots, Kostas pulled a chair next to Maria and held up the front page of the *Boston Globe.* "Look at this!" He read the headline. "*Boston Charlie Whacked!*"

Maria put a hand to her mouth, her eyes wide. "Oh, no, Kostas! What happened?"

Kostas' hands shook as he read the article. "It says, *Bullets sang the requiem of Cocoanut Grove owner Charles 'King' Solomon yesterday and wiped forever from his face the smile that thousands knew.*" He paused to silently read more, then summarized, "Apparently he was supposed to testify in federal court tomorrow."

Maria's brow furrowed. "Do they think the Feds killed him? That can't be right!"

"No, no! It was the damned Italians who whacked him. He was at the Cocoanut Grove, then went with some friends to the Cotton Club." Kostas rubbed his glum face. "Looks like some thugs followed him into the bathroom. The paper says, *Witnesses reported hearing an argument about a 'double-crossing, no good rat,' with Solomon saying something to the effect of, 'You got my roll, now what do you want?' The reply: 'You've had this coming for a long time.' Shots rang out. The men looked like Italian Americans who applied the multiple shots to Solomon's chest, abdomen and neck, as Solomon staggered out. 'The rats got me,' he grunted before being rushed to the hospital, where he died.*"

Kostas ran his fingers through his hair, sighed, and stared at Maria.

Maria touched her husband's trembling hand. "I'm so sorry, Kostas. I know you were friends, and had an exclusive deal with Charlie to deliver your rum to the Grove. Now what are you doing to do?"

Kostas shook his head. "I don't know. Depends on who takes over for him. But it wasn't just my rum deliveries to the Grove. Charlie also greased the skids with Mayor Tobin to keep the Feds from inspecting my ships. Without Charlie's graft, and with the Italians moving in on his territory, I'm at a much greater risk for my rum to be raided!"

Robbie's heart leaped into her throat as she listened to the conversation. *What if Kostas gets whacked? What if he loses his shipping business because of Prohibition? Will we end up on the streets with the bums on the dole? Oh, Dear God, please keep us all safe!* Her hands trembling, she set the book on the side table and let Grace slip from her lap. The little girl ran to her daddy.

Kostas lifted Grace onto his knee and gave her a quick kiss on the cheek.

Maria asked, "So, are you going to the Cocoanut Grove to find out what's going on?"

He looked at Maria. "Not today. I need to give this a few days to settle down." He held the paper out in front of him and read more. "Some witness said, '*I believe Boston Charlie was put on the spot to seal his lips—*' *about the rum running ring. Mob watchers speculate the Italian mob in the North End ordered the hit to eliminate a rival.*" Kostas pounded his fist. "Well, they sure as hell succeeded!"

"Kostas, I'm worried this is going to start a gang war, and you're going to be caught in the middle," Maria said. "You know I just want you to be safe."

Kostas gripped her hand. "Yeah, I know. I'm sure Charlie's guys are already scouring the North End looking for the killers." He set the paper aside and peered at Maria. "I know you worry about me, but I won't do anything stupid. All I know is I'm going to have to make a new deal to get our ships safely into the harbor, and not lose our loads to the Feds." He shook his head. "I wonder who else has close ties with Mayor Tobin."

Robbie sat rooted to her chair, imagining the worst but praying desperately for Kostas' safety.

A month later, Kostas and his associate sat at the dining table sipping rum, while Maria and the girls ate their dinner in the kitchen.

Dressed in a loose house dress, covered with a dirty apron, Robbie entered the dining room with plates of dinner for the men. Her long braid fell over her shoulder as curly wisps escaped around her face.

The visitor, who was slouched back in his chair, hands folded over his stout belly, took a long look at Robbie and let out a low whistle. "Well, well now! Who is this young lass?"

"This is our nanny, Robbie," answered Kostas. "Robbie, I'd like you to meet Barney Welansky, the new owner of the Cocoanut Grove."

"Nice to meet you, Mister Welansky." She nodded at the man as she set their plates on the table.

"You can call me Barney," he winked, taking in her long legs. "Tell me, Sweetheart, do you like to dance?"

Robbie paused and looked more closely at his bloated face and slicked, black hair. "I'm not sure. I don't think I know how."

"Well it's pretty easy to learn. Would you be interested?"

"What do you mean?" *Is he flirting with me? How odd.*

"I'm asking if you'd like to come to work for me at the Grove as a dancer. I think you'd be a big hit."

"Barney, are you serious?" Kostas chuckled.

"Hell yeah!" He sat forward in his chair. "You know how guys love the redheads these days!" Barney bellowed.

Robbie protested. "But I told you, I don't know how—"

Barney swung a hand in the air. "That doesn't matter. My girls can teach you the steps. I'm sure you'll pick it up in no time."

"I...I...I don't know." Robbie twisted her braid as she looked to Kostas for help. "Can I think about it?" *I'm sure he's not serious. He's probably just drunk.*

"Of course, Honey. I don't want to push, but *do* think about it. You'll have a lot of fun and get paid pretty damn good, too!"

Robbie returned to the kitchen to have her dinner with Maria and the girls and considered Barney's offer. *Dance at the Cocoanut Grove? Could I do that? I've heard it's a fancy place with lots of celebrities. What if I don't fit in? And will I still have time to care for the girls?* She fretted in silence as she picked at her food. *What will my family in Maine think if I do this? Probably that I'm a no-good sinner. But I bet it'd be fun, too. Gosh, I'm just not sure.*

Robbie rose to go into the dining room to retrieve the men's dinner plates, but stopped short of the door, as she overheard their conversation.

"Tell you what, Kostas," Barney's deep voice resonated. "If you can get your bombshell to come work for me, I'll give you the exclusive rum distribution rights at the club for the next two years."

Kostas responded, "She doesn't think she's a bombshell, Barney. Take a look at her—and she admits she can't dance."

"Ahhh, but I see a diamond in the rough just needing a little polishing," Barney chortled.

He thinks I'm a bombshell? The man must be drunker than I thought!

"Will you smooth the way with Mayor Tobin and still let us use Charlie's secret radio stations to make port undetected?" Kostas countered.

"I think all of that can be arranged."

"I'll tell you what," Kostas' voice rose. "Make it a five-year exclusive at the Grove, and I'll see what I can do!"

"Deal!" answered Barney.

Oh my goodness. They've made a deal over me. Now what am I going to do?

Reluctantly, Robbie entered the room. The two men were grinning and toasting with their glasses of rum.

Later that evening, after Barney had left and the children were put to bed, Kostas sat at the kitchen table with Maria and Robbie.

"Robbie, I'd really like you to consider Barney's offer to dance at the club."

"But Kostas, I don't know how to dance!" Robbie said, exasperated. She twisted the end of her braid, pursed her lips, and stared at the tabletop. *What should I do?* Her eyes flicked from Maria's good-natured face to Kostas' raised brows as he sat across from her, leaning back in his chair, his arms crossed over his chest.

"I can teach you. I cut a pretty mean rug, don't I, Honey?" He grinned at Maria.

"Well, he did once in his day. Don't know about now; he is getting pretty old." Maria winked at Robbie.

"What about the girls? I won't have time for them if I decide to be a dancer." Robbie's first priority was taking care of the children she loved.

"I'm sure we can work something out," Maria said. "I think it'd be fun for you to give it a try at least."

Having overheard the deal Kostas had made with Barney, Robbie knew the family's livelihood depended upon her agreeing to dance. She also felt obliged for all Kostas and Maria had done for her. She turned to Kostas. "Okay, I guess if you'll teach me to dance, I'll try to learn."

The following week, the Tsoukanis household became a whirlwind of activity. Maria sewed Robbie three new dance dresses, while Robbie kept the girls occupied. On Saturday, with the girls in tow, they went shopping for a new pair of high-heeled dance shoes. Robbie had never worn such a fancy pair before.

Then Maria led her entourage into her hairdresser's salon. Robbie stood behind the family when a middle-aged lady in a pinned-up hairdo greeted them. "Hello, Maria! Wonderful to see you. And how are these beautiful girls?" She waved at the children.

Elena, the oldest, spoke up, "We're great! And Robbie is going to be a dancer!"

Robbie blushed at Elena's outburst. Maria grasped Robbie's hand and pulled her forward. "Selena, I'd like you to meet our nanny, Robbie."

Robbie shook the woman's hand. "Nice to meet you."

The hairdresser turned back to Mrs. Tsoukanis. "And what can I do for you, Maria?"

"Well, Robbie is taking a second job at the Cocoanut Grove. So she needs a new, pretty hairstyle." Maria smiled up at Robbie.

Selena touched Robbie's long braid draped over her shoulder. "My, you have a lot of hair. And what a gorgeous shade of red! I think I know the perfect style. Here, come sit in my chair, and let's get to work."

Robbie hesitated. *I've never been to a salon in my life. What if I come out looking like a crazed squirrel?*

Maria touched Robbie's arm and directed her to the salon chair, then sat with the girls along the wall. "You'll be fine, Robbie. I trust Selena!"

Robbie peered through the mirror at the family behind her. Elena and Grace were giggling as they watched her. Maria nodded.

With the first few clips of the scissors, Robbie cringed at seeing her long, red locks falling to the floor. *Oh, God. Why did I ever agree to any of this?* She closed her eyes and tried to relax as her hair was yanked and pulled in different directions. When she opened her eyes, she was amazed to see her now shoulder-length hair, curled and bobbed like the fancy ladies she'd seen in magazines. *Wow! Is that me? I look so different. I hope I can do this again at home.*

Selena seemed to read her thoughts. "Here, let me show you how to do this." She straightened one curl in front, then wrapped it around her finger and pinned it tight to Robbie's head. "It's pretty easy, right? And Maria can help, too."

Robbie saw Maria grinning at her in the mirror. She rose from her seat and turned to face the family.

"You look gorgeous, Honey!" Maria gushed. Elena and Grace clapped, and Isis joined in their merriment.

Robbie blushed and did a little bow to the girls. Maria rose and hugged Selena, then paid her fee. "Thank you, Selena. I knew you'd do a great job. What do you think, Robbie?"

Smiling, Robbie said, "I think it's going to take some getting used to. But I like it!"

After dinner, Kostas tuned the radio to popular swing music and began the task of teaching Robbie to dance.

Taking her hand and beginning to lead her around the room, Kostas laughed. "Robbie, you need to relax and feel the rhythm of the beat."

Embarrassed, she responded, "I'm sorry for stepping on you, Kostas. I just feel like I have two left feet. I don't know if I can do this!" *Why in God's name did I ever agree to be a dancer? I'm just too clumsy, and I'm going to make a stupid fool of myself.*

Maria, resting in her wingback chair, her legs propped on an ottoman said, "You're doing fine, Robbie. Look! Even the girls are dancing with you!" She pointed to her daughters, laughing and swinging each other around in the corner.

"Here, let's try it again." Kostas took her hands and led her once more through the eight-step count of the Charleston. "One, two, three— kick! One, two, three— kick! There you go, you're getting it!"

After several rounds of repetition, she finally started to relax and felt her body swaying to the rhythm of the dance. *I guess it's not so hard. I just hope I don't step on anybody's feet!*

The next day, Maria showed Robbie how to apply makeup to cover most of her freckles. With some eyeshadow, rouge, and lipstick, Robbie was stunned at how grown-up she looked. She couldn't believe that within a week, she had been transformed from a children's nanny to a glamorous dance-hall girl.

I wonder what my big sisters, Pauline and Marjorie, would think of me now. Probably that I'm a godless sinner! She couldn't help but chuckle.

COCOANUT GROVE

Getting ready for her first night of work, Robbie's hands trembled as she donned her new dress and dancing shoes. She did her best to cover her freckles with makeup, as Maria had taught her. Taking a deep breath, she smiled into the mirror. *I hope I don't make a total fool of myself!*

Leaving her room, she walked down the staircase and presented herself to the family waiting in the living room.

Kostas rose and offered his hand as she descended the final steps. "You look beautiful, Robbie!" He guided her to Maria, who was sitting in her easy chair. The girls rushed around Robbie.

Maria smiled and took her hand. "Kostas is right. You are gorgeous, Honey. How do you feel?"

Robbie shook her head. "I don't know. Nervous and a little excited, I guess."

Elena, the oldest said, "You'll do great Robbie, I just know it! I hope you have fun!"

Robbie hugged the sisters. "Thanks, Elena. I'll tell you all about it tomorrow."

Kostas pulled their coats from the closet and handed one to Robbie. "We best be going." He quickly kissed Maria on the cheek. "I'll be back soon." Then he ushered Robbie out the door to his car parked along the side of the house. A cold wind caused Robbie to pull up her coat collar. Her heels sunk into the crusted snowbanks lining the driveway as she climbed into the front seat of the car. She remained mostly silent as Kostas prattled about the Cocoanut Grove during their three-mile drive from Dorchester Heights to Piedmont Street in downtown Boston.

Finally, Kostas stopped his car just beyond the club entrance. Robbie stared up at the brick two-story building. To the left of the entrance, signs announced *Dining and Dancing* and *Cocoanut Grove*. To the right of the revolving door, a sign said *Melody Lounge*. Kostas opened the car door for Robbie and helped her to the closed door, where he knocked. A sliding window in the door opened and a man peered out at them.

"It's Kostas!" he said. "And I have a guest." He gestured toward Robbie.

The door opened and Kostas escorted her inside. Robbie looked at the muscular doorman in awe. *I wouldn't want to pick a fight with him!* Then she surveyed the enormous room dotted with cocktail tables. "Kostas! This place is huge."

Kostas grinned. "Yeah, the owners converted an old warehouse. I think it's the biggest nightclub in Boston. This is the Melody Lounge."

To her right, Robbie saw a curved mahogany bar stretching the length of the room, where patrons were drinking and laughing. Behind the bar, bottles of illegal booze were lined up, their reflections glowing in the mirrored wall. A middle-aged Negro man played an upbeat jazz tune at the piano centered in the room. Several patrons leaned on the piano, singing a song Robbie had never heard. Couples sitting at round tables laughed and joked loudly. It was smoky in the room, and Robbie coughed to clear her throat.

A broad-shouldered man dressed in a fine suit approached them. "Kostas! Good to see you!" The man smacked his shoulder. "What can we do for you this evening?"

"Good evening, Jim. We're here to see Barney." He pulled Robbie next to him. "I have a new dancer with me."

Jim gave Robbie an intense look, making her uncomfortable. Then he pointed to the staircase. "He's upstairs. I'm sure you can find him."

"Thanks." Kostas grasped Robbie's hand and led her up the narrow stairway.

The large main dining room of the second-floor Broadway Lounge had a shiny wooden dance floor in the middle. Surrounding it on three sides were round tables covered in white tablecloths, set with fine silverware and linen napkins. On this mid-week night the room was busy as waiters catered to the diners, but it wasn't packed. In the front was the stage for the orchestra, who were tuning their instruments. Kostas pointed to a raised platform overlooking the dance floor, with similarly decorated tables.

"That section is reserved for celebrities. The band leader usually announces them when they arrive." Kostas swung his arm to the left. "This is the Caricature Bar." Robbie glanced at the long wooden bar, and noticed four well-dressed ladies standing at the end. *Those must be the Taxi Dancers!*

Suddenly, Robbie saw Barney's stout figure rushing toward them from the stage. Barney let out his famous low whistle as he took Robbie in his arms and kissed both of her cheeks. "Welcome to the Cocoanut Grove! You look ravishing, Sweetheart!"

"Thanks." Robbie's voice trembled. She tried to calm her shaking hands.

"Sweetie, don't worry. We'll take good care of you. Won't we, Kostas?" Barney said as he winked at his friend. With his arm around Robbie's back, Barney guided her to the line of girls waiting to dance. He stopped in front of an attractive brunette, older but shorter than Robbie, wearing red lipstick. "Robbie, I'd like you to meet Shirley Mason. She's my best dancer. She'll show you the ropes," he said as he introduced the women.

Shirley hugged Robbie and whispered in her ear. "Don't worry, Honey, you'll be fine, and we'll have a lot of fun."

Robbie immediately took a liking to Shirley, and started to relax.

Kostas touched Robbie's shoulder. "I'll be back to pick you up at eleven. Meet me out front."

Robbie nodded.

Shirley replied, "We'll make sure she's there, Kostas. Nice to see you again."

Three months later, in May 1933, Robbie stood with other young ladies along the wall, waiting for a dance partner. Each man paid ten cents—the price of a taxi ride, to the money collector, and received a dance ticket. He could then choose from the ladies in waiting. Each dancer received fifty percent of her ticket earnings, and the other half went to the club.

Robbie had quietly celebrated her seventeenth birthday in March. As she smoothed her green taffeta dress, a color that matched her eyes, she thought about the various compliments she had received from her dance partners. They said her long legs were sexy. Some called her "a tall drink of water." Others said her red hair reminded them of a fire engine. Most thought she was older than her years.

As she casually scanned the single men lingering around the room, she noticed a sharp-dressed man with black, slicked-back hair parted on the side, strolling across the dance floor toward the girls. He wore a brown pinstriped suit, yellow tie, and polished shoes. Robbie's heart beat faster as he made eye contact with her and smiled. *What a handsome man!*

"A ticket for a dance, Red?" he said.

Robbie blushed. She was captivated by his olive complexion, dark eyes, and strong jaw. *For once, a dance partner who is taller than me!*

"I'd love to," Robbie said, as she extended her hand. Of all the dances Robbie had learned: Foxtrot, Charleston, Jitterbug, Lindy Hop, and Swing—the Charleston was her favorite.

As they took their place on the dance floor among other couples, Robbie admired the South Seas-like "tropical paradise" created by artificial palm trees, rattan and bamboo, heavy draperies and swanky satin canopies suspended from the ceilings. *I wonder what it would be like to be swept away to such exotic lands.*

"What's your name, Red?" her dance partner asked.

"Robbie," she replied. "What's yours?"

"I'm Joe. Nice to meet you. But can I call you Red, anyway?" He laughed.

"Sure, why not," she replied.

They began the eight-count steps of the Charleston, kicking up their heels to the beat of the orchestra.

As they danced, Joe pointed to the canopy-draped ceiling. "Did you know they roll back the roof in the summer, so you can dance under the stars?"

"Oh, that sounds wonderful! I would love to see it sometime," Robbie responded, as she kept in step with Joe.

The orchestra's piece came to an end, and Joe escorted Robbie across the floor to the line of waiting dancers. "Can I buy you a pop, Red?" he asked.

"Oh, yes, thank you. I'd love one," she said, catching her breath. She smiled as she admired his tall, handsome form, strolling away. *I hope he asks me to dance again.* She patted her mussed hair back into place and straightened her dress in anticipation.

COTTON CLUB

Over the ensuing months, Robbie continued to live with the Tsoukanis family, caring for the house and girls during the day. Once the dinner dishes were put away, Robbie would change into her party dress and work until eleven as a taxi dancer at the Grove. Then Kostas would be waiting to drive her home. Her dancing skills had improved with practice, and her long legs had grown strong and shapely. Although she had many admirers, Joe Podusky had become her almost-exclusive dance partner. She often daydreamed they might become as famous as Ginger Rogers and Fred Astaire someday.

One Sunday afternoon in June, Robbie and Joe went to a Red Sox game at Fenway Park. Never having attended a game before, Robbie was amazed at the size of the ballpark, especially after they found their seats in the second deck. The big green wall in the outfield seemed enormous. With Robbie not knowing much about baseball, Joe patiently explained the umpire's calls of balls, strikes, and outs. Robbie stood and cheered when one of the Red Sox players hit a home run over what fans called The Green Monster.

As they munched on hot dogs, Joe turned to her. "Hey, Red! I've got an idea. Tomorrow is your night off. How would you like to go on a date to the Cotton Club in Roxbury?"

Her heart fluttered as she remembered Kostas being furious when Boston Charlie had been gunned down at the Cotton Club. "Gosh, Joe. I don't know. Is it dangerous to go there? Would we be safe?"

Joe looked at her with curiosity. "Why would you say that, Robbie? What makes you think it's not safe?"

"Well," Robbie wished she hadn't brought it up. "Isn't the Cotton Club where Boston Charlie got whacked?"

Joe chuckled. "Oh! Boston Charlie made a lot of enemies. That's just where they tracked him down. He could've been killed anywhere. Doesn't mean the Cotton Club isn't safe. And we don't have any enemies after us!"

Although apprehensive, Robbie nodded. "Okay, sure. I think it'll be fun."

The next night, Robbie dressed in one of the dresses Maria had made for her, and Joe picked her up at Kostas' house at seven. "We won't be late," Joe said to Maria, as he escorted Robbie down the steps.

Joe parked his car at an angle in front of a brick two-story building on Tremont Street. A small black-and-white sign attached to the side of the building advertised *Boston's Cotton Club*. Drapes covered the windows on both floors. Joe helped Robbie from the car, and they entered the club.

To her right, Robbie saw a dining room with about a dozen tables and booths, occupied by nicely dressed patrons eating their meals. The sounds of live music blared down to them from the upper level. Joe pointed to the stairs and held Robbie's arm as they ascended. Robbie noticed the upper room was considerably larger than the downstairs restaurant. At the far end, a Negro jazz band played a raucous tune. A shapely female singer, wearing a colorful head bandanna, swayed and crooned to the dancers directly in front of her.

A waiter appeared at their side. "Table for two, Sir?"

Joe nodded. "Yes. Thank you." They were led to a table against the right-hand wall. Joe sat next to Robbie as they faced the side of the dance floor.

"Drinks for you and the lady?"

Joe turned to Robbie. "What do you like to drink, other than pop?"

Robbie shrugged. "I don't know. I guess I don't drink much."

"Two beers," Joe said to the waiter, who retreated to bring their order.

Robbie watched the dancers, many of them Negro couples. She was mesmerized by their unfamiliar dance rhythms as she tracked their intricate footwork.

Joe put an arm around Robbie's shoulder. "So, what do you think?"

She smiled. "I like the music, and their dancing is wonderful. I doubt I could do it, though!"

"Oh, sure you could. You're a great dancer. It'd only take a little practice to get the rhythm." Joe grinned and bussed her cheek.

"Hmmm. Maybe in a while. I want to just relax and enjoy the show."

"Sure, Red, fine with me." Joe squeezed her shoulder.

After finishing dinner and second beers, Joe grasped Robbie's hand. "It's now or never. Let's dance!"

On the dance floor, Joe led Robbie through some slow footwork, then picked up their pace to keep time with the jazz band. Before long they were stomping their feet and swinging their hips along with the other dancers. Breathless and sweating, Robbie finally said, "I've got to stop, Joe! I need to take a break!"

Returning to their table, Joe ordered two more beers. "You were great, Red! I'm glad you decided to dance. We should come here again sometime!"

Catching her breath, Robbie smiled. "Yes. I'd like that very much."

As they finished their beers, Joe checked his pocket watch. "About time to get you home. It's getting late." He paid their check, rose from the table, and offered Robbie his hand. As she stood, she staggered in her heels, but Joe caught her by the arm before she fell.

"Oh! I'm so sorry. Guess I don't drink much!" She slightly slurred her words.

"Red, I think you're a little drunk. I'm going to take you back to my place so you can sleep it off, then I'll get you home in the morning," Joe said as he wrapped an arm around her back to steady her.

"Oh, gosh! I don't know, Joe. Maria and Kostas will be worried about me. And what about your landlord? Do you think it'd be all right?"

"Yeah, we'll be fine. My landlord likes me and keeps to himself anyway."

"Well, if you think so. I don't really want Maria to see me tipsy," Robbie agreed as they walked arm-in-arm to Joe's car.

When they arrived fifteen minutes later, Joe unlocked the door to his second-floor apartment and guided Robbie to a chair, where she plopped down, kicked off her heels and grinned. "Nice place you got here, Joe."

"Thanks. It's small, but I like it." Joe offered her a glass of water. "You can sleep in my bed tonight, and I'll sleep here on the sofa."

"Oh, no! I couldn't do that. I don't want to put you out."

"It's not a problem, Red. Now go on in there and get comfortable. You'll feel better in the morning." Robbie wobbled as she tried to stand, and Joe caught her in his arms.

"Can I use your toilet first?" She blushed, uncomfortable being in a man's apartment for the first time.

"Oh, sure. Door over there on the left." He pointed.

Robbie rose and steadied herself in her stocking feet. She closed the door and used the commode. *What am I doing here? I should just go home. But it's late and I don't want to take the trolley by myself. What if someone finds out I spent the night at Joe's apartment? I'll tell Maria in the morning, because she'll be worried. But I'll let her know nothing happened.* Robbie pushed stray hairs out of her face, fretting, as she stared into the mirror.

She remembered the talk she had had with Maria shortly after she had moved in.

Before they went to bed one night, Robbie and Maria chatted at the kitchen table. She had noticed Maria usually slept in a separate bedroom, instead of with Kostas. Robbie asked, "Maria, why do you sleep in a different room than Kostas?"

Maria smiled. "Because I don't want to have any more babies."

Robbie looked confused. "What do you mean?"

"Oh, Honey! You do know where babies come from, don't you?"

"Well, yeah, I suppose I do." Robbie blushed, not really sure how to answer the question.

"You get your 'little friend' every month, right?"

"Yeah. Mamma said it was the curse God gives to every girl. She told me to stay away from boys, or God would punish me with a baby."

"Robbie, it's when you're not having your 'little friend' that you can get pregnant," Maria explained. "Your body produces an egg, and when a man releases his manhood into you, that's what makes a baby. Just like you can't get baby chicks unless there's a rooster in the henhouse!"

Robbie flushed bright red, her forehead crinkled, and she began to cry.

"What's wrong?" Maria asked, touching Robbie's arm. Robbie's sobs became louder as she gulped for breath.

"Tell me, Honey, what's wrong?" Maria prodded. She poured Robbie a glass of water.

Robbie's hand trembled as she took several drinks. *Should I tell her? What if Leroy hurts Helen? Does he even know where Helen is? He might. But Maria is my best friend, and I don't think she'd tell Leroy.* Summoning her courage, she told Maria about that terrible day.

"When I was nine, Uncle George and Cousin Leroy came to visit. Leroy was a lot older than me." Robbie paused and took a drink, her face flushed. "I was feeding the chickens..." Robbie stared at the wall, the horrible memory flooding back. "He told me to go to the hayloft and throw down some hay." She scrunched her face and took a deep breath. "When I got to the loft, Leroy grabbed my ankle, and I fell forward." She took another drink of water, hands shaking. "The ne—next thing I...I knew...," Robbie was breathing hard, trying to get the words out. "He was...on top of me! I was so scared! I screamed for help—he slapped me," Robbie wailed. "Then he covered my mouth—and...and...told me to shut up or he'd kill me!" Robbie sobbed and took a big gulp of water as her whole body shook.

"It's okay, Honey. It's okay." Maria held Robbie's hand. "It was a terrible thing he did, but he can't hurt you now."

Maria's soothing voice calmed Robbie a little. She blew her nose and took a deep breath.

"Oh, Maria, I was just so scared! Leroy was a lot bigger than me—he had me pinned beneath him. He pulled up my dress...unzipped his pants. I didn't know what to do—it was so big! I tried to kick him—he squeezed my leg really hard—said if I screamed again...he'd hurt baby Helen." Her tears flowed as she recounted the terrible story for the first time. "He forced my legs open—and...and...thrust into me!" She gasped. "There was horrible pain—I tried to scream—Leroy covered my mouth, and I couldn't breathe. I thought I was going to die!"

Robbie took big gulps of air as she continued her story. "He rammed my body into the hay—over and over! I was crying and couldn't fight him. Why was he hurting me? I didn't do anything wrong," Robbie stared at Maria. "Then...then...he let out a loud groan and fell on top of me. It hurt so much, I screamed, and he slapped me again." Maria grasped both of Robbie's hands. "Leroy told me...it was all my fault, and if I ever told anyone, he'd hurt Helen. I didn't want anything to happen to the baby, so...so...I told Mamma I fell down when she asked about the bruises." The words tumbled out as Robbie finished recalling the rest of the horrible memory.

"Oh, Honey! He raped you, and you were so young!" Maria crossed herself, eyes fixed on Robbie. "Robbie, listen to me. It wasn't your fault. Don't you believe his lies for a moment. And no one will know you told me, so Helen is safe," Maria said earnestly.

"Thank you, Maria. You don't know how much that means to me. But…but…why didn't I get pregnant?—if that's how babies are made."

"Because you were too young, and your 'little friend' hadn't come to visit yet," Maria said. "Leroy never should have hurt you that way, and he was being a very bad young man. He should've been punished for taking advantage of you!" Maria soothed Robbie and gave her a big hug as Robbie's sobs subsided.

"Honey, you need to listen to me," Maria warned. "You can get pregnant now, so you need to be very careful around any man who wants to take you for a ride or offers to take you to his home. It would be very bad for you to get pregnant if you're not married."

Robbie took a deep breath and steadied herself as she left the bathroom and entered the living room. Joe guided her through the door into the small bedroom, which had a window overlooking the street, a single bed against the wall, a closet, a dresser, and a chair in the corner.

"Here, let me help you with your dress," Joe said as he unzipped the back. The flowered red dress that matched her hair slipped off Robbie's shoulders and puddled around her feet. Silently she stepped out of it. She was embarrassed for Joe to see her in her undergarments and dropped her gaze. Joe picked up her dress and laid it on the chair. Then he pulled back the covers, helped Robbie lie down, and kissed her cheek. "You get some rest now, and I'll wake you up in the morning."

"Hmmmm, thanks," Robbie said as she drifted off to sleep. *He's such a gentleman. I can trust him.*

A strange sensation awoke Robbie. She felt an arm draped over her waist and a hand caressing her breast, causing it to tingle. She heard a low mumble and sensed warm breath on her neck. Rolling partially on her back, she felt Joe's naked body pressed against her and jumped in surprise.

"Joe! Whad'ya doing? Get away from me!" She bunched her arms beneath his sweaty chest and pushed him from her.

"It's okay, Red. Just relax, we're gonna have a little fun." Joe guided her back onto the bed and kissed her. "You're a beautiful woman, and I want you all for myself tonight," Joe murmured in her ear, caressing her breast more firmly. She stiffened and tried to pull away from him. Then she felt a strange tingling begin down *there.*

ROBBIE IS DAMNED

As Joe caressed her, Robbie was surprised at her body's reaction. She had never felt anything like this before, and she was scared. *Should I let him continue? Or should I get up and stop this right now? What if it hurts, like with Leroy?* Maria's warning echoed in her mind: *Don't go home with a man. Don't get pregnant if you're not married. Oh, God, what should I do?*

Although surprised at her passionate response to Joe's gentle touch, she couldn't relax. Joe sensed her reluctance, stopped and gave her a puzzled look.

"I'm sorry, Joe. I'm just afraid it's going to hurt," Robbie admitted.

"I'll be as gentle as I can, Red. Trust me."

Despite her misgivings, and because she knew Joe really wanted this, she reluctantly let him help her remove her undergarments and continue stroking her naked body. For the first time she made love, discovering it wasn't as horrible as she had expected. *I just hope to God I don't get pregnant!* The thought haunted her as she joined with Joe, preventing her from fully relaxing.

One October morning, Robbie awoke feeling sick. She ran to the toilet and vomited. *Oh, gosh. What brought this on? I hope I'm not getting the flu. I don't want to make the girls sick.* She cleaned herself up, dressed, and went downstairs to begin making breakfast. Maria was already in the kitchen, and Robbie helped with the preparations. As Maria fried ham steaks, the aroma made Robbie's stomach churn, and she put a hand to her mouth.

Maria, watching Robbie's reaction, asked, "Are you getting sick, Robbie?"

"I don't know." Robbie took a deep breath. "I threw up this morning. I hope I'm not getting the flu."

"Why don't you go sit at the table, and I'll finish making breakfast." Standing at the stove, with her back to Robbie, Maria continued, "Honey, I don't want to pry. But I've noticed there have been some nights that you haven't come home. I presume you've been with Joe."

"Yes. I've spent some nights with him."

Maria turned to face Robbie. "When was the last time you had your little friend come visit?"

Robbie blanched. "Oh, gosh! I really don't know. I've been so busy, I haven't been paying attention."

"Do you think it's been more than a month?"

Robbie thought about the past few months and her whirlwind romance with Joe. "I think it was during the summer, maybe August?" Robbie's voice trembled.

Maria sat at the table with Robbie and held her hand. "Robbie, Honey. There's a good chance you might be pregnant."

Robbie stared at Maria as the words washed over her. *How could I have been so stupid not to notice I missed a period? Damn!* "Pregnant? You think I'm pregnant? Oh, Maria. What should I do?"

Maria nodded as she grasped Robbie's hand. "I'm sorry. But, yes I think you are. The first thing you should do is tell Joe. Then you'll have to decide when to get married. You don't want to have a bastard child."

Robbie gasped. "Married? I don't know if Joe wants to marry me. What if he says no?"

Maria looked sympathetically at Robbie. "Honey, the first thing you need to do is tell him. Then we'll see what happens. But you know we'll be here to support you."

"Thank you, Maria. You've been such a good friend."

Robbie leaned back in her chair as the girls arrived in the kitchen for breakfast. *A baby? I'm going to have a baby? Oh, my goodness! I hope Joe doesn't desert me like I've seen happen to some of the girls who have gotten in a bad way. But he's a gentleman, so I hope he will do the right thing.*

The following night at the club, Robbie worked up her courage and asked Joe to step outside with her after their dance. *How am I going to tell him? What if he leaves me? What will I do?* She fretted as they made their way down the stairs and out the front door.

Leaning against the wall, Robbie took deep breaths and stared at the man she'd come to love. "Joe, I'm pregnant." She watched for his reaction.

Joe stared back. "What! Oh, geez! Are you sure?"

"Yeah, I'm sure. Maria recognized my symptoms."

"And it's my baby?" Joe said, rubbing his chin as he paced in front of her.

"Joe, I haven't been with anyone else. Of course it's your baby," Robbie said, wringing her hands together, worried about Joe's reaction. "We have to decide what we're going to do."

"This is big news, Red," Joe said as he paced in front of her. "I need some time to think about it."

Tears sparkled in Robbie's eyes at Joe's less-than-enthusiastic response to her news. *What am I going to do now? Maria was right: we have to get married. But will he want to?*

"Joe, I think we should get married. I don't want to have a bastard child."

"Well…let's not rush into anything, Red."

Robbie's face distorted and Joe wrapped his arms around her as she sobbed. "It's okay, Red. We'll figure something out. Don't worry."

Over the next month, Joe didn't leave Robbie as she had expected. Instead, he rented a vacant two-bedroom apartment in the same building where he lived. Kostas helped Robbie move her sparse belongings into the new apartment, where Robbie and Joe set up housekeeping. Robbie continued to help Maria care for the girls, who were excited about the prospect of having a baby to dote on.

After moving in with Joe, Robbie met with Shirley Mason in the ladies' dressing room at the Grove.

"Shirley," Robbie said to her friend. "I'm going to have to quit dancing because I'm pregnant." Robbie's heart was heavy at telling Shirley of her predicament because she hated to quit the job she loved.

"Oh, Sweetie! I'm happy for you! When are you and Joe getting married?" Shirley hugged her.

Robbie shrugged. "I don't know. He got an apartment for us, so I would think soon. I'm so sorry to leave. You know I love working here with you. You've been like a sister to me." Robbie wiped back tears.

Several other dancers in the dressing room overheard the conversation. "We're going to miss you, Robbie," one said. "You've been a great friend," another chimed in.

Robbie did her best to hold back her tears.

Shirley grabbed her hand. "Let's go find Barney and let him know." They left the dressing room, walked by the stage, and spotted Barney sitting at the bar.

Shirley tapped his shoulder. "Barney, Robbie and I need to talk to you." After he turned to face the women, she added, "Looks like Robbie will be leaving us. She and Joe are going to have a baby."

Barney glared at Robbie. "When did you get married?"

Robbie squirmed. "We haven't yet. But we will soon."

Barney hefted his portly figure off the bar stool and stood facing Robbie. "Well, I'm very sorry to see you go. The men like dancing with you, and you've been quite a draw for the club. Now I'm going to have to find another redhead to replace you."

"I'm sorry, Barney. I really am. I have enjoyed working for you, and I love all the girls who have taken care of me. I will miss you." Robbie trembled, gulping tears.

Shirley touched Robbie's arm. "Let me walk you out, Honey." As the two women walked to the stairs, Barney called after them. "You make sure Joe makes an honest woman out of you!"

Robbie's heart twisted into a knot at Barney's outburst.

On the sidewalk, Shirley hugged her. "If you need anything, you be sure to call me. You know I'm always here for you, Robbie. I mean it!"

When she pulled from the embrace, Robbie said, "Thanks. You've been a good friend and I appreciate it. I don't know what I would have done without you."

"You be good to yourself now!" Shirley commanded, as Robbie walked along the sidewalk to the trolley stop.

When Robbie was five months pregnant, she received a letter from her older sisters in Maine. Her hands trembled as she opened the envelope.

Dear Robena,

We have recently been informed you are with-child outside of the sanctuary of matrimony and have committed a grievous sin. It is our faith in the Lord that guides us through this world and the decisions we make to stay strong in His grace. We are appalled at your decision to have this baby out of wedlock. We can no longer accept you as our sister or part of this family, as you have disgraced us with your actions. You are a sinner and a harlot in the eyes of God, and mark our words, you will be punished for having a bastard child. May God forgive you one day, as we will not.

Pauline and Marjorie

Robbie collapsed in the easy chair as she read the note and sobbed. *Who told them about the baby? Dammit, it must have been Gladys! Why would she betray me after all I've done to care for her all these years? She should've known how the sisters would react. Kicked out of the family? A sinner and a harlot? Oh, God, now what am I going to do? We need to get married before the baby is born.* Robbie loved Joe, and was going to have this baby to love, no matter what her sisters thought of her. *To hell with them!* She crushed the letter in both hands.

Joe came home from work and saw Robbie slumped in the chair, holding the crumpled letter, crying.

"Red, what's wrong?"

Robbie took a couple big gulps of air to calm herself. "Joe, we need to get married. My sisters said they've disowned me, and I've disgraced the family because I'm a harlot and a sinner for being pregnant out of wedlock."

"Your sisters are wrong. You're a beautiful woman, and they're just jealous."

"But Joe, I don't want to have a bastard child. It's not fair to me or to the baby," she pleaded. "Let's go to the courthouse and get married."

"I'll tell you what, Red. If we live together for six months, we'll have a common law marriage. We've been together for three months already. Another three months and we can claim we are husband and wife, and you can take my last name. That way the baby will be legal in the eyes of the state and the eyes of God."

"I don't know, Joe. It doesn't seem right to me, unless we're properly married."

"It'll be fine, Red. Trust me. I know people who do it all the time."

ROBBIE AND JOE FIGHT

In July of 1936, at age twenty and an unwed mother, Robbie gave birth to her daughter, Joan. The baby had Joe's black hair and olive complexion. But in a strange twist of genes, she had inherited Robbie's cat-green eyes. The combination was startling, giving the baby an eerie, almost other-worldly appearance.

At the beginning of their parenthood, Joe was loving and attentive to Robbie and the baby. He came directly home from his job at the bread factory, bringing little gifts and favors for them. Robbie diligently had dinner waiting for him. On weekends, they took Joan to the Boston Commons.

There they enjoyed riding the Swan Boats through the lush, serene public gardens, while Joan squealed at the ducks splash-landing nearby.

Then came the week when Joan was about a year old, when Joe came home late—not just once, but three times. Robbie was furious because his dinner had turned cold.

"Joe, why are you even going to the Grove?" Robbie demanded. "You tell me we're married in the eyes of the law, but you're still going to the club! What for?"

Joe held his palm face up towards Robbie. "I just had a few drinks with the guys after work. Calm down, all right?"

"I'm not stupid—I used to work there, remember? I don't want you getting involved with those girls. It's not fair to me and Joan!"

"Red, I'm not involved with anyone at the club. Trust me."

"Trust you! I've heard that before—why should I trust you? We're still not officially married, even though you said we would be."

"I'm sorry, Red. I just lost track of time." Joe reached for her arm, but Robbie swung away from his grasp.

"It's the third time this week, Joe, and I'm getting fed up with cooking dinner and not having you show up." Robbie went to the kitchen, grabbed the plate of food and tossed it onto the table. "Here, you can eat it cold! I'm going to bed."

Robbie closed their bedroom door and checked on baby Joan, sleeping soundly in her crib. Then she fell on their bed and cried until she fell asleep.

One night, less than a year later, Robbie heard Joe slam the door and let out a loud curse as he bumped into the furniture. It was after midnight, and Robbie was furious. She donned her robe and went into the living room, where she turned on a lamp.

"Joe, you're drunk!" Robbie hissed. "Keep your voice down or you'll wake the baby."

"I don't giv'a damn if she wakes up. I wan' you both outta here and outta my life!" Joe slurred his words, and reeked of rum. "I've met someone else, and you need to leave."

Oh, God, no! I can't believe this! How can he betray both of us just like that? What a fool I was to trust him! Robbie collapsed into a chair, feeling as if she'd been gut-punched. *How am I going to survive and support Joan?*

The little money I've got saved won't last long. And I'll be damned if I have to go on the dole!

Robbie stared up at Joe through watery eyes. "Joe, are you crazy? What am I going to do? Where will we go? What will I do for money?"

Her Poppa's voice rang in her head: *Those damned bums on the dole…they've got two good hands and can make an honest living.* Her thoughts raced wildly. *I'll have to get a job, but the only things I can do are cook, clean, and dance. I can't go back to dancing at night because no one will babysit Joan at that hour. And where will we live? Move back in with Maria and Kostas, or with Aunt Jeannette? If I do find a job, who can care for Joan?*

Tears flowed as her face reddened and fear gripped her heart. "Joe! Please—I beg you! Please don't do this!" She stood and grabbed his arm. "You know I love you! Can't we make this work for Joan's sake?"

Joe yanked from her grip and turned away. "Look, I'll try to find you a place, but that's it! I want to be done with both of you."

"What about Joan? Don't you love her?" Robbie circled in front of Joe and faced him. "She's your daughter, and she looks just like you! How can you disown her? And you need to help me pay for her upbringing!"

"She's your damned responsibility, Red! I never wanted a kid to begin with, so you take care of her!"

Joe's words slammed Robbie, ripping her heart out. She staggered and slumped back into the easy chair, dropping her head into her hands as sobs racked her body.

My sisters' warnings are coming true: God is punishing me for my sins!

BABYSITTERS

The day after her fight with Joe, Robbie called her friend, Shirley Mason, at the Grove.

"Shirley, I don't know what I'm going to do! Joe said he's got a new girlfriend and wants us to move out!" Robbie's voice quivered.

"Oh, Honey! I'm so sorry to hear that. What can I do to help you?"

Shirley's soothing voice helped calm Robbie's nerves. "Well, first I have to find a place to live, and then get a job. Do you know anyone who might have a room for rent I could afford?"

After a thoughtful pause, Shirley answered, "I might. Let me ask around, and I'll call you back."

"Shirley, wait. Can I ask you something?" Robbie took a deep breath.

"Sure, Honey. What is it?"

"Did you know Joe was cheating on me? He's at the Grove constantly. You must have seen something!"

Shirley let out a long sigh. "Aaugh, Robbie! You know I don't like to meddle in people's affairs. But I can tell you Joe dances with a few of my girls. I don't ask what they do on their personal time." She paused. "I'm so sorry! This must be so tough on you, with a young child to raise."

"I really wish you would have told me, Shirley! I really do." Robbie exhaled a gulping sob.

Shirley replied. "Listen, Robbie. You know I love you, and I'll do whatever I can to help. You need to stay strong for Joan. I'll be back in touch real soon."

"Thanks, Shirley. I appreciate any help I can get right now." Robbie hung up and stared blankly at her apartment wall. *Of course Shirley knew about Joe! She's there every night. God! I just wish she had warned me, so I could have been more prepared.*

Two days later, Robbie called the number Shirley had provided her for a boarding house. She was able to rent a small room for herself and Joan, for one dollar a day. She had mixed emotions, watching Joe help her move her meager belongings. She hated him for kicking her and Joan out of his life, but deep down, she knew she would always love him.

A few days after moving in, Robbie was pushing Joan in her stroller down Tremont Street. Passing by Bill's Diner, she noticed a *Help Wanted* sign in the window. Peering through the window, she saw several people sitting at tables and two men at the lunch counter. She bit her lip as she stared at the sign. *God knows I need a job. I could probably do whatever they need. How hard could it be?*

Taking a breath, she opened the door and pushed the stroller inside.

Bill Van Dyne was broad-shouldered and stocky, with thick, wavy blond hair, blue eyes and a ruddy complexion. Robbie thought he looked about her age, maybe a few years older. He hired Robbie on the spot to waitress at the diner, but she still had to make arrangements for someone to babysit Joan. Robbie had patched up her relationship with her sister Gladys, when they determined it was Aunt Jeannette who had written to the sisters in Maine about Robbie's pregnancy. So Gladys agreed to babysit Joan during the day.

Within the year, however, Gladys married an Irish fireman, Sean O'Neal, who lived in Southie, and began a family of her own. Having lost her babysitter, Robbie made arrangements for Joan to stay with an elderly woman, Mrs. Kantor, who lived in the same rooming house.

One day in June, Robbie returned from work to retrieve her daughter and knocked on Mrs. Kantor's door.

There was no answer.

She knocked harder. "Missus Kantor, are you there?" Robbie could hear whimpering coming from the room. She slowly opened the unlocked door. "Joan, where are you?"

Joan let out a squeal as she ran into her arms. The stench of dirty diaper engulfed Robbie as she lifted her daughter.

"It's okay, Honey. Mommy's here." Joan clung to her neck, as Robbie rubbed her back to comfort her. Raising her voice, Robbie called, "Missus Kantor, where are you?" She slowly walked toward the large over-stuffed chair facing the front window. As the side of the chair came into view, Robbie saw Mrs. Kantor—head slumped to her chest.

She reached out to shake the old woman's arm. "Missus Kantor? Are you all right? Wake up."

From Robbie's shaking, the body rolled and pitched forward in the chair.

Still supporting Joan in the crook of her arm, Robbie squealed and jumped back from the chair. "Oh, God! Oh, no! Is she dead?" Robbie staggered back, trembling from shock and the weight of Joan in her arms. She dropped into a kitchen chair, grasping Joan to her. *Oh, God! Now what do I do? Is she really dead? I need to get her help. The landlord—he has a phone.*

"Mommy, what's wrong? I'm scared." Joan sobbed as she grasped Robbie's neck.

She hugged her daughter. "It's all right, Honey. We need to leave right now." Taking deep breaths, Robbie grunted as she lifted Joan and backed out of the apartment, kicking the door shut.

She struggled down two flights of stairs and banged on the door of the landlord's apartment. When the door finally opened, Robbie recoiled at the sight of the heavyset man. Tufts of hair erupted at different angles from his head. He wore a stained white T-shirt that barely covered his broad, dirty belly. It appeared he hadn't shaved in days and his foul body odor engulfed her. A radio blared in the background.

"Yeah? Whad'ya want?" His small eyes squinted at her, as he pulled a cigarette from his lips.

"Mister Cohen. Please—call the doctor. I think Missus Kantor—is…is…dead!" Robbie gasped, trembling.

Cohen flicked his cigarette ash. "Whad'ya mean she's dead? What the hell you talkin' 'bout?" He stepped aggressively toward Robbie. She took another step back.

"I was just there to pick up Joan." Robbie tried to catch her breath. "Missus Kantor's slumped in her chair—I don't think she's breathing. Please—you need to get her some help!"

"Oh, Christ almighty! You're a mad woman." He swung an arm in the air. "Leave me be. I'll take care of it," Cohen groused, then slammed the door in Robbie's face.

Robbie hurried down the hallway to her room at the back of the house, unlocked her door, closed it behind her, and collapsed into a chair. She hugged Joan tight and cried wracking sobs, causing Joan to cry as well.

"Mommy, what happened? Is the lady sick?" Joan said, as she held tight to Robbie.

"Yes, Honey. She's sick, and we're getting a doctor for her." The stench of diaper reminded Robbie that Joan was dirty. "Let's get you into a bath, shall we?" She got her daughter undressed and into a bath, soothing her child by singing silly songs.

"Oh, I'm broke and badly bent…and I haven't got a cent. I'm so clean you'd think that I was washed in Lux."

Joan giggled as Robbie immersed herself in scrubbing her daughter, trying to make the woes of the world go away. *How can I work and care for Joan? Who else can babysit, and how much will it cost? I can barely pay for this room and food for us. I can't afford a babysitter every day.*

Robbie heard commotion on the stairway as Mr. Cohen barked directions to Mrs. Kantor's room. Hard footfalls and men's voices echoed up the stairwell.

Robbie dried Joan from the bath, put on a new diaper, got her dressed in her pajamas, sat her on the sofa with her favorite doll, then turned the radio on low. As she was preparing a light dinner for them, Robbie heard men's voices outside her door.

"Careful. Don't drop her!"

Then came several thumps on the staircase.

"I ain't dropping her!"

She heard Cohen holler, "Well, is she dead, or what?"

"Yes, she's dead. We're takin' her to the undertaker."

Robbie turned her attention to her cooking, trying to ignore what was happening in the hallway. Her stomach in knots, she fed Joan, but couldn't eat anything herself. She finally put Joan down in the bed they shared, and tried to sing her Mamma's favorite song: "Lullaby…and good night…thy mother's delight…" But it did nothing to calm her own nerves.

Sitting back at the kitchen table and drinking a glass of milk, Robbie allowed the darkness to envelop her. She twisted her clasped fingers and considered her options. *What am I going to do? Quit my job and go on the dole? And have both of us be damned to hell? I won't do it!* She heard Poppa's admonishments ringing in her head. *Who else can help me? I wonder if Marjorie or Pauline might have a change of heart, and be willing to take Joan for a short time—just until I can get back on my feet. I think Marjorie might be more forgiving. It's worth a try.*

Robbie gathered a pen and paper and began to write.

June, 1939

Dear Marjorie and Arthur,

This is a difficult letter for me to write, and I hope you will not judge me too harshly for what I am about to ask. I have fallen on hard times because Joe walked out on us for another woman! I must work to support Joan, but cannot afford a babysitter. It is my hope you could bring Joan to live with you on your farm for a short period of time. It would just be until I can get back on my feet and I can afford to support both of us again.

I will send you what money I can to help care for her. I hope your Christian faith will forgive me for my sins, and you would be sympathetic to providing temporary care of Joan.

I thank you for your love and support and anxiously wait for your reply.

Your Sister,
Robbie

Robbie dropped the pen and rubbed her tired eyes. *What if she doesn't answer my letter? What if she refuses to take Joan?*

Over the next week, Robbie fretted over what Marjorie's response would be. She had no choice but to take Joan with her to the diner, to Bill's disapproval. But what else could she do? She kept Joan busy at a back table with coloring books and her favorite doll.

The letter from Marjorie finally arrived. Robbie dropped to the sofa, the tremor in her right hand making it difficult to open the letter. *Do I even dare open this? What if the answer is no? Then what will I do?*

Robena,

Although you know we disapprove of you having a bastard child, the Lord has directed me to give this child a proper upbringing you obviously cannot provide. It is with great reluctance Arthur and I have agreed to let Joan come live with us. We will raise her as a proper God-fearing Christian. We hope your sinful ways have not spoiled her to reject the Word of the Lord. We will arrive by bus in Boston this Sunday hence to retrieve the child.

Your Sister,
Marjorie

Robbie cringed at Marjorie's harsh words, but let out a sigh of relief they would care for Joan on their farm, at least for a little while. It broke Robbie's heart to have to send away her beautiful daughter, whom she loved so much, but there were no other options. *I hope Marjorie won't punish her for my mistakes.*

The following Sunday, Robbie's heart broke as she packed Joan's clothes and favorite doll in a suitcase for her journey.

"That's enough! The suitcase will break," Marjorie admonished, as she stood in the bedroom, arms folded, watching Robbie's every move.

Robbie cringed as she heard Arthur call from the living room, "Hurry up in there, will you? We're gonna miss the bus!"

How can I send my daughter away? What kind of a heartless mother am I? But what other choice do I have? I just want what's best for her, and for her to be happy. "You know this is just until I can get back on my feet," Robbie pleaded with Marjorie, hoping for her sympathy. "I'll send you money every month to help with Joan. Once I get enough saved, I'll come and get her, I promise."

"Well, we'll just see about that now, won't we?" Marjorie stomped out of the bedroom and gave Arthur a withering look. "Let's go!"

Holding Joan's hand and carrying her suitcase in the other, Robbie walked with Marjorie and Arthur to the bus station. When the bus was ready to leave, Robbie choked back tears. Before Marjorie's disapproving glare, she crouched down in front of her daughter and held both of her hands.

"Joan, Honey, listen to me. You're going on a special trip to visit with Aunt Marjorie and Uncle Arthur, and it'll be a lot of fun."

"Aren't you coming, Mommy?"

"No, Honey. Not right now. But I'll come visit you real soon," Robbie said, trying to keep her voice cheery, despite the tight knot in her stomach. Joan's third birthday was just a month away, and Robbie hoped to be able to celebrate the day with her in Maine.

"No, Mommy! I want you to come, too. Don't make me go!" Joan clutched Robbie's neck in a death grip.

Robbie's heart broke as she remembered the pain of having to leave her younger brothers and sisters not that long ago. *Why am I being punished by losing the children I love so much?*

"I can't right now, Honey. I'm so sorry," Robbie let out a sob knowing how much she'd miss her precious daughter. "You know I love you. Don't you ever forget!" Robbie kissed Joan on her head. "You be a real good girl and mind your Aunt Marjorie now. I'll come see you real soon, I promise." Robbie hugged her daughter tight, not wanting to let her go. She hoped against all odds she could keep her promise, but was afraid it might be a long time before she would see Joan again.

Marjorie grasped Joan's arm, although the child struggled to stay connected to her mother. "Okay! Enough! Come along, child. The bus is leaving." Marjorie dragged Joan, screaming and crying, onto the bus.

Robbie stopped Arthur as he carried Joan's suitcase. "Please! Don't punish her for my mistakes. She's just an innocent little girl. Please!"

Arthur glared at her. "You brought this on yourself, Robbie. Not my doin'—can't be helped." He boarded the bus and didn't look back.

Robbie watched in agony as they took their seats. The last image she saw was her daughter's crying face pressed against the bus window mouthing the words, *Mommy! Mommy!* as it pulled out of the terminal.

Robbie collapsed to her knees, covered her flushed face and cried. "Oh, Dear Lord, what have I done? I'm a failure as a mother. I only want what's best for my daughter. Please watch over her and keep her safe." She desperately hoped one day Joan would forgive her.

That night, Robbie cried herself to sleep and dreamed of her own Mamma.

Robbie was in the field picking potatoes. She saw her Mamma struggling to lift a full basket of potatoes several rows away, with a baby slung on her back. Robbie rushed to help her mother by taking the baby off her back. The baby had the face of both her sister Helen and baby Joan. Mamma dropped the basket and swung her arm at Robbie, knocking her to the ground.

"You can't have this baby, you can't have any baby. You're a sinner!" Mamma scolded her.

"Please, Mamma! I promise I'll take good care of her," Robbie pleaded.

"You broke your promise, and God will punish you forever!" Mamma screamed at her.

Robbie awoke in a sweat, sobbing.

Mamma will never forgive me for breaking my promise to take care of the young'uns. But it wasn't my fault I was sent away. I wanted to keep my promise, I really did.

Now God is punishing me, just as my sisters predicted. Will I ever be forgiven for abandoning my own daughter? I am such a failure!

HORRIFIC MEMORIES

After Robbie's disastrous relationship with Joe, she swore off getting involved with men. For the next three years, she worked hard as a waitress at Bill's Diner serving customers, bussing tables, and working as a short-order cook beside Bill when they got busy. She had her own small apartment within walking distance of the diner. Depressed over losing Joan, she had little appetite, so her clothes hung haphazardly on her tall, thin frame. Her hollowed cheeks and the dark circles under her eyes made her look much older than her twenty-six years.

It was late Saturday night on November 28th, 1942, Thanksgiving weekend—the date seared forever into Robbie's mind. She had spent Thanksgiving Day with Gladys, Sean and their four-year old son Liam, in Southie. Liam was an adorable little boy, but being near him left Robbie sad and heartbroken over the loss of Joan. Boston was busy that weekend with visitors, football fans, and servicemen home on leave from the wars being fought in Europe and the Pacific.

Robbie had worked a double shift at the diner, and she was exhausted. After taking a long, hot bath, she donned her robe, put her feet up in the living room, and relaxed to the sounds of big band music. Her mind drifted to the bittersweet days of dancing with Joe at the Grove, and how she imagined they were like Fred Astaire and Ginger Rogers. Robbie was startled from her musings when the telephone rang. *Who could be calling me at this hour?*

"Hello?"

"Robbie, it's me." She heard anxiety in her sister Gladys' voice.

"Gladys? What's wrong? Why are you calling so late?"

"Robbie, Sean got called in. There's a fire at the Cocoanut Grove."

It took Robbie a moment to process what Gladys had said. "Wait! What do you mean? At the Grove? How bad is it?"

"I think it's pretty bad. Sean said they'd called all-hands-on-deck at his firehouse. He said they wouldn't bring the Southie guys downtown unless they were short-handed." Gladys' voice trembled.

"Oh, Dear Lord!" Robbie gasped, as the news sunk in. "What should we do?" *I hope Shirley is safe.*

"You're not far away. Can you go down there and see what's going on?" Gladys asked.

"Oh, Honey, I don't know. I'm exhausted, and my feet are killing me."

"Please, Robbie," Gladys' voice broke with strain. "I'm worried about Sean—I need to know he's all right."

"Okay, okay! I'll get dressed and try to get down there," responded Robbie wearily.

"Call me when you get back, no matter what time it is. I'll be waiting up."

Robbie dressed in a wool dress, working shoes, warm sweater, brimmed wool hat, and her winter coat. She remembered to grab her gloves as she rushed from her apartment, walking two blocks to Tremont Street. A cold wind pushed against her while she waited to board the trolley. Once aboard, she was surprised to hear folks talking about the fire.

"Everyone's gotten kilt'—that's what I heard!" a middle-aged man in a tatty fedora hat said from across the aisle.

"What? No one got out? Are you sure?" Robbie jerked to the edge of her seat, eyes intent on the stranger slouching in his seat opposite her.

"Nah!" cried a long-jawed young man hardly out of his teens, wearing threadbare overalls. "The band 'scaped outta the side door."

"No, it was the back door," a plump lady with a round, red face interjected. "An' only half 'em got out!" She folded her arms and glared at the young man.

Robbie faced front, hugged her arms to her chest, and stared at the tracks slowly disappearing under the trolley, wishing it would move faster.

Robbie exited the trolley on Arlington Street, one block from Piedmont, where the Cocoanut Grove was located. She smelled acrid smoke and saw a dark plume rising into the night sky. Wailing sirens and screaming voices contributed to the unfolding disaster. She hurried down Piedmont toward the scene with a rush of onlookers.

Stunned, Robbie watched more than a dozen firemen fighting the inferno, their hoses overlapping in the street. Injured patrons were on the ground, bloodied, being treated for their wounds. Some bodies were completely covered with scorched tablecloths. Her stomach lurched as she watched burned bodies being passed through windows that had been broken out by the firemen. Customers who had escaped the inferno helped those who were injured. Some attempted to go back into the building, but were forcibly turned back by the officials. Policemen yelled at the crowd to stay back. As more flames erupted, firefighters hollered at one another and scrambled to redirect their hoses. It was a war zone of total chaos.

Watching the mayhem, Robbie spotted Gladys' husband, Sean. She watched in shock as he and others dismantled the revolving door at the entrance to the club. Inside, unidentifiable bodies were tangled on top of one another, and blood smeared the glass.

Bile rose in Robbie's throat as she covered her mouth to keep her stomach from erupting. Frantically, she moved through the crowd searching for Shirley in the melee. A tall figure, dragging an injured man, one arm over his shoulder, caught Robbie's attention. The figure helped the burned man to the ground and motioned for a fireman to come help. The tall man straightened and ran his fingers through his tangled black hair as he turned to stare at the onlookers.

Robbie gasped. *It's Joe!* His face was dark with soot and blood stains spotted his white shirt. His hands were cut and bloody. Robbie remembered the last time she'd talked to him, when she told him she had sent Joan to live with her sister Marjorie.

"How could you abandon your only child? What the hell were you thinking?" Joe had chastised her. She was furious he would judge her because it was he, after all, who had abandoned them, leaving her with no financial support.

"I didn't abandon her!" she had shot back. "I sent her to stay with Marjorie for a little while. What was I supposed to do? I couldn't afford to work and pay a babysitter. And you weren't helping in any way whatsoever. So don't you criticize me! I did what I thought was best for OUR daughter!"

Robbie realized Joe was staring at her. *Should I approach him? Will he talk to me? Maybe he's seen Shirley.* She slowly parted from the crowd and walked toward him. He watched her approach. She reached out and touched his arm. "Joe? Are you all right?" His clothes reeked of smoke.

"Red, what are you doing here?" Joe said, frowning as he wiped his face on his sleeve.

"Gladys called. Sean's firehouse got called up from Southie. She was worried about him. What happened?"

He stared past her, then said, "I'm not sure…I saw a flash of light…then the palm trees were on fire—it spread to the canopies," he paused. "I was at the Melody Bar and got out quickly. Everyone panicked and tried to push through the revolving doors, but it got jammed. I think the other exits might have been blocked!" He shook his head.

"Have you seen Shirley? I can't find her—I'm sure she was here tonight." Robbie paced, her heart racing as she scanned the injured and dead spread on the ground.

Joe glanced at the chaos ensuing around them. "No. The last time I saw her, she was upstairs on the dance floor, talking to the girls. I haven't seen her since," he said, trying to stem the bleeding on his hand, visibly shaken by the scene in front of him. "Red, you shouldn't be here. Go home. There's nothing you can do—I'll call you tomorrow. I should go help where I can…" Joe mumbled, stumbling away.

"Joe! Wait!" There were so many things she wanted to say to him, to ask him. She realized even after all that had happened, she still had feelings for him. But now wasn't the time.

I'm not leaving until I find Shirley! Robbie huddled with the crowd, shivering, witnessing the disaster unfolding around her.

As the temperature dropped, the cobblestones froze into a sheet of ice, and the horde of serpent-like hoses stuck to the ground. Servicemen in uniform rushed from nearby bars to help with the wounded. Newspaper trucks were used to transport the injured to nearby hospitals. Firemen lugged out smoldering bodies, living and dead, and hosed them down. Some badly injured patrons died on the spot when they inhaled the icy cold air.

Where is Shirley? Why can't I find her? Dear Lord, please let her be alive and safe! Robbie paced, staring into the faces of the injured.

As the night wore on, cold and despair overtook Robbie. Her heart was heavy as she feared the worst for her dear friend. Robbie remembered the day, about a month after she'd started working at the Grove, when Shirley cajoled her: "Let's have our pictures made!"

Mike Fischer, one of Shirley's regulars, had offered her a special deal if she'd come to his studio. Not wanting to go alone, she had persuaded Robbie to join her. One Saturday, they dressed in their best dance outfits. Robbie wore her Mamma's special cameo pendant. The two women went to the Fischer Photography Studio to have their glamor shots taken. They giggled as they struck dance poses together, and had more pictures taken separately. Robbie had thought the photographs were wonderful, and was very proud of how grown-up she looked.

Oh, we were so young then, Robbie thought as she stared at Boston's premiere nightclub, now reduced to smoldering ruins.

Dawn broke and the sun-splashed ice steamed from the weak rays. Weary and numbed to the bone, and unable to locate Shirley, Robbie took the first trolley on Tremont Street back home. She wouldn't be able to work, so she stopped off at the diner to let Bill know. She was surprised to see the *Closed* sign on the door. Peering in the window, she saw Bill and his dishwasher, Charlie, sitting at a table. She rapped on the door, and Bill let her in.

"Jesus, Robbie! You look like hell. Where have you been?" Bill asked.

"There was a fire at the Grove—I had to go find Shirley," Robbie said, exhausted as she dropped into a chair. "But I'm afraid she didn't make it out." Robbie shook her head in dismay.

"I heard about the fire, that's why I'm closing the diner for the day," Bill said. "Let me get you a cup of coffee. I'm sure Shirley will be fine, so don't worry. She's a strong lady."

Robbie relayed the scene she'd witnessed to Bill and Charlie. As she warmed up, exhaustion overtook her. When she talked about Shirley, she felt hot tears well up, despite her determination not to cry. But she was so tired, she couldn't fight it any longer, and the sobs overtook her. Bill held her in his arms and let her cry until she finally stopped shaking.

"I've got to go call Gladys, and then I'm going to bed," Robbie told Bill as she rose from the table to leave.

In her apartment, she removed her coat and boots and called her sister. "Honey, I just got back from the fire. It was the—the most horrible thing—I've ever seen!" Her voice trembled. "I saw Sean and he's fine. But I couldn't find Shirley—I don't think she made it out."

"Oh, Robbie, I'm so sorry to hear that," Gladys said. "I know you and Shirley were close. But I'm afraid I have more bad news. Maria called this morning. Kostas didn't come home last night, and she's frantic with worry—he was at the club."

"Oh, good Lord! Not Kostas, too!" Robbie said, stunned. "He's a tough guy. I'm sure he made it out. He's probably in a hospital somewhere," she said, hoping it was true. *What would Maria and the girls do without Kostas?*

"Theo's with Maria right now, helping her try to locate Kostas. But nobody knows who's been taken where—it's all a big mess!" Gladys' voice broke.

"Honey, I'm exhausted. I'll say a prayer for Kostas, but right now I'm going to take a hot bath, have a little breakfast, and go to bed. Call me tonight and let me know if you've got any news."

"Yeah, okay, I'll call you later." Gladys said, then hung up.

Robbie didn't believe Kostas was dead, and prayed he would be found safe and alive. But she feared the worst for the loving husband and father, who had once taught her to dance.

FRIENDS ARE GONE

Robbie heard Kostas' body was found in the ruins of the Cocoanut Grove. As the flames quickly spread, apparently he had led panicked patrons into the basement to the entrance he had used to deliver rum barrels to the club. But the exit had been blocked from the outside and the crush of bodies made it impossible to find another route out. Kostas was found at the bottom of the grisly heap.

Robbie joined Gladys and her family in the funeral procession, along with Aunt Jeannette, Uncle Seamus and their four boys. Kostas' brother, Theo, and father, Constantine, were there to support Maria and her girls.

Elena, Maria's oldest, now fifteen, pushed her mother in a wheelchair. Maria had been too frail and exhausted from the ordeal to walk on her bad leg.

Kostas was laid to rest at the Greek Orthodox cemetery in South Boston, amid the anguished mourners, including mob bosses and dock workers. Robbie watched Barney Welansky walking with a cane next to Boston Mayor Maurice Tobin, whom she recognized from his pictures in the paper.

For Robbie, the horrible aftermath of the fire continued with more bad news. Shirley Mason's body was found in the cloakroom at the rear of the ladies' dressing room, huddled over the bodies of three dancers. She had perished trying to protect the girls she loved until the bitter end. Robbie was beside herself with grief over the loss of her friend.

Two days after Kostas' funeral, Robbie attended Shirley's service at St. Luke's Episcopal Church on Boylston Street. Robbie was surprised when Sally, one of the girls who had been a taxi dancer, sang "Ave Maria" in a sweet, soprano voice. The Latin phrases both swelled and soothed Robbie's heart. She prayed her dear friend's soul would find a special resting place in heaven. *I wonder if Shirley can hear Sally's angelic voice echoing through the church. I think she'd love it.*

The following Sunday, Maria invited Robbie to their house for dinner. As was their custom, the two women and three girls sat at the kitchen table, instead of using the formal dining room.

"Robbie, we have some news for you," Maria said, gently touching Robbie's hand.

Robbie felt a pull of dread as she stared at her friend.

"We've decided to sell the house." Maria informed her.

"What? Oh, no! Where will you go?" Maria seemed to have made the decision so quickly.

"I want to take the girls home to my village in Greece," Maria continued, taking a drink. "They've never been to the old country, and it's time they got to know their relatives."

"Oh, Maria! I'm so sorry. I'll miss you and the girls terribly! You know how much I love you all!"

Maria gripped Robbie's hand tight. "Honey, I knew you'd be upset. That's why I wanted to tell you in person."

"We're going on a big ship, and it's gonna be a lot of fun!" Isis, Maria's youngest daughter said, her eyes alight.

Robbie put on a brave face. "Yes, I'll bet it will be fun!" She winked at the young girl.

Maria sighed. "I can't stay here without Kostas. It's just too painful for me. I need to be with my family, so they can help raise my girls. I so hope you understand, Robbie." Maria's saddened eyes looked to Robbie for her approval.

"I know. I miss Kostas, too. I understand why you want to go home. But, gosh, you know I hate to see you leave!"

"It's what's best for the girls. Kostas' brother Theo will travel with us, and then he'll come back to Boston to continue the family business with my father-in law Constantine. This way we'll have a chaperone to protect us on our voyage," Maria explained.

"I'm glad Theo will be with you to keep you safe. It makes me feel much better," Robbie said, devastated, but trying to be strong.

Within a month, the Tsoukanis mansion in Dorchester Heights was sold, and the family's bags were packed for their transatlantic voyage.

Robbie accompanied Theo, Maria, and her girls to the dock to board the ocean liner. The massive ship blocked the view of the horizon. A hub of activity filled the boarding area. Baggage porters moved about quickly, directing passengers and loading cargo. Horns blew from ships docked farther up the port. Large cranes squealed as cargo containers were unloaded, and dock workers hollered instructions. Seagulls swooped and squawked around the masts of the ships. The smells of smoke and kerosene filled the air. Families embraced and said their farewells to loved ones who were boarding the ship.

Maria rose from her wheelchair and hugged Robbie. "Don't forget all the things I taught you when you were young. Get your hair done, and wear some makeup now and then. It'll cheer you up and make you feel better. Promise me you'll do that!" Maria's quick smile lifted Robbie's spirit.

Robbie laughed. "Okay! I promise. I'll cover those darned freckles as best I can!"

"Good!" Maria chuckled. "You take care of yourself, Robbie. We'll write to you as soon as we get home and let you know about our big adventure." Maria turned to her daughters. "Won't we girls?"

"Yeah, we sure will!" Isis said, giving Robbie a hug. Elena and Grace each took turns hugging Robbie and saying their goodbyes.

"We'll miss you, Robbie," Grace said, as tears filled her eyes.

Robbie's heart lurched. "You take real good care of your mother, now," she said to Elena, trying to keep her voice steady. "She needs you to be strong and help out with your sisters."

Robbie gathered the three girls in one last hug. "Don't forget I love all of you, and I can't wait to hear from you again."

"We love you, too, Robbie!" they yelled, as they followed Theo, who pushed Maria's wheelchair up the gangplank.

Why is God taking away the children I love so dearly? What have I ever done to deserve this life of loss and heartache?

While the ship slowly left the harbor, Robbie wept as she waved to the girls on the deck.

What will I do without my dear friends, Shirley and Maria, in my life? They loved me without judgment, unlike my older sisters. I am so grateful for their friendship and guidance as they helped me grow up. I already miss them terribly.

Months later, Robbie read in *The Boston Globe* Barney Welansky had been recovering from a heart attack at Massachusetts General, where many of the wounded were taken the night of the fire. He had been convicted on nineteen counts of manslaughter for fire victims who were randomly selected to represent the almost five hundred patrons who had perished. Welansky had been charged with allowing the nightclub to run in violation of the loose standards of the day, a practice begun by Boston Charlie Solomon. Exits had been locked, others concealed with draperies, and one emergency exit was bricked up to prevent customers from leaving without paying.

If I hadn't gotten pregnant with Joan, I could have died in the fire, too.

Putting the paper down, she shook uncontrollably, horrified, thinking about what might have been her fate.

WAR YEARS AND THE CANDIDATE

Robbie arrived at the diner before dawn on a Friday in late March of 1943. She shook the rain from her winter coat and opened the door. She heard Bill and his dishwasher, Charlie, talking in hushed tones in the kitchen. Robbie hung her coat in the back storage room and began her chores of refilling the salt and pepper shakers and napkin holders. A tap on her shoulder caused her to jump and swing around.

"Bill! Jesus, you scared me!" She took a step back.

"Sorry, Robbie. Didn't mean to sneak up on you, but I've got to talk to you. Can you come out to the table?" The look on his face made her worry.

Sitting at a back table, Bill had poured them each a cup of black coffee. Robbie sat and stared at her employer.

Bill reached into his pocket and placed an envelope on the table. He stared at it for a few seconds, then lifted his gaze. "The letter came this week, Robbie. I've been drafted into the Army."

"What!" Robbie began to tremble. "How can that be? I thought the cutoff age was twenty-eight, and you're twenty-nine! It must be some mistake!"

Bill shrugged. "Yeah, that's what I thought, too. But Charlie heard they've raised the draft age to thirty-seven, in order to recruit more men. Guess my time is up!" He sipped his coffee and looked away. "Believe me, Robbie, I am not at all happy about this."

"Can't you try to get a deferment because you own the diner?"

Bill shook his head. "I went to the Army recruitment office on Wednesday and explained my situation with the diner. My request for deferment was denied. They said I would have to find somebody to run the restaurant during my absence or close it down."

Robbie's stomach tied in knots as Bill stared at her. "So who's going to run the place while you're gone? Charlie?"

"No. Charlie said he'd be willing to do some cooking and continue with the dishes, but he prefers to stay in the back." Bill glanced toward the kitchen, then back at Robbie. "I was thinking you could take over for me. What do you think, Robbie?"

"Me? You think I could run the restaurant? I don't know, Bill. It's a huge responsibility." She squeezed her trembling hands together on the table. "What if I can't do it? What if I fail?"

Bill grinned and touched her clenched fist. "Robbie, I've seen you in action when I've taken you on shopping trips to the marketplace at Faneuil Hall. Your smile entices the fishermen to sell you their best catch of the day. You seem to have a knack for finding the freshest produce from the farmers, and those butchers give you special deals because they love your red hair."

Robbie blushed at Bill's description, both pleased and a little embarrassed he had taken notice of her bargaining skills. *I guess I learned a lot from Shirley about using my looks to get what I want. I think she would be proud!* "But Bill, that's a lot different from running the whole diner. I don't know if I can do it alone."

"You won't be alone, Robbie. Charlie can handle the kitchen, with you running the grill. Since Richard is over fifty and won't be drafted, he's agreed to stay on as my bookkeeper. And Karen said she would ask her adult daughter, Kim, to waitress with her." He swung his arm around the empty room. "The only difference is I won't be here. But I think all of you will do just fine!" Bill leaned forward in his chair. "So, what do you think? Will you do it?"

She paused, thinking of the extra work. "Will I get a raise?"

Bill sat back in his chair and laughed. "Sure! I'll make sure Richard takes care of it!"

"When do you leave?"

"I have to report for duty on Monday."

"In three days? You've known about this all week, and you're just telling me now!"

Bill reached for her hands, but she pulled them away. "I'm sorry, Robbie. I had a lot of things to work out, and I was pretty sure you would say yes." He raised an eyebrow. "I really need your help, and I'm sure everything will be fine. Please say yes."

She thought about her financial situation. "Well, the extra money would be nice. Would you mind if I moved into your spare bedroom upstairs? It would help me out a lot."

Bill grinned. "Sure! You can stay there. Then your answer is yes?"

Robbie smiled. "You drive a hard bargain. But, yes, I'll run the diner for you." Her smile faded. "Bill, what happens if you don't return from the war? Have you thought of that?"

Bill rubbed a hand through his thick, blond hair. "Well, according to the recruiter, I'm being sent to Bora Bora with the Construction Battalion Maintenance Unit, to work as their chef. Apparently they're building a naval fuel depot on the island. So I doubt I'll see any combat, unless someone tries to shoot me over my cooking!"

"Bill! Don't joke about war!"

"Sorry! I just don't want you to worry, because I'll be home as soon as my deployment is done."

Oh, God! What have I gotten myself into? A raise, a more convenient place to live. But so much responsibility! Please guide me with your loving grace, so I don't let Bill down.

After Bill shipped out, Robbie moved her meager belongings into the spare bedroom at the back of the apartment above the diner. She was relieved she no longer had to pay rent. At the beginning of every month, Robbie diligently sent money to Marjorie to support Joan, who was now seven years old. Along with the money, Robbie always included a letter to Joan telling her how much she loved and missed her, and asking Joan to write back about her school activities and friends. Robbie waited expectantly every day for a letter from Joan, but none ever arrived.

I hope Joan is getting my letters and knows how much I miss her. Why doesn't she write to me? I hope Marjorie and Arthur haven't turned her against me. Maybe I can save enough money to go visit her soon.

For the next two-and-a-half years, Robbie worked twelve-to-fifteen-hour days as the manager at Bill's Diner on Tremont Street in Boston. Charlie was indispensable in helping her address the many problems that arose. And Richard was doing a fine job of managing the cash flow. True to his word, Bill arranged for her raise. Her weekly paycheck was now a good deal more than she had been making, and she was able to increase her savings account.

Occasionally, she went on a date to the movies with a patron. She thought Jimmy Stewart was wonderful, as he reminded her of her older brother, Wilmot. *I'm thankful I'm too busy to get seriously involved with any men right now.*

When she could get an occasional break from the diner, she also enjoyed going to Red Sox games at Fenway Park with her sister Gladys, Sean, and their son, Liam. Liam was a big Sox fan, and Robbie loved to watch him cheering in the stands. *Oh, how I wish I could bring Joan with us to the ballpark. I think she'd really have a lot of fun with her cousin.*

In August of 1945, Robbie was shocked when she saw pictures on the front page of *The Boston Globe* showing total devastation in Japan. The news stated U.S. troops had dropped atomic bombs on Nagasaki and Hiroshima.

Memories of her next younger brother, Paul, flashed through her mind. He had hugged and consoled her after their Poppa and Mamma had died. He had been a sweet, sensitive boy who always worried about others. She remembered the letter she had received from him in March of 1941.

Dear Robbie,

You'll never guess where I am! I'm serving on the USS Oklahoma and we're stationed at Pearl Harbor in Hawaii. Can you believe a poor farm boy like me has made his way to such a glorious paradise?

You wouldn't believe how big the palm trees are here. And the local girls are quite exotic doing their hula dancing. Sure ain't like old Maine!

Well, gotta get to my station. Just wanted you to know where I am. Hope you are staying well. Will write again soon.

Your loving brother,
Paul

After Roosevelt's speech describing the Japanese attack on Pearl Harbor on December 7th, 1941 as "a date which will live in infamy," Robbie and Gladys had agonized for months over Paul's whereabouts. *What happened to his ship? Had he survived? Why hadn't he written? Where could he be?* The lack of any specific news about the attack was maddening.

The following February, Gladys called Robbie to tell her Pauline, their oldest sister, had received a letter from the War Department. Paul's ship, the *U.S.S. Oklahoma*, had been sunk by Japanese torpedoes in Pearl Harbor, and Paul had died in the attack. Robbie was devastated at hearing the fate of her favorite brother. *Why must I lose everyone I love so dearly?*

As she stared at the newspaper photographs of incinerated Japanese buildings, her emotions whip-lashed. *I feel sorry for the innocent people. But those bastard Jap pilots killed my brother, so it's their own damned fault they got what they deserved. Maybe these bombings will finally end this horrible war!*

Not long after the bombs had been dropped, Japan surrendered, and the war was over.

Bill returned from his deployment, and moved back into his apartment, with Robbie still living in the back room. He took over where he had left off managing the diner, with Robbie working as the head chef.

One Friday afternoon, in early June of 1946, there was a larger-than-normal lunch crowd at the diner, many of whom were in town to attend graduation ceremonies at nearby Boston College. Robbie was serving customers at the counter when she watched four men enter, dressed in suits. Leading the group was a short, rotund, elderly gentleman with a ruddy complexion, sporting a toothy grin. Beside him was a tall, good looking, lanky young man Robbie guessed was about her age. He had a wind-blown shock of thick, brown hair, and a grin that matched the old man's. Robbie saw the family resemblance immediately. The other two men, in their mid-forties, had somber expressions, as if they were providing protection for the older man.

Several men jumped up from their tables and rushed to greet the old fellow. They shook his hand, patted him on the back, and kissed him on both cheeks. The noise level increased as some folks began to sing "Sweet Adeline." Then the jolly gent joined the crowd with a sweet singing voice in his thick Irish brogue. He began making the rounds of the tables, shaking hands and introducing the slim young man at his side. *Must be a local politician drumming up votes,* Robbie surmised, even though she couldn't hear the conversations.

Out of the corner of her eye, Robbie saw Bill rush out of the kitchen through the swinging doors, and he joined Robbie behind the counter.

"Who's that guy?" Robbie nodded toward the rotund gentlemen, whose florid face was perspiring from exertion.

"Why, it's Honey Fitzgerald! He was the Mayor of Boston twice and a Senator for our great state!" Bill puffed up his chest and grinned. "I can't believe he's here!"

"Who's the guy with him?" Robbie asked, fascinated by the handsome man's appearance.

"Not sure—obviously a relative. You can see the resemblance," Bill noted. "I'm sure Honey Fitz is trying to get him elected to something—always the politician!" Bill chuckled with admiration.

The men made their way along the counter, shaking hands with patrons. Finally they arrived at the end where Bill and Robbie stood.

The young man leaned in toward Robbie and offered his hand. "Hi! I'm Jack Kennedy. I'm running for Congress for the great Commonwealth of Massachusetts!" He shook Robbie's hand, and flashed his wide, toothy grin.

"Nice to meet you, Jack," Robbie said, smiling into his young, handsome face. She was mesmerized by the flecks of light dancing in his greenish-gray eyes.

"With that fiery red hair, you must be an Irish lass!"

Robbie swiped straggles of hair from her face, blushing from his direct soul-piercing gaze. "Actually—Dutch and Irish," she stammered.

"Well, as long as I get your vote, it's good enough for me!" Jack laughed, his eyes crinkling. "So, what's your name, Miss Irish Lass?"

"Robbie."

"Robbie?" Jack grinned. "But that's a man's name. What's your God-given name?"

Looking down at the counter, she said quietly, "Robena. My parents named me Robena."

"What a beautiful Irish name!" Jack slapped his hand on the counter, making Robbie jerk slightly.

Jack turned to one of his assistants, who carried a leather folio under one arm. "Henry, pass me some handbills, would ya?"

Henry placed several on the counter. The top headline announced: *The New Generation Offers a Leader*. Below it was a photo of Jack from the shoulders up. With a slight smile, he was looking straight into the camera. He wore a dark suit, white shirt, and striped tie. His now-mussed hair was parted on the left, and combed back into a tight wave over his forehead. Beneath the picture it stated: *John F. Kennedy for Congress, 11th District, 1946.*

Henry passed Jack a pen. Jack smiled at Robbie, then leaned on the counter. She watched him write something next to his picture. Then he slowly straightened and passed her the poster.

Robbie read the inscription: *To Robena, a true Irish Lass. I need your vote! - Jack Kennedy*

She smiled back at the charming man, her heart pounding. "Thanks! I'll be sure to vote for you, Jack!"

Then he leaned across the counter and kissed her cheek. "You'd better!" he chided.

She gasped.

Bill chatted amiably with Honey Fitz for a few minutes, then the entourage left the restaurant. Jack turned back, waving at Robbie, and winked.

I wonder what it would be like to be married to such a charming man. She shook her head. *But then again, Joe was charming, and that ended horribly!*

I bet Jack Kennedy has a roving eye for the ladies, too. But with his good looks, I have no doubt he could get elected to whatever office he ran for.

ELLIE AND BARBARA

Living under the same roof and working together eventually led to romance between Robbie and Bill. Even though Robbie felt no sexual attraction toward him, when Bill showed an interest, she felt obliged to him for keeping her employed at his diner all these years. During Christmas of 1946, at the age of thirty, Robbie realized she was pregnant again. *Oh, God! Another baby? I can't have this child out of wedlock, because I know God will do something horrible to break my heart again! But I would like to have another baby to love and raise. I miss Joan so much, and wish she were with me.*

Robbie had noticed Bill's demeanor had changed when he returned from the war. He was spending more nights out with his buddies drinking after the diner closed. She was concerned since his drinking tended to bring out an angry side of him. *How is Bill going to take the news, when I tell him I'm pregnant?*

On the day before New Year's, when the lunch crowd had left, Robbie approached Bill behind the counter. "Bill, I need to talk to you. Will you come sit with me?"

"What is it? Can't you see I'm busy?" He continued to wipe crumbs from the countertop.

Robbie blanched at his curt reply. "Can you take a break and sit down for a minute?"

Bill grunted and tossed his rag into the sink. "Okay. But make it quick!"

Robbie led the way to a table at the back of the diner. She sat, with Bill opposite her, and paused. *I hope he doesn't decide to kick me out on the street!*

Bill stared at her. "Well? What is it?"

Taking a deep breath, she blurted, "Bill, I'm pregnant."

Bill slumped back into his chair and ran his hand over his shorn head. "Ahhhh shit, Robbie! Are you sure?"

She nodded. "Yes."

"And you're sure it's my kid?"

"Yes, Bill. I haven't been with anyone else. It's yours."

"Christ, Robbie. I hate kids! I don't know the first thing about being a father!" He sighed and shook his head. "My old man was a son-of-a-bitch! He drank constantly, beat my mother, and made my life miserable. What kind of a father would I be with that example?" He slumped back in his chair and crossed his arms.

"Well, I think if you cut back on your drinking some, you'd be a great father."

"But I like going out with the guys! It's the only break I get from the diner." He waved his hand toward the kitchen. "And they're all war vets."

She sighed and placed her hands on the table. "Bill, please listen to me. I had my daughter Joan out of wedlock, and God punished me by making me send her away. I don't want it to happen again!" Her voice broke and her stomach churned.

Bill turned and rubbed his eyes. "So you want me to marry you. Is that it?"

Echoes of Joe's response a decade ago, when she told him she was pregnant, ripped through her mind. *Oh, God! How do I get myself into these relationships?* Her heart pounded. "Yes. It's what I was hoping."

Bill sat back and stared at her. Then he leaned forward. "Robbie, I don't exactly know how to say this. I like you as a friend, and you're a hard worker. I appreciate your having taken over while I was in the Army." He paused and rubbed his face. "But…well…I don't love you. I'm sorry! I never wanted to have a kid, and this has caught me by surprise." He twisted in his chair. "Let me think about this, and we can decide what to do, okay?" He rose from the table and strode through the swinging door into the kitchen, leaving Robbie at the table in desolate silence.

The following August, with Robbie in her ninth month of pregnancy, she once again confronted Bill as they sat at a back table in the diner. "Bill, this baby is due any day. We have to get married before it's born, or God will punish both of us!" Her husky voice rose in frustration over Bill's procrastination.

Bill waved his hand in the air. "Jesus, Robbie! You've been nagging me about this since you got pregnant. All right! If that's what you want, then let's go!"

Robbie reached over and touched his hand. "Thank you. It means a lot to me!" *I cannot have another bastard child and face God's wrath again.*

The next day, Bill and Robbie were married in a civil ceremony at the Boston courthouse. Robbie's sister Gladys, and their kitchen helper, Charlie, were their witnesses.

In late August of 1947, Robbie gave birth to a baby girl. She named her Eleanor after First Lady Eleanor Roosevelt, whom she admired for her strength and independence, and Maria, after her dear friend Maria Tsoukanis, now gone from her life. To Robbie's surprise, the baby had inherited her Poppa Frank's thick, dark hair and brown eyes.

Robbie juggled working at the restaurant and caring for baby Ellie, whom she kept in a crib in the back storeroom during the day. *I'm glad I don't have to hire a babysitter. And our waitresses, Karen and Kim, have been such a big help with the baby! And Bill even seems to be interested in his daughter, which I'm grateful for.*

On Robbie's thirty-second birthday, in March of 1948, Karen and her daughter Kim surprised her by bringing a birthday cake to the diner.

"We didn't want to forget your birthday, Robbie!" Karen grinned as she set the decorated cake on a table.

"Oh, my! Well, this is a surprise," Robbie blushed. "I don't usually make a to-do about my birthday. Thank you!" She turned toward the back of the diner. "Let me get Ellie, so she can join us."

Robbie pulled seven-month-old Ellie from her playpen and returned to the table, where she perched her daughter on her lap. Kim set plates and forks when Bill and Charlie joined them. Several lunch patrons watched the celebration.

Karen passed Robbie a sharp knife. "Here you go, Robbie. You get to cut the cake."

Robbie leaned around Ellie and sliced through half the round cake. Suddenly, Ellie reached out and grabbed a fistful of pink frosting, smearing it on her face. Everyone laughed.

"No, no, Ellie! You have to wait!" Robbie pulled the girl's hand away from the cake then slid the confection away from the baby's reach. "I think you need to finish this." She handed the knife to Karen.

After Robbie had shared her cake slice with Ellie, she felt her stomach lurch. She swallowed hard to keep down the bile, but it erupted again. *Oh, no!* She turned to Kim, now in her mid-twenties, sitting to her left. "Will you hold Ellie for a minute? I'll be right back." She handed her daughter over, rose, and rushed to the bathroom at the back of the diner.

Robbie quickly lifted the toilet seat and vomited once, and then again. She grunted, wiping her mouth with the back of her hand. *What in heaven's name brought this on? I don't have time to be sick.* Straightening, she went to the sink and splashed water on her face, then wiped it with a towel. Taking deep breaths seemed to calm her nausea. She patted stray hairs from her face, then went back to the table to join the small celebration.

It was a cold, blustery day on November 9th, 1948, when Robbie went into labor with her third child. Bill called their neighbor, Mrs. Billings, to care for Ellie, then drove Robbie to the hospital, where she was admitted to a room with other expectant mothers. Robbie gasped at each new labor pain, her contractions coming quickly. She was both sweating and chilled.

Finally, the obstetrician entered the room and came to her bedside.

"Missus Van Dyne, how are you feeling?" Doctor Rogers asked.

"I feel like this baby wants to be born right now!" Robbie gasped, as another contraction ripped through her.

"Let me check your progress." The doctor sat on a stool at the end of the bed, pulled back the covers, and gently spread her legs. "You've got a little while yet before this baby is born. Try to relax and don't push when the contractions come until I'm here with you."

A nurse rushed into the room. "Doctor, come quick! You're needed in the next room."

"I'll be back soon, Missus Van Dyne. You're doing just fine," he said as he quickly left the room.

Robbie lay back in bed and tried to relax, but the contractions were coming swiftly now. The pain spiked and she felt the need to push. The young nurse in the room held Robbie's hand and mopped the sweat from her brow. Gasping for breath, Robbie squeezed the nurse's hand as the throbbing partially subsided. Minutes later, another round of contractions swept through her, and Robbie was helpless to stop the baby's progress.

The nurse rushed to the bottom of the bed and lifted the blanket. "Oh, no! I see the baby's head! Stop pushing!—Stop pushing! The doctor's not here!" she screamed. Panicked, she pressed her hands on the baby's head and pushed it back into the birth canal.

Robbie screamed.

"Get the doctor! Help me! Get the doctor!" the novice yelled at another nurse. "This baby is being born right now!"

Robbie could no longer fight, as contractions wracked her body. "Oh, Dear Lord!" she pleaded. "Why is this so hard? Why isn't this baby moving? Please help me and save my baby!" Robbie began to lose consciousness, as the room went gray around the edges of her vision.

Suddenly, Robbie saw her Mamma standing in front of a small cabin surrounded by a copse of pine trees. Robbie had never seen the cabin before. Holding Mamma's hand was a small girl about three years old, with red hair. Robbie instinctively knew it was her oldest sister, Mae, whom her family had only discussed in hushed tones. But there was something wrong—the girl's head was badly misshapen: huge at the top tapering to a pointy chin, and looked to be way too big for her tiny body. One arm ended at the elbow, where a tiny, deformed hand protruded. The girl wore a light cotton dress and no shoes. It was snowing.

"She's damaged. We can't keep her," Mamma led the girl through the door of the cabin. Inside, Mamma built a fire in the small wood stove. Next to the stove was an old wash basin. Against the opposite wall was a wood-framed

cot with one woolen blanket. The girl crouched in front of the stove, poking her tiny, deformed hands out for warmth, and smiled up at her mother. Mamma patted the girl on the head, walked out the door, bolted it shut from the outside and walked away.

"No! Mamma! You can't leave her there!" Robbie shouted in her mind. "She'll freeze!" Snow piled up around the cabin, until it was no longer visible amongst the trees. Inside, as the warmth escaped, the girl wrapped herself in the thin blanket and curled into a fetal position on the cot. Her breath billowed around her, until it was no more.

"Mamma! Mamma! Why did you leave her to die?"

"She's a monster. It's better this way!" Mamma said as she trudged through the knee-deep snow and disappeared into the woods.

"Mamma, wait!"

Robbie became aware of someone yelling at her to stop pushing, but she had no control of her body. This baby wanted to be born, and she was helpless to stop it. Blinking to clear her eyes, she saw Doctor Rogers suddenly burst into the room, grab the nurse and push her to the floor.

A second, older nurse rushed into the room, pulled the sobbing novice to her feet, shoved her out the door, then returned to assist Robbie.

"Missus Van Dyne!" Doctor Rogers called. "I want you to give me a big push with all you've got."

She felt someone squeezing her hand. "Robbie! Robbie!" the older nurse yelled at her. "You have to push now. Now! Big breath. All right…puuuuush!"

Robbie took a deep breath and squeezed down hard with as much strength as she had left. She felt the baby's head emerging and she screamed in pain.

"That's it…that's it…" the doctor guided. "One more big push, you can do it."

She gave one last grunt and felt the baby's body finally moving through her birth canal. Gasping for air, she fell back on the bed, exhausted.

An urgency in the doctor's voice prompted Robbie to lift her head and peer down to the end of the bed. "Nurse! Cut the cord. She's not breathing."

The nurse clamped the umbilical cord and cut it away from the baby, who was covered in a blackish/green fluid. Robbie watched in agony as Doctor Rogers cleared the baby's nose and mouth of placental fluid, grabbed her feet, held her upside down and slapped her bottom. The baby didn't respond.

Oh, Dear Lord! Please save my baby!

The doctor rushed the baby to a table, where he pulsed her chest several times, then lifted her again to smack her bottom. The baby finally let out a small mewl and began breathing on her own.

Robbie exhaled heavily, and slumped back onto the bed. *Thank you for not letting her die!* she thought, and slipped into darkness.

BILL IS FURIOUS

"I'm afraid the news isn't good." Doctor Worton, Barbara's pediatrician, said as he stared at the report on his desk. He paused to run his fingers through his graying hair.

Robbie and Bill sat in the doctor's office, waiting for the results of tests performed on Barbara, now a month old. Fifteen-month-old Ellie was squirming to get down from Bill's lap. Robbie held the baby, who was lying limp, staring up at the ceiling.

Something went terribly wrong during the delivery. I just can't remember everything, and no one has talked to us since Barbara's birth.

When Robbie had brought the baby home and tried to nurse her, Barbara would suckle for a few seconds, then her head would roll back and she'd lose interest. Concerned she wasn't getting enough nourishment, Robbie resorted to force-feeding her with a bottle. She thought it was odd when Barbara was wet or hungry, instead of letting out a healthy wail as Ellie had, she would just mewl quietly in her crib like a kitten. Robbie had to attend to the baby's needs much more frequently than she had Ellie at that age. *What if there's a serious problem with this sweet baby? Then what am I going to do?*

"Something bad happened during the delivery, didn't it?" Robbie asked the doctor, hoping he would tell her the truth.

The doctor looked up from his report. "I'm so sorry, Missus Van Dyne. A new nurse in the delivery room panicked when Doctor Rogers was called from the room." He shook his head. "Unfortunately, she held the baby's head from being born for several minutes," he explained. A look of deep concern and sadness crossed his aging face. "After conferring with Doctor Rogers, we have concluded Barbara suffered loss of oxygen to her brain during the delivery. It was an accident, and I want you to know the nurse has been disciplined."

Loss of oxygen? What does that do to the baby? The stupid nurse! That's why the baby wouldn't move. Why in heaven's name would she have done such a thing? The excruciating pain that had caused Robbie to pass out was still fresh in her memory. She hugged Barbara closer to her chest.

Doctor Worton scanned the papers. "From the tests we've done on the baby's progress, we believe she has irreversible brain damage. I'm so sorry to tell you this, but she is afflicted with cerebral palsy." He peered at Barbara, lolling in Robbie's arms.

Robbie gasped and her heart thumped in her chest. *Oh, dear Lord! This poor baby. How am I ever going to care for her?*

Bill's face flushed and he threw his hands into the air. "How the hell did that happen?" he raged. "Where the fuck was the doctor while all this was going on?"

"As I said, it was a terrible accident—"

"Accident? This was no goddamned accident! This is bullshit! How could you let this happen? Now what the hell are we supposed to do?" At his outburst, Ellie squirmed in Bill's lap and started to whimper.

The doctor's face went ashen as he absentmindedly ran his fingers through his mussed hair. "Mister and Missus Van Dyne, you must understand—this baby will never lead a normal life. She'll never walk, she'll never talk, and she'll never be able to care for herself. She may live a few years at best, considering her condition," he said, staring down at his desk. "I'm sorry to tell you this, but she'll require constant care and supervision for the rest of her short life."

Robbie stared at the slack infant in her arms. *Oh, you poor, innocent child. What have they done to you? I love you more than you could know.* She gently wiped the drool from Barbara's cheek.

"So what are we supposed to do with her? How the hell are we going to take care of her?" Bill yelled at the doctor. "I can't deal with a retarded kid!" He swung his arm and pointed at the lolling infant.

The doctor leaned forward in his chair. "Mister and Missus Van Dyne. I understand this news puts you in a difficult family position. But you should know there are some very good institutions in Boston that care for retarded children." He pulled a pamphlet from his desk drawer. "I would recommend you place the baby in one of these, where she can live out her life under professional care."

Bill took the pamphlet from the doctor. "And how much is this going to cost us? What if she lives longer than you expect? Then what?"

"It won't cost you anything, Sir." He nodded toward the baby. "We'll make arrangements for Barbara to become a ward of the state, and then her living expenses will be covered."

Robbie spoke up. "I don't understand. What does it mean if she's a ward of the state?"

"It means you give up your parental rights regarding decisions about her health treatments. It will be up to the doctors and nurses at the facility to decide what's best for the baby." He pointed to the brochure. "You will have visitation rights, so I recommend you select one close to your home."

Bill turned in his seat to face Robbie. Ellie whimpered and reached for her mother. In his agitated state, Bill had squeezed his daughter too tight, cutting off her cries. "Robbie, listen to me. The doctor is right. This baby is damaged. We can't keep her and care for her."

Robbie froze in her chair and stared at Bill. She was stunned at how Bill's comment so eerily echoed her Mamma's words from her vision about her sister Mae. She pictured the deformed little girl curled up on the cot, taking her last breaths. *Was it just a dream, or did it really happen? Is that why Mamma never talked about sister Mae? Did the whole family know what Mamma had done? How could she ever forgive herself for doing such a horrible thing?* A shiver ran through Robbie, making her whole body shudder.

Robbie glared at Bill. "Get rid of her like a piece of trash? Put her in an asylum? Let her die?" Robbie cried, still in shock over the diagnosis of her sweet daughter. "I won't do it! I can't do it! She's my daughter, and I will *not* turn her over to strangers who don't love her!" She caressed the baby's head. "Please, Bill! I can't bear to lose another child, no matter what her condition. Don't let them take her away from me!" Her voice cracked as she choked back tears and dropped her head.

Bill squeezed Robbie's hand, forcing her to look him in the eye. "Look, Robbie. We still have Ellie, who is normal. She'll keep you plenty busy. This baby is badly damaged. It's better this way—we need to give her up. We don't know how to take care of a retarded kid!"

Robbie was devastated at how callous Bill was being about the future of their baby.

"Plus, we could always have more kids someday, if you wanted."

Robbie pulled away from Bill's grasp and clutched Barbara. "No! No! No! I will *not* do it! She's my child, and I will love and take care of her for the rest of my life. I'll do whatever it takes!" She shook in fury as she rose from the chair, and cradled Barbara in her arms.

As Robbie stormed out of the office, she heard Doctor Worton say, "'I'm so sorry, Mister Van Dyne. If your wife changes her mind, please call me and we can make the arrangements."

Bill grabbed Ellie, who was now wailing, and followed Robbie out the door.

Later that evening, after putting Ellie to bed, Robbie slumped in her rocking chair, exhausted from the emotional day. She cradled her sweet, damaged baby girl in her arms and pondered the life ahead of them. *How can I care for this child? And what will happen to her when I'm gone? Did I make a mistake? Should we put her in an asylum? Why, oh why is God punishing me again? What have I ever done to deserve this life of constant pain and heartache?*

"God, please give me the strength and courage to care for this special child you have bestowed upon me, and still be a good mother for Ellie," she prayed. "I cannot bear to give up another child, no matter what the cost."

Robbie rested her head against the rocking chair, closed her eyes, and sang:

Lul-la-by and good night
Thy mother's delight
Bright angels beside
My darling abide.
Lay thee down now and rest
May thy slumber be blessed
Lay thee down now and rest
May thy slumber be blessed.

Barbara mewled in her arms as Robbie drifted to sleep.

BURNED STEW, BARBARA SPEAKS

One night, when Barbara wasn't quite a year old, Robbie had cooked a beef stew. She fed herself and Ellie, then spoon-fed Barbara baby food. Bill was out drinking with his buddies, as usual, after the diner closed. She set the pot of stew on the back burner to keep it warm for him until he came home.

She bathed both girls, and Ellie went right to bed and fell asleep. But Barbara was agitated and fussy. Robbie thought she might be teething. When Robbie tried to pin a diaper on her, Barbara kicked and fussed, crying her mewling sounds, making it hard for Robbie to hold her down. Robbie finally got a diaper and pajamas on her and cradled the baby in the rocking chair, trying to sing her to sleep. No sooner had she gotten settled, when the stench of poop filled the air. Robbie sighed, frustrated. She put the baby back on the changing table, removed the dirty diaper, cleaned her bottom, pinned on a clean diaper and put the pajamas back on. Once more, Robbie settled into rocking chair with Barbara in her arms, and started singing the baby to sleep.

Bill's voice bellowing from the kitchen shook Robbie awake in the rocking chair. "What the hell is burning in here? Robbie, where the hell are you?"

Robbie quickly laid Barbara in her crib and ran into the kitchen.

"I'm so sorry. I left the burner on to keep the stew warm, and I must've fallen asleep," she explained. She stepped to the stove and turned off the burner. The acrid smell of burnt stew permeated the kitchen.

"What the hell kind of a stupid wife are you? You can't even have a decent supper ready for me when I come home?" Bill staggered and slurred his words.

Why does he have to get so drunk? As she turned to face him, there was something about Bill's expression that made the hairs on her neck prickle. "I'm sorry," she said as she held her palms towards him in the way of an apology.

For a brief moment Bill stood there and glared, forehead knotted, looking confused. Then without warning, as if some demon possessed him, his face contorted. "I'll show you sorry!"

Before Robbie could react, Bill swung his right hand and slapped her across the face. Robbie stumbled backward, tripping over a dining chair. She fell hard, her head slamming against the kitchen floor. She squeezed her eyes shut as pain smashed through her head and lightning bolts flashed.

"Get the hell up and fix me something to eat!" Bill kicked her in the ribs and staggered around the kitchen. "You're worthless as a goddamned wife." He grabbed a beer from the refrigerator, stomped into the living room, turned the radio up full blast, and plopped into his easy chair.

Robbie curled up on the floor and grasped her pounding head. *I can't believe he hit me! What the hell is wrong with him? He gets so damned mean when he drinks. What am I going to do if he goes after the girls? I have to make sure they stay out of his way when he's drinking.*

With some effort, she raised herself to the kitchen chair and sat for a while, clearing her head of the ringing and dizziness. After taking two aspirins, she fixed Bill a sandwich and brought it to him in the living room, avoiding his gaze.

The following afternoon, Robbie had settled the two girls on the sofa and was cleaning the kitchen. A light knock on her door startled her. *Who could that be? I'm not expecting anyone.* She wiped her hands on a towel and opened the door, surprised to see her sister.

"Gladys! I wasn't expecting you. Come on in." Robbie held the door for her.

Gladys paused, staring at Robbie, then entered.

"Join me in the kitchen. I'll make us some tea." As Robbie walked to the stove, Gladys stopped at the sofa and kissed each of the girls' cheeks.

Gladys sat at the table while Robbie put the teapot on to heat, then joined her sister.

"So what brings you here today?" Robbie asked.

"Jesus, Robbie! What happened to you?" Gladys touched her own cheek, then pointed to Robbie's swollen face and bruised eye.

Should I tell her the truth, or lie? Will she think less of me as her sister if she knows the truth? Robbie dropped her head, then looked up. "I slipped and fell here in the kitchen. It's nothing, really."

Gladys leaned across the table and grasped Robbie's hand. "Robbie, I'm your sister. Be honest with me. Did Bill do this? I know how much he drinks, and I worry about you and the girls."

Robbie stared at the table and nodded. "Gladys, please don't tell anyone! It was my fault. I put the stew on the burner to keep it warm and fell asleep. It was burned by the time he got home." The odor still lingered in the kitchen.

"So what happened?"

"He said I was worthless as a wife, then he hit me. I fell over the chair and landed hard, hitting my head on the floor. I still have a headache." Robbie lightly rubbed her bruised cheek.

Gladys squinted at her sister. "Oh, Jesus! Has he done this before? I'm going to kill that sonofabitch, I swear!"

"No, no! This was the first time. Like I said, it was my fault! Please don't tell anyone. I'm just embarrassed, that's all."

"Robbie, this was *not* your fault. There's no excuse for him hitting you. Has he ever threatened the girls?" Gladys swung her arm toward the sofa.

Robbie shook her head. "No. Bill is good with Ellie, and he basically ignores Barbara. I just wish he wouldn't drink so much." The tea kettle whistled. Robbie rose, brought the kettle to the table, and started to pour the steaming water into their teacups. Her right hand shook so violently the water splashed onto the table.

Gladys stood and took the kettle from her sister. "Robbie, sit. Let me do that." She filled their cups, then returned the kettle to the stove. Sitting back at the table, she reached over and grasped Robbie's hand. "Robbie, if Bill ever lifts a hand to you again, I want you to tell me immediately. I'm really worried about you and the girls. Will you promise me?"

Robbie choked back her tears and looked up at her younger sister, who had always been her closest friend. "I'm sure it won't happen again. I just need to be more careful." She grasped her trembling right hand. "But yes, I will tell you if he does. I promise."

Ever since Bill's first attack seven years earlier, Robbie frequently experienced migraines and blurred vision. Sometimes the headaches were so severe she had no choice but to lie down in a dark room until the worst of the pain subsided. When she was overly tired, her right hand trembled uncontrollably. *I probably should go see a doctor, but I've got too much to do right now.*

By now Robbie had been at the mercy of Bill's drunken rants too many times, and she had the bruises and scars to show for it. He had never touched Ellie, but Robbie had had to put herself in harm's way on other occasions when Bill went into a rage, threatening to hurt Barbara—because she was a "freak," as he called her. Robbie did her best to hide her bruises from her sister Gladys, for fear of what she would think of her for enduring Bill's abuse.

I wish I could take the girls and leave. But I have nowhere to go and no money to support us. I have to protect my girls from harm, no matter what happens to me.

Juggling the responsibilities of mothering two young girls—one of them mentally challenged—working at the diner, and trying to avoid Bill's temper, had engulfed Robbie's life over the preceding years.

Her devotion to teaching Barbara how to accomplish the basic life functions was exhausting. From feeding herself to using the toilet, every act Barbara attempted was a challenge. When Robbie tried to help her, Barbara expressed her frustration by screaming, biting her own knuckles until they bled, slapping herself in the face, pulling out clumps of her own hair, or slapping others nearby. As Barbara grew older, she became stronger and heavier. Robbie needed all the strength and will she could muster to control the child's tantrums. Mrs. Billings, their neighbor, now in her sixties, babysat when Robbie went to work. Because Barbara needed constant supervision so she wouldn't injure herself, it became increasingly more difficult for the older woman to handle her.

Determined to prove the doctor wrong, Robbie had painstakingly taught Barbara how to walk. When Barbara was three, Robbie came up with a plan. She had Ellie stand on the second step from the bottom of the stairs, and hold Barbara's hands. Then Robbie crouched behind and lifted one of Barbara's legs up, saying: "Left." Robbie would then lift the other leg, saying, "Right," up to the same stair. Ellie pulled Barbara's weight up to the step. Sometimes Barbara would rebel, start screaming, and just plop down on the stairs. Robbie let her have her fit, then would gently lift the child to start up again. Robbie and Ellie repeated this process with Barbara climbing the stairway twice a day.

In their apartment, Robbie would stand behind Barbara, holding the child's hands in the air, and push Barbara's left foot forward saying, "Left." Then Robbie would push the child's right foot forward saying, "Right." Back and forth they would go. Through sheer force of repetition and determination on Robbie's part, Barbara learned to walk in a shuffling gate on her own at the age of seven.

I knew Barbara could do it. It just takes her longer than others to learn the skills. She's not stupid, she's just slow. I'm so proud of her, even if it did take four years!

Again, through endless repetition, Barbara learned to feed herself with a spoon. But it was a hit-and-miss operation, so Robbie always put a bib on her before meals.

Bill's voice rang in her mind. "I can't stand to eat at the same table with that child. She makes such a goddamned mess!" On those few occasions when Bill actually came home for dinner, Robbie served his meals in the living room.

Robbie and Ellie had also tried to teach Barbara to speak by holding objects in front of her and repeating their names: "ball," "shoe," "spoon." But Barbara never repeated any of the words, only stared at the objects, or screamed and threw them wildly around the room.

Although Robbie was often frustrated at Barbara's slow progress, she took joy in watching her older daughter. Ellie had grown into a sweet, caring girl who showed extraordinary patience helping and protecting her younger, challenged sister.

Ellie reminds me so much of my Poppa. He was so kind to everyone. And she looks like him, too, with her thick hair and gentle brown eyes.

Barbara had also inherited her Poppa's thick, brown, hair, but had Bill's piercing blue eyes, which always caught Robbie by surprise, whenever she looked at her younger daughter.

One September evening, when Barbara was eight years old, Robbie was cooking supper. The girls were playing on the sofa in the living room behind her. She heard Ellie say, "Boo," then giggle. *They sound like they're having fun.*

"Mommy, Mommy! Barb just said *boo*," Ellie yelled into the kitchen.

What did Ellie just say? Robbie rushed into the living room. "What do you mean she said *boo?*" Robbie's eyes went wide as she stared at her mute daughter.

"Here, watch." Ellie put her hands over Barbara's eyes, released them quickly, and said, "Boo!"

"Boo!' Barbara replied again, laughing, as she flung her arms in the air.

"Oh, dear Lord! That's the first word I've ever heard her say. Thank you!" Robbie whispered as she collapsed into a chair.

It was the only word Barbara would ever learn to speak.

BILL GETS AN OFFER

It was mid-morning on a beautiful autumn day in early October of 1955, when Robbie noticed a tall, well-dressed man enter the diner alone. His gray, pinstriped suit was nicely tailored, and complemented the graying hair at his temples. He carried a brown leather briefcase.

She approached him. "Table for one, Sir?"

He shook his head and peered at her. "Not just yet. Actually I'm looking for Bill Van Dyne. This is his diner, isn't it?"

Robbie nodded. "Yes, it is. He's in the back. Hold on, I'll get him for you." Robbie stepped behind the counter, and called through the window opening into the kitchen. "Bill! There's someone here to see you."

"Who is it? I'm busy," Bill groused from the kitchen.

Robbie shrugged. "I don't know." She tilted her head in the stranger's direction. "That guy."

Bill glared through the window. Then Robbie watched his expression change to one of recognition. He hurried through the kitchen door, bolted around the counter, and addressed the man. "John! How the hell are you? What brings you here? Hey, what can I get for you?" Bill gushed as he patted the man on the back.

Robbie had followed Bill at a short distance to where the stranger stood.

"Bill—long-time no see." The men shook hands. "Coffee would be fine, if you have a few minutes," John said.

"Sure. Have a seat." Bill motioned at a table toward the back of the diner. "Oh, this is my wife, Robbie." He patted her arm. "Robbie, this is John Fleming from my Army unit. I haven't seen him in years!" Bill turned to Robbie as he sat down with John. "Bring us a couple of joes, would'ya?"

A few moments later, Robbie returned with two cups of black coffee and set them on the table. "I'll leave you two alone. Nice to meet you, John," she said, as she went to the storeroom.

As Robbie waited on the few customers in the restaurant, she couldn't help but watch Bill and John, their heads bent close in intense conversation.

Robbie had noticed Bill's drinking, constant rants and perpetually bad mood had sent their regular customers fleeing. Now in his early forties, Bill's blond hair was tinged with gray. His naturally florid face was bloated from his constant alcohol use. Eating most of his meals at the diner had caused his weight to balloon over fifty pounds since he'd returned from the war a decade ago. Carrying the extra weight caused him constant back pain, which made him even more difficult to live with.

I wonder what they're talking about. I'm not going to ask, because I don't want to make Bill mad. But I hope he tells me sooner or later.

About a half-hour later, Robbie stood behind the counter and watched Bill and John rise from the table and shake hands. Then John left the diner. Bill had a smile on his face. He walked past Robbie and went directly into the kitchen. Curious, Robbie peered through the serving window and saw Bill and his dishwasher Charlie standing by the back door, talking in hushed tones. *Something's up. This worries me.*

Within a few minutes, two customers entered the diner and sat at the counter. Robbie wrote down their order, then clipped the slip over the window and rang the small bell to get Charlie's attention.

"Be right there!" Charlie hollered.

Robbie saw the two men still standing at the back, their heads almost touching. Then Bill nodded and shook Charlie's hand. Robbie stepped away and poured two cups of coffee for the new patrons. When she turned back, Bill was standing next to her.

"Will you come sit down with me? We need to talk," Bill said as he moved to the same table where he and John had sat. Robbie tried to read Bill's expression as she sat opposite him and clasped her hands on the table.

"So, you met John. Well, it turns out he's the East Coast regional manager with Saga Foods. They do food service for institutions like colleges." Bill rubbed a hand through his hair. "John said his chef at a college in Vermont has quit, and he's offered me the job."

"What!" Robbie's breath caught in her throat. "What did you tell him?"

Bill looked down at the table, then back at Robbie. "I told him I'd take the job. He needs someone to take over as soon as possible because the school year has already started."

"Bill, are you out of your mind? What are you going to do with the diner? I can't run it and still care for the girls. You know that!" Just thinking about how exhausted she had been managing the place while Bill was in the Army made her want to run.

"Look, Robbie. John said he'd pay me in advance, and there's a house near the college we could rent. It'd be good for the kids." He gestured toward the kitchen. "I just talked with Charlie. He said he'd take over, and he knows a good short-order cook he can hire. Plus, the diner just isn't busy anymore and I'm tired of it. I need a change!" He sat back in his chair and stared at her. "So I've decided we're moving to Vermont."

"*You* decided? Don't *I* have anything to say about this? What if I don't want to move?" Robbie's mind was reeling. *Move to Vermont? But my life is here in Boston! I can't leave Gladys and her family, especially now that she has her adorable twin girls. Aunt Jeannette and Uncle Seamus are here. They're my whole life! And what about Barbara? I'd have to find a new babysitter— someone who can handle her temper tantrums.*

Bill slammed his hand on the table, making Robbie jump. "No, you really *don't* have anything to say about this! You're my wife, and you and the girls will go where I tell you to go!"

Robbie glared at Bill. *Damn him all to hell!* "So when do you plan to leave?"

"I'll have to attend a three-day training session, then John needs me there within a week afterward."

"A week? We're moving in a week?" Robbie said, trying to get her mind around everything that would need to be done in such a short period of time.

"I'll see if Gladys' husband, Sean and their boy, Liam can help us move." Bill stood and stepped away from the table. "Now get upstairs and start packing," he ordered. "I'm going to celebrate with the boys tonight!"

Later in the evening, after finally getting the girls to bed, Robbie sat on the sofa in the living room, exhausted. Her mind sorted over the million things she'd have to do to get ready to move. Barbara had been difficult and fought Robbie throughout the day, throwing temper tantrums. She had tried to cajole and reason with her stubborn daughter, with little success. And uncharacteristically for her, Ellie had been in a whiny mood.

I'm probably not giving Ellie enough of my time because Barbara is so demanding. I'll have to make it up to Ellie somehow.

Then she heard Bill's heavy footsteps on the stairs leading up to their apartment. She sighed and braced herself for whatever foul mood he might be in after drinking with his buddies.

Bill walked into the living room, bent over and forced a kiss on Robbie, his breath reeking of beer.

Robbie pushed him away. "Jesus, Bill! You stink to high heaven!"

Bill threw his jacket off and plopped onto the sofa next to her. "Well, you should know the guys are happy for me. They said I made the right decision and congratulated me on my new job." He grinned.

"Good for them," Robbie said off-handedly, as she slid away from Bill.

"And you wanna know what else?" Bill slurred his words. "My buddy Doug was complaining his wife never wants him to touch her anymore. She says she's too tired from dealing with the kids." A strange laugh escaped him.

Robbie's heart thumped in her chest as she stared at Bill's distorted face. He had a strange expression in his eyes, one she'd never seen before. She started to rise.

"So that got me to thinkin'—it's been a damned long time since you and me had any fun."

Bill grasped her arm, but she pulled it from his grip and stepped away from him. "Bill, it's been a long day and I really *am* exhausted. Can't we just leave this for another time?"

Then Bill leaped from the couch, grabbed her, and yanked her toward the bedroom. She struggled to get away, but Bill outweighed her, and she was unable to free herself from his strong grip. "What are you doing? Cut it out. Leave me alone!"

He growled, "No! This can't wait. You're my wife, goddammit, now act like one!"

In the bedroom, as Robbie continued to struggle from his grip, Bill slapped her across the face and knocked her to the bed, then slammed the door behind them. "Don't fight me, goddammit!"

Robbie scrambled and rolled off the bed. "Bill! Stop it! You'll wake the girls!"

Bill yanked her back onto the bed. She kicked him in his ample stomach to push him away.

Bill howled, "You bitch!" He pinned her arms and straddled her midsection.

"Get off me! I don't want to do this. Leave me alone! You're drunk!" She squirmed beneath him trying to buck his heavy body off her.

The more she struggled, the more aroused he got. "You're my wife! Now do your duty!" Spittle sprang from his mouth as he slapped her again.

The force of his blow caused Robbie to bite her lip hard, and blood trickled down her cheek. She gasped as pain shot through her head. Holding her by one arm, Bill unzipped his pants and pulled out his engorged penis.

She flailed her legs, kneeing him in the rump, trying to topple him. "Stop it! Don't do this. You're hurting me!" Robbie turned her head away, sobbing.

Bill ripped through her blouse and bra and squeezed her bare breasts. She gasped in pain. Then he lifted her skirt and tore off her underwear. Robbie kicked and tried to roll away from him, but he pinned her against the bed.

"Stop fighting! You owe this to me!" Bill grabbed her legs and yanked them apart, positioned his rigid penis above her and rammed into her body. A guttural noise escaped him.

Robbie screamed as the pain ripped through her. Memories of Leroy's abuse when she was a child came flooding back to her.

"Now that's what a wife's for!" Bill growled, as he pumped her harder and harder, slamming her against the headboard.

Robbie could no longer fight and surrendered to Bill's grindings. She shut her eyes so she didn't have to look into his drunken, contorted face.

With a hard thrust, Bill growled and arched his back. "Ahhhhhh, Jeeez—zussssss!" Then his bulk collapsed on top of her.

"Get off of me!" she gasped, his weight crushing her.

Finally, Bill grasped his lower back and slid off the bed. He put on his trousers and left the room without looking back or saying another word.

Robbie sobbed, curling into a fetal position, and caressed her throbbing cheek. *Damn him all to hell! Why is he so violent? I just don't understand. I'm probably going to look horrible in the morning. I don't know how much more of this I can take.*

The following morning, Robbie went into the girls' bedroom to wake them. She shook Ellie lightly. Ellie's eyes went wide as she stared at her mother's bruised, swollen face. Robbie blushed, turned her head away, and tried to hide her face with her hair.

Ellie's eyes went wide. "Mommy? Are you okay?" she whispered. "I heard you and Daddy fighting last night. Then I heard him pounding on the wall."

Robbie touched Ellie's cheek. *She's a very perceptive girl for only being eight. She knows something's wrong, but what do I tell her?* "Honey, I'm all right. We just had a little argument," Robbie answered, a tremor in her voice.

"Mommy? Why is Daddy so mean?" Tears leaked down Ellie's cheeks.

Robbie shook her head. "I don't know. Sometimes he just gets mad." Robbie tried vainly to explain away his abuse.

Ellie sat up in bed and crossed her arms. "Is he going to hurt me and Barb, too?"

Robbie's heart ached. "No, Honey! I would never let him hurt either one of you. I promise!"

"Well I think he's mean, and I hate him! I hate him!" Ellie cried in her mother's arms.

"Now, Ellie, the Lord says it's a sin to hate anyone," Robbie said as she comforted her daughter. *But I can't say I disagree with her!*

I'd love to take the girls and run—but where to? Or maybe we could stay here and not go to Vermont. Would he let me do that? But then again, maybe a move would be good for all of us and Bill will stop drinking. I can only hope and pray.

Dear Lord, please give me your guidance, as I am a lost lamb.

VERMONT

NOVEMBER, 1955

MOVE TO VERMONT

"**I**'M GOING NEXT DOOR to see the Swansons' new television set," Bill announced, walking out the front door.

Since this was Thanksgiving Day, Bill had a rare day off. His regular routine was to leave for work at the college kitchen at 4:00 a.m., and he was usually home by dinner time.

Getting away from his drinking buddies has given Bill a new lease on life. I'm grateful he's cut back on his drinking, and has been treating me and the girls so much better since we moved.

Having been in Poultney, Vermont, for less than two months, Robbie hadn't gotten to know many people. *I'm glad Bill has taken a liking to the neighbors. I need to visit them more when I get some free time.*

"Dinner will be ready in about an hour. I'll send Ellie over to get you when it's ready," Robbie replied, as she prepared the first holiday dinner in their new home. She hummed to the music wafting from the radio in the background.

Robbie smiled listening to her daughters playing in the family room. "Patty cake…patty cake…baker's man…bake me a cake as fast as you can…" She heard hands slap together.

"Booooooo!" cried Barbara, her big laugh echoing off the walls.

This house is like a mansion compared to our two-bedroom apartment in Boston. Their meager furnishings barely made a dent in the spacious rooms. Three stone steps led up to a covered porch that stretched along the front of the house. There was a large entry foyer and a long hall leading to a well-equipped kitchen in the rear of the house. To the left of the foyer was a mahogany stairway going up to the second floor, where there were four bedrooms. Ellie and Barbara each had their own room, although sparsely furnished. Ellie was very happy with this arrangement. Beyond the stairway was a formal parlor and dining room, both empty of furniture. The dining room extended to the back of the house, where a door opened into the kitchen. To the right of the foyer was a family living room with windows opening to the porch. Their old furniture and radio barely filled the room. Halfway down the hallway a door gave access to the large family bathroom, complete with a deep, claw-footed tub, which Robbie loved to soak in when she got the chance. The backyard conjoined with other neighbors' yards—no fences, providing plenty of room for kids to run and play.

Shortly after their arrival, Robbie had taken the girls to Mass at St. Raphael's Catholic Church. She sat in the back pew in case Barbara started acting up, which she did. That prompted Robbie to move to the vestibule with the girls until the service was over. After the parishioners left, Robbie introduced herself to Father Tolin.

"Good morning, Father. I'm Missus Van Dyne."

Father Tolin shook her hand. "Welcome to Saint Raphael's Parish. I presume you are new in town." In his mid-thirties, with dark hair parted on the side, he was not a handsome man. His flushed, angular face was scarred with pockmarks from a severe case of acne.

Robbie nodded, trying not to stare at his disfigured face. *The poor guy must have had a terrible time finding dates. That's probably why he became a priest.* Robbie nodded. "Yes. We've been here a couple of weeks. My husband works at Green Mountain College. If you have a moment, I'd like to speak with you about something."

"Certainly," Father Tolin said, eying both girls. But his gaze lingered on Barbara.

"This is Ellie," Robbie said, laying her hand on Ellie's shoulder. Ellie smiled at the priest as she held Barbara's hand. "And this is Barbara. She was born with cerebral palsy."

Barbara reached out to touch the priest's robes. Father Tolin took a quick step back from her grasping hand. A look of revulsion crossed his face. "I see. So, what can I do for you, Missus Van Dyne?" he said, frowning at Barbara.

"Well, I was wondering if you knew anyone in the parish who might be able to help babysit Barbara. She needs a lot of supervision, and we had a wonderful woman in Boston who helped us. I was hoping you could give me a recommendation."

Father Tolin flashed a sheepish grin, as if somewhat relieved by her request. "Actually, there is someone I can recommend. Her name is Missus Davis. She's a registered nurse with four children. She works part-time until her two youngest graduate from high school. I think she'd be available to give you a hand. Hold on, let me get her number from my office." He scurried back into the church nave.

Barbara, now almost eight, squirmed holding Ellie's hand. She stomped her feet and made guttural sounds, agitated at having been in the same place for so long.

Robbie knelt on one knee, looked Barbara in the eye, held her index finger in front of the child's face and said, "Barbara! Stop!"

Barbara immediately stopped prancing. A grin spread across her crooked face and she yelled, "Boo!" in Robbie's face.

"Yeah, boo to you, too!" Robbie laughed. She stood up when she heard footsteps echoing in the church.

"Here you are, Missus Van Dyne." Father Tolin stood several steps away and passed her a piece of paper with a name and phone number. "I do hope you and your husband will join us for mass each week. We are happy to welcome new parishioners."

"We'd like that, Father. But it depends upon how Barbara is doing on any given day. Some are better than others," she explained.

"Oh, yes, of course. I understand," he said, glowering once again at Barbara. "I do hope things work out for you with Missus Davis. Good day," he said. His vestments swished behind him as he abruptly exited into the church chamber.

How strange. He seems so uncomfortable around Barbara. Odd reaction for a priest. Isn't he supposed to show unconditional love for all of God's children?

She dismissed her concerns and was grateful for the recommendation. She would call Missus Davis as soon as she got the girls home.

Robbie stirred the potatoes and squash boiling on the stove. As she bent over and opened the oven to check on the turkey, a wave of nausea overcame her and she felt herself getting lightheaded. Closing the oven door, she grabbed the counter to steady herself. The aroma of the turkey engulfed her, bringing up nasty bile in her throat. She took several deep breaths to steady herself. *What brought this on? Did I catch something from Ellie or her classmates?* She drank a glass of water, which seemed to settle her stomach.

Catching her breath, Robbie yelled down the hall, "Ellie, will you go get your father next door? Tell him dinner's ready." Robbie put place settings on their small kitchen table and made room for the side dishes. She hoped with Bill's increased salary, she'd be able to save enough money before next Thanksgiving to buy a nice table set to fill the empty dining room. She pulled the turkey from the oven and left it resting on the stove, waiting for Bill to carve it.

"Their television set is really nice," Bill said, as he and Ellie entered the kitchen. "I'd like to get one soon. I think the girls would have a great time watching it." Bill wielded a sharp knife and fork and began slicing parts from the roasted turkey.

Ellie tied a bib around Barbara's neck and helped her get seated. Robbie cut Barbara's food into spoon-sized bites, as Bill laid a platter of carved turkey in the middle of the small table.

Robbie held each of her girls' hands as she prayed, "Bless us, oh Lord, for these thy gifts, which we are about to receive, from thy bounty, through Christ, Our Lord, Amen." Bill didn't join in.

Robbie helped Barbara grasp her spoon and begin eating her meal, then filled her own plate with the feast. She was famished after cooking all day. But no sooner had she taken a bite of the succulent turkey breast, her stomach rebelled. A wave of nausea flooded over her. Ignoring Bill and Ellie's exclamations, she spit the turkey into her napkin and ran down the hall to the bathroom, where she heaved what little was in her empty stomach into the toilet.

Gasping for breath, the bile grating her throat, she dropped to her knees and rested her head on the toilet bowl. *What's wrong with me? What in heaven's name brought this on? I can't get sick now! I have too much to do.* She slurped some water from the tap, cleaned herself up, then went back to the table.

"What's the matter with you?" Bill asked.

"I don't know. Probably picked up a bug from somewhere," Robbie said as she ate a bite of mashed potatoes. They seemed to stay down, so she ate a little squash and a dinner roll, but didn't dare eat any more.

When dinner was over, she put the leftovers away, washed and dried the dishes, and went into the living room, where Bill and the girls were relaxing. "I'm going to lie down for a while. I'm exhausted," she told her family.

She poured herself a glass of water and climbed the stairs. Setting the water on her nightstand, she curled up on her side, trying to understand what was making her so ill all of a sudden, as her mind drifted.

Robbie was in the kitchen at her family farm in Maine. Mamma was holding baby Helen in her arms, feeding her porridge. Mamma turned, smiled, rubbed her tummy and pointed to Robbie.

Robbie awoke with a start from the dream. *Was that real?* And a sudden thought hit her—*Oh, dear Lord! What if I'm pregnant?* The memory of the horrible night when Bill forced her to have sex before they left Boston came flooding back.

I've been so busy with the move, I haven't been paying attention to my flow. If it's true, this is terrible news. I'm almost forty—too damned old to have another baby. How in the world can I care for an infant with Ellie and Barbara taking all of my time? And what if this baby is damaged, too? Oh, God! Please don't let it be true!

Robbie remembered when she worked at the Cocoanut Grove, Shirley would make arrangements for girls who had "gotten into trouble," to take care of the problem. Some of the girls returned to work, some she never saw again. Robbie never asked what happened to them—she didn't want to know.

Should I get rid of this child? I don't know that many people here. I wonder if I could find someone who could do it safely? I wish Shirley was still alive— she'd know what to do. But how could I possibly do such a thing? I don't think I could ever forgive myself. How badly will I be punished if I abort this child? God's already made me suffer with Barbara because I had Joan out of wedlock. She shivered to think of the dire consequences as she cried herself into a fitful sleep.

Bill came in sometime later and woke her to put the girls to bed.

"How the hell did this happen?" Bill said a week later, after Robbie had confirmed her pregnancy with her doctor. Robbie sat on their bed as she gave Bill the news. She had been afraid of how he would react. "You're too goddamned old to get pregnant!" he said, pacing in front of her.

"Well, Bill, you're the one who forced yourself on me, so you're partially to blame!" Robbie shot back.

"That's bullshit and you know it. It's your own goddamned fault!" He pointed a finger at her as he stormed out of their bedroom.

I hope he doesn't start drinking again. He's been doing so well since we moved here. Will I have to protect myself and the girls from his rage if he gets drunk again?

DEEDEE IS BORN

As Robbie's due date in July of 1956 approached, daily chores quickly tired her and her back ached from the weight of her pregnant belly. Thankfully, Ellie was out of school for the summer and was a big help with Barbara's daily needs.

After the horror of Barbara's delivery, Robbie couldn't help but worry about the upcoming birth. *What if I'm too old to have this baby? What if things go wrong again? What will I do if the baby is damaged like Barbara? And how will Bill react if something goes wrong? Will he start drinking again? Oh, dear Lord, please help me deliver a healthy baby with no complications.*

Before they moved to Vermont, Robbie had received a terse letter from her sister Marjorie informing her that Joan, aged nineteen, had married a young man named Darrel Fountain. He was from Connecticut, and his family spent summers in Maine. Robbie was heartbroken she hadn't been invited to the wedding. *I guess Joan didn't want to explain two mothers to her wedding guests.* She had sent a congratulations card to Margie's address in hopes it would reach Joan and Darrel. But she'd never received any response, just as Joan had never replied to any of Robbie's letters sent over the years. *I sincerely hope Joan finds love and happiness in her new life.*

In the card Robbie had received that past Christmas, Marjorie told her Joan was pregnant. *What a strange coincidence Joan and I are both pregnant at the same time. It just doesn't seem possible how much time has passed. It sure does make me feel old. I hope Joan is doing well with her pregnancy, and wish I could be closer to give her my love and support.*

In March, Robbie had quietly celebrated her fortieth birthday with a simple dinner and cake. Sitting at the table, the baby had kicked her ribs, making her uncomfortable.

Finishing his cake, Bill had said, "John called me today. He's sending an assistant chef up from Boca Raton, Florida, he wants me to train."

"Will you have time to train, with everything else you're responsible for?" Robbie asked.

Bill nodded. "Yeah, I think so. Plus John said he'd pay me extra during the training time. I'm hoping to buy a new car, 'cause the old wagon is on its last legs."

For the past several months, Bill had worked late most nights, and Robbie thought the new guy must need a good deal of guidance. In the back of her mind, she worried Bill had gone back to drinking, but she didn't smell the evidence on him when he came home. So she had to trust he was working as he said. She made a point to ensure his dinner was warm (not burnt), waiting for him.

On the last day of July, Robbie was fixing breakfast for the girls when a sharp cramp caused her to gasp and double over in pain. Then she felt a gush of water flow down her leg. "Oh, God!" She quickly turned off the burners and rushed to the bathroom, hoping most of the void would reach the toilet.

Moments later, Ellie knocked on the bathroom door. "Mommy? Are you all right?"

"Ellie, call your father. Tell him to come home right away. This baby is coming! Then call Missus Davis and ask her to come over to babysit. Hurry!" Robbie instructed her daughter, as a contraction gripped her.

"Okay, Mommy!" Ellie cried.

Bill drove his old Chevy wagon as fast as he could on the rough, winding roads to the Rutland Hospital, some twenty miles away. The car bounced and rattled over each pothole, gripping Robbie with pain, her involuntary moans adding to the cacophony of the ride.

"I hope it's a boy," Bill said as he concentrated on the road. "I'd like to name him Henry, after my younger brother. I guess if it's another girl, you can pick out whatever name you want."

Robbie took a deep breath as another contraction washed through her. "Yeah—okay—we'll figure out something. . ." she gasped, trying to get more comfortable in her seat.

After what seemed like an eternity, they finally pulled up to the hospital emergency entrance. Bill jumped out of the car and ran in to find a nurse.

"Help us! My wife's in labor!"

Two nurses exited the double doors pushing a stretcher. A doctor followed them. They helped Robbie out of the car and lifted her onto the gurney. She grunted with the movement. Her contractions were coming fast now.

"Take her to labor and delivery, quickly!" the doctor instructed the nurses.

In the labor room, the nurses quickly removed Robbie's clothing and put a hospital gown on her. They checked her vital signs. Her blood pressure was elevated, but all else looked normal. The doctor entered and positioned himself at the end of the bed. He checked her progress as a wave of contractions racked her belly. They moved her immediately to the delivery table and positioned her in the stirrups. Robbie was breathing hard and sweating. *Please Lord, let this baby be born normally!*

"Missus Van Dyne? I need you to take a deep breath and push now," called the doctor.

A deep guttural sound escaped her as she bore down. Pain ripped through her belly and lower back, causing her to squeeze her eyes shut. She felt the baby moving.

"One more time. We're almost there," guided the doctor.

Another deep breath, another big push, another grip of pain, and the baby slid out of her body.

"That's it, that's it," said the doctor as he cradled the baby. "It's a girl!" he announced as he slapped the baby's bottom to elicit a cry to get her lungs working. He passed the baby to the nurse, clamped the umbilical cord, then cut it away from Robbie. The nurse took the baby to a nearby table, cleaned her up, and weighed her.

"She's a healthy eight-and-a-half pounds," the nurse announced. As Robbie watched closely, the nurse bundled the baby in pink swaddling wrap.

She's healthy! Oh, thank God! Robbie gasped as her uterine muscles contracted again, expelling the afterbirth. The swaddled baby girl was placed in her arms. She had a full head of wispy blond hair, blue eyes, and was the spitting image of Bill. Since the baby was a girl, Robbie didn't need to consult with Bill. She decided to name her DeeDee Helen, the middle name in honor of her baby sister.

After Robbie and the baby were moved to a post-partum room, Bill was ushered in by the nurse. "Mister Van Dyne. Congratulations, you have a healthy baby girl," the nurse exclaimed.

He turned to the nurse. "You said the baby is healthy, right?"

"Yes, Sir, as far as we can tell. She weighed in at over eight pounds. She seems very healthy." The nurse exited the room.

Bill turned to Robbie. "Well, I guess it will make it easier for you to raise this child. But I will say I'm disappointed it's not a boy."

Robbie, exhausted from giving birth, frowned at her husband. "It'll be better for the whole family she's healthy, right?"

Bill stared out the window and didn't respond.

BILL'S MISSING

"Where in the world could he be?" Robbie muttered to herself.

It was eleven-thirty at night, and Robbie was worried because Bill hadn't come home from work yet. She had called his office several times, but there was no answer. *I can't imagine what might have happened to him. I know the old car is in bad shape, but even if it broke down, he can still walk home in about twenty minutes. I can't go looking for him at this hour and leave the girls alone. Should I call the police? Or just wait and see what happens?* There wasn't much she could do other than go to bed.

Having been up and down all night tending to her three-month-old baby's needs, Robbie finally got out of bed at day-break, still exhausted. Bill still wasn't home, and now she was really worried something terrible had happened. *Did he drink all night and pass out in a ditch somewhere? Is he injured and in the hospital?* The possibilities swirled through her head.

Robbie fed and changed the baby, fixed the girls their breakfast, and sent Ellie off to school. She wanted to go to the college to see if she could find Bill, but didn't want to take Barbara and DeeDee with her. She called Mrs. Davis and asked if she could come and sit with the girls while she ran an important errand. An agonizing hour later, Mrs. Davis arrived to babysit. Robbie grabbed her coat and purse and ran out the front door.

The stiff breeze of the crisp October morning slapped her face and swirled her gray-streaked red hair. She barely noticed the typical Vermont homes on streets lined with sugar maples, blazing red and gold with their final salute to the season. Leaves tumbled around her feet, and Robbie realized it had been just a year since they had arrived in Poultney. For the most part, she enjoyed living here, but never imagined a year ago she would have another baby to care for at her age. She missed Gladys and her family back in Southie, along with all the activities in Boston. *I can't imagine what's happened to Bill. Maybe he just fell asleep on a sofa somewhere.*

Robbie entered the college kitchen and saw workers rushing here and there preparing for lunch. She tried to find Bill amongst the staff, but there was no sign of him. She checked his office. Empty. Then she spotted Mr. Reynolds, the accountant, in his office next to Bill's. He was balding, in his late forties, wearing thick, black-rimmed glasses. She knocked on his door.

"Missus Van Dyne?" said Reynolds, lifting an eyebrow. "Please come in. What can I do for you?"

"I'm sorry to bother you, Mister Reynolds, but I'm trying to find Bill. I'm worried something's happened to him, because he didn't come home last night," Robbie said as she took a seat in front of his desk.

"You mean he didn't…" Reynolds cleared his throat, cleaned his glasses on his handkerchief and rubbed his nose, stalling. "Yes…well…hmmm …I believe Mister Van Dyne left yesterday morning to drive Miss Wells to Florida. He was concerned about her driving that distance alone and wanted to keep her company. He said he would be back in a couple of days." He peered over his glasses.

"Miss Wells?" Robbie gasped. The breath seeped out of her lungs.

"Yes, his assistant chef, Sandy Wells. He's been training her to take over as head chef in Boca Raton," answered Reynolds.

Robbie's heart beat wildly; she had a very bad feeling about this. Her head pounded as her face turned white. A bout of dizziness overcame her. Her stomach knotted and she felt the tremor in her right hand growing stronger as she gripped the arm of the chair. *His assistant is a* woman? *Why didn't I know that? Had he ever mentioned her name? Maybe, maybe not, I haven't been paying much attention, being so busy with the girls.*

Reynolds shuffled papers on his desk, not looking up. "I'm sorry, Missus Van Dyne. I assumed he had already told you. I'm sure it's just some misunderstanding, and he'll call you as soon as he can."

"Yes, yes. I'm sure you're right, Mister Reynolds. Thank you." She stood on shaky legs, then groped her way out of the kitchen.

Robbie collapsed on the steps outside the dining hall. Her body trembled so violently she was afraid she'd fall down the stairs. She dropped her head into her hands, sobbing. *Has Bill left me for good? Is he coming back in a few days as Reynolds said? How could I not know his assistant was a woman? How stupid can I be? Has he been having an affair with the woman all those nights he came home late? Did I ever smell perfume on him?*

She couldn't be sure of her doubts, since the smells of the kitchen always clung to his chef's whites. *Oh, Dear Lord! If this is true, what am I going to do now? How will I take care of my girls?* Her body shook with sobs as her mind raced in a million directions. She finally gathered herself together and walked home, her mind in a numb state of despair.

Robbie stumbled into the house and went directly to their bedroom. She checked Bill's side of their closet and saw the only clothes left were old ones he no longer wore. She yanked out his dresser drawers to find them mostly empty. Frantically she checked under the bed and saw both of his suitcases were gone.

How could I have not noticed his clothes were missing? He must have been taking them in to work in the morning, before I was up. He's been planning this, but for how long? Before DeeDee was born?

She searched the nightstands for a note, anything that would give her a clue, and found nothing. He was gone, truly gone. *How could I have been so stupid to trust him?* She collapsed on her bed and wailed, bringing Mrs. Davis to the doorway.

"Robbie? What's wrong?"

"Bill's gone—he left us!" Robbie stammered.

"Are you sure?"

"Yes. He left yesterday to drive Miss Wells, his assistant, to Florida—all his clothes are gone!" Robbie sobbed into her pillow. "I don't think he's coming back. He must have been having an affair with her for months—even while I was pregnant!"

"Oh, my Dear! I am so sorry. What can I do to help you?" Mrs. Davis sat on the bed and rubbed Robbie's back.

"I don't know. I don't know what to do! How am I going to support my girls?" Robbie gulped her breaths.

"I'll tell you what: let's get DeeDee and Barbara dressed and I'll drive you over to the church. We can talk to Father Tolin. I'm sure he'll know what to do," said Mrs. Davis.

An hour later, they arrived at the rectory of St. Raphael's parish. Robbie had DeeDee in her arms, and Mrs. Davis walked slowly up the stairs holding Barbara's hand. Mrs. Davis knocked on the door of Father Tolin's rectory, and he opened the door immediately.

Mrs. Davis took the lead. "Father, if you have the time, we have an urgent matter we need to discuss with you."

"Of course, please come in," said Father Tolin, his eyes wide as he stared at Robbie's disheveled hair and flushed, tear-stained face. The women and children entered the priest's chambers. Two chairs were positioned in front of a big mahogany desk. Robbie sat in one chair, cradling DeeDee in her arms. Mrs. Davis sat in the other chair. Barbara circled and whimpered, with no place to sit.

"Father, would you have another chair for Barbara?" Mrs. Davis asked.

Father Tolin glared at the girl, disgust showing on his face. "Yeah, sure," he stammered as he pulled a third chair to his desk so Barbara could sit down. "Now, how can I help you?" he said, taking his seat behind the desk.

"Father, I'm sorry to bother you, but I think Bill has left us and run off to Florida with another woman." Robbie's face was red with shame.

"Oh, my goodness! Are you sure?" The priest sat forward in his chair, his elbows resting on the desk.

"Pretty sure. He left yesterday, and all his clothes are gone," Robbie said, with a tremor in her voice.

"I'm so sorry to hear that, Missus Van Dyne," the priest replied. "Let me see what we can do to help you."

Barbara was getting fidgety, pounding her arms on the chair and stomping her feet. She bit down hard on her calloused fist and grunted her frustration, unable to express her needs. Her agitation grew as she slapped her own face and shouted, "Boo, boo, boooo!" At Barbara's outburst, DeeDee started fussing, so Robbie pulled a bottle out of her bag to quiet the baby.

"I'm sorry, Father. I think Barbara needs to use the toilet," Robbie said.

"Here, I'll take her," said Mrs. Davis. "Where is your bathroom?" she asked the priest.

Father Tolin hesitated, glaring at Barbara.

"Father?" asked Mrs. Davis again.

The priest cleared this throat. "Ahhh, yes, of course. It's the first door on the right down the hall." His face pinched as he watched their slow procession toward his private chamber.

Over the next several hours, they discussed Robbie's situation. She had a couple of hundred dollars saved, but couldn't afford the rent on the house—she'd have to move. She could get a job as a waitress or a cook, but would need to hire a babysitter: someone who was trained and strong enough to handle Barbara's temper tantrums. Mrs. Davis offered her help until they could find someone more permanently. And how would Robbie be able to afford that? Her despair deepened as they considered her options.

"One of the first things we can do is to sign you up for welfare assistance," the priest recommended.

Poppa's words echoed in her mind. She was adamant. "I will not go on welfare! I will not subject myself and my girls to the sin and shame of being on the dole! We are not going to burn in hell for accepting charity!"

Father Tolin looked taken aback by her vehement response. "I suggest you at least think about it." He leaned forward once again. "The situation you're in is not your fault, and certainly not your sin." He paused, staring at Barbara. "You know," continued the priest, "there's a training school in Brandon for retarded people. It's well run and I know several families who have children there. You might consider placing Barbara there for a short time. At least it would give you a chance to find a job and get some things in your life straightened out."

Put Barbara in an institution? How can I possibly do that? I've spent the last eight years raising and training her to live as normal a life as possible. What will happen to her if she's put into an institution? Robbie recalled horror stories she'd heard about other institutions. *Would she be mistreated? Would she be ignored and left to wallow in her own squalor? Would she even remember I'm her mother?*

"I really don't think I can send her away, Father," Robbie lamented. "I've cared for Barbara her whole life. I'm afraid of what will happen to her if I give her up to strangers."

"Well, I think you should consider what's best for the *child*." His voice grew peevish. "She would obviously be much better off in an institution where they can care for her!" He glared at the mentally challenged girl. "I can help you make the arrangements should you change your mind," the priest persisted. "It's really your only option."

Robbie was surprised by the priest's attitude. *Why does he think I can't care for Barbara? I've been doing a pretty good job so far. Lord knows what will happen to her in an institution. I don't think I can send her there and give up another child! It would break my heart.*

"Robbie," said Mrs. Davis, having returned with a much calmer Barbara in tow. "Here's something you might consider. I know a family who owns a large farm outside of Fair Haven. They have three boys, and Missus Granger has a serious heart condition. They've been looking for someone to help her with the household chores. I believe they could offer you and DeeDee room and board and a small salary for your work."

"And what about Ellie? What would I do with her?" Robbie asked. The situation was getting more desperate as she considered her dismal options. *Will I have to break up my family and send my daughters away from me again?* The thought of having to send away the children she loved so dearly was like a dagger piercing her heart. *Why is God punishing me again? What have I ever done to deserve such grief and heartache?*

"Do you have any relatives Ellie could stay with for a while?" asked Mrs. Davis. "At least until you can afford to get a place of your own?"

Robbie thought about the estranged relationship she had with most of her siblings, and whether or not any of them could help her. Her closest sister, Gladys, first came to mind. She remembered their cramped apartment in Southie with the three kids. Sean didn't make much money as a fireman, and they probably couldn't afford another mouth to feed, much less make room for one more child.

The other option was her oldest, judgmental sister, Pauline, and her husband Charles, who now owned the Scribner family farm in Monticello, Maine. They had a son, Charles Jr.—Charlie, who was several years older than Ellie. *Maybe it would be good for Ellie to go live on the farm until I can get my life back on track.*

"Oh, God! I just don't know," she sobbed, wiping her eyes. "I'm so confused right now, I don't know which way to turn!" DeeDee squirmed and whimpered in her arms.

"It's okay, Missus Van Dyne. You don't have to make any decisions today. But know that God loves you. He never gives us more challenges in life then He thinks we can handle," Father Tolin said pompously, crossing his arms.

Robbie seriously doubted whether that was true.

ROBBIE SURVIVES

"What do you mean I have to give up my parental rights?" Robbie glared at Father Tolin, furious he had deceived her. "You never told me that!" she yelled at the priest sitting across the conference table from her. "If I had known, I never would have agreed to send Barbara here!" The school administrator, sitting next to the priest, looked surprised at Robbie's outburst.

"I thought you knew when you signed the papers," Father Tolin said in a petulant voice, his pockmarked face flushed. "It's what's best for the child, anyway."

Robbie pointed behind her. "That *child's* name is Barbara!"

A few days after Robbie and Mrs. Davis had first visited the priest, Father Tolin had convinced Robbie enrolling Barbara in the Brandon Training School for retarded children was the best course of action for Barbara's continued care. Against her better judgment, and with a heavy heart at having to send another child away, Robbie reluctantly signed the papers in the priest's chambers. She had glanced through the dense legal wording, but thought she would have remembered if it had said anything about signing away her parental rights.

After Robbie's application was approved by the administration, Mrs. Davis drove Robbie and her girls to the training school some forty miles away, to enroll Barbara. Father Tolin had met them in the conference room with the school administrator, Mr. James, who looked as slick as a used-car salesman. Robbie took a seat at the table while Mrs. Davis sat on a sofa against the wall cradling baby DeeDee in her arms. Barbara and Ellie held hands sitting next to Mrs. Davis.

"Missus Van Dyne," Mr. James explained. "You must understand. Barbara is now a ward of the state of Vermont, and we run this training school. You've signed the papers, and we now have full custody over Barbara's care."

"But it's just a temporary situation. I'm going to come back and take Barbara with me as soon as I can get things straightened out! Why do I have to give up my parental rights? She's my daughter. It's just not right!" Robbie's right hand trembled and she clasped it in her lap as she scowled at Mr. James.

The sound of Robbie's raised voice started Barbara chewing on her calloused knuckles. She rocked back and forth on the sofa with increasing velocity until she was slamming her body against the backrest.

"Ellie," Mrs. Davis said to Robbie's oldest daughter. "Here, hold DeeDee so I can help Barbara." She passed the infant to the young girl. Mrs. Davis put her arm around Barbara's back and started rubbing slowly. Simultaneously, Robbie jumped from her chair to attend to her agitated daughter. Robbie dropped to both knees and gently pulled Barbara's fist from the girl's mouth. Saliva dripped down Barbara's chin and slid along her wrist. Mrs. Davis hugged Barbara to her chest as Robbie stroked her daughter's head.

"It's okay! It's okay, Honey. Mommy's here," Robbie said in a soothing voice. Robbie's stomach ached at the prospect of leaving her sweet, damaged daughter in the care of strangers. Barbara's rocking slowed as she lifted her slimy hand and touched her mother's face. "Shhhhh, shhhhh, now," Robbie comforted. "You're fine, Barbara."

Oh, God. I can't do this! I can't walk away from her!

"You see, it's just this type of behavior that proves this child needs to be in an institution!" Father Tolin declared unctuously.

Robbie stood up and swung around, her eyes shooting daggers at the sanctimonious priest. "Would you just shut the hell up!" she yelled at him.

"Please, please! Missus Van Dyne. Come and sit down." Mr. James pointed to her vacant seat. "Father, maybe it's best if you keep your opinions quiet for the time being," the administrator admonished the priest, who flushed a brighter shade of red at the rebuke.

Robbie sat and crossed her arms over her chest, frowning at the impeccably dressed man. *I wonder how much money he gets from the state. Looks like he's doing quite well for himself.*

"Missus Van Dyne, I'm sorry you're upset about your parental rights. But it is the law and has to be this way." Mr. James pushed a straggle of gray hair back into place. "There are some other rules you need to know about as well," he informed her. "Family visiting hours are limited to Sunday afternoons from noon until five. And no one under the age of twelve is allowed on the premises. We've made an exception today because you're enrolling Barbara. But in the future, neither of your girls will be allowed on campus until they reach that age."

"What! I won't have my girls growing up to be strangers! That's ridiculous. And you're telling me I can only see Barbara once a week? Well, I'm going to bring my daughters to visit their sister whenever I can make the trip. To hell with your rules!" Robbie exploded as her fury rose. "Damn you all to hell, Father Tolin!" she pointed an accusing finger at him. "You *lied* to me!"

The priest blanched, his scarred face scrunched as he shrank back in his chair, looking shocked at Robbie's attack.

Her hand shook. "You never told me any of this! How do I know Barbara will be properly taken care of, and not abused, if I don't have any say over her care?"

Mr. James lifted a hand toward Robbie in appeasement. "Missus Van Dyne, please be assured our mission is to provide the best possible care and training for our students as their abilities allow. Your daughter will not be mistreated in any way."

"Well, I'm going to fight your damn rules to make sure my daughters grow up knowing each other. This is totally unreasonable!" Robbie shuddered as her tears let loose. Mrs. Davis rose from the sofa and joined Robbie at the table, where she hugged the distraught mother to her.

"It'll be all right, Robbie," she said. "We'll come see Barbara every week and I'm sure she'll be well cared for. We just have to trust what they're telling us."

Dear Lord, please watch over Barbara, and don't let anyone mistreat her. Robbie sobbed into Mrs. Davis' shoulder.

"Let's get Barbara settled, shall we?" Mr. James said as he rose from the table and lifted Barbara's suitcase.

Robbie glared at Father Tolin, who slouched in his chair pouting, his arms crossed. He did not join them.

Robbie and Ellie each took one of Barbara's hands as they led her, with her shuffling gait, down the hallway to the dorm rooms. Mrs. Davis followed with a diaper bag slung over her shoulder, cradling baby DeeDee in her arms.

The group was led to a small room with beige walls, sparsely furnished with two twin beds, two chairs, two dressers and one closet. A window at the end of the room looked out to the mountains, now losing their fall color as the chill of winter approached.

"This is Barbara's room and she has a roommate, whom I'll introduce you to shortly," said Mr. James. "She will receive three meals a day, and will be monitored and educated by our trained staff. I hope in time you will approve of our care, Missus Van Dyne." Ellie helped Barbara, who was biting her knuckles in frustration, to sit on the bed. They waited for Robbie to arrange Barbara's clothes in the dresser and closet.

"Please follow me to the dayroom," Mr. James said as he exited the bedroom. Ellie helped Barbara to her feet and they followed Robbie and Mrs. Davis out the door, and down a corridor. In the large, sunny dayroom, about twenty girls and women of different ages were engaged in various activities. Suddenly, a high-pitched scream from the back of the room rose above the din of voices, bringing the group to a halt.

"Mommy! Help!" Ellie cried. Robbie turned to see Barbara howl, slap herself in the face, then bite hard on her fist. The agitated girl dropped to the floor, kicking her legs in different directions.

Robbie rushed over to her writhing daughter and sat on the floor, pulling Barbara backwards into her lap. "It's okay, Honey! I'm here!" She rubbed Barbara's back and gently pulled the calloused fist from her daughter's mouth.

Oh God! How can I leave her here? She's going to be scared to death without me! My poor, sweet, girl. She doesn't understand what's happening. I just want to take her home with me and love her as I've always done. Oh, Dear Lord! What have I done?

Two male orderlies, dressed in white, appeared at Robbie's side. "Let us help you," one of the young men said. One gripped Barbara under her arms as the other lifted her feet. Barbara howled and fought their grip. The men carried her to a large leather chair with wooden arms where they gently set her down.

"Do you have a doll? Any doll!" Panicked, Robbie yelled at the orderlies. "It usually calms her down."

One of the young men rushed to a nearby basket and grabbed a doll that he placed in Barbara's hands. Barbara immediately started picking at the doll's eyes, and calmed considerably. Robbie's hands shook as she sat on the arm of Barbara's chair and stroked her daughter's hair.

"I think she's going to be fine," Mrs. Davis said as she rubbed Robbie's arm. Robbie took a deep breath and stared into Mrs. Davis' face for reassurance.

A few moments later, Mr. James approached, holding the hand of a girl about Barbara's age. A chill ran down Robbie's spine as she stared at the child. The girl's head was enormous in comparison to her small body. Robbie's vision of her sister, Mae, being left to die alone in a snow-covered cabin, flashed through her mind. Her sister had looked almost identical to the girl walking toward them except this girl had normal arms. *Why, oh why, did Mamma have to let Mae die?*

Mrs. Davis leaned toward Robbie and whispered, "She has water on the brain. How very sad."

Mr. James stood in front of the women. "Missus Van Dyne, I'd like you to meet Cindy Wilson. She's Barbara's roommate."

The young girl broke into a big grin, her protruding forehead creasing under her stringy blond hair. Her bulging eyes twinkled as she hugged Robbie around the waist. "Hi! I'm Cindy! Nice ta mee'cha!"

The girl's high-pitched voice caught Robbie by surprise, but her infectious enthusiasm made Robbie smile. "Nice to meet you too, Cindy. This is my daughter Barbara," Robbie said. Cindy reached out to touch Barbara, but Barbara slapped Cindy's hand away from her doll.

"Oooowww!" Cindy cried as she backed away with a scowl on her face.

"I'm sorry, Cindy. Barbara doesn't like anyone touching her dolls. Can you remember that and still be nice?" Robbie said, trying to soothe the child's indignation. *I hope the girls can get along together. I know how temperamental Barbara is. I'm afraid this isn't going to work.*

Cindy put both hands on her hips and glared at Barbara, "Well! I suppose I can be nice if she's nice to me!"

Mr. James put a hand on Cindy's shoulder. "We'll get you your own doll, then you and Barbara can play together. Would you like that?"

Cindy nodded vigorously. "Yessssss! I'd like that." Her grin returned.

Mr. James addressed Robbie. "I think the girls will be fine together, once they get to know one another. Please don't worry. Barbara will be well cared for."

Robbie looked from Cindy to Barbara, who was intent on mangling her doll. "I can't help but worry. But I have to trust you and your staff will do the right thing for her."

DeeDee was fussy and crying in Mrs. Davis' arms. "Robbie, I'm going to change the baby's diapers. Then we should be leaving soon."

She's right. The longer we stay, the harder it will be to leave. "Ellie, say goodbye to your sister," Robbie instructed her daughter.

Ellie tried to give Barbara a hug, but Barbara was intently focused on pulling the doll's hair out and ignored her sister. Robbie went down on one knee. "Barbara!" she said with a stern voice as she lifted her index finger to Barbara's face to get her attention.

"Boo!" Barbara said, and laughed.

"Boo to you!" Robbie said, her heart breaking. "You be a good girl!" Robbie stood and kissed Barbara's head. "I love you!" she murmured into her daughter's hair.

Holding Ellie's hand, Robbie met Mrs. Davis carrying baby DeeDee at the door. They walked to the car.

Dear Lord. Please watch over Barbara and don't let her be mistreated.

Robbie's stomach knotted and her tears flowed as she shut the car door behind her.

ROBBIE REACHES OUT

Shortly after the first meeting with Father Tolin, when Robbie discovered Bill had left, she swallowed her pride and called her oldest sister, Pauline. She knew Pauline treated her like the black sheep of the family, but she was desperate to find a safe place for Ellie to live. Robbie asked Pauline if Ellie could stay with them on the Scribner family farm. She had bitten her tongue and endured Pauline's tirade about her sinful ways. Robbie assured Pauline it would just be for a short while, and then Robbie would come to retrieve Ellie. After much wrangling, Pauline had finally agreed to their arrangement.

After their phone call, Robbie joined Ellie in her bedroom. "Honey, your Daddy has left us, and I need to get a job. Right now, I can't afford to support all of us. Do you understand what that means?"

"Yes, Mommy, I think so," Ellie said with a sad look on her face.

"Your sister Barbara is going to live at a special school. And I thought you'd have fun visiting your grandpa's farm. Would you like that?" Robbie's heart broke over how grown-up her nine-year-old daughter was trying to be.

"Would I live with Aunt Pauline and Uncle Charles? How long would I be there?"

"Yes, and your cousin Charlie will be there for you to play with," Robbie said, trying to stay upbeat. "I'll come and get you as soon as I can, I promise!" Painful memories of saying those same words to another daughter, now lost to her, wracked Robbie. *I hope I can keep this promise. I don't want to lose Ellie's love and respect. She's such a smart, loving and compassionate little girl.*

"All right, Mommy. If it's what you want me to do, I'll go visit them." Robbie's heart ached because Ellie was being so brave.

"You're a good girl, Ellie. You know I love you, right?" Robbie said as she hugged her daughter.

"Yes, Mommy! I know! I love you, too!" Ellie squeezed her as Robbie held back sobs.

"Mommy?" Ellie said, as she pulled from their hug, a serious look in her face.

"Yes, Honey?"

"I'm glad Daddy's gone. He was mean, and I hate him!"

Robbie had done her best to shield the girls from Bill's abuse, but Ellie was a smart girl and knew about her father's temper. "I'm so sorry your daddy scared you. But he won't hurt us ever again, I promise you." Robbie hugged Ellie to her and let her sensitive child cry on her shoulder.

Two days after enrolling Barbara at the training school, Mrs. Davis drove Robbie, Ellie and DeeDee from Poultney to the bus terminal in Rutland, some twenty miles away.

With her daughter's suitcase loaded onto the bus, Robbie escorted Ellie up the stairs and had her sit in the first seat behind the driver. Robbie turned to the man, dressed in his Greyhound uniform. "Sir, my daughter Ellie is traveling alone, so I'd appreciate it if you could keep an eye on her and make sure she arrives safely."

"Yes, Ma'am," said the older, portly driver. "I'd be more than happy to do that. We'll be driving straight to Houlton, Maine, so it should be an easy trip." He tipped his hat to her.

"Thank you so much! My sister Pauline will be there to pick her up when you arrive. I really appreciate it," Robbie said, relieved. She turned to Ellie. "You behave for the driver, now, and do as he tells you, okay? I'll call you tomorrow, and you can tell me all about your trip."

"I will, Mommy. I promise!" Ellie said bravely as they hugged goodbye.

Robbie stepped off the bus, and the double doors slapped closed behind her. Donning a courageous smile, she waved at her daughter as the bus left the terminal. Once the bus had rolled out of sight, she slid heavily onto Mrs. Davis' shoulder, her legs crumpling beneath her, and sobbed over her loss of another child.

Mrs. Davis rubbed her back. "You did the right thing, Robbie. What else could you do? I'm sure Ellie will be fine."

But Robbie couldn't stop crying. *Why? Why? Why do I have to keep giving up the children I love? It's just not fair!*

In early November, with both of Robbie's older girls now gone from her care, Mrs. Davis arranged for Robbie and baby DeeDee to move into a small, dark upstairs bedroom tucked beneath the eaves of the Grangers' farmhouse, located several miles outside the town of Fair Haven, the next town north from Poultney. Robbie's old furniture and meager belongings were stored in the Grangers' hay barn.

Mrs. Davis had been Maureen Granger's visiting nurse for several years, as Maureen, in her early fifties, had degenerative heart disease. The arrangement for Robbie to help Mrs. Granger with the daily farm chores benefited all three women. Mrs. Davis had asked Robbie to contact her immediately should Maureen show any symptoms of heart palpitations or shortness of breath. Grateful for a place for her and DeeDee to live, Robbie readily agreed to Mrs. Davis' request.

Robbie was determined Barbara and DeeDee would not grow up to be strangers. She immediately wrote a letter to the governor's office requesting the law be changed to allow family members of any age to visit their relatives in Vermont-run institutions. Every month, in between managing her chores at the farm, she diligently re-wrote and sent her same plea to the governor. But she never received a response. Disheartened and frustrated, Robbie feared DeeDee would grow up not knowing her older sister, Barbara.

One cold November evening, two years after moving in with the Grangers, Robbie put DeeDee to bed. Then she joined Maureen, Brad, and their three sons in the living room to watch the evening news.

As Robbie got comfortable, the middle-aged male news anchor announced, "And in other news, the governor has signed a bill authorizing visitation rights to all family members, regardless of age, to those people held in Vermont-run institutions. This includes jails, prisons and state-run institutions."

Robbie gasped as her hand flew to her mouth. She turned to Maureen. "Did I hear him right? Did he just say the governor changed the law, and I can take DeeDee to visit Barbara?" Robbie's whole body trembled.

Maureen touched Robbie's arm. "Yes, Honey! That's what he said. Oh, I'm so happy for you! Looks like he got your letters after all. I always thought he was a good man, and would do the right thing."

Tears flowed down Robbie's cheeks as she heard the newsman say, "The law will go into effect on January first of the new year."

On those Sundays when Mrs. Davis was otherwise occupied, Robbie hitchhiked to see Barbara in Brandon, thirty miles away. Once the visitation restriction was lifted, despite Maureen's disapproval, she had taken little DeeDee with her on her perilous journey. Robbie had feared for their safety, standing along the side of the road, bumming rides from strangers. She prayed they would make the sixty-mile round trip without any trouble. But she was determined her daughters would grow up knowing each other, despite the perils.

Since moving to the Granger farm, DeeDee had grown into a robust, healthy three-year-old, with long blond curls. The older she got, the more it amazed Robbie how much she resembled her father, Bill. Maureen Granger had become like a sister to Robbie as Robbie had taken over most of her workload—cooking for the family; cleaning the house; handling the chickens; feeding the dogs; tending the garden; and boiling the sap in the sugaring house from the tapped maples and bottling the syrup, which they sold. Robbie also worked with the boys in the cheese house to make the sharp cheddar the Granger farm was famous for, and generally did the chores needed to keep a farm running in Vermont year-round. Maureen doted on DeeDee as if she were her own daughter, teaching her the alphabet and reading her books in the evening. The two adult women enjoyed much camaraderie and laughter as they lived and worked side by side.

Each night before she went to bed, Robbie dropped to her knees, made the sign of the cross, and prayed. "Dear Lord, thank you for my good fortune. Please keep Maureen healthy and in your good grace. And please watch over Joan, Ellie and Barbara, and make sure they are being well cared for. Let them know I love them. This I pray in your name, Jesus Christ, Amen."

In the spring of the following year, Robbie helped Maureen plan the wedding of her eldest son, Vincent, now twenty, to his high school sweetheart, Lynn. On a beautiful day in May, they were married in the backyard of the farmhouse. The heady aroma of purple lilacs mixed with the drafts of pungent farm odors. Robbie quietly cried as she watched them say their vows. *I wish I could have attended my daughter Joan's wedding as the mother of the bride.* After a brief honeymoon to Montreal, Vince and Lynn moved into a small cottage at the back of the farm that had previously been used by the farm manager.

The spring turned into summer. One muggy, late August afternoon, black thunderclouds stacked over the Green Mountains. All the windows in the farmhouse were open, but no breeze penetrated the stifling rooms. Maureen, Robbie and DeeDee sat at the kitchen table, de-stemming and snapping peas from the garden.

"Gosh, it's just so hot! I need to get some fresh air," Maureen said, fanning herself. She rose and balanced herself against the table. "Whew! I just hate this heat," she grumbled as she wiped the sweat from her brow. She opened the screen door and stepped onto the porch.

"Mommy, I hate those chickens! One of them bit me in the leg," DeeDee complained. "I don't want to get eggs—"

Suddenly, Robbie heard a loud thud-thud on the porch. She jumped from her seat and ran out the door. Maureen was lying at the bottom of the stairs. Robbie let out a cry and stumbled down the steps to her friend. She lifted Maureen's bleeding head onto her lap, as DeeDee ran out behind her. Maureen was grasping her chest, barely conscious.

"DeeDee," Robbie yelled at her daughter. "Run to the cow barn and tell Vince his mother is hurt and to come quick!" Another peal of thunder rumbled overhead. "Maureen? Maureen? Can you hear me?" asked Robbie, shaking her lightly. "Dear Lord! Please don't let her die!" Robbie looked to the sky as white lightning flashed across the clouds and fat raindrops began to fall. "She's my dearest friend in the world. Please save her!" she pleaded, as she began to sob.

"Maureen, open your eyes? Can you hear me?"

Maureen's eyes fluttered open. She whispered, "I'm…so…sorry," and her eyes closed again.

"Don't die on me Maureen; I love you!" Robbie cried as Vince and his father Brad arrived from the barn out of breath, followed by DeeDee.

"I think she's had a heart attack. We need to get her to the hospital!" Robbie hollered over a crack of thunder.

"Vince, help me carry her to the car," Brad said. He lifted the top of Maureen's torso, and Vince held his mother's legs. Robbie supported her back, as they moved to the car. Vince climbed into the backseat and pulled Maureen's unconscious body toward him, cradling her head against his shoulder.

Brad got into the driver's seat and started the engine. "Get the boys into the house!" he shouted at Robbie, then tore off down the driveway.

Robbie said another fervent prayer: *Please, PLEASE save the life of my dear friend!*

Hopper Family Farm
Fair Haven, Vermont
August, 1959

BERT HOPPER

AFTER MAUREEN'S FUNERAL, in August of 1959, Vince and Lynn moved into the farmhouse and Lynn took over managing the chores, so Robbie's services were no longer needed. Robbie and DeeDee were homeless again, and Robbie was without a job. She packed all her worldly belongings in two suitcases, and DeeDee's in one. Desperate, not knowing where to turn, she asked Brad to drive her to St. Mary's Church in Fair Haven, where she had become a parishioner.

Robbie set their luggage on the porch of the rectory, as Brad drove away. Father Sebastian answered the doorbell quickly. Robust, in his fifties, and with thinning hair, he escorted Robbie and DeeDee into his office.

"What brings you here today, Missus Van Dyne?" he asked, sitting behind his desk.

Robbie looked down at her trembling hands. "Father, I'm sorry to bother you, but I need some help." She swallowed her pride, hating to ask for charity, but she had to do what she could to provide for DeeDee. "My daughter and I need a place to live, and I need a job to support us. Would you happen to have any recommendations?"

Father Sebastian smiled at Robbie. "Missus Van Dyne, I do believe the Lord's grace is shining upon you today!" The priest blessed himself with the sign of the cross. "There's an elderly gentleman I know who needs a housekeeper. He lives about a mile south of town. His name is Bert Hopper. I believe he would have room for you and your daughter to stay at his house."

"What is his current physical situation?" Robbie asked.

"Well, he's in his eighties and slowing down. I believe he suffers from pulmonary edema he contracted working in the local slate quarries."

"I see," Robbie said, trying to picture the old man.

"Bert can still get around pretty well on his own. But he runs short of breath quickly, so he has to pace his activities," Father Sebastian said. "I know he loves his garden, but it's getting to be more than he can handle and I know he could use some help with it."

"I'm sure I can help Bert with his needs. I'm so glad I came to see you, Father! Thank you. When do you think I could start?" Robbie blushed at her forward behavior, as it was unlike her. But even though she had some money saved, she was desperate for a place for her and DeeDee to live.

At least we'll have a roof over our heads. Maybe someone is looking out for me after all. Thank You!

The priest nodded. "Let me call Bert and see if he's up for visitors." The priest flipped through his Rolodex and dialed the phone.

"Bert? Hello, this is Father Sebastian," the priest said into the receiver.

"I'm doing pretty well," the priest answered. "Listen, I think I may have found someone who can help you around the house."

Robbie could hear a deep male voice on the other end of the line, but couldn't make out his side of the conversation.

"Her name is Robbie, and she has a young daughter named DeeDee. They need a place to stay, and I thought you'd have room at your place," the priest explained.

More muffled conversation Robbie couldn't hear.

"How old is DeeDee?" the priest asked.

"She's three," Robbie answered. *I hope Bert doesn't have a problem with children. Please, Lord!*

"Okay, thanks Bert. We'll see you in a few minutes." Father Sebastian hung up the phone. "Bert says he'd like to meet you and DeeDee and to come by for a visit. I can drive you there now, if that's all right with you?" Father Sebastian smiled as he rose from his leather chair.

On the porch, Robbie grabbed one suitcase, while Father Sebastian lifted the other two. They stowed the cases in the trunk of the priest's Chevy. Robbie got DeeDee settled into the backseat, then joined the priest in the front. They drove around the park, through town, down the hill, across the bridge, then up another hill, to the south side of town. Father Sebastian pulled into the driveway of a white, clapboard two-story farmhouse. A covered porch extended along the front of the house, where two rocking chairs rested.

Father Sebastian knocked on the front door, with Robbie and DeeDee standing behind him. A tall, thin elderly gentleman, hunched at the shoulders, opened the door. Robbie noticed he was wearing a heavy sweater on this warm summer day. The man smiled, revealing an incomplete set of teeth. "Please come in," he said, his voice low and mellow.

Robbie held DeeDee's hand as they followed the priest into the main room.

"Bert, I'd like you to meet Robbie Van Dyne." Robbie leaned forward and shook Bert's bony hand. "And this is her daughter DeeDee," the priest said as he laid a hand on the child's head.

Bert leaned over to peer into the girl's eyes. "Well, hello there, Little One." He reached over to touch her golden curls causing DeeDee to retreat behind her mother's back.

"I'm sorry, Bert. DeeDee's a little shy around strangers," Robbie said, feeling DeeDee squeezing her hand.

"S'okay! I imagine a craggy ol' man like me would scare the daylights outta most livin' creatures," the old man laughed as he lowered himself into a rocking chair.

"So, Father Sebastian tells me you need a job and a place to live. Do you think this old place would do?" He grinned as he swept a hand around the cluttered room with a wood stove braced against one wall.

"Yes, Bert. I think it would do just fine!" Robbie smiled, taken by the old man's sweet nature and gentle humor. She was already mentally cleaning the room of its mess.

"I don't have a lot of money. But I can afford to pay you a hundred dollars a week, if that's acceptable to you." Bert looked from the priest to Robbie.

All I wanted was a roof over our heads. "Yes, that's more than generous. Thank you!" Robbie smiled at the elderly gentleman.

Father Sebastian walked to the door. "Well, it's settled then. Let me get your suitcases." The priest exited, then returned within a few moments and delivered the three suitcases to the front room.

Robbie gave the priest a hug. "Thank you so much, Father. You don't know how much this means to me and DeeDee."

The priest blushed at Robbie's unexpected display of affection. "May the good Lord bless you, Missus Van Dyne. Please call me if you need anything." He quickly left the house and drove back toward town.

Bert rose from his rocking chair. "Leave your cases and let me show you around the place." Sweeping his hand around the main room, Bert said, "This is the main part of the house built by my ancestors back in the eighteen-twenties."

Robbie noticed seven doors leading to other parts of the house, leaving little room for furniture in the main room. Bert pointed to a room to the left of the front door. "This is my room."

Robbie looked in to see a small bedroom at the corner of the house. A window looked onto the porch and another looked north. A twin bed was tucked into the corner away from the windows, with a nightstand and chair next to it. A mahogany dresser, holding a mirror surrounded by a wooden frame, sat against one wall. A free-standing, dark wooden chifforobe stood in the corner next to the front window and almost touched the ceiling.

Bert stepped down into the kitchen, and Robbie followed, holding DeeDee's hand. "The kitchen hasn't changed much from the original house. Obviously, we have electricity now," he pointed to the refrigerator tucked into a corner. "And I've replaced the old wood cook stove with a gas range."

To her right, Robbie saw the kitchen sink, the counter holding a dish rack. A small wooden table with four chairs sat in front of the window that faced the backyard. The window was framed with dusty, flowery curtains. Along the left of the window, custom-built cabinets lined the wall.

"It's lovely, Bert. I'm sure I can make you some great meals here." Robbie peered out the window and saw a two-story hay barn, some thirty yards from the house. A chill ran down Robbie's spine as she peered at the barn, which surprised her on this warm day. She turned to the old man. "So Bert, tell me about your ancestors who built the house."

Bert chuckled as he stepped back into the main room, with Robbie and DeeDee following. He led them through the door to his right and Robbie saw a long sitting room with a sofa and two comfortable armchairs. At the back of the room against the window facing south was a wooden, floor-model radio. Robbie smiled as she remembered her parents having a similar radio at their farm in Maine.

As they looked out the window to the back field, Bert said, "My ancestors. Well, it's a long story, so I'll make it brief." He chuckled. "Gabe and Emma Hopper built the original house, which contained the main room, kitchen and a loft upstairs." He pointed above him. "This half of the house we're in now was added on by my grandfather in the early nineteen hundreds."

They walked through a wide opening to a formal parlor at the front south side of the house. Robbie noticed pocket sliding doors tucked into the wall on each side. In the middle of the ceiling hung a crystal chandelier. Two windows in front and one on the side allowed a good deal of natural light to flow in. More formal seating was arranged in this room, and Robbie noticed a thick layer of dust on the furniture.

Bert chuckled, noticing Robbie's reaction. "I don't use this room much 'cause I don't have many visitors these days. So I guess it could use a good dusting, if you don't mind."

Robbie followed Bert through the single door at the left of the parlor, which led them to the stairway.

Bert paused, looking up the stairs. "When Gabe and Emma owned the farm, its twenty-plus acres stretched across the entire block." He took a few steps up and paused to catch his breath. "There were horse stables and a carriage barn…" He went up two more steps and paused. "A cow barn and sugaring house…" Robbie followed him slowly. ". . . are all gone now. The hay barn and chicken coop…" Bert reached the top of the stairs and wheezed to catch his breath. "…are still here." Robbie and DeeDee stood at the top of the landing with him. "Most of the land has been sold off…and is now family homes."

"I'm sorry to hear you had to sell off most of your land. That's a shame."

Bert flipped his hand in the air, a resigned look on his face. "Ah, well. It's just progress, I guess. I still have the chickens and my garden to keep me busy, so that's fine with me."

DeeDee tugged on Robbie's sleeve. "Mommy. I don't like chickens. They bite me!"

Bert patted the girl on the head and smiled. "It's okay, Little One. We'll keep you out of the chicken coop!"

Then Robbie followed Bert into the large bedroom to the left of the stairs. Suddenly, a deep chill coursed through her body again. She glanced around the room and noticed the two windows facing the street and the one facing south were closed. The room was stifling hot, with no air moving. *That's strange. Why am I getting chilled? I hope I'm not getting sick.* Robbie dismissed it as she looked around the room. Metal-framed twin beds with bare mattresses extended from one wall. A nightstand between them held a lamp. Another antique dresser, similar to the one in Bert's room, sat against the opposite wall.

"You can have this room, if you'd like," Bert said, sweeping his arm around. "I think it would work for you and DeeDee. This room was used by my parents and grandparents, so it's larger than the others. There's pillows in the closet." He pointed to a door on the left. "And the linens are in the bathroom."

Robbie opened the door and was surprised to see a deep walk-in closet. Empty hangers hung haphazardly on rods along both sides. Four pillows were stacked on a top shelf. Positioned against the back wall were two wooden-slat steamer trunks with rounded tops. A heavy padlock securely held the latch on the front of each trunk. *I wonder who those belonged to.*

She closed the door and turned back to Bert. "Oh yes, I think this is perfect, Bert. Thank you!" One of the first things she planned to do was open the windows and air the room out.

Bert stepped back into the hallway and showed Robbie the long, narrow middle bedroom that stretched along the back of the house. "This was my room when I was a kid, but it's too hard to climb the stairs now."

Tucked into the far south corner was another metal-framed bed with no mattress. In the corner next to the window was a wooden Victrola record player, standing about four feet high.

DeeDee walked to the unit, opened the two doors at her eye level and exclaimed, "Look, Mommy! There's toys!"

Robbie peered into the cabinet and saw stacks of 78 records, in yellowed parchment sleeves, arranged on the shelves. "No, no. DeeDee, don't touch!" She pulled her daughter's hand away.

Bert laughed. "Oh, my. I haven't used that old thing in years." He lifted the dusty, rounded cover and slowly turned the crank. The album bed began to revolve. "Ha! Look at that, would'ya? I think the old girl may have some life left in her yet! Maybe we can fire her up one of these days and see how she sounds."

Robbie smiled into the old man's crinkled, kind eyes. "I'd like that, Bert. I think it would be fun to listen to your records." *I'll bet he has some fond memories of listening to this old Victrola.*

Then Bert turned toward the rooms on the right. "Watch your step here," he said as he stepped down into the loft of the original house and chuckled. "They didn't do such a great job of building this addition, so the floors aren't level."

They traversed through an adjoining room with no windows to reach the original loft. A single window faced north. The ceilings on both sides sloped along the roofline. Bert pulled the string of the bare light bulb hanging from the ceiling to add more light in the darkened room. An old, beat-up dresser slumped forlornly against one wall. Next to the dresser Bert opened a door and Robbie peered into another long, walk-in closet. The left side of the ceiling followed the roof slope. Unlike the closet in the other room, this one was almost full. Robbie noticed more steamer trunks, metal trunks and boxes stacked willy-nilly.

She turned back to Bert. "My goodness. Who does all this stuff belong to?"

Bert shrugged. "Don't rightly know. My family I guess. No one's bothered to come claim it or clean it out." He pulled the light string and walked toward the stairs, with Robbie and DeeDee following. "Well, I guess that's the grand tour. I hope you like it here."

At the top of the stairs, Bert grinned, his wrinkles more pronounced. "Would you like to see the garden? It's my crowning achievement!"

"Of course," Robbie nodded. "Let's go take a look!"

Along the south side of the house, Bert directed Robbie and DeeDee along the garden paths. "Back in my ancestors' day, the stables and cow barn were located here." He swept his hand from the road to the end of the long garden. Then he pointed to an open spot along the trees in the back field. "And over there was our maple-sugaring house. It caught on fire during sugaring season when I was a kid, and had to be demolished. Sure do miss our homemade syrup, I can tell you that!"

On that late August day, Robbie noticed many of the vegetables were ripe or overripe and needed to be harvested. She remembered Father Sebastian saying he thought Bert could use some help in his garden. *I wonder if Bert has any canning jars. We can't let this go to waste.*

Robbie had lost her grip on DeeDee and turned to see her daughter climbing a lilac tree with low-hanging branches. The girl gripped a horizontal branch with her hands and let her legs swing beneath her, a couple of feet off the ground. Then she yelled, "Bert! Come help me. I'm hung. I'm hung!"

"DeeDee!" Robbie yelled. Then she was surprised to see Bert, his tall frame bent at the shoulders, shuffle over to the tree and grasp DeeDee by the waist.

"It's okay, I got'cha. You're safe now," he said, as he gently set her on the ground. The old man and the little girl both laughed with delight.

Over the summer and fall months, Robbie stayed busy helping Bert harvest his garden and preserve the vegetables. She tended to the chickens and sold the eggs to Bert's regular customers. Robbie would often look out the kitchen window and see DeeDee and Bert playing their "hanging" game, laughing together, and a smile would cross her face. *DeeDee needs a father*

I can't provide. I think Bert's the closest she'll ever get. Robbie also cooked Bert's meals, did his laundry, kept the house clean and administered his medications.

In the evenings, DeeDee would climb on the bed and cuddle against Bert's side as Robbie read them Bible stories, which always brought a smile to the old man's face.

In early winter, about six months after they had moved in, Bert's condition worsened, and he became bed-ridden. Robbie received instruction from Bert's visiting doctor on how to care for the invalid man. She gave him his medications, elevated him in bed to relieve his labored breathing, and learned to bathe him in bed. As his appetite failed and his swallowing became more difficult, she would make special dinners soft enough he could swallow easily.

Please, dear Lord. Let Bert recover from this terrible illness. He's so sweet and loves DeeDee as if she were his own granddaughter. I don't know what will happen to us if he passes away.

One frigid-cold morning in early January, Robbie arose before dawn and fed wood into the dying embers of the stove in the main room to warm the house. She put a pot of coffee on the kitchen stove to percolate, and prepared Bert's morning medications. She entered his small room next to the front door and turned on the lamp. As she shook Bert's arm to wake him in the dim light of the room, Robbie realized his lips were purple. She gently laid a hand over his mouth, but could feel no breath.

Oh, no! Oh, no! Oh, no! He can't be gone so soon. In her grief, she collapsed onto her knees and held Bert's cold hand to her heart.

"Dear Lord, please take this gentle soul into your loving arms. He was a wonderful man and I will miss him deeply." Robbie kissed Bert's stiff hand as her tears flowed. "Rest in peace, Dear Bert. We loved you."

Robbie grieved Bert's death as the country ushered in the new decade of the 1960s. She had grown very fond of the old man, with his wry sense of humor, and how he had doted upon her daughter. DeeDee was devastated at his loss and had grown sullen and withdrawn in the days that followed.

What's going to happen to us after his estate is settled? Bert said he had two wives who died, but didn't have any children. He never wanted to talk about his past much. I wonder if some long-lost relative will come forward and claim the property. Then we'll have to move, and I'll have to find another job. With my luck, I should have known this was too good to last very long. Please, Lord. Provide us your loving guidance so we don't end up as freezing bums on the street!

A month after Bert's funeral, on a snowy February day, there was a knock on the front door. Robbie answered it and saw a middle-aged man dressed in a suit, carrying a briefcase.

"Are you Missus Van Dyne?" he asked.

"Yes," Robbie replied, her heart thumping in her chest. *Oh, God! Here we go!*

"I'm Ralph Durkee. I'm the attorney for Mister Hopper's estate. May I come in?"

That was fast. They settled the estate quicker than I expected. Her mind raced, trying to figure out where she and DeeDee would go now. *Will they kick us out into the street in the middle of winter? Or will we be allowed to stay until spring?* "Please come in," she said with trepidation, then led him to the kitchen table, where he took a seat.

"Can I get you some tea, Mister Durkee?" Robbie stood next to him, wringing her hands.

"No, thank you. Please sit with me." He motioned to the chair next to him.

"Yes, of course." Robbie sat.

"Missus Van Dyne, I'm not sure if you're aware of this, but Mister Hopper made a new will before he died."

"No, I wasn't aware of that," she said, concerned.

"Well, he was very fond of your daughter, DeeDee, and he had no children of his own. Bert told me he wanted to provide for her future, and yours," Durkee continued.

Robbie's heart began beating very fast. *Oh, my! What did dear old Bert do?*

"Missus Van Dyne, I'm here to inform you Mister Hopper has named you as his sole beneficiary." He pulled papers from his briefcase and read: "You have inherited this property at 78 South Main Street, Fair Haven, Vermont, free of encumbrances; all of Mister Hopper's possessions; a 1955 Chevy Sedan, and the balance of two thousand, nine hundred and ten dollars and twenty-three cents in his savings account," the lawyer explained.

Robbie stared at the man, speechless. Her heart slammed in her chest, blood drained from her head and she felt dizzy. Her mind raced in a million directions.

Did I hear him right? Bert left me everything? Could this really be happening to someone like me? I've always had such rotten luck! Will I actually have a home to call my own for the first time in my life? DeeDee can grow up here, and I can have Ellie come live with us. Maybe, just maybe, I can get Barbara back, too. Please, dear Lord, don't let this be some horrible mistake!

"Missus Van Dyne? Did you understand what I said?"

"Ummm, I'm not sure." Robbie trembled. "Could you explain it to me again?" Her tongue stumbled over her words.

Mr. Durkee went over the inheritance with her again, step by step. He required her to sign papers that transferred the Hopper family farm into her name. He explained the papers would be filed with the court, and he would notify her when the estate was settled, then he bade his goodbyes.

DeeDee ran into the kitchen and tugged on her mother's arm. "Mommy, who was that man?" she asked.

Robbie pulled her daughter onto her lap and hugged her tightly. "Oh, Honey! He's the man who just saved our lives and gave you a real home," she said breathlessly, tears of joy running down her face.

LYNN COMES TO VISIT

"Hellooooo…Robbie?…you home?" A female voice called from the front porch. Lynn Granger balanced the casserole dish with her left hand, and used her right hand to reach through the rip in the screen door to unlock it from the inside. She let herself in, and saw Robbie dozing in her wing-back chair in the television room. Since Robbie's hip surgery, Lynn had been a regular visitor, stopping by daily to make sure Robbie was safe, often bringing her dinner. Ever since Robbie had cared for Lynn's mother-in-law, Maureen, some thirty-five years ago, Lynn and Vince had treated Robbie as their adopted grandmother. They made a point to include her in all their family events and celebrations with their three children.

Lynn set the casserole on the coffee table and gently shook the snoozing woman. "Robbie? It's Lynn. How are you doing?"

Robbie awoke from her nap, groggy, trying to clear her head from the memories of her life. "Oh! Hi Lynn! I didn't hear you come in. What time is it?"

"It's about seven. I brought you a shepherd's pie for dinner, just the way you like it, with the potatoes nicely browned on top," Lynn said.

"Oh, thank you, Dear. That's wonderful. Will you stay and join me?"

"Sure, I can stay for a little while before I need to get back to the farm."

Robbie scooted forward in her chair, grabbed her walker, and attempted to lift herself to a standing position. A sharp pain in her hip forced her to drop back into the chair. "Ahhh, that old devil's got me again. I've been sitting here too long. Looks like I'll need a little help."

Lynn leaned behind Robbie in the chair and placed both hands under the elderly woman's armpits. "Okay, on three: one…two…three…" Lynn lifted as Robbie pushed herself up and balanced over the walker.

"Let's get you walking a little before we have supper," Lynn said, as she helped Robbie navigate into the main room and out onto the porch, where twilight was fast approaching on this mid-September eve.

Over the previous year, DeeDee had hired a contractor to remove the old wooden steps up to the porch and replace them with wide, low-rise concrete steps, covered by a portico. A concrete walkway had also been laid leading to the driveway to make it easier for Robbie to move around with her walker. The bathroom had been remodeled with a handicapped shower and grab bars put in around the toilet for easier access.

Lynn helped Robbie down the wide steps and guided her walk along the pathway and back several times to get her hip loosened up. "How's the hip—feeling a little better?"

"Yes, it's better now I've walked a bit," said Robbie. "Let's go eat some of that great shepherd's pie before it gets cold!"

They made their way back into the house, and Lynn helped Robbie step down to the kitchen. Robbie sat at the table while Lynn served two big helpings of the layered hamburger, corn, and browned mashed potato casserole.

Robbie took a bite of the food and tried to swallow. The reality hit her all at once she would have to leave her home soon. She tried to hold back the tears, but grief overcame her. She scrunched up her face and began to cry.

"Robbie, what's the matter?" Lynn asked concerned. "Are you sick?"

"Oh, Lynn. I'm just so upset. DeeDee called me today." Her right hand trembled smacking the table. "She and Ellie are putting me into a nursing home! I can't believe it! I don't want to leave my home. I'm fine taking care of myself, and the nurse comes by to help me. Why do I have to leave? It's not fair!" Robbie sobbed, shaking in her chair.

Lynn pulled her chair close to Robbie and hugged the distraught woman to her chest.

"Oh, I'm so sorry, Robbie. I know how much you love this place. You must feel terrible, so you have every right to cry," Lynn said as she caressed

Robbie's back. "You know? Maybe it's for the best. You gotta admit, this big old house is much more than you can handle these days." Lynn swung her arm toward the main room. "And you'll have plenty of folks around to visit with every day. Maybe it won't be so bad after all. What d'ya think?"

When her sobs subsided, Robbie pulled from Lynn's embrace, and blew her nose on a napkin. "Gosh, Lynn, I just don't know. This is the only place I've called home for almost forty years. How can I just up and leave?" Robbie took a drink of water to clear her throat. "DeeDee said she's coming home for a visit to clean out the place and help me move. She'll be here Wednesday." Both of Robbie's hands now trembled uncontrollably as she spoke.

Lynn grasped both of the old woman's hands. "Well, I think it's going to take some time to get this place cleaned out. I mean, after all, Robbie, you gotta admit, you are a pack rat!" Lynn smiled as she swept her arm toward the piles in the kitchen. "That'll give you some time to think about things, and plan for your move."

"Yes, yes. I'm sure you're right. And you know how I hate to throw things out because I might be able to use them someday," Robbie responded with a slight smile.

"When DeeDee gets home, have her give me a call, and I'll come over," Lynn said. "I'm sure she'll be needing all the help she can get. Now, let's finish our supper, shall we?" she said, squeezing Robbie's hands.

After Lynn left, Robbie put on her nightgown, climbed into bed and said her prayers. She used to pray on her knees, but was afraid if she did that now, she wouldn't be able to get back up.

Robbie prayed out loud. "Dear Lord, please watch over DeeDee so she has a safe flight home. Thank you for bringing Lynn into my life. She's a wonderful girl who has taken good care of me over the years. And please help me to be strong so I don't become a burden to my daughters. When the time comes, Lord, please take me swiftly into your loving arms. Amen."

Robbie fell asleep weeping.

Gabe stands next to Robbie's bed as she grumbles in her fitful sleep. He reaches out and caresses her back.

"Thee is a good, God-fearing woman and has comforted my descendant, Bert, in his final days. I shall always be grateful for thy true kindness. May thee find eternal peace."

DEEDEE

HOPPER FAMILY FARM
FAIR HAVEN, VERMONT
SEPTEMBER, 1999

FIRST ENCOUNTER

THREE DAYS AFTER THE EMOTIONAL CALL to my mom, Robbie, I settled into my window seat as the flight lifted off from the San Jose airport at 6:00 a.m. for the first leg of my journey to Chicago O'Hare. I'm definitely not a morning person, and it was a challenge for me to make this morning flight. Even after landing in Burlington, Vermont at 6:00 p.m., I still had a two-hour drive south to reach my family homestead in Fair Haven. It was an exhausting day. I tried to count the many times I'd gone through O'Hare—once or twice a year for more than twenty years, yet had never actually been to the city of Chicago. One day, I'd have to schedule a layover so I could visit the downtown area.

As my flight began its long, eastward trek, I thought back over my life since I had left my mom in Fair Haven, and moved away at the age of eighteen.

After graduating from high school, I couldn't wait to get out of that small Vermont town where everyone knew your business, so I hightailed it to the nearest big city, Boston, to go to college. Four years later, armed with a Computer Science degree, I got hired at a computer manufacturing firm outside the city. At the wedding of a co-worker, I met a man from California named Dave, with whom I became completely smitten. We carried on a long-distance romance for many months, and Dave even flew me to California for a two-week vacation. Then he invited me to move in with him. I was torn about what to do. The allure of moving West was very enticing. But I had guilt and reservations about leaving Mom and moving across the country.

On a visit home, I told Mom my concerns.

"You need to do what you think is best for your life," Mom said, holding my hand at the kitchen table. "I hate to see you move so far away, but I'll be fine. And Ellie is close by if I need anything." She had put on a brave face, trying not to show her disappointment and heartache over my pending decision. "And don't forget, Dear, no matter where we are in the world, we'll both be looking at the same full moon."

I smiled, remembering our many evenings in the backyard gazing at the constellations and talking to the man in the moon. "I know, Mom. I'm sure the 'man' will relay my thoughts and love to you always." Trying not to cry I asked, "If I move, will you come to California and visit me?"

"Of course, Honey! I'd love to see the West Coast," she said with some feigned enthusiasm.

"And I'll come home for Christmas, Mom. I promise!"

"Well, we'll see how the weather is, Dear. I don't want you to fly in a storm," she said, always concerned about my well-being.

At the impressionable age of twenty-four, in October of 1980, I packed two suitcases and moved to Silicon Valley to live with Dave, and work as a programmer in the high-tech industry. Bill Gates, Steve Jobs, and Steve Wozniak were fledgling young-bucks then, with different strategic views of how the infancy of the personal computer industry should evolve. Gates' view was focused on all-encompassing software that would run any machine. Jobs' and Wozniak's vision was focused on the design, function, and simplicity of the entire computer. Both companies would evolve into highly successful computer firms, Microsoft and Apple.

With technological innovations oozing out of engineers' garages, it was a heady time to be in what truly was the futuristic Wild-Wild West. In comparison to the white-collar, buttoned-down, male-dominated business atmosphere of the East Coast, this was a sprawling valley of free-spirited men and women engineers with the motto: "anything-and-everything-goes." As a tech-savvy woman, I was swept up by the myriad possibilities for my burgeoning career.

The summer after I moved in with Dave, we had decided to buy a cabin on a ridge in the Santa Cruz Mountains, about twenty-five miles west of the valley. It was a long commute every day on a two-lane, steep, winding road. But I didn't mind, since I enjoyed living in the mountains.

For Christmas, we flew back East to spend holidays with our families. When we returned, it was raining hard, and we were disappointed our luggage had not arrived with us. What we didn't realize was this was the third day unprecedented, torrential rains had been battering the Bay Area. After picking up our animals at the shelter, we arrived to our cabin surrounded by swaying redwoods. I hit the light switch and nothing happened. Our electricity was out.

It didn't take long before all hell started breaking loose. Trees started falling around our cabin from the gale-force winds. We stayed up all night, scared to death a mighty tree would crush our cabin. The creek running behind our house overflowed and ripped out our road; hillsides slid taking homes and people with them, blocking the main road. We got stranded for a week with no fresh food, electricity, heat or running water in what was considered the worst disaster in the Santa Cruz mountains, where six people died.

Although we survived the ordeal, our relationship did not. The following spring, we sold the cabin back to the original owner, and Dave and I parted ways. At that point, I considered moving back East to be closer to Mom. But I loved my job and had grown accustomed to the usually mild climate, so I decided to stay. I moved into a studio apartment in the valley with my cats.

I lived the single life for a number of years and focused on my career. One Saturday night, after attending a wedding with friends who went home early to relieve their babysitter, I decided to go to a nightclub alone, which I had never done before. As I cruised the club, I noticed two guys sitting at the bar, chatting. One was blond and clean-shaven. The other was bearded with light brown hair and baby-blue eyes. The bearded guy kept flashing me a big grin each time I walked past. I finally went over and said hello. Big-smile, bearded guy introduced himself as Mark, bought me a drink, and asked me to dance.

Two years later, I married Mark, a native of San Jose, on his thirty-fifth birthday, April 2nd, in an intimate chapel in Los Altos Hills. I was happy I could afford Mom's plane ticket, so she could attend my wedding. She beamed with pride as she held my arm, and we walked down the aisle together. My older sister, Ellie, wasn't able to attend the wedding because she was pregnant with her second child. So at the old-maid age of thirty-one, I became a wife and stepmother to Mark's six-year-old daughter,

Sabrina, from his previous marriage. I have lived and worked in Silicon Valley ever since.

As I continued my journey to Vermont, I changed planes in Chicago and squeezed into the smaller commuter plane for the final flight to Burlington. My mind was a jumble of all the coordination I'd have to do once I reached my childhood home.

Ultimately, my plan was to clean out the house and barn, and put the property up for rent. But it wasn't going to be an easy task. Bert Hopper was the last in the Hopper family lineage. His ancestors had built the farm in the early 1820s. The property had been passed down through the Hopper family until Mom inherited it, and it had never been cleaned out. The place was full of a combination of junk, antiques, and who knew what else. Sorting through it would be a monumental task. I tried to prepare myself emotionally for what would be a gut-wrenching chore. A flood of memories of Mom and I living alone in that big old house whirled through my mind.

And then there was the sometimes-not-so-benevolent spirit, who shared the house with us.

I was about five years old the first time I encountered our ghost. My bedroom was in what was originally the front parlor, and the door to my bedroom was at the base of the stairs. At night, I would often hear the creaking of floorboards, as if footsteps moved across the upstairs bedroom. I wondered who else lived with us in the house. One cold night in November, I decided to find out.

The thumping of footsteps moving back and forth across the ceiling awoke me. I got out of bed, put on my slippers, and opened my door to the base of the stairs. I could hear Mom snoring lightly in her small room next to the front door. It was dark and chilly in the house, and I shivered as I took the first step up. I gripped the wooden banister and took another step. The wood shifted under my weight. I stopped, heart pounding, not wanting to wake Mom. Three more steps up—creak—my heart thudded louder.

Should I keep going up, or go back to bed? What if there's a monster or a bogeyman? Will it eat me?

My legs trembled as I took another step, gripping the banister, and another, and another. Finally I was at the top of the stairs, where I faced the closed doorway of the bedroom directly above mine.

We kept the upstairs bedroom doors closed to save on heat. I faced the door and tried to catch my breath. I heard floorboards creak on the other side. I was shaking as I bolstered my courage.

I want to know who else lives here with us.

I grasped the cold doorknob and slowly turned it to the right. The door unlatched. Despite my fear, I forced myself to crack open the door. I took one step into the room. It was dark, but glow from the streetlight came in through the front windows. I could just make out a dark figure standing there. I stood very still, willing my heart to calm down, as I tried to figure out what I was seeing.

Suddenly, an old man was standing in front of me. I jumped and let out a squeal. I hadn't seen him move. A deep chill flowed through me. My limbs seemed frozen and immobile. The figure had an eerie, greenish glow around him, but I could see his features clearly. He was tall and thin with hunched shoulders, a deeply wrinkled face, balding but with longish gray hair that flowed over his shoulders, with a big, gray beard. He wore a red flannel shirt that hung over dark, baggy trousers. On his feet were a set of rubber, knee-high boots, of a kind I'd never seen before. He seemed to be hovering just above the floor. A strange odor seemed to emanate from him that reminded me of the Granger farm, where we had lived for a short time. My heart slammed in my chest. I was glued to the spot.

"Do not be afraid. I shan't hurt thee. I shall protect thee and thy mother," I heard him say, thinking he was talking funny.

My mouth was dry as sandpaper, but I managed to whisper, "Who are you?"

"I am Gabe, and this is my house," he said. His gravelly voice was barely audible. "I have always been here, and I shall protect thee from evil. Go to bed and sleep well, my wee child."

Then Gabe waved his wrinkled hand over my head, and my shivering subsided immediately. I felt a warmth flush through my body. I stared as he glided back to the window. The streetlight illuminated his figure, which slowly faded into the darkness. I willed my legs to run, but I was rooted to the floor.

Is this real? I know I'm not dreaming because I remember getting up. At least now I know who else lives here with us!

After what seemed like an eternity, I backed out of the room, closed the door, and slowly made my way down the stairs in the dark. I climbed into bed wondering who Gabe was, and how long he'd been here. I felt warm and safe and fell asleep quickly. I was no longer afraid.

The next morning at breakfast I asked Mom, "Mommy, who is Gabe?" She wiped her hands on her apron, and whipped around from the stove. Her brow crinkled as she stared me. I was startled at her reaction.

"Honey, what are you talking about?" Mom's voice rose as she approached me at the table.

Not sure if I should tell her the truth, I mumbled, "I went upstairs last night—to see who else lives here—and I met Gabe," I replied tentatively.

Mom sat down at the table and held my hand. "Dee, I don't know who Gabe is, other than he's a spirit who's here to protect us," she said. "He appeared to me not long ago, right here in the kitchen. Scared the living daylights out of me!" Mom laughed. "He told me not to be afraid, that this was his house, and he is protecting it from evil."

"That's what he told me, too! I think Gabe's a good ghost." I squeezed Mom's hand.

"Yes, Honey! I think he's a good ghost, too. We're very lucky to have him and the good Lord watching over us," she reassured me.

It wouldn't be long before we realized our "good ghost" had a darker side.

Gabe watches Robbie and DeeDee sitting at the kitchen table, holding hands.

I am pleased to have good, honest, God-fearing people living in my house. I shall do everything in my power to protect them from any dishonorable brethren who may enter my premises.

NIGHTMARES

I arrived at my family homestead after a two-hour drive from the Burlington airport. I lugged my big suitcase and travel bag along the new concrete walkway and up the steps, where the porch light was on. Mom came out with her walker to greet me.

"How was your trip, Dear?" she asked as I hugged her. I thought she looked pretty good, despite her age of eighty.

"It was long, as usual. You know how I hate getting up so early to catch that flight."

"Oh, yes I do!" She began to sing, "Oh how I hate to get up in the mor-nin'. Oh how I long to be staying in bed. When my heart is full of yorn, I can hear the bugler's horn. Ya gotta get up, ya gotta get up, ya gotta get up this mor-nin'."

I laughed. "I always hated it when you sang me that song, because you knew I wanted to sleep longer." Leaving my suitcases in the main room I followed Mom as she made her way to the kitchen.

She bustled around and placed toasted tuna and cheese sandwiches with potato salad in front of us. I opened the refrigerator to get something to drink and was surprised to see a cold bottle of California chardonnay—thank God! I was exhausted and needed a drink. I popped the cork and poured two glasses for us.

Mom chuckled, "Lynn brought the wine over for you yesterday. She said she thought you'd need a drink after your long trip."

"Well bless her heart! She's a good girl," I exclaimed.

"Here's to your new life, Mom," I said, as upbeat as possible. I knew my visit home was going to be tough on both of us. I wanted to be as brave and strong for Mom, as she had been for me her whole life.

Mom looked at me with sadness in her eyes, and I thought she was about to cry. But she held it back as we clinked glasses. I was sad too, but too tired to get into that discussion. We'd have plenty of time to talk about her future during my visit.

After we finished eating, I dragged my cases into my old childhood bedroom on the south side of the house, next to the stairway. Suddenly, a sharp pain shot up my right leg, which caused me to stumble and drop onto the bed, rubbing my shinbone. Memories flooded back of the horrifying night in this room, on the eve of my thirteenth birthday.

It is my thirteenth birthday party and all my friends are in the backyard at the picnic table with Mom. Everyone is dressed in black, wearing party hats, laughing and talking. A birthday cake is on the table. The candles drip onto the cake because there is no one there to blow them out.

Next to the table is a coffin, and I am in it—alive. I try to lift the lid but my hands sink into the thick, silky lining. I can't get traction. I kick and push as hard as I can on the lid, but it won't budge.

I scream to Mom, "I'm here! I'm alive! Please let me out!" No one hears me.

I awake gasping for air, thrashing in my bed, trying to get out of the coffin.

After several occurrences of this nightmare, I became convinced I wasn't going to live to see my thirteenth birthday on the last day of July.

The day before my birthday, a Sunday, was hot and muggy. We opened all the windows in the house, but there was no breeze blowing, and the humidity was stifling. Mom decided to take me and my friends to the State Park at Lake Bomoseen, a few miles away, for a swim and birthday picnic.

After several hours at the lake, thunderclouds started stacking up over the mountains, and lightning flashed in the distance. Mom ushered us out of the lake, despite our howls of protest. She packed up the picnic and drove back to town to drop off the other kids. As we pulled into our driveway, thunder roared over our heads, and the heavens let loose. We grabbed the picnic gear from the car and dashed into the house, getting soaked. Then we rushed around the house closing the windows before the rain could get in.

Mom thought this would probably be a quick afternoon thunderstorm, so frequent in New England during the summer, and hoped it would finally cool things off a bit. But the winds picked up and the storm wailed into the evening. Then the power went out. Weather forecasting wasn't very accurate back then, and we were unaware we were getting hit with the tail end of a powerful hurricane.

We lit a couple of oil lamps and candles, then sat at the kitchen table playing cards. We listened to the rain pelting the windows and the wind howling through the trees. Suddenly, the candles on the table blew out. Goose bumps ran up my spine.

"Hmmm…must have been a gust from these darn drafty windows," Mom said as she re-lit the candles.

But I wasn't so sure. I felt a cold chill pass along my neck that didn't come from the window. I turned my head to look behind me. What appeared as a small ball of light glowed, then disappeared into the main room. A shiver ran through the rest of my body. I hugged myself to stop shaking. I stared at Mom to see if she had felt anything, but she was dealing the cards and didn't seem to have noticed. As we continued our card game, I was grateful to have a solid roof over my head in such a big storm. I felt sad for any homeless people out there who weren't so fortunate.

We finally decided to go to bed. I took a lantern to my room to light my way. The head of my bed was against the window on the south side of the house, and the bed extended into the middle of the room. I put on a nightgown, climbed into bed, and snuffed the lantern on the nightstand. The storm was very loud, driving pelting rain against the window above my head. It took me a long time to fall asleep.

I dreamed I was in the middle of an earthquake as I woke up to my bed shaking.

What the hell's going on? We don't have earthquakes in Vermont.

When I opened my eyes, a dark figure, strangely illuminated by a greenish-white glow, loomed above me. It appeared to be grasping the headboard. I screamed, and struck out with both arms to push it away from my bed, but my hands flailed at empty air.

The figure moved to the side of my bed, and I could see it more clearly. It took me a moment to realize it was Gabe.

"Tur rou bet," I heard him mumble in his low voice.

"What? What do you want? Leave me alone," I grumbled as I tried to go back to sleep.

"Turn around in bed," I heard more clearly.

"What are you talking about?" I didn't know why I'd been awakened, but I was starting to get frightened.

"Sleep with thy head there," Gabe said. A lightening flash illuminated a bony finger pointing toward the foot of the bed.

"Why? I'm fine here," I argued, hoping he'd just disappear.

"Thee must move!" he said firmly, and much louder. I was now fully awake and scared.

"Okay. Okay. I'll move!" I said, exasperated. As I lifted the covers, I started to say something else to him, but he was gone. Grumbling, I got up, groped the sheets out from the foot of the bed, moved my pillow, and felt around in the dark to tuck the sheets into the top of the bed where my head had been. I crawled back into bed with my head next to the footboard.

This is stupid! Why do I have to sleep with my head down here? I tried to go back to sleep while the storm raged.

What sounded like the roar of thunder awoke me up again, but this was different. When I looked up, I saw a huge chunk of the ceiling next to the window rip away from the wall. Before I could react, it slammed into the headboard and landed on my legs. I heard a crack under the sheets and a second later, a searing white-hot pain shot up my right leg. I screamed, then clenched my teeth to ward off the pain. Another chunk of ceiling fell to my left, spreading plaster dust, lath and debris over me and the room. Gasping from the pain in my leg, I breathed in the dust and started choking.

What's happening! Why is the house falling down on top of me? Am I dreaming? If I was dreaming, it was a very painful nightmare.

I watched the crystal chandelier directly above my head sway wildly. Glass shards sprayed around the room like manic fireflies. Then I heard a ripping sound, and saw the chandelier tip sideways as it dangled by its wires, its weight pulling at the last nail that held the base to the ceiling. I covered my head with the sheet as the chandelier crashed to the floor to my right, partially landing on my bed. I felt something pierce my right arm, and I screamed again. The whole house was shaking. The sound of the wind coming through the gaping hole in the ceiling was like a demon's howl. It felt like my entire world was collapsing around me, which it was.

"Mommy! Mommy! Help me!" I yelled.

A few moments later I heard Mom's voice from the doorway. "Oh God! What's happening? DeeDee! DeeDee! Are you hurt?" She shined a flashlight on my bed. I peeked out from under the sheet as she started to enter the room. More lath and plaster crashed between us, exploding on the floor, forcing her back. I looked toward the window above the headboard and saw a torrent of water flowing down the wall like some menacing serpent from hell.

The old house growled like a hungry bear waking too early from hibernation, as the ceiling support beams shifted in their moorings. Fortunately, they didn't completely collapse from the assault of water flowing through them. More lath and plaster rained down upon me. I quickly covered my head, choking and using my pillow for protection. I desperately wanted to crawl under the bed, but I was trapped when I tried to move as the searing pain shot up my leg again.

Unable to make her way across the debris to reach me, Mom yelled from the doorway, "I'm going to get some help!" Then she was gone.

As more of the ceiling collapsed around me, I realized it was the morning of my thirteenth birthday. My worst nightmare was coming true! I was going to die with the solid roof of my house, I was so thankful for just hours earlier, crushing me to death.

I began to pray, "Now I lay me down to sleep. I pray the Lord my soul to keep. Should I die before I wake, I pray the Lord my soul to take."

I hoped my death would be swift, and I wouldn't suffer any more pain. My mind tumbled down the rabbit hole into darkness and silence.

Gabe watches the rain pour into the open windows of the upstairs bedroom, which had not been closed earlier in the day. He tries to warn them as they are playing cards, by blowing out the candles. His warning goes unheeded because mother and daughter are distracted by the storm. As he watches, the water soaks into the carpet and oozes into the floorboards, turning the plaster into a heavy cement.

The ceiling is going to collapse where the girl is sleeping. I must warn her.

Stubborn little girl, she almost didn't listen to me! I am thankful she finally obeyed my command to change her position in bed. At least she will survive.

Gabe is devastated as he watches the ceiling of his house collapse around the young girl, but there is nothing he can do to stop the destruction.

THE STORM BREAKS

"DeeDee, can you hear me?" A man's deep voice echoed in my head.

Am I dead? Is this God? Where are the angels?

"DeeDee, can you hear me?"

I felt a pressure on my arm, and someone shaking me. I realized I wasn't dead as my mind swam up from oblivion, and the most horrible nightmare—that the world had collapsed around me. I felt something funny on my face and started to reach for it, but someone held my arm down. Opening my eyes I saw a dark shirt with a patch on the chest hovering over me. A plastic mask covered my nose and mouth. I became aware there were other people in the room, yelling and moving debris out of the way. So it was real—my world really did collapse, I realized in horror.

I heard Mom's voice. "You're going to be all right, Honey." My view shifted to see her standing next to the dark-shirt man.

He explained, "DeeDee, we're going to get you onto a stretcher. It's going to hurt a little when we move you, but we'll give you something for the pain when we get you to the ambulance, okay?" I nodded because it was hard to talk with the mask over my face. I felt hands go under my armpits, more hands under my back, and other hands under my left leg. But strangely, I couldn't feel my right leg.

The paramedic ordered, "Okay. On three: one…two…three!"

As I felt myself being lifted, a searing pain shot through my right leg. I gasped and screamed as I was laid on the stretcher. I looked down and saw a brace wrapped around my leg. My mind flashed back to the ceiling collapsing on top of me, and tears flooded my eyes. Mom held my hand as they wheeled the stretcher to the ambulance. A ray of early morning sunlight illuminated her face as she bent down to kiss my forehead. The storm had broken.

"I'll meet you at the hospital," Mom said. Then she smiled. "Happy birthday, Honey." I realized I would live to see thirteen after all.

I was in the hospital for two days. The doctor said I was lucky I had a clean break in my tibia, and it would heal nicely. The gash in my arm from the chandelier glass had taken ten stitches, leaving a zig-zag scar. I had to wear a leg cast for eight weeks. So I started eighth grade on crutches, which was a total pain in the ass—taking the bus and going up and down stairs in the three-story schoolhouse. But I managed to cope.

During my stay in the hospital, I had time to replay that night in my head. How much was a nightmare, and how much was real? I remembered Gabe telling me to change position in bed, which I did, reluctantly. Had I not moved, the first chunk of ceiling would have landed on my head and probably killed me.

I sent a silent prayer to Gabe, and thanked him for saving my life.

ELLIE MOVES IN AND OUT

The day after I arrived at my family homestead in Vermont, I made arrangements for a large dumpster to be parked next to the driveway to collect the refuse coming out of the house. I contacted the people Lynn Granger had recommended at the Fair Haven Historical Society and the auction house. I informed them we were cleaning out the house, and would contact them when we needed their assistance.

The first week included the arduous task of clearing out all the junk Mom had accumulated. She grew up in the Great Depression, and never wanted to throw anything out because she "could use it someday." Despite Mom's emotional protests, I convinced her we needed to throw out stacks of old newspapers, magazines, junk mail, phone books, church programs, coupons, and broken pieces of odds and ends. It all went into the dumpster.

Then we focused our attention on the upstairs bedrooms. I helped Mom up the stairs with her walker, and we started with the bedroom on the left above my room. This was the room where Gabe liked to hang out. It contained dented, metal-framed twin beds, which I planned to toss. But a beautifully carved, ornate mahogany dresser with a swinging mirror stood against one wall, and I guessed it would be popular at the auction. Two locked steamer trunks in the back of the walk-in closet had been there as long as I could remember. I knew I would need some strong help to move them. Then I'd have to figure out how to open them and inspect their contents.

This was also the room where my older sister, Ellie, had lived for a year.

When Ellie graduated from high school in Maine, she decided to go to Castleton State College, near Fair Haven, and she came to live with us. She was eighteen at the time, and I was nine.

Ellie had grown up with my Aunt Pauline and Uncle Charles on their potato farm in Maine, about fifteen miles outside the town of Houlton, where she attended school. My aunt and uncle were devoutly religious and very strict with Ellie's upbringing. Their son, Charlie Jr., was also kept under strict supervision, and worked the farm. Ellie was never allowed to date, and could only play with friends who were her close neighbors.

On the other hand, I basically raised myself and did whatever I wanted, since Mom worked two jobs and didn't have the energy to discipline me much.

Before Ellie moved in, Mom's first of two jobs was working the eleven-to-seven night shift at a nursing home a few blocks from our house. She would bring me with her, and I'd sleep on the sofa in the dayroom. In the morning we would go home, and she'd get me off to school. Then she would sleep during the day, get up around 4:00 p.m., and make dinner for me to heat up later. At five, she would leave to waitress at the NoWhere restaurant across the street from our house until 10:00 p.m. Then she'd come home, take a bath, change her clothes, gather me up in my pajamas, and we would go back to the nursing home for the night shift.

When Mom took the job cooking at the college to help Ellie pay for tuition, she quit her shift at the nursing home because she had to be at the kitchen by 5:00 a.m. She would phone me every morning at six-thirty to wake me up, so I could get myself dressed and to the bus on time. Then she would come home around four in the afternoon, make dinner, change clothes, and go to work at the restaurant.

A few months after Mom started working in the kitchen, she slipped and fell on some grease and hit her head on the cement floor. They rushed her to the hospital, where Ellie and I went to see her. We dreaded to hear her prognosis. The doctor said she had Parkinson's disease, and said it could be managed with medications. But he recommended she find a less dangerous line of work. So she ended up working as a cleaning lady in the college girls' dorms.

With Mom gone most of the time, I had plenty of freedom to ride my bike three blocks to visit my best friend, Marie, or my other friends, Katie and Leslie, and stay as long as I wanted. Mom always wanted me home before dark, but sometimes I would stay for dinner and ride my bike at night, not thinking twice about it in our small, safe town.

When Ellie moved in, my freedom as an only child was immediately threatened. It didn't take Ellie long to realize I was an unsupervised wild-child who needed "discipline." She decided she was going to be the one to impose it.

Being a know-it-all nine-year-old, the last thing I wanted was a big sister showing up on my doorstep, bossing me around. So I fought it tooth and nail. One rainy fall afternoon, after Ellie had been living with us for a couple of months, I got off the school bus and dumped my books in the house. Then I started to head out the door to get my bike and ride to Marie's house.

"Where are you going?" Ellie demanded.

"None of your goddamned business!" I said. This was not the first time she had attempted to stop me from my outings.

"It's raining. You can't go out on your bike," Ellie scolded.

"The hell I can't! You can't stop me, and you can't tell me what to do! You're not my mother, so leave me the fuck alone!" Without warning, Ellie slapped me across the face, sending me reeling backward onto the sofa. I was stunned. The stinging in my cheek brought tears to my eyes.

She hit me? I can't believe she hit me! Mom never hits me.

"Don't you talk to me that way! I'm your sister. You need to start behaving yourself."

"You bitch! I'm telling Mom you hit me when she gets home. Fuck you! You're gonna be in big trouble!" I ran to my room sobbing, giving up my plans to go out.

Later that night, Mom walked through the door after working at the restaurant, and we both accosted her.

"Mom! Ellie hit me—"

"DeeDee swore at me and called me a bitch—"

"Ellie wouldn't let me go over to Marie's—"

"She wouldn't listen to me when I told her not to go out in the rain—"

Mom slung her purse down and dropped into a chair at the kitchen table. She let out a long sigh and stared at us as if we were aliens. Groaning as she kicked off her shoes, she bent to rub the bottom of one foot, then the other. Then she put a hand on her lower back and straightened up slowly.

"Sit down, both of you," she said quietly. "Now, what happened?"

Ellie jumped in first. "DeeDee wanted to ride her bike over to Marie's in the rain, and I told her she couldn't go."

"She's not my mother. She can't tell me what to do!" I said, glaring at Mom.

"DeeDee runs around and does whatever the hell she wants with no one watching out for her. Someone's got to get her under control."

"No they don't. I can control myself! Just because you were raised in a nunnery, doesn't mean I have to be!" I knew it would hit home when I criticized my aunt who had raised her.

"Okay! Okay! Enough!" Mom snapped, after pouring herself a glass of water. "DeeDee, I know I haven't been the best mother to you because I work so much, and you spend a lot of time alone. I'm sorry for that. Ellie loves you and is just trying to look out for your safety. When she tells you not to go out in the rain, you should listen to her when I'm not here."

I didn't like what I was hearing: Mom was siding with Ellie against me! I felt betrayed and angry. "But Mom, she *hit* me!" I pleaded.

"I hit her because she swore at me!" Ellie yelled back.

Mom rubbed her tired eyes. "DeeDee, you need to watch your mouth and quit swearing. It isn't lady-like." She turned to my sister. "Ellie, please don't hit her again no matter how mad you are. It just makes matters worse." Mom admonished us both.

"She's not *your* mother, she's *my* mother," I screamed at Ellie. "Why did you ever come to live with us? I hate you, and wish you'd just leave me alone!" I cried as I ran out of the kitchen, into my room, and slammed the door.

Ellie stomped up the stairs to her room above me, and slammed her door. I heard Mom running bath water, and quiet sobbing coming from the kitchen. It made me feel sad we had made Mom cry.

The next afternoon, when Mom came home from work, I was doing my homework at the kitchen table, and I heard Ellie tell Mom she wanted to talk to her. They came into the kitchen and sat down at the table with me.

Ellie said somewhat sheepishly, "Mom, I know this sounds crazy, but there was an old man in my room last night."

Mom and I exchanged glances.

I egged her on. "Really? What'd he look like?"

Her face was ashen. "Well…gray hair…beard…flannel shirt…baggy pants." She looked like she hadn't slept well.

"Ohhhh! That was Gabe!" I exclaimed.

"Who's Gabe?"

"Well, Dear," Mom explained, "he's the spirit who lives in this house. He said he's here to protect us."

Ellie's eyes went wide. "There's a ghost haunting this place! Why didn't you warn me?"

I jumped in. "Gabe's a good ghost, except to people he doesn't like."

Ellie glared at me. "He told me he didn't want me in his house and I needed to leave. Doesn't sound like he's trying to protect *me!*" she grumped.

"Oh, shit! You'd better pack up and leave right now, otherwise Gabe will *kill* you!" I said, trying to get Ellie mad.

Mom scolded. "Now DeeDee, stop that! You're scaring your sister!"

With as much gravity as I could muster, I stared at Ellie. "No, I'm serious! If he told you to leave, you better get the hell outta here. Gabe doesn't mess around with people he doesn't like."

"That's nonsense," said Mom. "Ellie, you're perfectly safe to stay here. Gabe won't hurt you."

Ellie shook her head, looking first to me, then to Mom.

Trying my hardest not to giggle, I warned, "I don't know…I'd watch out if I was you! Those stairs can be pretty slippery." I saw a possible way out of my big-sister-imposed imprisonment. I didn't realize how prescient my warning might become.

Not long after her encounter with Gabe, I think Ellie gave up on me as a hopeless, spoiled brat, destined for nothing but a life of crime. A year after she had moved in with us, Ellie decided to live in the girls' dorm on campus for the next three years, until she graduated. I was thrilled I had "won," and had gotten my house and freedom back.

Ahhh…but what's the old saying? *Revenge is a dish best served cold.*

The first day of the second half of my eighth-grade year, and Ellie's last semester before graduation, our English teacher announced we would have a new student teacher. The door opened, and in walked Ellie with a big grin, giving me the evil-eye. I just about fell out of my desk because I knew my "gig" was up.

And oh, how she delighted in making my life miserable for the remainder of the school year, getting her just revenge. Of course, my friends loved it because they got off scot-free while I was tormented daily. There is no doubt one of the happiest days of my childhood was when I finally graduated from eighth grade.

GABE AND OLD JOHN

With a sigh, I concluded my remembrances about the year Ellie had lived with us, brought my mind back to the present, and took another look around what I considered to be Gabe's room. *There's still a lot of work to be done here.*

After Mom and I tagged the dresser for auction, and the beds for the dumpster, we moved to the middle bedroom at the top of the stairs. In the corner an old mahogany Victrola record cabinet stood about four feet high. The rounded top lifted up and provided access to the swing arm and turntable. As a kid, my friends and I used to get a kick out of cranking it up and playing the weird, scratchy old 78 rpm records stored in the cabinet. But as with all novelties, we got tired of it, and it had been sitting gathering dust where we left it all those years ago. I thought some collector would pay good money for it at the auction, and I tagged it. Full boxes stacked haphazardly around over the room probably belonged to renters who had stayed here at one time or another.

When I was growing up, although Mom worked two jobs, we basically lived in poverty, and money was always tight. Mom refused to go on welfare, because she said she didn't want the shame on her or her children of "being on the dole." Mom's opinion was "being on the dole" meant you were nothing but a worthless bum in the eyes of God. To get a little extra income, Mom rented this middle room out to elderly people needing a place to stay before they had to make the final trip to a nursing home. Two old ladies, Nellie and Gracie, lived with us at separate times throughout my childhood. But then they were gone.

One day, Mom came home from work and told me she was going to rent the room to Old John, a farm hand who worked on the Granger farm. John Topanski was a Polish immigrant who had survived a Nazi concentration camp. When John immigrated to the U.S., Maureen Granger's husband, Brad, had hired John as a favor to an old Army buddy. John was now an old, bent man, and they needed to use his space at the bunkhouse for younger workers. So Brad asked Mom if he could stay with us. The only problem was, Old John was crazier than a bat out of hell.

I was eleven when Old John lived with us. This was before the ceiling collapsed. My best friend was Marie Welch, who had six brothers. Marie had Native American ancestry from her mother's side, and I always thought she looked like an exotic Indian princess. She had a petite build, long, straight, glossy-black hair parted in the middle, so long that she could sit on it. She usually wore it in two braids draped over her shoulders. Her darker complexion glowed in the sun.

I, on the other hand, always felt like a gigantic Amazon girl standing next to Marie. With my robust Irish/Dutch heritage, a ruddy complexion that burned in the sun, and a tendency to gain weight—we were physically the exact opposites. I always wished I had inherited my mother's slim, statuesque figure instead of my father's broad-shouldered, stocky one. To me, Marie was like a delicate specimen from another world, and I loved her dearly as the soul-sister I never had.

Marie liked to come over after school to get away from the constant fighting of her brothers, and we would hang out in the yard. We often laughed and made fun of Old John pacing in the garden, yelling in Polish, and gesticulating wildly with both hands. Every once in a while we'd hear the word "Hitler" blurt out of his mouth.

I can only assume now he was probably having flashbacks of the concentration camp. But all we knew back then was he talked to himself in a weird language and was crazier than the Mad Hatter.

Old John preferred to use the two-seater outhouse attached to the back of the barn instead of the indoor bathroom. One day we watched as he made his way into the barn. We sneaked to the back of the outhouse and started banging on the wall, hollering in gibberish, doing our best to mimic Polish. Old John started yelling, and we ran and hid behind a tree. We watched him come running out of the barn hollering my name, fumbling to pull up his overalls. We giggled hysterically as girls of that age are wont to do.

One warm September afternoon, Marie rode her bike over after school, and came into the house. Mom was working, so it was just the two of us. We grabbed a blanket, a couple of Cokes, and some teen magazines, and went out back to lie on the lawn. We were fantasizing over which of the teen idols we'd most like to date when we grew up. My big crush was on Davy Jones of the Monkees. Marie thought Peter Noone, of Herman's Hermits, was totally rad, and knew all the words to "I'm Henery the Eighth, I Am."

"Where's Old John?" Marie asked, as we lay on the lawn.

"I don't know. I haven't seen him since I got home. Maybe he's up in his room," I replied.

We continued to discuss teen idols when suddenly we heard a blood-curdling scream.

"Aaaahhhhheeee!…I keeeiiiiill yooooou!"

We looked up to see Old John hurtling toward us, wielding a pitchfork like a battering ram, intent on doing some serious damage.

"Oh, shit!" cried Marie. "Run!"

We scrambled up from the blanket and ran in our bare feet into the back field. Old John chased us, pitchfork waving in the air, screaming like a banshee. The back field led to a path in the woods, which broke out onto the back edge of the baseball diamond at the South School. We ran to the school's swingset and looked back to the woods but there was no sign of Old John.

"Holy shit, he was trying to kill us!" Marie gasped, doubling over to catch her breath.

"I know, the guy's a fucking nut case. I'm definitely telling Mom about this when she gets home. He scares the shit outta me when I'm there alone with him," I said.

Being devout Catholic girls from St. Mary's, we had learned all the good swear words long before our public school friends, thanks to Marie's brothers. We caught our breath and walked another block to Marie's house, then hung out there for a couple of hours until I thought Mom would be home. We enlisted Marie's oldest brother, Jimmy, to come back to the house with us to get Marie's bike—and protect us from Old John, in case he was still on a rampage.

After Jimmy and Marie left, I sat at the kitchen table and told Mom, "Old John attacked me and Marie today! He came charging at us with a pitchfork, screaming he wanted to kill us."

Mom looked aghast. "Oh, DeeDee! I'm so sorry. What did you girls do?"

I swung my arm toward the backyard. "We took off running into the field, and went over to Marie's house. I'm scared of him, Mom! I don't like being alone in the house with him. Who knows what the hell he's going to do next!"

Mom's hand trembled as she grasped mine. "Honey, I know Old John is a little unstable. I'll go have a talk with him and tell him not to bother you. Then I'll see if I can find someplace else for him to live. It may take some time, but I'll do what I can." She gently touched my cheek. "I don't want you to be afraid in your own home."

I stood and hugged her. "Thanks, Mom. I love you."

"I love you too, Dear," she said, hugging me back.

The next day, I came home from school and went into my room to do homework. It was a rainy day, so Marie didn't come to visit. I was reading my social studies book when I heard Old John grumbling in Polish in his room at the top of the stairs. I didn't think much of it at first. Then his voice became louder and higher pitched, almost frantic. I couldn't understand what he was saying, but it scared me enough to get off my bed and look up to the top of the stairs.

I was shocked to see Old John teetering on the edge of the top step, and Gabe's glowing, spectral figure twisting John's right arm behind him. A shiver ran up my spine and down my arms. As I watched, Gabe twisted his arm tighter, and Old John let out a high-pitched wail. Then Gabe gave him a shove. John fell onto his back, his head hit the stairs hard, and his arm caught in the rungs of the banister. As the weight of his body pulled him down the stairs, I heard a crack and saw his arm twist at an awkward angle. His body thumped down the stairs head over heels, where he landed directly in front of me. Blood gushed from his nose and mouth as he moaned.

I covered my mouth to suppress a scream.

I looked up at the top of the stairs, and heard Gabe's gravelly voice. "*He shan't hurt thee again!*" Then the spirit was gone.

Then I did scream and began sobbing and shaking. *Oh, God! Is Old John dead? Did Gabe kill him? What if I get blamed? Now what am I going to do?*

Trapped in my room with John blocking my way, the only way I could get out was to step over him, which I was terrified to do. I sat on my bed for several minutes trying to gather my wits. I watched John, unconscious, bleeding heavily onto the carpet in front of me. I desperately wished Ellie was still living with us, because she'd know what to do. What's that old saying? "Be careful what you wish for; you just might get it." I regretted being such a brat to my big sister, and hoped she would forgive me someday.

Finally, I mustered my courage and gingerly stepped over his body, trying to avoid the blood. I stumbled my way into the kitchen, found the ambulance number on the list Mom had taped to the wall, and frantically called them for help.

Old John was in the hospital for a time, then sent to a nursing home.

About a month after the incident, I came home from school, irritated my math teacher had marked down my latest test grade for not showing the work. Math always came easy to me, and it'd just seemed easier to solve the equations in my head.

"Mom, look what the math teacher did!" I waved the test paper at her, as she sat at the kitchen table, eyes downcast and chin propped in her hands.

"Mom, what's wrong?" I let my test paper fall to my side.

Mom had hardly even glanced at me. "It's Old John," she answered softly.

I took a step closer to the table. "What about him? Is he still in the nur—"

Mom sighed. "He died earlier today. The nursing home just called me a couple of minutes ago, Honey." Mom pushed herself to her feet, chair scraping behind her. "He had such a bad fall—I've got to do something about those stairs." Mom gave me a wan smile. Her eyes flicked to the paper in my hand. "What's that you've got?"

"It's nothing important. Never mind." I felt a shiver and all at once the air seemed to go out of me. *Old John, dead…* "I'm going to my room."

I reluctantly concluded our "good ghost" did indeed have a dark side. Not only had I witnessed him commit acts that ended a man's life, but I had jokingly predicted it to scare Ellie, two years earlier. Had Gabe acted upon my rash words?

A deep chill ran through me.

BERT'S LINEAGE

I got Mom into the old part of the house by helping her manage the step-down into the two-part bedroom to the right of the stairs. Twin beds were tucked against both walls under the sloping ceiling, and a beat-up, light green, three-drawer dresser leaned against one wall. I didn't think it'd be worth much, so tagged it to go to the dump. A small desk and two chairs sat in front of the window facing north, where Mom had taken a seat.

The room had a large walk-in closet with a sloped ceiling on one side. Along with a bunch of boxes, three old wooden trunks with rounded tops and locked latches sat against the wall. I'd always wondered what was in those trunks. Not wanting to damage them, I went downstairs and called Danny, a local locksmith. He came by within the hour. He popped the locks on the two trunks in the closet in Gabe's room and the three in the loft closet. Then he helped me drag one of the trunks out, and set it up in front of the desk. I paid Danny for his time, and he was off to his next job.

When I opened the trunk, the heady aroma of cedar filled the room. On top of the pile, we found baby clothes intricately detailed with lace; a beautiful white silk layette embroidered with rosettes; a bonnet and other baby items that had all been hand-stitched. I wondered whose baby had worn these clothes, as they seemed almost brand new. I didn't detect the usual stains of well-used baby clothes. Deeper in the trunk we found women's clothing of a style probably favored by younger women of days gone by. There were a number of dresses with tight bodices, buttons up the back, poufy shoulders, long sleeves, and light-colored fabrics. A couple of the dresses were of a blousy variety, and appeared to be maternity dresses. Below those, we found other dresses that were more matronly, with darker colors and high collars. Several pair of well-worn, lace-up shoes were tucked beneath the dresses.

At the bottom of the trunk I saw a black, leather-bound book, and I pulled it out. Inscribed on the cover was *Holy Bible*.

I quickly passed my thumb over the pages. Hairs raised on my arms as the book fell open to the back cover. On the last page, I saw a handwritten title: *Hopper Family Bible*. A number of entries listed below it were hard to read in the dim light of the room.

"Mom, how much did you know about Old Bert's family?" I asked.

"Well, not much, Dear. He told me his ancestors built this farm back in the 1820s. It was much bigger back then, but they sold off a lot of the land."

"And he didn't have any kids, right?"

"Not that I know of," she said.

"Mom, I'm going downstairs to get a closer look at these inscriptions. Would you fold up these clothes and we'll put them back into the trunk?"

At the kitchen table, I re-opened the Bible to the last page to read the handwritten entries of the Hopper family lineage:

George b. 1850 d. 1916
m. 1875 - Emily Hastings b. 1857, d. 1912
   sons: Bert b. 1877
      George II b. 1880, d. 1884
      Claude b. 1882, d. 1893

   Bert m. 8/4/1908 Anna Franklin - b. 4/2/1884, d. 3/21/1910
      son: baby boy b. 3/20/1910, d. 3/21/1910

   Bert m. 6/1/1913 Faith Goodlaw - b. *5/16/1883, d. 11/25/1935*

Those simple entries bespoke the tragedy and grief of Bert's family history. Both of Bert's brothers had died at a young age and it must have been devastating for Bert. I wondered what had caused their deaths—illness or accident?

The first entries were written in a tight, flourishing script, almost hard to read, probably a woman's. The last entries were written in a more elementary, bold, perpendicular style, probably written by a man, who I guessed was Bert. As I stared at the dates, my heart broke when I calculated Bert was thirty-one—old for a first marriage in those days. He had married Anna, twenty-four, who died in childbirth just two years later, along with their infant son, who apparently was never named.

Old Bert must have been inconsolable when he lost both his young wife and baby boy during childbirth, after marrying so late in life. I couldn't imagine how much heartache he must have endured, first losing his younger brothers, and then his wife and child. That explained why the baby clothes in the trunk looked brand new; they had never been worn. *Maybe his second wife, Faith, gave him comfort. I wonder why they never had children.*

To honor his memory, and keep his family Bible complete, next to Bert's name, I wrote his death date, *d. 1960.*

Flipping to the preceding page I looked for more family entries, searching for a reference to a Gabe or Gabriel in the family tree, but the page was blank. Mom said the family built the farm in the 1820s, so I hoped I would find more evidence of Bert's lineage.

I wish I knew who our ghost was in real life. And more importantly, is he still here?

I returned to the upstairs bedroom with the Bible and sat next to Mom. "Did you know Bert's first wife and baby son died in childbirth?"

Mom's face scrunched. "Oh, dear. No, I didn't. He did tell me he was married twice, and both of his wives had died. I never pressed him, as he didn't seem to want to discuss it."

"He also had two younger brothers who died at early ages. How sad for him."

Mom had a melancholy look on her face. "I know he loved you as if you were his own grandchild. I think you gave him some joy at the end of his long life."

My love went out to the dear old man who had treated me like a princess. I fondly remembered swinging from the lilac tree, with Bert catching me. He was the closest thing to a father and grandfather I ever had.

After we stowed everything back in these trunks, I helped Mom maneuver to what I considered Gabe's room. I moved two chairs into the big walk-in closet and pulled the string of the bare-bulb fixture hanging from the ceiling. We planned to inspect the two trunks Danny had unlocked for us. I hefted the heavy, rounded wooden top of the trunk on the right, its hinges protesting the intrusion. Then I opened the top of the second one situated in front of Mom.

Mom reached into its cavernous base and pulled out a doll. "Dee, look at this!" she exclaimed.

The handmade doll had a stuffed Raggedy Ann quality, with yarn for hair, and wore a faded, yellow-patterned gingham dress. "This is very old, Dear. You can see where it was hand-stitched. I'm surprised it's in such good shape."

I peered into the trunk and found several hand-carved wooden toys. One of them was in the shape of a wagon, with wheels still attached. Lying next to it was a whittled horse. "These are cool. Whoever made these had some skill in woodworking." We returned the toys and doll to the trunk and closed the lid.

Then I sat down and started pulling items out of the second trunk. They ranged from baby clothes to a young girl's dresses and bonnets. As I compared the items, I realized the sizes didn't get progressively larger. It seemed like the girl didn't grow to be any older than a young child. Or clothes from her older years were stored elsewhere.

I was confused and turned to Mom. "I wonder who these belonged to. Bert didn't have any children. Do you think this was a daughter of one of his ancestors?"

Mom shrugged. "Could be. We really don't know much more than what we found in his Bible."

Then I noticed a faded yellow gingham dress made of the same fabric the doll was dressed in. The garment was folded in half. When I attempted to unfold it, the fabric stuck together. I gently eased the upper section from the lower part. Along the bodice of the long-sleeve, button-down dress was a large, dark-brownish stain splattered across the front. Then I saw another big, dark blotch spread along what would have been the girl's lap. It instantly gave me the creeps.

I passed it to Mom. "What do you think that stain is?"

She lifted the wrinkled material to her nose and sniffed. "It's got a faint odor. It could be blood."

I gasped. "Blood? Really?" I too sniffed the fabric. A very faint smell of iron rose from it. "Wow, if it's blood, there's a lot of it! I wonder what happened to her."

"Well, kids do get sick," Mom said matter-of-factly.

My mind raced. *Whose daughter was this? Did she die at a young age? If so, from what? And why would someone keep the bloodstained dress? Was it the girl's favorite because it matched her doll?*

I felt like I had jumped into the middle of one of the Nancy Drew stories I had loved reading as a kid. I was determined to find more answers to these perplexing mysteries of Bert's family lineage.

INSURANCE AGENT

We decided to clear out Mom's bedroom last, so my next plan was to attack the junk in the barn. The hay barn, built in the 1820s, was in rough shape—it listed to the right like a shipwreck moored on a rocky shore. The hand-hewn floorboards lifted unevenly, which made it tricky to walk around. The sliding doors creaked on their iron wheels. Some of the door slats hung loose, so the sagging doors no longer latched together. Being concerned about renting the property with the barn in such bad shape, I made an appointment with our insurance agent in town, Frank Rizzolo, to discuss options. I arrived at his office at our appointed time of 1:00 p.m.

Frank saw me walk into the office and rose from his chair, his rotund belly protruding against his buttoned shirt. With a big grin on his face, he engulfed me in a bear hug, kissing me on both cheeks in his flamboyant Italian manner. I laughed as I hugged him back. Frank had been an insurance agent for as long as I could remember, and he had the "dirt" on everyone in town. So no one in their right mind messed with him.

Frank's idol was J. Edgar Hoover. There was an autographed photo on the wall of Frank as a young man shaking hands with Hoover in what appeared to be Hoover's office. I didn't know the story of how this meeting took place, but I was sure it was a doozy. You couldn't miss Frank in town: his stocky build, purposeful stride, slicked black hair—now graying, and boisterous voice, always attracted attention.

"DeeDee!" Frank exclaimed. "It's so good to see you. You're looking great! How's Robbie doing these days? I haven't seen her in a dog's age!"

"Hi, Frank. Good to see you too," I replied, grinning.

"Please, come sit down." He gestured toward his desk as he settled heavily into a well-worn leather office chair.

"So, how's your Mom?" he asked again.

"Well, things are getting rough for her to live alone. You know the Parkinson's disease is getting the best of her, and she can't stay in the big old house by herself anymore. And that's what I needed to talk to you about." I took a deep breath. "My sister Ellie and I have made arrangements to move Mom to a nursing home in Rutland."

"Oh, I'm so sorry to hear that!" Frank said, genuinely sympathetic. "Robbie's a grand lady and was a hard worker all her life. She loves that house. I'm sure she's devastated to have to move."

His words sliced through my heart like a dagger.

Pushing past the hurt, I explained, "I'm here for a few weeks to get the house and barn cleaned out. I'm working with Monique and Jacques at the Historical Society, and John Barstow at the auction house, to figure out what we're going to do with most of the stuff. I'm hoping to rent the place after we get it fixed up, but I'm worried about the old barn out back possibly being a problem."

"I haven't seen the old barn in years. What kind of shape is it in?" Frank asked.

"Well, it's pretty rough and it's leaning to the right for some reason I can't figure out."

Frank glanced at his watch. "I've got some time. Let's go take a look at it, and I can give you a better idea of our options." He grabbed his keys off the desk.

I followed Frank to the house in my rental car. Mom came out on the porch with her walker to greet us.

Frank galloped up the stairs and gently moved her walker out of the way. "Robbie, my sweet girl!" He gave her a big bear hug, lifting her off her feet as he kissed both her cheeks.

Mom giggled like a school girl, blushing. "Oh, Frank, you're always such a flirt!"

"You know I have a soft spot for the redheads, Robbie, and you've always been my favorite!" He grinned as he gently set her down and retrieved her walker, then helped her into the house.

Apparently Frank hadn't noticed Mom's hair was now white. No doubt he remembered her as a younger woman when she first moved to Fair Haven.

"Mom, Frank and I are going to take a look at the barn. Can you make us some tea, and we'll come back in and talk when we're done?" We walked through the kitchen where I grabbed a flashlight. Going out the back door, Frank and I followed the slate stepping stones toward the barn. Frank stopped halfway and stared at it, his head tilting slightly to the right, as he tried to level the barn in his sights.

"Hmmm, that's odd it's tilting," he said. "This is all level ground. I wonder what's causing it." We continued around to the back of the barn, where the old two-seater outhouse was detaching itself from the wall.

Frank pointed to the decrepit structure. "Man, I'd hate to be taking a crap in there when it finally lets loose—talk about scaring the shit outta ya!" He laughed heartily at his ribald humor. We continued around to the right side of the barn, where Frank kicked up dirt and inspected the foundation.

"It's definitely sinking…look here…you can see where the slate stones in the foundation have shifted." He pointed to the jagged slate slabs. "Might just be soft sand in this area causing it," he speculated.

"Let's take a look inside, Frank." I partially opened one sliding door and began to step into the shadowed interior of the barn, then stopped with a gasp. Cobwebs! Thick, nasty cobwebs—probably the kind Black Widows make, I thought, shuddering. Long, shimmering, silvery filaments stretched into the dark interior. *I should have turned on the flashlight before walking in here.*

Retreating, I handed Frank the light. "Here, Frank. I'll let you go first. I can't stand spiders!" I moved to one side, then followed him into the gloomy interior, my arms swiping the webs away from my head.

The flashlight illuminated the junk stored there. I had no idea where most of it came from; probably Mom being a good Samaritan and offering storage to people to help them out. There were old appliances, a rusted sink, lawn mowers, wheelbarrows, boxes, old farm implements hanging from the walls, and plenty of unidentifiable stuff.

As we picked our way to the back of the barn, Frank noted the floorboards creaking under his feet. "What's in the loft?" he asked, peering up the stairs.

"I'm not sure anymore. There used to be old trunks up there when I was a kid." The sound of a critter scurrying overhead made me jump.

Frank shined the flashlight up and climbed the rickety stairs, pushing webs out of his way as he ascended. I watched closely to see where they landed. Once he was on solid footing, I followed him to the loft. I opened the square door in the wall on my right to let in more light. The pungent stench of mouse droppings littering the floor assaulted me.

Just as I had remembered, five black, foot-locker-type trunks were strewn across the floor, covered with decades of dust, bugs, and poop. I thought most of them were locked, but I remembered one wasn't. In there, my childhood friends and I had discovered old-fashioned men's clothes, with which we used to play dress-up. There was a rack against one wall, with moth-eaten dresses hanging from it. Broken-down wooden chairs were strewn around the floor.

"It's going to take some work to get this place cleaned out," Frank said, almost to himself. "Before you get Barstow in here for the auction, let me get some guys out here to help you, so at least we can see what you're up against," he offered.

"Oh! That'd be great, Frank. I would really appreciate some strong help." I squeezed his hand, grateful for his friendship.

We made our way down the stairs and out of the barn, where we did our best to slide the door closed. Back in the kitchen, Mom had tea and cookies waiting for us.

"Here's what I'm thinking," Frank began. "The barn will definitely be a liability if you rent the house. All it would take is one snot-nosed kid to get banged up in there, and you'll have a lawsuit on your hands before you can say lickety-split," he said, confirming my thoughts. "To make it safe, you'd have to get the floorboards fixed, put in new stairs, completely remove the old doors and install new ones that close and lock tight. We're talking a pretty penny here. And then there's the issue of why the barn is leaning in the first place, which probably can't be fixed."

"Yeah, that's pretty much what I thought, too," I said. "So what can we do? Tear it down?"

Mom listened intently to our discussion, sipping her tea.

"There's another option, Dee." He stared through the window at the listing barn. "I'm the Chief of the Volunteer Fire Department."

Why am I not surprised?

Frank continued, "We could burn the barn down, and use it as a training exercise for my firemen," he offered.

"Really? Is that legal?"

"As long as we have the homeowner's written permission, being you, then yes, it's legal. We do it on occasion, with just these types of circumstances," Frank told us. "As I mentioned, I can get some men out here to help you clean the place out. Then you can go through the stuff and figure out what you want to go to auction and what the Historical Society might want. I can tell you from what I saw, people love collecting old farm equipment, and they always fetch a good price at auction."

"Well, what do you think, Mom? Do you want to have a good old-fashioned barn-burning?" I asked.

Mom gave Frank a long look. "As long as it's safe, and you won't catch Mister Greene's barn on fire," Mom said, referring to our neighbor's barn, built recently, in the 1970s.

Frank peered out the window at the neighbor's barn about ten feet away from the listing right side of our barn. "We can shore up the leaning side. Then we'll set the fire so it burns heavily on the left, and falls away from Greene's barn," he assured her. "Too bad he built it so close to yours." He shook his head. "The first thing we'll have to do is get the slate tiles removed from the roof."

Mom nodded. "Vince Granger's cousin Dave has his slate business in Granville. I'm sure he'd be happy to pull the tiles for us."

"Oh, sure, I know Dave. He'll give you a good price for the slates. I'll give him a call," replied Frank.

"So, are you good with this idea, Mom, to burn the barn down?" I asked again to make sure.

She paused to look at Frank, then at me. "Yes, Dear. I trust Frank, and I don't want it to cause you any problems," she replied, always thinking about my welfare.

"Well then, let me make some calls, and we'll get things in motion," Frank said. He got up to leave, kissing Mom goodbye on both cheeks.

Mom blushed from his attention.

SHOTGUN

Frank was good to his word, and the next day Randy Wright and three workers showed up in two pickups to help us clean out the barn. I knew Randy from town. He was a tall, burly guy in his forties, with an infectious laugh, and I was happy to see him again. Lynn and Vince Granger brought over a pop-up tarp they used on the farm, and set it up in the backyard. We laid out two folding tables and chairs, so we were in business.

One of the men brought out an interesting wooden box, made of slats, found in the rearmost hay stall. It caught my interest. The top of the box sat wedged into the sides. I pried the top off. Lying inside was a flattened scroll. I carefully opened it to discover Bert and Anna Hopper's marriage certificate from 1908. The entire document had been hand painted with pinks, blues, greens and golden tones. At the top of the document was a painting of a wedding couple, standing in a rowboat with their wedding party seated around them. Guests on the bank of the river watched the ceremony. Bouquets of roses draped down each side the certificate. Swags of flowers swept along the bottom into a heart shaped form entwined with cupid holding interlocked wedding rings. In the middle was a curled banner which read "Holy Matrimony."

Names of the bride and groom, dates, wedding location, witnesses and the preacher's name were written on the lines below the matrimony banner. It was absolutely beautiful. My modern, computer-generated wedding certificate paled in comparison. I decided to keep the certificate along with Bert's family Bible as mementos of my benefactor. The rest of the box appeared to be full of letters, receipts, envelopes and whatnot, and I put a sticker on it to go through it later in hopes of finding more information on Bert's family.

As I was sorting through the box I heard one of the helpers call out, "Hey Randy, check out this old double-barreled shotgun! This is cool."

Randy walked over, took the gun and inspected it. He held it up to his eye, as if to shoot, then pointed the muzzle to the ground. "This is an old gun. I'd say at least from the late eighteen-eighties, maybe earlier." He took a closer look at the barrels. "That second barrel is cracked." Randy ran his hand over a dent in the middle of the barrel. "Doubt it's been shot in quite some time."

"Randy, can I see that?" I asked.

He brought the gun over and set it on the table, safely pointing the barrel away from us.

"Mom, do you remember this shotgun?" I asked her.

She nodded. "Well, Dear, I never shot it because Bert told me the barrel was cracked. But I always kept it propped behind the door in case we had any unwanted visitors from the NoWhere restaurant across the road."

Gabe watches the man cradle his shotgun. Horrible memories flood him of the night his wagon slid off the bridge during the slave posse attack. He recalls crossing the river, losing his balance, and slamming the double-barreled shotgun into a huge boulder to stop his fall. By the time he reached Luke, his son was dead. His anguish over the fateful night flared.

That night forever changed my life and my destiny!

ORPHANAGE

AUGUST, 1964

IT WAS RAINING again outside.

"Mom! It's not supposed to rain. It's summer!" I stopped looking out the window, then plopped down at the table in a huff. It was the week after my eighth birthday, and the weather had been bad for four days in a row. Mom had already cleared off the breakfast things, and I wanted to play outside.

"I know, Honey." Something about Mom's tone of voice made me look at her more closely. She focused on her task as she washed the dishes. Then Mom looked up and saw me watching her.

Her brow knitted as she joined me at the table. "DeeDee, Honey, I've got something to tell you."

I didn't like her tone of voice, nor the sad look on her face. I had a feeling this wasn't going to be good news.

"Do you remember when you were you had your tonsils out last winter?"

My heartbeat quickened when I remembered Mom taking me from the doctor's office to the emergency room because my tonsils were so swollen I could barely swallow. "Yeah, some of it."

Mom touched my hand. "There were some problems after the surgery, and you had to stay in the hospital until you got well."

I sighed. "I know. It seemed like I was there *forever.*"

"Well, I don't want you to worry, but I owe money on the doctor bills." She peered out the rain-splashed window pane, then back at me. "I went to visit Father Sebastian to see if he could help us." She paused, staring at the table, then continued, "So here's the good news. You're going to go to a new school in September, and I think it'll be fun for you."

"Where are we going, Mommy?"

She gripped her hands tightly. "The priest has made arrangements for me to work as the housekeeper for a rectory in Boston. It pays well and will give me a chance to pay off our bills." She unclenched her hands and touched mine. "There's just one problem," her voice shook. "I'm so sorry, Honey, but you can't come with me."

I stared at her, unsure of what I was hearing, my heart pounding. "What do you mean? Why can't I come with you? Where will I go? I want to be with you!" I sobbed.

She slowly shook her head. "I'm really sorry. The church rules say no children can live at the rectory."

I thumped back in my chair and folded my arms, glaring at her. "That's not fair! I hate rules! I won't cause any problems, I promise. You know I'm a good girl!"

Mom reached over and stroked my hair. "I know you are, Dear. So I'm sure you'll have fun living with the other children in Burlington. The sisters will take very good care of you." Mom sighed, her eyes glistening in turn.

"Mommy, I don't want to be a burden for you. Don't send me away like you did my sisters. Please! I want to stay with you." I cried at the thought of being left alone. "Don't you love me anymore?" I sobbed, hoping I could change her mind.

"Of course I love you! I hope it won't be for long, then I'll come get you. I promise!"

I saw the pained look on Mom's face. She covered her face with her hands, and began to cry. Then she lifted her head and wiped her eyes. "I need you to be a big girl for me and stop crying. Okay?" She gently touched my arm. "We'll find a way to manage."

At that age, all I could think was, *I got sick, went to the hospital, and now I'm being sent away because I'm too much of a burden for Mom to handle.* I was despondent over what my future held.

A few weeks later, Mom closed up the house and made arrangements for our neighbors, Betty and Howard Greene, to look after the place. We packed our suitcases, and she drove me to St. Augustine's Orphanage in Burlington. I cried and hugged Mom for dear life before she left me with the hovering nuns.

Despite my protests over Mom leaving me, I settled into the routine of the orphanage after a few weeks. The building was a big, brick four-story monstrosity. The first floor contained classrooms, a chapel with stained-glass windows, and confessionals. On the left half of the second floor, the dayroom housed tables, desks, chairs, a ping-pong table, books, and other stuff for kids. On the other half, a door led to a long hallway that divided the girls' dorm on the right, and the boys' dorm on the left. At the end of the hall were boys' and girls' bathrooms with tubs and showers.

The dorms were long, open rooms with bunks lined side-by-side along both walls. Each student had an old, metal army locker at the end of the bed to hold their clothes and belongings. The third floor was where the nuns and some lay staff lived. The dining hall was attached to the main building, and was partially below ground, with the windows very high up near the ceiling. A short staircase led from the dayroom to the flat roof of the dining hall. A three-foot railing had been installed around the edge of the roof and a "playground" of sorts had been installed. This included two swingsets, a slide, a teeter-totter, and a basketball hoop. I often wondered if any kids ever fell off the roof, especially in the winter.

I cried myself to sleep almost every night because I missed Mom, my home, and my protector, Gabe. On some nights, I heard heavy footsteps in the hall, and men's voices. Then the door to the boys' dorm opened. Muffled cries reached me, and what sounded like bare feet being marched down the hall. Later at night, I became aware of the heavy footsteps again, and the quiet crying of boys being brought back to their dorm. I didn't understand why the boys were being punished in the middle of the night, when most of the kids got punished in front of everyone during the day. I was scared that one night, I might be dragged from my bed and punished, too.

My worst experience at the orphanage started at lunch one day. The nuns served green pea soup, which I hated, and didn't want to eat. One nun, who was particularly nasty, stood over me and forced me to eat every bite. She slapped my head and screamed at me whenever I slowed down, sobbing and gagging on the goop. All the other kids had left the dining hall by the time I finished, and the nuns released me. I staggered down the middle of the hall. Suddenly, my stomach erupted. I doubled over and vomited a long projectile of green glop. A blow to the back of my head sent me sprawling, terrified and crying, face-first into the muck, my body sliding through the slimy mess.

"You horrible child!" Nasty Nun screamed. She stomped on my back and slammed my face into the vile, stinking vomit. "Lick it off the floor," she commanded. I lay on the floor for several minutes crying, trying to breathe. Nasty grabbed me by the back of my uniform, and hauled me to my feet. A nun grabbed a hold of each arm, and they marched me to the dayroom.

"Attention! Attention!" Nasty yelled at the children. The room went silent as heads turned to the sound of her voice. I saw the looks of shock, disgust, and pity on the faces staring back at me as I was presented for inspection. Snot ran from my nose and mixed with the bile in my mouth that dribbled down my chin. Slime dripped from my uniform as I heaved giant sobs, humiliated in front of my classmates.

"This child didn't want to eat her lunch, and you can see God has punished her for her disobedience. If any of you think you want to waste your food, God will punish you, too! Let this be a lesson to all of you!" Nasty preached to the kids.

The nuns dragged me through the middle of the large room as the kids scurried aside to let us pass. My focus stayed on the door to my right leading to the dorm rooms, avoiding the stares of my classmates. I desperately wanted to take a bath, put on a clean uniform and join the other kids. I thought about how much I hated pea soup, and hated the nuns even more.

Why am I even here? I'm only eight and I'm not an orphan—I have a mother! Why can't I just go home?

Instead of taking me to the dorm, to my great dismay, the nuns veered to the left. Nasty Nun unlocked the door to the cubbyhole closet tucked beneath the short flight of stairs rising to the flat playground roof. I had seen other kids thrown into this dank hole, and it terrified me. Determined not to go in there, I twisted my body against my captors. But they had me in a death grip and I was unable to pull away. I kicked the sister on my right in her shin. She howled and grabbed her leg, releasing my arm. With my free hand, I punched at the other nun's arm, but she moved into me and I hit her in the gut instead. She grunted and doubled over, but didn't release her hold. I kicked her in the knee. Then an arm pulled me into a choke hold. I gagged as my wind was cut off.

"Get a hold of her, don't let her get away!" Nasty screamed.

I caught a glimpse of a couple of the kids with their hands over their mouths, wide-eyed that I was fighting back against authority. My arms were pinned behind my back. I kicked violently at anyone in my path. A hand grabbed my foot and pulled me off my feet. I twisted my body back and forth trying to escape my attackers, but then I started to black out. The arm around my neck released and the nun grabbed my shoulders. I gasped for breath. Someone had my other foot, and now I was being carried to the cubbyhole. I was dropped to the floor and my arms released as they tried to shove me through the door. I grabbed the sides of the opening, trying to stall the inevitable. My hands were wrenched free from the door jamb, and my body shoved into the pitch-black hole. The door slammed shut, just missing my foot. A loud clunk echoed in that dank space as the key locked the deadbolt. The blackness enveloped me.

I screamed and screamed to be let out, pounding on the door.

"You shut up in there, or I'll beat you to within an inch of your life!" Nasty yelled at me. I curled up in a fetal position, and wailed for my mommy to come take me home.

When my sobs subsided, I felt a stinging sensation on my arm, and then another, and another. I brushed at the sting, and felt something crawl on my hand. I screamed. Something slithered up my neck and onto my face, and I swiped at it before it could sting me. Then I realized my clothes, soaked with sticky-sweet vomit, were covered with spiders. I jumped up in the cramped space, hitting my head on the bottom of the staircase. I frantically tried to get them off of me. I felt spiders in my hair, stinging my scalp. Breathing hard, I fought the monsters, spinning in circles until I was dizzy, screaming with what voice I had left to be let out of that black hell.

I collapsed to my knees, made the sign of the cross, pressed my palms together facing heaven and prayed, "Dear Baby Jesus, please help me! I'm so sorry for my sins. Please don't let me die in here! I love you. Amen."

Then I crawled on my hands and knees, feeling for anything that could help me, and found a bucket with greasy cleaning rags. I used one rag to shake the spiders out of my hair and covered my head with it. With another rag, I scraped at my chest to remove the spiders and as much of the vomit as I could from my uniform. Other rags I used to swipe the spiders from my legs and arms and wrapped one around each arm. I was out of rags, so I used the vomit rag to swipe at the spiders crawling on me until I was exhausted, barely whimpering. Mommy's face floated in my mind and I must have passed out.

A woman's loud voice woke me. The door opened and a light pierced my eyes. I squinted, recognizing Mother Superior crouched on her knees outside the open door.

"Oh, Dear Lord! What has happened to you, child?" she said, aghast.

Hands grabbed my shoulders and my body was dragged from the nest.

"Quick, Sister Nicholas, get a broom!" she commanded. "This poor child is covered with spiders."

With my eyes scrunched shut, I felt the broom scrape against my head, chest, arms and legs. Mother Superior lifted me in her arms, and took me directly to the girl's bathroom, where she stripped off my uniform and underpants, and dropped me into a tub of scalding water. I screamed in pain as the hot water collided with the hundreds of stings. She scrubbed my body, and made me lie back in the tub as she vigorously shampooed my hair. My scalp stung from the scrubbing and bites. Spiders, dead and alive, floated in the tub with me, and I frantically tried to push them away.

"Stop squirming!" Mother Superior scolded me.

"Sister Nicholas, go to the medicine chest in my office and get the salve, then get her pajamas," the head nun ordered.

She helped me out of the tub, dried me off and slathered my face and body with a stinky salve that cooled the stings, then she helped me into my pajamas. I stared in shock as hordes of black spiders swirled down the drain. My legs were shaky from the bites, and I had a hard time keeping my balance. Mother Superior lifted me in her arms, and carried me to the dorm room. The other girls, awake in their beds, had apparently heard my screams. They gaped at us as she put me to bed. I curled into a fetal position, pulled the blanket over my head and cried for Mommy to take me home, until I fell asleep…to nightmares of gigantic spiders trying to devour me.

At Christmas, Mom finally came to visit. When I saw her come into the dayroom, I ran and squeezed her. "Mommy, please, please take me home. I hate it here! The nuns are mean to me!" I sobbed into her belly.

"DeeDee, what's wrong?" Mom said, concerned.

"Mommy, they put me in the spiders' nest, and it was awful. The spiders crawled all over me and tried to eat me!" I wailed.

Nasty Nun, who was hovering nearby, came over to us with a fake smile plastered on her face. "Now Missus Van Dyne, don't believe a word she says. You know how kids love to make up stories," she cooed.

"Mommy! I'm telling the truth…why would I lie?" I pleaded.

"DeeDee, are you sure you didn't just have a nightmare?" Mom asked.

"Noooo, I'm telling the truth!" I insisted.

Nasty glared at me, then smiled back at Mom. "Well now, you know DeeDee has quite an imagination. I'm sure she just made up this story to scare the other kids. Of course we would never let anything like that happen!" She took Mom by the arm. "Let's have some punch and open our Christmas presents, shall we?"

After several hours, Mom rose and told me she had to leave. I hugged her as hard as I could. "Mommy, I want to go with you! Please take me home. I hate it here! The nuns are mean to me."

"DeeDee, I can't right now. I'm sorry, Honey. But I'll be back as soon as I can to visit you. Always remember I love you. Now you be a good girl and mind the sisters." Mom gave me a big hug and kiss, and walked out of the dayroom door, to my great anguish.

I collapsed on the floor and sobbed.

Someone grabbed the back of my uniform and yanked me to my feet. I tried to look behind me, but my right arm was twisted behind my back, just about yanking my shoulder out of the socket. I cried out in pain.

"You stupid child!" Nasty scolded. "How dare you tell your mother about anything that happens here! You're going to be punished for opening your big mouth."

"Take your hands off my daughter!" a familiar voice yelled from the door.

Nasty Nun released me, and I fell to my knees.

"What do you think you're doing?" Mom yelled, marching to Nasty and yanking her away from me.

"This child needs discipline, and I'm the one she has to answer to," Nasty said haughtily.

"Not anymore she doesn't! Get me Mother Superior, right now!" Mom was inches from Nasty's face.

Nasty Nun glared at Mom, not moving.

"*Now!*" Mom insisted. Nasty Nun scurried out of the room.

Once we had packed up my few belongings, Mother Superior followed us out the door, apologizing profusely. We got into the car, where we both sat silently.

Finally I said, "Mommy, why did you come back and get me?" I was grateful beyond belief to be out of that nightmare.

Mom reached across the seat and hugged me to her. "I looked into the nun's eyes and knew she was lying. I just couldn't leave you here any longer. It broke my heart, because I love you so much," Mom said.

I cried, shaking against her bosom, so thankful she actually believed me and loved me enough to rescue me.

We drove late into the night all the way to Boston as snow fell around us. In January, I was enrolled in the Catholic school next to the rectory where

Mom worked. Thankfully, these nuns were much more pleasant, and I enjoyed the rest of the school year, which ended with my First Communion ceremony. In June, when school was out, the priests fired Mom, because she had me living with her in the rectory against parish rules. We moved back home to Fair Haven, where I settled into the house once again with Mom, and my "good ghost," Gabe.

For years after I was "paroled" from the orphanage and reunited with Mom, I refused to tell her when I was sick, for fear of being sent back to that horrible place. Of course, the nuns at St. Mary's would get furious when I would come to school sick. So they would send me home. But with no adult to come pick me up, because Mom was working, it meant I had to walk two miles home, scared out of my mind, often in bad weather. Even now, years later, I still remember the long, weary journey…

…head south on Washington Street, make the sign of the cross as I pass the marble steps leading to the towering brick Catholic church; hope the barking German Shepard straining on his leash won't get free; look both ways, don't get splashed by cars, cross Park Place; walk to the middle of the park; go to the right of the circular slate fountain; walk faster to avoid the guys hanging out on the railing cat-calling me; exit the park; salute the black Revolutionary War cannon; wipe my runny nose on my sleeve, cough; wait for cars to pass, cross Main Street; walk along the sidewalk of the L-shaped brick business district; almost jump out of my skin as the noon whistle wails; see if I know anybody in Calvi's Ice Cream Shop; pass Ray's Five-and-Dime, wish I had money for some penny candy; dream about the soft, plush new sofas in Mallory's Furniture store; squeal and sidestep the old drunk slumped against the laundromat door as he lunges for my leg; imagine being dressed like the fancy mannequins in the window of Carl Durfee's clothing store across the street; stop at the corner in front of the Wooden Soldier restaurant, smell the delicious aromas as a customer opens the door, feel my stomach growl; continue to the bottom of the hill; cross the bridge over the Castleton River; listen to the thunderous waterfall roiling past the old slate mill, wonder what the cold water would feel like if I jumped over the falls; cough and wipe my nose; climb the steep hill to the railroad tracks; catch my breath, listen for a train whistle; cross the tracks; cross the street to the sidewalk; follow the rutted, broken slate slabs, try not to trip and fall; pass the scary house with the boarded-up windows, hope nothing jumps out at me; walk another block; jump as two dogs run to their gate, teeth bared, trying to eat me; walk faster; cross another side street; almost home, panting hard; run up onto our porch; sigh, home safe; unlock both doors, go inside, lock both doors from the inside like Mom taught me; take two baby aspirin and a swig of nasty cough syrup; hang up my blouse and uniform; get into my pajamas, crawl into bed, and pass out, coughing and exhausted.

To say the least, it was a challenge growing up as an unsupervised child.

Although being back at school was better than the orphanage, it was still no picnic. Kids who knew I didn't have a father would call me a bastard. Then there was my older sister, Barbara, born with cerebral palsy—called "retarded" in those days. I can't even count the number of times those "good" Catholic kids called me "retard" to my face, making spastic gestures along with their slurs.

Despite Mom's working two jobs, we were still poor, and received a monthly food basket donated by the parish. Those church ladies were more than happy to discuss which families were getting the baskets and, of course, their kids overheard their gossip. Along with all the other names, I earned the moniker "basket case" as a result of those donations.

And to top it all off, I lived in a haunted house, which I never talked about to anyone except my best friend, Marie, whom I trusted with my life not to reveal my deep-dark secrets. My childhood was lived at the end of a very long, dark, lonely road, far from Ozzie and Harriet's idyllic neighborhood.

Between being called a bastard, retard, or basket case on any given day, and the bullies not being reprimanded whatsoever by the nuns, I learned not to talk about myself or my family. And I came to loathe the hypocrites in the Catholic Church at an early age. There were plenty of times I pleaded with Gabe to strike my tormentors dead-as-doornails to relieve my humiliation at their hands.

It amazes me I actually survived Catholic school. But my stint in the orphanage would haunt me for the rest of my life.

Early one evening, many decades later, my husband, Mark and I were watching the local evening news at our home in California, when I received an intriguing phone call.

"Hello, may I speak with Missus DeeDee Williams?" a deep male voice said.

I muted the television and replied, "Yes, this is she."

"Missus Williams, my name is George Granter, and I'm an attorney from Connecticut. I'm sorry to bother you, but I think you may be able to assist me with the case of two clients I'm representing," he explained.

I replied, "I'm sorry, but I'm confused. I live in California. You must have the wrong person. How could I possibly be of any help with your clients in Connecticut?"

"Missus Williams, if I may ask, were you a resident at Saint Augustine's Orphanage in Burlington, Vermont, between the years of Nineteen Fifty-Five and Nineteen Seventy-Four?"

At the mention of the orphanage my body immediately went into fight-or-flight mode. My heart beat faster, my skin began to crawl, and bile rose in my throat at the long-ago memory of pea soup and black spiders. I hesitated answering his question, instead taking a gulp of wine to calm myself.

"Missus Williams, are you still there?"

"Yes…I'm here…sorry. Ummm—yes, I was at Saint Augustine's during that period—in the early sixties. So why are you calling again?"

"Well, I can't really discuss further details of the case until I verify your identity, I hope you understand," the lawyer told me. "Would you mind answering a few personal questions?"

"Ummmm," I hesitated. "I guess not."

"What is your maiden name?"

"DeeDee Helen Van Dyne."

"What was your mother's name?"

"Robbie Van Dyne."

"And was she alive at the time you were in the orphanage?"

I thought it an odd question. "Yes, she was the one who put me there."

"Okay. I can confirm you are on the student roster. It says you were enrolled in August, Nineteen Sixty-Four. Is that right?"

"Yeah, that sounds about right," I said, doing a quick calculation from my date of birth.

"And you left in December? So you were only there about four months."

"Yes, Mom pulled me out just before Christmas."

Granter paused, and cleared his throat. "If you don't mind my asking, what were the circumstances that led you to be in the orphanage?"

Oh, boy! How much of the complicated story of Mom's life did I want to get into with him? I quickly summarized Robbie was a single mother who fell on hard times, and put me in the orphanage so she could work.

He replied, "You know, DeeDee, a number of the students I've contacted have said the same thing. Their families had financial hardships, and sent them to the orphanage."

"Wow, I'm surprised to hear that. I always assumed I was the only one who wasn't an orphan." I wondered how many other kids I'd gotten to know during my short incarceration weren't orphans either.

Granter continued, "Yeah, it surprised me, too. So, my clients were boys at Saint Augustine's Orphanage during that time period. They are filing a class action lawsuit against the Catholic Diocese in Burlington, for pain and suffering they claim was incurred at the hands of the priests who molested them."

I gasped. I remembered those nights when I would hear boys being dragged out of their dorm room, and returned later in the night, whimpering and crying. I couldn't understand then why they were being punished in the middle of the night. Now I understood.

Granter said, "Through a court order, I have received class rosters of residents at the orphanage over a twenty-year period. I've been contacting as many as I can find who might be interested in being a part of this litigation," he explained. "Would you mind telling me, did you suffer any abuse at the hands of the nuns or priests at the orphanage?"

My hand shook as I held the phone; my heart beating wildly. Mark gave me a worried look, as if he wanted me to hang up.

"Whew," I said, my voice trembling. "Where do I begin?" I recounted my experience of vomiting pea soup, and Nasty Nun locking me in the spiders' nest. I also told him about the boys being dragged out of their rooms in the middle of the night, whimpering and crying. When I finished, I did my best to hold back tears, my skin still crawling. There was silence on the other end of the phone. "Mister Granter?"

"Yes, yes, sorry—I was taking notes. That's a horrific story," he said sympathetically. "I'm sorry you had to retell it, as I can hear it upsets you. But I appreciate your candor."

I took a big gulp of wine. "So what happens now?"

"DeeDee, with your consent, I would like to include your story in this class action lawsuit. I will mail you all the necessary paperwork for you to sign if you are interested."

"Would I have to fly back to Vermont to testify in court?" The thought terrified me.

"Probably not. I will ask you to write your story as you remember it, and have it notarized. That document, along with those of others in the lawsuit, will be used as corroborating evidence against the diocese." He cleared his throat. "Just so you know, we are suing for the amount of three million dollars in damages: one million for each of my two clients, and one million for the other complainants in the lawsuit, which will be distributed after attorney fees."

"Holy shit!" I blurted.

"Most likely the diocese will try to settle this out of court to avoid the negative publicity, but I'm going to do all I can to push for full compensation."

"Can I ask, how many people are included in the lawsuit?"

"I'm still tracking students down, but so far we have over a hundred involved."

"Wow, that many!" I had no idea of the extent of abuse that had occurred at that horrendous institution.

"Yeah, it's a big one, and it'll probably make headlines, at least in Burlington," he continued. "I appreciate your help with this. You'll be receiving a packet from me within the next few days. I'd appreciate it if you could return it as soon as you can. We're on the court docket in three months." He wrote down my mailing address, then bade me a good night and hung up.

Mark saw me shaking as I hung up the phone. He came over and held my hands. "What was that all about?"

"Two men are filing a class action lawsuit against the orphanage for child abuse, and they want me to be part of it," I summarized. "Those nasty nuns and that damned orphanage are finally getting what's coming to them after all those years of terrorizing us poor kids!" I said with relief, as my tears erupted.

A few months later, I was watching the national evening news when the anchor announced a breaking story. "A class action lawsuit has been filed against the Catholic Diocese in Burlington, Vermont, claiming child abuse by the priests and nuns who ran Saint Augustine's Orphanage, over a twenty-year period. The orphanage closed in Nineteen-Seventy-Four. The church is denying all allegations, and vows to fight the charges in court. As far as we know, this is the first lawsuit of its kind ever filed against the Catholic Church alleging abuse."

Oh, my God! I can't believe this made national news. I ran into the kitchen to tell Mark. I hoped Granter would be successful in his litigation, as I didn't want the perpetrators to walk away unscathed.

Six months later, I received a certified check in the mail for $5,000 from the successful lawsuit. It was quite a surprise, but small compensation for the terror I had experienced at the hands of those nasty nuns.

I've always had a raspy voice as a result of that botched tonsil surgery. I have a jagged scar on my left nostril from them packing my throat so I didn't bleed out, and large slash scars on both ankles from the blood transfusions.

But the lasting effect of "doing time" in the orphanage is I have a life-long, deathly fear of dark, cramped spaces, spiders, and green pea soup.

CIVIL WAR

We spent the next couple of days clearing out most of the junk from the floor of the barn. The helpers Frank sent delivered the old appliances and other debris to the dump in their trucks. They decided the stairs to the hayloft were too rickety to hold the weight of two men, much less with them carrying heavy trunks. On Saturday, Randy, the leader, rigged up a rope-and-pulley system outside the front, open hayloft window, so the trunks and other items could be lowered easily to the ground. Randy and his men said they would return Monday to get the stuff down from the hayloft, then bade their goodbyes.

Monday morning dawned cool and overcast and I hoped it wouldn't rain. Randy and his crew arrived around eight. Mom and I watched from the kitchen window as they began lowering heavy trunks, wrapped in ropes, from the hayloft to the ground.

"Let's go join them," I said to Mom. We bundled up against the chill, grabbed our cups of coffee, and went to the backyard. We positioned ourselves at the tables under the pop-up cover to examine the stuff being pulled from the barn.

Each trunk was deposited at our feet for further inspection. The round, embedded latches were locked and I didn't want to do damage by prying them open. I went into the kitchen and called Danny, the locksmith, who had opened the latches on the trunks we had found in the upstairs bedrooms. He said he would stop by the house on his way to another call. Within the hour, Danny arrived with his toolbox. After trying a couple of different tools, he finally hit the right one and released the latches on the trunks. I paid him twenty dollars, and he was off to his next appointment.

In the first trunk we found a jumble of mid-nineteenth-century boys' clothing in gradually increasing sizes. We spread out the various pieces on the table. What we found next surprised me. I removed a flattened dark blue wool cap with a dulled, crossed-sword, brass insignia above the bill. Then I pulled out a pair of well-worn, black leather, knee-high boots and laid them on the table.

I turned to Mom. "What do you think of these? Do you think they were Old Bert's?"

Mom put her hand into the cap and unflattened it. "I don't think so. They look like they were from before Bert's time. This hat looks like it might be military."

"Wow! Look at this, Mom," I said as I removed a bayonet from the trunk. I stepped away from the table and unsheathed it from its scabbard. "This is very cool." I swung the sword in a small circle.

Mom chuckled. "Be careful with that, Dear! Don't hurt yourself."

I slid the bayonet back into its sheath and laid it on the table. At the very bottom of the trunk, I retrieved a small, covered wooden box, which I gently set on the table. Unhitching the simple latch, I opened the box. A folded envelope sat on top. I set it to one side, and saw the box contained two military medals, pinned onto a velvet backing.

Unfolding the envelope, I saw it was postmarked from the U.S. War Department. I carefully removed the delicate parchment inside and unfolded the letter, which I read aloud to Mom:

Sixteenth December, in the Year of Our Lord, eighteen hundred and sixty-two

Dear Mrs. Mary Hopper,

It is with deepest regret I must inform you your son, Infantryman Brian Hopper, fought valiantly at the battle of Fredericksburg, Virginia. He gave his life on the 13th of December, 1862, for the cause of this great civil strife to keep our country united. His ultimate sacrifice should bring honor to your family.

My sincerest sympathies on your loss of this Patriot.
General Edwin H. Stoughton
2nd Vermont Regiment
United States Army

"Oh, my God, Mom! This is amazing!" My hands were shaking as I realized what an incredible piece of history we had discovered. I was shocked and saddened to learn the fate of one of Bert's ancestors. "This must be what was left of Brian's uniform. How very sad." I looked back at Mom. "Did you have any idea Bert's family fought and died in the Civil War?"

She shook her head. "No. Bert never mentioned anything to me about it. Guess he was just humble that way."

Excited about what other treasures we might find, I opened the second, almost identical, black trunk. As with the first, we pulled out a jumble of male clothing of various sizes. As we laid the pieces out on the table, I began to notice many of the articles of clothing were identical to the ones we'd pulled from the previous trunk. I matched up two vests, two sets of breeches, two identical shirts and jackets.

Below the clothes, I was surprised to discover a folded, dark blue, knee-length, wool uniform jacket. It was adorned with a high collar and brass buttons in a single line down the front. A light blue, V-shaped, three-striped chevron was attached to each sleeve. I then retrieved a pair of gray, crumpled trousers; a crushed, black cap with a floppy crown; a waist belt with a brass buckle containing the letters *U S*, and well-worn boots. Mom moved the boys' clothing to one side and I arranged these items on the table. Digging deeper into the trunk, I pulled out a bayonet in a scabbard, and a long-barreled revolver. I carefully laid the arms next to the uniform pieces.

"Holy shit!" I said, amazed at what was on the table. "This looks like a complete uniform. I'll bet this is from the Civil War, too."

Mom touched my hand. "No need to swear, Dear. The Lord is listening."

I blushed at being properly chastised.

At the very bottom of the trunk, I discovered a covered wooden box, slightly larger than the one in the first trunk, and set it on the table. I unlatched and opened the top. As before, I discovered a letter from the U.S. War Department, and my heart sank. Beneath the letter, attached to velvet, were four military medals. *Oh, no! This won't be good news.*

I carefully removed and unfolded the parchment, and read this second letter to Mom.

Second September, in the Year of Our Lord, eighteen hundred and sixty-three

Dear Mrs. Mary Hopper,

I am deeply saddened to inform you your gallant son, Sergeant Bernard Hopper, has succumbed of his mortal wounds sustained on the twenty-eighth of August, eighteen sixty-three, at the Battle of Gettysburg, Pennsylvania.

I felt my throat constrict as I realized another of Bert's ancestors had died in the war. How heartbreaking for the family. I took a breath and kept reading to Mom.

Several of Sergeant Hopper's men owe him their life, as he valiantly removed them from the battlefield. His heroic efforts will not be forgotten. It is my hope you will rest proud in the knowledge he served his country well, and is now in the arms of the Almighty Lord.

With My Deepest Regrets,
General George J. Stannard
Vermont Brigade
United States Army

Mom cleared her throat. "Sounds like he was a hero for rescuing some of his men from the battle."

"Yeah, that's amazing. It looks like Bernard worked his way up to sergeant, as he was in the war a year longer than his brother Brian, before he was killed," I said.

I wondered if they were twins. If so, then that might explain the duplicate articles of clothing we had found. And how old were they when they died? Probably pretty young, I surmised. How tragic for their parents to lose both of their sons in the war. I wondered what their ancestry to Bert would have been, as I had yet to find more of the Hopper family tree.

"Mom, this is so gut-wrenching. It looks like Brian and Bernard were brothers, and both died in the war. That must have been really tough on Bert's family."

She touched the medals in the box. "You know, Dee. Bert was a very private man, and rarely talked about his family. I wonder if he even knew his ancestors fought in the Civil War."

My heart ached thinking of sweet Old Bert and all the heartbreak he had endured in his life. Then I casually sorted through two more trunks, which contained an odd collection of men's, women's, and children's clothing in various sizes. I was at a loss to explain or understand to whom the contents might have belonged.

A few days before Mom and I discovered the trunks, I had paid a visit to the Fair Haven Historical Society. The curators were a lively husband and wife team, Monique and Jacques Roubillard. Being Canadian ex-pats, they preferred to be called by their American nicknames, Moni and Jack. I had met them a number of years earlier on one of my visits to Mom. Moni knew a bit of the history of the Hopper family, and said if I ever planned to clean the place out, to let her know. On my most recent visit to the historical society, Moni had been excited to hear I was staying for a while. She said to call anytime I needed their help.

Wanting to validate our findings, I went into the kitchen and called the historical society office. Moni answered the phone, and I quickly explained what we had found. I asked if she and Jack were available to come over. She was excited and said they'd be there.

About a half-hour later, I heard a car pull into the driveway. I rose and went to greet them.

Moni was a petite woman, barely five feet tall. Her long, black, curly hair, when worn loose, made her head look gigantic on her diminutive frame. On this day, she had corralled her mane into a ponytail, but tendrils still swirled around her face. She wore an oversized blue-and-yellow-striped sweater over blue pants tucked into hiking boots. Jack, not much taller than Moni, had short cropped black hair, sprinkled with gray. He wore a denim peacoat over his jeans and boots, and had a satchel slung over his shoulder. I wondered if Jack had ever considered being a jockey, as he was the perfect size for the job.

Approaching the couple, I hugged Moni, and shook Jack's hand. "Thanks for coming over on such short notice." I led them to the tables and swept my hand over the uniforms and artifacts. "Look what we've uncovered!"

Jack's deep blue eyes went wide as he scanned the items. "Well, well! What have we here?" In his excitement, his Canadian accent became more pronounced.

Jack pulled white gloves from his satchel and put them on, then he gingerly studied the front of the tattered uniform jacket. In deep concentration, he ran one hand over the blue-gray, three-striped chevron on the sleeve, then inspected the back of the jacket. He laid the jacket on the table, then lifted the crumpled trousers. Holding the pant waist with his left hand, he ran his other hand through a rip in the right pant leg. He pulled the fabric to his face and peered at it closely.

Moni and I exchanged glances as we watched Jack work.

"Hmmm," Jack mumbled. "The sergeant unlucky enough to wear this uniform probably didn't fare too well." He laid the trousers on the table and spread the material of the ripped pant leg. "See here," he pointed at the frayed, darkly blotched cloth edges toward the top of the leg. "It's been ripped apart. But the rest of the pant leg has been cut with a sharp object, probably a knife or sword." He pointed to the straight edges of the two sides of the opening.

Jack lifted his head and stared past Moni and me, as if his mind was in a far-off place.

Moni got his attention. "Jack! What are you thinking?"

Jack shook his head and his stare focused on us. "The good news is I believe this is an authentic Civil War uniform, and an amazing find, Dee!" He nodded toward the other artifacts on the table. "And I have no doubt the other items will prove genuine as well, but I will inspect them." He touched the chevrons on the jacket sleeve. "The bad news is this sergeant was shot in his thigh." He gently fingered the trousers. "Surgery procedures during the Civil War were rudimentary, at best. I suspect the pant leg was cut by someone in the field, to initially bandage the wound. But once he got to a medical tent, his leg most likely would have been sawed off—literally!"

I cringed at the thought of Bernard's leg being cut off with a saw, and my stomach twisted into a knot.

I told Jack, "The letter I found from the War Department said Sergeant Bernard Hopper died of his mortal wounds. Does that make sense?"

Jack nodded. "Yeah. Unfortunately, penicillin hadn't been invented yet, so there was no treatment for infection. Once a limb was amputated, the infection could run rampant in the body." Jack wiped his face. "It's a horrible way to die."

My legs were weak, and I sat next to Mom at the table. "Oh, my gosh, how awful," I murmured.

Mom reached her trembling right hand over and grasped mine.

Jack shook his head. "This is one of those nasty little secrets the Civil War generals didn't want the families of the soldiers to know about. They kept their inept medical procedures under wraps for a very long time."

I handed Jack the two letters I'd discovered so he could read them. Once he'd finished reading, I asked, "Do you know any more about the Second Vermont Regiment or the Vermont Brigade in the Civil War? What battles were they in, and what kinds of losses they incurred?"

"I know the First and Second Regiments mustered-in early during the war, in eighteen sixty-one. By sixty-three, many of the smaller regiments had been combined to form the larger Vermont Brigade." Jack handed the fragile letters back to me.

Jack swept his hand over the artifacts and looked at me. "Dee, I have a special request. I know these belong to you, but would you be interested in loaning them to the historical society? I'd love to put them on display in the museum." He pulled a notebook from his satchel and began carefully cataloging the uniforms and weapons.

I squeezed Mom's hand. "What do you think, Mom? Would Old Bert have wanted the world to know about his ancestors?"

Her chin quivered and she nodded. "Yes, Dee. I think it's a wonderful idea. Old Bert would have been proud of his family."

"Jack, I'd be willing to loan all of this to the museum, but I'd like copies of the letters from the War Department and your inventory list for my own records, if it's not too much trouble."

Moni chimed in, "Of course it's not too much trouble. We'd be happy to do that for you, right, Jack?"

Jack grunted and nodded, distracted with his work.

I was happy we could make a small contribution to the town archives to document the heretofore unknown history of our benefactors, the Hopper family.

As Jack was cataloging the uniforms, Moni sat at the other end of the table next to Mom and started sorting through the two trunks with the assortment of odd clothing. After a few minutes, Moni turned to me and asked, "Do you know anything about the Hopper family lineage?"

"Not much," I said. "I found Bert's family Bible, but it only goes back two generations. What do you think of these other clothes?"

Moni shrugged. "I have a suspicion of what they were used for," she said mysteriously. "But I need to do some research on this area of town before I can explain further."

Now I was curious about what Moni was thinking. Hearing voices, I turned toward the barn. I watched as Randy balanced three round hat boxes, one atop the other, and approached the table. When he set the boxes down they made a thud, which I thought strange.

Before he turned back to the barn, I asked, "Randy, are those heavy? They're just hat boxes, right?"

Randy shrugged. "Yeah, seems a bit heavy. Ya might wanna check 'em out."

I handed the top box to Moni, set the second box in front of me and slid the bottom box to Mom to inspect. In Moni's box was an off-white, well-worn, wide-brimmed, moth-eaten bonnet. When I opened my box, I discovered a blue bonnet with white lace embellishments. It seemed to be for a special occasion—possibly church services. Sitting next to Mom, I watched her open the box in front of her. She removed a black bonnet, again adorned with white lace.

Removing a layer of old paper Mom peered into the bottom of the deep, round container. "There's something else in here, Dee." With both hands she reached into the box and with some effort removed a bulky, square object wrapped in brown paper, tied with a cloth bow. It slipped from her hands and thumped onto the table.

"Oh, my! That's heavy!" Mom exclaimed, her right hand shaking.

"Hmmm, I wonder what this is," I said as I stood to inspect the package. Moni came around the table to join me.

I carefully untied the cloth ribbon and flipped the object several times to unwrap it from the fragile, brown paper. My heart thumped as I saw five dark, leather-bound notebooks, tied together with another ribbon. I untied this ribbon and laid the topmost book from the stack on the table. I carefully opened the brittle cover.

Moni leaned over my shoulder as Mom looked on.

Written on the first page was:

This is the diary of Emma Saunders Hopper, begun in the Year of Our Lord, eighteen hundred and twenty-one.

Moni laid her hand on my shoulder and grinned her impish smile. "Well, well! Isn't this something special you don't find every day? How wonderful!"

I became excited as I realized this could be the Hopper family history I'd been seeking. I squinted at the petite, slanted handwriting as I slowly read the first entry aloud:

"On this fifth day of June, in the Year of Our Lord, eighteen hundred and twenty-one, I, Emma Oriana Saunders, of eighteen years, from Sandy Hill, New York, am married to Gabriel Aaron Hopper, of twenty-one years, from

Fairhaven, Vermont. We begin our lives together as committed husband and wife in the name of our Lord and Savior, Jesus Christ."

Bingo! We had found our ghost! Not wanting to reveal our secret to outsiders, I smiled and winked at Mom. She nodded and smiled back, grasping my hand. I desperately wanted to sit there and read Emma's journals start to finish, but needed to finish my business with Moni and Jack first.

I turned to Moni and said, "Maybe we can find a family tree listed in here. What do you think?"

Moni, ever the curator, pulled a pair of white gloves from her pocket and covered her hands. "Dee, these journals are very fragile and it's best not to get oil from our hands on them." She reached for the open book. "Here, let me take a look."

"Oh, yeah. Of course. I didn't even think about that," I admitted. I was so thrilled to see the journals, I had forgotten they were over one hundred and fifty years old.

Moni carefully flipped through the pages of the first book, then gently closed the cover and laid it on the table. I watched her closely as she repeated the process with each journal, perusing the last pages. She put the fifth journal on the table and shook her head. "Sorry, Dee. I'm not finding any family lineage to speak of."

I was disappointed, but vowed to keep digging. I lifted the rounded top of the last unopened trunk. Wooden slats braced its sides. A beige removable tray sat on top where several old books lay, covers down, in the shallow compartments. The brown, leather-bound one caught my attention. I lifted and turned the cover to read it. The words *Holy Bible* jumped out at me.

"Moni, look!" I held the cover up so she could see it. "Another Bible. If the family tradition holds true, I'll bet this is where we'll find more of the family line!"

Moni held out a gloved hand and said, "May I?"

I carefully handed her the thick, well-worn tome.

Flipping to the final pages of the Bible, Moni gasped, "Dee, you were right. Here it is!"

There, on the last two pages, were the members of the Hopper Family lineage:

Gabriel Aaron Hopper b. 1800 d. 1863
   m. 1821 Emma Saunders b. 1803 d. 1868
      Children: Luke b.1822 d. 1850
         Adam b. 1825 d. *1897*
         Ruth b. 1827 d. 1832

Luke Hopper
m. 1840 Mary Egan b. 1823 d. *1896*
   Children: Brian b. 1842 d. 1862
      Bernard b. 1842 d. 1863
      Martha b. 1847 d. *1910*
      George b. 1850 d. *1916*

Perusing the terse entries, I recognized Emma's handwriting on most of them. But the dates entered after her death in 1868 were written in another hand.

I pointed this out to Moni. "I think another family member kept the records up-to-date after Emma's death. These later dates are in a different script."

Moni nodded. "Sure, it would be common for the family Bible to be passed down through the generations—usually kept by the women."

As I read the last name, a chill ran down my spine. "Moni! Oh, my God! George, the youngest child of Luke and Mary, was Bert's father!" I pointed to the last entry as I tied the lineage to what I had discovered in Bert's family Bible. "Luke died in eighteen-fifty, the same year George was born. I wonder how Luke died. It was more than a decade before the war, and he was quite young, only twenty-eight," I said, quickly subtracting to get his age. "And what about Adam? No mention of him marrying or having a family, nor of Martha either," I said, trying to piece the family puzzle together.

Scanning the dates, Moni said, "And it looks like Brian and Bernard *were* twins, as you suspected, Dee. That would explain the duplicated boys' clothing you found. How sad they both died in the war."

I was so distracted by the story of Brian and Bernard I hadn't looked closely at the other family members. All of a sudden, something jumped out at me. "Mom, look!" I pointed out the entry. "Gabe and Emma's daughter, Ruth, was only five years old when she died. I'll bet those were her clothes we found in the trunk upstairs."

Mom nodded. "Yes, I think you could be right, Dee. How very sad for them."

Moni turned to me. "What are you talking about?"

"Mom and I sorted through some trunks upstairs. We found one with hand-carved children's toys, and another with a young girl's hand-sewn clothing. When I unfolded one dress, there were blotchy dark-brown stains on it." I glanced at Mom. "Mom thought it might have been blood."

Jack looked up from his note-taking, his interest piqued by our conversation. "A common cause of death in children in the eighteen-hundreds was consumption. Does it say what month she died?"

Moni peered at the entry. "No. It just says 1832."

"Hmmmm," Jack frowned. "I would guess she died in the winter, as the cold weather would have made her condition worse."

I asked, "So what is consumption, exactly?"

Jack said, "Well, we know it in modern terms as tuberculosis. It's a highly contagious disease of the lungs, and it was called consumption, because it caused severe weight loss, and appeared to literally consume the body." He shook his head. "Back in those days, there was no cure, and children were highly susceptible to acquiring it."

I pictured the stained dress. "So would that explain the possible blood stains we found?"

Jack nodded. "If the little girl had consumption, she would have been coughing considerably as the disease progressed. It's highly likely she coughed up blood."

"Oh, gosh. That must have been so heartbreaking for the family to see their young daughter die that way," I said. The Hopper family had endured such grief.

Moni touched my hand. "Yes, it's just so sad." She peered at me. "When you have some time, Dee, I'd like to see what's in those trunks upstairs."

"Of course," I said. "The next time you come over, we can go through them. You're welcome to take whatever you'd like for the museum."

Then Moni turned her attention back to the trunks with the odd clothing assortment. "You know, Dee, the family tree still doesn't explain this strange collection of clothes. I think there was something more going on here."

Now Moni really had me intrigued. "What do you mean? What could have happened?"

She laughed and waved me away. "I need to do some research, then I'll let you know what I'm thinking."

As Moni and I were mulling over the Hopper family tree, Randy hollered from the barn door, "DeeDee, co'mere! You gotta see this. You ain't gonna believe what we found!"

I noticed the guys had rolled out into the yard two big, round, wooden grain storage bins that had sat against the right wall of the barn. As I walked to the barn, I heard Moni ask Jack if he wanted to join us.

"Naw, go ahead," he grumbled as he continued making notes.

The barn was dark as I entered, so I waited for my eyes to adjust to the dim light, always on the lookout for cobwebs. Moni followed me inside. On the right side of barn, I saw what appeared to be a dark hole in the floor. Some of the floorboards had been lifted and were resting against the wall.

Suddenly a head popped up from the hole and I jumped. It was one of the smaller guys who worked for Randy. "This is totally cool!" the young man said. "There's a room down here with all sorts of junk in it."

Randy explained, "When we moved the grain bins, we saw a rusted ring attached to the floorboards." He pointed to the upended hatch leaning against the wall. "When Bobby yanked on it, that trapdoor swung open. Surprised the hell out of us!" Randy let out a raucous laugh. "Bobby, come on out of there and bring the flashlight. Let DeeDee and Moni take a look."

Moni and I exchanged glances as her face broke into a grin. She accepted the flashlight from Bobby.

"What?" I asked her.

"Let's go see, shall we?" She moved toward the gaping black hole.

ARTIFACTS

I peered over Moni's shoulder as she shined her light down the dark passage. A dusty, cobweb-infested, rickety ladder led into the underground chamber. My heartbeat quickened, and my hands began to sweat. Dank holes full of spiders were definitely not my thing.

I waved my hand toward the opening. "After you," I said to Moni.

As Moni descended, I felt a pressure on my arm which startled me.

"Here, Dee. You'll probably need this," Randy said, giving me an odd look. He handed me a black, long-handled, lit flashlight which had apparently been in his tool belt.

I steadied my hand as I grasped the heavy light. "Thanks," I said, trying to keep my voice calm.

Moni called up to me. "Come on down, Dee, but watch your head."

Balancing the flashlight, I turned backward and eased my way down the six steps, cringing as I felt webs brush against my hand. I landed on a hard-packed dirt floor, and did indeed have to duck to avoid the low-hanging, hand-hewn beams along the underground ceiling. Cobwebs brushed my face, and I stifled a scream, swiping them away. *Breathe,* I told myself. *Just breathe!* But the musty, foul odor in the room kept me from inhaling too deeply.

The chamber was about ten feet wide and extended the entire length of the barn. The three outside walls were constructed of slate slabs stacked horizontally upon each other, in the local tradition of foundation cellars. I noticed mud had flowed between the slates and pooled on the floor along the right-side wall. The mortar between many of the slates had collapsed, thus causing the weight of the barn to tilt on this section of the foundation. I made a mental note to let our agent, Frank, know what we'd found. Then I turned around, the flashlight illuminating a dirt wall crisscrossed with long pieces of timber at the far end of the room.

Along the right wall was an old wooden kitchen table covered with dirt and rodent droppings. Four wooden chairs were nearby, one toppled over due to a broken leg. To the left of the table was a small, potbellied wood stove, the pipe venting through the ceiling. To the right of the table was a rough-hewn set of wooden shelves that contained dust-encased dishes, cups, silverware and what appeared to be jars of canned goods, covered in spider webs. My skin crawled. I hated to think of what was in those jars and how long they'd been there.

Turning to my left, I directed the light toward the back of the room. Three cots with rotted straw mattresses, covered with rodent droppings, were positioned against the walls in a horseshoe shape. Along the inner dirt wall were a chair and two black trunks, similar to those we'd retrieved from the hayloft.

Moni was making noises behind me, and I trained the light in her direction toward the front of the barn. She was inspecting a round, wooden bathtub. Some of the wooden slats had rotted, leaving large gaps between the round hoops. A small stand in one corner held a pitcher perched inside a wash bowl. A swirl pattern on the porcelain was barely visible through the layers of dirt. An apparently matching chamber pot sat in the opposite corner. Hooks hung from the low rafters in a rough semicircle around the area. A rotted cloth draped from one hook.

I asked Moni, "Who do you thi—"

Suddenly my heart began racing, and a pain shot down my left arm. My skin felt like shrink-wrap over my veins, and my breathing took on an unnatural, low huffing. I felt hot and clammy, with sweat dripping down my face. Needing to take a deep breath, I instinctively straightened, but slammed my head against the low-hanging rafter. Bile erupted in my throat, and the ground seemed to lurch beneath me. The close, dark walls tilted toward me. I dropped the flashlight and reached for the outer slate wall, yet it appeared to undulate away from my grasp. Losing my balance, my shoulder hit hard against the foundation. The room spun, then the mattress came up to meet me with a thump, and I collapsed upon it. A dust cloud engulfed me, making me gag.

"Dee! You all right?" Moni asked, immediately by my side.

Childhood memories flashed through my mind: nasty nuns throwing me into a black hole full of spiders; a ceiling collapsing and almost killing me. Woozy, I slowly sat up. I envisioned a hoard of rats swarming from the dingy mattress, their bared, pointy teeth attacking my flesh.

Moni's face swam in and out of focus.

"Tight spaces…scare the hell…outta me," I huffed. "Will you…help me out of here?" I coughed out the grime in my throat, embarrassed to admit my spider phobia.

Moni helped me stand and stabilized me on my feet and I kept my head low, still breathing hard. She guided my hips as I staggered up the ladder, gasping for air. Stumbling out of the barn, I braced myself against the outside wall and pushed my way behind the outhouse, where I vomited, emptying my stomach. I hoped Mom hadn't seen me, because I didn't want to have to explain my reaction to her.

After wiping my mouth and taking some deep breaths, I walked the long way behind the trees to the kitchen, where I poured myself a glass of water. Sitting at the table, I wiped the sweat from my brow and dropped my head into my hands. *This is the worst panic attack I've ever had. I thought I was having a heart attack! I can't believe after all these years, my body still reacts in such a violent manner to cobwebs and spiders!*

I took another sip of water, my heartbeat slowing to a more normal pace. *How in the world will I ever overcome this childhood phobia? I can't live my life like this! Maybe I can find a therapist who deals with this kind of stuff when I return home to California.* I tried to visualize anything but big, black spiders crawling on me.

As I was berating myself for being such a weakling, I peered out the window to the activity in the backyard. Jack sat alone at one table, using a magnifying glass to inspect the long-barreled revolver we had pulled from one trunk. Mom's back was to me, but it looked like she was folding clothes. A couple of Randy's helpers were loading the old grain barrels into a pickup truck. Then I saw Moni scurry from the barn clutching something under her arm. She laid the item on the table in front of Mom. Moni seemed very animated, and it piqued my curiosity.

Moving to the sink, I rinsed my mouth with a swig of water and spat it out. I stood up straight, ran my fingers though my hair, and took another deep breath. *I'm fine,* I tried to convince myself. *Just stay away from the dark holes!*

About fifteen minutes after I had entered the kitchen, I returned to the backyard to see what was happening. Moni sat next to Mom, perusing a long book lying open between them. I looked over their shoulder to see lined pages with neat, slanted script filling each line.

"What's this?" I asked.

Mom turned to me with a concerned look, but I avoided her gaze.

Moni looked up at me with her impish grin. "Well, Dee. When you hit the wall, I noticed two of the slates got pushed in. I thought it odd the other slates didn't move."

"Hit the wall?" Mom's head jerked up. "Dee, what happened?"

"Oh, nothing really." Turning back to Moni, I half-heartedly joked, "Guess I'm not quite strong enough to bring down an entire slate wall."

"I asked Randy for his help," Moni explained. "He came down with his tool belt, and we were able to wiggle the slates back and forth until they both came out of the wall. When I pointed the flashlight into the hole I saw something in the cavity. This is what I pulled out," she said as she closed the book so I could see the hardbound, dusty, gray-blue cover.

"A ledger book? Was this for the farm? Why was it hidden?" I asked.

"Not for the farm exactly," Moni said, her eyes sparkling. "I think we've found the equivalent of the Holy Grail!"

Now I was even more confused. "What are you talking about?"

Moni pointed to the leaning right side of the barn. "Based upon the artifacts in there, it looks like your hidden room was used to harbor slaves as part of the Underground Railroad migration north. This book is the proof!" She had donned a clean pair of white gloves, and carefully flipped a few pages. "There are names and ages of fugitives who passed through here, where they came from, and who their masters were. Whoever kept track of these travelers hid this ledger on purpose, as they probably feared repercussions for their involvement. This is an amazing piece of history!" Moni said, her face animated.

It took me a minute to process what she had just said. "Wow! You're kidding me! I had no idea." I was amazed the hidden room had been here for over one hundred and fifty years. Mom and I had had no knowledge of the history of the property. I felt quite uninformed for not knowing more about the local lore of the Underground Railroad in my own neighborhood.

Seeing Emma's journals on the table, I said to Moni, "I'll bet it was Emma who kept the ledger. She seemed to be a prolific writer."

Moni nodded. "Yeah, I'll bet you're right. We'll have to read her diaries to be sure."

"So what can you tell me about the history of the Underground Railroad around here? I remember being taught Revolutionary War history, but I don't remember any mention of this."

Jack set his magnifying glass down and joined the conversation. "Well, Dee, the network was maintained through word of mouth and not much was documented." He peered across the table at the ledger. "Slaves came through Vermont from the eighteen-twenties through the Civil War in the eighteen-sixties. From Fair Haven they were usually taken to Whitehall, to board ships on Lake Champlain and make their trek to Canada."

Then Moni pointed to the clothes Mom had been folding. "That's what I suspected when I saw those trunks full of odd clothes."

Surprised and exasperated, I said, "So why didn't you mention this to me before?"

Moni swung her hand over the ledger. "Because I needed more evidence—and here it is!" She continued, "Families who harbored fugitives often provided them with extra food and clothing before they were sent farther on their journey. Donations came from church members and included a wide variety of their cast-offs." She nodded toward the trunks.

Jack rose and stood behind Mom to view the ledger more closely. "The brick house at the corner of Academy Street, a block away, was owned by Zenas C. Ellis. It's a well-documented station on the railroad. I'm guessing the Ellis and Hopper families, being neighbors, probably worked together to help transport the fugitives. But the Hopper family's involvement had been lost to history until now," Jack said. "This is truly an amazing find, and a great addition to Fair Haven's history of participation in the Underground Railroad migration!" Jack patted my shoulder, then returned to his seat and continued his revolver inspection.

A childhood memory when I was ten, flashed back to me. I turned to Moni. "You know what? Now that you mention it, I remember the old lady who lived in the Ellis house once took me and my friends into her basement. She showed us a passage that led under the road to the sugaring house that once stood on the other side." I shuddered at the long-ago feeling of crawling in the oppressive underground passage. "I had forgotten until just now."

Moni nodded. "Yes. Missus Katherine Atwater and her family owned the Ellis property for several generations."

I continued, "I remember when we climbed back up to the kitchen, she told us the passage was used to hide slaves a very long time ago. My friends thought it was very cool." I recalled them giggling at the mention of slaves. But I had envisioned a bloody, chained gang crawling through the passage. I cringed at the memory. "It never occurred to me our property could've been part of the same network."

And is that house haunted, too? If so, by whom?

Chills ran down my spine as I thought about Bert's ancestors opening their hearts and home to fugitives coming through their land. The risks they took required a lot of courage and faith in their convictions. And they even gave their lives for the cause in the Civil War. The dry history lessons I'd learned in school now took on a whole new meaning.

"I'd like to spend time reading through the ledger before I donate it to the museum, if you don't mind," I said to Moni.

"Oh, no, of course not. It belongs to you so you're entitled to do with it as you wish."

"I'm really glad we found that room before we burned the barn down," I said, and grasped Mom's hand.

"Oh, yeah, me too!" Moni said, chuckling.

I ran my hand over the coarse surface of the blue-gray ledger. My skin prickled to the touch.

Time to discover what secrets this holds.

THE LEDGER

Moni and Jack spent the rest of Monday afternoon at the property. They wanted to photograph the underground room before any other artifacts were removed. Not wanting a repeat performance of my panic attack, I declined to go back down into the cobweb-infested chamber. As items were delivered to the table under the pop-up awning, Mom and I cataloged them into Jack's notebook.

When a cardboard box containing the jars of canned goods was brought to the table, my stomach churned. The odor that had permeated the chamber still clung to the jars and wafted around us. God only knew what unearthly creatures were growing in there.

I touched Mom's arm. "Mom, don't touch this stuff. I'll be right back." Trotting into the kitchen, I retrieved two pairs of yellow rubber gloves from under the sink, and brought them back to the table.

Handing a pair to Mom, I said, "Here, put these on. We don't want to get anything gross on our skin."

We both donned the cleaning gloves that stretched almost to our elbows.

I gingerly pulled a glass jar from the box. It had a flat, rusted, tin lid, and what appeared to be crumbling sealing wax securing the lid to the glass. I used a bit of Windex and a paper towel to gently wipe the crud from the jar. Then I slid the jar to Mom so she could take a look. Having canned vegetables her whole life, she was our resident expert.

"Be careful with this. It might not be sealed well," I cautioned her. "So what do you think is in there?"

Mom looked closely at something dark, blood-red in the container. "I think these were probably pickled beets." She slid the jar aside.

I passed her another jar I had finished cleaning. It had something chunky floating in a milky liquid.

"These look like they were once dill pickles. The brine has gone bad, though." Mom wrinkled her nose and moved it away.

As I cleaned the next jar, I noticed faint scratches in the tin lid. Turning it to the light, I could barely make out the numbers *1*, *8*, and *4*. Angling it a bit more, I saw what looked like a *9*. Chuckling, I turned to Mom. "Yeah, I think they would've gone bad by now because they were canned in eighteen-forty-nine! Imagine that!"

Mom laughed. "It's probably best we don't open them, Dear."

I couldn't have agreed with her more.

We finished wiping and replacing the nasty jars back into the box. I had no idea whether Moni wanted to take these to the museum or the dump. Either way, I wanted them *gone.*

Turning my attention to the ledger unearthed from the slate wall, I began reading what I recognized as Emma's small, slanted handwriting. The first entry for a visitor was dated 1825. I remembered Emma's diary began in 1821, when she was eighteen and married Gabe. I was amazed at how young they were, in their early twenties, when they started harboring fugitives. Scanning through pages of entries, I noted a number of families with children making the trek north. How difficult that journey must have been for those poor, scared kids. When I flipped through to the last page of the ledger, I realized for more than two decades, Emma and Gabe had harbored hundreds of fugitives in their barn.

Was it illegal to transport slaves during that time period? How were they able to help so many and not get caught or arrested? I'll have to do some more research.

The last entries in the ledger, dated October 1850, were of a family named Prescott. The family consisted of a grandmother, her son, daughter, and grandson. I presumed the grandson was the daughter's son, due to her age. There was something about the date of 1850 that seemed familiar. "Will you pass me the family Bible?" I asked Mom. "I need to check something."

Mom reached to her left and handed me the brown leather Bible. I flipped to the last pages to review the family lineage. I read again that Luke, Gabe and Emma's oldest son, had died in 1850, and Luke's youngest son, George, was born in 1850. It seemed Luke didn't have much time to spend with his newborn son, if any at all.

A number of questions swirled in my head. *What had happened in 1850? Jack said fugitives made their treks north through the Civil War, a good decade or so later. And how did Luke die? Did his death have anything to do with the reason Emma and Gabe stopped harboring escaping slaves?*

I was getting cold from being in the chilly air all day, and the cloudy afternoon light was waning. I could tell Mom was cold, too. I desperately wanted to curl up with a spiked cup of coffee and immerse myself in Emma's diary to get some answers to my questions.

Just about then, Moni and Jack returned to the table and began wrapping up their work for the day.

Moni turned to us. "Well, we've photographed and cataloged all the items in the underground chamber. We'll return another day and get the guys to help us hoist the artifacts out of there, if that's okay with you, Dee."

"Sure. Do you think they'll go into the museum?"

Jack bundled the uniform artifacts into one trunk. "Possibly. We'll have to see what we have room for. Some may go into storage for now." He lifted one end of the trunk. "Moni, can you give me a hand?" They carried the heavy trunk to their car, then returned to the table.

Moni stuffed the assortment of boys' clothing into the second trunk. "We'll come back tomorrow to get these, if that's all right."

"Yes, that's fine," I replied, then pointed to the box containing the jars of canned goods. "And you're taking these creatures, too, right?" I scrunched my face.

Moni laughed. "Yup. We may display a couple, but most will go to the dump. Guess they are pretty nasty, aren't they?"

"You think?" I said, laughing along with her.

Mom and I bade Moni and Jack farewell. Then Randy came to the table and said he and his helpers were on the way to the dump. They would be back in the morning to finish the barn cleanup. Their fully loaded pickups followed the Roubillards' car out of the driveway.

I helped Mom to her feet and grabbed the Bible, ledger, and Emma's journals. We made our way into the kitchen. "Mom, would you mind brewing a pot of coffee? I don't know about you, but I'm chilled to the bone."

"Of course, Dear. And I'll fix us a snack. I'm kinda hungry." She bustled around the kitchen.

"Thanks. Love you, Mom." I bent and kissed her cheek, then went into the living room and got comfortable in the easy chair, eager to begin reading Emma's diary.

EMMA'S DIARY

After reading the first few pages of Emma's diary, which began in 1821 when she and Gabe were married, I smelled the coffee brewing. Entering the kitchen, I saw Mom had fixed us a plate of crackers and Vermont Sharp Cheddar, topped with peanut butter and jelly. Yummy—a childhood favorite! My stomach gurgled as I realized we had completely skipped lunch. I grabbed a mug, splashed a generous shot of brandy into the bottom, and topped it off with coffee and cream. Carrying the plate of crackers into the living room, I set it on the coffee table and placed the cup next to me on the lamp table. I helped Mom sit in her wingback chair next to the window, then turned on the television to her favorite channel.

Settling into the easy chair next to her, I gulped a mouthful of spiked coffee. The brandy burned all the way down and warmed my innards. I sighed and perused more of Emma's diaries. I was particularly interested in discovering what had happened in 1850, as that seemed like a pivotal year in her life and the year Luke had died.

In the fourth journal, this entry caught my attention:

10 mo. 11th, Friday, early morning, 1850

A new group of travelers have arrived during the night seeking refuge from the storm. I thank Thee, Lord for guiding these weary souls to our doorstep. We shall provide them shelter and sustenance, as Thee would have done. Please shine Thy light upon Miss Elsie, Sarah, Samuel and Jonah so they may travel in Thy good graces to the land of Canaan. I ask this in Thy name, Jesus Christ, our Savior. Amen.

I recognized the names as those belonging to the Prescott family, the last entry in the slave ledger. *Why were they the last family the Hoppers had helped?* I hoped Emma had documented more.

I scanned the pages where Emma wrote about the horrific plight of the slave family and how they came to arrive at her farm. It was obvious Emma had great admiration and empathy for the grandmother, Miss Elsie, in leading her family on their perilous journey to gain their freedom. The Prescotts' escape story was terrifying, and I stifled tears as I learned about the inexcusable treatment inflicted upon them by their master.

Turning another page, I read the following:

10 mo. 13th, Sunday morning, 1850

Father and Luke have left on their journey to deliver the Prescott family to the canal in Whitehall. I pray the good Lord shines His guiding light upon the family and delivers them safely to freedom in the Promised Land. Yet, I cannot help but worry. I do not believe Father has been forthcoming about the risk that surrounds us because of this infernal new slave law.

'Tis not like them to travel armed when transporting fugitives. Mayhap they expected trouble and did not want to worry me. I can only pray they are successful in their mission to do God's will on this earth to help His downtrodden children. May the Lord hold and keep the travelers in His ever-loving grace and guide Gabe and Luke home safely. Amen.

This confirmed what Jack had said about the Underground Railroad conductors transporting fugitives to the Lake Champlain canal in Whitehall. I wasn't sure what new slave law had gone into effect in 1850, and made a mental note to find out. But whatever it was, Emma worried about the men traveling armed, which wasn't their normal mode. Something or someone had prompted Gabe and Luke to feel they had to be extra protective of their charges on this occasion. Emma sensed trouble might be coming.

I popped a loaded cracker into my mouth. As the sweet peanut butter and jelly oozed onto my tongue and mixed with the tangy cheese, I read Emma's next entry, dated a day later:

10 mo. 14th, Monday afternoon, 1850

My son is dead! Why? Why, Lord, has Thee taken Luke from my arms? I am beyond despair! He and Gabe were doing Thy will on this earth to help Thy downtrodden children. Why has Thee brought this terrible wrath upon our family?

I gasped, "Oh, God! No!"

Yesterday morning, only a short time after I had written here, our good neighbor, Friend Zenas C. Ellis, and his sons, brought Luke's body home to me. Our wagon was attacked by slave hunters and Luke was shot! Why would Thee allow such evil to exist in this world? And now, Gabe is in jail for transporting fugitives.

What shall I do? I cannot manage the farm alone. And how long will Gabe be in jail? The Lord warned me in my dream this would happen. I should have stopped them from transporting the fugitives and listened to my heart! This is all my fault, and now I have lost both Luke and Gabe. Oh Dear Lord, please forgive my trespasses!

Mom turned to look at me. "What is it, Dear?"

I shook my head, trying to shut out visions of the attack. "The Hopper family was transporting slaves to Whitehall. Their wagon was besieged, and Luke, Gabe and Emma's son, was murdered." I felt my voice break as I gave Mom a quick synopsis. "But Gabe got arrested for breaking the law. No wonder they stopped helping fugitives after this horrible event!" I removed my glasses to wipe my tears.

Mom's lower jaw trembled. "I'm so sorry to hear that, Dear." She reached and grasped my hand. "I wonder if Old Bert knew about this. That's so sad for their family. Poor Emma!" I continued reading:

I am overwhelmed with grief over such a horrible onslaught on these good, God-fearing people. And what will become of Luke's wife, Mary, and their children? Her unborn child shall never know their loving father. 'Tis an unbearable burden Thee has struck upon our family, from which our lives will be forever changed.

My thoughts wandered. *Oh, my gosh! So Mary was pregnant when Luke died. His death must have devastated her!*

I have dispatched a letter to my son Adam, in New York City, informing him of our family tragedy, and urgently requested him to return home.

*I shall need his help to manage the farm without Luke and Gabe. I do
not know how long Gabe will be in jail, nor where I shall get the money
for his bail. And what if he is not released for Luke's burial? I need the
strength of my husband by my side!*

*Oh, Dear Lord! Gabe will be furious over this ambush on our wagon.
I must visit him in jail so we can determine our future. My heart is
irretrievably broken. I do not know where to turn.*

Mom was right—poor Emma! I wanted to reach back through the ages
to give her a hug and let her cry on my shoulder. What a tough situation
she had been put in. With her son dead and her husband in jail, I could
imagine her angst over what she would do next, and how she would manage the farm. Hopefully Adam came home quickly to help her.

I continued on to Emma's next entry that same evening:

10 mo. 14th, Monday evening, 1850

*What a heart-breaking day. As if losing Luke is not bad enough, our
neighbor and Friend Paree Guildersleeve paid me a visit this afternoon.
She said she helped Samuel and Jonah travel in secret to Whitehall. Our
Friend, Titus Battis, shall stow the boys away on the steamship going to
Burlington. But Miss Elsie is dead! I am shocked and bereaved to learn of
this news! I prayed so fervently this determined, God-fearing woman and
her family would reach the Promised Land. Paree found Miss Elsie's body
in the river—drowned! She carried the body to her house, and has come
to discuss burial arrangements.*

*I would very much like Miss Elsie to be buried in our family plot, but
do not have the wherewithal to pay for both her funeral and Luke's, plus
post Gabe's bail. I am forever grateful Paree has offered to contribute
to Miss Elsie's burial expenses. May Miss Elsie find the freedom she so
desperately sought, in her Lord's arms.*

I sipped my cooled coffee and thought about Emma's plight. As a kid, I
had visited Old Bert's family plot in the Cedar Grove Cemetery, just a block
from our house on the south side of town. My friends and I liked to pick
wildflowers, and lay them on his gravestone. I had told them he was my
grandfather. Through all the years I had played and hung out in the cemetery, I never remembered seeing the graves of any other Hopper family. I

made another mental note to talk to Moni to see if she could help me locate Emma's family plot. I was very curious as to whether a slave woman named Elsie was also buried there.

I kept reading as Mom watched television.

10 mo. 15th, Tuesday evening, 1850

As I suspected, Gabe is torn with grief over Luke's death. He said the Lord has forsaken us. I pray 'tis not true! Our grandsons, Brian and Bernard, helped me hitch the carriage, and we went to town to visit Gabe in jail. Father insists Edward Allen shot Luke in a blind rage. I am shocked! Edward is just a boy! What would have compelled him to commit such an evil act? Apparently Enos Adams, our farm hand, shot Edward in the leg to stop him from committing more carnage. Oh, Dear Lord! What has this world come to, where neighbor is shooting neighbor? How could Thee let this evil loose in our town? What have we done to bring such unholy wrath upon us?

Wow! It sounded like all hell broke loose during the posse attack. No wonder Gabe was mad and thought the Lord had forsaken them. Now his son was dead, and he was in jail. What a terrible predicament!

When I whispered to Gabe that Miss Elsie was drowned, he wept in his cell. But he was encouraged to hear Samuel and Jonah were delivered to the canal safely by Friend Paree. Father told Brian and Bernard they must be men now, and double their work on the farm until he is released, and Adam arrives home. I was proud of our boys, who at eight years old, stood tall and agreed to their grandfather's orders.

Emma had a lot of faith in her young grandsons, that they would be able to take over the men's farm chores. It must have been really tough on them.

While we were visiting, Friend Zenas arrived at the sheriff's office. He graciously offered to post Father's bail, to my great chagrin. How will we repay his kindness? But Friend Zenas said it was his honor to release Gabe from jail. I am forever thankful for his goodness and generosity.
Now at home, Father and I must make arrangements to bury our dear Luke and Miss Elsie. Our hearts are leaden with such onerous tasks.

Thank goodness for Emma that Zenas bailed Gabe out of jail. His act of kindness must have taken a big load off her shoulders, along with Paree paying for Miss Elsie's burial expenses. But they still had the heartbreaking task of arranging two funerals.

I sipped my coffee and continued reading Emma's next entry, dated several days later.

10 mo. 19th, Saturday evening, 1850

Has been a heart-rending and difficult week as we have buried our first son, Luke, and freedom-seeker, Miss Elsie Prescott, in our family plot. I am highly offended our pious Methodist church members objected to Miss Elsie being buried in the white people's cemetery. The hypocrisy of those who opposed her internment baffles me. With the help of our dear Friend, Paree, we were able to convince the minister Miss Elsie deserved nothing less than a proper Christian burial, since she was a devout follower of Our Lord and Savior, Jesus Christ. I am thankful for Paree's persistence, and grateful Minister Sheldon finally agreed to our request.

Luke and Elsie now travel side-by-side as they continue their journey in the afterlife to the Promised Land, to reside at the Lord's right hand. May their spirits forever shine their guiding light upon us mortals until we can join them in heaven.

"I love it when a plan comes together!"

The deep, male voice booming from the television yanked me back into the present century. Mom was watching her favorite show, *The A Team*, and Mr. T, clad in his trademark gold chains, had it all figured out. If only real life were so simple, then and now. I took a deep breath as I thought about all the anguish Emma and Gabe had endured. It's no wonder Gabe questioned his faith after such terrible events had befallen their lives.

I glanced over at Mom. She was intently watching Mr. T and his A Team chase the bad guys.

I continued reading Emma's next diary entry, dated almost two weeks later:

11 mo. 1st, Friday afternoon, 1850

What a terrible day it has been! Sheriff Wardwell arrived at our doorstep before dawn to inform us our dear neighbor and Friend, Paree

*Guildersleeve, has been murdered along with one of her beautiful dogs!
Oh! The tragedy of it all! When will it end?*

*My heart grieves at such horrendous death and destruction brought
upon our town, because of those evil slave hunters!*

*Lord! Why has Thee allowed such vengeful wrath upon this wonderful
woman? I shall never forget her help when we stood our ground against
the townsfolk who opposed Miss Elsie being buried in our family plot.
May Paree and her beloved dog, Hilde, find peace in Thy Eternal
Kingdom. And please, dear Lord, stop the killing! So many good people
have passed from our lives, whose only mission was to do Thy will. My
heart cannot break any further!*

"Oh, no! How horrible!" I shook my head at all she had endured.

"What is it, Dear?" Mom asked.

I hadn't realized I had spoken aloud. I closed Emma's journal and stared
at the action on the television, not really seeing it. My mind raced at all the
carnage that had taken place in this sleepy little farm town over a century
ago—good people like Gabe and Emma having their lives turned upside
down, just for helping their fellow human beings to have a chance at freedom. My stomach soured as the brandy fought its way back up. I swallowed
hard, holding back tears, then turned to Mom, who was starting to doze
in her chair.

"It's a really sad story, Mom, with a tragic ending. Maybe I'll save it for
another day." I sighed, reached across to her wingback chair, and squeezed
her hand.

CEMETERY SEARCH

The following morning, Tuesday, Randy and his crew arrived around eight-
thirty. When I saw them in the backyard, I told Mom to stay inside, as the
weather was overcast and drizzly. I didn't want her catching a cold. I threw
on my boots and a raincoat and went out to meet them.

I approached Randy, who was dressed in hunting garb. His tall, bulky
frame was clad in green/brown camouflage, complete with a cap with the
flaps pulled over his ears.

"Hey Randy. How's it looking in there?" I nodded toward the barn. Two
of his helpers were pushing the irritably squealing sliding doors open.

He rubbed his bearded chin. "Took a good haul to the dump yesterday. I'm thinking we should be able to get most of the rest of the junk out today." He looked toward the barn, pondering. "You're probably gonna have a hefty dump bill when it's all said and done—just lettin' ya know."

I nodded. "Yeah, I figured that. Just give me your bill when you're finished up. If you find anything you think I might be interested in, Robbie's in the house, so bring it in to her. I need to take a trip into town in a little bit."

Randy proudly saluted. "Yes, Ma'am!" He chuckled as he entered the barn behind his helpers.

Back in the kitchen, Mom was washing up our few breakfast dishes. I put my arm around her hunched shoulders. "Mom, I told Randy if he found anything of interest, to bring it in to you. I want you to stay inside because the weather's getting nasty."

She turned to look up at me. "Are you going somewhere?"

"Yes. I'm going to town to see Moni and Jack. I want Moni to help me research something."

Mom smiled at me. "Okay, Dear. Drive carefully."

Gathering the Hopper Bible, ledger, and five volumes of Emma's journal, I placed them in a plastic bag so they wouldn't get wet. I kissed Mom on the cheek, then went into the yard to find Randy.

Waiting until he dropped an armload of old wood into the bed of his truck, I asked, "Randy, would you do me a favor? I'm going to meet Moni and I wanted to get this to her." I pointed at the trunk containing the two sets of boys' clothing, sitting next to the table. "Would you mind carrying this to the car for me?"

"Nope. No problem." He lifted the heavy, black metal trunk as if it were empty.

Ahhh, to be a strong, burly man, I thought, envying his strength. I opened the back door of my rental car so Randy could slide the trunk onto the seat.

"Thanks, Randy. I really appreciate your help."

He saluted again and sauntered around the back of the house toward the barn.

Then I drove into town and parked in front of the three-story, red-brick building on the north side of the park. What had been the town high school now housed the fire department and municipal offices on the ground floor.

The historical society and museum were on the second floor. As far as I knew, the third floor was used for storage.

Grabbing the plastic bag, I scurried through the rain, which was coming down heavier now, and pushed through the front door. At the top the first set of stairs, I turned left at the center hallway and went into Monique's office. She was bent over her desk, reading something through a magnifying glass.

Moni turned her head and smiled at hearing my footsteps. "Hey, Dee! What's up?" Laying the glass down, she waved me to her desk. "Have a seat." She pointed to the wooden armchair next to her desk.

I handed her the plastic bag. "I've brought the books we discovered yesterday, and I wanted to ask a favor."

Moni peered into the bag, then looked at me. "Sure, Dee. What can I do for you?"

"Well, I read through most of Emma's diaries last night. I was wondering if you could make copies of her entries dated in the eighteen-fifties. There's probably about twenty pages or so."

Moni nodded. "Of course. Anything else?"

"Yeah, actually. I'd like a copy of the last page of the ledger and the family tree at the end of the Bible, if it's not too much trouble. It's a fascinating family history, and I'd like to keep some of it for my records."

"That's no problem. I understand. I'll drop them by the house tomorrow."

"Thanks, Moni. Oh, I almost forgot. I brought the trunk of boys' clothing for you. Can you get someone to get it out of my car and bring it up?"

"Sure. When Jack's done in the war room, I'll have him get it." She paused and looked at me. "There's something on your mind. What is it?"

I laughed, not realizing I was frowning. "Do you happen to know when Cedar Grove Cemetery was first put into use?"

She wrinkled her nose. "Not off the top of my head. Why?"

"When I was reading Emma's diary, she mentioned a Hopper family plot. I know Old Bert is buried in Cedar Grove, but don't remember ever seeing any other Hopper stones. I wondered where Emma and Gabe might be buried." And I also wanted to see if Miss Elsie was buried nearby.

Moni donned a pair of white cotton gloves she pulled from a desk drawer and rose. "Follow me."

I walked behind her down the central aisle, with converted classrooms on each side. I noticed Jack, head bent, in the room dedicated to local wars, inspecting an object. I followed Moni into the last room on the left. Floor-to-ceiling shelves lined three walls where hundreds of books of varying sizes were neatly stacked. Rectangular tables with folding chairs sat in the middle of the makeshift library.

Moni crouched to view the spines of tall, leather-bound ledgers on the bottom of one stack. After a few seconds, she pulled one out and hefted it to the closest table. I joined her and raised an eyebrow.

Showing me the cover, Moni said, "These are the earliest records of Cedar Grove Cemetery. Let's take a look." She opened the heavy front cover and blank first page. Affixed to the second page was a document written in block printing. I started reading:

"At the annual meeting in March, 1870, a new committee, consisting of Thomas E. Wakefield, Edward L. Allen and John J. Williams, was chosen to look up and purchase a site for a new cemetery."

A chill ran through me. "Edward Allen?" I gasped. "Oh, my God, Moni! According to Gabe, that's who shot Luke!"

Moni gave me a confused look. "What are you talking about? Is this something you read in Emma's diary?"

"Yes! Emma said they were transporting the Prescott family to Whitehall, and their wagon was attacked by slave catchers. Her son Luke was killed, and Gabe was arrested. When she went to see Gabe in jail, he told her Edward Allen had gone mad and shot Luke. She said Gabe was furious. I can only imagine!"

Moni put her hand to her mouth. "Oh, my! How tragic! It probably explains why the Hoppers didn't continue to help fugitives after the attack."

I nodded. "Yeah, that's what I thought, too." I looked back at the parchment. "You know, if Edward was on the cemetery committee twenty years later, he must not have been convicted! And even if he was, it doesn't look like he served a very long sentence." My hands trembled as I wiped my brow. "Gosh, I wonder if Gabe and Emma ever got justice for Luke's killing."

I finished reading the rest of the document:

"This committee purchased, on the 8th of June, of the administrators of Israel Davey's estate, 22 acres of land lying on the south side of Davey Street, along the margin of the cedar swamp, paying $3,253.50 for the same.

The question of accepting a legacy of $1000 from Mrs. Hannah H. Dyer, deceased, for the adornment of the cemeteries of the town was presented to the annual meeting in March, 1870, and a committee, consisting of Colonel Alonson Allen, Joseph Adams, Samuel W. Bailey and Zenas H. Ellis was chosen to examine and report at an adjourned meeting what action it was advisable for the town to take. The committee reported, May 10th, recommending the acceptance of the bequest, and a vote of thankful acknowledgement for the same—and the legacy was accepted."

I looked over to Moni. "Was Zenas H. Ellis related to Zenas C. Ellis, the Hoppers' neighbor?"

She replied, "Yes. Zenas H. was the oldest son, and Barnaby the second oldest. If I remember my history correctly, Barnaby married and moved to Philadelphia. The Ellis family continued to harbor and transport fugitives, with Barnaby sending the travelers north to Vermont, throughout the Civil War."

I wondered how Gabe and Emma had felt about their neighbor continuing to work for the cause, after the Hopper family had suffered such tragedy and discontinued their involvement.

"And what about Edward Allen and Colonel Alonson Allen? Were they related?"

Moni smiled. "You have a good eye, Dee. Yes, Edward was the colonel's son. Colonel Allen and Joseph Adams were the leaders of the Vermont Temperance Society. So they were actively involved in the abolitionist movement. But what you said about Edward shooting Luke doesn't make sense." She pushed stray curls away from her face. "If the Allens were part of the Underground Railroad, why on earth would Edward shoot Luke?"

I nodded. "Yeah, good question. That's what I'd like to know, too. Is there a way we could find out?"

Moni glanced around at the bookshelves lining the room. "There might be some old records from the constable's office that could shed some light on it. If there was a trial, the courtroom documents may be in the archives." She pointed to a shelf along the front side of the room. "I'll have to do some digging, and let you know what I find."

"Thanks, Moni. I appreciate it." I returned my attention to the Cedar Grove Cemetery ledger. "Okay. So the original Hopper family plot wouldn't be here, because the cemetery didn't exist until eighteen-seventy. So where would they have been buried in eighteen-fifty?"

"The only cemetery in town then was West Street Cemetery." Moni closed and hefted the heavy journal, then replaced it on the bottom row.

Moving several steps to her left, she retrieved a second tall, leather-bound ledger. It made a thud as she laid it in on the table.

Moni pointed to the writing on the spine. "This is the first West Street Cemetery Ledger. It begins in seventeen sixty-five and goes through the late eighteen hundreds." Moni opened to the middle of the volume. Bending close to the book, she read the slanted script of names and dates. After flipping through several pages, she stopped and pointed. "Here we go." She read: "*Gabriel A. Hopper family plot. Eighteen thirty-two. Price: Eighty dollars. I N T: eight. Buried: Ruth Ann Hopper, eighteen thirty two. Aged five.*"

I remembered the girl's bloodstained dress we had found in a trunk. "It's so sad they lost their daughter at such a young age. Emma must have been heartbroken." I squinted at the ledger line and turned to Moni. "What does *I N T: eight* mean?"

"It indicates they had a plot big enough to intern eight family members. The price was based upon ten dollars per person. A pretty typical family plot size back in the day." Moni pulled a piece of scratch paper from a pile in the middle of the table and jotted down some numbers from the ledger line. "This is the plot location. Let's go take a look."

Moni returned the ledger to the bottom shelf, and I followed her partway down the hallway, where she stopped at the entrance to the war room. Jack sat at a table covered with artifacts. Wearing a magnifying eyepiece, he was inspecting a small revolver.

"Jack!" Moni raised her voice to get his attention.

Jack turned toward us and waved. "Hey, Dee! Didn't hear you come in."

Moni responded, "Dee brought the trunk of boys' clothes from the house. Can you get someone to help you bring it up from her car? We're taking a drive over to West Street Cemetery. We'll be back soon."

Jack nodded. "Yeah, sure. I'll get one of the guys downstairs to help me." He waved and went back to his task at hand.

Moni grabbed her jacket and purse from a hook in her office, and we headed down the stairs. Outside, the rain had let up, but heavy mist hung over us. We climbed into Moni's SUV and drove along West Street, away from the park.

I turned to Moni. "I wanted to ask you something. Emma mentioned a new slave law that went into effect in eighteen-fifty. Do you know what that was?"

She nodded. "Oh, sure. That was the Federal Fugitive Slave Act. I think it was passed around September of that year."

"So that was about a month before the Prescotts arrived at the Hopper farm. What did the law do?"

Moni sighed. "It offered a bounty to catch escaped slaves. But unfortunately, there was no distinction between free blacks and fugitives. Any blacks caught were arrested, and they had no recourse to a trial to prove their identity."

"Oh, my gosh, how unfair! How in the world could our government pass such a law?"

"I know. It was horrible. And get this: anyone who refused to help an official arrest an alleged runaway could be fined up to a thousand dollars!"

"Holy cow! That was a lot of money back then." I thought about Emma being worried about Gabe and Luke being armed as they transported the Prescotts. "That must have been what prompted the posse to attack the Hopper wagon. No wonder Emma was concerned."

Moni nodded. "Yeah, until eighteen-fifty, Northerners moved black fugitives in the open on their trek to Canada. Southern masters usually didn't bother to send trackers north to retrieve their property." She pulled the car off the road and parked in front of the closed cemetery gate. Turning off the engine, Moni continued. "But the Fugitive Slave Act suddenly turned the law-abiding abolitionists into criminals, causing major turmoil in their ranks. It was a terribly unjust law."

"Okay. That explains why Gabe was arrested for transporting them," I lamented. "It sounds like the bounty may have also turned neighbor against neighbor. How tragic."

She plopped the keys into her purse. "Yeah, it was a very dark time in this country's history."

Moni exited the vehicle, and I followed her through the pedestrian entrance. Dirt roads crisscrossing the cemetery were marked with letter posts, while rows of graves were marked with number posts. The grave plots were neatly mowed, but many of the unkempt stones had weeds growing around them. I followed Moni down the center drive as she searched for the grave coordinates she had written down. A gust of wind sighed through the trees, and I tightened my collar.

About a quarter of the way from the gate, Moni stopped and pointed. "There's the Hopper family plot," she said.

I saw an eight-foot-high, four-sided gray granite obelisk with the name HOPPER engraved in the center. The outer edges of the plot were marked with low granite posts. We walked to the headstones and inspected the names of the interred. The first, small stone, with an eroded angel engraved on the top, was Ruth's. Next to Ruth was Luke. A tingle ran through me as I looked upon his grave, knowing how he had died. To the right of Luke were Gabe and Emma's stones. Behind the obelisk I saw headstones for Emma's twin grandsons, Brian and Bernard. Next to them, and directly opposite Luke, was the marker for his wife, Mary. Doing a quick calculation, I noted Mary had lived into her seventies.

I remembered Emma mentioning in her diary Mary was pregnant with their son, George, when Luke was killed. Having experienced firsthand the difficulty of being raised by a single mother, I could only imagine the challenges she had faced raising her children without their father. And she must have been utterly despondent to lose her twin sons at such a young age, in the Civil War. I couldn't help but admire her strength.

The Hopper women had great fortitude and courage to endure such a life of grief and hardship.

Moni stood beside me. "So what do you think? Is this what you were looking for?"

I scanned the plot, looking for one more grave. "Yes, more or less. Just give me a minute." I turned to my right and stood at the corner marker, looking toward the road. I noticed a slightly raised headstone positioned a bit away from the family members, splitting the boundary of the plot. Reaching the front of the stone, I saw the inscription was faint and weathered. I crouched and used my sleeve to wipe away some of the grime. I squinted at the etching, which slowly became legible.

Miss Elsie Prescott, d. 1850.

She found freedom in her Lord's arms

I gasped. "Moni! Come look at this!"

Moni peered at the stone. "Elsie Prescott? She was one of the names listed on the last page of the ledger, wasn't she?"

"Yes! She was the grandmother. According to Emma, Elsie drowned when their wagon was attacked. Some lady named Paree found Elsie's body and paid for her funeral expenses." My hand was shaking as I recalled the story. "Apparently the townsfolk had an issue with burying a slave in the Christian cemetery, even within the Hopper family plot."

Moni crouched next to me and laid her hand on the small, elevated gravestone. "I'm not completely surprised to hear that. For all the good the abolitionists did, there was an undercurrent of prejudice throughout

New England. Most folks didn't mind helping the travelers move along their way, but often objected to having blacks as neighbors or members of their church communities." She shook her head. "It was a terrible double-standard."

I stood, and my knees creaked. "Well, I'm glad Paree helped Emma stand her ground, and Miss Elsie got a proper Christian burial. The really sad thing is, Emma said Paree was murdered for her involvement in helping the two boys escape to Whitehall."

Moni rose to her feet and hugged her arms to her chest. "Oh, that's horrible! Paree sounds like she was a good woman. I wonder if she's buried here, too. Do you happen to know her last name?"

I thought about it for a minute. "Sorry, not sure. I think Emma may have mentioned it in her diary, but I don't remember. Guess it's something we can research another time."

Moni pulled a steno notebook from her purse. "If you don't mind, Dee, I'm going to document the names and dates on the Hopper stones. I want to make sure they coincide with our records."

"Sure, go ahead," I said. "I'll just have a look around."

Having been enamored with cemeteries since I was a kid, and the stories brought forth from the epitaphs, I wandered around the graves behind the Hopper plot. About thirty yards away, my eyes rested on a square, elevated black granite stone, partially encrusted with lichen. The back of the stone bulged from the rough-hewn section of original rock. The name *Hopper* jumped out at me. I popped off the lichen growth with my fingernail and saw the name *Adam*. A chill ran through me. The death date of 1897 seemed to jibe with what I remembered from the Hopper lineage in the family Bible. *Oh, my God! I'll bet this is Emma's son, Adam!* Being obsessed with learning more about Luke's demise, I had forgotten about Adam. *But why is he buried way out here, and not in the family plot?* I thought that was very strange, as there would have been room for one more internment.

Dropping to my knees in front of the headstone, I felt the soggy ground immediately wet my jeans. Squinting, I could see there was an epitaph scrawled along the bottom. Bending closer and scraping the lichen with my thumbnail as I went, I finally deciphered the two-line inscription: *'Tis no sin in God's eyes to love another human being through eternity.*

Wow! That's pretty heavy. Why would Adam have thought it a sin to love another person? And why such a powerful statement on his headstone? Laying my palm against the polished stone front, the cool wetness seeped into my fingertips and chilled me to the bone.

"Hi, Adam. I'm DeeDee," I whispered. "It's nice to meet you." A wind gust swirled my hair. I looked toward the general location of the Hopper family plot, then back at Adam's stone. "What are you doing out here, so far away from the rest of your family?"

No answer.

Grimacing from the dampness sinking into my arthritic knees, I got to my feet and walked a few steps to my left. A family plot of Murphys contained several generations. Then I went to the right of Adam's plot, and saw a single grave directly adjacent. It was a square, elevated, black granite headstone, and the original rock bulged out the back. The name on the grave was Thomas Rogers, with his death date of 1900. Below the name was a two-line inscription, close to ground level. Kneeling again, I moved the weeds aside and scraped away the growth. Just as I finished deciphering the epitaph, a tap on my shoulder made me yelp. I collapsed onto my butt in front of Thomas' grave. The wet grass immediately soaked through my jeans.

Moni chuckled. "Sorry, Dee! Didn't mean to scare you. What are you looking at?"

A shot of electricity ran through my body. I wasn't exactly sure how to articulate what I was thinking. I looked up at Moni. "Do you remember the Hopper lineage in the family Bible?"

Moni nodded. "Yeah, sure."

I continued, "Gabe and Emma had three children. Ruth and Luke are in the family plot. But what happened to Adam?"

Moni shrugged. "Don't know. Moved away, maybe?"

I struggled to my feet and took a few steps to my left. I pointed at the stone. "Nope, here's Adam right here!" Nodding to Moni I said, "Read the epitaph."

She knelt and slowly read the engraved script, then peered up at me with a questioning look.

I walked back to Thomas' stone and pointed. "Now read his."

Moni obliged. Bending in front of the second, almost identical stone, she silently read the inscription. She gasped, covering her mouth with her hands. Moni stood and stared at me.

"It says: *'Tis no sin in God's eyes to love another human being through eternity.*"

My heart raced. "Moni, they're identical! I bet they planned this together to have the same epitaph. I think they were gay. Why else would they be buried so far away from the Hopper family plot?" My thoughts raced. "And the reference to the fact it isn't a sin in God's eyes to love another human being. That's really powerful, especially back then!"

Moni's eyes went wide. "Wow, Dee! I think you may be right. Homosexuality was certainly forbidden by the churches as being an abomination of God's law. They probably had to keep their relationship secret." She glanced back toward the Hopper obelisk. "It could be Adam may have decided to get a separate plot for himself and Thomas, to not embarrass his family."

"Or it could be they were discovered and banished from the family," I lamented. "How very sad for everyone—through eternity!"

My heart again reached out to dear, sweet Emma, wanting to give her a hug. I imagined she had prayed and anguished over Adam's well-being, just as she had with Luke's.

THE BARN

Driving home from my meeting with Moni, I kept thinking about Emma and her family. They had suffered such heartache and tragedy as they followed their faith and convictions to help slaves escape cruel bondage. And if Adam and Thomas were gay, how would they have been treated back then? Would they have been ostracized in their own community? Or did they hide their secret from society? I thought Emma would have turned a blind eye to any criticism, loving and supporting her son Adam, no matter what. I would have cherished having Emma as a friend.

By the next day, Wednesday, the rains had passed, and Randy and his crew finished mucking out the rest of the debris in the barn. After his last trip to the dump, Randy returned alone and gave me his bill, including dump fees, for three hundred and seventy-five dollars. I wrote him a check, then hugged his broad chest and thanked him for his help.

Randy blushed at my affection. "Gosh, Dee! It was the least I could do. Robbie's always been real good to me and my family. She's a real keeper." He swept his arm toward the house. "You take good care of her, now. You hear me?"

I felt a lump in my throat realizing Mom was so well-loved in town. I hated the task I had in front of me of moving her out of what she called "the only home I've ever known."

"I will, I promise!" I called to Randy as he waved, jumped into his truck, and drove off.

I took a deep breath and braced myself for the next phase of our move: burning down the old barn.

Back in the house, I called Dave Granger, who owned a slate mill, asking if he could remove the barn roof slates. Dave was Vince Granger's cousin. Vince and his wife, Lynn, looked after Mom daily.

"Sure, Dee," Dave said over the phone. "You know I would do anything to help Robbie. She's one great lady!"

I smiled at his enthusiasm. "We appreciate your help. So when do you think you could come by, and how long does it take to remove barn slates?"

"Let's see," Dave paused. "Looks like I can get my crew over there tomorrow, if that works for you. And it usually takes us pretty much the whole day to remove the slates. It'll depend upon what shape they are in."

"Wow! That'd be great," I said, thinking of my diminishing time line to be in Vermont.

"Okay. Then we'll see you tomorrow morning. Bye, Dee," Dave said, hanging up.

I spent the rest of the afternoon clearing the backyard of the makeshift office we had set up. The two trunks of assorted clothing were still on the lawn, and I dragged them into the house. I made a mental note to contact Moni to see if she wanted them for the museum.

Thursday morning, Dave Granger and his crew arrived with two crane trucks to remove the slate roof tiles. One crane hoisted two workers onto the barn roof. The second crane positioned two large wooden boxes next to the men on the roof. Each box was partitioned by wooden slots to hold the slate tiles and roof caps.

Hours later, when the workers were done, I noticed the wooden roof underlayment looked naked, raw, and exposed without its protective covering. It made me sad.

As I stared forlornly at the rain-blotched roof, I felt a presence by my side. I glanced up at Dave's angular, clean-shaven face. Now middle-aged, his tall, lanky form still reflected his younger days as a local basketball star.

Dave touched my arm. "You know, Dee. It never ceases to amaze me how well slate survives over the centuries." He followed my gaze to the roof. "It looks like we'll be able to salvage about seventy percent of these tiles, and re-use them for other purposes." He swept his hand toward the heavily laden boxes on the truck. "The broken ones will be crushed and used for stepping stones or decorative fill."

"That's great," I said. My voice wavered as I held back tears. "It's nice to know they won't just be going into a landfill."

"Oh, no! These weathered slates are in high demand. We'll be able to sell them quickly to our customers," Dave said as he went to the cab of his truck.

A few minutes later, he handed me a check for four hundred dollars for the slates, which I thought was a good price. I figured he'd probably more than double his money on their resale. At least this money covered my expenses for Randy and his team cleaning out the barn. With that step done, it was now time to burn down the barn.

The following day, Friday, Frank Rizzolo, our insurance agent and the volunteer fire chief, arrived with several of his firefighters to prep the barn. Because of its slant to the right, and being less than ten feet from our neighbor Howard's barn, the men propped two-by-fours against the side as a precautionary measure. Red X's were painted on the floor in multiple places indicating where kerosene-soaked rags would be placed. The sliding barn doors and rails, hayloft doors, and outhouse door were removed. The trapdoor to the underground room was nailed shut, so the barn could burn at an even rate without the flames rushing into the cavern, causing the barn to collapse prematurely.

Once the barn was prepped, Frank came into the kitchen and sat at the table to talk to Mom and me.

"Okay, we're ready to go," he told us. "We'll be here tomorrow around four in the afternoon to get things going. It's better to do this in the evening hours, as the winds are usually calmest then." Frank glanced at the barn through the kitchen window. "DeeDee, because you're the property owner, legally you have to start the fire. We'll be videotaping you for insurance purposes."

I must have blanched at the thought, and Frank read my expression.

"Don't worry, it won't be dangerous," he continued. "We'll place a metal bucket in the middle of the barn full of newspapers. We'll give you a lighted torch, and here's what we want you to say." Frank handed me a typed piece of paper.

I read the statement, which was pretty straightforward. "Okay, that seems simple enough."

"Once you've lit the newspapers, we'll take the torch from you and you can leave the barn. One of my boys will then start in the loft and light the rags one by one, working his way out the front," Frank explained. "Then it's just a matter of managing the burn as it progresses and hope it falls the way we want it to go."

"Sounds scary. I hope your guys know what they're doing," I said. *And you don't burn down Howard's barn in the process!*

Frank leaned back in his chair and laughed. I noticed his ample belly protruding against his buttoned shirt. "They've done this before, so you have nothing to worry about." Then he rubbed his chin. "Oh, and by the way, you should notify your neighbors today of what we've got planned. We don't want a bunch of calls coming into the firehouse reporting the fire. The more folks who know about it in advance, the easier it will be on our dispatchers, because calls *will* come in."

"Oh, I never thought about that. I'll go contact the neighbors as soon as you leave. Might as well invite a few folks over and have a little barn-burning party while we're at it," I suggested, looking at Mom.

"Well, if you're going to do that, Dee, make sure no one blocks the driveway for our trucks, and you all stay a good distance away," Frank warned. "That old barn will be putting out a lot of heat!"

"Yeah, sure. I'll let everyone know," I promised.

Frank and his team left Mom and me sitting at the kitchen table. We looked out at the skeleton of the old barn that had stood proudly across two centuries. She had endured all the hardships the Vermont weather could throw at her, and had harbored hundreds of fugitives along the way. She was now going to take her final bow. I couldn't help but think about all the stories that "old girl" could tell about the families who had passed through her squeaky doors. It broke my heart to be the one responsible for her destruction. I looked at Mom and saw her chin tremble. A pained expression spread across her face. I figured she was thinking the same thing.

I grasped her shaking hand. "Well, Mom. Are you ready to have a barn-burning tomorrow?" I asked, trying to lighten our moods.

She nodded. "Yes, Dear, I guess so. But I'm sorry to see it go." Her husky voice cracked as she fought back tears.

"Yeah, me too, Mom. It makes me very sad," I said, wiping my eyes. "Let's invite some folks over and make a little party out of it. It'll make us feel better. I'll go to the store and get some drinks and snacks."

Mom smiled wanly, and shook her head. "I have a better idea," she glanced around her tiny kitchen. "Why don't I make a pan of lasagna? And we can serve salad, so folks can have something decent to eat."

"Sure. If you feel up for making it, I'll go get what we need." Even though Mom was a great cook, on the other hand, I really hated to cook. I'm thankful my husband, Mark, loves the kitchen. Otherwise, left to my own devices, I'd be the proverbial "junk-food junkie."

"Yes, that would be fine, Dear." Mom stood and pulled a deep-dish pan from the cupboard.

I spent the next hour or so walking around the neighborhood informing our neighbors of the barn-burning, and inviting a few over for refreshments. Then I drove to the Grand Union market on the other side of town to get lasagna ingredients, salad, bread, beer, wine, sodas, and other munchies for the gathering. Mom and I spent the rest of the afternoon making lasagna, tantalized by the smell of it cooking. Fortunately, we also made a small pan for us, which we devoured straight out of the oven.

Burn day! A clear, brisk October Saturday. The sugar maples swayed gently, ablaze in their crimson cloaks, paying homage to the changing of the season. Perfect.

Mom's good friends, Lynn and Vince Granger, and their three children, came by early to help us set up. We placed folding tables and chairs near the big garden patch along the south side of the house. I figured we would be far enough away from the barn but still have a good view. We finished setting out picnic ware, a big pan of reheated lasagna, salad, garlic bread, and a cooler with drinks. Shortly thereafter neighbors began to arrive carrying lawn chairs. It was a festive atmosphere and the beer and wine flowed freely.

While I was chatting, I noticed our elderly next-door neighbor, Howard Greene, hosing down the roof of his barn, built just ten feet to the right of ours. I guessed Howard, being a hardheaded Vermonter, didn't place much trust in our volunteer fire brigade. Never having been involved in a barn-burning before, I believed Chief Frank and his crew knew what they were doing.

Folks helped themselves to dinner as the sun sank behind the trees. They settled in to watch the main event as the firetrucks arrived. Once the engines, firemen, and hoses were in place, it was "game time." I saw Frank waving me over to the barn, and I walked slowly to join him. I knew what was coming, and I was nervous with all the neighbors watching.

Frank touched my arm. "Are you ready for your command performance?" He laughed jovially.

I pulled the script from my pocket and showed it to him. "I guess so. Let's get this over with!"

We walked to the center of the darkening barn. I was surprised at how big it looked with all the debris removed. I couldn't help but glance over to the nailed-shut trapdoor. Thoughts of Emma and Gabe, and the Prescott family, swirled through my mind. What would they think of us burning down their sanctuary? I hoped they wouldn't haunt me to hell and back!

Frank positioned me in front of a metal bucket full of newspapers. I watched the cameraman fiddle with some settings. Suddenly, bright lights blinded me, and I heard the cameraman say, "Go!"

My heart thumped, and I cleared my throat. My voice cracked a bit as I began. "My name is DeeDee Williams. I am the owner of the property at One-Seventy-Nine South Main Street in Fair Haven, Vermont." I paused to read the paper rattling in my hand. "I am willingly starting this fire to burn down my barn as a training exercise for the Fair Haven Volunteer Fire Department. Today's date is October sixteenth, nineteen ninety-nine." My legs shook as I finished the script.

Then Chief Frank handed me a flaming torch and my hand dropped. I wasn't expecting it to be so heavy. Gaining control of the torch, I stepped forward and touched the flame into the bucket. The lighter fluid-soaked newspapers ignited with a whump, causing me to yelp and jump back. I was embarrassed the cameraman was still tracking my movements. The papers flared, then died down in the bucket, and the camera lights went out.

"You okay, DeeDee?" Frank looked concerned as he retrieved the torch from me and passed it to a waiting fireman.

I nodded, unable to speak, shaking.

Frank touched my arm. "You did fine. Good job. Now you are officially burning your barn down!"

The thought made me cringe as I watched the fireman slowly climb the loft stairs, torch held high.

Frank pointed toward the yard. "Go keep an eye on Robbie now, and make sure no one gets too close," he directed.

I walked quickly out of the barn to join Mom and the neighbors by the garden, already watching the event.

Within minutes, smoke started to drift out of the front hayloft window. Moments later, the torch-man rushed from the barn, smoke trailing him, as he took his station at one of the hoses. Black, acrid smoke billowed from the barn openings for some time. Suddenly, with a loud whoosh, huge flames shot through the roof, blazing into the early evening sky. A cheer rose from our audience.

My heart pounded as I watched the orange-yellow flames snake across the naked roof, denuded of its slate tiles. I took a couple of gulps of wine to calm my nerves. My stomach was in knots watching the conflagration. *Please don't let anything go wrong!*

Firemen, some still inside the burning barn, aimed water at the right wall, forcing it to burn away from Howard's barn. The darkening sky reflected the rosy glow of the leaping flames.

"You see, Mom," I pointed to the flame-engorged barn roof, while putting a protective arm around her shoulders. "Any minute now, it'll start falling to the left."

Then the roof joists screeched. Although flames engulfed the entire roof and left wall, the structure began to shudder. The scream of heat-deformed joists tearing loose intensified. To my horror, the barn jolted and jerked, shifting to the right, not the left!

Nearby a fireman cried, "Frank! The roof—" The rest of his words were drowned out by the thunder of rending timbers. The men inside scrambled out of the opening, and aimed their hoses on the conflagration.

"Oh, God!" I exclaimed softly. I heard Mom gasp, putting a hand to her mouth.

Despite the elaborate precautions and planning, the barn slowly slumped to its right, joists and wall studs cracking with explosive force. Then the right wall and roof began to violently separate.

Our neighbor, Howard, his face apoplectic, frantically hosed down his barn. Shaking his fists at the firefighters, he screamed, "Ga'damn! You sonsabitches!"

Suddenly, the flaming right wall, along with the supporting two-by-fours, careened into Howard's barn. Glass shattered as his barn side window exploded from the impact. The firemen scrambled to get their hoses on the collapsed wall and Howard's barn, which was starting to smolder.

Even though I was horror-struck at the calamity unfolding, I figured that "old girl" was doing it her way—defiant to the very end!

Lynn's husband, Vince, who was sitting beside me, jumped up, catching me by surprise. "Oh, shit! That wasn't supposed to happen!" he yelled as he dropped his beer, and rushed over to help Howard.

Chief Frank, who stood in the middle of the melee directing the firemen like General Patton, shouted at Vince, while pointing at Howard. "Get'im outta the way!"

Vince grabbed Howard by both arms, and tried to pull him back from his barn. Howard resisted, still screaming, trying to keep his hose on the barn. Struggling with Vince, Howard's hose went wild, and he sprayed two firemen, forcing them to jump out of the way. Vince, being younger and stronger, wrestled Howard to the ground and yanked the hose from his hands. He pulled Howard to a safer spot and held him down, while Howard tried to break his grip.

"Oh, dear! Oh, dear!" Mom gasped as she squeezed my hand, watching the events unfold. I was afraid if the firemen couldn't save Howard's barn, I might have to build him a new one, which I definitely could not afford.

Two firemen grabbed axes and started chopping at the opposite edges of the flaming wall leaning against Howard's barn. A loud crack echoed across the yard as the wall buckled. The broken, burning timbers screeched as they slid down the side of Howard's barn. Two of the firefighters doused the still-standing structure, while others trained their hoses on the burning rubble on the ground next to it. Those old timbers emitted a foul, black smoke, and my nose stung from the acrid odor.

Because Howard had wet his barn down earlier, it never did catch fire— it was only braised a bit. But I could tell the dark scorch marks and broken window made Howard furious as he gestured wildly at the fire brigade. I would have to talk to Chief Frank about how we could make amends with Howard, after things calmed down.

I released Mom's hand and clenched my own, afraid I might break her bones from my nervous anxiety.

Just as I was taking a deep breath, a loud crash came from behind the barn. Someone yelled, "The outhouse just fell!" Two firemen ran to the back with a hose to manage the area.

And that "old girl" still wasn't done with those pesky firemen.

"Watch the roof!" one of the guys shouted.

The back wall section collapsed, slamming into the middle of the barn. The impact caused the rest of the attached roof to buckle forward, forcing the front wall to crash toward the firemen.

As flaming timbers rained down around them, Chief Frank leaped to the side, and the other men retreated in a mad rush behind the trucks. Those old hand-hewn timbers blazed hot and bright, and the heat was intense, even at our distance. The left wall that was supposed to fall first, still stood at an odd angle. With one last bow, it slowly nodded its head into the flames, as the "old girl" gave her final curtsy into eternity.

Now it was just a pile of burning rubble, which the firemen let burn at will. They kept a hose trained on Howard's barn, just in case anything erupted.

Vince helped Howard to his feet, brushed off the old man's clothes, put an arm around his hunched shoulders, and talked with him for a while. I watched Vince point our way, as he if was inviting Howard to come over for a beer. Howard shook his head, which was just as well. I'd have to go apologize to him tomorrow, as I felt bad for what had happened. But I was more than relieved the firemen had saved his barn.

Gus, one of our more "seasoned" neighbors hooted, "Now that's a good ga'dam'd piss-ant bahn burnin' if I evah done seen one!" He raised his beer in salute to the conflagration.

Still shaking, I chuckled along with everyone else, now that the worst had passed. I looked at Mom and saw her tears glistening. I hugged her close to me, and let her cry on my shoulder, my own tears mingling with hers. "It's okay, Mom. It's over." I rubbed her back to calm her.

Glancing to the upstairs window, I thought I saw in the glow of the firelight a stooped, shadowy figure, peering down upon the gathering. A deep chill ran through me. In the sighing of the slowly diminishing flames, I thought I could hear the whispers of the souls who had sought freedom from oppression, echo around me. Those travelers had found a safe harbor in the hidden chamber of that "old girl." And joining the chorus, I felt the indomitable spirit of Old Bert's ancestors, who had risked their own lives helping the fugitives along their way.

I imagined Gabe shed a tear as he watched the final outbuilding of his once-prosperous farm go up in flames.

A big part of our family history, and the legacy of those who had passed before us long ago, was now in ashes.

ROBBIE'S ROOM

While we were waiting for the barn rubble to cool, Moni and Jack enlisted Randy's workers to transport the heavy trunks in the upstairs bedrooms to the historical museum.

Three days after burning down the barn, Frank sent in two dump trucks to remove the debris. When they finished, a truckload of sand was dumped into what remained of the cellar hole and smoothed over to fill in the gaps. The sand pit looked strange and out of place in the backyard. I was amazed at how much our view from the kitchen window had changed now the barn was gone. We could see all the way through the backyard to the thicket of forest separating our property from the neighbors on the next block. It was quite beautiful, with the fall foliage at full color contrasting with the green pines.

Now we were at the final and toughest stage of cleaning out the house—Mom's room. I knew this was going to be very emotional for her, so I tried to go slow and tread lightly as we packed up her personal belongings.

We sorted through her closet first, deciding what to keep and what to throw out or donate. In the back of her closet I pulled out several brightly colored square-dance dresses, complete with petticoats.

Mom grinned when she saw them. "Oh, I sure did love square dancing with those handsome men swirling me around!"

After she retired from the college, Mom had joined a square-dancing group, and loved to travel around New England dancing with other "squares." I had seen her group dance twice when I was home visiting, and they were very good indeed. I felt bad Mom could no longer kick up her heels as she'd once done in her younger years. We would donate the outfits to our local clothing drive.

Then I pulled down a cardboard box from the top shelf, and set it on the bed to sort through. On the top was an aged manila envelope with Mom's maiden name on it, and the return address of Fischer Photography Studio, Boston, Massachusetts. Inside were a handful of eight-by-ten glossy photographs of two young women, finely dressed, staged in dance poses.

"Hey, Mom, who's this?" I asked, staring at the photos.

Mom blushed. "Why, that's me and my friend Shirley in our glamor photos! It was many years ago, Dear."

"That's you?" I exclaimed as I took a closer look at my mother in what looked like her early twenties. I was astounded at how beautiful she was. "So tell me about this. Who's Shirley, and why were you guys all dressed up?"

I realized I actually knew very little about my mother's life before I was born, when she was in her forties. It occurred to me Mom had lived half of her life before I was in the picture, and I had never really talked with her about it. I guess like most kids, we don't think of our parents as having separate lives before us. We just assume their lives began when they became our parents.

"Well, Dear. Shirley was my best friend, and we were dancers at the Cocoanut Grove in Boston," she recalled.

"You were a dancer? I had no idea!" For some reason, the old movies of bawdy burlesque dancers popped into my mind. "What kind of dancer were you?"

"We were called Taxi Dancers," Mom said, getting a faraway look in her eyes. "Men would pay ten cents to have one dance with us, and we got to keep half of the money. That's where I met my first husband, Joe. Oh, he was so handsome and such a marvelous dancer! We loved doing the Charleston!" A sad smile crossed her face.

It gave me a bit of a shock to picture the hard-working, domestic mother I grew up with, as a dolled-up young woman. I could picture Mom, with her long shapely legs and flaming red hair, dancing the night away to the Charleston, with dashing men at her side.

Good for her! She did have a life before she had kids.

Mom continued, "Shirley asked me to go to the studio with her to have our glamor shots made. We got all gussied up, and posed like silly school girls for the pictures. I was eighteen at the time, but I thought the pictures made me look very grown-up. I've always been proud of them." Mom blushed again.

"You should be proud of them," I said looking at the single posed shot of her. "You're beautiful."

"Thank you, Dear. But I'm afraid I'm just an old lady now."

"Mom, you'll always be beautiful to me," I replied, holding her trembling hand. Then something occurred to me. "Wait! Did you say you danced at the Cocoanut Grove? Wasn't there a bad fire there, and a bunch of people died?" I vaguely remembered the little history I had heard about the place.

Mom nodded solemnly. "The fire broke out years after I had worked there. It's something I'll never forget."

"Do you know what happened?"

She took a breath and stared at me. "Well, it was the Saturday night after Thanksgiving in nineteen forty-two. I'll never forget that date! I had worked a double shift at the diner, and I was exhausted. I had just put my feet up after taking a bath, and your Aunt Gladys called me. She was worried because your Uncle Sean's firehouse in Southie had been called into town to help fight the fire," Mom had a pained expression on her face. "I didn't want to go down there, but Gladys insisted, and I was worried about Shirley because she still worked there."

Something about Mom's tone gave me a bad feeling about her friend Shirley.

"I got dressed and took the trolley as close to the Grove as I could. The smell of smoke was terrible. When I got to the club there was a huge crowd of onlookers. I could see burned bodies crumpled on the ground." Mom grasped my hand, her arm shaking. "People were screaming and choking from the smoke. Firemen were everywhere trying to put out the fire. A bunch of people got jammed up against the revolving doors and died right there. It was the most—the most horrifying thing I've ever seen! I never really wanted to talk about it."

I was astonished that not only had she actually witnessed this incredible history, but she had never talked about it before. I hugged her to me. "Oh, Mom! I'm so sorry. What a terrible thing to have witnessed! I can see why you didn't want to talk about it. So what happened to Shirley?"

Mom straightened up then looked down at her shaking hands. "She died in the fire. I tried all night to find her, but she never made it out. I was heartbroken to lose my best friend." Mom paused and wiped her eyes.

Now I knew why she had cherished those lovely photos for all these years.

"You know, Dee, I also lost another person I loved in the fire that night, which made it even more unbearable." She sniffled.

"You don't have to tell me this if you don't want to, Mom. It's okay."

"No, no, it's time you knew, Dear," she continued. "After my Mamma and Poppa died, I worked as a nanny for a Greek couple in Boston—Maria and Kostas Tsoukanis. They had three lovely daughters. Kostas delivered rum to the Grove during Prohibition, and he was there the night of the fire. Apparently he had tried to lead a group down into the basement to escape, but the door was blocked and they couldn't get out. When Gladys told me they found his body, I was devastated. He was such a kind man with a great sense of humor. He even taught me how to dance! I'll always remember him fondly."

Now Mom was sobbing. I handed her some tissues I pulled from her dresser. "Oh, God, Mom! I'm so very sorry. I had no idea you went through this. How horrible that must have been for you."

She wiped her eyes and nodded. "The hardest part was when Maria and her daughters moved back to Greece after Kostas' funeral. It broke my heart to have to say goodbye to them, as I loved those girls dearly, and they'd all been so good to me."

I pulled her toward me and let her cry on my shoulder, as I was saddened over the heartbreaking losses Mom had endured in her life.

Mom dried her tears, lifted herself to her walker, and shuffled over to her dresser. She opened her jewelry box and pulled out something wrapped in faded beige linen. With the object in her hand, she came back to the bed and handed it to me. "Here, I want you to have this," she said.

I unwrapped the linen and saw a beautiful, ivory, cameo pendant on a filigree chain. "This is gorgeous. It's the one you're wearing in the photo, isn't it?"

"Yes, Dear. It belonged to my mother, and came from her mother in Ireland. When Mamma died, I took it out of her jewelry box, so I would have something to remember her by," she said, her voice cracking.

"Mom, I can't take this. It means so much to you. You should keep it."

She shook her head. "I don't think anything will be safe from thieves where I'm going, so I want you to have it for safekeeping. Maybe you can give it to your own daughter someday, if you have one."

"Okay, if you're sure," I said. I hugged Mom and tucked the cameo into my purse.

Returning to the bedroom, I sorted through more of the box. Then a familiar face caught my attention. I pulled out a faded political handbill. The top banner read: *The New Generation Offers a Leader.* A photograph of a young, slender man, his thick brown hair parted on the side and swept from his face, stared back at me with a pensive look. On the bottom it read: *John F. Kennedy for Congress, 11th District, 1946.*

"Mom! This is JFK! Where did you get this?" Then I noticed a faded, sprawling note next to his picture that read:

To Robena, a true Irish Lass. I need your vote! - Jack Kennedy

"And he even signed it! Mom, I bet this is worth a fortune!"

She chuckled. "Well, I guess it could be, Dear. I never really thought about it. But you know I met him once!" She grinned.

"You never told me that! Where did you meet him?" I wondered how many other secrets Mom had kept about her life.

"He and his grandfather, Honey Fitzgerald, came into our diner when Jack was campaigning for Congress. He shook my hand and asked if I was an Irish lass with my red hair," she recalled, with a fond look on her face.

"He asked my name, and I said it was Robbie. Jack shook his head and asked if it was my given name. I said no, it was Robena." I noticed color rise in her cheeks. "Then he said Robena sounded like a good Irish name." Mom chuckled. "He signed this campaign poster and presented it to me when they left." Her eyes twinkled. "Oh, he was such a handsome man!"

"Wow! You were smitten with him, weren't you?" I joshed her, glad to see her mood improving.

"Well, Dear, yes, I guess you could say I was. We were the same age, you know." Mom poked my arm. "But I knew he was way out of my league! I was thrilled when he became the first Irish-Catholic to be elected president."

"How did you feel when he got shot?" I only had a vague memory of Kennedy's assassination, as I had been just seven at the time.

"Of course I was devastated when I heard the news. Who could do such a horrendous thing to a wonderful, young man in the prime of his life? I thought Jack was a great president. And I worried about what would happen to his lovely wife, Jackie, and their two young children, left without a father." There was a deep sadness in her eyes, perhaps a reflection of how she, too, had struggled bringing up children without their father. "Do you remember when we watched the funeral on television? I cried when I saw young John-John salute his father's casket. It was all so very tragic. I often wondered what wonderful things Jack could have done for our country had he lived a long, fruitful life." Mom's melancholy gripped me as she remembered those tragic events.

"Oh, Mom, I feel bad for you. I don't remember his funeral very well, but I do remember you crying. You said a great man had been taken from us before his time. It made me sad." I hugged her to me.

"Well, Dear. Death is a part of life, and you just have to move on in your grief."

Her sage words ripped at my heart, knowing her years were numbered.

When we had finished the sorting and packing of items in her bedroom, it was supper time, and we were both famished. Because there was very little food left in the house, I drove into town and picked up Chinese takeout and a cold bottle of wine. Then we sat down at the kitchen table for the last time to eat our feast.

"Hey, Mom, I wanted to ask you something. Do you know if Gabe is still here? I haven't heard him stomping around since I've been home."

Mom nodded. "Oh, yes, he's still here. I hear his footsteps upstairs quite often. You know he's been protecting me for a long time, and I sure hate leaving him here alone," she said, with melancholy in her voice.

I hope Gabe doesn't cause any problems for my new tenants.

"Well, Mom. This is your last night here. How do you feel?"

"You know I'm sad, Dear. This is the only place I've ever called home, and I hate to leave it. But I know you're doing this for my own good, and I don't blame you," Mom added, being brave, her chin trembling. "Dee, I want you to promise me something." She grasped my hand. "I want you to promise me you won't ever sell this house, because I want you to always have a home to come back to. I don't want you to ever be homeless like I once was!" She stared at me intently.

"Okay, Mom, I promise," I said, holding her trembling hand.

I hoped I could keep my promise.

ROBBIE LEAVES

The next day our good friends, Vince and Lynn Granger, arrived in their pickup truck. We loaded Mom's suitcases, a few boxes, and her favorite caned rocking chair into the truck bed for the trip to the nursing home.

Lynn and I helped Mom down the porch steps so she could maneuver her walker along the concrete pathway. About halfway to the car, Mom stopped.

"Are you all right, Mom?" I asked.

Her face looked pained, her chin trembling. "You know I'm sad to be leaving the only place I've ever called home. I so wish I could stay." Tears gleamed in her eyes.

I hugged her. "Yeah, I know, Mom. I wish you could, too. It breaks my heart to have to make you move, believe me."

Mom nodded. "Well, you're doing it for my own good, so I don't blame you, DeeDee. I just hate getting old. I would love to be young again and kicking up my heels at the Grove." A wistful expression crossed her face.

"We best be going, Mom," I said, directing her toward the car.

She paused, then glanced toward the upstairs windows and waved.

I smiled, wondering if Gabe was watching.

Gabe peers out the upstairs bedroom window, and sees the elderly woman wave.

She is a good, God-fearing woman who showed love and compassion to my descendant. I am eternally sad to see her leave. I hope she shall be well cared for in her final years.

He watches the vehicles leave the driveway.

Now I must be diligent to protect my property from those who harbor the devil's ill will!

The Grangers followed Mom and me as we drove in my rental car to Rutland, fifteen miles away. When we arrived, Ellie and the nursing home director, Sharon, were there to meet us. Ellie had made all the administrative arrangements to have Mom admitted.

Sharon, tall and lean, with short-cropped gray hair, led our entourage down a long hallway. A number of residents, sitting in their wheelchairs in front of their rooms, greeted us as we passed by. I steadied Mom's arm as she negotiated the gauntlet with her walker. Ellie, Lynn and Vince followed. Then we entered a room at the end of the hall, where an elderly lady sat, propped up in her bed next to the window.

Sharon walked to the lady's bed. "This is Miriam Caples," she said. "Miriam, this is your new roommate, Robbie Van Dyne." She directed Mom over to the bed to shake hands.

"Nice to meet you, Miriam," Mom said, being gracious. "I hope we'll be good friends."

"Humph, we'll see," grumbled Miriam.

Uh, oh, this isn't starting off well.

Sharon said, "Miriam had somewhat of a rough night, so she's a bit out of sorts." She touched the elderly woman's shoulder. "You're usually a very pleasant lady, aren't you Miriam?"

Miriam stared at her. "Yeah, I guess so. Just not feeling so good today."

Mom sat on the edge of her new bed and sighed. She grasped her palsied hands in her lap. Next to the bed sat a nightstand and a comfortable visitor's armchair. A hospital curtain was pinned against the wall behind the bed. Against the opposite wall were two identical dressers, and one had Mom's name on it. The walls were painted a faint yellow, and I noticed the room had a freshly cleaned smell, which made me happy.

"Guess we'll go get Robbie's stuff," Vince said, as he and Lynn left the room.

Sharon turned to Mom. "We're here to make you as comfortable as possible, Missus Van Dyne." She lifted a button attached to a cable. "This is your call button. We'd prefer residents only use it if necessary, but please don't hesitate to call if you need something." Then the director turned to me and Ellie. "If you'd like to have a phone put in, please see me in the office before you leave, and we can make the arrangements. You have to pay for the line of course, but most residents like having their own phone."

Ellie responded, "Yes, we'll want Mom to have a phone. We'll see you before we leave."

Sharon said, "Missus Van Dyne, if you're up for it, I'd love to give you and your family a tour of the facilities." She moved toward the door.

Mom assented, and we walked through the spacious dining room on the second floor surrounded with windows showing a magnificent view of the mountains in full foliage. Then we went into the kitchen, where the industrial stoves especially interested Mom. We peeked into the women's bath and shower area, and were introduced to several residents in the dayroom on the first floor, where a piano sat in the corner.

"We have musical groups who like to come and perform for us," the director informed us. "Many of our residents love to dance."

I watched Mom's expression perk up.

"Oh, do they do square dancing?" Mom asked with enthusiasm.

"We do have squares that perform for us, and sometimes our residents join in." Sharon smiled at Mom. "Do you like to square dance?"

"Oh, yes, I love it, Dear. But I haven't danced in years," she lamented.

"Well, we'll have to see what we can do to get you up dancing again!" Sharon gently held Mom's elbow and led us from the dayroom.

We finished the tour in the basement, where we were shown the arts and crafts room. Large prints of colorful Vermont scenes hung on the light green walls. The wall to the left had floor-to-ceiling shelves holding boxes of craft supplies. On the opposite side was a beverage counter holding a coffee maker, water bubbler and instant drink packets. Long tables spread around the room, and a few residents were busy with their creations. Mellow music from the ceiling speakers evoked a relaxing atmosphere. Next to the crafts room was a small auditorium, where they showed movies, held bingo, and hosted other group activities.

Everything we'd seen was clean and immaculately maintained, which made me feel a little better about having Mom live there.

Sharon ushered us back to Mom's room, where Vince and Lynn were unpacking her suitcases. The director said, "We begin serving lunch at eleven-thirty, and your family is welcome to join us. I'll see you in the dining room," she said as she left.

Once Mom's stuff was unpacked, and her rocking chair placed near the bed, Vince and Lynn hugged Mom and bade their farewells, promising to visit her soon.

Mom, Ellie, and I made our way to the dining room, where we found seats at the end of one table. We were served a lunch of ham, mashed potatoes, vegetables, and bread, which was quite good. We joined in the conversation with other residents as they introduced themselves and told us where they were from. One lady knew folks in Fair Haven whom Mom also knew, so I think that made her feel better.

After lunch, we walked with Mom to the dayroom, where she wanted to join the lady from lunch to discuss who else they knew in town. Ellie and I reluctantly hugged Mom goodbye.

"Are you going to be okay?" I asked her, guilt ripping at my heart.

"Yes, Dear, I'll be fine," she said, keeping a brave face, but I saw her chin quiver. I hugged her tight.

"I'll be back tomorrow to visit, so you be good!" I said.

Then Ellie and I went to the office to get her phone line set up.

When I arrived home, I went into the silent, mostly empty, lonely house, sat on the sofa, and cried my heart out.

Then footsteps thumped upstairs, and I froze!

AUCTION

John Barstow, the auctioneer, and his crew, spent the next two days tagging, cataloging and moving furniture from the house. I made a deal with him to buy the antiques and what was salvageable from the barn. He would earn thirty percent of the proceeds from the auction, and we would get seventy. Anything that didn't sell immediately would either be held for future auctions or disposed of. The money from the auction would go into Mom's account for her expenses at the nursing home.

I hired Arlene Sutton, a local real estate agent and old friend of Ellie and Mom's, to be our property manager. I left it up to Arlene's discretion to screen applicants and find suitable tenants.

Then I packed my suitcases, since I would be spending the rest of my visit in a hotel nearby. I took one last walk through the empty house, remembering scenes from my life. I expected I would never spend another night in my childhood home. I made a special stop in Gabe's bedroom, above my old one.

"Gabe, this is DeeDee," I said. "There's going to be new people living here, and I want you to be nice to them, okay?"

No response.

"I know this is your house, and you protect it from evil, but I would appreciate it if you didn't hurt anyone again. Thanks." I hoped he heard me.

I could feel Mom's presence follow me as I made my exit. Although I would be back to oversee the cleaners and carpet layers getting the house ready to rent, this felt like a final goodbye. I gulped back tears as I locked the front door.

Over the next two weeks, the house was cleaned, necessary repairs made, walls were patched and painted, and carpet installed. Based on insurance requirements, we affixed new smoke and carbon monoxide detectors in all the rooms.

During this time, I met with our insurance agent, Frank, and signed all the necessary papers to cover the house as a rental unit. A few days after we burned the barn, he and I had paid Howard Greene a visit. We reimbursed my neighbor to have a new window installed and his barn repainted. Although it appeared Howard appreciated the money, I could tell he was still unhappy with Frank about the way the barn-burning had gone down. I figured at least he still *had* a barn, so, no harm, no foul.

Now my vacation time was up, and I had to fly back to California to go back to work. On my way to the airport in Burlington, I stopped to visit Mom again at the nursing home in Rutland. After checking her room and the dayroom, I found her downstairs in the arts and crafts area. She was sitting at a table with three other ladies. An array of craft items spread across the table between them. Mom's back was to me as I entered, and I overheard part of their conversation.

"...and then Old Lady Eisley beat those poor deacons with her cane as they carried her ass out of church!" Mom laughed, removing her glasses and wiping tears from her eyes.

I remembered chuckling when Mom had first told me the story over the phone just a few weeks earlier.

"Hoooo, Lordy! That old broad is goin' to hell in a handbasket, ya mark my words!" the lady sitting next to Mom declared, her false teeth clacking.

All four ladies laughed heartily.

I walked in and kissed Mom on the cheek, interrupting their merriment. "Hi, Mom. Are you telling tales out of school again?" I moved her walker to the side, and pulled up a chair to join the group.

Mom blushed and grinned at me. "Well, Dear." She put her glasses back on. "We're just having a nice ladies' chat."

"Hi, everyone," I said, greeting the women.

Mom turned to the group. "DeeDee, these are my friends. This is Mildred," she touched the lady to her left, who had made the handbasket comment. "This is Sheila." She indicated the woman directly across from her in a wheelchair. "And this is Dotty," she said, pointing to the other lady across the table, also in a wheelchair.

I recognized Dotty as the woman we had met in the lunch room, who knew folks from Fair Haven.

"Nice to meet you all," I said, looking at the crafts on the table. "So, what are you making here?"

Mom lifted an item. "We're making masks for everyone to wear at our Halloween party." Then she placed the brightly colored, plastic mask over her eyes, and turned to me. "What do you think?"

"I think it's splendid!" I said, laughing.

Dotty chimed in, pointing to a row of blank masks. "So we paint these any way we want. Then we punch holes in each side, and insert these stretchy strings so we can slide them over our heads." She grasped a handful of equal-length strings crimped with plastic ends that were inserted on each side of the mask.

Mom touched my hand and laughed. "That's my job! They won't let me paint because they don't like my wobbly lines!"

Mildred leaned to Mom. "Now, Robbie! You know that's not true. It's for Halloween—the scarier the better!" she exclaimed.

All the ladies cackled.

I thought Mom looked quite content, and it made my heart a little lighter to see her enjoying herself. "Well, Mom, the house is all cleaned out, and I'm on my way to the airport. I wanted to get your new phone number before I leave. Do you know what it is?"

"Oh, yes, Dear. I memorized it."

"Okay, hold on." I pulled a notepad from my purse. "Go ahead."

She recited her number, and I jotted it down. I checked my watch. "I've got to get on the road, Mom." I rose from the table.

Mom pushed out her chair, propped her hands on the table, and rose beside me. She gave me a big hug and whispered, "I love you! Don't worry about me, I'm fine."

The guilt of leaving her welled in my heart, and I choked back tears.

Then I helped her sit back down. Taking a breath and turning to the ladies I said, "Y'all take good care of Robbie, now, you hear me? Otherwise I'll be back to haunt every one of you!"

They all laughed. I bent and kissed Mom's cheek. "I'll call you Sunday, same time as always."

"Okay, Dear. I'll be waiting for your call. Have a good flight home. I love you," Mom said as she waved goodbye.

I walked out of the nursing home with a heavy heart, not knowing when I would see her again.

TENANTS

Our first tenants bolted in the middle of the night with no warning! They were a husband and wife with two young daughters, and had caused me considerable angst during the nine months they had rented the house. Against the terms of the lease, which explicitly prohibited it, they used both a portable dishwasher and washing machine that blew up the tiny 600-gallon septic tank. It had cost us over three thousand dollars to replace it with a larger tank, and I was furious.

Then my property manager, Arlene, told me they managed to trash the place with their hasty exit, and I was even more pissed. I could hear my husband Mark's disapproving voice: *I told you so!* I didn't know what the hell had happened to those people, but I had no doubt Gabe was somehow involved. I was somewhat thankful Gabe had probably forced them to leave, so I wouldn't have to evict them. But now I had a decision to make.

Should I re-rent the place or not? Is Gabe going to terrorize whoever is living in his house? And what if someone DOES die? Will I get blamed as the landlord?

Shit! What a mess.

After getting the damage to the house repaired, most of which was covered by insurance, we reluctantly decided to find new tenants. I insisted Arlene check and double-check all previous rental references. I was a bit paranoid about her competence, but decided I would give her another chance, as property managers were scarce. However, I didn't want another debacle like with the previous occupants.

My next tenants were Darcy and Bob Anthony, parents of three school-aged boys. Bob was from Rutland and worked in construction. Darcy was from Fair Haven and held two low-income jobs to support the family. Everything went pretty well with these tenants for a couple of years. They paid the rent on time and kept the place pretty well picked up, according to Arlene.

Then late one afternoon, I got a call from Katie, my old childhood friend from the south side of town. We had stayed in touch over the years, and she was now a teacher at the elementary school.

"Hi, Katie. It's good to hear from you. So what's up in your busy world?" I was happy to hear my friend's voice, and curious as to why she was calling.

She chuckled, "Well, there's never a dull moment, that's for sure." She paused. I waited. "So, Dee. The reason I'm calling is because there's some stuff going on you should know about."

"Really? What kind of stuff? About whom?"

"Well, the Anthonys are renting your place, right?"

I braced myself. I didn't think this was going to be good news. "Yeah, that's right. What's up?"

"The two younger boys, Sean and Harry, showed up at school yesterday with bruises to their faces and arms." She sighed. "When I questioned them, they said they had been wrestling with each other. But looking at the extent of the bruises, I didn't believe their story."

"So, what do you think happened?"

"I've seen my fair share of abused kids over my years of teaching," Katie replied. "Those black eyes weren't caused from wrestling. Someone hit them, and hard!"

I had a bad feeling about what Katie was telling me.

"And there's more," Katie said. "I heard through the teacher grapevine the oldest boy, Bobby, got into a fight on the high school grounds. He's been suspended for three days."

"Oh, no!" I lamented. "That doesn't sound good. Do you have any idea what's happening with Bob and Darcy? Are they having problems?"

Katie sighed. "Could be. Apparently Bob injured his back on the job, and he's home on disability, maybe permanently. Rumor is he's been drinking a lot. I heard Darcy has been spotted around town wearing big sunglasses. I guess she has quite a shiner underneath."

"Oh, man! This sucks." Now I was starting to get worried. If Bob was at home drinking and beating his wife and kids, I knew Gabe wouldn't stand for it. I had the horrible feeling something bad was about to happen.

"I'm sorry to bring you bad news, Dee. But I thought you'd want to know what is happening at your house."

"Yeah, I do. Thanks. I appreciate you being a good friend and letting me know, Katie. If you hear anything else, feel free to call anytime."

"Sure will," she said, and hung up.

One of the things I had hated about living in a small town was that everyone knew your business: good, bad, and ugly. At least the tradition now came in handy to keep me informed about my tenants.

After ending my call with Katie, I called my property manager. "Arlene, have you been over to check on the house lately?" I asked her.

"No, why?" Her voice seemed a bit testy.

"Well, I've been hearing rumors Bob's been drinking, and possibly hitting his wife and kids. I don't want them trashing the house. I'd like you to pay them a visit to see what's going on."

Arlene complained. "By law, I have to give them twenty-four hours' notice before I can enter the premises."

"Okay, then call and tell them you'll be there tomorrow!"

"Well, I'm pretty booked up all week," she whined. "The earliest I could get there would be Friday."

Today was Tuesday. Once again Arlene wasn't moving as quickly as I wanted her to. I had to remind myself life moved slower in Vermont than in fast-paced Silicon Valley, and to try to be more patient. "All right, tell them you'll be there on Friday to do an inspection. I want you to walk through the entire house and report back to me what you find," I directed her. I wanted to light a bonfire under her ass.

"Why? What do you think I'm going to find?" Her voice rose. I could tell she was getting annoyed with my insistence.

"I don't know, Arlene!" I said, exasperated. "That's why I want you to go over there. Based on the rumors I've heard, all is not right in the house. I want you to go check it out."

"Well, you know how I hate to stick my nose in other people's business," she grumped.

"Arlene! It's your job!" My anger rose. "We have a right to inspect the house on a regular basis to see if there are any problems." I took a breath. "Now would you please contact them and tell them you'll be there Friday?"

"Okay! I'll take care of it!"

The phone slammed in my ear. It was obvious she wasn't happy with the assignment.

Arlene called me the following Saturday to report what she'd found.

"I went over there yesterday afternoon," she said. "Bob was the only one home, and he was drunk in the living room watching television." She paused and took a breath. "He didn't want me there, and swore at me to get the hell out. You're not going to like this, but the house is a total mess."

"Oh, goddammit! What did you do?" Visions of the mess we had to clean up from the unexpected exit of my first tenants swept through my mind.

"I told Bob I was there to do an inspection, and if he gave me any grief, I'd call the sheriff. When I walked through the house I saw a big problem. They had newspapers stacked up everywhere, and electrical outlets overloaded in the living room. It looked like a fire hazard to me," Arlene recounted. "I called the fire marshal and had him come meet me at the house."

"Good!" I was happy to hear Arlene had taken some initiative. "So, what happened?"

"The marshal said there was a definite fire hazard and issued them a warning to get the place cleaned up within thirty days, or they'd face a fine." Arlene sounded quite proud of herself.

"Thirty days! They could burn down the whole damn house by then! Dammit! I want you to write them a certified letter and tell them they have exactly seven days to get the house cleaned up, or they face eviction." I was sorely tempted to jump on a plane and fly back to take care of the business myself. I took a deep breath. "And I want you to talk to Darcy when she gets home from work, and explain the situation to her. Hopefully she'll get the place straightened up, despite Bob being an asshole."

"Yeah, all right. I'll get the letter off Monday." Arlene's heavy sigh rumbled through the phone before she hung up.

I lamented being a long-distance landlord was indeed a total pain in the ass.

NURSING HOME

"Okay, Mom. I'll call you next week, same time, same station. I love you."

"I love you too, Dear. I'll be here waiting for your call."

Robbie hung up after her weekly phone call from DeeDee, and wiped her tears. Even though DeeDee flew to Vermont to visit her every year, she missed her youngest daughter terribly.

I want to give her a hug and tell her I love her. I'm glad DeeDee stuck to her homework when I was working. It helped her get scholarships for college. I'm proud she has become so successful with computers. I sure as heck don't know anything about them! I wish Dee didn't live so far away and could come visit me more often.

But I am grateful Ellie brings my granddaughters to visit. They are so adorable. I just love them to pieces! And I appreciate Ellie driving me to their house for Sunday dinners and holidays. If it wasn't for them and the Grangers, I wouldn't have any visitors at all!

Now at the age of eighty-four, Robbie had been in the nursing home for more than four years, and she was tired of it.

I just want to go home, and die where I belong.

Although the staff at the nursing home were pleasant, she hated having to wait for someone to come help her with the basic necessities of life: going to the bathroom, getting in and out of bed, dressing and undressing, showering, and even eating her meals.

I've been fighting that damned Parkinson's for over thirty years, and the old devil is winning the war! It makes me so mad! As independent as I've been my whole life, this is no way to live.

As she choked back tears from her phone call, another coughing fit racked her body. She grabbed for a Kleenex next to her chair, and coughed deeply into it, bringing up phlegm spotted with blood. She tried to take a deep breath, but there just didn't seem to be enough air, and she gasped. She swiped her eyes, and tried to suppress the nasty cough she'd been fighting for weeks.

There's usually some kind of sickness going around this place, and I always seem to catch it. If I could just lie down for a while, I'm sure I'll feel better.

She pushed her call button and slumped back into her armchair to wait for an attendant. Then Robbie felt someone shaking her arm. *I must have dozed off.*

"Robbie, did you need something?" Kathy, a blond, blue-eyed, young attendant asked her.

"Oh, yes, Dear. Would you help me into bed? I'd like to take a little nap."

Kathy eyes went wide as she put her hand on Robbie's forehead. "Jesus, Robbie, you're burning up! Here, let me take your temperature." She extracted a thermometer from her uniform pocket. Robbie opened her mouth and the thermometer was stuck under her tongue.

"Try to hold it there as long as you can," Kathy said.

Robbie nodded.

In a few moments, Kathy removed the thermometer and held it to the light. As she did, Robbie watched her eyes go wide.

"One hundred three point two! Oh, God! I'm sorry Robbie, but you're not going to bed. We need to get you to the hospital, because we can't treat this fever here. I need to get the head nurse to take a look at you," Kathy said, rushing from the room.

The head nurse, in her mid-forties, was strong and lanky, with short brown hair. She entered the room flanked by two attendants. As the nurse inserted the thermometer into Robbie's mouth again, it triggered a gag reflex, and Robbie started coughing uncontrollably, spitting up again into a Kleenex.

"Let me see that," the head nurse said, reaching for and unraveling the crumpled tissue. A gob of dark blood stuck to the fibers. Turning to Kathy, the head nurse ordered, "Call the ambulance!"

"Robbie, Honey, I think you have pneumonia. You have a very high fever and a horrible cough," the nurse said, resting her hand on Robbie's forehead. "We need to have the doctor examine you. We're getting the ambulance right now. Since the hospital is just across the street, we'll have you over there and comfortable in no time."

"Oh, my! Is it really that bad?" Robbie asked, her hands trembling uncontrollably. "Will you call my daughter, Ellie, and tell her I'm going to the hospital? She'll be worried about me."

"Yes, we'll call her as soon as we get you into the ambulance. Here, let's get your slippers on," the head nurse said as she helped Robbie with one foot and then the other. She went to the closet and selected a jacket so Robbie wouldn't get a chill on this overcast day in early May. The nurse helped Robbie slide the jacket over her arms, and pulled it down her back as Robbie leaned forward in her chair.

Shortly, two paramedics arrived with a stretcher. The men got on each side of Robbie, with one hand under her thighs and one on her back. On the count of three, they lifted her in unison and laid her gently on the stretcher, where she was covered with a blanket.

"I've already given the hospital your information, so they're ready to admit you," Kathy said, returning to the room. "You take care of yourself, Robbie." She held Robbie's hand as she was wheeled out of the room. "We'll be waiting for you when you get back."

"Thank you, Dear." Robbie smiled at the nice young attendant she'd become fond of, who reminded her so much of DeeDee.

DEEDEE FLIES TO VERMONT

I came home from work Monday afternoon in early May. I was changing into comfortable clothes when the phone rang.

I heard my sister's voice. "Dee, it's Ellie."

"Hi, what's up?" I asked, immediately fearing bad news.

"I wanted to let you know Mom's in the hospital. They took her in last night. The doctors say she has pneumonia."

My heart pounded, my hands trembling.

"What do you mean? I just talked to her yesterday, and she seemed all right. She was coughing a bit, but it didn't seem that bad. How could she have gotten pneumonia so fast?" I had a terrible feeling in the pit of my stomach.

"Well, she's had a bad cough for a while, and when the nurse checked her temperature yesterday, it was over a hundred and three. So, they called an ambulance and took her to the hospital. I went to see her today. They have her on antibiotics, pain meds, and an oxygen mask to help her breathe," Ellie said.

"Dammit! I wish she would have told me she wasn't feeling well." I was angry at Mom for not being more forthcoming about her health.

"Oh, I'm sure she didn't want you to worry. You know how she is about stuff like that," Ellie reminded me.

"Yeah, I know. But it makes me nuts! Is there anything I can do?" I asked.

"I guess not right now. Let's see how she responds to the meds. But you should maybe think about making a trip home to see her soon."

"Yeah, I will. Thanks for letting me know. Keep me posted on her progress," I said. I mentally reviewed my pending workload, and said a silent prayer she would recover quickly.

"Okay, I'll call you tomorrow with what I find out from the doctors." Ellie hung up.

Three days later, I was on a plane flying to Vermont to see Mom. This was the hardest trip home I had ever made. In our many phone calls over the past few days, Ellie informed me Mom had taken a turn for the worse. Her organs were shutting down, and she had slipped into a coma. In other words, she was dying, and the doctors were just keeping her comfortable. I sincerely hoped they could keep Mom alive until I arrived.

By some twist of fate, I ended up sitting in first class to Chicago, where I spent the flight weeping, thinking of Mom, and willing the plane to fly faster. The flight attendants were very sympathetic, plying me with free cocktails.

When Ellie and I walked into Mom's hospital room, the first thing I noticed was her hands were still, lying by her side. In my whole life, I could never remember a time when her hands didn't have a tremor from Parkinson's disease. It was then it hit me she was really dying. I collapsed into the visitor's chair, took her hand in mine and cried.

"Hi Mom, it's DeeDee. I love you. How are you doing?" I hoped she could hear me.

COMA

Robbie heard DeeDee's voice. It seemed very far away, yet close at the same time. She felt someone holding her hand.

DeeDee, I hear you. Why can't I see you? Darling, is that you holding my hand?

Gradually Robbie realized she was not speaking aloud, but only in her mind.

I want to talk to DeeDee. Why can't I open my eyes? Why can't I move? I want to see my daughter!

She struggled to swim up from the deep hole she was in, but felt as though she were mired in concrete.

Her mind drifted to one of the many trips she had taken to California. She and DeeDee went on a ferry ride on San Francisco Bay. She felt the stiff breeze blowing through her hair, and saw the fog layer, like a tidal wave, washing over the Golden Gate Bridge. She was amazed at the enormity of the bridge when they cruised beneath it. From pictures she had seen, she thought it would be smaller. She laughed at the barking seals sunning themselves on the wharf at Pier 39. She and DeeDee toured the dank cells at Alcatraz Island. She remembered the headlines when Al Capone, *Public Enemy Number One*, was sent there back in the thirties.

Then they went camping in Yosemite Valley. She was in awe of the magnificence of Half Dome, with its sheer cliff rising from the valley floor to the heavens. The power of God and Mother Nature humbled her.

Oh, how I wish I could make one more trip to California. DeeDee, can you hear me?

VIGIL

Because Ellie worked as an elementary school administrator, and had to care for her family, we traded off keeping a vigil at Mom's bedside. On the third night I was there, we both went to the hospital after dinner to be with her. The nurses came in several times to check her machines. They told us her breathing was slowing down.

"You've been a good mother, Mom. You know we love you. You did the best you could for your daughters," I said through my tears as I held her still hand. "You should be proud of us and yourself. You worked hard to give us everything you had, and we love you for it." I didn't want to let her go. I knew her passing would leave a huge void in my heart. But I also knew it was her time, and she was ready to meet her Lord.

"Go find your Mamma and Poppa, Mom. They're waiting for you in the light, and will welcome you home." I whispered in her ear.

The hospital room door opened, and a priest entered the room. I jerked upright in the chair next to Mom's bed.

"I'm Father O'Malley," he said as he shook my hand and Ellie's. "I understand Missus Van Dyne is Catholic. I'm here to administer the sacrament of Last Rites."

I gulped at the finality of his words.

Ellie and I held hands, and we each placed a hand on Mom's head. The priest spread holy water in the form of a cross on Mom's forehead and blessed her. We joined him to recite the Our Father and Hail Mary over Mom's gently undulating body. The priest continued his prayers and incantations as my tears flowed steadily. Ellie, too, was crying. We watched as Mom's breathing slowed…slowed…and then, with a serene look on her face, there were no more breaths.

The machine monitoring her heart buzzed, and a flat line appeared.

"We love you, Mom," we both said in unison. "Rest in peace." We kissed her on the forehead as our tears dripped on her face. I leaned over and put my head on her chest to give her one last hug. She was gone from this earth, on to whatever the next world held for her.

The priest blessed himself and Mom one more time. "May you go with God," he said as he bowed over her body.

Two nurses entered the room and gently ushered us aside. They checked Mom's vital signs. One nurse checked her watch. "Time of death, nine-for-ty-five p.m.," she said quietly.

Ellie and I hugged and cried over the loss of this strong, independent, feisty redhead, who had endured unfathomable hardships to give her daughters a better life than she had lived. We would miss her terribly.

ROBBIE'S VISION

DeeDee's faraway voice entered Robbie's consciousness. "Go find your Mamma and Poppa, Mom. They're waiting for you in the light, and will welcome you home."

Robbie sees her beloved Mamma, her long red braid draped over her shoulder, sitting at the kitchen table at their farm in Maine. At the opposite end is Poppa, his hair snowy white. To Mamma's left sits her younger brother Paul, who died at Pearl Harbor.

He looks so young and handsome in his Navy uniform. Oh, how I've missed his wonderful sense of humor!

Next to Paul is Robbie's brother Frank Jr., dressed in Army fatigues.

I was so sad when Frank lost his life on the beaches of Normandy. They were both so brave to give their lives defending our country.

Sitting to Poppa's right is Robbie's oldest brother, Wilmot. He looks the same as Robbie remembered him, when she and Gladys were sent to Boston. Two years after Mamma and Poppa died, Wilmot and his buddy Clyde were deer hunting. When they tried to cross a swollen stream, Clyde lost his footing and his gun discharged, shooting Wilmot in the back, killing him.

I was stunned when Wilmot died. But I was still grieving Mamma and Poppa's loss and I couldn't accept Wilmot was gone. He always protected me from the wrath of my older sisters. I loved him and should have prayed for his soul.

Robbie's sister Gladys sits to Mamma's right. Still middle-aged, Gladys looks up and smiles at Robbie.

That damned cancer took her way too young. I was devastated when she passed away. She was my closest friend in the whole world. I have missed her every day since!

Baby sister Helen, now an old lady with gray hair, sits next to Gladys. She blows Robbie a kiss and imitates a hug. Robbie's heart melts.

I wish I could have protected baby Helen after Mamma died, but I wasn't given the chance! I broke my promise to Mamma, and I am eternally sorry.

Her older sisters, Pauline and Marjorie, both old, bent, forlorn women, sit next to Helen. Neither acknowledges Robbie's presence.

I am forever grateful they helped raise Joan and Ellie during my difficult times. But they always resented me, so I guess it doesn't matter much now.

The sweet smell of cinnamon porridge, bubbling on the stove, wafts through the kitchen.

Then Robbie notices Mamma cradling a young girl in her arms. Bright red curls sprout from the child's oversized head. Her stubby, deformed right arm rests against Mamma's bosom.

"I'm your sister, Mae," the girl says, waving with her good hand. "Please come join us!"

Oh, Mamma! Did you really leave Mae to die alone in the cabin in the snowy woods? I hope the good Lord has forgiven you!

Poppa raises an arm, smiles, and beckons to her. A gentle glow surrounds the gathering, and Robbie is drawn to the warmth of the light. At the age of eighty-four, she is the last living sibling.

I've missed them so much! I just want to give them all hugs.

Robbie starts to join her family, when a familiar voice pulls her back.

"You've been a good mother, Mom."

She recognizes DeeDee's voice, and hears her continue, "You know we love you. You did the best you could for your daughters."

Robbie's heart swells.

All I ever wanted was to be a good mother to my girls. I wish my life had turned out differently, and I could have kept them all with me. I hope they know I will love them forever.

Then another vision appears and Robbie sees her home in Fair Haven she loves so dearly.

Old Bert is standing in his abundant garden, engulfed in bright sunlight. He smiles and waves at her to come join him. The purple lilacs are in bloom, and Robbie inhales their heady fragrance.

The house smelled so wonderful in the spring with those bouquets in every room!

Then Robbie notices an old man with a gray beard, wearing a red flannel shirt and dark trousers, held up by suspenders. The figure hovers several feet off the ground, near the garden.

That's Gabe! I would recognize him anywhere. I am so grateful he was watching over me in my old age.

Gabe nods. He, too, beckons her to the verdant yard.

Oh, it's so beautiful!

Robbie feels the bonds of the earthly grip loosen, as she senses herself rising above the bed.

I love you, Joan. I love you, Ellie. I love you, Barbara. I love you, DeeDee. I will always be with you! Please don't cry, my darlings. There is a better place that awaits me.

All the pain, heartache, joy, and sorrow of Robbie's life is replaced by the peace and wonder of the vision she seeks. The welcoming light engulfs her, and Robbie follows her heart into the world beyond.

THE FAMILY GRIEVES

Ellie, Rob, and I arrived at the funeral parlor in Fair Haven in the early evening for the viewing. Local folks greeted us and expressed their condolences at Mom's passing. I noticed Betty and Howard Greene, our longtime neighbors, go to the casket and pay their respects. Howard, now in his late seventies, looked distraught. I knew he and Mom had had great respect for one another.

I walked slowly down the center aisle and approached the open, mauve casket embellished with pink roses. My heart was heavy. I reached down to touch Mom's still, cold hand. She looked serene and peaceful dressed in a cream-colored dress embellished with tiny pearlesque beads. Her long, snow-white hair draped over her shoulders and cascaded down her arms like wings. Her Mamma's cherished cameo pendant rested on her heart. Mom looked like a beautiful guardian angel, and I felt her spirit would always be by my side.

"Rest in peace, Mom. I love you," I whispered.

When I turned back to the gathering, I noticed my older half-sister, Joan, and her husband, Darrel, standing alone at the side of the parlor. I hadn't realized they planned to travel from Maine for Mom's service.

At age sixty-five, Joan's once jet-black hair had turned completely gray and was close-cropped. She had inherited Mom's long legs and tall, lanky figure. Dressed in a calf-length, black, long-sleeve dress accented with a string of pearls, she resembled an austere nun. Darrel, who stood a head taller than Joan, was dressed in a black suit and muted tie. His arm was casually draped around her waist. I thought they looked like CIA agents, scanning the roomful of unfamiliar people as if searching for a prime suspect.

Over the years, Mom and I had visited Joan and her family twice at their home, where I met my nephew and nieces, all about my age. And I recalled

Joan and Darrel had visited us once in Fair Haven. So, I really didn't know my half-sister, who was twenty years my senior. But I did know her relationship with Mom had always been strained.

Joan caught my eye and motioned me to come join them. As I walked toward her, she said something to Darrel, and he left her side.

When I reached her, I said, "I didn't know you were coming. This is a surprise."

Joan stood rigid and tight-lipped. "Well, I guess it was only *proper* for us to be here." She paused, peered around the room, then back at me. "You know, Dee, I always thought *you* were the only daughter Robbie ever loved, because she was never a mother to me!"

I stared, stunned by her vitriol, figuring she had more to get off her mind. *I know Joan resents me because I was the only daughter Robbie managed to raise. And I wasn't even born when Mom sent her to live with Aunt Marjorie. Maybe it would have been better if she hadn't shown up.*

Joan continued, "After Aunt Marjorie died, I cleaned out her closet, and I was surprised to find shoe boxes full of unopened letters from Robbie." She checked to see if anyone was close by, then held her head high. "I have no idea why Marjorie never gave them to me. I thought Robbie had abandoned me and didn't love me."

I felt bad for Joan, who had never really gotten to know her birth mother. "Oh, my gosh! That's so sad for you."

Her strained face softened. "I spent a week reading those letters, and it just ripped me apart." She glanced toward the casket. "I'm still trying to forgive Robbie for giving me up, but I don't think I can ever forgive Marjorie for keeping her letters from me!" She looked away. "It would have made such a difference in my life, if I had known Robbie cared for me." She turned away, her face pinched.

I nodded, feeling her pain. "Well, you know Mom had a rough life and bad luck with husbands. She did what she thought was best for each of us to have a better life." I glanced at Ellie, who was talking to our neighbor, Howard. "And I'm sure she loved all of her daughters with her whole heart!" I looked at Joan, struggling with her conflicting emotions. "I hope you can forgive her because she did the best she could under difficult circumstances."

Joan glared at me. "I'm working on it, but it's hard after all these years."

I didn't know what else to say, so I reached out and hugged her. Joan stood perfectly still, then turned and walked away.

May you find peace in your heart someday.

Then the funeral director announced we should all be seated, as the eulogy would begin shortly. As folks shuffled to take their seats, I noticed the outside parlor door open. I was surprised to see my sister, Barbara, flanked by her caretakers, Kim and Larry.

Oh, no! I don't think Barb is going to handle this very well.

Barbara, now in her mid-fifties, her auburn hair streaked with gray, still looked young, with few lines on her face. Her diminutive figure hunched slightly at the shoulders. She was dressed in stretch-waist black pants and a white button-up blouse. I thought she looked healthy. I went to greet them and gave Barb a hug. She patted my face in greeting, a lopsided grin on her face. I was glad she remembered me.

As Kim led Barb slowly up the aisle with Ellie and me following, the onlookers grew quiet. Kim stopped in front of the open casket. Barb reached down and tapped Mom's cheek to say hello. When Mom didn't move, Barbara lightly slapped her again. "Booooo!" Barb called to Mom. Rustling and murmuring arose from some in the audience.

Kim gently pulled Barbara's hand from the casket and tried to lead her away, but Barb was having none of it. She started screaming and banging on the casket, trying to reach Mom. Ellie and I put our arms around her, trying to calm her. Then Barb collapsed to the floor, wailing, throwing her arms in all directions. I took a pretty good punch to my neck as I went down on my knees next to her. Kim sat on the floor behind Barb and pulled the writhing woman to her chest. Ellie and I each grasped one of Barbara's hands.

I said through my tears, "It's okay, Barbara. It's okay. We're here, and we love you." I knew exactly how she felt. I wanted to throw a temper tantrum, too, at Mom's loss.

"Oh, my goodness! What's wrong with her?" I heard a woman gasp behind me.

Our good friends, Lynn and Vince Granger, were immediately by our side. "Here, let me get her up," Vince said.

Kim moved to the side, and Vince crouched down, put one arm under Barbara's knees and supported her back with the other. With little effort, he lifted her from the floor and carried her down the aisle. I saw the stares of folks gathered around us. The funeral director led Vince into an adjacent room, where he laid Barbara on a sofa. She wailed, stuck her fist into her mouth and bit down hard, drawing blood.

"We should take her home. I'll go get the car," Kim's husband Larry said as he rushed out the door.

Kim looked at Ellie and me as we hovered over my distraught sister. She gently ran a hand over Barb's head. "Larry said we shouldn't bring her to the wake, but I thought she'd be able to handle it." She shook her head. "I guess I was wrong. I'm so sorry."

"It's alright, Kim," Ellie said. "I thought it was important for Barb to see Mom one last time." Ellie reached down and held Barb's free hand.

My heart wept for my sweet, brain-damaged older sister, who would never comprehend what had happened to her mother.

We heard a horn toot outside and through a window saw Larry's car idling. Ellie and I helped Barb to her feet as Kim opened the door. Keeping pace with Barb's shuffling gate, each of us held one arm and guided her to the backseat of the waiting car. Kim helped slide Barb's legs into the seat and fastened her seatbelt. Ellie leaned in and kissed her on the cheek. When she stepped away, I did the same and gave Barb a hug.

As I pulled away, Barb smacked me on the cheek. "Booo—oooo!" she wailed, her face scrunched in anguish.

The morning of Mom's funeral dawned with thunderstorms and heavy rain. The funeral director assured us he had plenty of umbrellas for all who would need them. Since Mom was no longer Catholic, the service was held in the funeral parlor. Ellie had enlisted her minister, Mrs. Stanton, who knew Mom well, to perform the service.

In the front row beside me were Ellie, her husband, Rob, and their two teenage daughters. Across the aisle from us Joan sat stoic, with her husband, Darrel, by her side. Barbara was not in attendance.

Lynn and Vince Granger and their three children, who had loved Mom as their adopted grandmother, sat behind us. I did my best to be brave during the funeral service, trying not cry as I accepted the condolences of the townsfolk and friends.

When the stanzas of Bette Midler's "The Rose" wafted through the parlor, I let grief wash over me.

I thought about the heartache Mom had experienced as she loved deeply all those who had been a part of her life. She had been my flower, my guide, and my soul-mate. I was the seed she had nurtured. Mom had danced, dreamed, and taken chances. She had unselfishly given to others. She had *lived!*

Mom had traveled a long, often lonely road, showing us all her strength, courage. and unconditional love. I thought she was now a beautiful spring red rose in God's garden. When Bette's soulful voice came to an end, Ellie pulled me to her, and I sobbed against her shoulder.

Just then, a ray of sunshine burst through the window and beamed on Mom's casket. I knew it was her spirit saying a final farewell to all of us, still tethered to this earth.

When we stepped outside, the sun sparkled through parting rain clouds, and the umbrellas were no longer needed.

Mom was buried in the Cedar Grove Cemetery, a block away from her house, just three days before Mother's Day. Her grave was not far from the Hopper family plot, where she'd be close to dear Old Bert, in her afterlife.

The left half of the heart-shaped, granite headstone was engraved with Mom's name and her birth and death dates. Her epitaph read simply: *A true believer.*

Inscribed on the right lobe of the heart was my sister Barbara's name and her date of birth.

SLIPPERY STAIRS

Gabe seethes as he watches the man hit his wife in the face, knocking her to the floor. Then the man chases his sons, whipping them on the back with his belt strap.

He is evil, abusing his God-given sons and his beloved wife. Those boys do not deserve such a beating. What kind of man inflicts pain on his family? He is the devil incarnate! I must make him leave!

The following day, Gabe's disgust grows as he watches the man, alone in the house, drinking the devil's elixir. The drunk rises, staggers up the stairs, and lands with a thud on his bed.

Two hours later, the man grabs his crotch, and mutters, "I gotta pee." He rises and stumbles toward the stairs.

Gabe seizes his opportunity. Summoning his energy, he appears in front of the disheveled man.

"Thee is evil, and must leave my house!"

The man yelps. His eyes widen as he stares at the visage of an old, bearded man wearing a red flannel shirt and baggy trousers. Hungover and groggy from his nap, he hollers, "What the hell? Who the fuck are you?"

"This is my house, and thee is not welcome. Thee must go now!" Gabe's deep voice reverberates in the stairway.

"Fuck that! I'm not going anywhere! Leave me the hell alone." The man grumbles, halting at the top of the staircase. He runs a hand through his mussed hair. "Had too much fuckin' drink. I'm just imaginin' this ol' bastard. The hell with this shit!"

Gabe's fury fuels his energy. He gives the evil man a mighty shove.

The man misses the top step, causing his foot to land sideways, snapping his ankle bone. He howls in pain, grasping for the banister and simultaneously reaching for his injured foot. Losing his precarious grip, his momentum sends him careening down the stairs.

"Aaargh! Sonofabitch!" the man wails from the bottom of the stairs. Blood spurts from his broken nose. The jagged ankle bone lances through his skin, with more blood gushing from the wound.

"Thee must leave! Now!" Gabe bellows as he floats down the stairs, shaking his fist at the man. *This evil one must heed my warning.*

"Fuck! Help me, someone help me!" the injured man wails, splayed at the base of the stairway. A ragged wet patch spreads across the front of his jeans.

I had just come home from work on a hot August afternoon in 2004 when the phone rang. I ran to answer it.

"DeeDee, it's Arlene in Vermont," the caller said.

My heart sank. Arlene never called me with good news. I immediately braced myself for the worst.

"Hi, Arlene. What's up?" I asked with resignation.

"There's been an accident at the house. Bob fell down the stairs and broke his ankle and busted his nose," Arlene explained. "Darcy just called to say he's in the hospital right now."

I had a very bad feeling about this. I remembered another time, many years ago, when I had watched an old man fall down those stairs, landing in front of me, with disastrous consequences. "Damn! What happened?" I asked.

"Well, here's the thing. Bob swears some old man with a beard pushed him down the stairs," Arlene said, her voice trembling.

"So, what are you saying, Arlene—that there's some old man stalking my tenants? That's ridiculous!" I reprimanded. I had to head off any notion of a ghost theory. "And besides, how loaded was Bob at the time? He was probably hallucinating, or just fell in a drunken stupor."

Arlene paused, and I could hear her breathing. "Yeah, I guess you're right. He was probably drunk. But Bob's really freaked out. He's convinced Darcy they have to move right away. Darcy doesn't know what to do. She was hysterical when she called me from the hospital!" Arlene was starting to sound frantic.

Shit. This isn't good! "Arlene!" I raised my voice. "Give Darcy a couple of days to calm down. Tell her if they want to move, they have to give us thirty days' notice. That's what's in the lease. If they don't, they'll lose their security deposit." Knowing how tight money was for their family, I figured Darcy wouldn't want to forfeit their deposit.

"Okay, I'll talk to her, but I can't guarantee anything. She's pretty upset," Arlene grumbled.

"Keep me posted as soon as you hear from them one way or the other." I hung up.

Dammit! Gabe's up to his old tricks again. Now what the hell am I going to do?

PROPERTY MANAGER

In late August, a week after Bob's fall, he, Darcy, and their boys packed up their belongings and moved out of the house. Although they technically forfeited their rental deposit, I refunded half of it to Darcy as a goodwill gesture, because I knew she'd need the money.

Just three months after Mom's funeral, my manager was none too happy when I told her I had to fly back to Vermont to take care of family business. And I wasn't thrilled with having to make the trip so soon, either. I planned to stay for only a week to make minor repairs to the house and rent it once again. I brought my laptop computer, so I could log in and work from my sister Ellie's house while I was there.

The day after I arrived in Vermont, I met Arlene Sutton, my property manager, at her office.

"What kind of shape is the house in?" I asked.

Arlene leaned her plump body back into her desk chair and said, "It's actually looking pretty good. Darcy did a good job of cleaning it after they moved out. I'm glad we gave her half the deposit back. It was the right thing to do."

"Yeah, Darcy's a hard-working girl. Too bad she's hooked up with a jerk like Bob. She deserves better," I lamented. "Are there any repairs I need to get done before we find new tenants?"

"Ummm…about finding new tenants…" Arlene hesitated, pushing her teased bouffant away from her face.

"Yeah, what about it?" *What is she up to now?*

"Well, Dee," she cleared her throat. "I've decided I cannot be your property manager any longer. My real estate business is keeping me very busy, and I just don't have the time to manage the property," Arlene paused, fidgeting with the pens on her desk.

I raised an eyebrow, since I could tell she had more to say.

"DeeDee, I think there is evil in that house! As a Christian woman, I don't want to be a part of it anymore!" she blurted, her face reddening.

Oh great! This is just what I don't need right now. "Arlene, what the hell are you talking about?" I wanted to project a healthy skepticism, as well as find out exactly how much she knew.

"Well, since all of your tenants have left under suspicious circumstances and injuries were involved, I can't help but wonder if there's an evil spirit in that house who doesn't want people living there." Beads of sweat formed on Arlene's brow as she spoke.

"Arlene, that's just crazy! I grew up in the house. Don't you think I'd know if there was a spirit living there? I mean, really! Accidents do happen, you know?" I waved my hand in the air. "Bob was a sloppy drunk so it's not surprising there were problems! It doesn't mean there was some nefarious force at work." I shook my head.

"Well, did you ever see or feel a spirit in the house?" she asked, staring at me.

"No! I never did. And if I had, I would have told you about it before we rented the place." Time to dig out the lies. "Arlene, look at all the times you've been there. Did *you* feel any evil spirits? You would have been the first to tell me if you had, wouldn't you? So, come on, now!"

She crossed her arms. "Well, no, I can't say I did for sure. But anyway, I've made up my mind. You'll have to find someone else to manage the property for you." Her annoying, petulant voice grated on me.

Even though Arlene had driven me crazy over the past years, she was the only person I knew in the area who managed properties. "I'm sorry to hear that, Arlene. But it's up to you," I said, exasperated with her. "Is there anyone else you could recommend who could manage the rental for me?"

"No, no, not really. I know there are property management companies in Killington who handle the ski-resort condos, but I don't think they'll manage private residences like this." The pens got rearranged again.

"Well, shit, Arlene! What the hell am I supposed to do now?" I was more than frustrated with her and the situation. I was being backed into a corner.

"You want my honest opinion?" she asked.

I really didn't, but nodded my head.

"I think you should burn the place down and get rid of the evil spirits once and for all!" she blurted, her cheeks burning red.

I just stared at her. I wondered how many people she had talked to about her suspicions. I imagined it was a lively topic of discussion at her ladies' Bible study sessions, so it was probably all over our little town by now. "That's a little extreme, don't you think?" I said in a quiet voice.

Arlene blushed brighter and stammered, "Oh, gosh!…well…maybe… yes…I guess it is a bit. It's your house, and I suppose you can do what you want with it. But you should think about it." She fiddled with her rats-nest hair. "I just don't want to be involved anymore!"

My stomach was in a knot at the prospects of the dwindling options with the property. I just wanted to get away from this pain in the ass before I reached across her desk and strangled her. "Okay, Arlene, I got it! Give me the house keys. I want you to gather up all of our business files and have them ready for me. I'll come pick them up tomorrow." I grabbed the keys off her desk and rose to leave.

"I'm sorry, DeeDee. But I think this is the right thing for me to do," she whined.

I exited the door, my fist clenched tight.

On the five-mile drive back to the house in Fair Haven, my mind was racing.

This is my responsibility. There's no one else who can take care of this but me. But now what am I going to do? I can't rent the place without a local property manager. How am I ever going to get this figured out in a week? What a goddamned mess!

I unlocked the front door and went inside to do an inspection. The house was decently clean. Some furniture had been left behind that wasn't broken. I presumed Darcy and Bob didn't have room for it in the trailer park they had moved to. There were a few garbage bags left in the backyard, which I could take to the dump. I silently thanked Darcy for her efforts. I took out a notepad from my purse and jotted down things that would need to be done before I could re-rent, if that was even going to be possible: new carpet in the main room, deep cleaning, new shower curtain, and so on.

And then the issue of Gabe reared its ugly head.

He's obviously still active in the house and has scared off my tenants. If I rent the place again, then what? Is he going to force them to leave, too?

I worried again about what would happen if someone died in the house at Gabe's hand. What kind of liability would I have as the landlord and would I be blamed? That really scared me. But how could I get rid of him? Maybe I could contact a local priest or medium, and see if they would do an exorcism, seance, or ritual cleansing to scare off spirits. I wasn't sure if that stuff even worked other than in the movies. Visions of *The Exorcist* flashed through my mind. That movie had scared the living shit out of me! One thing I did know for sure was if an exorcism was performed in the house, the news would be all over town in a heartbeat! I just couldn't get my head straight as to what to do next, and I hated not having a plan. Where was Mr. T when I needed him most?

I'll have to talk it over with Ellie. Grinding my teeth, I aimed the car for her house in Killington.

DEEDEE'S DILEMMA

My sister, Ellie and I sat at her kitchen table drinking wine. On this humid August afternoon, her teenage daughters lounged on the back deck, sunning themselves and listening to music.

Ellie yawned. "Sorry, it's been a hectic day with school starting in a couple weeks. So, how did things go with Arlene?"

I sighed. "You're not going to believe this—she fucking quit on me! Said she was too busy with her real estate business to manage the place—and of course, couldn't recommend anyone else to take over." I didn't want to get into Gabe's escapades, even though Ellie knew of his presence, because it was just too complicated.

"Well, that's probably just as well, don't you think?" Ellie asked. "From what I've seen, she hasn't done a very good job managing the place." She paused, staring at me. "Have you thought about selling it?"

Other than bulldozing it, which was what Mark was pushing me to do, I knew selling was an option I had to consider. "Phew…I don't know. Mom made me promise her before she went into the nursing home I'd never sell the place. She wanted me to always have a home to come back to."

Ellie took a sip of wine. "Realistically, do you think you would ever move back here?"

I shook my head. "Probably not. Mark would hate the winters, and so would I, now that I've become a California girl. But it *is* the house I grew up in, and I do have a pretty big emotional attachment to it. I don't know if I'm ready to make such a big decision just yet."

"Yeah, I know," Ellie sympathized. "But before you do anything else, you should probably get an inspection done. The house is old and pretty beat-up. At least this way you'll know what you're dealing with, one way or the other."

"That's a good idea. Anyone you can recommend?"

She nodded. "Actually, I know a guy who used to work for the state as a building inspector and now has his own business. Let me get you his number. I imagine he can help us out." Ellie went into her office and came back a few minutes later with a business card for Charles Turpin. His business address was in Brandon, some twenty-five miles north of Fair Haven.

I removed myself to Ellie's office, and immediately called Charles. He informed me the earliest he could meet me would be the following week. I explained the dire situation I was in: I was only planning to be in Vermont until the following Sunday. Since today was Monday, it gave me less than a week to figure out my options. Charles seemed sympathetic to my situation, and said he would check his schedule and get back to me.

Back in the kitchen, I relayed our conversation to Ellie, then slugged a gulp of wine.

Ellie grinned as I drank, then turned serious. "Dee, I know you're only planning to be here for a week. But I think to make the right decision, it's going to take a whole lot longer than you had planned."

Reluctantly, I knew deep down she was right. This was a milestone decision in my life: to sell my family homestead or not. I'd have to step up and deal with it, no matter what. "Yeah, I'm beginning to realize that. So, what do you suggest?"

She swung her hand toward the living room. "Of course, you're welcome to stay here, but I know the pull-out sofa isn't very comfortable. Have you thought about moving into the house yourself? Then you could stay a while, and give yourself time to think things through to decide what you want to do. Rob and I could help you scrounge up some basic furniture."

Move back into the house and live there alone? Now that's scary! Me and Gabe together again in the big old house after all these years? Would he even remember me? I don't want him pushing ME down the stairs! And for how long? Would I have to survive the harsh Vermont winter alone?

Staying through the winter frightened me even more than having an encounter with Gabe. Plus, I figured my manager would throw a major hissy fit and possibly fire me, if I told her I was staying in Vermont for an unknown period of time.

For my first full day back in my hometown, I'd had a lot thrown at me all at once.

I finished my glass of wine. "I hadn't really thought about it, but I guess it's a possibility. I'd have to get a phone line hooked up so I could dial in to work, and probably cable television, so I wouldn't go crazy," I said. "Let me sleep on it tonight, and we can figure it out in the morning. My mind is just going in too many directions to make any decisions right now."

Ellie patted my hand. "I'm sure whatever you decide, it will all work out fine."

I could only hope she was right.

INSPECTOR

Fortunately Charles Turpin was able to rearrange his schedule. He and his crew met me the following day at the house to do the inspection. Charles was balding, of medium build, in his mid-fifties. I greeted him at the door, then led him to the kitchen where I had set up a card table and folding lawn chairs I borrowed from Ellie.

Charles sat and placed a yellow notepad on the table.

"Thank you for meeting me on such short notice," I said. "I really appreciate it."

He nodded. "Yeah, it sounds like you're under a tight time schedule. I hope we can help you out." He pulled a pen from his breast pocket, and continued, "So, have you ever had an inspection done on this house before?"

"I've had one done on our home in California, but I don't think we've ever had one done on this house."

"So, you didn't have the house inspected before you rented it?"

"No, why?"

"How did you get a state rental permit, if you didn't have it signed off by an inspector?" he asked, his tone ominous.

My heart jumped a beat. I was speechless. *I needed a permit to rent the place? Why didn't I know that?…and why hadn't Arlene told me? She must have known, being a real estate agent! Shit!* I could've kicked her prissy, fat ass once again.

"Oh, I hired a real estate agent as my property manager. I just assumed she had taken care of it. She never mentioned to me we needed a permit," I admitted.

Charles shook his head as he wrote. "It means you've been renting this place illegally. Did you know if any of your tenants had realized this, they could've turned you in to the state and refused to pay rent?"

My thoughts immediately went to my first horrible tenants. *Thankfully they weren't as smart as they thought, or I would have been in big trouble!*

"No, I guess I didn't." I began to shake, cursing Arlene under my breath.

"You could have faced some serious fines as an illegal landlord. It's just as well you're not planning to rent it now," Charles scolded. "You got real lucky."

"I'm sorry. I wasn't fully aware of the rental laws, not living in Vermont," I said as contritely as possible. "I was relying on my property manager to inform me of the process, which she did not do!"

Charles nodded. "Okay. Well, what's done is done. So here's how the inspection will work. My guys will start on the roof and work their way through the entire house including the cellar. We'll document everything we see, good and bad. It'll probably take us about eight hours to complete the inspection. Then I'll meet you back here on Friday, and we'll review the report."

Uh-oh! This is going to take the rest of the week, and my flight is on Sunday. Ellie's right—nothing is going to happen quickly. Shit! "Fine," I responded. *I'm sure the report will be nothing but bad news.*

Reviewing his notes, Charles said, "The total cost of the inspection and report will be nine hundred and fifty dollars. You can pay me on Friday, and I do take credit cards."

Ouch! I wasn't expecting it to be that expensive. *I know it's needed, so I'll just have to do it. But Mark is not going to be happy about the cash outlay.*

He continued, "If you do plan to rent the house again, there will probably be a number of items on the report you'll have to address, and then you'll need another inspection to ensure everything is up to code."

"I understand," I said, my mind reeling.

To rent or not to rent? To sell or not to sell? How much will I need to fix if I put it on the market? I had no idea. *And what will the bottom line be? And what is Mark going to think about all of this?*

"You don't need to stick around. We'll lock up when we leave," Charles said.

I knew the results weren't going to be good. One way or another, I was going to have to deal with it. *It looks like I'm going to have to cancel my plane ticket and move into the house after all. Damn! I hope Gabe won't mess with me.*

DEEDEE MAKES A MOVE

Back at Ellie's, I poured myself a glass of wine and got comfortable in her office to call my husband, Mark.

"Arlene quit on me!" I complained. "And the house isn't in very good shape. There's a guy there now doing an inspection. But he won't have the report to me until Friday." I took a sip of wine. "He said the house can't be rented until all the repairs are up to code."

"Oh, I'm sorry to hear that, Babe." Mark paused. "Sounds like this could get expensive. So what do you want to do?"

"Well, this is going to take a whole lot longer to figure out than I originally planned." I dreaded the thought. "Ellie suggested I might consider moving into the house until we decide on a plan of action."

Mark groaned. "How long do you think it would be for?"

"I don't know! Believe me, I don't really want to do this. But I don't see I have many options at this point."

"Will you be all right living there alone?"

"Good question! I certainly hope so." My thoughts went to Gabe and his antics. "And I sure as hell don't want to be here all winter. That would totally suck!"

"Yup, I agree!" Mark paused. "So, what about your work? What is your manager going to say?"

I figured that was going to be a rough conversation. "Well, she's probably going to be pissed. But if I can get a phone line hooked up, then I could still log in to work and stay up with things." It would be tough, but I was sure I could do it. "I'm not going to contact her until I see the inspection report. Then I'll tell her what's going on."

"Okay, Babe. Well, I'm sorry to hear this. I know you'll do what you think is best. Just hang in there."

"Thanks. I'll let you know what the inspection report says at the end of the week. Love you."

"Love you, too," Mark said, and hung up.

Over the next couple of days, Ellie and her husband Rob helped me procure from their neighbors a bed, nightstand, dresser, small kitchen table and chairs, desk, some basic living room furniture, and a small television with a stand. The previous tenants had left behind an old sofa, which was still pretty comfortable. I put the sparse bedroom furniture in Mom's old room to the right of the front door, then arranged the sofa and an easy chair, along with the television, in the main room. The old potbelly wood stove, which had once stood prominently against one wall, had long since been removed and replaced by the furnace in the cellar. I set up a small office of sorts in front of the kitchen window facing the backyard. The wooden kitchen table and chairs were placed to the left of the desk. I had effectively made myself a small apartment in what had been the original farmhouse. I closed the doors to the upstairs addition, as I had no intention of spending any time there, if I could avoid it. I knew Gabe roamed those rooms, and I didn't want to trigger any unnecessary confrontations.

Then I arranged to have a phone and internet line installed, and went to the local cable company to get television service hooked up. They insisted I sign a one-year contract even though I insisted (hoped!) I wouldn't be staying that long. Since they wouldn't budge on their rules, I figured I'd just deal with the penalties when I left. Because the end of August was quickly fading into fall, I had the furnace serviced and the heating oil tank filled. Since I had originally planned to be in Vermont for only a week, I had traveled with just lightweight summer clothes. My next stop was at the mall in Rutland to buy more layers, a jacket, and sturdy boots.

On Friday, Charles met me at the house to review the inspection report.

"I have some good news," Charles said as we sat at my upgraded kitchen table, with the report open in front of us.

My heart leapt a beat. *Maybe this won't be as bad as I initially thought.*

"You passed windows!" He smiled.

Several years before Mom moved out, we had replaced all the old windows with double-paned storm windows to keep the house warmer in the winter. It was an expensive upgrade, but now I was glad we had had it done.

"That's great!" I said.

"Now for the bad news." He paused, looking straight at me. "You flunked everything else."

My stomach churned. *Oh, shit! I knew the other shoe was going to drop!* "Oh, that's not good!" My mind was already running through calculations of the worst-case scenarios.

We spent the next two hours going through the report page by page: slate tiles on the roof were broken and needed to be replaced; flashing and gutters needed to be repaired; I should consider putting a whole new roof on. The floorboards in the upstairs bedrooms were rotted and needed to be replaced; other floorboards downstairs had similar problems. The plumbing in the bathroom was leaking because the pipes were corroded. The cellar dirt floor needed to be covered with something more permanent. The foundation slate walls were seeping mud and needed to be remortared. Bees, wasps, termites, mice, and a host of other creepy-crawlies infested the house. He recommended I should have it tented and completely fumigated.

Would that get rid of a ghost as well?... Probably not.

But the worst of all was the old tube-and-knob wiring in the cellar had live wires hanging from the ceiling. Charles informed me it would only take a simple spark from those wires, and the furnace or the water heater could explode. Now he definitely had my attention!

"Phew! That's a lot to take in all at once," I said, as panic started to set in. Where would I even begin?

"I know, I'm sorry," Charles said. "This is an old house with three separate sections, and each one has its own issues."

My mind raced. *This is going to cost us a fortune!* "So, the bottom line? If I was going to fix everything on the list, what do you think it would cost me?"

Charles took a few minutes to look back through the report, jotting some calculations on his notepad. "I'd say your biggest expenses would be the roof and foundation. Then of course, you need to get an electrician in here to get the wiring upgraded. Altogether, I think you're probably looking at a hundred thousand, maybe more."

A hundred grand! Is the house even worth that much? I doubted it. *Do I really want to spend that kind of money just to take the chance of new tenants possibly trashing the place again?* Mark's disapproving voice rang in my head...*bulldoze it!*

If I had any realistic intentions of us moving back to Vermont, it might be worth the investment, but not to set it up as a rental again. My options were limited: I would probably have to sell the house, and go back on my promise to Mom. It broke my heart to think about it.

I let out a breath. "Wow! That's a boatload of money."

Charles nodded sympathetically. "Yeah, it is. If you want my personal opinion, I'd put the house up for sale as-is, and let the new owners decide what repairs to make. I don't think it'd be worth it for you to put that kind of money into this place just to rent it out again," he added, confirming what I was thinking.

"Well, I'm going to stay here for a while, so I can decide what to do next," I told him.

He shook his head and said, "If you're going to do that, Dee, you need to have an electrician come in right away and tie off those live wires for your own safety." He pulled a business card from a folio in his briefcase. "Here's a good electrician in Fair Haven I can recommend. He's reasonable, so it shouldn't cost you a lot to get the wiring repaired."

"Thanks, Charles. I appreciate your honest feedback," I said. I handed him my credit card so we could complete our business.

"Well, good luck, Dee. I hope everything works out for you." Charles shook my hand.

I hope everything works out for me, too!

Instinctively I went to the refrigerator to pour myself a glass of wine to settle my nerves. But I hadn't gone grocery shopping yet, since I wasn't officially moved in, and the shelves were bare. Shit! I poured a glass of water, sat back down at the table, and stared at the report, pondering my options.

If I do major repairs, I can't live in the house. But I'd have to stay local to manage the contractors. So, I would have to rent an apartment somewhere. And how long will the repairs take? A year? Maybe longer?

I knew it was almost impossible to line up contractors in Vermont in the fall, as they all took time off for deer-hunting season through Thanksgiving. Then with the winter setting in, no work would probably begin until spring. *I came home for a week, and now it looks like I may have to spend the next year of my life here to get this old house fixed up. This sucks!*

But I had also made a promise to Mom not to sell the place. The emotional turmoil of the week was taking its toll.

As my mind swirled, an idea formed. *Maybe I can subdivide the three acres, sell the house, and keep some of the land, just in case I ever want to move back here. Then I could technically keep my promise to Mom and still get out from underneath the house. It just might work.*

I grabbed the report, closed up the house, and drove back to Ellie's so we could discuss the possibilities. Ellie thought my idea of subdividing the property and selling the house was probably the best way to go. She recommended a realtor, Bill Graybert, in Castleton, a few miles from Fair Haven, with whom she had gone to college. She said Bill had thought highly of Mom and would probably do a good job putting the house on the market.

That night, I called Mark and recounted the many issues on the report. He groaned when I told him Charles' estimate to complete the repairs. We agreed it was too much to spend on a rental. Mark again recommended bulldozing, and I vetoed his suggestion. We ultimately decided subdividing the property and selling the house as-is was our best option. My heart was heavy over the decision.

The next morning, I contacted Bill Graybert and set the wheels in motion to have the property surveyed, so we could draw new boundary lines to subdivide the land.

The last long-term issue I had to deal with was my rental car. I couldn't afford to continue to pay the hefty weekly rental fee, but I had to have transportation. On Saturday, Ellie followed me to Burlington, an hour-and-a-half drive, where I turned in the rental at the airport. Then we went to Rent-a-Wreck, where I procured a used car for a more affordable monthly fee.

On Sunday, instead of boarding a plane to go home to my husband and kitties in California, I packed my suitcase, gathered my laptop and work files, left Ellie's house, hit the grocery store, and moved back into my childhood homestead alone.

All I could think was: *What the hell have I gotten myself into?*

A RUDE AWAKENING

I took a deep breath as I entered the dark, quiet house. Turning on the lights, I peered around. Not seeing any spectral images, I proceeded to put my groceries away, and unpacked my suitcase. After preparing a light dinner and watching some television, I decided to go to bed.

It felt strange sleeping in Mom's old room, next to the front door. This was also the room where Old Bert had died. *Is his ghost still here, too?*

Lying in bed in the darkness, I considered all the things I would have to deal with in the coming days. Suddenly a scurrying sound came from the wall next to my head. I bolted up in bed. *What the hell was that?* I turned on the bedside lamp and looked around the small room. No ghostly figure lurked nearby. Then I heard the scratching again, and what I thought were chirps.

You should have the house fumigated. Charles' words flooded back to me.

Oh, God! Are there mice in the walls? How did they get in there? And can they get into this room? I don't want to wake up with critters gnawing on me!

I got up and pounded on the wall, hoping they would skitter away. Then I reluctantly climbed back into bed, turned off the light and lay rigid, listening. The wind had increased, and the windows rattled ever so slightly. I curled up under the blankets, trying to will myself to sleep.

Thumps on the porch just outside my window broke my twilight sleep. I bolted up in bed. Footsteps thudded again. *What the hell? Are there more mice out there? They sound pretty damned big!*

Tired and frustrated, I got up, went to the door, and turned on the porch light, then peered through the glass in the top of the door. The backside of a black-and-white varmint, tail high in the air, pounced down the steps into the yard. Then another skunk followed in hot pursuit. *Shit! Were they mating on my porch?* I didn't dare open the door to investigate. I turned off the light and went back into the bedroom, where I saw the clock read 3:30. *Damn! I'm never going to get a good night's sleep in this house!*

I nodded off, hoping Gabe wouldn't mess with me, along with the nocturnal creatures at my doorstep.

I was cranky Monday from my restless night, and dreaded having to call my manager in California to explain my situation to her. Later that morning, when I told her I would be staying in Vermont for an indefinite period, she wasn't at all happy. I assured her I would be able to continue my work remotely and attend necessary meetings. Our team was working on a massive data migration project, and I was managing the Notebook PC section. Our deadline was fiscal year end—October 31st. I knew we were under the gun, and I would have to do the best I could to focus on work, along with handling all the issues with the house. I could feel my stress level percolating.

During my second week home, I dreamed there were fire engines surrounding the house, with sirens blazing. As I became more fully awake, I realized the cacophony was coming from inside. *What the hell? Where is all this noise coming from?* My heart raced, and I couldn't get my mind around it. I glanced at my beside clock and the digits read 2:01. *Shit! What the hell is going on?*

Shaking and unsteady, I got out of bed, put my slippers on, and listened more carefully. The noise was deafening and reverberated all over the house. I walked into the kitchen and realized the smoke detectors were wailing. But why? I didn't smell smoke. Because of my rental insurance requirements, I had installed smoke and carbon monoxide detectors in all the rooms. It seemed as if all the detectors in the house were going off at once.

What set them off? Does carbon monoxide have an odor? I had no idea. *Am I being poisoned because of a leak?* I opened the cellar door, turned on the light, walked down a few steps and peered into the dank space. I wasn't sure what I was looking for, but didn't see any warning lights flashing on the furnace, or anything else out of the ordinary.

Don't smoke detectors chirp when the batteries are going dead? I didn't think they went into full alarm mode, though. *What are the chances of every detector in the house going off at exactly the same time?* Now I was starting to panic. *Shit! I hate being here alone! It's times like this when husbands come in very handy!*

I climbed the step-stool and unscrewed the caps of the two detectors in the kitchen. It was a stretch to reach, but I managed to remove the batteries, and the wailing abruptly stopped. But the rest of the detectors in the house still screamed, and my nerves were on end.

After I removed the batteries from the detectors in the downstairs rooms, I hesitated at the bottom of the stairs. If I was going to have any chance of going back to sleep, I'd have to deal with the detectors in the upstairs rooms. I dragged the step-stool up the staircase and went into the room on the left—Gabe's room. I immediately felt a chill run through my body. The wailing echoed off the walls and seemed much louder in this enclosed, empty space. I gritted my teeth, climbed the stool, and removed the batteries from the detectors on the ceiling. They stopped squealing. I made my way to the other two bedrooms and repeated the process.

The silence was deafening once the wailing finally stopped. I collapsed, shaking, onto the stool seat, my heart thumping. *What the hell just happened? Why in the world did all these detectors go off all at once?* I had no idea and didn't like the possibilities swirling through my mind. I made a mental note to go to the store in the morning to buy new batteries.

With adrenaline coursing through my body, I knew I was too wired-up to go back to bed. I went to the kitchen and brewed myself a pot of coffee, then got comfortable in my easy chair and turned on the television. Scrolling through the channels, I settled on an old black-and-white Western, with no notable stars I recognized. I could have used a good dose of John Wayne right about then to boost my courage!

The phone ringing made me jump from my dream. My first thought was the smoke detectors were going off again. I was slumped at an odd angle in my chair where I'd fallen asleep, and my neck was stiff. I cringed as I moved to answer the phone on the table next to me.

"Hi, DeeDee, this is George Standard. I hope I didn't wake you," the man said. Bill had hired George to survey the property. I looked at the clock; it was almost 9:30 in the morning. *Damn it! I need to get moving!*

"Hi George, it's okay. I just had a rough night. What's up?"

"I'd like to come by today to start the survey. Would that work for you?"

"Yeah, sure, that'd be fine. What time will you be here?"

"In about an hour, if it's all right," George said.

I was exhausted from the previous night, but knew I couldn't sleep any longer. "Yeah, that's be fine. I'll see you then," I said, and hung up. I took a quick shower, dried my hair, dressed, and picked up the house and kitchen a bit. Then George was at the doorstep.

We reviewed the current property boundaries. The parcel was shaped like a long rectangle, starting at the road and stretching back to the middle of the block. It measured a total of 2.59 acres. Looking at the property from the road, the house sat in the lower right-hand corner of the rectangle. George drew a square extending all the way around the house, leaving a long, narrow access lane to the back field.

"If we include the point-five-nine acres with the house, that would leave you a thirty-foot-wide easement from the road to access the back of the property. You'd still keep two acres," George informed me.

"It seems reasonable to me. Sell the house with a half an acre, and then I can still keep most of the land."

"Okay, then. Let me get the exact measurements and stake boundary markers. When I'm done, I'll have you come take a look." George left the kitchen, and his assistant joined him outside as they began their work.

I logged in to the office, answered emails, and continued working on my data migration project. In mid-afternoon, the phone rang. It was the electrician I had contacted to fix the wiring in the cellar. He wanted to come over right away to get the work done before dark. I agreed to meet him. When he arrived, he informed me he would have to shut off the main breaker to do the work. I realized I was supposed to call in to a meeting in an hour. I asked him to wait a few minutes while I contacted my boss. I told her my electricity was being turned off and I wouldn't be able to make the meeting. She was not happy. So be it.

While the electrician worked, I joined George in the yard and watched as he took measurements. The land extended back into the wooded area of the block, and he was having a tough time keeping his lines straight, so I offered to help by moving bushes out of his way. As we were finishing, I saw the lights go on in the house, which was great, as it was almost dark. I excused myself from George and his assistant, and went to find the electrician.

He told me, "I tied off all the live wires and stapled them to the ceiling so they won't be in the way. I also made some repairs at the junction box which is pretty old. You might want to consider getting a new one soon."

Oh, great! One more thing to put on my to-do list.

"It's a good thing you did this," he said. "You had a real dangerous situation in the cellar."

I thanked him and wrote him a check for a hundred bucks. *A good deal to keep the house from blowing up around me!*

Then George returned to the house. I approved the lines he had staked out on the property. He explained he would now file the new survey report with the town, and then we'd have to wait for their approval, as well as get a legal sign-off, to complete the subdivision. He would bring me the final paperwork and survey in about a week to ten days, when I could pay him. I thanked him for his help.

I went back to my computer and logged back in to work for several hours until my stomach started growling. I made myself some dinner, poured a glass of wine, and settled in to watch television for a while. Soon I was exhausted and climbed into bed.

Fire engines with wailing sirens surrounded the house. I jolted awake from my dream. *What the hell?* The noise was everywhere, but how could that be? It dawned on me I had forgotten to buy batteries during the day, since I'd gotten busy. *The smoke detectors are completely disabled! How could they all be clanging again?* I glanced at my bedside clock: 2:01 a.m. *You've got to be kidding me! Am I dreaming?* I lay in bed shaking, my heart slamming in my chest, not wanting to get up and investigate.

I hesitated to turn on the lamp, because I didn't want to face whatever might be lurking in the shadows. When I pulled my bare arm out of the covers, I realized the room was very cold. It was getting chilly at night as fall was setting in, but it wasn't below freezing. And I kept the thermostat set at fifty-five degrees—so unless the furnace had gone out, I couldn't figure out why it was so frigid in the room. When the light came on, I could see my breath exhale in front of me. I put on my glasses and they immediately fogged up from my hot breath; my vision went white. I pulled off my glasses and my gaze traveled to the end of the room. In the doorway was the glowing apparition of an old man. I blinked rapidly. *Is he really there, or are my eyes playing tricks on me?* I struggled to focus, as the steam from my heavy breathing billowed around me.

The ethereal figure had a long, gray beard and was wearing a red flannel shirt tucked into dark, baggy trousers, held up by suspenders. He stared at me.

Oh, shit! It's Gabe! So he IS still here! He looked the same as I remembered as a kid—hovering in his heavy rubber boots. *Will he remember me as the little girl who grew up in this house, or will he try to kill me, like he did my tenants?*

I lay frozen to the bed, the cacophony around me deafening.

CLOSE ENCOUNTER

I slowly propped myself up in bed, gathering the covers around me. "Gabe! I'm DeeDee, the little girl who grew up in this house. Do you remember me?" My voice trembled. "You promised to protect me from evil." I stared at the wavering apparition hovering in the doorway, my heart pounding. "Are you doing this? Are you making all this noise?" My hot breath billowed in the frigid room. "Can you please turn it off? I can't sleep!"

No movement.

"I'm not here to cause any problems, Gabe. I'm just here for a visit." I hoped to appeal to his gentler side.

The shrill clanging echoed louder and I covered my ears. The moments ticked off as if eternity had come to a screeching halt. I stared at Gabe. He peered at me. Neither of us moved.

"Please!" I desperately whispered.

As I watched, his bright visage slowly faded, and I could see through the doorway to the room beyond.

Then silence. The echo of the alarms still reverberated in my mind.

"Thank you!" I said, shaking all over. I let out the breath I didn't realize I was holding. I could no longer see the vapor.

I fell back on the bed and lay still as death for several minutes, willing my heart to calm down. Finally, I put my glasses back on, got out of bed, and wrapped myself in a robe. I peered around the main room as I made my way to the kitchen. No spectral images hovered nearby. Not wanting to stay up the rest of the night, I poured a glass of milk instead of making coffee, and sat at the table trying to get my mind around what had just happened.

So Gabe is still here, but he wasn't aggressive—other than waking me up two nights in a row. I heaved a sigh and took a sip of milk. *Does he even remember me? I sure hope so. But what about any new owners? How will he react to them? And will I have to disclose the house is haunted when I put it on the market?*

I knew there were a lot of crazy people who were ghost hunters and loved haunted houses. On the other hand, I figured most normal people would avoid a haunted house like the plague. *Is there a way to get rid of him? A seance? Spiritual cleansing? Fumigation?* How would I even find anyone around here who could do something like that? And how fast would the news fly around town? *Like a whirlwind, no doubt. Shit! Probably best not to mention it at all.*

I went back to bed with critters and ghosts swirling in mind.

The next morning, as I was brewing a pot of coffee, I noticed little black droppings on the countertop. Following the trail led me to the bowl of Halloween mini-chocolates I had put out. Several of the wrappers had been chewed through.

Oh great! Now I've got a mouse in the kitchen. Like I don't have enough stuff to worry about! I poured a cup of coffee, unplugged the machine, and moved everything on the counter to the kitchen table. I scrubbed the counter with disinfectant, slightly grossed out a mouse had been running around.

My previous tenants had managed to shatter the glass window in the oven door. With three active boys and a drunken father, I could only imagine how it had happened. My guess was the mouse or mice were living in the oven, since it was no longer being used.

After getting dressed, I drove to the local hardware store, now managed by Karen, an old school friend. I had made several trips to the store since I had been living at the house, and she had become a great help.

"Hey, Dee!" Karen smiled as I walked in. Her once-blond hair was sporting streaks of gray. Several inches shorter than me, she tilted her head up to talk. "How are things going out at the old house?"

I shook my head. "Not good…looks like I've got mice in the kitchen. What's your best recommendation for getting rid of them?"

"Well, you've got two choices: poison or traps," she explained. "Personally, I don't like to use poison, because the mice go back into their nest to die, then stink to high heaven, and they're usually impossible to find!" She scrunched her nose as she laughed.

I cringed. "Okay, so that's gross. Probably not what I want to do. What's the deal with traps, and how do they work?" I asked, wishing once again Mark was here to take care of this "manly" chore.

"Here, let me show you." Karen led me along an aisle, scanning shelves, then she pulled out several packages of traps. I followed her back to the counter.

She unwrapped one package to demonstrate how to set the trap without hurting myself. She recommended placing peanut butter in the holder to attract the mice. Then she showed me how to release the mouse and drop it into the garbage.

"At least with traps, you can dispose of the critter before he scurries back to his lair," she chuckled.

Even though I had grown up a country girl, I had been suburbanized for almost thirty years. The thought of wildlife invading my living space really creeped me out. I bought a package of six traps and batteries for the smoke detectors, then thanked Karen for her help. She wished me good luck. I figured I'd need it. Next door at the grocery store, I bought a big jar of peanut butter and a package of rubber gloves. Before I went to bed that night, I set all six traps on the stove and countertop, hoping to catch the varmint.

Sure enough, when I got up the next morning, there was a dead mouse in one of the traps. Donning the rubber gloves, I gingerly lifted the trap, took it outside, released the catch as Karen had directed, dropped the mouse into the garbage bin and closed the lid. *Who says I can't live here alone without a man?* I was quite proud of myself.

That night before I went to bed, I repeated the process, setting the traps.

Bam! Bam! Bam!

Instantly I awoke. *Jesus! What the hell is that? Is Gabe messing with me again?*

Bam! Bam! Bam!

My heart pounded as I glanced at the clock—5:35 a.m. *Well, at least it's not 2:01!* And the room didn't seem unusually cold. But what the hell was causing the noise? I turned on the lamp, put on my glasses, threw on my robe and slippers, and slowly edged out of the bedroom to investigate.

Okay! Maybe a brave husband would come in handy right about now!

Bam! Bam!

The noise led me to the kitchen. When I turned on the light, the source of the banging was apparent. A mouse had been caught in a trap on the countertop, but wasn't dead. It was using its hind legs to lift the trap up and down, caught on its head. It propelled its body across the counter, leaving a trail of slime, guts, and poop in its wake.

I gagged. *How disgusting!* As I inched closer to the counter, I saw tiny forms squirming in the slime. *Oh, God! It's a female and she's expelling her babies!*

Being too much for me to handle before having my morning coffee, I ran to the bathroom and vomited. *God, I hate living here alone! I wish Mark was here to take care of this gross stuff.*

I gathered my courage, put on rubber gloves, gingerly lifted the trap and wrapped the whole mess in paper towels. I threw the trap and squirming mouse together into the outdoor garbage bin. Bending over, retching, I gulped the chilly morning air.

The next hour or more was spent cleaning the slime from the counter and stove. The smell of bleach stung my nose and made my eyes water as I made sure it was completely disinfected. Then I brewed myself a much-needed pot of coffee and collapsed.

This day certainly wasn't starting off well, and it wasn't even 7:00 a.m.

HOUSE GOES ON THE MARKET

A few days later, with the smoke detectors now silenced and no new mice caught in my traps, Bill Graybert came by with the real estate contract, and the newly approved subdivision survey.

"Here's the house inspection report I had done a couple of weeks ago," I said, sliding the report across the table.

"Dee, I can't look at the report," Bill said, which surprised me. "If I see anything amiss, I'll have to legally disclose it on the listing. It's for your eyes only. The potential new owners can have their own inspection done."

"Oh, I didn't realize that's how it works," I responded. "I would have thought the new owners would appreciate seeing it, since I paid a lot of money for it."

"You're being too nice!" Bill admonished me. "This is business. You don't show your cards until you're ready to make a deal."

At this point I had to make a decision about Gabe. Should I tell Bill about him or not? Based on what he'd just told me, if he knew about the ghost (and believed me in the first place—another pitfall I preferred avoiding), he would probably have to legally disclose it. I decided to keep Gabe under wraps, at least for now. I signed the papers to get the process rolling. Bill stuck a For Sale sign on the lawn as he left. It made me sad to see the sign waving in the breeze, beckoning travelers as they whizzed along the road. A big chapter in my family's life was coming to an end.

For the next couple of weeks, I puttered around the house making small improvements. A childhood friend who owned a local plant nursery came over and dressed up the front of the house with fall mums and hanging baskets. The flowers gave the old house a bit of "curb appeal," and made the real estate pictures look more inviting.

During that time, Bill brought by several prospective buyers and showed them around the property. He had admonished me not to talk to the visitors, since I was too forthcoming. He feared I would give them more information than they needed for submitting an offer. Properly chastised, I focused on my work, trying my best to ignore the visitors. No one made an offer, because the house had issues.

I flipped the calendar to October 2004, and had an ominous feeling I was going to be stuck here all winter.

As a diversion from focusing on all the issues running through my head and the stress of keeping up with work requirements, I settled in every evening to watch the baseball post-season playoffs.

As things would have it, my favorite team, the Red Sox, were actually doing quite well. I recalled Mom's lifelong devotion to the team.

Saturdays had been Mom's day to clean the house. She would put the Red Sox game on and go about her chores. One day when I had been watching the game, a Sox player was called out at home plate. Mom ran into the room and shook her fist, almost cold-cocking the portable, black-and-white television, and yelled, "Open your eyes, Ump! He's safe!" She put her hands on her hips, glaring at the set. Muttering under her breath, "Damned umpires!" she went back to her chores.

I was always amazed at her ability to keep one eye on the game the whole time.

As I reminisced, I thought about the Red Sox having a bad history with the World Series. In fact, the team hadn't won the championship since 1918, when Babe Ruth was traded to the New York Yankees, thus bringing on the dreaded "Curse of the Bambino"—never winning a World Series since that infamous trade.

This year the Yankees had won their division over the Sox, but the Sox had squeaked into the playoffs as the Wild Card team. After winning the early playoff rounds, the Sox now faced their dreaded nemesis, the Yankees, in the American League Championship Series. Winner of the best of seven games would go to the World Series.

"Hey, Mom!" I reached out to her spirit. "The Sox are playing the Yanks again. Let's hope we can beat those devils this year!"

But the Series wasn't going in the Sox's favor. Game four was being played at Fenway, and our boys were down three games to none. This was a do-or-die game for the Sox. If the Yankees won, they moved on to the World Series, and the Sox would go home empty-handed—again. Statistics said it was practically impossible for a team to come back and win the final four games.

I fixed myself a quick dinner, poured my ever-present glass of wine, and settled into my easy chair to watch what I figured would be the Sox's last game of the season.

"Well, here we go, Mom. We gotta win this one! Cross your fingers!"

By the ninth inning, my nerves were on edge, as the Sox were down by one run.

"It's not looking good for our guys, Mom! Do you think that old Curse is getting them again?"

No answer from above.

I sighed and sipped my wine. *The Sox can't seem to shake their Curse any more than I can shake Gabe from his house!*

Then, suddenly, a hit into the outfield sent the man on second base heading for home. A tight play at the plate—safe!

"Good call, Ump!" I pumped my fist, channeling Mom's enthusiasm.

The Sox had tied the score, and the game went into extra innings.

"Hey, Mom! Our Sox are making a comeback. What do you think of that?"

No response.

With the hour approaching midnight, I felt drowsy from the wine, but I was determined to see the outcome. I paced the house to wake up a bit, then got comfortable again to watch the rest of the game.

In the twelfth inning, David Ortiz, "Big Papi," hit a walk-off home run to win the game for the Sox. The crowd went wild. I jumped up, cheered and clapped like a crazy person. If Gabe was watching he probably thought I had gone mad.

The following night, still in Fenway, the Sox took it to fourteen innings, again playing until long after midnight. Unbelievably, "Big Papi" drove in the winning run again. Now the series was Yankees three, Red Sox two. But the final two games would move back to Yankee Stadium. I figured our boys were doomed.

"Our Sox are going to enemy territory, Mom. Going to be tough to win two there. Let's keep our fingers crossed!" I could feel her spirit willing them on to victory.

Game six had Curt Schilling pitching for the Sox. During his performance, the stitches from a recent ankle surgery broke loose. I was fascinated watching the blood stain on his sock grow as the game stretched on. It gave a whole new meaning to the name "Red Sox." Schilling pitched an amazing game, giving up only one run.

Then things got ugly in the eighth. Fans erupted after a disputed call went against a Yankee player, and a run was erased. Debris was thrown on the field, and several guys who rushed the pitcher's mound had to be forcibly removed. The game was halted while the umpires restored order. The Sox won four to two, silencing the hostile crowd.

"They tied the Series, Mom! Can you believe this? Maybe this year they'll reverse the Curse!"

The following night, in game seven, the "big bats" of the Red Sox players came out swinging early, putting several runs on the board. But the Yankees roared back and tied the game at three each. Then the Boston sluggers rallied, adding seven more runs, to win the game in a blowout.

I jumped up hollering, "Mom, they won! They beat those damned Yankees! Can you believe it? Our Sox are finally going to the World Series! I wish you could be here to enjoy it with me." I felt her spirit surround me.

Red Sox players rushed the field, ending up in a human heap in the infield. Sox fans in the stands went wild, as disgruntled Yankee fans quickly exited the stadium. The Sox had done the impossible: coming back from a three-to-zero Series deficit, to defeat the dreaded Yankees. It was an incredibly proud moment for our Red Sox Nation!

Now the Red Sox faced the St. Louis Cardinals in the World Series. The Boston men won the first two games at Fenway, then swept the Series with two more wins in St. Louis. It was anti-climactic after their big comeback win over the Yanks, but still amazing to see them become World Champions for the first time in almost one hundred years.

I put my jacket on and went to our favorite spot in the backyard, where the Hunter's full moon glowed bright across the landscape. "Mom! They did it! Our boys won the World Series. They finally reversed the Curse! Can you believe that? I bet you were cheering the whole way!" I smiled, remembering how Mom would jump up clapping every time a Sox player hit a home run, and hoping the "man in the moon" would relay my conversation to Mom on the other side.

Two days later, I watched thousands of fans pack the roads and waterways of Boston, as the players rode the famous Duck Boats in their victory parade. The irony was not lost on me that Mom, a lifelong Red Sox fan, had never gotten to see her beloved team win the World Series. I thought it a strange coincidence the Sox finally won the same year Mom passed away, and wondered how much influence she had from her high perch.

"I'm so sorry you never got to see your favorite team win the World Series, Mom, because I know you would have loved it!" I wept over her passing, as I missed her dearly.

After the Series was over, I decided to compile a written history of the property, including all previous owners, old photographs, and what I had discovered about the role of our property in the Underground Railroad migration era. It was a labor of love; a way to say my goodbyes to the old house that had withstood the test of time, albeit almost killing me before I became a teenager. I thought potential new owners would appreciate knowing the amazing legacy of the property.

I had no indication at the time how important this report would turn out to be.

CHANTAL

MOREAU RESIDENCE
MONTREAL, QUEBEC, CANADA
OCTOBER, 2004

CHANTAL GETS A SURPRISE

"H EY, BABE! Come take a look at this one." Chantal Moreau heard her husband, Clay, shout from his office.

"Okay! Gimme a minute," she responded.

Chantal's younger daughter, Whitney, five, sat on the floor between her mother's legs while Chantal plaited tight, narrow rows of braids into her daughter's hair. Her older daughter, Charmaine, eight, sat on the sofa next to her mother, flipping pages of a magazine. "Honey," Chantal turned to Charmaine, "will you help me up? I've got to go see what Daddy wants."

Whitney scrambled out of the way. Charmaine rose and grasped her mother's hands. "Here, Mommy, hold my hands." Chantal grunted as she hefted her burgeoning belly, now six months pregnant, from the soft sofa.

As Chantal entered Clay's office, she glanced around the cramped space. The smallest of the three bedrooms in their apartment on the fourth floor of a six-story complex, it overflowed with a combination of office furniture, electronics, and exercise equipment. An elliptical trainer faced the window, blocking access to the small closet. Clay's weight bench directly behind it was haphazardly covered with technical manuals. His rarely used barbells sat in one corner.

I hope we can find a place with more room before this baby is born. The babe can't live in our bedroom forever. And it's going to take a herculean effort to clean this room out.

Clay Moreau, an I.T. manager for a bank in Montreal, had recently accepted a promotion and raise to transfer to Rutland, Vermont, where the bank was opening a new branch. Clay would manage the branch's new technology infrastructure. Having lived in an apartment in Montreal his entire married life, he was eager to find a big house with a yard for his growing family.

"Check this out," Clay said, leaning his broad shoulders back so Chantal could see the computer screen. "It's got four bedrooms and about a half an acre of land. And best of all, it's within our price range."

Chantal peered at the picture of a brown, two-story house with a big white porch supporting hanging flower baskets. A large lawn extended along the front and side of the house.

"That's kinda cute. Where's it located?" Chantal asked.

"In Fair Haven, about fifteen miles from Rutland. Not too far."

Something tugged at Chantal's memory. "Fair Haven? Huh. For some reason that name sounds familiar," she said, trying to recall where she had heard it before. With nothing coming immediately to mind, she let the thought slip.

Clay turned around in his chair and smiled up at his pregnant wife. "How about we take the girls on a road trip this weekend and go see it? Maybe I can find a hotel in Rutland with an indoor pool for the girls. We can do some sightseeing, since the foliage should be in full color right about now."

Chantal chuckled at her husband's enthusiasm. "Yeah, okay. That'd be fun. You know how the girls love road trips: 'I see a white car,' 'I see TWO red cars,'" Chantal laughed, mimicking her girls.

Clay laughed, "Yup, they love to outdo each other, don't they?"

The following Saturday morning, the Moreau family made the three-hour drive from Montreal through the Green Mountains, awash in autumn glory, to Rutland, Vermont. They checked into their hotel, with a pool, and contacted the property realtor, Bill Graybert. Bill gave them directions to the house in Fair Haven, and they agreed to meet him there at 2:30 p.m.

When Clay pulled into the driveway, Chantal saw two cars already parked. The door of the second car opened, and a slight, middle-aged man with graying hair, dressed in a casual suit, came to greet them.

The man approached Clay. "Hi. I'm Bill Graybert. You must be Clay. Nice to meet you. How was the drive down?" He and Clay walked to the passenger side of the car, where Chantal stood with their girls.

Chantal responded, "It's a gorgeous weekend to take in the foliage." She extended her hand. "Hi, I'm Chantal. Nice to meet you, Bill." She laid a hand on each girl's shoulder. "And these are our daughters, Charmaine and Whitney."

Bill bent slightly and shook both of the girls' hands. "It's a pleasure to meet you both."

Charmaine mumbled, "Merci," and cast her eyes to the ground. Whitney giggled.

"Please follow me," Bill said, leading the family across the front lawn.

Chantal inspected the hanging baskets. "Oh, I love the mums. They're so pretty this time of year." She walked up the steps onto the porch, with her family following.

"After you." Bill held the door and motioned for Chantal to enter.

As Chantal stepped through the front door, her skin began to tingle, her heart raced, and a warm flush ran through her body.

Oh, my gosh! What's happening? Am I getting sick? Having a heart attack?

She stood motionless in the doorway for several seconds, taking shallow breaths, waiting for the feeling to subside.

"Babe? You okay?" Clay asked, standing behind her.

"Yeah, yeah, sorry," Chantal said. She stepped into the main room, shaking off the unusual sensations.

Clay gave her an odd look, and she shook her head. The girls and Bill joined them inside.

Bill explained the house configuration. "Where we are standing is the center of the original farmhouse, which I believe was built in the eighteen-twenties." He pointed out the bathroom and small bedroom downstairs to the right of the front door. "The adjoining two-story addition was built in the early nineteen-hundreds."

Chantal followed Bill through a narrow hallway to a parlor and stairs leading to the second story. At the top of the stairs, Bill entered the large bedroom on the left. Following him into the room, Chantal's skin tingled and a warm flush rushed through her again. She marveled at the odd sensation.

This is so strange. What's causing this? Whatever it is, I feel safe and warm around it.

Walking through the room devoid of furniture, Chantal peered out the window facing the street. Bill and Clay chatted near the doorway, as the girls explored the other bedrooms. Chantal could hear them bickering as to who would get which room. A soft pressure on her shoulder made

Chantal turn. Expecting Clay, she was surprised to see he hadn't moved from his location across the room, chatting with Bill. No one was near her.

Is something or someone trying to get my attention? This is really odd! I'm not afraid, but I DO sense something. Why am I the only one feeling this? What can this be? I've never really believed in the afterworld, although Grandma once said she could feel the spirit passing from a dying person.

Bill called to her. Shrugging off a shiver, she dutifully followed him into the other upstairs bedrooms. She felt no odd tingling in these rooms. Then Bill led the way downstairs, the girls following, chatting loudly. Before she could start down the stairs, something grabbed her arm, making her jump. She turned to see Clay by her side.

"Honey? Are you all right?" Clay gave her a concerned look. "You've been in a strange mood since we walked in here."

She smiled appreciatively at her handsome husband. "Yeah, I think I'm okay. I'll tell you about it later." She waved toward the stairs. "Let's go see the rest of the house."

Clay gently guided her arm. "Be careful going down those stairs, now."

Chantal felt her legs wobble a bit. She grasped the worn, wooden banister as she descended each step. *What is making me so shaky? Must be the pregnancy.* She shook her head.

Bill and the girls stopped in the parlor. When Chantal and Clay joined them, Bill directed the family toward the kitchen, where the owner of the property waited.

A JOLT

On Saturday, I had been analyzing raw-data spreadsheets to compile a metrics report my manager in California wanted by Monday. The sound of Bill's voice talking to visitors in the main room got my attention, since I hadn't heard the door open.

Oh, boy, here we go again! I know I have to do this to sell the house, but it's getting old. I wish I could just close it up and go home to Cali. At this rate, with no offers, I'm probably going to end up here all winter, which would totally suck!

I sighed and rose from my desk to tidy up a couple of dirty dishes on the counter. Then I went back to my work, ignoring the visitors, as Bill had instructed me to do. Footsteps running through the upstairs rooms distracted me. I knew I wouldn't get any more work done while the looky-loos were in the house, so I saved my files and logged off the computer. Within a few moments, I heard children's excited voices nearing the kitchen, so I swung around in my office chair to greet the visitors.

I was pleasantly surprised when I saw this group. They were unlike most of the previous, disheveled, local "lookers" I had grown to expect.

Standing in front of me was a well-dressed black couple who looked to be in their mid-to-late thirties. They entered the kitchen behind Bill and two young girls.

The woman was tall and slender. Her protruding belly made it apparent a baby was due in a few months. She wore a multi-colored fall sweater of orange, yellow, and brown that nicely matched her creased brown trousers and leather, heeled boots. Her hair was straightened and shiny, about shoulder length, and formed a wispy frame around her face. The burnt-orange lipstick she wore picked up the colors of her sweater and complemented her dark skin tones.

The husband was about the woman's height, although she seemed taller in her heels. His hair was close-cropped, and he had a salt-and-pepper mustache. I noticed his bicep pressing against the long sleeve of his white Oxford shirt, tucked into pressed jeans. From the pointed alligator-skinned toes peeking out at me, it looked like he was wearing expensive cowboy boots. His smile revealed a perfect set of pearly white teeth.

Whoa! What a gorgeous hunk of man. I felt myself blush, and I arrested my mind from going any further down *that* slippery slope.

I looked at the two young girls, and guessed their ages to be about eight and five. Each girl's hairdo was styled in similar corn-row braids, ending in multiple pigtails wrapped in colorful bobbles. The older child wore a brightly colored top over black leggings, and sported black sneakers with neon-green stripes. Pink was obviously the younger girl's favorite color. From the pink flowered top to the pink tights, pink sneakers, and even pink bobbles in her hair, she looked like a huggable bowl of sherbet.

Bill introduced us. "DeeDee Williams, I'd like you to meet Chantal and Clay Moreau. They are here visiting from Montreal."

I rose to greet my visitors. *"Bonjour! Bienvenue chez moi."* I said, welcoming them to my home, hoping my French was passable.

"Tu parlez Francais?" the younger girl asked.

"Oui, un peu," I responded, making a small space between my outstretched thumb and forefinger.

The pink-clad munchkin giggled at my gesture.

"*Je m'appelle Chantal,*" the mother said to me. "*Et c'est mon mari, Clay,*" Chantal said, pointing to her husband. "*C'est Charmaine.*" Chantal laid a hand on her taller daughter's shoulder. "*Et c'est Whitney,*" she said, pointing to the younger child.

"*Ravi de vous rencontrer,*" I said, pleased to meet them. *Maybe my high school French will impress them.*

"*Merci,*" Chantal responded. Then she began to speak rapidly in French. *Uh-oh. Now I'm in trouble!*

I laughed and held up my hand. "*Je ne comprend pas, s'il vous plait!* You've gone way beyond my high school French!"

Both girls grinned at my response as they held hands.

Chantal laughed, too. "*Ce n'est-ce pas un problème. Nous parlons anglais,*" she said as she swept her arm across her family.

"*Merci beaucoup!*" I said, glad to be returning to English.

"How is it you speak French?" Clay asked, peering more closely at my laptop computer.

"Well, I was raised in parochial school here in Fair Haven. The nuns figured since Canada was our closest neighbor, we should be able to communicate in your language." I grinned, a little embarrassed. "I learned my first French phrase when I was in kindergarten, and loved the language. So I continued taking French lessons until I finished high school."

"That's quite impressive," Chantal said, her English lilting with her accent.

Shrugging, I said, "I don't get a chance to practice it much anymore. Where I live, Spanish and Cantonese are the main foreign languages." I turned to Charmaine, the older daughter, "I like your hair. I wish I could do that with mine."

Charmaine cast her eyes to the ground, and said a quiet, "*Merci.*"

The younger daughter, Whitney, grinned and met me eye to eye. "Mommy did it! Mommy loves to do braids and she's really, really good at it!" Her enthusiasm made me smile.

"Yes, she is. She's very good at it, indeed!" I said, winking at Chantal.

Chantal held out a slender hand to me, and I noticed her long, painted nails matched her lipstick. "It's nice to meet you, DeeDee," she said, grasping my hand.

"Nice—" What felt like a jolt of electricity shot up my arm, coursed through my body, and down my legs. Staring at Chantal, I noticed her dark eyes go wide.

Is she feeling this, too? What's going on? What is it about this woman that's drawing me to her? Her sense of peace and serenity are intriguing.

Our hands lingered a little longer than normal, then she broke free, still staring back at me. I stepped back and almost fell over my office chair. Regaining my composure, I turned and shook Clay's hand. No jolt.

I cleared my throat, a bit shaken from the encounter. "Nice to meet you both."

Just then, Whitney tugged at my sweater, and I peered down at her. "Bet you can't guess what my favorite color is," she giggled.

Grateful for the distraction, I noticed even her Chapstick was a shade of pink. "Hmmmm…let me think." I rubbed my chin. "Is it blue?" I said, giving her a serious look. From the corner of my eye, I noticed Chantal slowly grin.

"Nooooo! It's PINK!"

I exaggerated my surprise. "Pink? Why I never would have guessed that in a million years!"

Whitney put her hands on her hips and did a little twirl, her pigtails flying, to show off her outfit.

What a precocious kid!

"I think you look beautiful, Whitney."

Her big smile showed a front tooth missing, then she grabbed her mother's hand.

Clay's smile dazzled me. He asked, "You mentioned people speak Spanish and Cantonese where you live. So, you don't live here?" He waved his hand. "I noticed there's not much furniture in the house."

"Well, yes and no. I grew up in this house, but I live and work in Silicon Valley now. I'm just staying here temporarily, until we can sell the place," I explained, as Bill gave me his stern don't-say-anything-else look.

"And you're able to work from here?" Clay asked, motioning to my laptop.

"Yeah, I had a DSL line installed when I had the phone hooked up, so I can log on to work."

"It's good to know they have DSL available way out here," he said.

I laughed. "Well, it's a bit slower than what I'm used to in the Bay Area, but it's sufficient to get my work done." I glanced at my laptop, remembering my impatience at waiting for big files to download. But Clay didn't need to know that. "So, what brings you here from Montreal?"

Clay said, "My bank is opening a branch in Rutland, and I'm being transferred to manage their I.T. department. We live in an apartment now, and we're looking for a place with some land where the kids can grow up."

As Clay and I were having our discussion, I felt Chantal's gaze on me. It felt like she was trying to figure me out, as much as I was trying to do the same with her.

Clay waved his hand toward the kitchen window. "Bill told us you had more land, but subdivided it to sell the house."

I glanced at Bill. He nodded, giving me approval to discuss it further. "Since this was my childhood home, I wasn't ready to give up the entire property all at once. So I kept the two acres that stretch out into the back woods. But there won't be any fences, so the girls are more than welcome to play out there, if, by chance, you decide to buy the place."

Clay tucked his hands into his tight jeans pockets. "Do you think you'd ever do anything with the back property?"

"Oh, gosh, I don't know. I suppose if the Big One ever hit, and California slid into the ocean, I'd have a place to escape. But right now I don't have any specific plans."

Bill opened the back door in the kitchen. "Clay, Chantal, let's take a walk outside, and I'll show you the property boundaries." Bill led the way to the backyard, followed by Clay and the two girls, who were chatting in French. Chantal hung back, giving me a curious look, as if she wanted to say something but then thought better of it.

I looked into her soulful, dark eyes, and felt her warmth radiate. "It was very nice to meet you, Chantal." Before she could step through the door, something compelled me to add, "I think this would be a great place for your kids to grow up. I know I had a lot of fun here when I was young." I glanced at her tummy. "Do you know if the new baby is a boy or girl?"

Chantal touched her belly. "Nope! It's going to be a surprise for the whole family. Of course, Whitney wants a baby sister so she can dress her in pink!" She laughed, her eyes crinkling.

We shook hands again, no jolt this time, and grinned at one another. Something had definitely bonded us that I couldn't put my finger on.

Why is it the Moreau family strikes such a chord with me? How interesting!

UNEXPECTED VISITOR

On Sunday morning I was gathering my dirty clothes to do a stint at the laundromat downtown, when I heard a knock on the front door. Not expecting visitors, I was surprised to see Chantal on the porch.

"I'm sorry to bother you, DeeDee, but do you have a few minutes we could talk?" Noticing me glancing over her shoulder toward the driveway, Chantal added, "Clay took the girls for ice cream and to play in the park for a little while. I wanted to talk to you alone. Do you mind if I come in?"

This is a surprise! I wonder what's on her mind. Maybe she wants to buy the house. That'd be really cool if she did.

I opened the screen door, welcoming her inside. "No, no, of course not!" I laughed as I led her to the kitchen. "I was just heading to town to do laundry. I'd love any excuse to avoid *that* like the plague! Cup of coffee?"

"Sure, I'd love one," she said as she removed her coat and sat down. I poured two cups of coffee and put out sugar and cream, not knowing how she liked her coffee, then joined her at the table. I smiled watching her pour three teaspoons of sugar into her cup.

She gave me an inquisitive look.

I told her, "You remind me of my mom. She liked three sugars in her coffee, too."

"Is she still alive?"

I shook my head. "No. Her name was Robbie, and she passed away earlier this year. She'd been in a nursing home for a few years, and died of complications from Parkinson's disease." I looked away and swallowed hard to hold back the unexpected tears welling up. Talking about mom's passing was still very raw for me.

Chantal saw my reaction and touched my hand. "Oh, I'm so sorry for your loss, Dee. That must be tough on you, especially being in this house alone now."

Her hand was warm on my skin.

Taking a breath, I said, "Yeah, it's been an emotional roller coaster deciding to sell my family property. It was just the two of us living here when I grew up, as she was a single mom."

I watched Chantal peer slowly around the dingy, old kitchen, then glance into the main room. She stirred her coffee, staring into the cup as the liquid swirled. Then her dark eyes looked up at me. I sat very still. *What's on her mind? She seems a million miles away.*

After rubbing her hand over her forehead, she laid her palm on the table. Then she said, "Dee, the reason I came back here alone is I want to ask you something, and I hope I'm not overstepping my bounds." Chantal grasped her cup, then released it.

I waited, raising an eyebrow.

When she continued, her voice was a bit more husky. "When I first came into the house yesterday, a very strange feeling came over me."

I swallowed hard. *Oh, shit! This isn't good. Is Gabe already messing with these nice people?* I tried to stay calm. "What kind of feeling?"

Chantal shook her head. "Well, it's hard to describe. It was like a tingling, and then a warm flush went through my body. It was actually very pleasant, like something I've never felt before." She stared at me. "And when I went into the upstairs bedroom on the left—I know this sounds crazy—but I had the distinct feeling there was a presence there, very close to me."

"Hmmm, that's interesting," I said, astounded by her admission and not wanting to give anything away.

Her description reminds me of the feeling that coursed through me the first time I met Gabe, when I was a little girl. I had felt very safe and warm.

Chantal fidgeted, her eyes flicking from the cup to me. Finally she seemed to overcome her embarrassment and looked hard at me. It felt like she was searching my soul. "I hope you don't mind...but I...I have to ask. You grew up here. Did you ever have any...any experiences you couldn't explain?"

I shuddered. Now was the moment of truth.

What should I tell her, and what should I not tell her? Probably shouldn't mention why my tenants left, or the horrible events I had witnessed as a child. Should I tell her about Gabe saving my life on my thirteenth birthday? Probably not.

I risked another glance at Chantal. *What is it about this woman's psyche that has tapped into Gabe's presence? And does Gabe like her? Does he want to protect her? Is that why she had a warm feeling engulf her?* I couldn't put the pieces together in my mind, and I felt Chantal's eyes pressing on me with every passing second.

She cleared her throat. "You don't have to give me an answer, Dee, if you don't want to. But from your expression, it looks like I may have hit a nerve." Her soft, polite, lilting voice didn't match the riveting focus of her gaze or the intense gleam in her eyes.

I stared at this lovely, gracious woman, asking me questions I really shouldn't be answering. I couldn't help but wonder if her pregnancy had made her more receptive to the spirit around us. The image of my real estate agent flashed through my mind, aghast I would even be having this conversation with a potential buyer. I ignored it.

Deciding to be forthright, I let out a long sigh. "His name is Gabe. He told me and Mom he was here to protect us and the house from evil," I admitted. "But, please! You have to promise you won't mention this to Bill, since I didn't disclose anything about the spirit when we put the house on the market."

"Oh, my goodness! You have my word, honest!" she said as she crossed her heart. "What do you know about Gabe? Who he is? Why is he here?" Chantal asked, her interest piqued.

I grinned at her excitement. "When I was little, my mother was the housekeeper for an elderly gentleman named Bert Hopper. We lived here with him. I was about three when he died, and he willed the property and all his belongings to Mom."

"Wow! That was fortunate for your mother and you."

I sipped my coffee. "Yeah, I guess it was. But it was tough on mom, because she worked two and three jobs to support us and keep the house up. But we managed." Fond memories of Mom flitting around the kitchen came back to me. "A few years ago, when I had to move her into a nursing home, I decided to rent the house. There was an old barn out back." I pointed out the window. "You can just make out the sandy area where it used to stand. My insurance agent said, because it was old and unstable, it would be a major liability in case anyone got hurt going in there."

Chantal gazed into the backyard, where the outline of the barn footprint was still visible.

"Well, as is typical in most small towns, my insurance agent, Frank, is also the Chief of the Fire Department." I watched Chantal smile and nod. "Frank convinced us it would be in our best interest to let him and his men burn the barn down as a training exercise." I chuckled, thinking of the debacle that almost consumed Howard's barn as well.

Chantal saw my reaction. "Oh, goodness! I've never heard of anyone doing that before. How did it go?"

I grinned. "Not exactly as planned. Let's just say I'm thankful my neighbor Howard's barn is still standing. If you look, you can still see the scorch marks along the side." I pointed out the window to Howard's white barn, still streaked black on the side facing our property, which he hadn't yet painted.

Chantal put her hand to her mouth to stifle a grin as she looked at the damaged barn. "Oops! Do you think your ghost was involved in any way?"

I turned back to my visitor and shrugged my shoulders. "Could be, but I can't say for sure. Anyway, the cool thing is, when we were cleaning out the barn, we actually discovered a hidden chamber underneath. Mom and I had owned the property for forty years, and we had no idea it was there!"

Chantal's eyes went wide. "Really! Did you go down into it? What did you find?"

My stomach lurched at the memory of my horrific visit to the underground cavity. "We found artifacts that indicated fugitives had once stayed there as they traveled through the Underground Railroad network."

Chantal gasped, leaning forward in her chair. "Wow! That's amazing. And what about the ghost?"

I continued, "So, Gabe Hopper, the conductor, was Bert's ancestor. From the documentation we found, we learned Gabe and his family helped fugitives escape to Canada from the eighteen-twenties through eighteen-fifty." I waved my hand toward the ceiling. "As to why Gabe's still here? Well, I can only guess he's still protecting his property."

Chantal's eyes were bright as she held my gaze. "*Mon Dieu!* That's an incredible history you've uncovered." She paused and sipped her coffee. Her hand trembled ever so slightly.

I nodded. "Yeah, we were really surprised, I can tell you! Mom and I enlisted the help of the curators at the Fair Haven Historical Society to catalog our finds. We actually found a ledger buried in the slate foundation of the chamber. It included the names and details of families who had traveled through the property." I smiled, remembering the excitement. "Monique, the curator, called it the 'Holy Grail.' She said it was more proof of the Underground Railroad migration coming through this neighborhood."

She glanced out the window, then back at me. "That really *is* wonderful! You must have been so excited when you discovered that chamber. What happened to the artifacts? Do you still have them?"

Chantal's enthusiasm caught me off guard. I shook my head. "No. I donated most everything to the museum. Moni and her husband, Jack, have put them on display. I'm honored I was able to contribute to our small-town historical society museum."

Chantal smiled. "That was very generous of you, Dee." She again glanced around the kitchen, her expression becoming serious. "You know, it was the strangest thing. When Clay first showed me this property on the internet, somehow the town of Fair Haven seemed familiar, but I couldn't figure out why."

"And now?" I asked.

Chantal shrugged. "I'm not sure. I think our family is descended from slaves who escaped to freedom in Canada. But I don't know much more about their journey. I need to ask my mother what she knows of our family history, because she has some of Grandma's things."

I nodded. "Now isn't that an interesting coincidence? According to the ledger entries, there were hundreds of fugitives who came through this property over the years. Apparently, Fair Haven was a busy waystation for the travelers to get to the canal in Whitehall, New York, which is only a few miles from here. The canal feeds into Lake Champlain, which ends in Canada, and freedom." I looked at Chantal's pensive expression and added, "Gosh, you never know! There just might be a family connection around here." *How amazing would that be?*

Voices and footsteps on the porch, then a knock at the front door, halted our conversation.

Chantal smiled when she heard her daughters' voices calling, "Mommy!" She pulled a business card from her purse and wrote a number on the back. "Here's my home number. I'd like to keep in touch with you." She pulled out another card, turned it over, and asked, "Would you mind if I called you? Can I have your number?"

"No, not at all," I said. I recited my number as she wrote it down. "I'd be interested to hear what your mother has to say about your ancestors."

Turning Chantal's card over, I saw she was an investment adviser for a three-partner firm in Montreal. "Looks like a high-stress job," I said, grinning at her.

"*Oui!* Keeps me busy. But I love it." She smiled.

We both rose from the table. Chantal grabbed her jacket, and we walked through the main room to greet her family.

The girls must have enjoyed their ice cream: gooey spots gave away the evidence—Charmaine chocolate, Whitney strawberry—of course. Chantal was not the least bit fazed. "Looks like those tops are heading for the laundry when we get home," she said with a laugh.

"You ready to go, Babe?" Clay asked, looking quite handsome in his black leather jacket.

"Yeah, I'm ready." Chantal turned to me. "DeeDee, it was a real pleasure to meet you. Thank you for letting me interrupt you today." She gave me a hug, and I felt a warm glow emanating from her.

I waved to the family as they walked to their car. Before the door shut behind her, I heard Chantal say to Clay, "Honey, you're not going to believe what..."

CHANTAL VISITS HER MOTHER

Chantal stared out the passenger-side window at the colorful foliage, but it was all just a blur. The girls played their car-color counting game in the backseat, each trying to outdo the other. Clay had put on a Ray Charles CD. On their journey back to Montreal, the music and swaying of the car lulled Chantal, and her mind wandered.

Something in that house seems to be reaching out to me. I wonder if DeeDee's ghost wants to protect us, too. And why does the town of Fair Haven seem familiar?

As she dozed in her seat, snippets of stories she had heard as a child from her grandmother, Emmaline, flashed in her mind.

"…family escaped from their master…"

"…missing fingers…"

What was Grandma's father's name? I remember her mentioning it, but I was so young, I wasn't really paying much attention.

With Ray Charles' soulful voice surrounding her, she dozed, recalling her grandmother's words:

"…Samuel and his family…harbored in Fair Haven…"

"…wagon attacked…Samuel escaped…"

Suddenly she opened her eyes and sat straighter. *That was his name! Samuel! And it WAS Fair Haven where they were sheltered! Hmmmm. What a strange coincidence we're looking at a house in the same town.*

Clay turned to her briefly. "You okay, Babe?"

She nodded. "Yeah, I just remembered something. I'll tell you about it when we get home." She stared at a fast-moving river, tumbling over boulders, running along the right side of the two-lane roadway. The breeze showered the car with a jumble of leaves that swept across their path.

I really don't remember much more of Grandma Emmaline's stories, since I was only eight when she died. Now I wish I had paid more attention! I'll have to talk to mother when I get home and see what she can tell me about our family history.

Monday, the following day, Chantal couldn't shake the feeling that had enveloped her at the house in Fair Haven. Back at work, she did her best to focus on her clients' business concerns, but her mind kept drifting. By mid-afternoon, she finished up the bulk of her office work and called her mother, Sophia. After three rings, she heard her mother's voice.

"Hi, Mom! It's me. What are you doing?"

"Oh! Hi, Honey. I was just working on a jigsaw puzzle before I start getting dinner. Where are you?"

Chantal straightened a few papers on her desk. "I'm at work. But I wanted to come by for a visit, if you're going to be home. I need to talk to you about something."

Sophia chuckled. "Sure. I'll be here. I'm anxious to hear about your trip to the States. Did the girls have a good time?"

Chantal smiled, thinking of their game. "Oh, yeah. I think they counted every car on the highway. You know how competitive they are!" Chantal heard her mother laugh. "I'll be by soon. See you then."

She placed a quick call to Clay, letting him know she was going to her mother's after work and would be a bit late arriving home.

After ending the call, Chantal logged off her computer, grabbed her jacket and rode the elevator from her tenth-floor office to the parking garage. Exiting the garage, she drove her black Audi north from Montreal's World Trade Centre office complex. Within minutes, Chantal turned onto Rue University. Driving along the thoroughfare of her alma mater, McGill University, Chantal smiled at the familiar sight of the iconic old-English, Tudor-style Art Building, the center of campus. As she watched students gather in groups on the manicured lawns, ride bikes along the boulevard, and rush to classes, she fondly remembered her time studying there. Thoughts of her favorite teacher, Mrs. Sheer, a cheerful, middle-aged black woman who taught economics, made Chantal wonder if the woman was still teaching. Chantal made a mental note to look her up one day.

Driving through the campus, Chantal turned right, drove two more blocks, and approached the grounds of the faculty condominiums. Chantal's older brother, Reggie, was a science professor at McGill, and his wife, Becky, worked in administration. They lived with their three sons in the condo complex. When Chantal's father, Lewis, had passed away ten years earlier, Sophia had sold the family home in Napierville, an hour's drive southeast from Montreal. Chantal was happy when Reggie had made arrangements for their mother to move into faculty housing, so Sophia could be closer to her children and grandchildren.

Stopping at the gate leading to the complex, she opened her driver's-side window, and punched a code into the keypad. The automatic gate swung slowly open. To her right was a large, well-maintained playground with brightly colored climbing apparatus. To the left was the main office and large recreation room. Four-story buildings lined both sides of the center road. Chantal took the first right and parked in front of the last condominium on the right. Beyond the complex was a soccer pitch stretching to a wooded copse peppered with pines, firs, and the bright foliage of maples.

Before Chantal could reach the walkway, the door leading to her mother's ground-floor apartment flew open. Chantal smiled at her tall, stately mother, now in her late sixties, standing in the doorway, her arms stretched wide. She was dressed in a colorful flowing caftan and wore a matching turban skillfully wrapped around her head. Chantal recalled how as a child she had thought her mother was an exotic African queen. Sophia had spent her life as a social worker with the Montreal Child and Family Protective Services, helping those in difficult circumstances find better lives. Sophia loved everyone as if they were her own children.

After being hugged and ushered into her mother's eclectically decorated parlor, Chantal waited as Sophia, placing tea and cookies on the coffee table, got comfortable on the sofa next to her.

After pouring tea into their cups, her mother grasped Chantal's hand. "So, tell me about your trip. Did you and Clay find a property you liked?"

Releasing her mother's hand, Chantal took a sip of tea. "I'm not sure. Maybe."

She glanced at her mother's collection of busts lining one shelf. The statues depicted prominent black figures through history, including Frederick Douglass, Harriet Tubman, Martin Luther King, Jr. and Rosa Parks. Chantal remembered during her childhood, how each time Sophia added a bust to her collection, Chantal had been tasked to learn about that historical figure. After dinner, Sophia would challenge Chantal to recite what she learned to the family.

I should find a fun way for my girls to learn history, like my mom did for me.

Sophia's voice got Chantal's attention. "So, where is the property? How big is it? What did you think? Tell me more."

Chantal chuckled at her mother's enthusiasm. "The house we looked at was in Fair Haven, Vermont. Does that town sound familiar to you at all?"

Sophia furrowed her brow, staring at her daughter. "It might. Why do you ask?"

"I sort of remember when I was a kid, Grandma Emmaline telling me stories about our ancestor, Samuel. For some reason the name of the town sticks in my mind."

Sophia put a hand to her mouth. "Oh, my gosh! You remember her stories? Those were meant to be family secrets, you know. Grandma probably thought you were too young to understand." Sophia's hand visibly trembled as she reached for a cookie.

Chantal recoiled. "Family secrets? Why are the stories secret? Shouldn't I know about our family history?"

Her mother nodded slowly. "Yes." She sighed. "I suppose you should. You're old enough now. But tell me about this house first."

Chantal watched her mother's expression closely. "Okay. So, this is odd: when I walked into the house, a very weird feeling came over me." She shook her head. "Sort of a warm chill went down my body. It stopped me in my tracks!"

"Hmmm. That's quite curious. What do you think brought it on?"

"I don't know." Chantal shrugged. "But when we went into the upstairs bedroom, I was looking out the window and felt a touch on my shoulder. When I turned, no one was close to me." She looked at Sophia. "I know it sounds strange, but it seemed something or someone was trying to get my attention."

Sophia's eyes grew wider. "How unusual. What happened next?"

"We went back downstairs and were introduced to the property owner, DeeDee. When I shook her hand, what felt like a jolt of electricity shot through me. It surprised the hell out of me!" Chantal shook her head. "From DeeDee's expression, she must have felt it, too. Now what do you think of that?" She reached for her teacup, only to slosh the tea into the saucer, and set the cup back down.

Sophia smiled and touched Chantal's hand. "Honey, you know you've always been very perceptive, especially when you were a child. Maybe you tapped into something other-worldly in the house."

Chewing on a cookie, Chantal said, "Yeah, that's what I thought, too. I wasn't scared, but I wanted to know more about who or what might be lingering there. So yesterday before we left, I sent Clay and the girls into town, and went back to talk to DeeDee." Chantal paused, watching her mother's gaze intensify. "Mom, she eventually admitted to me there was a spirit in the house, which she had known about since she was a young girl!"

Sophia's eyes were bright. "Wow! See? There you go, you did perceive something! What did DeeDee tell you? Is it a good or evil spirit?"

Chantal stared at the family portrait hanging above the mantel. It was taken just a year before Grandma Emmaline had died, at the ripe old age of eighty-eight. Emmaline sat primly in the center with Sophia and Chantal's father, Lewis, standing behind her. Chantal looked at her seven-year-old self, smiling at the camera, wearing a pretty yellow dress, one elbow propped on Grandma's knee. On the opposite side of Emmaline stood nine-year-old Reggie, looking grumpy and uncomfortable, having been forced to wear a suit for the photograph.

What family secrets has Mother kept from me all these years?

Turning back to her mother, Chantal said, "DeeDee told me the ghost's name is Gabe. She said he told her he was there to protect her and her mother from evil."

Smiling, Sophia said, "Ahhh. So, he's a benevolent spirit! Well, I guess that's good to know, especially if you decide to buy the house. You wouldn't want anything bad to happen to the girls."

Taking a sip of tea, Chantal said, "Yeah, I guess you're right. But here's the kicker. DeeDee recently discovered the barn on her property was used to harbor slaves as part of the Underground Railroad route. She said they uncovered documentation showing Gabe and his family were conductors on the line. Apparently for several decades during the eighteen-hundreds, they helped fugitives escape to Lake Champlain and travel to freedom in Canada."

Sophia looked away for several seconds, then turned to her daughter. "That's really amazing! Not much of the Underground movement was ever documented. And from what I know, what little was written was deliberately destroyed to not implicate any of the white folks."

"DeeDee said she donated all the artifacts to the local historical society, so at least they've been saved." Chantal sipped her tea, set down her cup, and grasped her mother's hand. "So, Mother. Why is our family history such a big secret? And *is* there some connection to Fair Haven?"

Sophia patted her daughter's hand. "Stay here. I'll be right back. There's something you need to see." She rose and drifted into her bedroom at the end of the hall.

Chantal rearranged her position on the sofa, since the baby was pressing uncomfortably against her bladder. Moments later, Sophia emerged from her bedroom carrying a thick scrapbook tied shut with a ribbon. Chantal moved aside the tea and cookies as Sophia sat next to her and laid the unopened book on the coffee table.

"What's this?" Chantal touched the unadorned, beige cloth cover.

Sophia glanced at the family portrait, then turned back to Chantal. "When your grandmother was young, she was a prolific writer. She wrote articles for the *Provincial Freeman* newspaper about families who escaped slavery and their flight to freedom. She used only her first initial to keep some sense of anonymity."

Chantal frowned. "I'm confused. I thought Grandma Emmaline was a school teacher for black kids."

He mother nodded. "Well, yes, eventually she was. But in her twenties, not only did she interview other families, but she documented her father Samuel's life in detail before he died. She published stories of his account of slave life on the tobacco plantation and their tragic journey traveling north to Canada." Sophia tapped the scrapbook. "All of her published articles are in here."

A chill ran down Chantal's spine. "Oh, my goodness! How come you never showed me this before?" She started to untie the bow.

Placing her hand on the cover, Sophia gave Chantal an imploring look. "Honey, please listen. There are secrets in here that could still bring harm to our family! So, I ask you to be very discreet with this information."

"Mother! What in the world are you talking about?"

Sophia stared into the distance, then said, "I remember the day, when I was about five, a white man came to our house." Her voice took on a husky timbre as she recollected the event. "Father was at work, and my big brother, James, and I were at home with Mama. I was scared, because a white man had never been in our home before. But mother graciously let him in and offered him tea, which he refused."

Chantal shifted on the sofa. "What did he want?"

"The man laid copies of your grandmother's articles on the table. He specifically pointed to ones describing Samuel's master, Mitchel Swaley, and his son, Chester." Sophia shook her head. "Mama never knew how he got copies of those articles, written for free blacks in Canada."

Watching her mother closely, Chantal waited for her to continue. *This was all so long ago. I don't see how it could possibly affect us now.*

"The white man said the grandson of Samuel's Master Swaley was out-raged the stories painted his family in a very damning light. The man yelled at Mama, and I got really scared!" Sophia wrung her hands. "He told her if she didn't stop publishing more articles, she and her family would be at great risk."

"Oh, my gosh! He threatened her?"

Sophia nodded. "Yes! I remember Mama being upset and shaking. The man told her Walter Swaley was a very powerful man, and he could find her and her children anytime he wanted. He made Mama swear on her Bible she would no longer write or publish any more articles about Samuel's life!"

"And did Grandma comply?"

"Yes. She had no choice. She was sobbing and swore on her Bible she would abide by his wishes," Sophia said, her voice breaking. "Then the white man left our house with a stern warning: *Remember, we can always find you!*" Sophia's face hardened. "It was then Mama decided to change her career from being a journalist to a school teacher. She said it was the only thing she could do to keep her children safe."

Chantal touched her mother's hand. "Oh, Mom, I had no idea! I'm so sorry! What did Grandma Emmaline write that was so upsetting to the Swaleys?"

Wiping her tears, Sophia said, "She kept all her articles in this scrapbook, and gave it to me for safekeeping before she died. She admonished me that secrets can be very dangerous when they are brought into the light." She lifted the heavy scrapbook and handed it to Chantal. Leaning close to her daughter, she spoke in a low voice, "I now pass you these family secrets to read and keep as you see fit. But I must warn you, I have reason to believe descendants of the Swaley family are still alive in the States! And who knows how they might react, should this information be made public?"

Exasperated by her mother's paranoia, Chantal's voice rose, "But Mom! It's the twenty-first century, and this is Canada. Surely there are no slave hunters left to threaten our family!"

Sophia lifted an eyebrow at her daughter's outburst. "Don't be naive, my dear daughter! Surely you know the white men in the Southern states have never stopped fighting the Civil War. It would not take much to raise their ire and have them come hunting for us again!" She touched the scrapbook cover. "Once you spend some time reading your Grandma Emmaline's account of Samuel's journey, you'll understand why it's so important to keep our family secrets."

After finishing her tea, Chantal gathered her coat, purse, and scrapbook, and hugged her mother goodbye. Sitting in her car with the engine off, her thoughts swirled.

What happened to Samuel? Why have we kept his secrets all these years? And what is drawing me to the house in Fair Haven? Is Samuel's story somehow linked to that property? And will our family be safe in a house with a ghost who protects a white family?

Starting her car, Chantal drove back through the McGill University campus toward her downtown apartment, eager to discover what secrets her family history held.

CHANTAL AND CLAY

When Chantal opened the door of her apartment, the smell of roasted garlic made her stomach gurgle.

"Mmmm, something smells good. What's cooking, Babe?" she called to Clay. Setting her purse and the scrapbook on the hall table, she hung her coat in the closet and kicked off her heels.

Stepping into the living room, she saw Charmaine and Whitney curled up on opposite ends of the sofa, watching an animated movie. "Hi, girls!" Chantal walked over and kissed each one on the cheek.

Charmaine responded, "Hi, Mom. Did you have a good day?"

Chantal said, "Well, it was busy—"

Whitney waved her arm in the air. "Mah-aam! You're in the *waaay!*"

Chantal swirled and pointed her index finger at her younger daughter. "Hey! Don't be rude. You can ask me nicely to move, can't you?"

Chastised, Whitney lowered her head and pouted. "Yes, Mom."

Out of the corner of her eye, Chantal saw Charmaine put her hand to her mouth to cover a giggle.

Leaving the girls, she walked into the kitchen and kissed Clay's cheek. His biceps bulged below the short sleeves of his black T-shirt, worn loose over jeans. "Hey, Babe," she said. "What're you cooking? It smells wonderful."

Clay poured Chantal a glass of fresh apple cider, her favorite fall drink. "I wasn't sure when you'd be home, so I'm baking garlic chicken breast with roasted potatoes." Pointing to the partially chopped tomatoes on the counter, he added, "Just getting a salad ready. How was your visit with Sophia?" Clay lifted a glass of red wine sitting near him on the counter and clinked Chantal's glass.

Chantal sipped her cider as she wistfully watched Clay drink his wine. "Well, it was interesting. I learned some things about Grandma Emmaline I didn't know—some of it rather startling."

Clay raised an eyebrow. "Oh? Such as?"

With a grunt, and a hand wrapped protectively around her protruding belly, Chantal sat on a bar stool opposite the center island, where Clay chopped vegetables. "Remember when I told you Emmaline was a school teacher?"

Clay nodded. "Yeah, she died when you were quite young, right?"

Chantal admired Clay's quick chopping skills as he powered through a green pepper. "Yes. I was eight when she died." She sipped her cider and paused, remembering her sweet grandmother's wrinkled face. "It was strange. After we left the house in Fair Haven yesterday, I vaguely remembered some of Grandma's stories she told me when I was a kid. I hadn't thought about them in years. When I told mother about the bits I remembered, she sort of freaked out. She said I shouldn't repeat them, because they were meant to be kept as family secrets."

Clay looked up from his work. "Really? That's odd. But you don't know all that much about your family history, do you? I don't remember you ever talking about it much."

Chantal shook her head. "No, not as much as I'd like. Mother was always very closed-lipped about our family whenever I asked her questions. She said she would tell me someday, when I was older. Her excuse was always 'loose lips sink ships.' I never quite understood what she meant."

"And now?" Clay returned his attention to his work.

"Well, apparently Grandma Emmaline was a journalist before she became a school teacher. According to mother, she interviewed black families who had escaped to freedom. She published their stories in a local newspaper called the *Provincial Freeman*."

Clay raised his brow and looked at Chantal. "No kidding? That was very brave of her back then."

"Yeah, I thought so too. But get this: she did extensive interviews with her father, Samuel, an escaped slave. She published his first-person accounts of his family's journey." Chantal took a drink of the sweet, tangy cider and stared at Clay. "I guess that's our family's history mother doesn't want to talk about."

Clay gathered the chopped vegetables into a bowl. "Hmmm. So, what did Sophia tell you tonight?"

Chantal was momentarily distracted by the sound of the girls giggling in the living room. "Mother remembered one time when she was a young girl, a white man came to their house. He had been sent by the family of Samuel's old slave master." Chantal's hand trembled. *I'd sure love to be drinking wine instead of cider.* "The nasty man warned Grandma if she didn't stop writing articles making the master's family look bad, she and her family would be in great danger!"

Clay stopped his chore, scowling. "Wow! He came all the way to Canada to threaten her? That's crazy! How in the hell did they see those articles in the States? And more importantly, why would the master's family even care so many years later?" He landed his hand with a thud on the countertop.

Chantal jerked at Clay's outburst, and shook her head. "I don't know! Mother remembers Grandma being very scared and crying after the man left. His threat was enough for Grandma to end her career as a journalist. She told the family she had to protect them, and she would do no more writing. I'm not sure how long afterward she began teaching."

Clay tossed the salad with a vigorous motion. "So what did Emmaline write that was so damning they sent a man to threaten her?"

Chantal sighed and rubbed her bulging tummy. "I'm not sure, but I'm going to find out. Mother gave me a scrapbook containing all of her articles." Chantal remembered her mother's warning. "She said there are secrets that could still bring harm to our family, and warned me to be careful who I shared the stories with."

Clay growled, "Oh, my God! That's ridiculous. In this day and age? Who could possibly bring us harm? Those goddamn masters are long since dead and buried!"

Chantal's heart thumped at the thought of danger coming to them or their girls. "That's what I told Mother. But she insisted there could be Swaley descendants down South who wouldn't take kindly to seeing Grandma's stories come to light."

Clay let out a blustery breath and wiped his brow. He gulped the rest of his wine. "This is unbelievable! Well, I guess you need to read Emmaline's articles and find out what these big family secrets are."

Chantal smiled and raised her cider glass. "That's exactly what I plan to do after dinner."

MISSING FINGERS

After her family finished dinner and the girls had gone to bed, Chantal left Clay watching television in the living room, and retreated to their master bedroom with the scrapbook. She set a refilled glass of fresh cider on the side table next to her cushioned rocker. After removing and hanging her work clothes, she donned her floor-length flannel nightgown. Sighing, she got comfortable in the rocker.

Memories of nursing both baby girls in that chair floated back to her. She smiled at the thought of a new, warm babe snuggling in her arms within a few months. *I hope we've found a new home by then.* Chantal propped her feet on the footstool and gently rested the scrapbook on her tummy.

Opening the beige cover, she saw a darkened newspaper sheet affixed to the first page. The masthead read: *The Provincial Freeman.* Below, in smaller text, it read: *The voices of freedom in a free land.* In the upper right corner was: *Province of Ontario.* The date in the upper left-hand corner read: *April 2, 1917.*

Multiple tight-set columns lined the page, interspersed with article titles. Moving her side lamp closer to read the cramped text, she scanned the articles, but nothing jumped out at her as being written by Emmaline Prescott.

Chantal's mother's words floated back to her: "*…she used her first initial to keep some anonymity…*"

Reading the titles more closely, one caught her attention: *Missing Fingers, by E. Shabot.*

Tingles ran down Chantal's spine. *Of course! She used her married name. That makes me wonder all the more how the master's family tracked her down so many years later.*

Chantal began reading Emmaline's article.

This is part one in a series of articles which describes the experiences of a young Negro boy fleeing oppression and finding freedom in Canada.

My father, Samuel, is missing the first two fingers on his right hand. When I was little and asked him what happened to those fingers, Papa told me this story.

"I was a young boy livin' on the tobacco plantation. One day, I took a basket and went to the woods to pick berries. When the basket was full, I turned to go home, but had lost my way. All of a sudden, I heard a deep growl. I stopped in my tracks, scared out of my wits. Then a big grizzly bear came out from behind the trees, stood on his hind legs and roared at me."

Papa pawed the air like a big bear and growled, scaring me, too.

"I was afraid the bear would eat me, so I offered him my berries. When the beast chomped down on the basket handle, he bit off my two fingers and ran off with them, along with the sweet berries."

Papa laughed and waved his mangled hand.

"But those were magic berries, so I rubbed the purple juice over the wounds and they healed…," he snapped the fingers on his left hand, "…just like that! So, my sweet daughter, if you ever come across a bear when you're pickin' berries, my advice is to drop your basket and run away as fast as you can!"

Chantal's heartbeat quickened. *So it WAS Samuel who had missing fingers! That's quite a fantastic story to tell a little girl. I wonder what really happened.* She sipped her cider and continued reading Emmaline's story.

My father is now approaching his 80th year on this earth. I have interviewed and published the stories of families who have found their freedom following the Drinking Gourd. I decided it was now time to interview my father, Samuel, an escaped slave, to learn the truth of our family history before he passes into the Good Lord's hands.

In the small town of Napierville I approached our family home. It's a solidly constructed two-story house with a steep roof, just two blocks from the train station. It looked much smaller than I remembered as a child. Similar houses in the predominantly black community nestled close to one another along the street. Fond memories of my three older brothers and me growing up here tugged at my heart. I regretted that I had not visited Papa in over a year. The tulip bulbs mother had planted along the front walkway were starting to pop their heads from the muddy ground, on this bright day at the end of March. Frail buds on the maples surrounding the house were emerging from their winter slumber.

I gently knocked on the heavy wooden front door, then let myself into the cramped living room. My mother, Catharine, had passed away several years ago, and the stale odor of an old man living alone overpowered me. I was thankful my next oldest brother, Josiah, and his family, lived in town and cared for father's daily well-being.

"Who goes there?" Papa's deep voice resonated from his big, cushioned chair with its back to the door. A wooden cane rested against one armrest. The radio on the shelf next to him played softly.

I removed my coat, set down my satchel, and walked around to face him. His eyesight had dwindled over the years, so I came close. I took in his silver hair, stubbly beard and hunched shoulders, as he sat slumped in his chair. "It's me, Papa." I squeezed his hands.

Papa grinned. "Ahhhh, my sweet girl. It's so good to see you. Have you come for a visit? How was the train trip from Montreal?"

Sitting on the footstool in front of him, I bemoaned my trip. "There were two boys who bickered the whole time. After four hours of their nonsense, I'm glad to be home here with you!"

Papa patted my hands and chuckled. "Yes. I imagine those boys were quite tryin' on your nerves. But you'll have children of your own one day and will have more patience, I presume." He laughed heartily. "So, what brings you here to visit your old Papa?"

I stared into his dark eyes, wondering if my trip had been a mistake. Maybe he doesn't want to tell me his story. "Well, Papa. You know I write

*about our people and their journey to freedom. There is a newspaper that
publishes my stories."*

*Papa smiled and nodded his head. "Yes. I think that's wonderful. Good
for you."*

*I plunged ahead. "I remember the story you told me about the bear
eating your fingers and the magic berries that saved you." I paused to see
Papa's reaction. He rubbed his bristly chin, in deep thought. "I was hoping
you would tell me the real truth about how you lost your fingers."*

*There, it was out. He could say yes or no. I waited, not knowing how he
would respond.*

*Papa raised his mangled right hand in front of his face and gave it a
hard look, then let it drop onto the chair. He squinted up at me and took
a deep breath. I waited. Then he said, "It's a sad tale, my sweet girl. But
you are a married woman now, and may soon have children of your own.
So . . . yes . . . you should know my truth."*

*I pulled a chair from the dining table up close to his, and gathered
my pen and notebook. After a bit of prodding, this is what Papa finally
revealed.*

*"I am the illegitimate son of my Master, Mitchel Swaley. My mother,
Miss Elsie, was his house cook. Master's legitimate son, Chester, was two
years older than me. The Master wanted both his sons to be educated, so
my half-brother and I took our lessons together. Chester's mother died
when he was very young, so Mama raised us and my older sister, Sarah,
in the Big House."*

Chantal re-read the passage. *Ahhh! So Samuel WAS educated on the
plantation.* Then she gasped. *But, wait! He was the master's son? Did the
master rape Samuel's mother, Miss Elsie? He must have! How else would
this have happened?* A feeling of dread spread through her as she continued reading.

*"So Papa, how did you lose your fingers?" I asked. He was starting to
ramble, which he was wont to do at his age.*

*Father nodded and rubbed his stubbly beard. "Yes, Yes. Well, one day,
when I was about five, Chester told me that if I was goin' to be a useful
niggah, I needed to learn a trade. I wanted to get Mama's permission,
but Chester said I had to obey him . . . or else! I admired him, but he also
scared me because he could get mean. Chester took me to the sawmill
where the workers were millin' lumber. When they took their midday*

*meal break, Chester and I snuck into the mill. He had me hold a piece of
lumber on the conveyor belt and showed me how to slide it through the
round saw."*

Papa took a deep breath.

*"Then Chester started the blade rotatin'. The noise was really loud
and I was scared. The wide plank looked enormous but I tried to guide it
along the belt. Then the board slid sideways and I reached out to push it
back in place." He paused, taking a breath. "I got really confused when I
saw it turnin' red. Suddenly my right hand felt hot. When I looked down,
I saw two fingers wedged into the sawdust, and realized they were mine."
His weary eyes stared up at me. "That's when I panicked!"*

Chantal gasped and threw her hand to her mouth. At her sudden movement, the baby kicked and changed position, causing her to gasp.

*Oh, my God! That must have been horrifying for Samuel. That poor little
boy! He was about the same age as Whitney is now.*

Adjusting her position to get more comfortable in the padded rocker
and fanning herself with her free hand, she continued reading Emmaline's
story.

*I was shocked at Papa's account, as this was a much different story from a
bear chomping his fingers. I asked him what he did next, and Papa gave
me a wan smile.*

*"At first I didn't feel any pain and couldn't understand why my fingers
were gone." Papa paused and shrugged his bony shoulders. "Then blood
was spurtin' from my hand and I started screamin'." Papa looked away
frowning, then continued. "Chester turned off the blade, and slammed his
hand over my mouth. He held me so tight I couldn't breathe!" Papa shook
his head, as if to shake off the memory. "Chester made me promise not
to tell anyone what happened. He said if I did, Miss Elsie, and my whole
family would be split up and sold down the river." Papa's voice broke. "He
choked me until I promised I would never tell a soul."*

Papa's dark, crinkly eyes bore down upon me.

Chantal's tears welled. *Chester blackmailed Samuel as the boy was bleeding to death! What a monstrous thing for that little shit, Chester, to do.* She
instinctively rubbed her protruding tummy. *If Samuel hadn't survived, I
wouldn't be here!* She took a sip of cider, then, hand shaking a little, turned
the page to read the remaining columns of the story.

I grasped his wrinkled, stumpy right hand. "Oh, Papa! I had no idea. I'm so sorry! What did you do?"

Father had a far-off look in his eyes as he recalled the event. "Chester threw me a rag to wrap around my bleedin' hand. I grasped it to my chest and ran to the kitchen, hollerin' to get Mama's help." Papa's cough rattled in his chest.

I was heartbroken to finally learn the real truth about my father's missing fingers. "What did your mama do when she saw your hand?"

Papa bowed his head. "She washed my hand in the basin, and kept scoldin' me to tell her what happened. But I didn't dare tell her nothin' 'cause Chester said she'd be sold away. Even when Master Swaley threatened to have me whupped, I held my promise to my brother, and kept my mouth shut." Papa stared at me with his sad, soulful eyes. "Don't you understand?" He raised his voice. "We would have ALL been sold... I just couldn't let that happen!"

I could still see the fear in my father's eyes as he recounted this horrible childhood event.

"Master sent for the doctor and he came and stitched up my stubs." Papa lifted his damaged hand. Wrinkled, blotched skin stretched over his thumb and two remaining bony fingers. "I was thankful Mama didn't ask me no more 'bout it. But I regret she never knew the truth before she died. I couldn't tell her because I wanted to save her!" Papa wiped his eyes, brimming with tears. "So now, all these years later, I guess I've finally broken my promise. I can only hope, my sweet daughter, you will hold this truth close to your heart."

When I asked Papa if I had his permission to tell his story in the paper, he smiled his almost-toothless grin and said, "I am an old man and have no more secrets to keep, so you do what you think is best."

With Papa Samuel's permission, this is the first of his stories I will share with our Provincial Freeman *community.*

Chantal wiped her tears and took a deep breath. The baby moved slightly, then settled.

Clay was right. Grandma was very brave to publish this story. Now I understand why mother wanted Samuel's history kept under wraps.

Chantal yawned as she quickly flipped through the yellowed, ragged-edged pages of the scrapbook. She saw a number of newspaper articles affixed to the sheets. Toward the back were sepia-toned photographs of various figures in stiff poses.

I guess these are my ancestors. I wonder what secrets they'll share with me tomorrow.

ESCAPE

"Get chur popcorn…get chur peanuts…get chur cotton candy…right here!" the man in the colorful hat barks.

Chantal strolls with Clay along the brightly lit midway, the girls between them, all holding hands. Laughing families and clusters of teens spill excitedly around them. Music blares from the adult rides whirling in the air to their right. On their left, they approach the animated kiddie rides.

"We's got bears…we's got elephants…we's got giraffes! Hey, Mister! Don'cha wanna win these beauties for those gorgeous girls?" Chantal watches the bearded man beckon Clay to throw some softballs at a target surrounded by huge stuffed animals.

Clay laughs and waves his hand dismissively at the carnival barker.

Chantal feels Whitney tugging her hand. "Mommy! I wanna ride the horsies!" Her daughter points to the merry-go-round. The garishly painted horses make their slow procession around the twirling carousel.

Whitney releases Chantal's hand and runs ahead of the family. As the carousel slows to a stop, Whitney jumps aboard the platform.

Chantal yells to Clay over the erratic music. "We need to catch up to her!"

As Chantal rushes to the ride, she sees Whitney reach up to touch a large, red heart painted on the forehead of a brown horse with white spots. Suddenly, the horse rears its head, whinnies, bares its teeth and chomps down on Whitney's hand. The carousel starts moving, and the pole-mounted horse lurches up, yanking a screaming, terrified Whitney by her trapped hand off the ground.

Chantal hears her daughter's screech. "Moooommmmmiiiie! Heellllp!"

She runs around the outer metal barrier trying to reach Whitney, but the carousel increases speed. Breathless, Chantal sprints after her daughter. Finally she reaches an opening in the barrier and throws herself aboard the rapidly spinning platform. Other children giggle and scream as they grip the center poles of the thumping, painted mounts. Clay and Charmaine stand outside the spinning ride, their horrified faces flashing by her. Struggling to keep her balance, Chantal braces herself between the pumping horses, trying to reach Whitney.

When she reaches her daughter, Whitney is in midair, her hand still in the grip of the horse's mouth. Chantal grabs her by the waist and wrestles her away from the sneering steed. Blood gushes from Whitney's wrist and splashes Chantal's face. She collapses onto the whirling carousel clutching her injured daughter. Peering up, Chantal sees Whitney's severed hand hanging from the horse's mouth, oozing blood.

"Oh, noooooo! Ohhhhhhh! Jeeeeesus! Heellllp!" Chantal screams, dizziness overcoming her as the carousel spins out of control…

"Babe! Honey! Chantal!" A deep voice and a shake to her body ousted Chantal from her nightmare. She opened her eyes to darkness and gasped. Turning her head, she saw Clay's face hovering above her. She felt his hand gripping her arm.

Wha—what?" she stammered.

She felt Clay shift position in bed, and suddenly light filled the dark room. "Babe! You were screaming." Clay leaned onto one elbow to peer down at her. "What in the world were you dreaming about?"

Chantal's heart beat rapidly. She took several deep breaths, then propped herself up against the headboard. "Oh, Clay! It was horrible. Whitney was on a merry-go-round and the horse bit her. I ran and ran to get to her, but it was spinning really fast! When I finally grabbed her, her hand was gone…the horse had it in its mouth!" Chantal let out a cry. "How could I let this happen?" She sobbed into her hands.

Clay put his arm around her neck. "Honey! Nothing happened! The girls are fine. You are fine. It was just a nightmare. Here, drink some water." Clay reached to his bedside stand and handed her a plastic bottle of water.

Chantal took a sip, coughed, then took a longer drink. She felt her heart starting to slow down.

Clay touched her arm. "Feel better?"

Chantal nodded slowly, the anguish still swirling in her mind.

Clay sat up in bed and propped himself against the headboard. "What do you think brought this on? That's a really bizarre dream."

Visions of Samuel's fingers being severed by the circular saw flashed before her. Chantal shook her head. "Oh, my gosh! I was reading one of Grandma Emmaline's articles before I went to bed." Her body trembled as she took another deep breath. "Her father, Samuel, was missing the first two fingers on his right hand. But Emmaline never knew what happened. When Samuel was old, he finally told her the truth."

Clay stared at Chantal, his interest piqued. "What did happen to his fingers?"

Chantal wiped her tears. "Apparently his half-brother, Chester, the master's son, talked Samuel into going to the sawmill. When Samuel tried to push a board through the moving blade, his fingers got cut off." Chantal gulped air. "All I could think was Samuel was about Whitney's age when he lost his fingers. What a horrible thing to happen to that poor little boy!"

Clay caressed Chantal's cheek. "It's okay, Honey. You know how sensitive you are to other people's feelings. It probably just stuck in your mind. Charmaine and Whitney are fine." He grasped her shaking hand. "Wait! You said Samuel had a half-brother who was the master's son?"

Chantal nodded. "Yes, I think that damned master raped Samuel's mother, and he was her bastard child."

A look of disgust crossed Clay's face. "Sonofabitch! I'd like to go back in time and have every one of those goddamned bastards strung up by their balls!"

Running her hand through her mussed hair, Chantal said, "I know! I guess since they owned the slaves, they felt they could do whatever they wanted with the help. It's so unfair!"

Clay got out of bed shaking his head, and turned to Chantal. "Babe, maybe you shouldn't be reading Emmaline's stories before you go to bed— they might give you more nightmares!"

Chantal saw the deep concern on Clay's face. "Yeah. You've got a good point." She squeezed his hand. "I'll be all right. It just really shook me, that's all. Can you help me up? I gotta use the bathroom."

Chantal awoke the following morning with a headache, scratchy throat, and stuffy nose.

Oh, great! Besides having a bad night, now I've got a damned cold coming on.

She waddled into the bathroom and took her temperature. The digits read ninety-nine point eight.

Damn! Guess I'm staying home today.

In the kitchen, Chantal saw the girls were already up, sitting at the table, while Clay fixed their breakfast. She poured a cup of coffee and sat at the counter.

"I'm coming down with a cold, so I'm calling in sick. Can you get the girls off to the bus?" Chantal sat down at the table and sipped her coffee.

Clay turned to her. "Oh, sorry to hear that, Babe. Yeah, I'll get the girls ready. Why don't you go and rest?"

Charmaine gave her mother a concerned look. "Anything I can do to help you, Mommy? I'll stay home from school if you'd like."

Chantal chuckled at her caring older daughter. "Nice try, Honey. But, no—you have to go to school. If you'd like, you can help Whit get dressed. Sometimes she has a problem with her shoes." Chantal grinned as she tilted her head toward her younger daughter.

Whitney piped up, "I can tie my own shoes. Honest I can!"

Chantal touched Whitney's arm. "And you can let your sister help you, too, can't you?"

Whitney pouted. "Yes, Mommy."

After Clay left, hustling the girls to the bus stop, Chantal called her office. The familiar voice of the department secretary greeted her.

Chantal explained, "Hi Maryann, it's Chantal." She moved the phone away as she stifled a cough.

"Geez, you don't sound too good," Maryann commented.

Chantal swallowed her urge to cough. "I'm not. I've got a nasty head cold coming on, so I'm not coming into the office today. Would you check my calendar and see what appointments are scheduled?"

"Sure. Hold on a minute."

Chantal could hear Maryann typing.

The secretary replied, "Let's see, two clients this morning. And Leland's staff meeting is this afternoon."

Chantal replied, "Oh, shoot! It's Tuesday. I forgot about the staff meeting." She sniffed and wiped her nose. "I imagine Leland will be pissed if I miss it, but I know he'll get himself worked into a royal tizzy if I even dare spread a germ in his vicinity."

Maryann laughed. "You know you got that right!"

Chantal envisioned her boss, Leland Cromwell, one of the firm's three partners. He was the epitome of a stiff, upper-crust, middle-aged British businessman. Dressed in impeccable suits, his starched, white handkerchief was always at the ready. Leland refused to touch anything with his bare hands that was used by the public masses. He used his hanky to open door handles, push elevator buttons, and even lean on the desks of his staff. Chantal often wondered how he even managed to tinkle by himself. His germ obsession was well-known in the office, so no one even bothered joking about it anymore.

Chantal responded to her secretary. "Maryann? Will you cancel both my morning clients and give Leland my apologies for missing his staff meeting? I'll come in tomorrow if I feel better."

"Sure, consider it done. Don't worry about Leland. You know how he hates being around sick people," Maryann chuckled. "Take care of yourself and get some rest."

"Will do, thanks." Chantal hung up the phone and swiped at her runny nose.

Brewing a pot of honey-lemon tea, Chantal pondered Leland's germ phobia. A few years earlier, one of Leland's close associates had confided to her a bit of her boss's history. Apparently as a child growing up outside of London, Leland had found an old book in his grandfather's library. In it, the impressionable boy had read detailed, gruesome accounts of the disfigurement of victims of the plague that had ravaged Europe in the Middle Ages. Leland, a math prodigy and social outcast, had become obsessed with the idea there were germs everywhere, trying to kill him. His friend said Leland never outgrew his phobia. Chantal couldn't help but feel sympathy for the brilliant man, living his life in such constant fear.

When the teapot whistled, she diluted in it a big tablespoon of cough syrup and an aspirin, to help tamp down her symptoms. Still dressed in her flannel nightgown, she carried a cup of tea into her bedroom and placed it on the side table. She retrieved a box of tissues from the bath counter and located it near her. After turning the clock radio to a soothing music station, she got comfortable in her padded rocker. The baby moved and squirmed, kicking her in the ribs, then finally settled.

I'll be glad when this babe is born. I think it'll be our last, because at thirty-four, I'm getting too old to handle another pregnancy.

Chantal sighed and lifted the scrapbook from the lower shelf of her side table. She gently balanced it upon her tummy, careful not to startle the baby.

I hope learning more about Samuel's life won't bring on another nightmare!

Opening the book to the second of Emmaline's articles, Chantal read the title:

"Escape" by E. Shabot. April 9, 1917.

This is part two in a series of articles which describes the experiences of a young Negro boy fleeing oppression and finding freedom in Canada.

After enjoying a light supper delivered by my brother, Josiah, Papa and I returned to the living room, where we both got comfortable and I continued my interview.

"Papa? Did you leave the plantation because your fingers got cut off?"

Papa shook his head. "No. Several years later, my older sister, Sarah, had a baby boy she named Jonah. Mama made sure Jonah was raised in the Big House, along with me and Chester. When Jonah was about three, Mama overheard Chester in the barn offerin' some men money to have Jonah killed!" Papa's eyes narrowed as he stared at me. "That night in our little house, Mama was frantic. She said we had to protect Jonah, and the only way to do that was to run away." He ran his hand over his beard. "I was scared and didn't want to leave 'cause I wanted to continue my lessons. But Mama said I could get more lessons in the land of Canaan, because Jonah's life was more important."

"Oh, my goodness. Why did they want to kill Jonah? He was just a little boy!" I asked him.

Chantal gasped. *That's what I want to know, too! Sounds like Chester was the instigator, but why? What could Jonah have possibly done at that age?* She blew her stuffy nose and continued reading.

Papa shrugged. "I don't know. Mama wouldn't tell me—said 'tweren't none of my business. But I think Sarah knew, because she and Mama would never let Jonah outta their sight."

I asked Papa, "So what did you do? How did you escape?"

Papa paused for a long while, staring at a painting on his wall. "Well, my girl, it took some time. And all the while, Mama was frantic about Jonah's safety. But we finally got a letter from Mama's brother, Robert, who had joined the Navy and earned his freedom. He told us when his ship would be in port, and we should meet him there. One night, we packed a few of our belongin's, bundled up Jonah, and then Mama, Sarah and I walked off the plantation."

I was surprised at Papa's casual re-telling of their escape. "Oh, my. That was very brave of you. Weren't you worried you'd be chased and captured?"

Papa grinned. "Oh sure! I didn't say it was easy. We spent three days on the run, wadin' through cold swamp water, hidin' from riders, and hopin' the hounds didn't find us. We were slowed up 'cause one of us always had to be carryin' Jonah so's he wouldn't drown." Papa gripped his hands. "When we made it to the dock at Chesapeake Bay, it was a nightmare. Ships were docked everywhere unloadin' cargo."

Papa coughed into his hand and took a deep breath.

"Slave hunters were chasin' and whippin' our folk, takin' 'em back in chains, screamin' and bleedin', to their masters. We ran through the crowd until we finally saw the Navy ship with the letters U S on it. Uncle Robert found us and helped us get on board."

Papa shook his head in dismay.

"I saw some of our people thrown off the gangplank. It was horrible. I was very scared 'cause none of us knew how to swim."

I asked, "And so you were able to get away?"

Papa nodded. "The sailors chased the posse off our ship, and we quickly set sail, despite the angry shouts from the men on the dock. We sailed for two days and finally landed in New York City. We were given an address to a safe house run by some very kind white men. I'll tell you, we all breathed a little easier being outta the South."

"Oh, Papa," I said. "You must have been so relieved to get away!"

"Yes, Honey. We were at the time. But we didn't know the devil was lyin' in wait for us!"

Papa dropped his head, and I saw a tear land on his hands. Then he looked up at me. "We stayed at safe farmhouses as we made our way to Vermont, where we were hidden under the barn of a kind, God-fearin' family in Fair Haven."

Chantal re-read the last paragraph, stunned. *Grandma was right! Samuel and his family* were *in Fair Haven. What are the chances of us looking at a house in the same town? And a property that once harbored fugitives in their barn? This is very bizarre indeed.*

She sipped her tea, now cooled a bit, to soothe her scratchy throat.

"Papa?" I asked. "Can you tell me their names?"

He shook his head. "I can, but I won't. Don't want 'em to be gettin' into trouble, now. I'll just call 'em Mister and Missus H."

Chantal's conversation with DeeDee the previous Sunday ran through her mind. *What was the name of the folks who had owned DeeDee's house? Houser? Hawker? No, that's not it. Hopper! That was it. Could they be the very same Mister and Missus H. Samuel refers to?*

She rubbed her scratchy eyes. *I think I'm imagining things. It's pretty far-fetched to think there might be a connection here.* Taking another sip of her tea, she continued reading.

Because I wanted more facts for my article, I said, "But Papa, they're all dead. What kind of trouble could come to them now?"

Papa shrugged. "Don't know. But their kin may still be around, and I don't wanna cause 'em no harm."

"So what happened in Fair Haven?" I waited while he cleared his throat and blew his nose on his hanky. His voice was husky when he began speaking again.

"Mistah H. told me he was worried about our safety, 'cause he'd seen slave hunters in town. So he and his son, Luke, covered a hay wagon for us to hide in. They was plannin' to take us to the canal in Whitehall, New York, so we could board a ship on Lake Champlain."

Papa bowed his head again. I touched his hand and waited.

He looked up at me, tears brimming. "Ahhhh, my sweet girl. It all went horribly bad!" Papa swiped at his eyes. "We were attacked by an armed group of vigilantes. I grabbed Jonah and escaped from the wagon before it fell off the bridge. We hid in the trees waitin' for Mama and Sarah to join us... but they never came!"

Chantal let out a small cry and covered her mouth. *Oh, no! Poor Samuel!*

"Oh, Papa! You must have been so scared."

"I was, Honey. And I've never really wanted to talk about it. Don't you see? It was my job as the man of the family to keep us all safe." Papa's voice cracked. "I failed miserably!"

"But Papa, you were just a boy! It wasn't your fault. What else could you have done?"

He looked up at me, his wrinkled face in anguish. "I suppose you're right. But you need to know our story, so I better tell it all. While Jonah and I were hidin', I heard Sarah screamin'—the men had captured her. I wanted to run and help her, but I had to protect little Jonah." Papa's hands trembled. "Then I heard a gunshot and I crouched over Jonah." Papa paused and wiped his nose. "I was afraid if we were seen, we'd get shot, too! So with all the commotion, I grabbed Jonah, and we ran through the trees away from the bridge."

"What happened to your Mama?"

Papa's body trembled as he sobbed into his hanky. "We lost her. She drowned in the river!" He sighed. "Jonah and I hid in a barn and we were found by a white lady who wanted to help us. She got us a horse and guided us across the river. It was then we found Mama's body." He gasped, his hands shaking. "It broke my heart! I had to hide it from Jonah 'cause I didn't want him yellin' out. The lady helped me pull Mama's body from the river. She said we had to keep movin', but she would make sure Mama got a proper Christian burial. I didn't even have time to say a proper goodbye. I still miss Mama every day!"

The baby shifted causing Chantal to adjust her position. *Oh, my gosh! Samuel endured so much tragedy at such a young age. He was so brave to carry on, protecting his little nephew, Jonah.* Her tears welled, making her nose run more. She blew her nose on a tissue and wiped her eyes, then read the rest of Emmaline's article.

Papa continued his tragic story. "When we got to Whitehall, we were hidden by a free black couple I'll call Mister and Missus B. They gave us clean clothes, and a satchel of food for our journey. Mister B. hid us on board a steamship named Saranac II, where he worked as a cook."

I asked Papa, "So the ship took you and Jonah to freedom in Canada?"

The deep sadness in Papa's eyes ripped at my heart. "No, Honey. I didn't make it to the Promised Land for another six months."

Papa yawned and rubbed his eyes. "I'm tired, my sweet daughter. Let's call it a night, and I'll tell you more in the morning."

Honoring Papa's wishes, I helped him to bed. Then I sat in his big, lumpy chair, feeling his energy. Despite his distress, I hoped telling his story would lift a heavy burden off his shoulders. I prayed for him to be at peace.

The continuing story of my Papa Samuel will be published in next week's edition.

Chantal sighed. *What in the world was Samuel doing for six months? Why did it take him so long to reach Canada?*

She yawned and felt herself getting drowsy. *Maybe I'll take Clay's advice and get some rest.*

Closing the scrapbook and laying it on the lower shelf, Chantal rose from her chair and stretched. Then she got comfortable in bed and turned down the radio volume.

I hope Samuel finally found the peace and freedom he fought so hard for.
She drifted into a restless sleep.

THE STORM

"Mommy! Mommy! Where are you?"

The sound of Whitney's voice startled Chantal from a troubled dream. Its stark, fleeting images floated in her mind. Late afternoon sunlight streamed between the closed window blinds.

Oh, my gosh! What time is it?

Peering at the alarm clock, she saw it was almost three in the afternoon. Sitting up in bed, Chantal rubbed her eyes. *I guess I was tired! I've slept most of the day.*

Before she could rise, there was a sharp knock on the door, then Whitney burst into the darkened bedroom. Charmaine walked in slowly behind her.

Whitney promptly stood in front of Chantal and thrust a colorful drawing toward her. "Mommy! Look what I made today! It's two dogs playing together in the park. See the trees! Don't they look really real? Can we get a dog?"

Chantal yawned and turned on the light, then reached out to take the drawing. "Whoa! Slow down, Whit. Let me take a look." Chantal peered at the artwork of two huge, awkward dogs chasing one another in front of miniature, spindly pine trees. She grinned at her five-year-old daughter, who was waiting impatiently with her hands on both hips. "It's lovely, Whitney. You did a great job! And, no, we are not getting a dog."

Charmaine sat next to Chantal on the bed and touched her mother's arm. "How are you feeling, Mom? Did you sleep all day?"

Taking a bit of inventory, Chantal realized her nose was no longer stuffy, her throat felt better, and she no longer had a pounding headache.

Just then, Clay appeared in the doorway, standing with an arm propped against it. "Hey, Babe? You feeling better?"

Chantal chuckled. "I thank you all for your concern. Yes, I'm feeling better. I need to get up and get dressed, so if you'd all leave me in peace, I'll do just that."

Clay grinned. "Okay. Come on, ladies. Let's leave your mother alone."

Whitney retrieved her drawing from Chantal, then did a little twirl, her corn-row braids flying behind her. Clay closed the door behind their daughters as they jogged down the hallway.

Chantal chuckled when she stepped into the shower. *Whit's got some work to do on perspective, but at least she's trying. I gotta give her credit.*

After her shower, Chantal donned a flowered maternity dress, slipped on her house shoes, and joined Clay and the family in the kitchen. House rules required the children to do their homework before they could watch television, or play with friends. Charmaine had a textbook opened on the table and was writing in her notebook. Whitney was practicing her alphabet.

Chantal poured herself a glass of cider. "How was work?" She perched on the bar stool, where she could talk to either Clay in the kitchen or the sisters at the table.

Clay poured himself a glass of red wine, then sat next to Chantal. "It was busy. I have to log in later to keep an eye on a system update we're running."

Chantal said, "Do you want me to cook dinner?"

Clay shook his head. "No. I want you to take it easy. I was going to cook a pork loin, which won't take too long. Then I'll go check work." Clay smiled and lowered his voice. "So, did you learn more about Samuel and your ancestors today?"

Chantal touched his hand, lowered her voice, and nodded. "I did. It was very sad. They had a tragic journey after they escaped the South. And for some reason, it took Samuel six months to reach Canada, even after he boarded a steamship on Lake Champlain." She tilted her head toward their daughters. "I'll tell you more when we're alone."

Clay sipped his wine. "Wow. That's unusual. What happened to him?"

She shrugged. "I don't know yet. I'm hoping I'll find out when I read more of Emmaline's stories.

After the family finished cleaning up from dinner, Clay retreated to his office. Once the girls got comfortable on the sofa watching television, Chantal took her cider and went back into the bedroom. Getting situated in her rocker, she propped the scrapbook gently on her tummy and turned to the next of Emmaline's articles.

"The Storm" by E. Shabot. April 16, 1917.

This is part three in a series of articles which describes the experiences of a young Negro boy fleeing oppression and finding freedom in Canada.

After Papa and I finished our breakfast the next morning, we took our tea cups and returned to the living room. Papa got comfortable in his big, lumpy chair, and I sat next to him. I was eager to learn about the next steps in his journey.

"So, Papa, last night you said it took you another six months to reach Canada after you boarded the ship in Whitehall. Where were you, and what were you doing the whole time?"

Papa clasped his bony hands together in his lap, and took a deep breath. "Ahhh, my sweet girl. This is so hard for me to talk about, so please excuse me if I dodder a bit."

"Take all the time you need, Papa," I told him.

Chantal smiled as she remembered sitting on her grandmother's lap, holding her weathered hands, as Emmaline told her stories. The old woman's crinkled face and dark, soulful eyes had kept Chantal enraptured as she listened to the tales of their ancestors. *Grandma was a smart and sympathetic woman her whole life. I hope I am living my life in her honor and making her proud.*

Finally, Papa nodded his head and looked deeply into my eyes. "Well, Jonah and I were stowed away on the ship. After we set sail, Mistah B. let us out of our hidin' place. But he told us to stay below on the bunks, which we did. Did I mention it was stormin' when we set sail? Well it was. And those winds rocked that big steamship back and forth somethin' fierce. It made both of us very sick."

Papa's hands trembled. I touched them to encourage him to continue.

"Suddenly I heard a loud screech and a thud comin' from below us. We felt the ship shudder. Then it came to an abrupt halt and we were thrown out of our bunks."

"Oh, no! The ship wrecked?" I asked.

Chantal exhaled a sharp gasp and covered her mouth with her hand.

Papa nodded. "Well, I didn't know for sure, but it sounded bad. Jonah and I huddled in the bunk room, waitin' for Mistah B. to come fetch us, but he never came. Not long after the thud, we felt the ship tippin' sideways. I grabbed Jonah, and we struggled to climb from the cargo hold to the top deck. What I saw there scared the daylights outta me! Remember I told you we couldn't swim?"

My stomach tightened as father struggled to tell his tale. "Yes, I remember. What was happening on deck?"

Samuel frantically looked around the tilting deck for something to hold onto that would keep him and Jonah afloat. He watched in horror as panicked passengers lost their grip and slid off the ship into the churning water. Jonah cried out in fear, and Samuel, his heart pounding, wrapped his arm around his nephew. *Dear Lord, please save us!* Samuel's arm burned from the strain of holding himself against the rising port railing. He crouched and swung his right arm around Jonah's waist. "Put your hands around my neck and hold on! Hold your breath as long as you can—we're going into the water."

Samuel released his grip on the railing and kicked his feet out in front of himself, so Jonah would land face down on Samuel's chest. As the two boys slid down the deck, a heavy object slammed into Samuel's leg. Samuel cried out as excruciating pain exploded in his ankle, and he almost lost his grip on Jonah. A large wave of water loomed over them.

Papa rubbed his left hand over his weathered face. "The right side of the ship was startin' to dip into the waves. Anythin' that wasn't tied down was fallin' into the water. People were screamin' as they fell off the ship. Papa scrubbed at his chin. "I was scared for my life and all I could think was I needed to keep Jonah safe!" He let out a small cry.

I grasped his right hand to comfort him. "It's okay, Papa. I've never heard you speak of what happened to Jonah before now. Did he survive?"

A high-pitched keening emanated from Papa, scaring me. He bent over and sobbed into his hands.

"Hold your breath!" Samuel screamed, and the boys were sucked into churning waves. Kicking with his uninjured foot, Samuel gripped Jonah with his right arm and used his left arm to push them away from the sinking ship. His lungs straining, he finally broached the surface, pulling Jonah up as they both gasped for air. Panicked shouts of the passengers and crew surrounded him, as debris continued to roll off the ship. Flailing, he turned and saw a plank that had fallen from the deck. Desperately, he wrapped his arm around it, pulling Jonah onto the board. "Hold on!" he yelled at his nephew.

A loud creak and metallic groan from behind him made Samuel look over his shoulder. He saw the ship's bow slide below a churning wake and he paddled furiously as the enormous wave from the submerging ship crashed over him. The plank they clung to rolled violently, and Samuel felt himself being sucked into the churning abyss. He instinctively reached out and grasped Jonah's collar, only to have it slip through the inadequate grip of his mangled right hand. *No! I can't lose Jonah! Loooord!*

I had never seen him this distraught before, and it greatly upset me. I stood and rubbed his back to give him comfort. He finally sat up and blew his nose. I passed him his cup of tea, and steadied his hands as he took a drink. His crumpled face and bloodshot eyes tore through my heart.

I set his teacup on the table and caressed his hands. "You don't need to tell me this story, Papa, since it upsets you so much."

Chantal paused to envision old Samuel, with his weathered face and scruffy beard, as he struggled to tell his story. *Grandma was so patient with him. I'm glad she finally got him to talk about his journey and the stories he had kept deep inside for all those years.*

Staring through me, as if I wasn't right beside him, Papa wailed, "Ahhh, God! I was the man of the family. It was my job to save Jonah, and I failed!"

I watched a wave of sorrow flow across his face. "Oh, Papa! I'm so, so sorry!"

He wiped his eyes and took a deep breath. I sat in my chair and waited.

After clearing his throat, he sat up a little straighter. "As we slid off the deck into the freezin' water, somethin' slammed my leg. Then we were churnin' under the surface." He swiped at his swollen eyes. "I pushed Jonah onto a plank of wood and held on behind him. I could see the shore in the distance, and I paddled hard toward it"

Papa reached for the tea. I helped him steady it as he took another drink.

"Then I heard the roar of the ship sinkin'. Suddenly, a huge wave rolled over us and threw us both off the plank. As I sank, I reached for Jonah and grasped his coat—but I couldn't hold on! I had to surface

because my lungs were burnin'." Papa raised his damaged right hand and squeezed it into a fist. "Damn you, Chester! Damn you for maimin' me!" He shook his thin arm toward the ceiling. "It's all your fault I couldn't save him!"

"Oh, Papa! You did the very best you could in a horrible situation."

His grief was palpable as he stared beyond me, engulfed in his memories.

Samuel felt his body being lifted by the surf as it crashed toward the rocky point. Losing his grip on the floating debris, he tumbled and rolled underwater, fighting the urge to scream. At last his head broke the surface, and he gasped for breath, struggling to stay above the splashing surf. Just visible through the pounding rain, Samuel saw a marshy inlet. Breathing hard, he struggled to wriggle toward the shore.

Another wave propelled his body farther up the reed-filled marsh, and he inched his body forward. Slowly he got onto his hands and knees, despite the searing pain in his leg. To his left he saw a scraggly bush growing out of a slanted rock formation. With retching breaths, he grabbed the bush and pulled himself up to the small ledge and collapsed.

Squinting toward the stormy lake, Samuel was stunned to see Jonah on the crest of a wave crashing toward him. "Jonah!" Samuel screamed as he reached out to grab the boy before his small body was dashed against the rocky shore. Before Samuel could reach his nephew, Elsie appeared on the wave next to Jonah. "Mama!" Samuel cried. "Jonah is going to drown!"

Elsie gathered the floating boy to her chest and smiled. "I's got'im, Samuel. No need to fret yo'self now. We's safe in the Lord's arms." The roiling clouds parted, and a brilliant light shown down upon the matriarch and her grandson. "We's see you in the Lord's Kingdom!"

Samuel watched in amazement as Elsie and Jonah rose above the waves, engulfed in the shaft of light, then the storm clouds closed behind them.

I gently touched Papa's arm. "Do you want to tell me more?"

He slowly raised his head and nodded. "The waves pushed me on shore and I landed on the rocks. Then I had an amazing vision! I saw Mama float down from the clouds and scoop Jonah from the churning waves into her arms. She told me not to fret, they were safe in the Lord's arms! Then they disappeared into the shaft of light." He paused and peered at the ceiling. "Ah, my sweet daughter, I just wanted to die because I had horribly failed them both!"

He dropped his gaze and shook his head. "My whole life I've blamed myself for not savin' Jonah. He deserved better. I just hope I can plead for forgiveness when I finally meet my Lord."

"But don't you see you were blessed to still be alive? I'm sure the Lord has already forgiven you. Look at what an amazing life you have lived. You will be welcomed in heaven with open arms!"

Dropping his head into his hands, Papa mumbled, "Yeah, I hope you're right. But I wish I could have done more!" After a moment of silence, his weary face peered up at me and he let out a long sigh. "That's enough for now…"

The continuing story of my Papa Samuel will be published in next week's edition.

Chantal sat motionless. *Oh, poor Samuel! As if he hadn't endured enough in his young life, for him to lose his nephew because of his mangled hand must have been devastating for him.* She wiped her tears. *I believe Grandma was right. Samuel was saved so he could do good in this world. He's God's witness to the horrors inflicted upon our people. May this tragic history never, ever repeat itself!*

ROKEBY FARM

After readjusting herself in the rocker, Chantal sipped her cider, and decided to read Emmaline's next article.

"Rokeby Farm" by E. Shabot. April 23, 1917.

This is part four in a series of articles which describes the experiences of a young Negro boy fleeing oppression and finding freedom in Canada.

Papa and I took a break for lunch, then returned to the living room for the afternoon. Once he got seated, Papa took a breath and looked up at me.

"Are you ready to go on?" I asked.

He nodded.

Then I asked, "What happened after Jonah drowned?"

Papa shrugged his bony shoulders. "I think I musta passed out, 'cause the next thing I knew men were hoverin' above me. I could hear people moanin'. One of the men said, 'He's alive. Let's take 'im to Rokeby.' Then they lifted me and I screamed, 'cause a sharp pain shot through my leg. They laid me in the back of a wagon, and I remember hollerin' every time we hit a bump. I think I probably fainted from the pain."

Chantal thought about Samuel being washed ashore after the shipwreck. *That poor injured boy must have been frightened to death when he heard people moving around him. He probably thought he would be found by the slave catchers at any moment.*

Papa paused and peered around the room, then continued. "When I awoke again, I thought I was with an angel! I asked her if I was in heaven and where Jonah was, but she didn't know." Papa sighed, swept up once more by his vision. "That lovely angel with blue eyes and golden skin touched my face and told me her name was Ester. She said I had been taken in by Rachel and Rowland T. Robinson, and I was at their farm called Rokeby. She told me I was safe, but I had a broken ankle, and I had to stay put while my bone healed."

Chantal smiled. *Samuel sure did like his angels. I wonder if the nurse was a mixed-race slave girl with blue eyes. That's quite unusual.* She continued reading.

I asked Papa. "Rachel and Rowland T. Robinson? Do I have your permission to publish their names?"

He nodded and smiled. "Yes, my girl. The Robinsons were well-known abolitionists. They hired our people to work on their farm, paid us a decent wage, then helped us on our journey along Lake Champlain to the Promised Land. They are good folks, and should be remembered fondly by history."

"And so you stayed at Rokeby for six months?"

Papa nodded. "Yep. While my leg was healin', I worked in the kitchen. Ester taught me how to cook and to spin wool. Her father, Justice, sheared the Merino sheep Mister Robinson raised on the farm." Papa grinned. "I must tell you, I was quite enamored with that girl, even though she was a bit older. I had grand visions of jumpin' the broom with Ester when I grew up!"

"Papa! You're such an old romantic!" I was happy to see his mood lighten as he reminisced about his time at Rokeby.

Chantal envisioned Samuel working in the kitchen with Ester. *After all the tragedy Samuel endured, he still had an eye for the ladies. He must have been quite a charming character.*

Papa chuckled. "When we were workin' in the kitchen one day, Ester mentioned she and her father, Justice, had also spent time with a family in Fair Haven." Papa looked away, then back at me. "She wouldn't tell me what had happened, but said there was an incident with the family's son, and they were forced to leave. I could tell it had really upset her. I felt bad 'cause I would've done anythin' to protect my beautiful, blue-eyed angel. That's when they came to work at Rokeby."

Chantal pondered. *Hmmm... how interesting... another fugitive family staying in Fair Haven. Sounds like there's probably quite a history there of the Underground Railroad, like DeeDee has discovered.* She felt a deep inner stirring to return to Fair Haven and find out more about the town.

I followed Papa's glance as he turned in his chair to stare at two framed, charcoal drawings, hung one above the other on the narrow wall between the window and front door. The two pictures had been there my whole life and were now smeared with years of dust and grime. I had never paid much attention to them as they were just part of the aging decor.

Papa turned back to me. "When I wasn't workin', Mister Robinson's son, Rowland Evans, taught me to draw and paint. Rowlie, as he was called, was a few years older than me, and was a talented artist." He smiled wistfully. "We became good friends over those long winter months, talkin' and paintin' by the fireplace."

Pointing at the drawings, Papa said, "The one on the top, of the three naked sheep emergin' from the shearin' shed, was drawn by Rowlie. You can just see Justice in the back gettin' ready to shear another. Rowlie gave me the drawin' as a gift when I left Rokeby, knowin' how I felt about Ester." Papa grinned. "The one below it, of a man and boy in the pasture tendin' the Merinos, is mine." He chuckled. "If you take a good look at the two pictures, you can see I still had a lot to learn!" Papa scratched his stubbly beard. "I am forever grateful to Rowlie for his lessons. Drawin' has given me such joy throughout my life. I was saddened to bid my friend farewell when it was time to leave."

I rose from my chair and took a closer look at the charcoal renditions of life on the farm. Despite what Papa said, I thought they were both very lifelike.

Chantal thought about her mother, Sophia, selling the family home in Napierville ten years earlier, after Chantal's father had died. *I wonder what happened to those drawings. I'll have to ask Mom if she still has them. I would love to see them.*

Returning to my chair, I said, "I always knew you liked to draw, but never knew how you learned. That's wonderful Rowlie took you on as his apprentice. So you left in the spring? What happened to Ester and Justice? Did they stay at Rokeby?"

Papa's look turned somber. "When the lake thawed in April, I had earned enough wages, so Mister Robinson booked my passage on a steamship bound for Canada. I was excited Ester and Justice had also booked passage on the same ship, along with two other farm hands seekin' their freedom. I was hopin' we'd all live together in the Promised Land!"

Papa slowly rose from his chair, his bones creaking as he stretched. "I need to walk and get some fresh air. Won't you join me?" He grasped his cane and walked toward the front door, where he grabbed his jacket.

"Of course, Papa. I'd love to!" I followed him into the bright spring day, the birds squawking raucously in the nearby trees.

The continuing story of my Papa Samuel will be published in next week's edition.

Chantal sighed. *What amazing fortitude Samuel had to continue his journey without his family. And he was so young, barely a teenager! I am proud to be his descendant.* As she glanced back over the article, the name of the farm Rokeby caught her eye. *I wonder if that farm is still there. I'll have to do some research. It would be fun to take Clay and the girls to go visit it sometime.*

She closed the scrapbook and returned it to the bottom shelf of her side table. Grunting as she rose, she felt the baby settle in her tummy. Then she walked along the hallway to her daughters' room. They had just gotten into bed and were chatting and laughing.

"Sweet dreams, girls. I love you."

"I love you, too, Mommy," they both chimed in.

Chantal turned off the bedroom light and closed the door behind her. She made her way toward Clay's office to tell him more of her discoveries.

When they're a little older, I'll tell them what an amazing man their ancestor was. They have no idea how lucky they are!

FREEDOM

The following evening Chantal returned home from work, exhausted. Still fighting her head cold, she had tried to focus on her clients' needs, but her mind kept wandering to Samuel's story.

She entered the living room to find her daughters had finished their homework. They sprawled on the sofa, watching television. She turned toward the kitchen, but didn't see Clay.

"Hi, girls, where's your daddy?"

Charmaine responded, "He's in his office, working on something."

"Thanks, Honey." Chantal said as she walked down the hallway to Clay's cramped office. She knocked lightly on the open door.

Clay turned in his office chair and smiled. "Hey, Babe! How was work? Did Leland wrap himself in a bubble when he saw you?" He chuckled.

Chantal playfully punched his arm. "Clay! That's mean! He's a nice man, he just…has a few *issues*." She couldn't help but laugh at remembering Leland scurrying into his office and shutting the door, when she had arrived at the office that morning.

Clay grasped her hand. "You look tired. Come, sit down." He removed books from the chair next to his desk.

She lowered herself into the chair and sighed. "I just can't shake this cold, and I probably should have stayed home today, too." She ran her hands through her hair and moaned. "Do you remember last night I told you Samuel had a broken ankle after the shipwreck, and he stayed at a farm in Vermont over the winter?"

"Yeah, that's why it took him six months to get to Canada, right?"

She nodded. "Well, the name of the farm was Rokeby, and it was owned by the Robinson family, who were abolitionists. I was thinking if by chance the farm is still there, it'd be interesting to take the girls to go see it sometime. Wouldn't it be a great history lesson for them to learn more about Samuel's life?"

Clay chuckled, "Well Babe, a hundred and fifty years later, chances are it's owned by someone else by now. They probably don't want visitors traipsing around their private land, if you know what I mean."

Chantal pursed her lips. "Yeah, you're probably right. But if we buy the house in Fair Haven, maybe one day we could locate it."

Clay's face turned serious. "And are we buying the house in Fair Haven?"

Chantal tilted her head to one side, as if struggling to find words. "I don't know. There's something about that house…I felt something there that has me intrigued." She sighed. "I realize Samuel and his family were harbored in Fair Haven, but so were other fugitive families. I know this sounds crazy." She paused and peered around the cramped office. "But what do you think the chances are this is the same property where my ancestors were sheltered?"

Clay laughed. "I think it's pretty far-fetched, if you want to know the truth. I mean, Babe, listen to yourself! We look at one house in a town where, just by sheer coincidence, your ancestors had traveled. You even said there were lots of other black folks passing through the town. The chances of this being *the* property where Samuel stayed are pretty slim, don't you think?"

Chantal remembered the strange feeling that overcame her when she had walked through the front door of the house in Fair Haven. *Was there indeed a spirit who vowed to protect the house from evil, as DeeDee reluctantly admitted?*

Chantal rubbed her tummy. "Yeah, I guess you have a point. I'm probably just imagining things, trying to connect the dots." She shook her head. "There's at least one more of Grandma's articles I want to read tonight. I'm hoping it sheds more light on Samuel's life."

Clay clasped her hand. "Honey, I don't want to discourage you. But we should buy a house that meets our needs as a growing family, and not just because there's a remote possibility it may have been visited by one of your ancestors over a century ago. What about the other places we've looked at?"

Chantal shook her head. "I don't know, perhaps."

He grinned his big, white smile and squeezed her hand. "Why don't you go get changed and relax for a while? I'll call you when dinner's ready. We're having burgers tonight, as per *your* demanding daughter Whitney's request!"

Smiling at Clay's description of their daughter when she was being insistent, Chantal left his office and went into their bedroom, where she changed from her office dress into a pair of maternity pants and a comfortable sweater. In the kitchen she drank a diluted glass of cough syrup, gagging a bit on the strong flavor. After pouring herself a glass of cider, she retreated to their bedroom, and got settled in her padded rocker. Moving the lamp closer, she retrieved the scrapbook from the bottom shelf and flipped the pages to the back of the book.

She began reading the next article.

"Freedom" by E. Shabot. April 30, 1917.

This is part five in a series of articles which describes the experiences of a young Negro boy fleeing oppression and finding freedom in Canada.

After Papa and I finished our afternoon walk, my brother, Josiah and his wife, Deneille, took us into town for a lovely dinner. Returning home, Papa went straight to bed, so the rest of my interview had to wait until the following morning.

After breakfast, we got comfortable in the living room. Papa, after reminding me how he, Ester, and her father, Justice had booked passage on the steamship to Canada, continued his story.

"Our steamer landed at Rouse's Point, New York, located just a mile from the Canadian border."

I asked, "What happened when you got there?"

Papa hitched himself up in his chair and sighed, his eyes getting a far-off look. "That was a day forever burned in my mind. . ."

The baby kicked, causing Chantal to change her position. She rubbed her tummy to quiet the infant. *I wonder if Samuel and his companions all made it safely to Canada that day.*

> A chill wind coming off Lake Champlain buffeted Samuel as he disembarked from the steamship arriving at Rouse's Point. The dock teemed with other passengers, sailors, cargo handlers, ships' crews, and a motley collection of idlers and bystanders. He tightly clutched his small carpet bag containing his few possessions, scanning the array of figures and faces surrounding him.
>
> *Someone's supposed to be here to meet me.* Another passenger accidentally bumped his shoulder, making him jump. *And there may be slave catchers here, too. I must be careful.* He took two tentative steps forward, only to have a tall, burly black man, dressed in dark clothing and wearing a top hat, grasp his arm.

"Are you Samuel Prescott?" the man asked, peering down upon him.

Samuel's legs trembled. *Is he friend or foe?* Staring at the stranger, Samuel slowly nodded.

"Let me see your papers," he demanded.

Samuel paused, looking around the busy dock. *Are we being watched?* His heart thumped as he handed the man his travel letter.

The breeze rattled the paper in the man's beefy hand as he read the missive from Mister Rowland T. Robinson. Then he nodded. "Very well. I am Reverend Cato Perkins, and I will accompany you to Canada. Follow me."

Releasing a deep breath, Samuel nodded. *I just might make it after all.* Surprised at how purposefully the reverend strode across the dock, Samuel dodged other harried travelers to keep up with his long-legged companion. They halted in front of several moored, smaller canal schooners, each with a sail hoisted on its double masts.

Where is Ester? I need to find her! Samuel frantically searched the faces of the jostling passengers, waiting to board the vessels.

"Come, Samuel. We must board!" the reverend insisted.

Just then, Samuel saw Ester's father, Justice, his head towering above the crowd, leading her onto the schooner moored in behind them.

A horn blasted, and a man yelled, "All aboard," directing passengers onto the steamship Samuel had just disembarked.

"Ester!" Samuel yelled and waved. *I hope she can hear me.*

To Samuel's surprise, Ester turned in his direction, smiled and waved back.

"I'll see you in the Promised Land!"

She nodded, then followed her father on board.

Reverend Perkins lifted Samuel's satchel from his arms, then helped Samuel jump down onto the crowded, rocking boat.

Chantal shifted in her rocker. Eagerly, she read more of Emmaline's article.

"Papa?" I lifted my voice slightly to get his attention.

His gaze slowly focused on me. "Reverend Cato Perkins met me at the dock and accepted my letter from Mistah Robinson. I was so relieved when he told me he would guide me to Canada. Just as I was boardin' the sailing schooner I saw Ester and Justice gettin' into a similar boat, moored along the dock."

Papa adjusted himself in the big chair and sighed. "I yelled to Ester and waved. She saw me and waved back. I told her I would meet her in the Promised Land." He paused, looking away. "But that, my dear girl, was the last time I ever saw the first love of my life!"

I saw the deep sadness in Papa's eyes. "Oh, Papa. Your heart must have been broken!"

He gave me a rueful smile. "Even though I loved your mother dearly, I often think of my sweet, blue-eyed angel, Ester, who nursed me back to health. I can only hope she has lived a wonderful, long life in this free land."

I could see Ester's bright blues eyes still burned in the old man's soul.

Chantal remembered her grandmother Emmaline's lined, loving face. *She certainly loved her father deeply. And poor Samuel, still so young. How did he face this new disappointment?*

The Reverend pushed his way through the throng of passengers and found a place to lean against the boat railing. Samuel wedged himself next to his large companion. The boat was unleashed from its mooring, and the sails flapped in the breeze, causing the boat to lurch side to side. Memories of him and Jonah being swept under the waves flashed through Samuel's mind. Grasping the railing, he cried out. "Please, dear Lord! Don't let this boat sink!"

Reverend Perkins, who had set the satchel on the deck between his feet, wrapped a strong arm around Samuel and pulled him close. "Hold on! It may get a bit rough!"

As the boat swung toward the middle of the channel where the water calmed, Samuel focused on the passing shoreline, his stomach churning.

Then the Reverend grasped Samuel's shoulder, making him jump. "Look!" To his left, the Reverend pointed to a large rock outcropping, with a flag on top. "That's the Royal Union Jack. We are now in Canada, my boy!" he bellowed.

Samuel and other passengers cheered lustily. He felt tension drain out of his taut muscles, and an unfamiliar, light feeling come over him. "I'm free! I'm finally free! No one can catch me now!" He watched the fluttering blue flag, emblazoned with diagonal and horizontal red and white crosses, pass behind them.

And then, despite his joy, his tears flowed. He collapsed to his knees and sobbed.

Chantal pictured young Samuel on a crowded boat, scared to death, being guided by a stranger. *But since he had come this far, what else could he do?* After sipping her cider, Chantal continued reading Emmaline's article.

I asked Papa, "So you and the Reverend made it to Canada together?"

Papa's glazed eyes focused on me, and he slowly nodded. "It was a bitter-sweet moment 'cause I was the only one of our family to reach the Promised Land. It broke my heart I didn't save them!"

I grasped his mangled right hand. "I know Papa, but you were very brave. Where did you come ashore?"

Papa smiled, "The Reverend pointed out landmarks as we crossed the Chambly Canal, and traveled up the Richelieu River. I remember the lovely apple trees sproutin' their pink and white blossoms. After about two hours on the big river, the boat slowed, and we turned west into the narrow mouth of a smaller river. It wasn't long before we landed in the town of Lacolle, the home of Reverend Perkins."

"Oh, I never knew where you lived before our family home."

Papa nodded. "Imagine my surprise when I entered the Perkins' house and discovered two other black boys livin' there. James was two years older than me, and Michael was about five when I moved in. Missus Perkins said they, like me, had been orphaned durin' their escape from slavery. I spent the next ten years livin' with the Perkins and growin' up with my adopted brothers."

I touched Papa's hand. "I'm so glad you had a family to live with who loved you. You were very lucky after all the tragic events in your life."

Chantal felt her eyes moisten and found herself breathing in quick gasps at reading Emmaline's account of Samuel's long flight to freedom. *Oh, Lord! So many things could have gone wrong—any one of them would have changed the whole course of his life, and Grandma Emmaline's, and my mother, and I...*

She smiled, offering a short but heartfelt thanks to God and the fates for shining their grace upon her ancestor. *Grandma Emmaline was right—the Lord was protecting that boy, after all the hardship he endured!*

Taking another sip of her drink, she resumed reading.

Papa nodded. "Yes, my dear girl. I believe the Good Lord was indeed watchin' over me. Despite my crushin' grief, I have been very fortunate."

I prodded for more details. "What was your life like living with the Perkins'?"

Papa sipped his tea and continued. "Missus Perkins was the headmaster at our school for Negro children. 'Cause I already knew how to read and write, she put me to work tutorin' the other kids after I attended my own lessons. During dinner at home, she often fretted over the conditions of our schools. She said they were greatly inferior to the common schools for the white kids. She railed about the unfair treatment our children received, and said somethin' needed to be done about it."

Papa stared off into the distance, then he turned to me.

"One evenin' after dinner, a white man came to visit, and Reverend asked me to join their discussion. He introduced the man as Mister Peter Matthews, a lawyer from Napierville, where the county courthouse, the Palais de Justice, was located. Reverend asked Mister Matthews if he could help us do somethin' about the awful conditions in our schools. The lawyer was an abolitionist, and sympathetic to our cause. He said he would help us file a lawsuit against the provincial legislature askin' them to provide books, desks, and heat at all the schools attended by Negro students. Wantin' to help, I asked Mister Matthews if I could assist with the legal briefs, and he agreed. Shortly thereafter, I became his apprentice."

"That was a wonderful opportunity for you! What happened with the lawsuit? Were you successful?" I asked Papa.

Papa frowned. "Well, in those days there were different opinions as to whether Negro students had the right to attend the common schools. In our school, as with many others in black neighborhoods, we were segregated. The opposin' argument was that we chose to have our own school and, even though there were no common schools close by, it was the responsibility of our people to support it." Papa shook his head. "It was a long, hard fight against unfair education practices in the province.

We argued our case for almost four years to convince the trustees the Negro schools deserved the same fundin' as the white common schools. But we finally prevailed and, at last, all of our kids were able to complete their lessons in warmth, on desks, with the same textbooks as the white children."

I smiled, but wasn't surprised, at hearing of Papa's involvement in challenging bigotry in the schools. It had happened before I was born, and Papa never liked to discuss his cases in front of us children. "Gosh, Papa. I had no idea you were so influential in changing the provincial school system in favor of our people. You're a hero!"

Chantal felt a wave of pride sweep over her. *Good for him! He was indeed a pioneer of his time, fighting against injustices.*

Papa chuckled and waved his hand dismissively. "Through my internship with Mister Matthews I learned a great deal about the law, and decided I wanted to become a lawyer. I was blessed and fortunate when Reverend Parsons and my mentor sponsored my studies at King's College at the University of Toronto. I had a job in the law library, and lived in a boardin' house with other Negro men. After I received my law certification," Papa pointed to the framed document hanging on the wall, "Mister Matthews asked me to join him in his practice in Napierville. I've spent the rest of my life livin' here and defendin' our people against unjust laws, so they could live good lives in this free land. I'm very proud of the work we've done."

When I grasped his hand, I saw him through my childhood eyes, when he allowed me to visit him in the courtroom at the Palais de Justice. There, he stood tall in his dark suit, his black wavy hair slicked back, as he ardently defended our people against unjust provincial laws. "I'm proud of you, too, Papa! I think you're amazing! And didn't you meet Mama at the university?"

Papa grinned sheepishly as he rotated the simple gold band on his left hand with his thumb. Then he stared at his diploma.

Chantal's breath hitched, and she let out a small moan. *Oh, my goodness. Samuel was a lawyer. That's a surprise!* She set the scrapbook aside, rose from her rocking chair, and stretched. *It's truly amazing Samuel devoted his life to supporting the black community in Canada. And even with all his hard work, it sounds like he still had romance in his heart.* After rubbing her tummy to ensure the baby was settled, she sat back down. *I wonder how difficult it was for Samuel to become a lawyer all those years ago.*

Samuel yawned as he read the dry legal passage. "…in such cases, a deposition is required of the defendant…" It was late, and as far as he knew, he was the only one still in the law library.

Suddenly voices reached his secluded study table.

"…well I think yo' fren' is wrong, and ya should stay away from her!"

"But Mama, I don't have that many—"

Samuel looked up from his textbook. Glancing at the clock, he noted it was after midnight. Rising, Samuel walked across the open center of the library where he saw two women mopping. One was an older black woman, bent from years of hard work, pointing her finger at a young black woman, who pouted, her eyes downcast.

The older woman scolded. "I don' care! You'se my daughter, and ya better mind me, ya hear?"

"*Bonsoir!*" Samuel hailed.

Both women froze, staring at their unexpected visitor.

"I'm Samuel. I was studying at my desk and I heard you talking."

The older woman's face scrunched. "I's sorry. We didn't mean to disturb ya, Sir."

When the daughter lifted her head, Samuel's breath caught in his throat. *She's just a petite, delicate flower that should be blooming in a beautiful garden!* Instinctively he felt the urge to reach out and protect her. Samuel stammered, "What—what are your names?"

Leaning her mop into the bucket, the bent woman said, "I's Constance." She waved her hand toward the girl. "And 'dis here's ma daughter, Catharine."

Catharine looked up briefly at Samuel, smiled, then cast her eyes to the ground.

Constance said, "We's sorry for botherin' ya. We's be quieter as we work."

Catharine put her hand to her mouth and nodded, but never looked up.

"Thank you, I appreciate it." Samuel smiled at both women, then returned to his study table. Staring at the textbook, the words blurred in front of him. His attention drifted to the working women. Samuel was mesmerized watching Catharine's spry figure efficiently covering the floor with her mopping motion. He noted she was about twice as fast as her mother.

After about a half-hour passed, with Samuel watching their every move, the women worked their way into another room. To his dismay, Samuel could no longer see them. *Guess it's time to leave. But I'll be back again tomorrow night. I must to get to know this young lady better!*

Chantal looked up from the article and glanced across the room. *How did Samuel meet his wife in college? Were they in the same classes? I know I'll never forget the first time I met Clay in the student center at McGill University. I thought he was so handsome!*

Papa's glance returned to me. "Yep. I was studyin' late one night in the law library, when I heard two women talkin' loudly, which surprised me."

Papa rubbed his chin. "I approached them and introduced myself. That's when I met Constance, and her daughter Catharine. My first impression of your mother was she looked like a beautiful, petite flower. All I wanted to do was protect her!" Papa flashed his almost toothless grin, seemingly lost in his pleasant reverie.

"I wonder what Mama thought of you. She never mentioned the first time you met," I said.

Papa shrugged. "She probably thought I was some crazy old man, because I was already thirty!" He laughed. "Constance apologized for disturbin' me, and said they would be quieter as they went about their work. I vowed to return every night, so I could get to know the lovely young Catharine better. And I did! Took me most of the year, and many sleepless nights, to get into their good graces. When she turned eighteen in the spring, I asked Catharine, in front of her mother, to marry me. She said yes! I can tell you, I was the happiest man on earth!"

Chantal smiled. *Samuel was patient and determined to get his lady. I'm glad Catharine said yes!* Then she continued reading.

Papa stared at their wedding picture hanging on the wall to his left, next to the over-crowded bookshelf.

"After I finished my studies in Toronto, Catharine and I moved here to Napierville, so I could work at the Matthews' law firm. Not long after, we bought this house. Over the years, Catharine gave birth to your brothers, Lemuel, John, and then Josiah. I love my sons dearly, but you can imagine how excited we were when you were born, and we finally had our baby girl!" Papa smiled and grasped my hand. "Did you know you were named after Missus H., the wonderful lady who harbored my family in Fair Haven?"

"Oh, my! Her name was Emmaline? I never knew this before."

Papa grinned, "Not exactly, but very close!"

Chantal gasped. *Emmaline was named after Missus H. in Fair Haven? I need to call DeeDee and ask her more about Gabe and his family. I wonder what Gabe's wife's name was. I don't remember DeeDee mentioning it. No matter what Clay says, I still feel there's a connection here!* She finished reading the end of the article.

Papa's expression of joy turned somber. "Since your mother was twelve years younger, I figured she'd outlive me by a country mile. But that damned cancer took her way too soon. I miss her beautiful smile, and sense of humor, every day. I only hope the Good Lord takes me soon, so I can join her in heaven, where my family is waitin' for me!"

I grasped his hand. "Well, Papa. I love you and hope you live for many more years!"

He grinned and clasped my hand with both of his.

From being a slave in the American South, to his tragic escape and loss of his family, to finding a new life of love and fulfillment in Canada, my Papa, Samuel, was an amazing spiritual man devoted to God, his family, and his adopted country.

I am forever grateful he told me his story, and I could share it with the readers of The Provincial Freeman.

Chantal thought about Samuel's amazing journey. *How sad for Samuel his wife died so many years earlier. I imagine he was lonely in his old age, even though his son was close by to care for him.*

She flipped through the next few pages of the scrapbook, filled with old sepia-toned photographs. There was Samuel, nicely dressed, sitting stiffly in an ornate, straight-backed chair. Catharine stood next to him, wearing a simple white dress and a bridal veil. Her hand rested gently on his shoulder. The next photograph showed Samuel, dressed in a dapper three-piece suit, standing to the left of an empty judge's bench. An older white gentleman, dressed similarly, with bushy sideburns, stood to the right of the bench. Behind them on the wall hung the great seal of Canada.

That must be Mister Matthews, Samuel's law partner.

On the following pages were photographs of Samuel's growing family. One showed petite Catharine, a slight smile on her face, sitting in the same gilded chair, her feet not touching the ground. Behind and to her left, Samuel, dressed in a dapper suit, towered above her. Two young boys of differing heights, their hands jammed into their trouser pockets, stood behind and to her right. Another boy, of about two years old, sat cross-legged on the floor in front of her dangling feet. A big smile was spread across his face.

The next photograph was similarly staged, but the three boys were several years older, and stood on either side of Catharine, who sat in the big chair. In her arms she cradled a baby girl dressed in a long, white christening dress. Samuel stood behind the chair, looking lovingly at the infant.

Ahhh. Grandma Emmaline as a baby. How adorable!

As Chantal studied the photographs, a chill ran through her. She noticed in every picture, Samuel had tactfully hidden his mangled right hand.

That was such a defining disfigurement for him. I imagine it was always in the back of his mind he might be identified and taken away from his family at a moment's notice!

As Chantal began to close the book, she noticed a one-column article affixed to the last page. She heard Clay calling from the kitchen, but decided to take a moment to read the story.

"Eternity" by E. Shabot. August 28, 1920.

Several years ago, I was privileged to have a series of articles published by this newspaper about my father, Samuel, who endured a tragic journey to escape oppression in the American South, and live a free life in Canada.

Papa had been reluctant his whole life to discuss his struggles to reach freedom. When questioned about it, he would only say that what was important was his life and family now. I was honored when he finally told me his life's story, as he approached his eightieth year. This is the final article about my dear father.

Last week, when my brother, Josiah, brought Papa his usual morning breakfast, he called Papa's name, but there was no answer. Upon entering Papa's bedroom, Josiah discovered our father had passed away in his sleep. Samuel Prescott was eighty-three years old.

Grasped in Papa's damaged right hand was his wedding photograph. To his left on the bed, were two charcoal drawings from Rokeby Farm. Josiah said Papa's eyes were open, and a soft smile had frozen on his face.

It is my sincere hope Papa's angels: his mama, Miss Elsie; nephew, Jonah; my mother, Catharine; and perhaps his special blue-eyed angel, Ester, were all there to welcome him with open arms into eternity.

May he forever find love, comfort and freedom in the Good Lord's arms. My kind, loving and courageous Papa Samuel will always be in my heart.

I miss and love you, Papa. Rest in peace, my dear, sweet soul!

Chantal wiped her flowing tears. *What an amazing life Samuel lived! I am so glad he told his story to Grandma Emmaline. I can only hope our little family has made him proud!* She slowly rose from her rocker to join Clay and her daughters in the kitchen for dinner.

DEEDEE GETS INTERRUPTED

As I sat working at my desk in the kitchen, I heard a car pull into the driveway. *Oh, boy. Here we go again. I'll bet that's Bill with more looky-loos. Maybe we'll get a winner this time.*

Peering out the window into the expansive backyard, I noticed dark clouds hovering overhead and the bare-limbed maples swaying in the breeze. The dim afternoon light was quickly fading to twilight. My mood was as grim as the brewing storm.

The front door opened, and I listened to my realtor go through his spiel welcoming our latest set of visitors. Since Chantal and Clay had visited the previous Saturday, this was the fourth set of potential buyers to traipse through the house. For only being Thursday, it had been a long, grueling and stressful week. Thus far, no offers had been made on the house. The weather was turning cold with snow flurries predicted overnight—not unusual for Vermont in October. To my great chagrin, I had been trying to mentally prepare myself to hunker down for a long New England winter. I couldn't remember the last time I had actually driven in snow, and it scared the hell out of me. Also, my manager in California was none too happy I couldn't give her a definite date to return to the office.

Chantal and Clay's visit with their daughters had been on my mind all week. I felt an unusual connection had formed between Chantal and me, and I was somewhat disappointed I hadn't heard back from her. I was hoping she and Clay might want to make an offer on the property.

Indistinct voices and the creaking of the stairway let me know the group was heading upstairs. Then I heard footfalls moving from one empty bedroom to another. Knowing it would only be a matter of minutes before they appeared in the kitchen, I saved my work and closed my laptop.

Soon I heard chatter in the parlor, then Bill appeared in the kitchen. Following him was a disheveled, sleep-deprived young mother, her long, unwashed hair swept back in a ponytail. An infant was strapped to her chest in one of those reverse backpack contraptions. Since I never had babies, for the life of me, I couldn't figure out how those things worked. A few steps behind her came a bearded man with longish, unkempt brown hair, probably mid-twenties. He was holding the hand of a fussy boy toddler. I figured they were looking for a first home to buy, and this place was probably in their price range. However, seeing the scowl on the man's face, I was pretty sure they weren't going to be potential buyers.

I greeted my visitors politely and answered their questions as generically as I could. Then Bill escorted them to the backyard to view the rest of the property. Since it was late in the afternoon, I felt my energy waning. So I brewed myself a cup of tea, went back to my desk, and opened my laptop. Not long afterward, I heard the car pulling out of the driveway. That old song by Queen, "Another One Bites the Dust," rolled through my head.

With the last vestiges of light fading, I noticed the yard turning white from big, fat snowflakes drifting down in the dusk. I groaned internally.

As I started to log in to work, the phone rang. I had been on a conference call earlier in the day with my project team, and several issues with my manager had gone unresolved. I figured this was her calling me back, probably in a bad mood. I reluctantly snapped on my headset and answered the call.

"Hallo? DeeDee?" the unfamiliar voice said. "This is Chantal Moreau, from Montreal."

With my mind on work, it took me a moment to register it wasn't my manager calling to chew me out. I was happy to hear her voice.

"Chantal! Hi!" I said. "It's nice to hear from you. This is a surprise. How are you?"

"I'm doing pretty well," Chantal said in her lilting accent. "Baby's growing and kicking up a storm." She laughed. "I hope I'm not bothering you."

Thankful for the diversion, I logged off and closed my laptop. "Nope. I need a break, so it's a good time to chat. What's up?" I prodded, hoping for good news.

Chantal sighed. "Oh, my gosh, where do I even begin?" I could hear the excitement in her voice. "No, no…never mind…I'll get to that later. I want to ask you something, and I hope you don't think I'm crazy, because Clay does!"

Uh-oh! This has got to be about Gabe. I wasn't sure how to respond. "Go ahead, Chantal. What's on your mind?"

"I remember you told me a man named Gabe helped the fugitives who had passed through your property, right?"

I nodded, though she couldn't see me. "Yeah, that's right. Gabe Hopper. He was the conductor who helped them travel to the canal in Whitehall. Why do you ask?"

Chantal asked, a bit breathless, "Gabe had a wife, right? Do you happen to know what her name was by any chance?"

This is odd. I wonder why she's asking. "Sure. Her name was Emma. It was because of her journals, we learned so much—"

A small squeal came through the phone. "DeeDee! Oh, God! You are not going to believe what I've found! I *knew* I was right!"

I laughed nervously, not sure whether to feel alarmed or amused by her excitement. "Chantal, slow down! What are you talking about? Is this about your family?"

"Yes!" she exclaimed. "Remember when I told you I thought the town of Fair Haven was familiar to me?"

"Yeah, but you weren't sure why. I think you were going to talk to your mother about your family history."

Chantal responded, "And I did! You're not going to believe this. She had a scrapbook with articles my Grandma Emmaline wrote about her father Samuel's escape from oppression. My mother told me she'd kept it hidden to protect our family secrets."

I gasped, "Wait! What? Your grandmother's name was *Emmaline*? And her father was Samuel? That's quite a coincidence."

A chill ran down my spine as I recalled the entries in Emma's diary about Miss Elsie, Samuel, and their family. Could Chantal's ancestors actually have been the *same* family Gabe and Emma had helped so many years ago? It seemed impossible.

Chantal's voice rose. "But don't you see, DeeDee? I don't think it's a coincidence at all!" She took a breath. "Samuel told Emmaline she was named after a Missus H, who had harbored his family in Fair Haven. I think it was Gabe's wife, Emma!"

I stared out the window as I processed what Chantal had said. If it was the same Samuel from Emma's diary, then it meant he actually made it to freedom, where he raised a family. What forces in the universe had conspired to bring his descendant, Chantal, here?

"Whoa! This is pretty crazy, Chantal. So, you're saying you have proof Samuel stayed in Fair Haven?"

"Yes! That's why it was familiar to me. I remembered Grandma telling me some of the stories when I was little. In one of her articles, she asked Samuel who had harbored his family in Fair Haven. But he refused to name them, because he didn't want them to get into trouble. He just called them Mister and Missus H. I think it was the Hoppers!"

The excitement in Chantal's voice was contagious. I was starting to be convinced her wild assertions just might be true. As I listened, I reached into my briefcase and found the folder with copies of the ledger and part of Emma's journal Moni had given me. I opened to the ledger page.

"Chantal, do you happen to know the names of Samuel's family members by any chance? I have copies of Emma's diary and a ledger she had hidden, which contains names of fugitives who passed through the property."

I heard Chantal gasp, "Oh, my gosh! You do? That's incredible!" She took a deep breath and added in a quieter voice, "Let's see, Samuel's mother was Miss Elsie, and he had a nephew named Jonah. He had a sister, too. I think her name was Sarah."

As she mentioned the familiar names from Emma's diary, my heartbeat quickened and I began to tremble. Someone, somewhere, somehow had drawn Chantal to this house. I was dumbfounded.

My voice quavered a bit as I asked, "Chantal, one more question. Was Samuel's last name Prescott?"

"Yes! How did you know that?"

I laughed at the strange, unbelievable circumstances unfolding between the two of us. "Because his entire family is well-documented in the ledger and Emma's diary!" I sighed. "And believe it or not, you have indeed found their hiding place in Fair Haven!" I heard some shuffling noises, then it sounded like Chantal blew her nose away from the phone. "Chantal? Are you still there?"

Chantal sniffled, and her voice was husky. "*Ah! Mon Dieu!* DeeDee! This is incredible. Clay kept trying to convince me I was making too much out of Grandma Emmaline's stories. But I just had a feeling, from the first time I stepped into your house, something there was calling me!"

A shiver ran through me as my thoughts whirled. *Who had orchestrated this? Gabe?…Samuel?…Emma?…or even Luke?* I knew Gabe was still hovering around the property, but were the others still here, too? I guessed anything was possible in the spirit world. I grabbed my phone handset, asked Chantal to hang on a moment, and took a few steps to the kitchen counter. My trusty bottle of brandy called out to me, and I needed a drink—now! I popped the cork, returned to my office chair, and dosed my cup of tea with a big splash from the bottle.

The spiked tea burned all the way down and helped calm my nerves. I gathered my thoughts, then said, "Chantal, you do realize how crazy this is, right? I mean, what are the chances that you and Clay just happened to look at a property where your ancestors were once sheltered as fugitives? I'd say like…one in a million!"

Chantal laughed. "I know! That's what Clay said, too. He thinks I'm just crazy hormonal with this baby." She chuckled. "But somehow I feel I'm being drawn to your property for a reason. I don't know if it's Samuel guiding me, or someone else. But I think it's all very strange and wonderful!"

I recalled Emma's account of the attack on the wagon. She was aware Samuel and Jonah had escaped the slave hunters. But there was never any mention of them afterward in her journals. *I wonder if she ever knew their fate.*

"Chantal, maybe you can help me fill in the gaps. According to Emma's diary, the wagon Gabe and Luke used to drive the Prescotts to Whitehall was attacked at the bridge, crossing the border to New York. Unfortunately, Gabe's son Luke was shot and killed, and Sarah was captured. Emma thought Samuel and Jonah had escaped, but she never mentioned them again. Do you happen to know about their travels?"

Chantal's voice rose as she responded, "Oh, my gosh, DeeDee! That's exactly the same story Emmaline wrote about. Samuel told her about the wagon attack, and how Luke had told them to run. So Samuel grabbed Jonah and ran through the woods until they found a barn to hide in. I guess a local lady found them and helped them get to Whitehall." She took a deep breath. Her voice shook slightly as she continued, "Apparently, along the way, they found Samuel's mother, Miss Elsie, drowned in the river. The lady told Samuel she would make sure Miss Elsie got a good Christian burial.

Then she made Samuel and Jonah hurry along. Samuel was distraught he never had the chance to say a proper goodbye to his mother."

Emma's sorrow over Miss Elsie's death came to mind. "Chantal, I want you to know Emma thought very highly of Miss Elsie. She wrote in her journal about her admiration of Elsie's courage and determination to bring her family to freedom, despite the perils." I scanned quickly through other passages of Emma's writing I had on my desk. "The local lady was named Paree, and she was good for her word. You'll be happy to know she and Emma made arrangements for Elsie to be buried in the Hopper family plot here in Fair Haven."

Chantal said, "Did they really? That was very kind of them! I'm sure Samuel would have liked to have known his mother was properly interred. I would love to visit her grave one day."

I remembered another entry in Emma's journal, where she described Paree being murdered by a vigilante gang, in retaliation for her shooting some of the slave hunters. But I decided now wasn't the time to mention it to Chantal.

"So, Chantal, tell me about Samuel's escape," I prodded. "Did he and Jonah make it to freedom in Canada?"

I heard her take a deep breath, then Chantal said, "Well, not exactly. It was all so very tragic for Samuel."

"Oh, no! What happened?"

Chantal sighed. "Well, they boarded a steamship in Whitehall. But there was a bad storm on the lake, and the ship wrecked." Her voice sounded weary. "Samuel and Jonah both went overboard. Samuel did his best to save Jonah, but ended up losing his nephew under the waves. Jonah drowned, and Samuel barely survived. He was washed ashore with the debris."

I was shocked at hearing of this turn in Samuel's fate for the first time, and surprised at how emotionally attached I had become to this family who had passed through here more than a hundred and fifty years earlier.

I took another gulp of my spiked tea. "Oh, Chantal. I am so sorry to hear this! Samuel must have been devastated, losing Jonah after all they'd been through."

"Yeah, he was. He blamed his mangled hand for not being able to hold onto the boy in the water. He was really upset over not being able to save Miss Elsie and Jonah, because he considered himself the man of the family."

"Oh, that's so sad! And he was just a boy himself. I believe he was about twelve at that time, wasn't he?"

"Yes, that's about what I figured," Chantal replied.

"But he did survive the shipwreck. Then what happened to him?"

"He was badly bruised and had a broken ankle," Chantal continued. "Some guys rescued him and took him to a farm called Rokeby, on the shore of the lake. It was owned by the Robinson family, who were abolitionists. Samuel stayed there for six months recuperating from his injuries. He was paid a wage for his work, as were other blacks on the farm. The next spring, he took another steamship to the border of New York and Canada. From there, a smaller boat took him to freedom in Canada."

I was relieved to hear Samuel finally gained his hard-fought freedom. "Wow! What an amazing, heart-wrenching journey he endured! He had the same courage and determination Emma so admired in his mother." I glanced at the copies of Emma's journal. "You know, Chantal, I don't think Emma or Gabe ever knew of Samuel's fate. I'm sure Emma would have been proud to learn he finally reached the Promised Land."

Chantal sniffled. "*Oui!* I think she would have been very proud, especially since Samuel eventually became a lawyer. He was an advocate for our people's quest for justice in Canada."

I said, "Really? Isn't that amazing? He must have been a very passionate soul."

Chantal sighed. "Yes, I think he was. I wish I had known him. He and my great-grandmother had four children. My grandmother, Emmaline, was their youngest, and their only girl. I guess that's why they decided to name her after Emma." She paused. "You know, after all Samuel endured escaping slavery, he lived to the ripe old age of eighty-three!"

Something Chantal had said earlier in the conversation leapt to my mind. "Chantal, didn't you say your mother hid your grandmother's articles to keep your family secrets? If you don't mind me asking, did you find out what those were?"

Chantal's voice grew heavy. "Yeah, I think so. When my mother was young, she said a white man came to their home. He said he represented the Swaley family, who had been Samuel's masters. Apparently the family had somehow gotten hold of Emmaline's articles. They weren't at all happy at how they were portrayed."

I was surprised. "Wow! I wonder how they found Emmaline's family in Canada?"

Chantal paused, then said, "I don't know, but they did! My mother remembers the man threatening our family if Emmaline continued to write about the Swaleys. Even though her articles had been published decades earlier, Grandma was very upset the man had found them. She promised on her Bible she would no longer write any more articles."

"Oh, my goodness, how awful! I don't blame Emmaline for being scared. I didn't think plantation owners would bother to send an emissary all the way to Canada."

"I guess if they had a purpose, it was worth it for them to make the trip," Chantal said. "You know after reading her stories, I think Samuel's description about how he lost his fingers at the hands of the master's son was the most damning. My mother is worried, even in this day and age, descendants of the Swaley family could still bring harm to our family."

"That seems unlikely, don't you think?"

"Clay said the same thing." Chantal paused. "He thinks my mother is a bit daft. But she obviously had her reasons to keep our family story under wraps." The excitement in Chantal's voice returned. "But now, not only do I know more of our family history, but because of you, DeeDee, I also know where they were once harbored!"

I laughed. "Chantal, I can assure you, I had nothing to do with this! But I do believe someone in the universe has paved the way for you to find this waystation where Samuel once stayed. I think it's truly amazing!"

"I can't wait to tell Clay and Mother about what we've figured out! I know they are going to be amazed, as well. Then I can prove to Clay I'm not crazy!" Chantal chuckled. "I'm hoping I can convince Clay to make another trip to Vermont, so we can come visit again—if that's all right with you?"

Remembering Chantal's gentle smile and regal nature, I said, "Of course, I'd love to have you come visit again. And please bring your daughters, if you can. They are such a delight!"

"Thanks again for all your help, DeeDee. This is all so unbelievable! I'll be back in touch soon. *A bientôt.*" Chantal hung up the phone.

I removed my headset and took the last drink of my spiked tea. Staring at the darkened kitchen window, I saw my disheveled reflection peering back at me. Our conversation replayed in my head.

So, Emma's Samuel and Chantal's Samuel were one and the same person! Chantal is right: this is pretty unbelievable. But how could this be happening? What or who in the world has guided Chantal and her family to this house? Is my childhood protector, Gabe, trying to help me move on? Or is the spirit of Samuel somehow leading Chantal to where he had once been sheltered? And why? Did either or both of them want Chantal to live here?

Suddenly, a bright flash moved behind my reflection in the window, and a deep chill ran through me. *What the hell?*

I turned in my chair and looked around the kitchen, then into the main room. Nothing there. Then the overhead fluorescent light flickered several times, and began buzzing. Rooted in my chair, I stared at the offending light fixture. After a few moments, the buzzing receded.

I rasped, "Gabe? Is that you? Are you trying to get my attention?"

I waited. No answer.

I wonder how much Gabe knows about Samuel's fate. Do spirits meet in the afterworld and share their life stories?

I could only ponder the many mysteries of the great universe beyond.

DEEDEE'S SURPRISE

The storm that blew through on Thursday night and Friday morning left about four inches of snow. I was thankful it wasn't more, as I was still able to get out of my driveway. Saturday dawned as a beautiful, sunny, fall day with temperatures in the fifties. I decided the house needed to be aired out, so I opened the windows downstairs to get a cross-breeze flowing.

After a week of people traipsing their muddy feet through the house, the dingy, threadbare carpets were filthy. Knowing it wouldn't make a huge difference, I figured at least I could vacuum the worst of the dirt. After finishing the downstairs rooms, I took a quick lunch break. Then I dragged the heavy vacuum up the steep stairs to attack the second floor.

Entering the bedroom on the left just past the landing, a familiar cold shiver ran through me. I stopped at the doorway and glanced around the empty room. I remembered standing in that same position as a young girl and seeing Gabe hovering by the front windows—my first encounter with our *other* house inhabitant. I saw no one here now.

Setting the machine in the middle of the room, I plugged it into a wall socket and vacuumed the dark carpet, stopping at the closed closet door. I switched off the vacuum and pulled it out of the way so I could enter the walk-in closet. When I opened the door, a warm flush engulfed me. Gasping, I took a step back. I hadn't felt that sensation since I was a child. I peered into the closet.

There, hovering in the gloom, was Gabe. His signature red flannel shirt covered his hunched visage. His long gray hair and beard glowed almost white against the dark background. Vaguely I noticed his worn trousers and rubber work boots that seemed to fade into near invisibility in the shadowed bottom of the closet.

With my heart pounding, I stood very still, watching and waiting. Catching my breath, I whispered, "Hi Gabe. It's DeeDee. I'm still here."

The ephemeral figure didn't move.

My mind raced. *Why is Gabe appearing to me now? What does he want? Does this have anything to do with my conversation with Chantal?* I figured it was as good a time as any to probe the mystery.

Taking a breath to steady myself, I asked, "Gabe? Did you bring Chantal and her family here?"

I waited. Then I heard a distinct, low moan, "Nooo…" then trailed off.

Surprised at Gabe's audible response, I asked, "Do you know who did?"

He shook his head slowly, then another low-pitched grumble, "Nooo…"

Confused, I took a step closer to the closet entrance. *If Gabe isn't responsible for leading Chantal here, then who is?*

Concerned about the family's safety, I asked, "Gabe, would Chantal and her family be welcome here?" I waited.

A few moments later, I heard a low hiss, "Yesss…" then faded away.

My knees were trembling and I took a breath. "And you will protect them?"

I felt his stare boring into me. Another hiss that sounded like yes, emanated from him. I stared at the softly glowing figure hovering at the back of the closet. Then his right arm lifted toward me, his palm open, in what I interpreted as a welcoming gesture.

"Thank you, Gabe," I whispered. "They are good people. I hope they decide to live here. And I feel better knowing you will protect them, like you did me and Mom."

Gabe slowly nodded his head over his hunched shoulders. Then his pale visage gradually faded into the dark recesses of the closet.

My legs were shaking so badly, I collapsed against the wall next to the closet. I took deep breaths to settle my pounding heart. It relieved me to know Gabe wouldn't cause Chantal and her family injury, as he had with some of the previous inhabitants. But I was still perplexed as to who had guided Chantal here, unless it had been only blind chance. And of course, I didn't know if, or when, Chantal might ever come back to the house, anyway. So, in the end it was probably just a moot point. But I still kept my hopes up she and Clay would return.

Sunday morning, I did my stint at the laundromat in town, feeling good about having a dresser full of clean clothes. After my cleaning spree on Saturday, I thought the old house looked about as good as it was ever going to get. Deciding to take advantage of the rest of the sunny day, I took a walk around the neighborhood. My route led me one block south to Cemetery Street, which I followed west, paralleling Cedar Grove Cemetery. I smiled, remembering many childhood escapades with friends in this place of departed souls. Rows of granite and marble headstones stood at frigid attention, rising above the surrounding patches of snow.

I made my way to Mom's heart-shaped grave, and cleared the dripping snow from her granite stone. Thankfully, my sister Barbara's name on the right half of the stone still had no death date engraved. Having been born with cerebral palsy, she was now in her late fifties, living a simple life where she was well cared for. I sent a special quiet thanks to her caregivers.

Laying my hand on Mom's stone, I said, "Hey, Mom! Well, you probably know I'm still here. Had a surprise visit from Gabe yesterday. Looks like he's still watching over me and the house." My emotions were raw as Mom's smiling face came to mind. "I'm hoping I can sell the house, Mom, even though you told me not to. I really don't want to spend the winter here. So, if there's anything you can do to make that happen, I'd certainly appreciate your help."

I lingered at her grave, taking deep breaths to quell my sadness. I hoped her spirit was hovering close by, and would direct the forces of the universe in my favor.

"I love and miss you, Mom, and wish I could give you a big hug." I bent and kissed the top of her gravestone, my tears dropping into the snow melt.

Walking across the center aisle and west a few paces, I came to Old Bert's grave. His wife Anna's stone was smaller than Bert's and sat directly to its right. Their son's stone, about the size of Anna's, and placed just to the right, said simply, *Baby Boy.* His birth and death dates were identical to Anna's death date. Any passer-by could instantly infer Anna had died in childbirth, as had her infant son. It made me sad to think of the type of life Old Bert could have enjoyed had his family lived.

I touched Bert's stone and said, "Hi, Old Bert. It's DeeDee. Remember me? I haven't been to visit you in a while. I'm living at the house, and have learned a lot about your family." Emma's stories filtered through my mind. "And guess what. Your ancestor, Gabe, is still keeping me company. Imagine that!" My distant memory of Old Bert "rescuing" me as a three-year-old gripping a limb in the lilac tree made me smile. "If there are any strings you can pull in your world to help me sell the old house, I sure would appreciate it!"

Invoking the spirits of my loved ones, I tipped my face up to the warm sunshine. A sense of peace and contentment washed over me. I felt something good was in the works; I just needed to be patient and let it play out.

Leaving Old Bert's grave site, I meandered through the cemetery, recognizing the familiar names of townsfolk, then I exited the west-end gate. In my mind, I kept replaying my conversation with Chantal about Samuel and his family. And my surprise encounter with Gabe yesterday was even more perplexing. *Maybe Chantal is right, and Samuel's spirit is indeed guiding her here.*

Following the uneven slate sidewalk, being cautious not to trip, I made my way past single-family homes lining the narrow streets. Front porches sported fall decorations of pumpkins, cornstalks, scarecrows, witches and other Halloween regalia. I lingered as I walked by the home of my childhood best friend, Marie, who had helped me escape crazy Old John's pitchfork attack. Marie had recently died from inoperable brain cancer—too young! I missed her terribly as I recalled her sweet smile and her long, black braids reaching to her waist. I wondered if her Indian spirit was shining her light down upon me.

Finishing the two-block circuit, I turned the corner for home and saw my realtor's car parked in the driveway. I was surprised he was at the house on Sunday, as he usually didn't bring clients on the Sabbath. I hurried my pace to catch him before he left. Just as he was backing out of the driveway, I yelled, waved, and got his attention. He stopped and turned off his car engine. I noticed he was alone as he came to meet me on the front lawn.

"Hi, Bill. What brings you over today?"

"Hey, Dee, beautiful afternoon for a walk. Do you have a few minutes? I need to talk to you about something."

Bill's stoic face gave nothing away. I felt that old: *Shit! I'm stuck here for the winter* dread creep back into my heart. Unlocking the front door, I ushered Bill into the kitchen. While hankering for something stronger, I poured myself a glass of water and offered one to Bill. He declined.

I joined him at the table and gave him a wan smile. "So, Bill, to what do I owe the honor of your company?"

He set his briefcase on the floor, opened it, pulled out a folder, and placed it on the table. From the folder, he retrieved an official-looking real estate form and slid it across the table to me.

I glanced at the document cramped with two columns of tight lines, interspersed with various dollar amounts. "What's this?" I asked.

"DeeDee! I'm excited to tell you the Moreaus from Montreal have made an offer on the house." He finally broke a smile.

My pulse increased and my hands began to tremble. *So, Chantal and Clay decided to move here after all!* I was happy for her and thrilled to hear the news, but wasn't completely surprised. After our enlightening talk a few days earlier, I imagined she had had quite an interesting conversation with Clay, explaining her suspicions about Samuel's family were indeed true.

"Oh, Bill!" I said. "I'm so glad to hear that! I think this'll be a great place for their kids to grow up."

Bill's smile had disappeared. "Yeah, well, their offer is ten thousand less than what we listed. I think we should counter-offer and see if they'll come up five thousand."

I had no interest in dickering with Chantal and Clay over the price of the house. Plus, it needed so much work, I figured they'd end up pouring a ton of money into the place anyway. And I knew, deep in my heart, this was where Chantal was supposed to be.

I shook my head. "No, Bill. I'm not going to counter-offer. I think it's a fair price for this old place."

"Dee, are you sure? We can always wait and see if more offers come in."

I figured he was calculating how much he would lose on his commission. "Bill, I really don't want to be here all winter," I said firmly. "And, with the condition the house is in, people aren't exactly knocking the door down to submit offers. I'm good with this, believe me!"

He stared at me for a long minute. "All right, if that's what you want. With the Moreaus' loan already approved and no mortgage on the house, we should be able to close within a week or so, if it works for you."

A week? Wow! My mind immediately went into list-mode, thinking of all the things I'd have to get done to extricate myself from the house. But that was fine—the sooner the better, as far as I was concerned.

I nodded. "Yeah. That'd be great if you could get the closing done in a week."

Bill shrugged. "I'll get the paperwork in order and schedule a time for us to meet with the Moreaus to finalize your signatures. I'll call you tomorrow with more details."

He closed his briefcase and rose from the table. Then he shook my hand. "You got real lucky on this one, Dee. I thought you'd enjoy spending the winter in your old hometown." He winked, and I heard him chuckle as he let himself out the front door.

I supposed he was right, but I didn't think luck had anything to do with it. Someone else was pulling the strings here and I was just a puppet in their marionette theater. I immediately called my husband, Mark, in California to give him the good news.

After hanging up, with thoughts of Chantal still swirling, it finally sank in—I had actually sold the house! The spirits of the universe were indeed conspiring to make this happen. It was a huge load off my mind!

But will Gabe keep his promise and protect Chantal and her family? I could only hope for the best.

HISTORICAL SOCIETY

After speaking with my husband, Mark, the previous evening, I had called my sister, Ellie, and enlisted her help to move the furniture out of the house. She and her husband, Rob, were excited we had sold the property. I figured I'd give Ellie the full scoop of what had transpired with Chantal once I saw her in person.

On Monday morning, Bill called to let me know we were scheduled to meet Chantal and Clay the following Friday to sign the closing papers. I sent my manager in California a quick email explaining my upcoming time line. I knew she would be happy I planned to return to the office soon. Realizing I didn't have any boxes to speak of, I made a quick drive to the U-Haul center in Rutland and bought packing materials. On the way home, I decided to pay a visit to the Historical Society in town.

"DeeDee!" Monique exclaimed, her face breaking into a grin as I walked into her office on the second floor.

I hadn't seen Monique since we had cleaned out the barn a couple of years earlier. I gave her a hug as she rose from her desk. Her petite frame was all but obscured by an oversized, pink, cable-knit sweater. Her long, naturally curly black hair was pulled into a ponytail. Unruly tendrils floated around her face. I noticed new streaks of gray along her temples.

Moni motioned for me to sit in the chair next to her desk. "I heard you were staying out at the old house," she said.

I laughed at her directness. "Boy, news sure travels fast around here, doesn't it?"

"Oh, you know this town—everyone knows everybody's business. And if they don't, they just make it up as they go!" She laughed heartily at her own joke. "Actually, I'm glad you dropped in." She pulled some folders from her bottom drawer.

"What do you have there?"

Moni opened the first folder. "We didn't get a chance to touch base after you cleaned out the property, so I wanted to let you know about some of my recent research."

"Really? That's great! What did you find?"

She lifted a copy of multiple handwritten journal pages. "Do you remember when you were trying to figure out when the Cedar Grove Cemetery was founded? You discovered Edward Allen was on the board of directors of the organizing committee?"

I nodded. "Yeah, I was surprised, because Gabe accused him of shooting Luke. I wondered if Edward had gone on trial for Luke's killing."

Moni waved her hand in the air. "Well, I spent time searching the court scribe's notes and Edward *did* go on trial for shooting Luke." Scanning the pages, she continued, "The judge was William C. Kittredge. But before the trial could even begin, the prosecuting attorney, James Pottle, accused the judge of having a conflict of interest and asked him to recuse himself. "

Moni read from the transcript. "Here's what Pottle said, *Sir, being you are a business partner with Colonel Alonson Allen, whose son is on trial, I believe your business interest in the Fairhaven Marbleized Slate Company makes you unfit to judge these proceedings!*"

"Wow, that's amazing," I said. "So the judge and Edward's father were business partners. Did the judge recuse himself?"

Moni responded, "Nope, the defense attorney, Ira C. Allen, didn't have an issue with him presiding, so the judge stayed."

"Oh, this doesn't bode well for Gabe getting a fair trial, does it?"

Moni shook her head. "Sure doesn't, but the other surprise is Ira C. Allen was Edward's first cousin!"

I chuckled. "Typical small town, everyone's connected one way or another—just like today!"

Moni shrugged, "Yeah, you could say that. But get this—a man named Enos Adams, who worked for Gabe and Emma, also joined the posse. Talk about being a traitor to your boss!"

"Oh, my goodness! Did he really betray them?" I felt sorry for all Emma and Gabe had endured.

Moni nodded. "It looks like Enos must have had a change of heart when the wagon was attacked. He was the first witness called to testify." She browsed several pages, then summarized. "James Pottle walked Enos through the events of the night the wagon was attacked. Apparently Edward had fired a shotgun early on, which spooked Gabe's horses as they tried to get across the bridge, then all hell broke loose. George, the deputy, took Edward into custody and tossed his shotgun."

"Really? So how did Edward get away?"

Moni said, "With all the commotion, no one was paying attention to Edward. Enos said Edward's horse reared, and he saw the boy slip off the back and scurry into the woods next to the stream. Enos followed him." She read another page. "When Enos came upon Edward along the riverbank, he testified Edward started screaming, pointed a revolver and shot Luke."

"Oh, wow. That's really dramatic," I said.

Moni looked up at me. "Well, when Enos accused Edward in the courtroom, apparently Edward freaked out, jumped up, lost his balance, slammed into his attorney, screaming and pointing at Enos: *You shot Luke! You shot Luke! You shot Luke!*"

"My gosh, you could've made a movie about this!"

Moni shook her head. "Yeah, you think? Well, Judge Kittredge was having none of Edward's outburst, so the bailiffs dragged the boy's sorry ass out of the courtroom!"

I laughed, "Is that what the transcript says?"

Moni's eyes crinkled, "More or less, with a little embellishment, of course!"

"Geez, Edward was one little creep, wasn't he?"

Moni nodded. "After the uproar in the courtroom calmed down, the judge called the defense attorney, Ira C. Allen, to question Enos."

"Here you go, take a look at the last few pages of the transcript." She slid the notes across her desk to me.

I pulled the papers closer and slowly started reading the tight, handwritten script.

JUDGE KITTREDGE: "Thy witness, Mister Allen."

IRA C. ALLEN (to Enos Adams): "Mister Adams, what do you do for work?"

ENOS: "I work with my father, Joseph Adams, who is the business man-
ager at the Marbleized Slate Factory."
ALLEN: "Is this your only job?"
POTTLE: "Objection, your Honor. Goes to relevance."
JUDGE: "Mister Allen?"
ALLEN: "If you will allow me, Judge, I'll get to the point presently."
JUDGE: "Very well, but make the point in the next few questions."
ALLEN: "As I asked, Enos, is working at the Slate Factory your only job?"
ENOS: "No. I also work for Mister Gabe Hopper on his farm."
ALLEN: "And is Gabe Hopper the father of the deceased Luke Hopper?"
ENOS: nodding.
ALLEN: "I need you to state your response."
ENOS: "Yes, Gabe is, ahhh, was Luke's father."
ALLEN: "So is it safe to say you and Luke worked together on the Hopper
farm?"
ENOS: "Yes."
ALLEN: "Then isn't it also safe to say you and Luke were friends?"
ENOS: "Yes, we were friends."
ALLEN: "So, if Luke was your friend, why did you join the slave posse to
capture him?"
POTTLE (standing): "Objection! My client's reasons for being with the
posse are irrelevant to these proceedings! And my objection as to rel-
evance still stands."
ALLEN: "Your Honor, both lines of questioning go to show motive for
the witness' actions. If you will allow me?"
JUDGE (to Pottle): "Objections overruled. Please continue, Mister Allen."
ALLEN: "Enos, isn't it true you were embarrassed at being part of the
posse chasing your friend, and you shot Luke so he wouldn't find out?
Then you shot Edward so there would be no witnesses?"
ENOS: "Yes…no! Wait. What did you say? I didn't shoot Luke!"
POTTLE: "Objection! Your honor, defense is leading the witness with
erroneous statements! And one question at a time should be put to
the witness."
JUDGE KITTREDGE (banged his gavel): "Order! Order, I say! Mister
Pottle, you know very well the defense may pose leading questions
to a prosecution witness. The objection is overruled. However, Mister
Allen, please state your questions one at a time and allow the witness
to answer appropriately."
ALLEN: "Enos, why did you join the posse to go after the Hoppers' wagon?"

ENOS: "I didn't want to, but Buster Slater convinced me. It was a terrible mistake! Sheriff Wardwell said he wanted to take Gabe and Luke into custody peaceably, and there would be no violence. But then Edward showed up and fired off his shotgun. It spooked their draft horses and caused the wagon to go over the bridge!"

ALLEN: "Your Honor! Witness' response contains multiple hearsays. Also, inadmissible opinion as to what might have spooked the horses or caused the wagon to go over the bridge. We request testimony be disregarded."

JUDGE (nodding): "Jury will disregard the witness' last statement. Move on, Mister Allen."

ALLEN: "Enos, did you shoot Luke, so he wouldn't know you were part of the hunting posse?"

ENOS: "No! I did not shoot Luke—Edward did!"

ALLEN: "And didn't you then shoot Edward so there would be no witnesses to your killing Luke?"

PROSECUTOR POTTLE: "Objection! Already asked and answered. Witness has already testified he shot Edward after Edward shot Luke!"

JUDGE: "Objection sustained. Mister Allen, restate your question."

ALLEN: "You admit to shooting Edward, is that correct?"

ENOS: "Yes! Edward yelled: 'Gonna kill me some niggahs!' then he shot Luke. I didn't want him to hurt anyone else, so I shot him in the leg."

ALLEN: "Enos, did anyone else witness Edward shooting Luke, as you so allege?"

ENOS: "I don't know, Sir. There was a lot of confusion near the bridge."

ALLEN: "In fact, the matter of who shot Luke boils down to your word against Edward's, isn't that right?"

ENOS: "Yes, I suppose so."

ALLEN: "And you didn't like Edward, did you?"

POTTLE: "Objection! Irrelevant, your Honor!"

JUDGE: "Overruled. The witness shall answer."

ENOS: "No, I didn't much like Edward, and I HATE him now for killing Luke!"

ALLEN: "No more questions, your Honor."

After digesting what I'd read, I looked up at Moni and shook my head. Then I passed the transcript back to her. "Uh oh, this doesn't bode well for Enos, does it?"

Moni shook her head, "Well, after Enos shot Edward, Edward's leg had to be amputated, and he walked with a peg-leg. Looks like the jury may have been sympathetic to his disfigurement."

"Oh, no! Are you kidding me?"

Moni frowned as she read the jury verdict. "Since there were no other witnesses, and Enos admitted to shooting Edward, Enos was found guilty of non-lethal assault with a firearm. He was sentenced to six months in jail. But Edward was found not guilty of shooting Luke due to lack of evidence and set free!"

I gasped. "So, Gabe and Emma never *did* get justice for Luke's death! How tragic!"

"Nope, they didn't, and I'm sure it was very traumatic for them," Moni said. "And that's probably why they didn't continue to harbor fugitives after the tragedy with the Prescotts."

"How unfair!" I said. "I feel so bad for the Hoppers. They were just trying to do the right thing based upon their beliefs." *And that explains why Gabe is still protecting his house from evil!*

Moni looked pained. "I agree. It was a really tragic time for many citizens of this town." She closed the folder and moved it aside, then opened the second folio on her desk. "When I was reading Emma's journal, I came across her note about Paree helping with Miss Elsie's funeral. And I found her later entry lamenting Paree's murder. Paree's last name, which you couldn't remember, was Guildersleeve."

I nodded. "Okay, that sounds familiar. I know Emma really appreciated Paree's help and was devastated when she died."

Holding another stack of copied court scribe entries, Moni said, "As I was researching Edward Allen's trial, I wondered whether anyone was convicted for killing Paree." She tapped the sheets of paper. "It took some digging, but I found the transcripts of the trial of Jeb Slater."

"Oh, my goodness, you did? So what happened?"

Scanning through the pages, Moni gave me the story. "Jeb Slater owned the town tavern. His son, Buster, was the farm hand for the Hoppers who convinced Enos to join the slave hunters!"

I gasped at hearing this. "So, did all of Gabe and Emma's workers turn against them? I wonder why they would do that."

Moni shrugged, then glanced at her transcript. "Yeah, more or less—probably for the bounty money. When the two fugitive boys escaped the broken wagon, Buster and a couple of other men took off chasing them on

Paree's property. Paree warned the posse they were trespassing and to get off her land."

"Uh, oh. I'll bet this didn't end well."

Moni shook her head. "No, it didn't. According to the testimony, Paree shot Buster, knocking him off his horse. Then one of her dogs attacked him, and ripped his throat out!"

"Man, that's just brutal all the way around!" I could just imagine the chaos that must have taken place.

Moni continued, "A man named Paul Yates, and his father Carl, were with Buster. Paul testified Carl shot Paree's dog in the head as he was attacking Buster."

"Oh, no! I bet Paree was furious!"

"She was! In fact, when she saw her dog was dead, she shot Carl point-blank in the chest with her shotgun, killing him!"

"Oh, shit! Seriously? She was one bad-ass woman!"

Moni broke a little smile at my ill-timed joke, then continued solemnly. "Apparently the sheriff refused to arrest Paree, because she was defending her property from the trespassers." Moni continued reading the scribe's notes. "Buster's father, Jeb, was none too happy about his son being man-gled and Paree not being charged with his murder!"

"I imagine he was probably pretty pissed!"

Moni flipped to a new page. "A couple weeks after the wagon attack, Jeb enlisted Paul Yates and six other vigilantes hell-bent on getting revenge on Paree." Moni paused. "Apparently, when they approached her house in the middle of the night, the outdoor dogs started barking, alerting Paree."

"Oh, man. Those guys were crazy to mess with her." I lamented.

"Yeah, looks like Paree was in her nightgown, but had her loaded guns ready."

Moni looked at me, then continued reading. "According to Jeb's state-ment, when he opened her back door, another dog jumped him, chomping down on his arm, causing him to drop his gun. As he tried to kick the dog off, he fell to the ground. The dog swung her head so violently, she ripped Jeb's arm out of its socket."

I said, "Wow, that's one strong dog!"

"Yeah, she was protecting her master." She read more, then continued, "Looks like the two outside dogs got free and attacked some of men sta-tioned around the house. Guess the vigilantes had some pretty serious wounds."

Moni paused, then looked up from the transcript. "Paul had followed Jeb through the door, and apparently shot the dog as she was attacking Jeb, which is how Jeb survived."

"Oh, how sad for the dog. I bet that set Paree into a rage!"

Moni said, "It sure did! Looks like a close-at-hand gun battle ensued in the living room. Paree shot and killed two men named Cyrus and Elmer, as they charged her. Then she and Paul shot each other pretty much at the same time. Both went down." Moni paused and blew out her breath.

"Good for her. She did fight back!" I thought Paree was very brave fighting off so many men invading her home.

Moni's eyes glistened as she looked at me. "Are you sure you want to hear the rest?"

"Probably not, but go ahead." My stomach tightened.

Moni stared at the transcript for a long minute. "Jeb testified Paree was only wounded, so he pulled his knife and slit her throat! Said it was his just revenge for her killing his son, Buster!"

I gasped. My hands were shaking as I envisioned the ambush. "Good Lord! What a terrible end for Paree, who seemed like a righteous woman, just protecting her land."

Moni wiped her eyes and took a breath, then peered at the next page of notes. "Well, get this—Jeb had the nerve to complain to the judge he no longer had the use of his right arm because of the dog's attack!"

"Did he really? Wow, what an asshole he was! So, did anyone get convicted?"

Moni grinned. "Yes! Jeb was found guilty of organizing an illegal vigilante party and first-degree murder for Paree's death. He was sentenced to life in prison."

"What about the other men involved? Were they ever charged?" I asked.

Moni nodded. "I did more digging. So Paul Yates survived the shooting, as he testified at the trial. But I discovered he was later convicted of being involved with Paree's murder, and also sentenced to prison."

My heart went out to Emma, who had lost her good friend under such horrific circumstances. "I wonder if Gabe and Emma found a small bit of solace that at least some justice was served from all the killings." I knew Gabe had never found peace, but I couldn't help wonder about Emma, who seemed to have steadfastly kept her faith.

Moni responded, "Who knows. I would hope so, too."

I thought about Paree's devotion to her pack. "Do you know whatever happened to the other two dogs?"

"Nope, no record I could find."

"How sad. I wonder if they survived."

Moni shrugged, then pulled out what I recognized as a copy of a portion of the cemetery ledger. "But, guess what—I found Paree's grave! She's in the West Street Cemetery, tucked into a shady corner not far from the Hopper plot."

"Wow, you did? That's amazing!"

Moni nodded. "Her epitaph reads: *A God-fearing woman who loved dogs.* And next to her is a small stone, with what looks like a German Shepherd carved on top. The name *Hilde* and *1850* are engraved on it."

"Oh, how touching! I remember Emma was distraught Paree's dog was killed at the same time."

Moni nodded. "Yeah, Paree's dogs did their best to protect her." She closed the folders and set them aside. Swiping at her runaway curls, she gave me an inquisitive look. "Enough of this sordid history. So how are things out at your place? You had it rented for a while, right?"

"Yeah, didn't work out real well," I said, not wanting to get into any details that could spread around town. "There are a lot of repairs needed, and it's just too much for me to deal with. So I decided to put it on the market."

Moni frowned. "Oh, I'm sorry, Dee. That must be tough for you, being your childhood home and all. Any interest so far?"

What should I tell her about Chantal and her ancestors? Moni's probably going to think Chantal and I are both crazy as loons!

"Actually, that's what I wanted to talk with you about. There's a black family from Montreal who have put in an offer."

Monique showed a keen interest. "Really?" She leaned closer, eyebrow raised. "We don't get many black folks looking for places around here."

"Yeah, I know. Kinda surprised me, too. The husband, Clay, works for a bank and is being transferred to Rutland. So they're looking for a place with some land for their kids. They have two daughters and a baby on the way. Very nice couple!"

"Okay. So, why are you telling me this?" Moni asked.

"Do you remember the ledger we found in the barn? The one with the names of the fugitives in it?"

"Of course. We have it on display in the Underground Railroad room, with the other artifacts we pulled from the barn. What about it?"

How do I explain this simply? "Well, I know this is going to sound odd, but Chantal, Clay's wife, thinks her ancestor Samuel was harbored in Fair Haven while he was escaping slavery."

Moni's eyes went wide. "Whoa! That's pretty incredible. What makes her think so?"

"Well, according to Chantal, her grandmother Emmaline published a series of articles about her father's amazing journey to freedom. Emmaline interviewed Chantal's great-grandfather when he was almost eighty years old. Chantal said her mother had kept the scrapbook of articles hidden until just recently."

Moni gaped. "Wait! This lady's grandmother was named Emmaline? That's awful close to Emma, don't you think?"

I laughed. "It sure is! Samuel told Emmaline she was named after a *Missus H.* from Fair Haven, who had sheltered his family."

Moni's forehead scrunched. "DeeDee! Do you really think this is the *same* Samuel from Emma's diary? That's really crazy—you do know that, right?"

I shrugged. "Based on what Chantal has told me, I think there's a very good chance the Prescotts are Chantal's ancestors."

Moni expelled a long breath and stared at me. "Seriously, Dee, what are the chances that someone would look at your property, and discover it had once harbored their ancestors? I'd say about one in a million. This is really unbelievable!"

Watching Moni's reaction, a shiver ran through me as I thought once again of this unexpected turn of events. "Yeah, that's what I said to Chantal, too. I guess that's why they decided to put an offer on the place."

Moni pushed stray wisps from her face, and sat back in her chair. "Oh, my goodness! So, how do I fit into this picture?"

"My realtor, Bill Graybert, is pushing to close on the house by the end of this week," I said. "I'd like to recommend to Chantal she come visit you. I was hoping you could show her Emma's ledger and journals. I think she would be interested in reading them."

"Of course!" Moni enthused. "I'd love to show them to her! As well as all the artifacts we pulled from the old barn." She paused and glanced around her cluttered office. "You know, we've had lots of folks come in looking for historical information about their families, but I'm pretty sure this is the first time we've ever had anyone with connections to the Underground Railroad here. I'm really excited to meet Chantal!"

I smiled. "You'll like her. She has a very sweet charm about her." I pictured her regal stature and calm demeanor. "I'll be moving out soon, and I probably won't have a chance to see you again before I leave. I want to thank you in advance for any help you can give Chantal and her family.

Oh, and she's mighty pregnant, too, so I'm sure you'll recognize her! I hope they'll enjoy living here."

"Sure! I'm happy to help. Anything for you, Dee!" Moni folded her arms and gazed at me.

Something was on her mind, so I waited.

In a quieter voice, she said, "Dee, I don't want to pry, but as a friend, can I ask you something?"

I had a feeling I knew where this was going. "Sure, what is it?"

"Ummm…well…" she hesitated. "I've heard rumors your house is haunted. What do you think?" Monique squirmed a bit in her chair. "And what about the new owners? Do you think they'll be okay?"

Oh, boy! Here we go. How much should I tell her? I stared back at the curator for a moment, trying to decide how to respond.

Moni grinned and shrugged her shoulders, seeming to sense my uncertainty. "What can I say? Your previous tenant had a big mouth."

I raised an eyebrow. "Oh yeah? What exactly did he say?"

Moni fidgeted, then sat up straighter. "Well…Bob Anthony said something or someone pushed him down the stairs."

Oh, shit! So my ex-tenant has been telling tales around town, probably in a drunken stupor.

"Moni, I have no idea what happened to Bob. My guess is he was drunk as usual, and tripped his own ass down the stairs. For all I know, he might have been so soused he was hallucinating! I'm sorry he got hurt, but I don't think any spirit was involved." I waved my hand in a dismissive fashion. "And I don't think Chantal and her family have anything to worry about!"

Moni held her hand up in defeat. "Okay! I get it. So, what do you think brought Chantal to your doorstep?"

The million-dollar question. "I have no idea. But I'm glad they are buying the place and hope they will be happy there. As much as I love Fair Haven, I really didn't want to spend the winter here!" I rose from my chair. "I've got to go pack. Thanks for all the updates and agreeing to show Chantal around. I appreciate it."

Moni nodded. "Sure, happy to. I look forward to meeting her." As she collected her folders, I noticed a frown cross her face. I could tell she was disappointed I wasn't dishing up all the juicy details.

DEEDEE MOVES ON

The rest of the week was a whirlwind of activity as I made arrangements to move out of the house. I boxed up items I wanted to keep, including an office printer as well as extra clothes that wouldn't fit into my suitcase, and shipped them all to California. I contacted the cable company and gave them a date to disconnect the service. They groused about canceling my contract early and said they'd charge me a fee. So be it. I scheduled disconnecting my phone and internet line for the following week. Bill had said he would manage transferring the other utility bills to the Moreaus' name. Then I called the airlines to book my one-way flight home.

My sister Ellie had saved Mom's favorite wingback chair and caned rocking chair, and I wanted to keep both of them. On Thursday, Ellie and Rob dropped the chairs off at the house. The moving company arrived in the afternoon to pack up the chairs and ship them cross-country. Ellie, Rob, and I loaded their pickup truck with most of the furniture and kitchenware I had borrowed, to be returned to the original owners. Leaving in place the bed, nightstand and lamp, one parlor chair, the television, and the kitchen table, I had what I needed to spend one last night at the house. I didn't tell Ellie about the discovery Chantal and I had made. I wanted to wait until we had some quiet time together to tell her the whole incredible story.

After my sister and brother-in-law left with the load, I poured myself a glass of wine in a red plastic Solo cup, then turned on the television to watch the early local nightly news.

As I half-listened to the talking heads, my thoughts ran through all that had happened since I had left California in August with plans to stay in Vermont for only "a week." It began with my tenants abruptly leaving, most likely because Gabe pushed Bob Anthony down the stairs. I had to chuckle imaging Bob's reaction when he saw Gabe glaring down upon him. Then my property manager, Arlene, had quit after advising me to burn the house down to get rid of "evil spirits."

I really don't think Gabe would have appreciated that much!

After being presented with the inspection report, I had realized I needed to make a critical decision—stay or go. Not having much choice, I stayed and dealt with all the issues of the old house. From my self-ascribed bravery in catching the wayward mice, to my heart-pounding interaction with Gabe on his first nightly visitation, I was proud to have survived in the house alone, and not completely freaking out!

I glanced into the parlor, which had been my childhood bedroom. Chills ran through me as I remembered Gabe ordering me to turn around in bed and me arguing back, just before the ceiling collapsed on me!

Then there had been the unusual connection Chantal and I had made the first time we met. After all the potential buyers who had come through the house, for Chantal—whose ancestors had actually been hidden here—to be *the* one to buy the property was absolutely amazing!

Through so much that had happened since I'd returned to my childhood home, I could now recognize Gabe's presence interceding in the events.

And of course, my mother, Robbie, was never far from my mind. Memories of us living in this house, both good and—through hazy recollections—not so good, filled my thoughts.

Mom, I hope you've found the peace and comfort in the afterworld that so eluded you on this earth. I thought about what a difficult life she had lived as a single mother, trying to do her best for her four daughters.

I sipped my wine as the national nightly news broadcast began. I was happy Chantal and Clay would be raising their children here. This was a good house for kids, as long as Gabe was there to protect them. But I was sad this was my last night in my childhood home. I hoped Mom had forgiven me for selling it, after I had promised her I wouldn't.

As I was musing, I heard the phone ring. I rose from my chair and trotted into the kitchen to answer it.

I heard the now-familiar, lilting voice say, "Hallo, DeeDee. This is Chantal."

"Chantal! It's great to hear from you." I paused, unsure of how to continue the conversation. "So, I was wondering…how did things go with Clay after we last talked?"

She sighed. "Well, it took a while to convince him Samuel's family had actually found safe harbor there." She paused. "Clay thought maybe you were just feeding me a line to sell the house."

I was shocked he had said that. His good looks aside, my opinion of Clay dropped a notch. I blurted, "Oh, my God, Chantal! I would never in a million years think of doing such a thing!"

"I know, I know!" Chantal replied quickly. "You know how men are—always thinking someone is trying to play an angle. But when I told him you had documentation on the Prescott family, he started to come around."

"Did you tell him both of us could confirm the exact same names of Samuel's family members?"

"Yes!" Chantal said. "That was the clincher. Clay had to admit as crazy as the whole story sounded, I was right about Samuel. He agreed buying the house was the right thing to do, and I did indeed belong there!"

I was a bit concerned over Chantal's story and hoped they wouldn't regret their decision. "Well, I'm really happy for you guys."

Chantal chuckled. "Thanks. I think it's going to be quite an adventure, to say the least."

I pictured her daughters, Charmaine and Whitney, playing in the big yard. "I think your girls are going to love growing up here. I know I did."

"You can bet they are both excited to have their own rooms for the first time, and they've each picked out their colors." Chantal laughed. "Can you guess what color Whitney has chosen?"

I smiled, remembering the first time I met Whitney. "Hmmm…let me think…blue?"

"No! It's pink!" Chantal said, mimicking Whitney's high voice. We both laughed at her precocious younger daughter's antics.

I said, "Chantal, once you get settled, I recommend you visit Monique Roubillard. She and her husband, Jacques, are the curators at the Historical Society."

"Actually, that's why I was calling. I'd love to go see Emma's ledger and journals. Do you know the museum hours? And would you happen to have their phone number?"

Having already packed away my local business directory, I quickly logged onto my computer to find the number. I responded, "The museum is closed for the winter, but the offices are open. I just saw Moni recently, and mentioned to her your ancestor, Samuel, had once been harbored on the property. As you can imagine, she was astonished to hear the story!" I chuckled.

Chantal laughed, "Yeah, I bet she was!"

"Moni said she's excited to meet you. I'm pretty sure if you call her, she'd be more than willing to give you and your family a private tour of the museum and show you Emma's artifacts. Do you have a pen handy? Here's the number." I recited the local number for her.

Chantal said, "Thanks, Dee. I appreciate your help—with everything!"

"Oh, you're very welcome! And by the way, Monique and Jacques are Canadian, so you have something in common!"

I heard Chantal laugh. "Small world, isn't it?"

"Yup, in more ways than any of us could have ever imagined!" I thought about the uncanny forces of the universe at work. "I'll see you tomorrow at Bill's office. Drive safely."

"Will do. I'm looking forward to seeing you again." Chantal ended the call.

Friday morning I awoke early, as it was going to be a busy day. Looking out the kitchen window as I brewed a pot of coffee, I saw a light rain falling and a breeze swaying the barren trees. *Guess it's a good day to be moving on.* After I drank my coffee with the last stale donut I had saved, I quickly showered and dressed in a warm work outfit.

I finished packing the last of my clothes and toiletries into my suitcase, and stowed it by the front door. Then I gathered the bed linens into a large plastic bag and propped it by my suitcase. While slugging down a second cup of coffee, I emptied the remains of the refrigerator, saving a few items in a small cooler to take to my sister's house. The rest went into garbage bags. The coffee pot and a few remaining kitchen items went into an empty box. I lugged everything into the main room and grouped them by the front windows.

Around eleven, Ellie and Rob arrived with their pickup truck. I gave them both a hug as I ushered them into the house.

Rob looked around the rooms and said, "It should be a pretty light load today. Let's get the bed out first."

As Rob led the way into the small bedroom, Ellie touched my arm and stopped me. "So, how does it feel to be leaving your old house for the last time?"

Looking at my sister, who looked so much like Mom, I felt the emotion rising in my chest. "I'm sad, but happy, too. You know I really didn't want to spend the winter here, so I'm glad to be going home where it's warm."

Ellie laughed, "Yeah, you sure did turn into a California girl, didn't you?"

I shrugged. "I guess the thing I regret most is promising Mom I'd never sell this old house. I broke my oath to her, and it makes me sad."

Ellie put her arm around my shoulder. "Dee, Mom never could have imagined all you've been through with this property! I'm sure she'd understand and forgive you if she were here."

I nodded. "I hope you're right. I'd hate to have her haunt me for the rest of my life."

She grinned, "Oh, hell! You know she's going to do that anyway!"

We both laughed as we helped Rob wrestle the mattress out of the bedroom, through the front door, and into the bed of the truck. Within an hour or so, we had finished loading everything but the garbage, and secured the load.

Before Ellie climbed into the truck, I said, "I've got a great story to tell you tonight about the new owners. I think you're going to be really surprised."

Ellie grinned. "Oh, really? Can you give me a hint?"

I said, "Nope! But we're going to need a big bottle of wine, believe me!"

Ellie shook her head and laughed as she climbed into her seat. "I can't wait. We'll see you later." They drove off with the last remains of my stay.

Back in the house, I decided to do one last walk-through. I opened all the kitchen cabinets and found a few things for the garbage. I went through the bedroom, checking the closet, and walked slowly through the parlor, looking out the windows at the front street. I said a mental goodbye to my old childhood bedroom.

Slowly climbing the creaking stairs, I entered the bedroom on the left and walked to the center of the room. I had left the door open to the large closet, and now I peered inside. No ethereal figure stared back at me. Instead, the deep silence echoed with fragments of memory.

"Okay, Gabe! This is it. I'm leaving for good," I said, figuring he was nearby. "I'm going to hold you to your promise! I want you to protect Chantal and her family, just like you did me and Mom."

I paused. "Do you hear me?"

Something thumped behind me and my heart leapt into my mouth. I turned just in time to glimpse a fledgling bird flop away from the window. "Shit! That almost gave me a heart attack!" I said to no one. "I better get the hell out of here, before my nerves are completely frayed!"

Stopping at the door, I looked back into the barren room and took a deep breath. "Take care, Gabe. I love you!"

I took a quick look into the smaller, middle bedroom, which I figured would become Whitney's. I envisioned it painted a bright pink, and chuckled. Then I stepped down into the two-part bedroom that was the loft of the old original farmhouse. I walked through the windowless adjoining room into the main bedroom. Peering out the side window, I looked into the upstairs windows of Howard Greene's house, directly next door. Visions of my elderly neighbor, frantically hosing down his barn, flicked through my mind.

Glancing around the room, my eyes fell on the opening to the walk-in closet. I remembered Mom and I sorting through the trunks we had pulled from there, finding Old Bert's family Bible.

For some reason, I felt compelled to look in the closet. Snapping on the overhead light, I took a couple of steps into the room, where the slanted left side of the ceiling followed the roofline. I stopped and looked around. Empty. As I turned to leave, a white glimmer on the back corner of the closet floor caught my eye. I bent and picked it up. It was a folded scrap of white paper. Thinking it must have been dropped by a visitor, I started to tuck it in my pocket, but something stopped me.

When I opened the paper, a deep chill ran through me, and I gasped. On it, written by a familiar, trembling hand, were the words: *I love you.*

My heart slammed in my chest. *How in the world…?*

I whirled around expecting to see—I didn't know what! But in that moment, instinctively, I knew—I had been forgiven! I felt Mom's love engulf me, and I began to cry.

I whispered, "Thanks, Mom! I love you, too!"

Back downstairs, I put on my coat, and loaded the garbage bags into the trunk of my car. I grabbed my purse and briefcase containing my laptop and business folders. In it was also the report on the house I had compiled over the past several weeks. I had bound it in a clear folio. On its cover was an enlarged photo of the house, looking quite festive with the fall mums in bloom.

I sighed. It was time to go. I turned off all the lights except the one on the porch. I gently closed and locked the front door. My heart was at peace leaving my childhood home for the last time.

After making a quick trip to the dump on the west side of town, I returned to the main downtown business block. I was a little early for our two o'clock meeting, but wanted to chat with Bill before the Moreaus arrived.

Bill stood and greeted me when I entered his office, which was tucked into the corner on the north end of the L-shaped business block. We shook hands.

"Hi, DeeDee," Bill said, looking at his watch. "You're a little early." He motioned to the three chairs positioned in front of his desk. I chose the one farthest to the left. He sat back down in his leather chair.

"Yeah, I know. I wanted to give you something before Chantal and Clay get here." I reached into my briefcase and presented Bill with the house inspection report. "You said you didn't want to look at this before we sold the house, but I want you to have it now."

Bill nodded, opened the report and read the summary on the first page. His expression went from mild interest to a more concerned frown. He looked up at me. "Wow, Dee! I had no idea there were so many problems with the place. Now I understand why you didn't want to dicker on the price."

I nodded. "I know. It's going to take a lot of work to get it fixed up. I'm hoping you can use this as a guide to help the Moreaus address some of the issues. You can decide whether or not you want to give them the report. But it means a lot to me they are happy there."

Bill cocked his head and gave me a curious look. "You really like them, don't you?"

"I do," I said. "Plus, it is my childhood home, and I want to make sure it's well cared for."

Bill smiled. "I'll work with them to have contractors get some work done before they move in. So, I don't want you to worry about it."

"Thanks, Bill. I really appreciate your help."

The tinkle of the bell jogged by the door opening caught my attention. I turned to see Clay, holding the door for Chantal as she entered the office, then following her inside.

Chantal looked lovely in a purple-flowered maternity dress topped with a solid purple blazer. Her belly had grown noticeably rounder since I'd seen her just a few weeks earlier. I figured the baby was probably due in a month or two.

Clay wore an impeccably tailored gray, pinstriped suit, white shirt, light yellow-and-purple-striped tie, and matching pocket square. He looked like he had just stepped off the cover of *GQ Magazine*.

I, on the other hand, was dressed in jeans, a heavy winter sweater, and hiking boots. I felt like country mouse meets city mice. I was disappointed their daughters weren't with them, as I had hoped to see them once again. But it was a school day, after all.

I stood and hugged Chantal. She kissed me on both cheeks, in the French custom, and we both giggled.

"Nice to see you again," I said to Chantal.

She grinned. "You, too!"

I reached behind her and shook Clay's hand.

"DeeDee," Clay said, acknowledging me with his bright smile.

Bill motioned to the chairs. "Please, take a seat."

Chantal settled into the middle seat between Clay and me. I caught a whiff of her delicate perfume.

When we finished signing the myriad pages of paperwork, I pulled the folio from my briefcase and passed it to Chantal. "I thought you'd like this. It's a history of the property I compiled, based on research I did at the town hall. It covers the property transfers, land sales and dates, throughout its history. I also included names and numbers of local contractors and the utility companies I thought you might need."

"Wow! Thanks so much, Dee! I really appreciate this," Chantal said as she flipped through the pages. "This is great to have as a keepsake for the girls."

Our eyes met. "I think there's probably more you can add to the beginning and ending of this story."

Out of the corner of my eye, I noticed Bill had a confused look on his face.

Chantal grinned and squeezed my hand.

"Oh, I almost forgot." I reached into my purse and laid the house keys on the desk. "Here you go."

Bill slid the keys to his side of the desk. "I'll hold these and get copies made for you."

Clay asked Bill, "So, when do you think we'll be able to move in?"

Bill held his hand up to Clay, and turned to me. "It looks like your business here is done. I need to discuss with Clay and Chantal what work they'd like to get done first."

Taking my cue, I rose from the table and grabbed my purse and briefcase. Clay and Chantal also stood to give me room to pass.

"Would you give me a minute?" Chantal said. "I'd like to see DeeDee out."

Clay held the door for us, and we exited to the sidewalk, where we hugged our goodbyes. I gave Chantal my business card. "Please keep in touch, and let me know how things are going at the house." I smiled. "You know I have a vested interest in your success."

"And you want to know if anything goes bump in the night!" she said, with a hearty laugh.

"Yup, that too!" I replied as I waved, then walked to my car.

Two days later, on Sunday, my brother-in-law, Rob, followed me for the drive to Rent-a-Wreck in Burlington. Low clouds swirled around us, making visibility problematic, so we took it slow. I dropped off my used car, then he drove me to the airport. We hugged at the curb, and I dragged my heavy suitcase to be checked in to my destination in San Jose. I was more than relieved to be going back to the temperate climes of the Bay Area, as it had started to snow here. I looked forward to hugging Mark and my kitties. This visit to my family homestead had been an emotionally exhausting, overwhelming, and bittersweet journey.

As I waited to board the plane, I noticed some children running through the terminal in costumes. It dawned on me it was Halloween.

Well Gabe, I thought, grinning at the cavorting monsters and princesses, *you could have come to see me off, and no one would have even noticed!*

HOPPER FAMILY FARM
FAIR HAVEN, VERMONT
THANKSGIVING, 2004

CHANTAL MOVES IN

THE MOVING VAN ARRIVED at the house in Fair Haven on the Wednesday before Thanksgiving. Snow flurries flitted through the barren trees.

Chantal rested on a kitchen chair positioned in the main room, while she directed the placement of furniture. She laughed as the girls ran up and down the stairs, cheering when sections of their bedroom furniture were put into place. Whitney was first to slide down the banister, despite Charmaine's admonishments. Chantal peered out the front window and saw Clay rubbing his hands together for warmth while he directed the unloading of their belongings from the moving van. Snowflakes sprinkled his black hair.

It's been a busy month. I'm glad we're finally here, Chantal thought as the baby shifted its position.

Clay's transfer had gone through, and he had been given Thanksgiving week as a holiday. Since they'd already celebrated Canadian Thanksgiving in October, there was no reason for them to repeat it, so it was the perfect time for them to move. Clay had rented an extended-stay suite in Rutland, while they waited for the movers to navigate U.S. Customs and arrive at the property.

Since they had signed the closing paperwork, Chantal had been in almost daily contact with realtor Bill Graybert, about getting work done at the house. A new electrical junction box was installed and the wiring upgraded throughout the house. The downstairs rooms were painted a soft shade of white. Whitney claimed the middle bedroom, and the soft pink walls glowed. Charmaine, the elder child, was awarded the two-part bedroom that was once the loft of the original farmhouse. She chose lavender and purple for her special colors. The connecting room would eventually become the nursery. The master bedroom, at the top left of the stairs, was painted a soothing turquoise. New carpets were installed throughout the house. In the kitchen, a new cooking range replaced the broken one, and new flooring had been laid. Corroded plumbing was replaced, and floor tile as well as a new toilet and vanity sink were installed in the bathroom. In the cellar, slate tiles were interlocked over the smoothed dirt floor. The furnace and water heater were serviced, and the heating oil drums filled.

Chantal smiled as she admired the upgrades. *Bill and his contractors did a great job! I think the house is very inviting.* Her thoughts turned to her conversation with DeeDee the first weekend they had met, when DeeDee had reluctantly admitted a spirit still resided in the house. *I hope Gabe approves of our changes, and he welcomes us to his home!* She peered around the room and sighed. *I guess we'll just have to wait and see what he thinks.*

By mid-December, once they'd gotten settled and the girls were attending their new school, Chantal decided to visit the Fair Haven Historical Society. She was eager to see the artifacts bearing witness to her ancestors' travels through the town. Arriving at the three-story brick building located across from the north end of the park, she was relieved to find an elevator inside the entrance.

Exiting on the second floor, she looked to her right and saw a closed, half-glass door. She peered down a long hallway that stretched along the middle of the building. Etched on the door window were the words: *Fair Haven Historical Society Museum.* She caught glimpses of the displays in the open classrooms on either side of the hall. Turning left, Chantal saw one office on each side of the short hall. The name plaques read: *Monique Robillard, Historical Society Curator* and *Jacques Robillard, Historical Society Archivist.*

Chantal entered Monique's office.

Hugging both walls of the narrow entryway, bookshelves reached floor to ceiling. As a musty odor enveloped her, Chantal glanced at the stacks of historical volumes. Moving into a cluttered, open office area, she saw a woman with long, curly black hair, sitting hunched over her desk.

"Hallo?" Chantal said apprehensively.

The woman, in her mid-forties, swung around in her chair, gave Chantal a long look, then grinned. "Hi there! You must be Chantal!" She rose quickly, her petite frame engulfed by a multi-colored sweater, and rushed to greet Chantal. "I'm so glad to meet you."

"Ahh, yes—yes, I am. How did you know my name?" Chantal asked.

"Well, there aren't too many pregnant black women in this town. In fact, I'll bet you're just about the only one!" she said with a hearty laugh. "Plus, DeeDee Williams told me you might stop by for a visit." She stretched her hand toward Chantal. "I'm Monique."

Chantal smiled at Monique's unabashed nature, and shook her hand. "Guess I do sort of stick out like a sore thumb, don't I?" Chantal felt a twinge of worry about her daughters. "Do you think our family will be welcome here?"

"Oh, heck, yeah!—don't see why not. Most folks around here are real friendly, and those that aren't? Well, they're just old curmudgeonly Vermonters, and you can ignore them anyway."

Chantal nodded, hoping Monique was right.

"But I gotta warn you, everybody's gonna want to know your business—just the way folks are around here." Monique grinned and shrugged her shoulders. "It's already 'round town you bought the old Hopper place out to south side, and your kids are enrolled in school."

"Wow, that was fast! You're not kidding, are you?" Chantal said, a bit surprised by the speed of the rumor mill in a small town.

"Nope. You're the talk of the town right now. But it'll die down when the next old geezer gets caught drunk in the park, so don't worry about it. Please, come sit." Monique motioned to the wooden armchair next to her desk. "Looks like you could take a load off."

Chantal grunted and her back twinged as she lowered herself into the chair.

Monique swiveled her chair toward Chantal. "So, when is the baby due?"

Chantal rested her closed hands on her protruding tummy. "Pretty soon, probably around the end of the year."

"You gonna deliver in Rutland?"

"Yeah. I met with the obstetrician last week, and we're all set."

"Let me give you a little advice. If there's a storm, you should call our local paramedics. They can get you to the hospital real quick in their rig—faster than taking a car." Monique reached into a desk drawer and handed Chantal a multi-page pamphlet. "This is a directory of all the businesses in town as well as emergency numbers. Just call the fire department, here."

Monique circled a number. "Those boys are on call twenty-four-seven, and they'll be at your house lickety-split to take care of you."

"Thanks for the advice. I just might do that. Can I keep this?" Chantal flipped through the pages.

"Oh, sure, I've got tons of them. So, what brings you to visit today, other than to see my pretty face?" Monique laughed as she pushed away some wild curls.

"DeeDee mentioned I should come visit you. She told me about Emma's journals you found in her old barn and thought I might like to see them."

Monique nodded. "Yeah, we were really excited to find those documents, I can tell you!" She paused and looked at Chantal. "I understand your grandmother was named Emmaline. What can you tell me about her?"

Chantal smiled, remembering her tall, stately grandmother. She realized how much her mother, Sophia, resembled her. "She was very sweet and loving. I was only eight when she passed away, but I remember sitting on her lap as she told me old family stories." Chantal chuckled. "Since then, I never really thought much about them, until I visited Fair Haven."

"Oh?" Monique said. "Why Fair Haven?"

"For some reason, the name of the town seemed familiar, but I couldn't figure out why." Chantal looked at the various books about Fair Haven's history, stacked on a shelf behind Monique. "When I mentioned the town to my mother, she reluctantly showed me Emmaline's articles which she had kept hidden."

"Oh, wow! That must have been quite a surprise for you." Monique said, her eyes wide.

Chantal nodded. "It was! I had no idea until then the scrapbook even existed."

"What did you discover from your grandmother's writings?

"Well, she interviewed her father, Samuel, when he was almost eighty. He had become a successful lawyer, but had been reluctant to tell his family about his escape." Chantal smiled. "Samuel was missing the first two fingers on his right hand, and Emmaline wanted to know the truth. Samuel finally told her the real story."

"Oh, my! Emma mentions in her diary the young boy, Samuel, was missing those exact same fingers!"

Chantal nodded. "Right! Quite a coincidence, isn't it? According to Emmaline, Samuel told her she was named after a lady he called *Missus H*, who harbored his family here."

Monique said, "And you think it was Emma Hopper?"

"I do! And after talking with DeeDee, she thinks so, too." Chantal paused, glancing around and lowering her voice. "In one of Emmaline's articles, Samuel recalls being in a hay wagon that was attacked on a bridge by slave hunters. He and his nephew escaped, but his mother died, and he never knew the fate of his sister."

Moni expelled a long breath. "Wow! It sounds like the same story in Emma's diary. Do you happen to know the names of Samuel's family members?"

Chantal nodded. "Yes. Samuel's mother was Miss Elsie. His sister was named Sarah, and Jonah was her son."

Monique gasped, then leaned back in her chair and stared at her visitor. "This is incredible! It sounds like they are indeed the same family Emma and Gabe once harbored." Monique chuckled. "I mean, really! What are the chances you would discover a connection to your ancestors along the Underground Railroad just by accident? It's gotta be one in a million at least!"

Chantal grinned. "I know, right? Believe me, I'm pretty blown away by all of this, too!" She paused and thought of her heated discussion with Clay. "It took some work to convince my husband Dee's property had once sheltered my ancestors. But then Dee was able to confirm the names of Samuel's family from Emma's diary. So there was no question in my mind."

Monique grasped one of Chantal's hands. "Chantal, I'm so glad you decided to buy the property. It really seems like you and your family belong here."

Chantal smiled. "Yeah, me too. I hope everything works out well." *And Gabe welcomes us.* She glanced over her shoulder. "I know the museum is closed, but I was hoping I could take a peek at Emma's journals." Chantal paused. "Would it be possible?"

"Oh, sure!" Monique said as she opened a desk drawer, where she extracted two pairs of white, cotton gloves. "Here, why don't you put these on? Our artifacts are delicate, and skin oil can cause damage." Monique donned her pair and retrieved her keys. After Chantal had donned the gloves, Monique came to her chair and put a hand under her arm. "Here, let me help you up."

Chantal grunted as she arose. "Thanks. This baby is getting awful big...be glad when it's born." As she followed Monique out of her office, Chantal casually scanned the titles of the tomes stacked on the bookshelves. Suddenly she stopped and gasped.

Monique whirled around in concern. "Chantal? What's going on?" Monique reached for Chantal's arm. "Are you all right?"

Chantal pointed a trembling finger at a brochure laying face-up at the end of one shelf. "Monique, what is this?"

Monique lifted the booklet and passed it to Chantal. On the cover was a picture of a light brown, two-story, Federal-style farmhouse with a covered front porch. "This is the visitors' guide to Rokeby Museum. It's in Ferrisburgh, just south of Burlington. Why do you ask?"

"Oh, my God! It's a museum!" Chantal half-whispered in disbelief.

Monique gave her visitor an inquisitive look. "Have you been there before?"

Chantal shook her head. "No! But Samuel has!"

"What! Are you kidding me? What makes you think so?" Monique stepped closer.

Chantal stared at the many windows in the farmhouse, wondering which room Samuel might have stayed in. Her voice turned husky. "Because Emmaline wrote about Samuel surviving a shipwreck on Lake Champlain. He was taken to a farm named Rokeby, where he stayed for six months while his broken ankle healed." Chantal held up the guide. "It *must* be the same place!"

Monique grinned. "Holy crap! This is crazy. The plot thickens!"

Chantal laughed. "Yeah, I guess you could say that."

Monique continued, "Well, Rokeby Farm was owned by four generations of the Rowland T. Robinson family. They were Quakers and staunch abolitionists. The family meticulously documented their farm life and the stories of fugitives who worked for them."

"Oh, my gosh! That's wonderful." Chantal sighed. "If it weren't for the Robinsons, who knows what might have happened to Samuel! I am so grateful they saved his life."

Monique smiled. "They were very kind people, and I'm sure Samuel was well cared for. In nineteen sixty-one, the remaining Robinson descendants donated the farm to become a non-profit museum. They've preserved many of the outbuildings, and there's a docent tour of the main house and grounds which is just amazing. You should go visit when it opens in May." Monique touched the cover. "Who knows, the curator may have archival records of Samuel's stay there!"

Chantal flipped through the booklet. "Wouldn't it be amazing if they did? I can't wait to tell Clay and my girls about this. I know they'll be excited to visit!" She started to slip the booklet back onto the shelf.

Monique touched her arm. "You can keep it if you'd like. I can always get more."

"Are you sure? I don't want to take your only copy."

Monique nodded. "I'm sure. I'm good friends with Rokeby's curator, so I can always ask her to send me a few more for my collection."

Chantal smiled. "Thank you so much! I'm looking forward to reading more about the farm."

Monique motioned for Chantal to follow. The curator unlocked the museum door and stepped into the hallway. As they proceeded down the aisle, Chantal glanced into rooms dedicated to specific local subjects: the Native American tribes, the slate industry, farming, and maple sugaring.

Monique stepped into the last room on the left, and Chantal followed. "This is our war room," Monique said, as she waved her arm toward the displays. "We cover the big ones from the Revolution and Civil War, through Vietnam and the Gulf War." Monique walked toward the tall windows along the side of the building. "I wanted to show you this."

Chantal saw two male mannequins dressed in historic military garb. When she looked closer, she noticed the trouser leg of one of the uniforms was ripped up to the thigh.

Monique gently touched the shoulder of one of the mannequins. "DeeDee found these Civil War uniforms when she cleaned out her barn." She turned to Chantal. "Let me introduce you." She patted the figure's arm. "This is Infantryman Brian Hopper." Monique stepped to the second military man. "And this is his twin brother, Sergeant Bernard Hopper."

Chantal took a quick breath at hearing the familiar surname. "Oh, my! Are they related to Emma and Gabe?"

Monique nodded. "Yes! These boys were their grandsons."

Chantal moved closer to inspect the intricate uniforms. A chill ran through her as she peered at the ripped trouser leg. "What happened to them? Did they survive the war?"

Monique guided Chantal to a nearby glass display case. "Unfortunately, no. Both died defending the Union." She pointed to two yellowed documents, each bearing the letterhead of the U.S. War Department. "These are the letters to their mother, Mary Hopper, informing her of their passing."

Chantal bent to read the brief letters. "Oh, dear! That's so heartbreaking for Mary to lose both of her sons. It sounds like they were brave war heroes."

Monique nodded. "Yes, that's what DeeDee and I surmised when we read the letters. According to Emma, I think Gabe took their deaths very hard. After all, he lost his son, Luke, the twins' father, when they were attacked by the posse."

Chantal momentarily bowed her head. "I remember DeeDee telling me about Luke. How tragic for the entire family." She thought about the spirit still dwelling at the house. *Poor Gabe! He was just trying to do the right thing, based upon his anti-slavery beliefs. I wonder if his grief over losing his son and grandsons has kept him tied to this earth.*

Monique touched Chantal's elbow. "Here, let me show you Emma's artifacts."

They crossed the aisle to the last room on the right. A large sign hanging on the side wall between the windows indicated this was the Underground Railroad Room. A shiver ran down Chantal's spine as she stepped in and peered around.

Glass display cases rimmed two sides of the room. The back wall supported a large, crowded bookcase. Chantal joined Monique, watching as the curator unlocked and lifted the hinged glass top of one of the cases. With her gloved hands, Monique lifted a long, bound ledger and placed it on a round table in the center of the room. Then she removed one of Emma's opened, leather-bound journals, and set it next to the ledger.

Monique motioned to a chair. "Please have a seat."

After removing her coat, Chantal settled herself onto the straight-back wooden chair and leaned close to the table. "I can't believe I'm actually seeing Emma's diary. This is amazing!"

Monique pointed to the larger, gray-blue, hard-covered book. "This is the final page of the ledger which identifies the Prescott family—the last ones Emma and Gabe harbored. I believe these are your ancestors, Chantal."

On the last four lines, Chantal read the names of her family: Elsie, Samuel, Sarah, and Jonah. *I so wish Grandma Emmaline could see this! It amazes me she grew up not knowing anything about Samuel's past. It wasn't until his old age, that he finally revealed his secrets. I am forever grateful to her for writing Samuel's stories, otherwise I never would have known about any of this. I love you, Grandma. Thank you!*

Monique continued, "We think the Hoppers stopped harboring fugitives, because of the tragic events that unfolded when their wagon was attacked. According to Emma, the aftermath was a very difficult time for them."

Chantal wiped a tear from her cheek. "I can only imagine what they must have gone through. It was all so very sad for everyone. I can't blame them for no longer wanting to be involved in the cause, after losing their son, Luke. Plus, they probably thought they had failed at saving the Prescotts."

Monique nodded and tapped Emma's journal. "We found five volumes of Emma's journals, dating back to the mid-eighteen-twenties." Moni grinned. "She was a very prolific writer! This one covers the eighteen-fifties, when they sheltered their last family." Moni turned to look at Chantal. "Emma thought very highly of Miss Elsie. I'm sure you'll find her writing fascinating." Monique rose from her chair and placed a hand on Chantal's shoulder. "Well, I'll leave you to it, then. If you need anything, just give me a holler. I'm right down the hall." She left Chantal alone in the room.

Trembling with anticipation, Chantal gently lifted the fragile journal and read the entry on the left page.

10 mo. 11th, Friday early morning, 1850

A new group of travelers has arrived during the night seeking refuge from the storm. I thank Thee, Lord, for guiding these weary souls to our doorstep. We shall provide them shelter and sustenance, as Thee would have done. Please shine Thy light upon Miss Elsie, Sarah, Samuel and Jonah, so they may travel safely in Thy good graces to the land of freedom. I ask this in Thy name, Jesus Christ our Savior. Amen."

She laid the journal on the table and thought about Samuel.

I can see why he had such respect for the Hoppers. Emma and Gabe were very brave to help strangers arriving at their door! It just breaks my heart their deep faith and convictions against slavery led to such a horrible outcome. I am forever indebted to them for trying to protect my ancestors against the evil men who sought their capture. Had Samuel not survived his ordeal, none of my family would even exist!

After reading several more journal entries, Chantal felt the baby shift, and a sharp kick jabbed her ribs. Her brows knitted as a pain shot up her back. Closing Emma's journal, she slowly rose, using the table as leverage. Leaving her white gloves on the table, she gathered her purse, coat, and the Rokeby Museum visitors' guide, and made her way back to Monique's office.

"Hi Chantal. Everything all right?" Monique rose from her desk.

Chantal rubbed her aching back. "The baby's telling me it's time to go, and I could use your bathroom. Looks like I'll have to come back another time to read more of Emma's journals," Chantal said, as she braced herself against the wall.

"Oh, sure. I understand. The toilet is downstairs on your left, behind the staircase. Here, can you come sit for a minute?" Monique motioned to the chair next to her desk.

Balancing the items in her arms, Chantal nodded and eased herself down to the chair.

Monique smiled. "You know, I've been thinking about this amazing story of how your ancestor Samuel came through the Hopper property. After DeeDee and I found Emma's documents, I gave Dee copies of sections of the journal and ledger to keep for her records. I'd be happy to make copies for you, too." Monique gently touched Chantal's hand. "Then you can read Emma's pages at your leisure. I know those old wooden chairs aren't very comfortable." She chuckled.

"Oh, my goodness! How very kind of you. You're right, I would be more comfortable in my easy chair." Chantal grimaced as her back twinged again. "Thank you so much, Monique! You don't know how much this means to me!" Chantal grasped Monique's hand.

"Great! Give me your number, and I'll call you when the copies are done. Shouldn't be long," Monique said.

Chantal recited her number as Monique jotted it down. Grasping the arms for leverage, Chantal slowly rose from the chair. Monique slid her arm under Chantal's elbow and guided her to the elevator.

"I'll talk to you soon. Please take care of yourself," Monique said, as Chantal entered the lift.

"Thanks again. I will." Chantal smiled at the petite woman, a head shorter than herself.

As the elevator door whirred shut, Chantal thought, *I wonder what surprises Emma has in store for me.*

PROPERTY HISTORY

Two days after visiting the historical society, Chantal rested in her recliner as music played softly on the stereo. With Clay at work and the girls at school, she had the house to herself. Reading the history of the property DeeDee had left her, she was surprised to learn the farm had once stretched over twenty acres, covering an entire town block. Besides the original two-story farmhouse, there had been barns for cows, horses, and hay, as well as a chicken coop, cheese house, and maple-sugaring shed. A substantial carriage barn and stables had stood next to the main road. Chantal tried to imagine what the Hoppers' daily life had been like in the 1800s.

I'm so glad I was born into the modern world. I probably wouldn't last a week cooking, scrubbing and milking cows…much less making my own cheese and syrup! She chuckled, envisioning her girls trying to collect eggs as hens chased them around the coop.

She read according to Gabe's family lineage, when his elder son Luke got married, a new house had been built directly next door to the original farmhouse. Luke, his wife, Mary, and eventually their children, lived just a few yards away from Gabe and Emma. That house was now owned by Howard Greene, whom Chantal had met shortly after they moved in. The spry, white-haired neighbor had regaled her with local stories, making her laugh. *He's quite a colorful native Vermonter, to say the least!*

It saddened Chantal to see how the property had been gradually sold off in parcels over the years, where newcomers had built homes. All the outbuildings had been demolished long ago, and only the enlarged original farmhouse still occupied the remainder of the once-sprawling Hopper farm.

A sharp stab in her back made Chantal cry out as the baby shifted position. Chantal massaged her rock-hard tummy and felt what she thought was a foot poking her hand.

This baby's getting restless. I hope he or she makes an appearance soon! She caressed her tummy on both sides, trying to soothe the infant.

"It's okay, Little One," she cooed. "Mommy's here and keeping you safe until you're ready to come into this world."

A knock at the front door pulled Chantal from her musings.

"Just a minute. Be right there!" she hollered from the parlor. Setting DeeDee's report down, she carefully got up from the recliner and shuffled into the main room.

As Chantal opened the front door, a blast of cold air assaulted her. "Monique! Please come in. It's freezing out there."

Monique stomped her snow-covered boots on the porch before entering. "Hi, Chantal. I was passing by and thought I'd drop off these copies for you, and save you a trip to town." She handed Chantal a folder.

"Oh, my gosh! How kind of you. Thank you so much." Chantal accepted the documents. "You're right! It is getting tough for me to drive, since this big old belly doesn't fit behind the steering wheel very well." Chantal smiled, and laid an arm over the top of her protruding tummy.

Monique laughed. "Well, it sure looks like a healthy baby!"

"Both my girls were over eight pounds," Chantal said, rubbing her tummy. "But I think this one is going to be twice that size if he or she waits any longer!"

Monique chuckled, touching the folder Chantal held. "Anyway, this is the last page of the ledger and a section of Emma's journals covering the eighteen-fifties and sixties. I hope this helps you learn more about your ancestors' travels."

"Well I hope so, too." Chantal smiled. "These documents are a wonderful legacy for my children. I want them to know the sacrifices their ancestors made to gain their freedom." Her voice trembled. "Kids these days don't have any idea how easy they have it. They need to learn they walk in the footsteps of giants, who paved the way for us."

Monique hugged Chantal, then stepped back and continued, "I forgot to mention something when you were at the office the other day. After DeeDee cleaned out her barn, she got curious about where Emma and Gabe were buried. We did some research and found their family plot—it's in the West Street Cemetery." Monique paused and smiled. "And we discovered your ancestor, Miss Elsie, is also buried there!"

"Oh, my gosh! With all that's been happening, I had forgotten DeeDee mentioned that." Chantal sighed. "Apparently a lady who helped Samuel and Jonah escape had found Elsie's body in the river. She promised Samuel Miss Elsie would get a good Christian burial. I guess Emma made sure it happened."

Monique nodded. "Yes, you have the history right. Emma mentions it in her writing. The neighbor lady's name was Paree Guildersleeve. It seems the two women may have encountered some resistance from their church to have Miss Elsie buried in the Hopper family plot. But they persisted and ultimately prevailed in their plan."

I guess not everyone in Vermont had a favorable view of our people back then. I shouldn't be surprised. "Oh, I didn't know that! I'm so glad the women stood their ground and defended their Christian beliefs. I imagine it probably wasn't easy for them."

Monique nodded. "Paree and Emma were pretty strong-willed women for their time. I think they had to be tough to survive during such turmoil in our country."

I wonder if I would have been strong enough to defend my own convictions in the face of that kind of adversity. "After the baby's born, I would very much like to visit the Hopper family plot. Can you give me directions to the cemetery?"

"Sure, it's easy to find. After you pass the historical society building on the right, go straight through the intersection at the end of the park, and you'll be on West Street. The cemetery is about a half-mile down on the right." Monique waved her hand in the direction of town. "But call me before you go, and I'll give you the exact coordinates of the family plot. The rows are marked by letters and numbers, so it'll be easier to find."

"Thanks, Monique. I really appreciate all you and DeeDee have done to help me learn more about my heritage. I'm sure I'll be seeing much more of you in the spring." Chantal grinned.

Monique said, "Oh, it's no problem! I'm more than happy to help. Please do keep me informed of what you discover. Who knows, maybe I'll write a story about your family someday, with your permission, of course!" Monique waved her hand in a devil-may-care manner.

Chantal laughed. "Now wouldn't that be something? I guess it is pretty incredible when I think about it. And I'll be sure to let you know what I find." She squeezed Monique's hand.

"Well, I gotta run," Monique edged toward the door. "I hope all goes well with your delivery. Don't forget to call the paramedics, if you need them. And Merry Christmas to you and your family!" She laughed as she closed the door behind her.

Chantal returned to her recliner in the parlor, put her feet up and opened the pages Monique had left.

Okay, Miss Emma! Let's have a little chat, shall we?

CHRISTMAS TREE

Clay kissed the top of Chantal's head. "Babe, I'm going to take the girls across the street to pick out a Christmas tree. Do you want to walk over with us?"

Saturday, the day after Monique's visit, Chantal was reading pages from Emma's diary when Clay interrupted her. Christmas music played softly from the stereo.

Resting the papers on her belly, Chantal smiled at her husband. "No, I'll stay here. I don't want to take the chance of slipping on the ice. Do you want to take the car to get the tree home?"

"No, Mommy! We can carry it," Whitney exclaimed with glee. "See!" The child grabbed her bicep. "I'm as strong as Popeye!"

Charmaine grinned broadly as Whitney twirled, her braids flying.

Clay winked at Chantal. "With both these strong girls, I think we can manage it. We won't get anything too big, I promise." He kissed her again. "C'mon, girls, let's go find our Christmas tree!"

"Yeah! We're strong!" Whitney exclaimed, as they left the house.

Across the street and about fifty yards south of their house stood the American Legion clubhouse. When Chantal had first met her elderly neighbor, Howard, she was surprised to hear a restaurant and bar, appropriately named The NoWhere, had once stood there. She chuckled, remembering Howard's colorful stories of the many parking lot brawls that broke out on Friday nights, while a local band played raucous country music inside.

I bet the sheriff had his hands full back then.

According to Howard, about ten years earlier, a grease fire in the kitchen had caused the place to burn to the ground. Shortly thereafter the Legion bought the property and built their meeting place.

I hope the Legion patrons are mellower than their predecessors.

Now, just days before Christmas, Chantal and Clay had been pleasantly surprised to see the Legionnaires selling fresh-cut Christmas trees from their parking lot. *It doesn't get any more convenient than that,* thought Chantal.

Before being interrupted, Chantal had been engrossed in Emma's descriptions of her daily life on the farm.

What a hard life they lived, but they didn't know it at the time. And Emma and Gabe helped so many families seeking shelter on their farm. Were people that much more open-hearted and willing to help others back then? I don't know if I would have opened my home to any stranger who came knocking. I guess the family's strong religious beliefs and hatred of oppression are what led them to treat their visitors with such kindness.

Chantal sighed, wishing for more empathy in this world, with Christmas approaching. She continued reading Emma's pages.

10 mo. 11th, Friday, mid-afternoon, 1850

I simply cannot imagine my heartache if one of my boys had lost two of his fingers at the tender age of five years. 'Tis mysterious Samuel will not reveal the truth. The pain and suffering of both the boy and his mother must have been unbearable. The good Lord was watching over Samuel, so he did not die that day. I pray Samuel lives a very long life, as the Almighty must have something very special in store for the young lad.

Chantal's stomach lurched as she remembered Emmaline's article describing how Samuel lost his fingers in the sawmill. Her heart went out to the young boy for the abuse he had endured at the hands of his evil half-brother, Chester. "Emma was right: Samuel could have died that day," she whispered to herself. "The good Lord did indeed have plans for Samuel, Emma. And you would have been proud to know he lived a good, long life!"

The soulful voice of Nat King Cole drifted from the stereo, *O holy night, the stars are brightly shining…*

Footfalls on the porch got Chantal's attention. "Mommy! We're home!" Chantal heard Charmaine's voice calling from the front door.

"Come see our tree, Mommy! It's beeeauuuutiiifullll!" Whitney cried.

Damn! I wanted to read more. Reluctantly, Chantal set the diary on her side table, dropped the footrest of her recliner, and heaved herself up with a grunt. "I'm coming. Just hold your horses!" she called toward the main room. Chantal stood and held the back of the chair, waiting for the baby to settle. *Any day now…*

When she entered the room, Chantal burst out laughing. Clay struggled with a hefty pine tree, the top bent sideways against the lowered ceiling. "I remember someone promising the tree wouldn't be too big!" The sight momentarily overcame her angst at reading Emma's sad diary entries.

"What can I say?" Clay said with a sheepish grin, grasping the unruly tree with both hands. "I was outvoted!"

"It's perfect! Don't you think so, Mommy?" Whitney asked, her hands on her hips.

Clay grinned at his daughter, then peered from behind the tree at Chantal. "I think it will fit fine in the parlor, because the ceiling is higher. Plus, I can always cut some off the bottom if we need to."

His dark eyes and bright smile melted Chantal's heart. She turned to Whitney, who grasped Charmaine's hand. "Girls, I think it's perfect! You picked out a very nice tree. Good job!" She gave them both high-fives. "Now, take off your coat and boots, and let's help Daddy get it decorated."

"Yay!" Whitney beamed. "Let's decorate our tree." She did her special twirl, braids flying, then hugged Chantal's belly. "We'll make a very special tree just for you, Baby Sister!"

As Clay predicted, once he cut a section from the bottom, the tree fitted nicely in the corner of the parlor, between the two windows facing the street. Clay retrieved the decorations from the cellar and put the girls to work unwrapping ornaments.

Chantal poured herself a glass of milk, before getting comfortable once more in her easy chair.

Nat was still crooning... *Fall on your knees... O hear the angel voices... O night divine...*

Chuckling at the antics of her family bickering over which ornaments should go where, she opened Emma's diary to where she had left off.

I am aghast at the appalling attack on Sarah Miss Elsie witnessed when she returned from her errands. Miss Elsie said she was in the kitchen of the big house, when she heard Sarah's muffled screams. She ran upstairs and burst into the guest bedroom. Rage overtook her at seeing her young, virgin daughter, naked and bloody on the bed, held down by Chester and another white boy, while being raped by Master Swaley!

Sarah was just a young girl to endure such a violent assault by those white men. And for her to get pregnant from the assault must have been horrifying for her! Why does the Lord allow bad things to happen to these good people? 'Tis not fair! No wonder Sarah is sullen and silent. Had I endured such an indignity, I probably would not speak my mind either.

Chantal's hand instinctively went to her mouth as she gasped. *What? The bastard raped Elsie's daughter, Sarah, too? And that little shit Chester helped hold her down! What a disgusting family! But the master was also Samuel's father. So, that means Sarah's baby, Jonah, was Samuel's nephew AND his brother! Oh, my God!*

A deep shiver ran through Chantal as she watched her daughters hang hand-colored ornaments.

Chantal recalled the story of the white man threatening Emmaline. *I thought Mother was being overly paranoid about the Swaley descendants tracking down our family. Now I'm not so sure.* Then a revelation swept over her. *Ah, Mon Dieu! That man wasn't worried about what happened to Samuel's hand. He didn't want it made public the despicable Master Swaley had raped a teenage, virgin slave girl, and she bore his son!*

Chantal shook her head in disbelief.

...God rest ye merry gentleman, let nothing you dismay...

I don't think Samuel ever knew the truth about Jonah's father. How very tragic it all was! Chantal's heart went out to her ancestor, Miss Elsie, for all the family had endured.

Whitney called, "Mommy? Do you like this angel here, or here?"

Chantal looked up to see Whitney place the ornament, first in front of the tree, then to the side. Distracted by thoughts of Sarah, she tried to focus on her daughter's request.

"Ummm…I like it in the front, Honey." *A guardian angel for our house…* Chantal's gaze lifted to the ceiling. *I guess the more, the better!* She smiled admiring the tree taking shape, then went back to reading:

Damn those men and their dominating oppression over God's children. I know 'tis not my place to judge, but may they burn in hell for their sins! …To save us all from Satan's power…when we were gone astray…

Chantal was a bit surprised at Emma's blasphemous thoughts. *I couldn't agree more, Emma!* She continued reading.

I cannot blame Miss Elsie for not telling Samuel who fathered Sarah's child. She was right to be worried if Samuel knew the truth, he might very well have reacted badly and faced dire consequences.

Chantal sighed. *Ahhh! I was right. Samuel did not know who Jonah's father was!* She shook her head. *It was probably best he didn't know the whole truth.*

Nat's deep voice resonated in the background…*Oh, tidings of comfort and joy…*

"Babe, did you hear me?" Clay stared at her.

Her husband's voice brought Chantal back to the present. "Oh, sorry, no! What did you say?" She took a drink of milk.

"What are you reading?" Clay asked from across the room.

"It's Emma's diary Monique dropped off yesterday. I'm reading the part about my ancestors. It's fascinating and so very sad." Chantal's voice trembled.

Clay walked to her chair and touched her arm. "Do you think now is a good time to be reading that? We're getting the tree decorated and some of our favorite Christmas music is playing." He peered into her eyes. "I don't want you getting upset."

Clay's look of concern warmed Chantal's heart. "You're probably right. But I want to learn more about my family from Emma's point of view, so please indulge me." She smiled at her handsome husband, again thankful for her supportive family. "You asked me something?"

"Oh, yeah. I was going to get some dinner going. Would you like hamburgers or chicken breast?"

"Hamb'gers, Daddy! Hamb'gers!" Whitney called from the side of the Christmas tree.

"And French fries!" Charmaine chimed in, as she untwisted garland to wrap around the tree.

Chantal grinned at Clay. "Guess you have your answer. Burgers will be fine. Would you mind refilling my milk while you're in the kitchen?"

Clay swung his right arm in front of himself and took a deep bow. "Your wish is my command, My Lady!" He headed for the kitchen, chuckling.

Chantal looked wistfully at the decorations Charmaine and Whitney were hanging on the tree. She remembered helping the girls make and color the ornaments over the past few years. *They're growing up so fast.*

…Silent night, holy night, all is calm, all is bright…

"Chantal! Girls! Dinner's ready!" Clay called from the kitchen.

…Holy infant so tender and mild…

Chantal tried to clear her mind of her ancestors' plight as she put the diary to the side. She realized her stomach had soured. Maybe Clay had been right. *Dinner? How can I eat after reading this!*

"Okay, Daddy! We'll be right there," Charmaine answered for all of them. Whitney sprinted toward the kitchen.

"Here, Mommy, let me help you up," Chantal's older daughter offered her hands. Chantal dropped the footrest of her recliner, slid to the end of the seat, and grabbed Charmaine's hands.

"Ready?" Charmaine asked. "On three. One…two…three!" Chantal held tight to her daughter's hands, and Charmaine took several steps backward, the momentum pulling Chantal to her feet.

"Thanks, Honey. You're a big help right now. You know I love you!" She kissed the top of her daughter's head and slowly made her way to the kitchen.

At dinner, Chantal tried to engage with her family's happy chatter. But with thoughts of Samuel and Sarah floating through her mind, she was only half-listening. She silently berated herself for not being in a more festive mood, as she just picked at her hamburger.

When the family retreated back to the parlor to continue their decorating, Clay spread strings of lights on the floor, plugging each into a socket to ensure they worked. One string was half-dead, and Chantal chuckled in her recliner, watching Clay trying to find the offending bulb.

Charmaine and Whitney giggled as they unwrapped more handmade ornaments.

Chantal sighed, basking in the warmth of her family. *And next year, we'll have another little one to share our holidays.*

…Joy to the world, the Lord is come…Let earth receive her King…

She flipped to the next page of Emma's diary. The tight, slanted script of Emma's hand was now familiar, and no longer a struggle to decipher.

10 mo. 11th, Friday, early-evening, 1850

Elsie told me about one day when she went to the coop to get eggs. She neared the stables when she recognized a familiar voice. She stopped alongside the barn, and heard Chester ask a stable hand if he could get one of the horses to trample Jonah! Chester said he wanted the boy dead, but wanted it to look like an accident. Elsie's heart leapt in her chest! She was frightened for her grandson's safety. She ran back to the big house without her eggs, where she told Sarah what she overheard. That night, back in their cabin, Elsie started planning their escape, even though they knew the great risk they would face on the run. I commend Elsie for her fierce determination to remove her grandson from the threat of grave harm.

Chantal's heart raced. *Chester was there when his father raped Sarah, so he knew who sired her child! That little shit couldn't stand having two black half-brothers. And he was so cruel as to want Jonah murdered! Makes me want to reach back in time and whip Chester's ass!*

She remembered her grandmother's story. *Samuel told Emmaline he didn't understand why Miss Elsie wanted to run, and what it had to do with Jonah. Now it all makes sense! Poor little Jonah! He must have been so frightened being on the run.*

Chantal looked up from her reading and watched Clay, sidestepping the girls, as he circled the tree to wrap the light strings from bottom to top.

…Oh, He rules the world with truth and grace…

Chantal was absorbed in Emma's account of how the Prescott family made their escape from Maryland on a Navy ship. Then they were harbored in New York City by Emma's son Adam, and Gabe's uncle Isaac T. Hopper.

A familiar name in the next passage caught Chantal's eye.

10 mo. 12th, Saturday, late-evening, 1850

When Mrs. Higgins and Miss Harriet brought Miss Elsie and her family to the canal dock in bright daylight, they encountered two men holding a broadside, looking for a slave family. Elsie was so scared, she said she wanted to jump into the river rather than be caught. The Lord was guiding their journey, since Samuel had disguised his injured hand, and the family was not recognized. Mrs. Higgins and Miss Harriet must have had tremendous courage to confront the slave hunters, and shepherd the Prescott family on board the canal barge safely.

Chantal rubbed her tired eyes and focused on the tree decorations taking shape. *Miss Harriet? Hmmm…I wonder if that was Harriet Tubman. What an incredible coincidence if she actually helped Miss Elsie and her family on their journey north!* She read Emma's next entry.

'Tis amazing Miss Harriet, a runaway slave herself, would risk her life to return south to guide others. I admire her bravery putting herself in grave danger to help kindred folk escaping bondage. May the Lord bless her perilous journey.

Chantal gasped and her skin tingled. "Oh, my gosh! It *was* Harriet Tubman!"

Memories flashed through Chantal's mind of the afternoon her mother had brought home a bust of Harriet for her collection of historical black figures. *I must have been about ten at the time. I knew I had to learn all I could about Harriet before dinner time, so I could recite what I had learned.* Chantal had gone to her father's study, lined with floor-to-ceiling bookshelves. Her father, Lewis, had been the headmaster at the Napierville Secondary School and had acquired an extensive collection of history books, predominantly about black figures.

She smiled, still recalling part of her memorized recitation. *"Harriet Tubman was born a slave in eighteen twenty-one, on the eastern shores of Maryland. She escaped the plantation in eighteen forty-nine, and successfully arrived in Philadelphia. Eventually she led groups of fugitives to freedom in Canada. Despite her fits of sleeping sickness, between eighteen forty-nine and eighteen-sixty, Harriet successfully helped over three hundred slaves escape to Canada."*

Chantal couldn't help but chuckle at remembering the description of Harriet being petite, stoop-shouldered and muscular. *I guess being small she could hide easily!*

Chantal's childhood oratory had continued, *"By eighteen-sixty, plantation owners had offered rewards of over sixty thousand dollars for her capture! Harriet's favorite saying to her followers was: 'Go free or die!' She famously claimed she never lost a passenger on the Underground Railroad."*

Chantal recalled Harriet's bust: her hair wrapped in a turban, her chin protruding. *I would love to have met that amazing woman!*

Her recitation of Harriet's life had concluded, *"During the Civil War, Harriet became a scout, a spy, and a nurse for the Union Forces. She died in nineteen-thirteen, at the ripe old age of ninety-two, at her home in Auburn, New York. She was widely considered the Moses of her time, for leading her people out of bondage to the Promised Land!"*

Chantal considered the time line. *So, if Harriet had helped Miss Elsie and her family escape through New York in 1850, this would have been long before there was a bounty on her head. Unbelievable! I can't wait to tell Mother. I know she'll be amazed!*

Chantal read Emma's last entry on the page.

I thank Thee, Dear Lord, for guiding the Prescotts on their journey and they have arrived safely into our care. We seek to do Thy will on this earth in Thy Loving Grace. Amen.

"Mommy, who's Harriet Tubman?" Whitney asked from the sofa. Ornaments splayed across the coffee table in front of the girls.

Whitney's question surprised Chantal as she hadn't realized she had spoken aloud. "Harriet Tubman was a very brave woman who helped our people escape to freedom a long time ago."

Nat began his signature "Christmas Song": *Chestnuts roasting on an open fire...*

"You all right, Babe?" Clay asked, as he placed the shining, white angel on the top bough.

Chantal hadn't noticed him bring in the step-stool. "Oh, my gosh, Clay! You'll have to read this. It's all so amazing and incredible." She wiped her eyes. "It's just too much to explain to the girls right now."

"What's too much, Mommy?" Charmaine asked.

"Do you remember when I told you your ancestor, Samuel, once came through this property with his family, trying to escape to Canada?" Chantal smiled at her older daughter.

"Yeah. That's pretty cool," Charmaine replied.

"Well, the lady who sheltered Samuel and his family at this farm was named Emma."

"Wow! Kinda like great-granny Emmaline?" Whitney asked, her eyes wide.

"Yep. Kinda like your great-granny," Chantal echoed. "Anyway, this Emma wrote a special story in her diary about our family, and that's what I'm reading." Chantal took a deep breath, then a sip of milk. "When you're both older, I'll let you read it. But not now."

... Yule-tide carols being sung by a choir...

Chantal inwardly cringed at the thought of letting either of her girls read the harrowing story. But she knew it was an integral part of their history, and sooner or later they should learn of their family's struggle and sacrifice to gain their freedom.

Clay stepped down from the stool, walked to Chantal, and grasped her hand. "Well, I think you should put the journal away for now. You can always read more tomorrow." He looked deeply into her bloodshot eyes. "Give it a rest. You need some sleep."

Chantal saw his love for her reflected in his concerned expression. "You're right. I am tired. Can you help me up the stairs?" She gripped her husband's hands as he assisted her up from the easy chair. "The tree looks amazing! You all did a wonderful job."

As she left the room, Chantal smiled at their beautiful, innocent, young girls. She could only imagine and shudder at what their lives would have been like more than a century earlier.

... tiny tots with their eyes all aglow ... will find it hard to sleep tonight ...

A PACKAGE ARRIVES

Although Clay had the week between Christmas and the New Year off from work, he was still "on call" in case of any technical emergencies. He had made arrangements with two co-workers to back him up when Chantal went into labor. For the first week of January, Clay's manager approved him to work from home. Written in big letters on a sheet attached to the refrigerator were the phone numbers of Chantal's doctor and the local paramedics.

A snowstorm blew into the region during the evening of December twenty-third. When it stopped snowing on the afternoon of Christmas Eve, over a foot of snow covered the yard. Throughout the storm, plows had continuously traversed the main roads to keep them clear for travelers.

Bill Graybert, the realtor, had referred Clay to Ralph Smith, who plowed driveways for forty dollars. Clay had a standing order with Ralph to plow them out whenever they received more than three inches. So just before dusk on Christmas Eve, Clay heard the sound of a truck in the driveway. He stood on the porch and watched as Ralph moved the snow first to one side, then the other. Earlier, Clay had shoveled the steps and a small section of the concrete walkway.

Once Ralph had the driveway cleared, he repositioned his truck and plowed along the walkway. When he met the area Clay had shoveled, Ralph turned the plow blade to push the snow away from the house. Stepping back into the house to retrieve two twenty-dollar bills from his wallet, Clay decided to add another twenty to recognize Ralph for helping them on a holiday.

After thanking Ralph for his work, Clay returned to the house and joined Chantal and the girls in the parlor, where they were watching television. "Looks like the snow has stopped, and we're plowed out for now."

"Oh, great! That was really sweet of Ralph to plow us out on Christmas Eve," Chantal said.

Chantal massaged the sides of her protruding tummy. *Okay, Baby. We're plowed out. Please make your appearance soon!* She hoped her thoughts would transfer to her unborn child.

Clay grinned. "Yeah. I gave him a little extra present for his efforts." Then he turned to his daughters, who were playing cards on the coffee table. "Go get dressed, girls. We don't want to be late for church services."

"Ahhhh, Daddy! Do we have to go?" Whitney whined.

Chantal shook her finger at her younger daughter. "Yes, you have to go! It's Christmas Eve, and it'll be fun. I'd go with you if I could move better, you know that. So say a special prayer for me and the baby, you hear? Now go get dressed!"

"Yes, Mommy!" Charmaine replied for both of them, as they finally scrambled up the stairs.

A half-hour later, Clay appeared in the parlor dressed in a black suit and white shirt, sporting a red-and-black-striped tie. A red pocket square sat neatly in the jacket breast pocket. His newly polished boots shined.

Damn! He looks so fine when he dresses up. Chantal mused as she watched her husband do a Whitney-style twirl in front of her.

"How do I look, Mommy?" He mimicked Whitney's voice.

Chantal laughed. "You look stunning, Honey! Wish I could go with you. Don't want any of those ladies in town dragging you off for their Christmas stocking."

Clay chuckled, then a concerned look crossed his face. "Will you be okay here alone? Do you want me to call someone to stay with you?"

Chantal shook her head. "I'll be fine for an hour or so. The baby's not due for a couple more weeks, anyway. Go and enjoy the service with the girls."

"Not to worry, my Lady. We shall be home in a flash." Clay bowed deeply and grinned at his very pregnant wife. "Let's go, girls!" he hollered up the stairs.

Footsteps thudded down the stairs, then both girls stood in front of Chantal for inspection. Charmaine wore a green, long-sleeved wool dress, and Whitney wore a pink dress with red roses. Both girls wore heavy black winter tights.

Whitney twirled. "How do we look, Mommy?"

Clay winked at Chantal, and they both laughed.

"You both look wonderful! Now, come give Mommy a kiss, and get moving before you're late."

Each girl bent over Chantal and kissed her on the cheek. Clay bussed Chantal's forehead.

"Merry Christmas, Honey. We'll be back soon," Clay said as he shepherded the girls into their coats and boots, then out the front door.

After the family left, Chantal made her way into the kitchen and poured herself a cup of virgin eggnog. *Next year, I'll be able to spike it a little.* She returned to her lounge chair in the parlor, grunting as she settled in, then continued reading more of Emma's diary.

10 mo. 13th, Sunday morning, 1850

Father and Luke have left on their journey to deliver the Prescott family to the canal in Whitehall. I pray the good Lord shines His guiding light upon the family and delivers them safely to freedom in the Promised Land. Yet,

I cannot help but worry. I do not believe Father has been forthcoming about the risks surrounding us because of this infernal new slave law.

Chantal sipped her drink. *Emma was right to be worried, as things went so terribly wrong for them. I wish I could reach out and give her a big hug!*

Christmas Day dawned sunny and bitterly cold. Both girls were up early and they squealed with delight when they saw what Santa had delivered. After the girls had gone to bed the previous evening, Clay had brought up the presents hidden in the cellar and spread them around the tree.

Chantal's thoughts wandered back to the terrible hardships of her ancestors, even as she delighted in watching the girls rip into their presents. *They have no idea how lucky and blessed they are.*

Then Clay came over to Chantal and handed her a small wrapped box. "This is for you, Babe." He smiled, dropping to one knee in front of her.

"Clay! What did you do?" She admonished. "We weren't going to get each other gifts, remember?"

"Well, I broke the rules! This is something I thought you'd like," he said, resting his elbows on his bent leg.

Chantal unwrapped and opened the small, square box. A jeweler's name was emblazoned on its cover. Inside was a slip of paper. She read: *This certificate entitles you to one gold mother's ring containing the three birthstones of your children. Love, Clay*

She choked back tears. *He's so thoughtful. I just love him to pieces!* "Oh, Honey! This is a wonderful idea. I never would have thought of it. Thank you so much!" Chantal wiped her eyes.

Clay bent forward and kissed her lips. "After the baby's born, we'll know the birthstone and have the ring made. It'll always remind you of your children." He squeezed Chantal's hand.

"I'll treasure it forever!" Chantal said, her voice breaking. "I love you."

"I love you, too, Babe. Merry Christmas!"

Both girls had received plastic sleds from Santa. After they finished a delicious breakfast of eggs, bacon, and pancakes with Vermont maple syrup, Clay took the girls into the backyard to play. Chantal got comfortable at the kitchen table and looked through the window at her family frolicking in the snow. Because she couldn't join the fun, she picked up

Emma's diary, and resumed reading where she had left off the previous evening.

Chantal gasped and let out an involuntary cry when she read Emma's heartbreaking account of Luke's dead body being brought home, and of Gabe being arrested for transporting fugitives. Chantal knew part of the story of the wagon attack from her grandmother, but experiencing it through Emma's eyes gave her a whole new perspective on the horrible incident. No longer able to hold her emotions in, her tears flowed. Wiping her eyes, she read the rest of Emma's entry.

10 mo. 14th, Monday afternoon, 1850

What shall I do? I cannot manage the farm alone. And how long will Gabe be in jail? The Lord warned me in my dream this would happen. I should have stopped them from transporting the fugitives and listened to my heart! This is all my fault, and now I have lost both Luke and Gabe. Oh Dear Lord, please forgive my trespasses!

Chantal stared out the window, thinking of Emma's dire situation. *That's so unfair Emma blamed herself for the tragedy. There was nothing she could have done to stop it. How in the world did she manage to keep the farm going without her menfolk? I could never have done it in a million years.* Chantal shuddered at the thought.

Absentmindedly, she watched Clay trying to pull Whitney on her sled. Then he stumbled and took a face-plant into the knee-deep snow. Charmaine jumped on top of him, and Whitney joined in the fray, with snow flying in every direction. Chantal couldn't help but laugh at their antics.

I wish I could join them. It looks like fun. Next year…

She went back to reading about the sad funeral of Luke and Miss Elsie. *I'm grateful Miss Elsie received a proper Christian burial in the Hopper family plot. Emma's grief must have consumed the poor woman.*

10 mo. 21st, Monday evening, 1850

Now that Luke and Elsie have gone to be with Our Lord, I worry Gabe has become bitter because of their deaths. To my great chagrin, Father has proclaimed he will never help our wayward visitors again. He swears in the grimmest manner he shall forever protect his property and family from evil. I pray for his everlasting soul!

Chantal abruptly put the diary down. She remembered the warm, tingling feeling that had engulfed her when she first walked through the door of the house, and hoped it was a good omen. *And Gabe is still here protecting his house. I hope he protects us from evil, too.*

Several days after Christmas, Chantal watched the weather report on television with trepidation. A major nor'easter was forecast to barrel down from Canada and hit Vermont on New Year's Eve.

She turned to Clay, sitting in his easy chair next to her. "That looks like a big storm coming. With the baby due any day, I hope we don't get snowed in."

Clay said, "We'll be fine. I talked to Ralph, and he said he'd be over to plow us out as soon as the snow stops. He said if you go into labor before then, to call him, and he'll be over immediately."

Charmaine and Whitney sat on the sofa, legs crossed, facing each other, playing Go Fish. Charmaine spoke up. "Mommy, why can't you have the baby at home? Didn't they used to do that in the olden days?"

Chantal cringed at the thought of birthing with no medical staff or pain relief. "Well, Honey, thank goodness this isn't the olden days! When women have babies now, it's a good thing to be in a hospital with doctors and nurses to help out. It's much safer."

Clay reached across the side table between them and grasped Chantal's hand. "And don't forget, if the roads are bad, we can always call the paramedics. We'll do everything possible to get you to the hospital in time."

Chantal smiled at his concern. "I know you will, Babe. Thanks. I've just never had a baby in the middle of winter before, and I can't help but be worried." She stared at the game show just starting on television.

Please, Lord. Help me get to the hospital safely so we can have a healthy baby. Thank you! Amen.

The morning of New Year's Eve, Chantal yawned and stared out the kitchen window. Heavy snow fell in the yard. She reluctantly admired its beauty, but hoped the forecasters' most recent predictions were wrong. The baby was restless and had kept her up most of the night. Plus, snowplows regularly rumbling along the main road made it difficult to get back to sleep. The girls were cranky, having been inside for two days, and were in the parlor bickering as they played a board game. Clay was in his office, remotely logged in to work from his computer.

As far as Chantal knew, once this storm passed, no new snow was predicted for the next several days. She caressed her taut abdomen and cooed, "Okay, little one. As soon as we're plowed out, I'd like you to make your appearance in this world. You're big enough now, and it's time for you to leave the nest. Doesn't that sound like a great idea, my love?"

By mid-afternoon on New Year's Day, the snowfall had lessened. Chantal was relaxing in her easy chair absentmindedly watching the Rose Bowl football game with Clay. Earlier in the day, she and the girls had admired the gorgeous flower-laden floats as they lumbered through sunny Pasadena. *Ahhh, I'd love to be in warm California right now,* she had lamented. Now, the rumble of a diesel engine caught her attention.

Clay rose from his chair and looked out the parlor window toward the road. "Oh, great! Ralph's here. I'll go out and give him a hand." Clay bent and kissed Chantal's cheek. "See, I told you we'd get plowed out. So do you think you could have a chat with that kid and tell him to get his butt moving?" He gently laid a hand on her bulging tummy and chuckled.

Chantal gave Clay a feigned scowl. "Hey! What makes you think the baby's a *he*?"

Clay flashed his big white smile. "Oh, I don't know. Just a hunch! We'll find out soon enough." He waved as he left the room.

An hour or so later, Chantal rose from her chair and peered out the window. She was surprised to see the snowbanks were at least four feet high, and she could barely see the road. But for now at least, the walkway and driveway were plowed.

Okay, sweet child, let's get this show on the road. You heard your daddy!

On January 3rd, 2005, Chantal finished dinner with the family and started to lower herself into the easy chair, when an intense pain gripped her abdomen. She let out an involuntary cry, as she felt her water break.

"Clay! Quick! I need your help!" she gasped. Balancing on the edge of her chair, she felt the fluid seep down her legs and soak her dress.

Within moments, Clay stood by her side, the girls hovering behind him, their faces somber. "Babe?" He grasped her hand.

"Help me to the bathroom. My water just broke." She reached for his hand. "Call the doctor, and get the girls ready. We have to get going!"

Clay helped Chantal stand and supported her back. She knew she left a dripping trail as Clay walked her to the bathroom and closed the door behind her. Another spasm rocked her. She braced herself against the sink and took several deep breaths, hoping to slow the labor. Cleaning herself up as best she could, she heard Clay barking commands at the girls.

When Chantal emerged from the bathroom, Clay quickly helped her into her boots and coat. "Charmaine, go open the car door for your mother, and *walk*—no running! I don't want anyone slipping and hurting themselves!" Clay turned back to his wife. "You okay to walk to the car?"

Chantal nodded, breathing heavily. She exited the front door, then Clay closed and locked it. He supported her back and guided her along the icy path to the car. She sat in the front seat with a grunt. Clay started to strap the seatbelt over her, but she pushed him away.

"No! I can't bear that right now. Just don't crash!" she said breathlessly.

Clay checked the backseat to make sure both girls had their seatbelts buckled, then got behind the wheel and started the car. He drove as fast as he dared on the icy roads, toward the Rutland Hospital fifteen miles away.

Chantal couldn't help but chuckle through her labor pains, listening to her daughters debate names for a new baby sister.

"I think we should name her, *Strawberry Pink*," Whitney said.

"That's not a real name—you can't name a kid *Strawberry*," Charmaine scolded her.

"Why not? I like strawberries, and pink is my favorite color! I think it's a great name!" Whitney exclaimed.

"I think we should name her Isabella…like the Queen! Now that's a *really* great name!" Charmaine shouted over Whitney.

"No, it isn't! I hate that name! Mommy, do we have to name her Isabella?" Whitney called, leaning forward against her straining seatbelt.

Chantal gasped and let out a breath as another labor pain squeezed her abdomen.

Clay gave his wife a worried glance, then kept his eyes on the road. "Girls, quiet down and leave your mother alone. She can't talk to you right now. We'll figure it out after the baby's born."

"Humpf…Well I don't like Isabella," Whitney groused, folding her arms and slumping back into the seat.

After Chantal was rushed into the hospital in a wheelchair, Clay, Charmaine, and Whitney were escorted to the maternity unit waiting area by a slim, dark-haired nurse, who introduced herself as Anne.

Clay asked her, "Can the girls stay here while I check on my wife?"

Anne smiled. "Of course!" Stepping to a large basket in the corner, she retrieved a deck of cards and several board games. She placed them on the table in front of the two girls, sitting on the edge of the sofa. "Here you go, young ladies. Have fun." Then she turned to Clay. "Don't worry, they'll be fine here. Let's go see Chantal."

Whitney crinkled her nose, then spoke up. "But, Daddy! Why can't we go see Mommy?"

Clay dropped to his knees in front of his daughters. He grasped a hand of each girl. "Your Mommy is having the baby, and the doctor is with her, so she can't talk to you right now. Do you understand?"

Whitney's face turned grave. "Yeah, I guess so." She looked at Charmaine for approval.

Charmaine smiled at her younger sister. "She'll be fine, Whit. We'll see our baby sister real soon. Right, Dad?"

Clay stood. "You're absolutely right, Honey! Now just relax, and I'll be back to see you soon."

Over the next two hours, Clay moved in and out of the labor room to check on his daughters. On his last visit, they looked eagerly at their father when he told them their sibling was about to be born.

In the delivery room, Clay was given surgical garb to wear. He sat by Chantal, whose legs were propped in the birthing position. Over the succeeding minutes, Clay alternately squeezed Chantal's hand, mopped her sweaty brow, and encouraged her as she fought through each contraction. Finally, Chantal gave one last, mighty push, and the baby was born.

The doctor cradled the newborn in his arms, then looked up at Chantal and Clay. Smiling, he said, "Congratulations! It's a boy!"

Clay laughed. "Oh, my God! It's a *boy*! Did I be knowin', or what?" With tears in his eyes, he gave the exhausted Chantal a loving kiss. "Great job, Honey!"

After the doctor cut the umbilical cord, Nurse Anne placed the baby on a nearby station, where she cleaned the child and weighed him. She turned to the couple and said, "He's a healthy eight pounds, seven ounces!"

Clay was happy to have a son, but was even more thrilled their newborn was healthy.

Chantal muttered, "Thank you, Lord, for blessing us with a healthy baby!" Then she turned to the nurse. "We'd like to be the ones to tell our daughters the baby's gender."

Anne nodded. "Of course!" She wrapped the cooing child in a white swaddling blanket, and placed him against Chantal's chest.

Cradling the infant, Chantal gently caressed her son's full head of curly black hair. Grinning at Clay, she said, "He's going to be a handsome lad, just like his daddy! But I think the girls are going to be disappointed at not having a baby sister. I wonder if Whitney will still want to dress him in pink!"

Clay laughed. "Oh, I have no doubt she'll try!"

Anne touched Clay's arm. "If you're ready, let's bring in your daughters." She held the door for Clay as they exited the room.

A few minutes later, Clay ushered the girls to Chantal's bedside. Still in awe of the miracle of birth he had just witnessed, he bent and kissed Chantal's cheek, then peered at the infant in her arms.

Wearily, yet feeling as if she floated on a cloud, Chantal smiled at Charmaine and Whitney. "Girls, I'd like you to meet your new baby brother!"

Charmaine squealed and turned to her sister. "See, Whitney! I told you *Strawberry Pink* was a dumb name!"

Whitney crossed her arms and pouted, taking several steps back from the bed.

Nurse Anne handed Clay a knitted blue cap. "Here you go, Dad. Would you like to do the honors? We need to keep the baby's head warm."

Chantal leaned forward so Clay could reach the baby. He gently fitted the cap over the infant's head, covering his thick, dark curls. Then he grinned and kissed his son's cheek. "Welcome to our family, Little Man!"

Whitney sidled up to the bed rail, watching intently as Clay fitted the baby's skull cap. Suddenly, her face brightened, and she clasped her hands. "I know! We can name him *Strawberry Blue!*"

THE ETERNAL CONDUCTOR

Gabe watches Chantal cradling the baby as she settles into her rocking chair in the main room. A light pressure on his right shoulder causes him to turn.

An elderly black man, bent and wizened, stands beside him. A broad grin accentuates his age-scored features. Gabe stares at the man's face—there is something familiar. Then he notices the first two fingers are missing from the wrinkled, blotched hand resting upon him. Suddenly the years melt away from the figure, revealing the youthful smile of the lad Gabe had sheltered in his barn.

"Samuel! 'Tis wonderful to see thee!" Gabe clasps the man's arm. "It appears thee lived a long life."

Samuel rubs his stubbled, gray beard, and nods. "Yes, Suh, I sure did! I found freedom in Canada and married my lovely wife, Catharine. We were blessed to raise four healthy children." He glances fondly at Chantal rocking her infant. "I learned the local law, and spent my years aidin' those of us who were less fortunate." Samuel pauses, looking into the eyes of the weary old man, now his equal, who had long ago provided him safety and comfort. "I am forever grateful to you for helpin' our family in our time of need. I only wish we had all reached the Promised Land."

"I am proud of all thee has accomplished in thy life, Samuel." Gabe tilts his head toward Chantal. "And did thee bring her here?"

Samuel nods. "Yes, Suh. I provided guidance to help her find a safe harbor, as I myself once did. I hope you don't mind."

Gabe touches Samuel's damaged hand, and shakes his head. "Of course not, Samuel. I felt she was connected to thee, when she stepped through my doorway. They are a fine family."

"Yes, Suh. I would agree with you there." Samuel smiles at the infant boy, then turns to Gabe. "But I must tell you: I come bearin' a message."

Gabe frowns at Samuel. "Oh? What message is that?"

Samuel peers into Gabe's grizzled face. "Miss Emma wants you to come home. She says your work on this earth is done. She is with Miss Elsie, your boy Luke, and the rest of our families." Samuel points above his head. "We've been waitin' a long time for you to join us, Suh."

Gabe looks to the heavens and sees the serene face of his wife, Emma, reflecting back to him. "Yes, I think Mother is right. I promised to protect my property from evil, and after what seems like an eternity, I have done my duty." He turns to Samuel. "I thank thee for guiding them to my home. I know now this is the family I have been protecting my property for!"

Samuel bows his head in a sign of respect. "You are quite welcome. But now 'tis time for us to move on, Suh."

"Yes, Son. I do believe it is." Gabe lifts an eyebrow and turns to the ethereal figure on his left. "Will thee join us?"

Her long, snowy-white hair ripples over her shoulders as she shakes her head. "No, Dear. I will stay here in the only place I've ever called home. After all, I do have more children to love and protect!"

Gabe nods in approval. "Yes, I believe thee does."

Then he places his arm protectively around Samuel's back. "Shall we, my dear friend?"

The men wave to the spectral vision left behind, as they glide into the glowing light that beckons from beyond.

The remaining figure, adorned in a cream-colored dress, embellished with tiny pearlesque beads, clasps the cameo pendant resting next to her heart. As she watches Chantal nurse the infant, the yearning to cuddle her own babies once again engulfs her, and she sings her Mamma's favorite song.

Lul-la-by and good night
Thy mother's delight
Bright angels beside
My darling abide.
Lay thee down now and rest
May thy slumber be blessed
Lay thee down now and rest
May thy slumber be blessed.

Chantal rested her head against the back of the rocking chair and closed her eyes. As her infant son, Samuel Gabriel Moreau suckled, a warm glow enveloped her, and a gentle smile crossed her face. She began to sing:

"Lul-la-by and good night…"

Epilogue

When the fair haven Historical Society Museum opened the following May, visitors were surprised to discover a remodeled version of the Underground Railroad room.

Welcoming the visitor is a framed, poster-sized photograph of a smartly dressed black family, posed around a petite woman sitting in an ornate chair and holding a christened babe in arms.

Three new glass-enclosed, tabletop dioramas line the wall. The first shows a wooden bridge spanning a churning river. On the bridge is a covered hay wagon, perched precariously, hanging over one edge. At the far end of the bridge is the figure of a gray-bearded man, straining to hold two draft horses, still attached to the toppling wagon. At the back of the wagon, a young black woman is being helped to the ground by a dark-haired white man. On the icy road leading to the bridge are four white men on horseback, all pointing guns at the wagon. One gray-haired man wears a wide-brimmed hat, and a sheriff's badge is pinned to his chest.

If the visitor looks closely along the riverbank, he can see two black boys, the younger clinging to the older, crouching beneath overhanging branches. Above them on the bank, a youthful white man, with a hate-filled glare, points his gun toward the figures exiting the back of the wagon.

The second diorama depicts an 1840s-era steamship, half-submerged near a rocky shoreline. The ship's cargo, debris, and passengers bob in the choppy waves. Among the debris can be spotted two young black boys, grasping a floating plank. The older boy's arm is in the air, as if waving for help.

The third new tabletop display shows the older black boy, blood splattered on his face and arms, his right leg bound in a makeshift splint, lying alone in the back of a wagon that is parked in front of a big red barn. The farm's name, R O K E B Y, is painted in large letters along the front wall. Standing behind the wagon is an elderly white couple, dressed in traditional Quaker garb. Their stern expressions contrast with their outstretched arms welcoming the injured black boy.

On the wall behind this display are two framed charcoal drawings, positioned side by side. The yellowed parchments are blotched with age. The portrait on the left depicts three naked Merino sheep, emerging from a shearing shed. In the background, a black man is preparing to shear another animal. The artist's skill, using depth and contours, brings the scene to life. Leaning closer, the visitor can see the artist's signature: *Rowlie,* scrawled with thin, white paint lines, in the lower right-hand corner.

The second drawing was created with darker, more elementary lines, with minimal contour and shading. But the scene of a black man and a boy in a pasture tending a flock of sheep is recognizable. In the lower right-hand corner is the sweeping signature: *Samuel.*

On the far side of the dioramas stands a second framed, poster-sized portrait. The tall black man from the family photograph, dressed in a dapper three-piece suit, stands to the left of an empty judge's bench. To the right of the bench, a similarly dressed, middle-aged white man, with long sideburns, poses with a hand on his hip.

Hanging high on the wall directly behind the judge's bench is the great seal of Canada.

In the glass display case along the adjoining wall, artifacts from travelers who escaped along the Vermont Underground Railroad are displayed. An aged, brown leather journal is propped open, and the visitor must squint to interpret the two pages of tight, slanted script. Thankfully, the writing has been transcribed to an enlarged, printed document, propped on the top of the display case. Told by the wife of the elderly wagon driver, it describes in agonizing detail the slave hunters' attack on the wagon, the arrest of her husband, and the murder of their son at the bridge.

Next to the fragile journal is a newer, beige, cloth-covered, three-ring scrapbook. It is opened to an article titled "Escape" by E. Shabot, dated April 9, 1917, from a Canadian newspaper, *The Provincial Freeman.*

Again, the visitor must struggle to decipher the article's dark type in the cramped columns. An enlarged excerpt is displayed on the glass case. It, too, describes the armed posse's attack on the wagon.

Only, this account is from the heart-wrenching memories of a proud man, who has lived a long life, recalling horrific events of his boyhood, as he evaded the pursuing men.

Large gold letters on the wall blaze:

SAMUEL'S STORY.

Somewhere, courageous, gentle souls, rest.

ACKNOWLEDGMENTS

Josiah Wedgwood (12 July 1730–3 January 1795) was an English potter and entrepreneur. He founded the Wedgwood Company. A prominent abolitionist, Wedgwood is remembered, too, for his "Am I Not a Man and a Brother?" anti-slavery medallion, featured on the front page. He was a member of the Darwin-Wedgwood family and he was the grandfather of Charles and Emma Darwin.

My sincerest gratitude goes to the fine folks at the **Fair Haven Historical Society**, the **Town Clerk's Office**, and the **Fair Haven Free Library** for their cordial assistance in helping me dig into the archives to research the town history going back to its founding in 1779.

Brahms' "Lullaby" — aka the "**Cradle Song**"
Originally written by Johannes Brahms in 1868, under the title of "Wiegenlied: Guten Abend, gute Nacht" ("Good evening, good night"), for his friend Bertha Faber, to commemorate the birth of her second son.

Johannes Brahms (7 May 1833–3 April 1897) was a German composer, pianist, and conductor of the Romantic period. Born in Hamburg into a Lutheran family, Brahms spent much of his professional life in Vienna.

Although the lyrics have evolved throughout the years, the basic tenet of the lullaby that begins, "Lullaby and good night…" is still sung to children today.

Rokeby Museum, Ferrisburgh, Vermont
www.rokeby.org
Thank you for your permission to include Rokeby Farm and Museum in this historical fiction novel. Your help in my research of the fugitive slave migration north through Vermont was invaluable.

Rokeby Museum presents a nationally significant Underground Railroad story tucked inside a quintessential Vermont experience.

A major exhibit—*Free & Safe: The Underground Railroad in Vermont*—brings the Underground Railroad vividly to life. Focused on Simon and Jesse, two fugitives from slavery who found shelter here in the 1830s, the exhibit traces their stories from slavery to freedom, introduces the abolitionist Robinson family who called Rokeby home, and explores the turbulent decades leading up to the Civil War.

North Star Underground Railroad Museum, Ausable Chasm, New York
www.northcountryundergroundrailroad.com
A tremendous resource to learn of the hidden history of the Lake Champlain Line of the Underground Railroad. Poignant exhibits portray compelling stories of fugitives from slavery who passed through Northeastern New York and the Champlain Valley on their way to Québec and Ontario, Canada. Runaway slaves who reached these waterways took steamboats, barges and canal boats as part of their northward journey.

My special thanks go to my devoted critique partners. **Peter Stafford**, for not being afraid to get his hands dirty, and compelling me to dig deeper. **Betsy Schwarzentraub**, for her theological guidance. **Simone Stein**, for her expert medical knowledge and additional feedback on our shared hometown. **Paul Stein**, for his always positive recommendations.

I wish to express my sincerest gratitude to my editor, **Kathleen Strattan**. Her insightful analysis, meticulous attention to detail, and continual enthusiasm for the story, kept me motivated to finish our editing process.

And a big shout-out goes to **John Reinhardt** of John Reinhardt Book Design, for his amazing work and patience in formatting the manuscript to get this book out to the world. You're the best!

I sincerely appreciate everyone's time and support!

About the Author

DEBBIE GARNEAU GRIFFIN grew up on a small farmstead in Fair Haven, Vermont. After moving her elderly mother to a nursing home, Debbie discovered their property had once been a waystation on the Underground Railroad for fugitive slaves seeking freedom in Canada.

Upon retiring from a successful high-tech career, Debbie was compelled to learn more about the lives of the refugees who had passed through her small Vermont town more than a century earlier. Out of her quest to research the Underground Railroad routes of the Northeast, came the genesis of *The Eternal Conductor*.

This is her first novel.

Debbie and her husband live in a historic gold-rush town in the California Sierra foothills, and coexist with all manner of critters. Lions and coyotes and bears and dogs and cats—oh, my!

www.theeternalconductor.com